NON SANZ DROICT.

William Shakespeare

Four Great Tragedies

Hamlet
Othello
King Lear
Macbeth

WITH AN INTRODUCTION BY
Sylvan Barnet

CL

A SIGNET CLASSIC

NEW AMERICAN LIBRARY

NEW YORK AND SCARBOROUGH, ONTARIO

Library of Congress Catalog Card Number: 81-85146

Hamlet, Othello, King Lear, and *Macbeth* are also available as
separate volumes in the Signet Classic Shakespeare editions.

SIGNET CLASSIC TRADEMARK REG. U.S. PAT. OFF. AND FOREIGN COUNTRIES
REGISTERED TRADEMARK—MARCA REGISTRADA
HECHO EN WINNIPEG, CANADA

SIGNET, SIGNET CLASSIC, MENTOR, PLUME, MERIDIAN AND NAL
BOOKS are published *in the United States* by
New American Library,
1633 Broadway, New York, New York 10019,
in Canada by The New American Library of Canada Limited,
81 Mack Avenue, Scarborough, Ontario M1L 1M8

First Printing, May, 1982

2 3 4 5 6 7 8 9 10

PRINTED IN CANADA

INTRODUCTION

Hundreds of books have been written about tragedy (indeed hundreds have been written about Shakespeare's tragedies), and it is fairly usual for them to begin by saying that there is no such thing as tragedy—there are only *tragedies*. We get the point; each play is different and ought not to be forced into a Procrustean bed, its special features lopped off or stretched so that it may be neatly confined within a label.

Still, Shakespeare's contemporaries certainly thought there was such a thing as tragedy; they used the word in talking about literature, and they defined it in their dictionaries. Here are some definitions. Thomas Cooper in 1568 (Shakespeare was four years old) defined tragedy as "a kind of plays representing personages of great estate, and matters of much trouble." The redundantly named Thomas Thomas, writing a dictionary at about the time that Shakespeare was probably beginning his theatrical career, i.e., the late 1580's, said that tragedy is

> a lofty kind of poetry, and representing personages of great state and matter of much trouble, a great broil or stir: it beginneth prosperously, it endeth unfortunately and doubtfully, contrary to comedy.

And, finally, a definition by John Florio, three of whose books Shakespeare undoubtedly knew—and he may have known Florio himself, since Florio tutored the man to whom Shakespeare dedicated *Venus and Adonis* (1593) and *The Rape of Lucrece* (1594). In his Italian-English dictionary of 1598 Florio defines tragedy thus:

> A tragedy or mournful play being a lofty kind of poetry and representing personages of great state and matter of much trouble, a great broil or stir: it beginneth prosper-

ously and endeth unfortunately or sometimes doubtfully, and is contrary to comedy.

These and similar definitions (to say nothing of the plays themselves) allow us to assert that the Elizabethans regarded a tragedy as a "lofty" play showing "personages of great state" engaged or caught up in a "lamentable" action that "beginneth prosperously and endeth unfortunately." The terms apply well to Shakespeare's tragedies; the only modification needed is that *Hamlet* does not begin prosperously, for Hamlet's father has already been killed, and his mother (in his view) has ignobly remarried. But the three other plays begin with the hero riding high on Fortune's wheel. Othello, the chief prop of Venice, is married to his heart's joy; Lear, full of years and power, is surrounded by an attentive court; Macbeth, victorious in battle, is given new honors by his grateful and gracious king. And of course all four of these tragic heroes will, in the course of the plays, go through nearly unendurable agonies and will, in the fifth act, die.

Behind the figures in Renaissance drama who fall from high place are medieval nondramatic tragedies, that is, narrative poems telling of the insubstantiality of high place in a world governed by Fortune. Chaucer's Monk knows a hundred such stories and recites fifteen of them to his fellow pilgrims before the Knight, bored stiff, interrupts him. The one interesting thing about the Monk's tedious narratives is that although he instances his tragic figures (correctly enough) as people deserted by Fortune, they are a mixed bag. King Peter of Cyprus is totally innocent—indeed, he is slain merely out of envy—yet Lucifer, on the other hand, "fel . . . for his synne," and Adam lost Paradise because of his "mysgovernaunce." So there are two explanations for the fall: capricious fortune, and man's vice. If we go beyond the four plays in this volume and look at the whole range of Shakespeare's tragedies, we can say that at one pole are Romeo and Juliet, attractive young people who are "star-crossed," i.e., who have bad luck and who can be regarded almost as sacrificial victims, and at the other pole is Macbeth, who knowingly embarks on a career of murder and who is, for his "mysgovernaunce," justly punished. Rejecting the view that Fortune governs capriciously or malevolently, Macbeth sees that "even-handed justice / Commends th' ingredients of our poisoned chalice / To our own lips." (I.vii. 10-12).

We can say, then, that for Shakespeare there was such a thing as tragedy (people in high estate fall into intense suffering and finally into death), and yet every play is unique; Shakespeare never repeated himself, but always filled the old bottles with new wine. The plays differ in countless ways: *Hamlet* and *Lear* are rich in pervasive bitter comedy but *Othello* has only two short, witless comic scenes; *Hamlet* is almost twice the length of *Macbeth;* *Lear* is unique in having a subplot (Gloucester and his sons) running parallel to the main plot (Lear and his daughters); the source of *Othello* is a short story that runs only a few pages, but the sources of *Lear* include an old play (in which, by the way, the king is restored to the throne) and a monstrously long prose romance, and the source of *Macbeth* is a long prose historical account. And, to return to the chief point, the degree of guilt of the tragic figures ranges greatly—from Hamlet, who initially finds himself in a wretched situation not at all of his own making, to Lear, who indeed bungles by giving his kingdom to two villainous daughters (but here his intentions are good, and, considering the hideous treatment he later receives, he can fairly say that he is "more sinned against than sinning"), to Othello, who is duped into murdering his wife, to Macbeth, who knows what is right but who nevertheless kills in order to gain the crown.

In 1615, four years after Shakespeare had retired from the theater, one John Greene published a blast against the theatrical profession. He took a survey of what he had seen and read—and although he does not name Shakespeare, there is no reason to assume that he was exempting Shakespeare—and he set down his thoughts.

> The matter of tragedies is haughtiness, arrogancy, ambition, pride, injury, anger, wrath, envy, hatred, contention, war, murder, cruelty, rapine, incest, rovings, depradations, piracies, spoils, robberies, rebellions, treasons, killing, hewing, stabbing, dagger-drawing, fighting, butchery, treachery, villainy, etc. and all kind of heroic evils whatever.

There is a good deal of redundancy here, but on the whole it is true. *Hamlet* (probably written 1600–01), to take the earliest play in our group, fits the description nicely, except perhaps for "rapine" (plunder). "Haughtiness, arrogancy": Hamlet bitterly speaks of the "insolence of office," perhaps

thinking of the usurper Claudius. "Ambition, pride": somewhat oddly, Hamlet characterizes himself as ambitious and
proud, and in any case in III.iii.55 Claudius specifically refers
to the "ambition" that prodded him to kill for a crown and a
queen. "Injury, anger, wrath, envy, hatred, contention": these
need scarcely to be documented. "War": the play is full of
talk of war between Norway and Denmark, and at the end
the Norwegian prince takes possession of Denmark. There is,
too, the battle between Hamlet and Claudius ("mighty opposites," in Hamlet's words). "Murder, cruelty": we need
hardly point out examples, but we should note that Hamlet
himself is, in various ways and for various reasons, "cruel."
For example, he says to his mother, "I must be cruel, only to
be kind"; his cruelty to Rosencrantz and Guildenstern (he
kills them) is understandable, for he is, in effect, at war, but
perhaps less understandable is his almost joyful contemplation of the trick by which he dispatches them. "Incest":
Hamlet is deeply disturbed that his mother has posted to
"incestuous sheets," i.e., married her former brother-in-law,
an incestuous act by Elizabethan standards. We need not go
through the rest of John Greene's catalog except to mention
that even "piracies" is present in *Hamlet*, for he escapes from
the ship bearing him to death in England by the fortunate appearance of a pirate vessel, which he boards. And yet
Greene's blast against tragedies, so right in all its details, is
somehow all wrong. One is reminded of the story that Mark
Twain's very proper wife, to cure him of his habit of cursing,
once repeated one of his foul outbursts word for word. He
listened, thought for a moment, and then patiently explained
to her that she had the words right but she didn't have the intonation. Greene argued that because tragedy is concerned
with evil, it corrupts the spectators. What he didn't see was
the vision behind the plays; we can almost say "the moral
vision." Hamlet, for example, *is* partly corrupted by the corrupt world around him; but heroically, and almost miracu-
lously, he finally accomplishes the stern task imposed upon
him by the ghost of his murdered father ("Revenge his foul
and most unnatural murder"), and he accomplishes it nobly,
not by any base scheme but by stabbing the murderer with a
poisoned foil that Laertes, Claudius's tool, had treacherously
prepared to use against Hamlet, and by forcing Claudius to
drink a cup of poison that Claudius had prepared for Hamlet. Hamlet has been sorely tried, and he has done things that
no decent person willingly does, but (despite the school of

criticism that sees him as a weakling who invents excuses for not getting on with the job) on the whole and finally he behaves heroically, meriting the military funeral that he is given at the end. When the cannon pay final tribute to him, we are audibly reminded that he has been a warrior and that against all odds he has done his duty. Indeed, our memories need not be especially keen to recall, when we hear this closing military salute, that earlier in the play cannon were used to salute Claudius as he downed his wine (I.iv.6–12); here, at the end of the play, they are put to fitter use, providing Hamlet with "the soldiers' music," in tribute to his tragic victory in a just cause.

This brief introduction has not touched on the two questions that many people think are central to *Hamlet*: Why does Hamlet delay? and, Is Hamlet mad or only pretending to be? Nor will it touch on them, except to say that they do not arise when one is deeply immersed in reading the play or in seeing it on the stage. Rather than go into these tedious matters, the limited space at hand will be used (before glancing at the three other tragedies printed in this book) to talk briefly about the languages of drama, drawing examples chiefly from *Hamlet*. Elizabeth Bowen has said that in fiction, *dialogue* is what the characters *do* to each other. A very shrewd observation. But a play is people moving about on the stage—engaging in dialogue, of course, but also wearing costumes, picking up props, making gestures, hearing sound effects—matters to keep in mind while we read the play.

Take the business of costumes: Hamlet at the start is dressed (according to his own words) in an "inky cloak," and this garment doubtless sets him apart from the opulently dressed court in I.ii. That is, the costume *says* something. It says that Hamlet is in mourning, and (by contrast with all the other courtly costumes) it says that he is isolated. And it also marks him as a figure of death, for we cannot overlook the fact that he deals in death: Rosencrantz and Guildenstern, Polonius, Laertes, and Claudius all meet death at his hands, and he bears some responsibility for Ophelia's death too. (This is not to say that he is a villain; that role is clearly reserved for Claudius, but only that this "sweet prince," forced into the role of avenger, is dressed accordingly.) Later, in his description of his activities while sailing for England, he speaks of wearing his "sea gown," and it may well be that when we first see him after the voyage (in the churchyard, in V.i) he is dressed in this gown, the change in costume indicating a change within, for from this point he is confirmed in his purpose.

When we turn to theatrical props, we think first perhaps of the prayerbook that Polonius, that meddlesome stage-manager, thrusts into Ophelia's hands, but we should also remember such things as the throne on which the usurping Claudius sits, the poisoned chalice, and, most important of all, the sword that Hamlet doubtless wears throughout the play—reminding us that he is in combat. We have already noticed the chief sound effects, the roar of cannon, but we should also recall the "flourish" of trumpets announcing the entry of Claudius, in I.ii.1 and elsewhere, and the "trumpets and kettledrums" that precede the dumbshow in III.ii.92.

But of course a play—especially a play by Shakespeare—chiefly makes use of words, and something must be said about Shakespeare's prose and verse. We think of Shakespeare primarily as a poetic dramatist, but only two of his plays (Richard II and King John) are written entirely in poetry. About half of the other plays are at least one-fourth in prose. Almost one-third of Hamlet, for example, is in prose, and the same is true of King Lear. It is sometimes said that in Shakespeare's tragedies the noble characters speak verse and the lower characters speak prose, but this generalization is far too simple, even when modified by such an amendment as the assertion that noble characters when mad speak prose. The fact is, Shakespeare's noble characters use prose in a wide variety of situations. Hamlet, for example, uses it in greeting his old school-friends Rosencrantz and Guildenstern (II.ii), in princely reflections on "What a piece of work is a man" (also II.ii), and in meditative comments on the impending duel with Laertes (V.ii). Let's look briefly at these passages. First, a sample of Hamlet with Rosencrantz and Guildenstern. When he sees them he says, "My excellent good friends! How dost thou, Guildenstern? Ah, Rosencrantz! Good lads, how do you both?" A moment earlier Hamlet had been taunting Polonius—in witty prose—but now, seeing his old schoolfriends, his genial nature and his sense of courtesy revive, and he expresses in simple language his heartfelt joy at their presence. But almost immediately he suspects that Claudius has sent them to spy on him, and his prose begins to hammer at them:

Were you not sent for? Is it your own inclining? Is it a

free visitation? Come, come, deal justly with me. Come, come; nay, speak. (II.ii.280-83)

When they confess that the king sent for them, Hamlet, secure in knowing that he has their number, can turn his thoughts away from them and to himself, and we get a speech that, although addressed to Rosencrantz and Guildenstern, sounds almost like a soliloquy:

> I have of late, but wherefore I know not, lost all my mirth, forgone all custom of exercises; and indeed, it goes so heavily with my disposition that this goodly frame, the earth, seems to me a sterile promontory; this most excellent canopy, the air, look you, this brave o'erhanging firmament, this majestical roof fretted with golden fire: why, it appeareth nothing to me but a foul and pestilent congregation of vapors. What a piece of work is a man, how noble in reason, how infinite in faculties, in form and moving how express and admirable, in action how like an angel, in apprehension how like a god: the beauty of the world, the paragon of animals; and yet to me, what is this quintessence of dust? Man delights not me; nor woman neither, though by your smiling you seem to say so.
>
> (II.ii.303-19)

Only in the last part of the last sentence (from "nor woman, neither") does the prose again become a weapon to use against the two spies.

Finally, let's look at Hamlet's response to Horatio's offer to make excuses if Hamlet wishes to avoid dueling with Laertes:

> Not a whit, we defy augury. There is special providence in the fall of a sparrow. If it be now, 'tis not to come; if it be not to come, it will be now; if it be not now, yet it will come. The readiness is all. Since no man of aught he leaves knows, what is't to leave betimes? Let be.
>
> (V.ii.220-25)

Of the sixty-two words in the speech, all but seven are monosyllabic. On the whole the diction is colloquial (e.g. "Not a whit"), but there is a solemn echo of the Bible ("special providence in the fall of a sparrow"), and the clauses are balanced. The speech is simple and meditative, yet strong-willed in the final "Let be."

Now for an equally brief discussion of the poetry. Some of the poetry is rhymed, but most is unrhymed, written in blank verse. We shall consider blank verse in a moment, but first we will dispose of the rhymed poetry. Sometimes the end of a blank verse speech is given emotional heightening by a couplet (a pair of rhyming lines). A particularly interesting variation of this device occurs in *Hamlet*, where, after conversing with the ghost, Hamlet rejoins his fellows, speaks blank verse, and then uses a couplet which (however bitter) seems by virtue of the rhyme emphatic or forceful—but then Hamlet adds a short unrhymed line; the effect of this addition is not only to indicate Hamlet's need for companionship (that is the gist or content of the line) but to indicate his exhaustion:

> Rest, rest, perturbèd spirit. So, gentlemen,
> With all my love I do commend me to you,
> And what so poor a man as Hamlet is
> May do t'express his love and friending to you,
> God willing, shall not lack. Let us go in together,
> And still your fingers on your lips, I pray.
> The time is out of joint. O cursèd spite,
> That ever I was born to set it right!
> Nay, come, let's go together.
>   (I.v.182-90)

Couplets are also sometimes used to end a scene or an act, to wrap it up before a new group of characters enters. Long speeches in rhyme may be used to indicate that these speeches are not normal discourse, for in the play, normal discourse is chiefly unrhymed poetry, or prose. An obvious example in *Hamlet* is the play-within-the-play in III.ii. And of course there are other uses for rhyme, such as Ophelia's mad songs in IV.v and Hamlet's poem in his letter to Ophelia in II.ii.

Having said that Shakespeare makes dramatic use of prose and of rhyme, we must of course recognize that his chief medium is blank verse, unrhymed iambic pentameter. In a mechanically exact line there are five iambic feet (each foot consisting of an unstressed syllable followed by a stressed syllable), so of the ten syllables every second is stressed. But the stresses are not all of equal weight, and in any case Shakespeare often departs from the pattern. One reads a passage according to the sense, not according to a fixed idea of meter. In the following passage, Claudius rather formally addresses his court:

> Though yet of Hamlet our dear brother's death
> The memory be green, and that it us befitted
> To bear out hearts in grief, and our whole kingdom
> To be contracted in one brow of woe,
> Yet so far hath discretion fought with nature
> That we with wisest sorrow think on him
> Together with remembrance of ourselves.
>
>   (I.ii.1-7)

But Claudius does not always sound so poised and kingly. To get an idea of the range of Shakespeare's blank verse, and of the ways in which it creates or reveals character, we can compare this speech with another passage from the same scene, where Claudius puts aside, to some degree, the ceremonious manner we have just heard, and speaks more intimately to Laertes:

> And now, Laertes, what's the news with you?
> You told us of some suit. What is't, Laertes?
> You cannot speak of reason to the Dane
> And lose your voice. What wouldst thou beg, Laertes,
> That shall not be my offer, not thy asking?
>
>   (I.ii.42-46)

Intimacy is here created not only by the shift from the royal "us" in the second line to the more human "my" in the last, and by the ingratiating repetition of "Laertes," but also by the short sentences: we get five sentences in five lines, as opposed to the single sentence seven lines long quoted in the previous example.

These comments on Shakespeare's language (nonverbal as well as verbal) have only scratched the surface, but they may serve to alert the reader to some of the subtleties and complexities of Shakespeare's art. On each rereading one will see and hear more, but this is not to say that on an initial encounter with a play one should worry about whether a passage is in rhyme, blank verse, or prose. Merely read the play carefully (it's no use speed-reading the speeches as though they are items in a newspaper), if not aloud at least so that they sound in the mind's ear, and they will do their work, or at least much of it. Once you are familiar with the plot and the characters, and indeed with Shakespeare's language, you can reread, paying closer attention to the artistry and thereby deriving yet greater pleasure from it. There is scarcely a speech which, if read aloud two or three times, will not in some way grow richer—perhaps funnier, perhaps more pathetic, perhaps more harrowing. Listening to good recordings of the plays (most libraries have them) will also greatly deepen understanding and enjoyment.

After writing *Hamlet*, Shakespeare probably wrote *The Merry Wives of Windsor, Troilus and Cressida,* and *All's Well that Ends Well,* and then, in 1604, *Othello,* the tragedy that next concerns us. *Hamlet* is a revenge play, which means that its structure is that of action and reaction, an eye for an eye, a tooth for a tooth. The initial action—the murder of Hamlet's father—took place before the play begins, but when Hamlet learns who the murderer is, his course of action, or, so to speak, his reaction, is clear, and from this point onward Hamlet and Claudius engage in a barely concealed battle. But in *Othello* we get a play with a different structure, largely because Othello does not clearly know, until the final scene, that he is being acted upon. This play, like *King Lear* and *Macbeth,* is indebted to a late medieval genre called the morality play (the most famous example is *Everyman*), specifically to the kind of morality play that shows a man tempted into sin. Iago is the tempter here, a sort of devil (he himself appeals to hell for inspiration in devising his scheme); at the other side of Othello stands "the divine Desdemona," a sort of good angel. Shakespeare derived his plot from a rather unimpressive story that would occupy about ten pages in this book, and he turned it into a play that is at once intensely human and yet rich in reverberations of mysterious powers. We have no ghost, as in *Hamlet,* and no witches, as in *Macbeth;* rather, we have only suggestions of mysterious powers, chiefly through imagery of angelic goodness on the one hand and diabolical evil on the other. Iago offers several motives for hating Othello—Othello has not promoted Iago, Iago suspects Othello has been to bed with Iago's wife, etc.—but the best comment on Iago's search for a motive is Coleridge's: "the motive-hunting of motiveless malignity." Why this malignity? As well ask why Judas betrayed Christ. Indeed, perhaps this gives us a clue: a mere hatred of the good. In any case Iago says of Cassio, another of his victims, "He hath a daily beauty in his life / That makes me ugly. . . ." (V.i.19-20).

But we can ask, To what degree is Othello himself at fault? His are the hands, after all, that kill Desdemona. And so critics have sought to find Othello's "tragic flaw." "The noble Moor" (thus he is characterized in the play) is said to be guilty of jealousy, or of stupidity, or of African barbarism covered with only a veneer of European civilization. Some evidence can be adduced in support of these charges; for example, although Othello often speaks nobly and behaves heroically, after Iago has poisoned his mind with the suggestion that Desdemona has slept with Cassio, Othello is capable of such barbarously crude utterances as "I will chop her into messes" and "I'll tear her all to pieces." This, from the man who has spoken with dignity and with splendor, as when (to take a very brief example) he said to old Brabantio, who was accompanied by an armed band prepared to attack Othello:

> Keep up your bright swords, for the dew will rust them.
> Good signior, you shall more command with years
> Than with your weapons.
>
> (I.ii.58-60)

Still, the idea of hunting for a flaw in Othello is misguided, for it puts the emphasis in the wrong place. Exactly what is it that leads to the terrible tragedy of Othello killing the thing he most values? It is not a weakness but a virtue, as Iago himself tells us, and here he is no deceiver. The Moor, he says, is "of a free and open nature / That thinks men honest that but seem to be so. . . ." (I.iii.390-91), and so Iago knows that Othello will not suspect him. (We might note, that Hamlet meets his death not because of a flaw but because he is high-minded. Laertes can with impunity use a poisoned foil in what is supposed to be a game because he knows that Hamlet, being "free from all contriving / Will not peruse the foils.") Iago knows, too, that he can turn Desdemona's "virtue into pitch, / And out of her own goodness make the net / That shall enmesh them all" (II.iii.360-62). Nobility or excellence, paradoxically, is by its nature vulnerable, and it is this fact as much as any other that causes tragedy to arouse (in the words of Shakespeare's slightly earlier contemporary, Sir Philip Sidney) "admiration [i.e. wonder] and commiseration." Wonder and pity. But, finally, at the end of the play there is more than wonder and pity; there is almost—we might say—joy at the end, for although Othello suffers beyond endurance when he learns that he has murdered his innocent wife, the news of her innocence is not simply the worst news he could hear; it is also the best news, reestablishing his belief in goodness. And so, in a long, dignified, beautiful speech he sums up his career, judges his horrible action scrupulously (he says he, "Like the base Judean, threw a pearl away / Richer than all his tribe"), and goes on to pronounce justice on himself. He speaks of an infidel, an enemy to the state, whom he killed, and so he now, once again, kills the infidel, himself. Iago has not, after all, destroyed Othello's moral sense. T. S. Eliot oddly said that in this moving speech Othello is adopting a sentimental attitude toward himself, "endeavoring to escape reality," and is "cheering himself up." Helen Gardner much more astutely suggests that Othello, by affirming the values by which he lived, is cheering *us* up.

In *King Lear* (1605-06) Shakespeare is again indebted to the morality pattern (Lear is flanked by the virtuous Cordelia and Kent on one side, and the wicked Goneril and Regan on the other), but the play is utterly unlike *Othello*. In this play the tragic action—Lear's banishment of the loving Cordelia and his entrusting of himself to the care of Goneril and Regan—takes place in the first scene. Goneril and Regan are monstrous hypocrites, but the action is clearly Lear's alone. The banishment of Cordelia brings immediate protests from Lear's true friend, Kent; Lear cannot claim later that he was a victim. We can wish that Cordelia had spoken more gently (though we cannot blame her for lacking the "glib and oily art" of her fawning sisters), and we can scarcely blame an eighty-year-old man who wishes to retire, but the foolish deed is Lear's. The upshot is that Lear suffers terribly for his egotism at the beginning, and, through suffering, comes to value the loving Cordelia, whom he had brutally rejected. We cannot say—and do not want to say—that through his trials Lear is purified and finally dies worthy of entering heaven. We need not say, with the great critic A. C. Bradley, that the play might be called "The Redemption of King Lear," but surely at the end of the play Lear is better and wiser. Perhaps he is happier too, and this point is worth discussing.

Bradley says that Lear dies overcome with joy in the belief that Cordelia is alive, but the text is ambiguous. Holding Cordelia in his arms, Lear dies with these words:

Do you see this? Look on her. Look, her lips.
Look there, look there.

(V.iii.312-13)

What does Lear see on her lips? Breath and motion, or life-
lessness? It will not do to assert dogmatically that Lear,
madly thinking Cordelia is alive, dies joyfully, or, on the
other hand, that he dies full of outrage that the virtuous Cordelia has been murdered. But we can say this: earlier in the
speech the agonized Lear, aware in a lucid moment that the
innocent Cordelia is dead, asks, "Why should a dog, a horse,
a rat have life, / And thou no breath at all?" Lear does not
formulate an answer, but our answer must be, "Because a human being, but not a lower animal, can choose (as Cordelia
chooses) to act out of love rather than out of self-interest."
The monstrous unfairness remains, but nothing further needs
to be said, and Lear, having already experienced the most intense suffering (as well as the most intense joy when, however briefly, he is reconciled with Cordelia) can scarcely go
on living. It is surely preposterous to say, with a recent critic,
that Lear's "final retreat to madness . . . makes it impossible
to retain *any* concept of an ordered universe." At the end of
the play, as at the beginning, Lear is wrong about some facts
(his infirm mind seems not to grasp, for example, the fact
that the loyal Kent has served him in disguise as Caius), but
he is right about Cordelia's love, and whether he dies
outraged at the fact of her death or overjoyed (surely the
more meaningful interpretation) in the mistaken belief that
she is alive matters less than that Cordelia loved him, that he
comes to see this, and that he is reunited with her. We joy in
her love, and we are immensely relieved that he is at last re-
leased from "the rack of this tough world." We can note, too,
without unctuously suggesting that all's right with the world,
that all of the villains are dead and that their deaths are not
accidental or casual but supremely appropriate: the villainous
Regan dies at the hand of her former partner in wickedness
and now her rival, the villainous Goneril; Goneril dies by her
own hand; Edmund dies by the hand of the brother whom he
wronged.

With *Macbeth* (1605–06) we come to the last of our four
great tragedies, though Shakespeare went on to write two
more *(Antony and Cleopatra* and *Coriolanus)* as well as
several comedies. It is Shakespeare's shortest tragedy, and the
one most clearly indebted to the structure and indeed the ob-

vious morality of the morality play. Macbeth, a sort of heroic Everyman, is tempted (his wife, and the witches); although he has at his side images of virtue (the noble King Duncan, Banquo), and he knows that he is doing wrong, he yields to temptation and then learns that he must pay the terrible price. Notice: he "knows" that he is doing wrong, but he must still "learn" that he must pay the price. And what is this price? Not simply death, but a loss of all sense of the value of life. In the fifth act he sees clearly the irony of his tragic action: he killed Duncan in order to increase his happiness, but he finds that he has lost all happiness, all of what was represented by Duncan's world:

> My way of life
> Is fall'n into the sear, the yellow leaf,
> And that which should accompany old age,
> As honor, love, obedience, troops of friends,
> I must not look to have; but, in their stead,
> Curses, not loud, but deep. . . .
> (V.iii.22-27)

This speech only states explicitly what spectators of the play see: they see, for example, that after Macbeth, encouraged by his wife, murders Duncan, Macbeth becomes gradually isolated even from her, his accomplice in this first crime. In III.ii he keeps from her his plan to murder Banquo and Fleance. She has already noticed his isolation and she asks him, "Why do you keep alone, / Of sorriest fancies your companions making?" and he replies by saying that he is tormented by the thought that Banquo and Fleance still live. To her question, "What's to be done?" he answers only, "Be innocent of the knowledge, dearest chuck;" the affection in "dearest chuck" (i.e., chick) and the desire to shield her from further evildoing only underscore the pain of the separation from the woman who earlier was his "dearest partner of greatness." After IV.i Macbeth is never again seen in the play with any of his former associates, not even Lady Macbeth, who dies offstage in V.vi and whose death evokes from him only the dead words, "She should have died hereafter; / There would have been a time for such a word." Whether these words mean, "She would have died sometime anyway" or "She ought to have died at a more opportune moment" does not much matter; it is clear from the view

expressed in the lines that follow—Macbeth's, not Shakespeare's—that life is now meaningless:

> Tomorrow, and tomorrow, and tomorrow
> Creeps in this petty pace from day to day,
> To the last syllable of recorded time;
> And all our yesterdays have lighted fools
> The way to dusty death. Out, out, brief candle!
> Life's but a walking shadow, a poor player
> That struts and frets his hour upon the stage
> And then is heard no more. It is a tale
> Told by an idiot, full of sound and fury
> Signifying nothing.
>
> (V.v.19-28)

Aristotle in his *Poetics* (composed almost two thousand
years before *Macbeth*) was the first to tell us that tragedy
evokes "pity" and "terror," and here, at the end of our brief
discussion of four great tragedies, we can see how these terms
apply to this play. The terror is obvious enough: that
Macbeth, receiver of Duncan's bounty, should murder his
benefactor, is terrifying. That he should go on to a career of
slaughter, killing not only those who are obviously his enemies but even the utterly innocent Lady Macduff and her
child, suggests that we live in a world where no one is safe
from the reaches of a madman. Terror, too, that *we*, like
Macbeth, might yield to temptations if the prize seemed
within easy reach, and terror that we would suffer Macbeth's
fate. And this gets us to the matter of pity, not only the obvious pity for Macbeth's victims but even for Macbeth himself,
for it is strange but true that although he is monstrous he
nevertheless evokes a degree of pity. Why do we feel any pity
for this man who, unlike all of Shakespeare's earlier tragic
heroes, knowingly does evil? A few answers may be suggested.
1) It is pitiful that a brave warrior who is, at first, a savior of his nation should become the enemy of his nation. 2)
He is in some degree the victim of the Witches and of Lady
Macbeth, i.e., of some destructive power-seeking force that
permeates the world. 3) Knowing that his deeds are evil, he
is tormented by his conscience. His punishment, as has already been suggested, is not merely that he dies but that his
conscience afflicts him with fear and guilt, with "terrible
dreams / That shake us nightly" (III.ii.18-19). 4) Finally, at
the end of the play he fights strongly, and we can only recall

sadly that, in contrast with the report of his courage and patriotism in I.i, he now fights for a wicked cause.

No reader of this introduction to four tragic masterpieces will be more aware than the writer that its assertions are too simple and that its omissions are great. Even if much more space were available it would be inadequate to these plays, which, on the page and in the theater, evoke infinitely complicated responses. I can end only with the words of Shakespeare's two fellow actors who wrote the preface to the first collection (1623) of Shakespeare's plays: "And so we leave you to other of his friends, whom if you need can be your guides. If you need them not, you can lead yourselves, and others. And such readers we wish him."

SYLVAN BARNET
Tufts University

The Tragedy of

Hamlet
Prince of Denmark

◆

EDITED BY
Edward Hubler

Dramatis Personae

Claudius, King of Denmark.
Hamlet, son to the late, and nephew to the present, King.
Polonius, Lord Chamberlain.
Horatio, Friend to Hamlet.
Laertes, son to Polonius.
Voltimand
Cornelius
Rosencrantz   courtiers
Guildenstern
Osric
A Gentleman.
A Priest.
Marcellus
Bernardo   officers
Francisco, a soldier.
Reynaldo, servant to Polonius.
Players.
Two Clowns, gravediggers.
Fortinbras, Prince of Norway.
A Norwegian Captain.
English Ambassadors.
Gertrude, Queen of Denmark, and mother to Hamlet.
Ophelia, daughter to Polonius.
Ghost of Hamlet's father.

Lords, Ladies, Officers, Soldiers, Sailors, Messengers, and Attendants.

Scene: Elsinore.

The Tragedy of Hamlet
Prince of Denmark

[ACT I

Scene I. *A guard platform of the castle.*]

Enter Barnardo and Francisco, two sentinels.

Barnardo. Who's there?

Francisco. Nay, answer me. Stand and unfold° ¹ yourself.

Barnardo. Long live the King!°

Francisco. Barnardo?

Barnardo. He.   5

Francisco. You come most carefully upon your hour.

Barnardo. 'Tis now struck twelve. Get thee to bed,
Francisco.

¹ The degree sign (°) indicates a footnote, which is keyed to the
text by the line number. Text references are printed in *italic* type;
the annotation follows in roman type.
1.i.2 *unfold* disclose   3 *Long live the King* (perhaps a password,
perhaps a greeting)

33

Francisco. For this relief much thanks. 'Tis bitter cold,
    And I am sick at heart.

Barnardo. Have you had quiet guard?

10   *Francisco.*   Not a mouse stirring.

Barnardo. Well, good night.
    If you do meet Horatio and Marcellus,
    The rivals° of my watch, bid them make haste.

                Enter Horatio and Marcellus.

Francisco. I think I hear them. Stand, ho! Who is
    there?

Horatio. Friends to this ground.

15   *Marcellus.*   And liegemen to the Dane.°

Francisco. Give you° good night.

Marcellus.   O, farewell, honest soldier.
    Who hath relieved you?

Francisco.   Barnardo hath my place.
    Give you good night.   *Exit Francisco.*

Marcellus.   Holla, Barnardo!

Barnardo.   Say——
    What, is Horatio there?

Horatio.   A piece of him.

20   *Barnardo.* Welcome, Horatio. Welcome, good Marcel-
    lus.

Marcellus. What, has this thing appeared again tonight?

Barnardo. I have seen nothing.

Marcellus. Horatio says 'tis but our fantasy,
    And will not let belief take hold of him
25   Touching this dreaded sight twice seen of us;
    Therefore I have entreated him along
    With us to watch the minutes of this night,
    That, if again this apparition come,
    He may approve° our eyes and speak to it.

13 *rivals* partners 15 *liegemen to the Dane* loyal subjects to the
King of Denmark 16 *Give you* God give you 29 *approve* confirm

Horatio. Tush, tush, 'twill not appear.

Barnardo.   Sit down awhile,   30
And let us once again assail your ears,
That are so fortified against our story,
What we have two nights seen.

Horatio.   Well, sit we down,
And let us hear Barnardo speak of this.

Barnardo. Last night of all,   35
When yond same star that's westward from the
    pole°
Had made his course t' illume that part of heaven
Where now it burns, Marcellus and myself,
The bell then beating one——

Enter Ghost.

Marcellus. Peace, break thee off. Look where it comes
again.   40

Barnardo. In the same figure like the king that's dead.

Marcellus. Thou art a scholar; speak to it, Horatio.

Barnardo. Looks 'a not like the king? Mark it, Horatio.

Horatio. Most like: it harrows me with fear and wonder.

Barnardo. It would be spoke to.

Marcellus.   Speak to it, Horatio.   45

Horatio. What art thou that usurp'st this time of night,
Together with that fair and warlike form
In which the majesty of buried Denmark°
Did sometimes march? By heaven I charge thee,
    speak.

Marcellus. It is offended.

Barnardo.   See, it stalks away.   50

Horatio. Stay! Speak, speak. I charge thee, speak.
                              Exit Ghost.

36 *pole* polestar   **48** *buried Denmark* the buried King of Denmark

Marcellus. 'Tis gone and will not answer.

Barnardo. How now, Horatio? You tremble and look
 pale.
 Is not this something more than fantasy?
55 What think you on't?

Horatio. Before my God, I might not this believe
 Without the sensible and true avouch°
 Of mine own eyes.

Marcellus.   Is it not like the King?

Horatio. As thou art to thyself.
60 Such was the very armor he had on
 When he the ambitious Norway° combated:
 So frowned he once, when, in an angry parle,°
 He smote the sledded Polacks° on the ice.
 'Tis strange.

Marcellus. Thus twice before, and jump° at this dead
65 hour,
 With martial stalk hath he gone by our watch.

Horatio. In what particular thought to work I know
 not;
 But, in the gross and scope° of my opinion,
 This bodes some strange eruption to our state.

Marcellus. Good now, sit down, and tell me he that
70 knows,
 Why this same strict and most observant watch
 So nightly toils the subject° of the land,
 And why such daily cast of brazen cannon
 And foreign mart° for implements of war,

57 *sensible and true avouch* sensory and true proof   61 *Norway*
King of Norway   62 *parle* parley   63 *sledded Polacks* Poles in
sledges   65 *jump* just   68 *gross and scope* general drift   72 *toils
the subject* makes the subjects toil   74 *mart* trading

Why such impress° of shipwrights, whose sore task   75
Does not divide the Sunday from the week,
What might be toward° that this sweaty haste
Doth make the night joint-laborer with the day?
Who is't that can inform me?

Horatio.   That can I.
At least the whisper goes so: our last king,   80
Whose image even but now appeared to us,
Was, as you know, by Fortinbras of Norway,
Thereto pricked on by a most emulate pride,
Dared to the combat; in which our valiant Hamlet
(For so this side of our known world esteemed him)   85
Did slay this Fortinbras, who, by a sealed compact
Well ratified by law and heraldry,°
Did forfeit, with his life, all those his lands
Which he stood seized° of, to the conqueror;
Against the which a moiety competent°   90
Was gagèd° by our King, which had returned
To the inheritance of Fortinbras,
Had he been vanquisher, as, by the same comart°
And carriage of the article designed,°
His fell to Hamlet. Now, sir, young Fortinbras,   95
Of unimprovèd° mettle hot and full,
Hath in the skirts° of Norway here and there
Sharked up° a list of lawless resolutes,°
For food and diet, to some enterprise
That hath a stomach in't;° which is no other,   100
As it doth well appear unto our state,
But to recover of us by strong hand
And terms compulsatory, those foresaid lands
So by his father lost; and this, I take it,
Is the main motive of our preparations,   105

75 *impress* forced service   77 *toward* in preparation   87 *law and heraldry* heraldic law (governing the combat)   89 *seized* possessed   90 *moiety competent* equal portion   91 *gagèd* engaged, pledged   93 *comart* agreement   94 *carriage of the article designed* import of the agreement drawn up   96 *unimprovèd* untried   97 *skirts* borders   98 *Sharked up* collected indiscriminately (as a shark gulps its prey)   98 *resolutes* desperadoes   100 *hath a stomach in't* i.e., requires courage

The source of this our watch, and the chief head°
Of this posthaste and romage° in the land.

Barnardo. I think it be no other but e'en so;
Well may it sort° that this portentous figure
110   Comes armèd through our watch so like the King
That was and is the question of these wars.

Horatio. A mote it is to trouble the mind's eye:
In the most high and palmy state of Rome,
A little ere the mightiest Julius fell,
115   The graves stood tenantless, and the sheeted dead
Did squeak and gibber in the Roman streets;°
As stars with trains of fire and dews of blood,
Disasters° in the sun; and the moist star,°
Upon whose influence Neptune's empire stands,
120   Was sick almost to doomsday with eclipse.
And even the like precurse° of feared events,
As harbingers° preceding still° the fates
And prologue to the omen° coming on,
Have heaven and earth together demonstrated
125   Unto our climatures° and countrymen.

Enter Ghost.

But soft, behold, lo where it comes again!
I'll cross it,° though it blast me.—Stay, illusion.

It spreads his° arms.

If thou hast any sound or use of voice,
Speak to me.
130   If there be any good thing to be done
That may to thee do ease and grace to me,
Speak to me.
If thou art privy to thy country's fate,
Which happily° foreknowing may avoid,

106 *head* fountainhead, origin   107 *romage* bustle   109 *sort* befit
116 *Did squeak . . . Roman streets* (the break in the sense which
follows this line suggests that a line has dropped out)   118 *Disasters* threatening signs   118 *moist star* moon   121 *precurse* precur-
sor, foreshadowing   122 *harbingers* forerunners   122 *still* always
123 *omen*   calamity   125 *climatures* regions   127 *cross it* (1)
cross its path, confront it (2) make the sign of the cross in front
of it   127 s.d. *his* i.e., its, the ghost's (though possibly what is
meant is that Horatio spreads his own arms, making a cross of
himself)   134 *happily* haply, perhaps

O, speak!   135
Or if thou hast uphoarded in thy life
Extorted° treasure in the womb of earth,
For which, they say, you spirits oft walk in death,

                                 The cock crows.

Speak of it. Stay and speak. Stop it, Marcellus.

Marcellus. Shall I strike at it with my partisan°?   140
Horatio. Do, if it will not stand.
Barnardo.   'Tis here.
Horatio.   'Tis here.
Marcellus. 'Tis gone.   *Exit Ghost.*
We do it wrong, being so majestical,
To offer it the show of violence,
For it is as the air, invulnerable,   145
And our vain blows malicious mockery.

Barnardo. It was about to speak when the cock crew.

Horatio. And then it started, like a guilty thing
Upon a fearful summons. I have heard,
The cock, that is the trumpet to the morn,   150
Doth with his lofty and shrill-sounding throat
Awake the god of day, and at his warning,
Whether in sea or fire, in earth or air,
Th' extravagant and erring° spirit hies
To his confine; and of the truth herein   155
This present object made probation.°

Marcellus. It faded on the crowing of the cock.
Some say that ever 'gainst° that season comes
Wherein our Savior's birth is celebrated,
This bird of dawning singeth all night long,   160
And then, they say, no spirit dare stir abroad,
The nights are wholesome, then no planets strike,°
No fairy takes,° nor witch hath power to charm:
So hallowed and so gracious is that time.

Horatio. So have I heard and do in part believe it.   165

137 *Extorted* ill-won   140 *partisan* pike (a long-handled weapon)
154 *extravagant and erring* out of bounds and wandering   156 *probation* proof   158 *'gainst* just before   162 *strike* exert an evil influence   163 *takes* bewitches

But look, the morn in russet mantle clad
Walks o'er the dew of yon high eastward hill.
Break we our watch up, and by my advice
Let us impart what we have seen tonight
170   Unto young Hamlet, for upon my life
This spirit, dumb to us, will speak to him.
Do you consent we shall acquaint him with it,
As needful in our loves, fitting our duty?

Marcellus. Let's do't, I pray, and I this morning know
175   Where we shall find him most convenient. *Exeunt.*

[Scene II. *The castle.*]

*Flourish.° Enter Claudius, King of Denmark, Gertrude
the Queen, Councilors, Polonius and his son Laertes,
Hamlet, cum aliis° [including Voltemand and Cor-
nelius].*

King. Though yet of Hamlet our dear brother's death
The memory be green, and that it us befitted
To bear our hearts in grief, and our whole kingdom
To be contracted in one brow of woe,
5   Yet so far hath discretion fought with nature
That we with wisest sorrow think on him
Together with remembrance of ourselves.
Therefore our sometime sister,° now our Queen,
Th' imperial jointress° to this warlike state,
10   Have we, as 'twere, with a defeated joy,
With an auspicious° and a dropping eye,
With mirth in funeral, and with dirge in marriage,
In equal scale weighing delight and dole,
Taken to wife. Nor have we herein barred
15   Your better wisdoms, which have freely gone

I.ii.s.d. *Flourish* fanfare of trumpets s.d. *cum aliis* with others
(Latin)   8 *our sometime sister* my (the royal "we") former sister-
in-law   9 *jointress* joint tenant, partner   11 *auspicious* joyful

With this affair along. For all, our thanks.
Now follows that you know young Fortinbras,
Holding a weak supposal of our worth,
Or thinking by our late dear brother's death
Our state to be disjoint and out of frame,°   20
Colleaguèd with this dream of his advantage,°
He hath not failed to pester us with message,
Importing the surrender of those lands
Lost by his father, with all bands of law,
To our most valiant brother. So much for him.   25
Now for ourself and for this time of meeting.
Thus much the business is: we have here writ
To Norway, uncle of young Fortinbras—
Who, impotent and bedrid, scarcely hears
Of this his nephew's purpose—to suppress   30
His further gait° herein, in that the levies,
The lists, and full proportions° are all made
Out of his subject;° and we here dispatch
You, good Cornelius, and you, Voltemand,
For bearers of this greeting to old Norway,   35
Giving to you no further personal power
To business with the King, more than the scope
Of these delated articles° allow.
Farewell, and let your haste commend your duty.

Cornelius, Voltemand. In that, and all things, will we
    show our duty.   40

King. We doubt it nothing. Heartily farewell.
                            Exit Voltemand and Cornelius.
And now, Laertes, what's the news with you?
You told us of some suit. What is't, Laertes?
You cannot speak of reason to the Dane
And lose your voice.° What wouldst thou beg,
    Laertes,   45
That shall not be my offer, not thy asking?
The head is not more native° to the heart,

20 *frame*   order 21 *advantage*   superiority 31 *gait*   proceeding
32 *proportions* supplies for war 33 *Out of his subject* i.e., out of
old Norway's subjects and realm 38 *delated articles* detailed documents 45 *lose your voice* waste your breath 47 *native* related

The hand more instrumental to the mouth,
Than is the throne of Denmark to thy father.
What wouldst thou have, Laertes?

50 *Laertes.*   My dread lord,
Your leave and favor to return to France,
From whence, though willingly I came to Denmark
To show my duty in your coronation,
Yet now I must confess, that duty done,
55 My thoughts and wishes bend again toward France
And bow them to your gracious leave and pardon.

King. Have you your father's leave? What says
Polonius?

Polonius. He hath, my lord, wrung from me my slow
leave
By laborsome petition, and at last
60 Upon his will I sealed my hard consent.°
I do beseech you give him leave to go.

King. Take thy fair hour, Laertes. Time be thine,
And thy best graces spend it at thy will.
But now, my cousin° Hamlet, and my son——

Hamlet. [*Aside*] A little more than kin, and less than
65 kind!°

King. How is it that the clouds still hang on you?

Hamlet. Not so, my lord. I am too much in the sun.°

Queen. Good Hamlet, cast thy nighted color off,
And let thine eye look like a friend on Denmark.
70 Do not forever with thy vailèd° lids
Seek for thy noble father in the dust.
Thou know'st 'tis common; all that lives must die,
Passing through nature to eternity.

---

60 *Upon his . . . hard consent* to his desire I gave my reluctant
consent   64 *cousin* kinsman   65 *kind* (pun on the meanings
"kindly" and "natural"; though doubly related—*more than kin*—
Hamlet asserts that he neither resembles Claudius in nature or feels
kindly toward him)   67 *sun* sunshine of royal favor (with a pun
on "son")   70 *vailèd* lowered

Hamlet. Ay, madam, it is common.°

Queen.   If it be,
　Why seems it so particular with thee?   75

Hamlet. Seems, madam? Nay, it is. I know not "seems."
　'Tis not alone my inky cloak, good mother,
　Nor customary suits of solemn black,
　Nor windy suspiration° of forced breath,
　No, nor the fruitful river in the eye,   80
　Nor the dejected havior of the visage,
　Together with all forms, moods, shapes of grief,
　That can denote me truly. These indeed seem,
　For they are actions that a man might play,
　But I have that within which passes show;   85
　These but the trappings and the suits of woe.

King. 'Tis sweet and commendable in your nature,
　　Hamlet,
　To give these mourning duties to your father,
　But you must know your father lost a father,
　That father lost, lost his, and the survivor bound   90
　In filial obligation for some term
　To do obsequious° sorrow. But to persever
　In obstinate condolement° is a course
　Of impious stubbornness. 'Tis unmanly grief.
　It shows a will most incorrect to heaven,   95
　A heart unfortified, a mind impatient,
　An understanding simple and unschooled.
　For what we know must be and is as common
　As any the most vulgar° thing to sense,
　Why should we in our peevish opposition   100
　Take it to heart? Fie, 'tis a fault to heaven,
　A fault against the dead, a fault to nature,
　To reason most absurd, whose common theme
　Is death of fathers, and who still hath cried,
　From the first corse° till he that died today,   105
　"This must be so." We pray you throw to earth

74 *common* (1) universal (2) vulgar 79 *windy suspiration* heavy
sighing 92 *obsequious* suitable to obsequies (funerals) 93 *con-
dolement* mourning 99 *vulgar* common 105 *corse* corpse

This unprevailing° woe, and think of us
As of a father, for let the world take note
You are the most immediate to our throne,
110 And with no less nobility of love
Than that which dearest father bears his son
Do I impart toward you. For your intent
In going back to school in Wittenberg,
It is most retrograde° to our desire,
115 And we beseech you, bend you° to remain
Here in the cheer and comfort of our eye,
Our chiefest courtier, cousin, and our son.

Queen. Let not thy mother lose her prayers, Hamlet.
I pray thee stay with us, go not to Wittenberg.

120 *Hamlet.* I shall in all my best obey you, madam.

King. Why, 'tis a loving and a fair reply.
Be as ourself in Denmark. Madam, come.
This gentle and unforced accord of Hamlet
Sits smiling to my heart, in grace whereof
125 No jocund health that Denmark drinks today,
But the great cannon to the clouds shall tell,
And the King's rouse° the heaven shall bruit° again,
Respeaking earthly thunder. Come away.
                    Flourish. Exeunt all but Hamlet.

Hamlet. O that this too too sullied° flesh would melt,
130 Thaw, and resolve itself into a dew,
Or that the Everlasting had not fixed
His canon° 'gainst self-slaughter. O God, God,
How weary, stale, flat, and unprofitable
Seem to me all the uses of this world!
135 Fie on't, ah, fie, 'tis an unweeded garden
That grows to seed. Things rank and gross in nature
Possess it merely.° That it should come to this:
But two months dead, nay, not so much, not two,

---

107 *unprevailing* unavailing 114 *retrograde* contrary 115 *bend
you* incline 127 *rouse* deep drink 127 *bruit* announce noisily
129 *sullied* (Q2 has *sallied*, here modernized to *sullied*, which
makes sense and is therefore given; but the Folio reading, *solid*,
which fits better with *melt*, is quite possibly correct) 132 *canon*
law 137 *merely* entirely

So excellent a king, that was to this
Hyperion° to a satyr, so loving to my mother   140
That he might not beteem° the winds of heaven
Visit her face too roughly. Heaven and earth,
Must I remember? Why, she would hang on him
As if increase of appetite had grown
By what it fed on; and yet within a month—   145
Let me not think on't; frailty, thy name is woman—
A little month, or ere those shoes were old
With which she followed my poor father's body
Like Niobe,° all tears, why she, even she—
O God, a beast that wants discourse of reason°   150
Would have mourned longer—married with my
    uncle,
My father's brother, but no more like my father
Than I to Hercules. Within a month,
Ere yet the salt of most unrighteous tears
Had left the flushing° in her gallèd eyes,   155
She married. O, most wicked speed, to post°
With such dexterity to incestuous° sheets!
It is not, nor it cannot come to good.
But break my heart, for I must hold my tongue.

Enter Horatio, Marcellus, and Barnardo.

Horatio. Hail to your lordship!

Hamlet.   I am glad to see you well.   160
    Horatio—or I do forget myself.

Horatio. The same, my lord, and your poor servant
    ever.

Hamlet. Sir, my good friend, I'll change° that name
    with you.
    And what make you from Wittenberg, Horatio?
    Marcellus.   165

140 *Hyperion* the sun god, a model of beauty   141 *beteem* allow
149 *Niobe* (a mother who wept profusely at the death of her
children)   150 *wants discourse of reason* lacks reasoning power
155 *left the flushing* stopped reddening   156 *post* hasten   157 *incestuous* (canon law considered marriage with a deceased brother's
widow to be incestuous)   163 *change* exchange

Marcellus. My good lord!

Hamlet. I am very glad to see you. [*To Barnardo*]
    Good even, sir.
But what, in faith, make you from Wittenberg?

Horatio. A truant disposition, good my lord.

170 *Hamlet.* I would not hear your enemy say so,
    Nor shall you do my ear that violence
    To make it truster° of your own report
    Against yourself. I know you are no truant.
    But what is your affair in Elsinore?
175   We'll teach you to drink deep ere you depart.

Horatio. My lord, I came to see your father's funeral.

Hamlet. I prithee do not mock me, fellow student.
    I think it was to see my mother's wedding.

Horatio. Indeed, my lord, it followed hard upon.

180 *Hamlet.* Thrift, thrift, Horatio. The funeral baked
    meats
    Did coldly furnish forth the marriage tables.
    Would I had met my dearest° foe in heaven
    Or ever I had seen that day, Horatio!
    My father, methinks I see my father.

Horatio. Where, my lord?

185 *Hamlet.*   In my mind's eye, Horatio.

Horatio. I saw him once. 'A° was a goodly king.

Hamlet. 'A was a man, take him for all in all,
    I shall not look upon his like again.

Horatio. My lord, I think I saw him yesternight.

190 *Hamlet.* Saw? Who?

Horatio. My lord, the King your father.

Hamlet.   The King my father?

Horatio. Season your admiration° for a while
    With an attent ear till I may deliver
    Upon the witness of these gentlemen

172 *truster* believer   182 *dearest* most intensely felt   186 *'A* he
192 *Season your admiration* control your wonder

    This marvel to you.

Hamlet.   For God's love let me hear!   *195*

Horatio. Two nights together had these gentlemen,
    Marcellus and Barnardo, on their watch
    In the dead waste and middle of the night
    Been thus encountered. A figure like your father,
    Armèd at point exactly, cap-a-pe,°   *200*
    Appears before them, and with solemn march
    Goes slow and stately by them. Thrice he walked
    By their oppressed and fear-surprisèd eyes,
    Within his truncheon's length,° whilst they, distilled°
    Almost to jelly with the act° of fear,   *205*
    Stand dumb and speak not to him. This to me
    In dreadful° secrecy impart they did,
    And I with them the third night kept the watch,
    Where, as they had delivered, both in time,
    Form of the thing, each word made true and good,   *210*
    The apparition comes. I knew your father.
    These hands are not more like.

Hamlet.   But where was this?

Marcellus. My lord, upon the platform where we
    watched.

Hamlet. Did you not speak to it?

Horatio.   My lord, I did;
    But answer made it none. Yet once methought   *215*
    It lifted up it° head and did address
    Itself to motion like as it would speak:
    But even then the morning cock crew loud,
    And at the sound it shrunk in haste away
    And vanished from our sight.

Hamlet.   'Tis very strange.   *220*

Horatio. As I do live, my honored lord, 'tis true,
    And we did think it writ down in our duty
    To let you know of it.

---

200 *cap-a-pe* head to foot   204 *truncheon's length* space of a short
staff   204 *distilled* reduced   205 *act* action   207 *dreadful* terrified
216 *it* its

Hamlet. Indeed, indeed, sirs, but this troubles me.
  Hold you the watch tonight?

225 *All.*   We do, my lord.

Hamlet. Armed, say you?

All. Armed, my lord.

Hamlet. From top to toe?

All.   My lord, from head to foot.

Hamlet. Then saw you not his face.

230 *Horatio.* O, yes, my lord. He wore his beaver° up.

Hamlet. What, looked he frowningly?

Horatio. A countenance more in sorrow than in anger.

Hamlet. Pale or red?

Horatio. Nay, very pale.

Hamlet.   And fixed his eyes upon you?

Horatio. Most constantly.

235 *Hamlet.*   I would I had been there.

Horatio. It would have much amazed you.

Hamlet. Very like, very like. Stayed it long?

Horatio. While one with moderate haste might tell° a
  hundred.

Both. Longer, longer.

Horatio. Not when I saw't.

240 *Hamlet.*   His beard was grizzled,° no?

Horatio. It was as I have seen it in his life,
  A sable silvered.°

Hamlet.   I will watch tonight.
  Perchance 'twill walk again.

Horatio.   I warr'nt it will.

Hamlet. If it assume my noble father's person,

230 *beaver* visor, face guard 238 *tell* count 240 *grizzled* gray
242 *sable silvered* black mingled with white

I'll speak to it though hell itself should gape   245
And bid me hold my peace. I pray you all,
If you have hitherto concealed this sight,
Let it be tenable° in your silence still,
And whatsomever else shall hap tonight,
Give it an understanding but no tongue;   250
I will requite your loves. So fare you well.
Upon the platform 'twixt eleven and twelve
I'll visit you.

All.   Our duty to your honor.

Hamlet. Your loves, as mine to you. Farewell.
                              Exeunt [all but Hamlet].
My father's spirit—in arms? All is not well.   255
I doubt° some foul play. Would the night were come!
Till then sit still, my soul. Foul deeds will rise,
Though all the earth o'erwhelm them, to men's eyes.
                                        Exit.

[Scene III. *A room.*]

Enter Laertes and Ophelia, his sister.

Laertes. My necessaries are embarked. Farewell.
And, sister, as the winds give benefit
And convoy° is assistant, do not sleep,
But let me hear from you.

Ophelia.   Do you doubt that?

Laertes. For Hamlet, and the trifling of his favor,   5
Hold it a fashion and a toy° in blood,
A violet in the youth of primy° nature,
Forward,° not permanent, sweet, not lasting,
The perfume and suppliance° of a minute,

248 *tenable* held   256 *doubt* suspect   I.iii.3 *convoy* conveyance
6 *toy* idle fancy   7 *primy* springlike   8 *Forward* premature   9 *suppliance* diversion

No more.

Ophelia. No more but so?

10 *Laertes.* Think it no more.
For nature crescent° does not grow alone
In thews° and bulk, but as this temple° waxes,
The inward service of the mind and soul
Grows wide withal. Perhaps he loves you now,
15 And now no soil nor cautel° doth besmirch
The virtue of his will; but you must fear,
His greatness weighed,° his will is not his own.
For he himself is subject to his birth.
He may not, as unvalued° persons do,
20 Carve for himself; for on his choice depends
The safety and health of this whole state;
And therefore must his choice be circumscribed
Unto the voice and yielding of that body
Whereof he is the head. Then if he says he loves you,
25 It fits your wisdom so far to believe it
As he in his particular act and place
May give his saying deed, which is no further
Than the main voice of Denmark goes withal.
Then weigh what loss your honor may sustain
30 If with too credent° ear you list his songs,
Or lose your heart, or your chaste treasure open
To his unmastered importunity.
Fear it, Ophelia, fear it, my dear sister,
And keep you in the rear of your affection,
35 Out of the shot and danger of desire.
The chariest maid is prodigal enough
If she unmask her beauty to the moon.
Virtue itself scapes not calumnious strokes.
The canker° galls the infants of the spring
40 Too oft before their buttons° be disclosed,
And in the morn and liquid dew of youth
Contagious blastments are most imminent.

11 *crescent* growing 12 *thews* muscles and sinews 12 *temple* i.e.,
the body 15 *cautel* deceit 17 *greatness weighed* high rank considered 19 *unvalued* of low rank 30 *credent* credulous 39 *can-
ker* cankerworm 40 *buttons* buds

Be wary then; best safety lies in fear;
Youth to itself rebels, though none else near.

Ophelia. I shall the effect of this good lesson keep   45
As watchman to my heart, but, good my brother,
Do not, as some ungracious° pastors do,
Show me the steep and thorny way to heaven,
Whiles, like a puffed and reckless libertine,
Himself the primrose path of dalliance treads   50
And recks not his own rede.°

Enter Polonius.

Laertes.   O, fear me not.
I stay too long. But here my father comes.
A double blessing is a double grace;
Occasion smiles upon a second leave.

Polonius. Yet here, Laertes? Aboard, aboard, for
    shame!   55
The wind sits in the shoulder of your sail,
And you are stayed for. There—my blessing with
    thee;
And these few precepts in thy memory
Look thou character.° Give thy thoughts no tongue,
Nor any unproportioned° thought his act.   60
Be thou familiar, but by no means vulgar.
Those friends thou hast, and their adoption tried,
Grapple them unto thy soul with hoops of steel,
But do not dull thy palm with entertainment
Of each new-hatched, unfledged courage.° Beware   65
Of entrance to a quarrel; but being in,
Bear't that th' opposèd may beware of thee.
Give every man thine ear, but few thy voice;
Take each man's censure,° but reserve thy judgment.
Costly thy habit as thy purse can buy,   70
But not expressed in fancy; rich, not gaudy,
For the apparel oft proclaims the man,
And they in France of the best rank and station

---

47 *ungracious* lacking grace **51** *recks not his own rede* does not
heed his own advice **59** *character* inscribe **60** *unproportioned*
unbalanced **65** *courage* gallant youth **69** *censure* opinion

Are of a most select and generous, chief in that.°
75   Neither a borrower nor a lender be,
For loan oft loses both itself and friend,
And borrowing dulleth edge of husbandry.°
This above all, to thine own self be true,
And it must follow, as the night the day,
80   Thou canst not then be false to any man.
Farewell. My blessing season this° in thee!

Laertes. Most humbly do I take my leave, my lord.

Polonius. The time invites you. Go, your servants
tend.°

Laertes. Farewell, Ophelia, and remember well
What I have said to you.

85   *Ophelia.*   'Tis in my memory locked,
And you yourself shall keep the key of it.

Laertes. Farewell.   *Exit Laertes.*

Polonius. What is't, Ophelia, he hath said to you?

Ophelia. So please you, something touching the Lord
Hamlet.

90   *Polonius.* Marry,° well bethought.
'Tis told me he hath very oft of late
Given private time to you, and you yourself
Have of your audience been most free and bounte-
ous.
If it be so—as so 'tis put on me,
95   And that in way of caution—I must tell you
You do not understand yourself so clearly
As it behooves my daughter and your honor.
What is between you? Give me up the truth.

Ophelia. He hath, my lord, of late made many tenders°
100 Of his affection to me.

---

74 *Are of . . . in that* show their fine taste and their gentlemanly
instincts more in that than in any other point of manners (Kitt-
redge)   77 *husbandry* thrift   81 *season this* make fruitful this (advice)   83 *tend* attend   90 *Marry* (a light oath, from "By the Virgin
Mary")   99 *tenders* offers (in line 103 it has the same meaning,
but in line 106 Polonius speaks of *tenders* in the sense of counters
or chips; in line 109 *Tend'ring* means "holding," and *tender* means
"give," "present")

Polonius. Affection pooh! You speak like a green girl,
  Unsifted° in such perilous circumstance.
  Do you believe his tenders, as you call them?

Ophelia. I do not know, my lord, what I should think.

Polonius. Marry, I will teach you. Think yourself a
    baby   *105*
  That you have ta'en these tenders for true pay
  Which are not sterling. Tender yourself more dearly,
  Or (not to crack the wind of the poor phrase)
  Tend'ring it thus you'll tender me a fool.°

Ophelia. My lord, he hath importuned me with love   *110*
  In honorable fashion.

Polonius. Ay, fashion you may call it. Go to, go to.

Ophelia. And hath given countenance to his speech, my
    lord,
  With almost all the holy vows of heaven.

Polonius. Ay, springes to catch woodcocks.° I do know, *115*
  When the blood burns, how prodigal the soul
  Lends the tongue vows. These blazes, daughter,
  Giving more light than heat, extinct in both,
  Even in their promise, as it is a-making,
  You must not take for fire. From this time   *120*
  Be something scanter of your maiden presence.
  Set your entreatments° at a higher rate
  Than a command to parley. For Lord Hamlet,
  Believe so much in him that he is young,
  And with a larger tether may he walk   *125*
  Than may be given you. In few, Ophelia,
  Do not believe his vows, for they are brokers,°
  Not of that dye° which their investments° show,
  But mere implorators° of unholy suits,
  Breathing like sanctified and pious bonds,°   *130*
  The better to beguile. This is for all:

102 *Unsifted* untried   109 *tender me a fool* (1) present me with a
fool (2) present me with a baby   115 *springes to catch wood-*
cocks snares to catch stupid birds   122 *entreatments* interviews
127 *brokers* procurers   128 *dye* i.e., kind   128 *investments* garments   129 *implorators* solicitors   130 *bonds* pledges

I would not, in plain terms, from this time forth
Have you so slander° any moment leisure
As to give words or talk with the Lord Hamlet.
135   Look to't, I charge you. Come your ways.
Ophelia. I shall obey, my lord.   *Exeunt.*

[Scene IV. *A guard platform.*]

Enter Hamlet, Horatio, and Marcellus.

Hamlet. The air bites shrewdly;° it is very cold.

Horatio. It is a nipping and an eager° air.

Hamlet. What hour now?

Horatio.   I think it lacks of twelve.

Marcellus. No, it is struck.

Horatio. Indeed? I heard it not. It then draws near the
5   season
Wherein the spirit held his wont to walk.
            A flourish of trumpets, and two pieces go off.
What does this mean, my lord?

Hamlet. The King doth wake° tonight and takes his
        rouse,°
Keeps wassail, and the swagg'ring upspring° reels,
10   And as he drains his draughts of Rhenish° down
The kettledrum and trumpet thus bray out
The triumph of his pledge.°

Horatio.   Is it a custom?

133 *slander* disgrace I.iv.1 *shrewdly* bitterly 2 *eager* sharp 8 *wake*
hold a revel by night 8 *takes his rouse* carouses 9 *upspring* (a
dance) 10 *Rhenish* Rhine wine 12 *The triumph of his pledge*
the achievement (of drinking a wine cup in one draught) of his
toast

Hamlet. Ay, marry, is't,
　　But to my mind, though I am native here
　　And to the manner born, it is a custom　　　　　　15
　　More honored in the breach than the observance.
　　This heavy-headed revel east and west
　　Makes us traduced and taxed of° other nations.
　　They clepe° us drunkards and with swinish phrase
　　Soil our addition,° and indeed it takes　　　　　　20
　　From our achievements, though performed at height,
　　The pith and marrow of our attribute.°
　　So oft it chances in particular men
　　That for some vicious mole° of nature in them,
　　As in their birth, wherein they are not guilty,　　　　25
　　(Since nature cannot choose his origin)
　　By the o'ergrowth of some complexion,°
　　Oft breaking down the pales° and forts of reason,
　　Or by some habit that too much o'erleavens°
　　The form of plausive° manners, that (these men,　　30
　　Carrying, I say, the stamp of one defect,
　　Being nature's livery, or fortune's star°)
　　Their virtues else, be they as pure as grace,
　　As infinite as man may undergo,
　　Shall in the general censure° take corruption　　　35
　　From that particular fault. The dram of evil
　　Doth all the noble substance of a doubt,
　　To his own scandal.°

　　　　　　　　　Enter Ghost.

Horatio.　　　　　　Look, my lord, it comes.

Hamlet. Angels and ministers of grace defend us!
　　Be thou a spirit of health° or goblin damned,　　40
　　Bring with thee airs from heaven or blasts from hell,
　　Be thy intents wicked or charitable,

18 *taxed of* blamed by　19 *clepe* call　20 *addition* reputation (literally, "title of honor")　22 *attribute* reputation　24 *mole* blemish　27 *complexion* natural disposition　28 *pales* enclosures　29 *o'erleavens* mixes with, corrupts　30 *plausive* pleasing　32 *nature's livery, or fortune's star* nature's equipment (i.e., "innate"), or a person's destiny determined by the stars　35 *general censure* popular judgment　36–38 *The dram . . . own scandal* (though the drift is clear, there is no agreement as to the exact meaning of these lines)　40 *spirit of health* good spirit

Thou com'st in such a questionable° shape
That I will speak to thee. I'll call thee Hamlet,
45   King, father, royal Dane. O, answer me!
Let me not burst in ignorance, but tell
Why thy canonized° bones, hearsèd in death,
Have burst their cerements,° why the sepulcher
Wherein we saw thee quietly interred
50   Hath oped his ponderous and marble jaws
To cast thee up again. What may this mean
That thou, dead corse, again in complete steel,
Revisits thus the glimpses of the moon,
Making night hideous, and we fools of nature
55   So horridly to shake our disposition°
With thoughts beyond the reaches of our souls?
Say, why is this? Wherefore? What should we do?
                        Ghost beckons Hamlet.

Horatio. It beckons you to go away with it,
As if it some impartment° did desire
To you alone.

60   *Marcellus.*   Look with what courteous action
It waves you to a more removèd ground.
But do not go with it.

Horatio.   No, by no means.

Hamlet. It will not speak. Then I will follow it.

Horatio. Do not, my lord.

Hamlet.   Why, what should be the fear?
65   I do not set my life at a pin's fee,
And for my soul, what can it do to that,
Being a thing immortal as itself?
It waves me forth again. I'll follow it.

Horatio. What if it tempt you toward the flood, my
        lord,
70   Or to the dreadful summit of the cliff

43 *questionable* (1) capable of discourse (2) dubious 47 *canon-*
ized buried according to the canon or ordinance of the church
48 *cerements* waxed linen shroud 55 *shake our disposition* disturb
us 59 *impartment* communication

That beetles° o'er his base into the sea,
And there assume some other horrible form,
Which might deprive your sovereignty of reason°
And draw you into madness? Think of it.
The very place puts toys° of desperation,   75
Without more motive, into every brain
That looks so many fathoms to the sea
And hears it roar beneath.

Hamlet.   It waves me still.
Go on; I'll follow thee.

Marcellus. You shall not go, my lord.

Hamlet.   Hold off your hands.   80

Horatio. Be ruled. You shall not go.

Hamlet.   My fate cries out
And makes each petty artere° in this body
As hardy as the Nemean lion's nerve.°
Still am I called! Unhand me, gentlemen.
By heaven, I'll make a ghost of him that lets° me!   85
I say, away! Go on. I'll follow thee.

                              Exit Ghost, and Hamlet.

Horatio. He waxes desperate with imagination.

Marcellus. Let's follow. 'Tis not fit thus to obey him.

Horatio. Have after! To what issue will this come?

Marcellus. Something is rotten in the state of Denmark.   90

Horatio. Heaven will direct it.

Marcellus.   Nay, let's follow him.   *Exeunt.*

---

71 *beetles* juts out   73 *deprive your sovereignty of reason* destroy
the sovereignty of your reason   75 *toys* whims, fancies   82 *artere*
artery   83 *Nemean lion's nerve* sinews of the mythical lion slain
by Hercules   85 *lets* hinders

[Scene V. *The battlements.*]

Enter Ghost and Hamlet.

Hamlet. Whither wilt thou lead me? Speak; I'll go no
    further.

Ghost. Mark me.

Hamlet.   I will.

Ghost.   My hour is almost come,
    When I to sulf'rous and tormenting flames
    Must render up myself.

Hamlet.   Alas, poor ghost.

5 *Ghost.* Pity me not, but lend thy serious hearing
    To what I shall unfold.

Hamlet.   Speak. I am bound to hear.

Ghost. So art thou to revenge, when thou shalt hear.

Hamlet. What?

Ghost. I am thy father's spirit,
10   Doomed for a certain term to walk the night,
    And for the day confined to fast in fires,
    Till the foul crimes° done in my days of nature
    Are burnt and purged away. But that I am forbid
    To tell the secrets of my prison house,
15   I could a tale unfold whose lightest word
    Would harrow up thy soul, freeze thy young blood,
    Make thy two eyes like stars start from their
        spheres,°
    Thy knotted and combinèd locks to part,
    And each particular hair to stand an end

I.v.12 *crimes* sins   17 *spheres* (in Ptolemaic astronomy, each planet
was fixed in a hollow transparent shell concentric with the earth)

Like quills upon the fearful porpentine.°   20
But this eternal blazon° must not be
To ears of flesh and blood. List, list, O, list!
If thou didst ever thy dear father love——

Hamlet. O God!

Ghost. Revenge his foul and most unnatural murder.   25

Hamlet. Murder?

Ghost. Murder most foul, as in the best it is,
But this most foul, strange, and unnatural.

Hamlet. Haste me to know't, that I, with wings as swift
As meditation° or the thoughts of love,   30
May sweep to my revenge.

Ghost.   I find thee apt,
And duller shouldst thou be than the fat weed
That roots itself in ease on Lethe wharf,°
Wouldst thou not stir in this. Now, Hamlet, hear.
'Tis given out that, sleeping in my orchard,   35
A serpent stung me. So the whole ear of Denmark
Is by a forgèd process° of my death
Rankly abused. But know, thou noble youth,
The serpent that did sting thy father's life
Now wears his crown.

Hamlet.   O my prophetic soul!   40
My uncle?

Ghost. Ay, that incestuous, that adulterate° beast,
With witchcraft of his wits, with traitorous gifts—
O wicked wit and gifts, that have the power
So to seduce!—won to his shameful lust   45
The will of my most seeming-virtuous queen.
O Hamlet, what a falling-off was there,
From me, whose love was of that dignity
That it went hand in hand even with the vow
I made to her in marriage, and to decline   50

20 *fearful porpentine* timid porcupine 21 *eternal blazon* revelation
of eternity 30 *meditation* thought 33 *Lethe wharf* bank of the
river of forgetfulness in Hades 37 *forgèd process* false account
42 *adulterate* adulterous

Upon a wretch whose natural gifts were poor
To those of mine.
But virtue, as it never will be moved,
Though lewdness° court it in a shape of heaven,
55   So lust, though to a radiant angel linked,
Will sate itself in a celestial bed
And prey on garbage.
But soft, methinks I scent the morning air;
Brief let me be. Sleeping within my orchard,
60   My custom always of the afternoon,
Upon my secure° hour thy uncle stole
With juice of cursed hebona° in a vial,
And in the porches of my ears did pour
The leperous distillment, whose effect
65   Holds such an enmity with blood of man
That swift as quicksilver it courses through
The natural gates and alleys of the body,
And with a sudden vigor it doth posset°
And curd, like eager° droppings into milk,
70   The thin and wholesome blood. So did it mine,
And a most instant tetter° barked about
Most lazarlike° with vile and loathsome crust
All my smooth body.
Thus was I, sleeping, by a brother's hand
75   Of life, of crown, of queen at once dispatched,
Cut off even in the blossoms of my sin,
Unhouseled, disappointed, unaneled,°
No reck'ning made, but sent to my account
With all my imperfections on my head.
80   O, horrible! O, horrible! Most horrible!
If thou hast nature in thee, bear it not.
Let not the royal bed of Denmark be
A couch for luxury° and damnèd incest.
But howsomever thou pursues this act,
85   Taint not thy mind, nor let thy soul contrive

54 *lewdness* lust   61 *secure* unsuspecting   62 *hebona* a poisonous
plant   68 *posset* curdle   69 *eager* acid   71 *tetter* scab   72 *lazar-
like* leperlike   77 *Unhouseled, disappointed, unaneled* without the
sacrament of communion, unabsolved, without extreme unction
83 *luxury* lust

    Against thy mother aught. Leave her to heaven
    And to those thorns that in her bosom lodge
    To prick and sting her. Fare thee well at once.
    The glowworm shows the matin° to be near
    And 'gins to pale his uneffectual fire.   *90*
    Adieu, adieu, adieu. Remember me.   *Exit.*

Hamlet. O all you host of heaven! O earth! What else?
    And shall I couple hell? O fie! Hold, hold, my heart,
    And you, my sinews, grow not instant old,
    But bear me stiffly up. Remember thee?   *95*
    Ay, thou poor ghost, whiles memory holds a seat
    In this distracted globe.° Remember thee?
    Yea, from the table° of my memory
    I'll wipe away all trivial fond° records,
    All saws° of books, all forms, all pressures° past   *100*
    That youth and observation copied there,
    And thy commandment all alone shall live
    Within the book and volume of my brain,
    Unmixed with baser matter. Yes, by heaven!
    O most pernicious woman!   *105*
    O villain, villain, smiling, damnèd villain!
    My tables—meet it is I set it down
    That one may smile, and smile, and be a villain.
    At least I am sure it may be so in Denmark. [*Writes.*]
    So, uncle, there you are. Now to my word: *110*
    It is "Adieu, adieu, remember me."
    I have sworn't.

Horatio and Marcellus. (*Within*) My lord, my lord!

        Enter Horatio and Marcellus.

Marcellus.   Lord Hamlet!

Horatio.   Heavens secure him!

Hamlet. So be it!

Marcellus. Illo, ho, ho,° my lord!   *115*

Hamlet. Hillo, ho, ho, boy! Come, bird, come.

---

89 *matin* morning 97 *globe* i.e., his head 98 *table* tablet, note-
book 99 *fond* foolish 100 *saws* maxims 100 *pressures* impres-
sions 115 *Illo, ho, ho* (falconer's call to his hawk)

Marcellus. How is't, my noble lord?

Horatio. What news, my lord?

Hamlet. O, wonderful!

Horatio. Good my lord, tell it.

Hamlet. No, you will reveal it.

Horatio. Not I, my lord, by heaven.

120 *Marcellus.* Nor I, my lord.

Hamlet. How say you then? Would heart of man once
　　think it?
　　But you'll be secret?

Both. Ay, by heaven, my lord.

Hamlet. There's never a villain dwelling in all Denmark
　　But he's an arrant knave.

Horatio. There needs no ghost, my lord, come from the
125　　grave
　　To tell us this.

Hamlet. Why, right, you are in the right;
　　And so, without more circumstance° at all,
　　I hold it fit that we shake hands and part:
　　You, as your business and desire shall point you,
130　　For every man hath business and desire
　　Such as it is, and for my own poor part,
　　Look you, I'll go pray.

Horatio. These are but wild and whirling words, my
　　lord.

Hamlet. I am sorry they offend you, heartily;
　　Yes, faith, heartily.

135 *Horatio.* There's no offense, my lord.

Hamlet. Yes, by Saint Patrick, but there is, Horatio,
　　And much offense too. Touching this vision here,
　　It is an honest ghost,° that let me tell you.
　　For your desire to know what is between us,
140　　O'ermaster't as you may. And now, good friends,

127 *circumstance* details　138 *honest ghost* i.e., not a demon in
his father's shape

As you are friends, scholars, and soldiers,
Give me one poor request.

Horatio. What is't, my lord? We will.

Hamlet. Never make known what you have seen tonight.

Both. My lord, we will not.

Hamlet.   Nay, but swear't.

Horatio.   In faith,   *145*
My lord, not I.

Marcellus.   Nor I, my lord—in faith.

Hamlet. Upon my sword.

Marcellus.   We have sworn, my lord, already.

Hamlet. Indeed, upon my sword, indeed.
                    Ghost cries under the stage.

Ghost. Swear.

Hamlet. Ha, ha, boy, say'st thou so? Art thou there,
truepenny?°   *150*
Come on. You hear this fellow in the cellarage.
Consent to swear.

Horatio.   Propose the oath, my lord.

Hamlet. Never to speak of this that you have seen.
Swear by my sword.

Ghost. [*Beneath*] Swear.   *155*

Hamlet. Hic et ubique?° Then we'll shift our ground;
Come hither, gentlemen,
And lay your hands again upon my sword.
Swear by my sword
Never to speak of this that you have heard.   *160*

Ghost. [*Beneath*] Swear by his sword.

Hamlet. Well said, old mole! Canst work i' th' earth so
fast?
A worthy pioner!° Once more remove, good friends.

150 *truepenny* honest fellow 156 *Hic et ubique* here and every-
where (Latin) 163 *pioner* digger of mines

Horatio. O day and night, but this is wondrous strange!

165 *Hamlet.* And therefore as a stranger give it welcome.
There are more things in heaven and earth, Horatio,
Than are dreamt of in your philosophy.
But come:
Here as before, never, so help you mercy,
170 How strange or odd some'er I bear myself
(As I perchance hereafter shall think meet
To put an antic disposition° on),
That you, at such times seeing me, never shall
With arms encumb'red° thus, or this headshake,
175 Or by pronouncing of some doubtful phrase,
As "Well, well, we know," or "We could, an if we
would,"
Or "If we list to speak," or "There be, an if they
might,"
Or such ambiguous giving out, to note
That you know aught of me—this do swear,
180 So grace and mercy at your most need help you.

Ghost. [*Beneath*] Swear.   [*They swear.*]

Hamlet. Rest, rest, perturbèd spirit. So, gentlemen,
With all my love I do commend me° to you,
And what so poor a man as Hamlet is
185 May do t' express his love and friending to you,
God willing, shall not lack. Let us go in together,
And still your fingers on your lips, I pray.
The time is out of joint. O cursèd spite,
That ever I was born to set it right!
190 Nay, come, let's go together.   *Exeunt.*

172 *antic disposition* fantastic behavior 174 *encumb'red* folded
183 *commend me* entrust myself

[ACT II

Scene I. *A room.*]

Enter old Polonius, with his man Reynaldo.

Polonius. Give him this money and these notes, Reynaldo.

Reynaldo. I will, my lord.

Polonius. You shall do marvell's° wisely, good Rey-
naldo,
Before you visit him, to make inquire
Of his behavior.

Reynaldo.   My lord, I did intend it.   5

Polonius. Marry, well said, very well said. Look you
sir,
Inquire me first what Danskers° are in Paris,
And how, and who, what means, and where they
keep,°
What company, at what expense; and finding
By this encompassment° and drift of question   10
That they do know my son, come you more nearer
Than your particular demands° will touch it.
Take you as 'twere some distant knowledge of him,
As thus, "I know his father and his friends,
And in part him." Do you mark this, Reynaldo?   15

Reynaldo. Ay, very well, my lord.

II.i.3 *marvell's* marvelous(ly) 7 *Danskers* Danes 8 *keep* dwell
10 *encompassment* circling 12 *demands* questions

Polonius. "And in part him, but," you may say, "not
   well,
   But if't be he I mean, he's very wild,
   Addicted so and so." And there put on him
20 What forgeries° you please; marry, none so rank
   As may dishonor him—take heed of that—
   But, sir, such wanton, wild, and usual slips
   As are companions noted and most known
   To youth and liberty.

Reynaldo.   As gaming, my lord.

Polonius. Ay, or drinking, fencing, swearing, quarrel-
25   ing,
   Drabbing.° You may go so far.

Reynaldo. My lord, that would dishonor him.

Polonius. Faith, no, as you may season it in the charge.
   You must not put another scandal on him,
30 That he is open to incontinency.°
   That's not my meaning. But breathe his faults so
      quaintly°
   That they may seem the taints of liberty,
   The flash and outbreak of a fiery mind,
   A savageness in unreclaimèd blood,
   Of general assault.°

35 *Reynaldo.*   But, my good lord——

Polonius. Wherefore should you do this?

Reynaldo.   Ay, my lord,
   I would know that.

Polonius.   Marry, sir, here's my drift,
   And I believe it is a fetch of warrant.°
   You laying these slight sullies on my son
40 As 'twere a thing a little soiled i' th' working,
   Mark you,
   Your party in converse, him you would sound,

20 *forgeries* inventions 26 *Drabbing* wenching 30 *incontinency*
habitual licentiousness 31 *quaintly* ingeniously, delicately 35 *Of
general assault* common to all men 38 *fetch of warrant* justifiable
device

Having ever seen in the prenominate crimes°
The youth you breathe of guilty, be assured
He closes with you in this consequence:°   *45*
"Good sir," or so, or "friend," or "gentleman"—
According to the phrase or the addition°
Of man and country—

Reynaldo.   Very good, my lord.

Polonius. And then, sir, does 'a° this—'a does—
What was I about to say? By the mass, I was about   *50*
to say something! Where did I leave?

Reynaldo. At "closes in the consequence," at "friend
or so," and "gentleman."

Polonius. At "closes in the consequence"—Ay, marry!
He closes thus: "I know the gentleman;   *55*
I saw him yesterday, or t'other day,
Or then, or then, with such or such, and, as you say,
There was 'a gaming, there o'ertook in's rouse,
There falling out at tennis"; or perchance,
"I saw him enter such a house of sale,"   *60*
Videlicet,° a brothel, or so forth.
See you now—
Your bait of falsehood take this carp of truth,
And thus do we of wisdom and of reach,°
With windlasses° and with assays of bias,°   *65*
By indirections find directions out.
So, by my former lecture and advice,
Shall you my son. You have me, have you not?

Reynaldo. My lord, I have.

Polonius.   God bye ye, fare ye well.

Reynaldo. Good my lord.   *70*

Polonius. Observe his inclination in yourself.°

43 *Having . . . crimes* if he has ever seen in the aforementioned
crimes 45 *He closes . . . this consequence* he falls in with you in
this conclusion 47 *addition* title 49 *'a* he 61 *Videlicet* namely
64 *reach* far-reaching awareness(?) 65 *windlasses* circuitous
courses 65 *assays of bias* indirect attempts (metaphor from bowl-
ing; *bias* = curved course) 71 *in yourself* for yourself

Reynaldo. I shall, my lord.

Polonius. And let him ply his music.

Reynaldo.   Well, my lord.

Polonius. Farewell.   *Exit Reynaldo*.

Enter Ophelia.

                    How now, Ophelia, what's the matter?

75 *Ophelia*. O my lord, my lord, I have been so affrighted!

Polonius. With what, i' th' name of God?

Ophelia. My lord, as I was sewing in my closet,°
Lord Hamlet, with his doublet all unbraced,°
No hat upon his head, his stockings fouled,
80 Ungartered, and down-gyvèd° to his ankle,
Pale as his shirt, his knees knocking each other,
And with a look so piteous in purport,°
As if he had been loosèd out of hell
To speak of horrors—he comes before me.

Polonius. Mad for thy love?

85 *Ophelia*.   My lord, I do not know,
But truly I do fear it.

Polonius.   What said he?

Ophelia. He took me by the wrist and held me hard;
Then goes he to the length of all his arm,
And with his other hand thus o'er his brow
90 He falls to such perusal of my face
As 'a would draw it. Long stayed he so.
At last, a little shaking of mine arm,
And thrice his head thus waving up and down,
He raised a sigh so piteous and profound
95 As it did seem to shatter all his bulk
And end his being. That done, he lets me go,
And, with his head over his shoulder turned,
He seemed to find his way without his eyes,

77 *closet* private room 78 *doublet all unbraced* jacket entirely
unlaced 80 *down-gyvèd* hanging down like fetters 82 *purport*
expression

For out o' doors he went without their helps,
And to the last bended their light on me.   *100*

Polonius. Come, go with me. I will go seek the King.
This is the very ecstasy° of love,
Whose violent property fordoes° itself
And leads the will to desperate undertakings
As oft as any passions under heaven   *105*
That does afflict our natures. I am sorry.
What, have you given him any hard words of late?

Ophelia. No, my good lord; but as you did command,
I did repel his letters and denied
His access to me.

Polonius.   That hath made him made.   *110*
I am sorry that with better heed and judgment
I had not quoted° him. I feared he did but trifle
And meant to wrack thee; but beshrew my jealousy.°
By heaven, it is as proper° to our age
To cast beyond ourselves° in our opinions   *115*
As it is common for the younger sort
To lack discretion. Come, go we to the King.
This must be known, which, being kept close, might
    move
More grief to hide than hate to utter love.°
Come.   *Exeunt.* *120*

---

102 *ecstasy* madness   103 *property fordoes* quality destroys
112 *quoted* noted   113 *beshrew my jealousy* curse on my suspicions
114 *proper* natural   115 *To cast beyond ourselves* to be over-
calculating   117–19 *Come, go . . . utter love* (the general meaning is that while telling the King of Hamlet's love may anger the
King, more grief would come from keeping it secret)

[Scene II. *The castle*.]

Flourish. Enter King and Queen, Rosencrantz, and
Guildenstern [with others].

  King. Welcome, dear Rosencrantz and Guildenstern.
    Moreover that° we much did long to see you,
    The need we have to use you did provoke
    Our hasty sending. Something have you heard
5   Of Hamlet's transformation: so call it,
    Sith° nor th' exterior nor the inward man
    Resembles that it was. What it should be,
    More than his father's death, that thus hath put him
    So much from th' understanding of himself,
10   I cannot dream of. I entreat you both
    That, being of so° young days brought up with him,
    And sith so neighbored to his youth and havior,°
    That you vouchsafe your rest° here in our court
    Some little time, so by your companies
15   To draw him on to pleasures, and to gather
    So much as from occasion you may glean,
    Whether aught to us unknown afflicts him thus,
    That opened° lies within our remedy.

  Queen. Good gentlemen, he hath much talked of you,
20   And sure I am, two men there is not living
    To whom he more adheres. If it will please you
    To show us so much gentry° and good will
    As to expend your time with us awhile
    For the supply and profit of our hope,
25   Your visitation shall receive such thanks
    As fits a king's remembrance.

Rosencrantz.   Both your Majesties

II.ii.2 *Moreover that* beside the fact that 6 *Sith* since 11 *of so*
from such 12 *youth and havior* behavior in his youth 13 *vouch-*
safe your rest consent to remain 18 *opened* revealed 22 *gentry*
courtesy

Might, by the sovereign power you have of us,
Put your dread pleasures more into command
Than to entreaty.

Guildenstern.   But we both obey,
And here give up ourselves in the full bent°   30
To lay our service freely at your feet,
To be commanded.

King. Thanks, Rosencrantz and gentle Guildenstern.

Queen. Thanks, Guildenstern and gentle Rosencrantz.
And I beseech you instantly to visit   35
My too much changèd son. Go, some of you,
And bring these gentlemen where Hamlet is.

Guildenstern. Heavens make our presence and our
    practices
Pleasant and helpful to him!

Queen.   Ay, amen!
        *Exeunt Rosencrantz and Guildenstern [with some
                                    Attendants].*

            Enter Polonius.

Polonius. Th' ambassadors from Norway, my good
    lord,
Are joyfully returned.   40

King. Thou still° hast been the father of good news.

Polonius. Have I, my lord? Assure you, my good liege,
I hold my duty, as I hold my soul,
Both to my God and to my gracious king;   45
And I do think, or else this brain of mine
Hunts not the trail of policy so sure°
As it hath used to do, that I have found
The very cause of Hamlet's lunacy.

King. O, speak of that! That do I long to hear.   50

Polonius. Give first admittance to th' ambassadors.
My news shall be the fruit to that great feast.

30 *in the full bent* entirely (the figure is of a bow bent to its
capacity)   42 *still* always   47 *Hunts not . . . so sure* does not
follow clues of political doings with such sureness

King. Thyself do grace to them and bring them in.
[*Exit Polonius.*]
He tells me, my dear Gertrude, he hath found
55 The head and source of all your son's distemper.

Queen. I doubt° it is no other but the main,°
His father's death and our o'erhasty marriage.

King. Well, we shall sift him.

Enter Polonius, Voltemand, and Cornelius.

Welcome, my good friends.
Say, Voltemand, what from our brother Norway?

60 *Voltemand.* Most fair return of greetings and desires.
Upon our first,° he sent out to suppress
His nephew's levies, which to him appeared
To be a preparation 'gainst the Polack;
But better looked into, he truly found
65 It was against your Highness, whereat grieved,
That so his sickness, age, and impotence
Was falsely borne in hand,° sends out arrests
On Fortinbras; which he, in brief, obeys,
Receives rebuke from Norway, and in fine,°
70 Makes vow before his uncle never more
To give th' assay° of arms against your Majesty.
Whereon old Norway, overcome with joy,
Gives him threescore thousand crowns in annual fee
And his commission to employ those soldiers,
75 So levied as before, against the Polack,
With an entreaty, herein further shown,
[*Gives a paper.*]
That it might please you to give quiet pass
Through your dominions for this enterprise,
On such regards of safety and allowance°
As therein are set down.

80 *King.*   It likes us well;
And at our more considered time° we'll read,
Answer, and think upon this business.

56 *doubt* suspect 56 *main* principal point 61 *first* first audience
67 *borne in hand* deceived 69 *in fine* finally 71 *assay* trial 79 *regards of safety and allowance* i.e., conditions 81 *considered time* time proper for considering

Meantime, we thank you for your well-took labor.
Go to your rest; at night we'll feast together.
Most welcome home!   *Exeunt Ambassadors.*

Polonius.   This business is well ended.   85
My liege and madam, to expostulate°
What majesty should be, what duty is,
Why day is day, night night, and time is time,
Were nothing but to waste night, day, and time.
Therefore, since brevity is the soul of wit,°   90
And tediousness the limbs and outward flourishes,
I will be brief. Your noble son is mad.
Mad call I it, for, to define true madness,
What is't but to be nothing else but mad?
But let that go.

Queen.   More matter, with less art.   95

Polonius. Madam, I swear I use no art at all.
That he's mad, 'tis true: 'tis true 'tis pity,
And pity 'tis 'tis true—a foolish figure.°
But farewell it, for I will use no art.
Mad let us grant him then; and now remains   100
That we find out the cause of this effect,
Or rather say, the cause of this defect,
For this effect defective comes by cause.
Thus it remains, and the remainder thus.
Perpend.°   105
I have a daughter: have, while she is mine,
Who in her duty and obedience, mark,
Hath given me this. Now gather, and surmise.
                    [*Reads*] *the letter.*
"To the celestial, and my soul's idol, the most
beautified Ophelia"—   110
That's an ill phrase, a vile phrase; "beautified" is a
vile phrase. But you shall hear. Thus:
"In her excellent white bosom, these, &c."

Queen. Came this from Hamlet to her?

Polonius. Good madam, stay awhile. I will be faithful.   115
          "Doubt thou the stars are fire,

---

86 *expostulate* discuss 90 *wit* wisdom, understanding 98 *figure*
figure of rhetoric 105 *Perpend* consider carefully

Doubt that the sun doth move;
Doubt° truth to be a liar,
But never doubt I love.

120   O dear Ophelia, I am ill at these numbers.° I have
not art to reckon my groans; but that I love thee
best, O most best, believe it. Adieu.

     Thine evermore, most dear lady, whilst this
machine° is to him, HAMLET."

125 This in obedience hath my daughter shown me,
And more above° hath his solicitings,
As they fell out by time, by means, and place,
All given to mine ear.

King.   But how hath she
Received his love?

Polonius.   What do you think of me?

130 *King.* As of a man faithful and honorable.

Polonius. I would fain prove so. But what might you
think,
When I had seen this hot love on the wing
(As I perceived it, I must tell you that,
Before my daughter told me), what might you,
135 Or my dear Majesty your Queen here, think,
If I had played the desk or table book,°
Or given my heart a winking,° mute and dumb,
Or looked upon this love with idle sight?
What might you think? No, I went round to work
140 And my young mistress thus I did bespeak:
"Lord Hamlet is a prince, out of thy star.°
This must not be." And then I prescripts gave her,
That she should lock herself from his resort,
Admit no messengers, receive no tokens.
145 Which done, she took the fruits of my advice,
And he, repellèd, a short tale to make,

118 *Doubt* suspect   120 *ill at these numbers* unskilled in verses
124 *machine* complex device (here, his body)   126 *more above* in
addition   136 *played the desk or table book* i.e., been a passive
recipient of secrets   137 *winking* closing of the eyes   141 *star*
sphere

Fell into a sadness, then into a fast,
Thence to a watch,° thence into a weakness,
Thence to a lightness,° and, by this declension,
Into the madness wherein now he raves,   150
And all we mourn for.

King.   Do you think 'tis this?

Queen. It may be, very like.

Polonius. Hath there been such a time, I would fain
    know that,
    That I have positively said " 'Tis so,"
    When it proved otherwise?

King.   Not that I know.   155

Polonius. [*Pointing to his head and shoulder*] Take
    this from this, if this be otherwise.
    If circumstances lead me, I will find
    Where truth is hid, though it were hid indeed
    Within the center.°

King.   How may we try it further?

Polonius. You know sometimes he walks four hours
    together   160
    Here in the lobby.

Queen.   So he does indeed.

Polonius. At such a time I'll loose my daughter to him.
    Be you and I behind an arras° then.
    Mark the encounter. If he love her not,
    And be not from his reason fall'n thereon,   165
    Let me be no assistant for a state
    But keep a farm and carters.

King.   We will try it.

                Enter Hamlet reading on a book.

Queen. But look where sadly the poor wretch comes
    reading.

Polonius. Away, I do beseech you both, away.

                          Exit King and Queen.

148 *watch* wakefulness   149 *lightness* mental   derangement
159 *center* center of the earth   163 *arras* tapestry hanging in front
of a wall

170 I'll board him presently.° O, give me leave.
How does my good Lord Hamlet?

Hamlet. Well, God-a-mercy.

Polonius. Do you know me, my lord?

Hamlet. Excellent well. You are a fishmonger.°

175 *Polonius.* Not I, my lord.

Hamlet. Then I would you were so honest a man.

Polonius. Honest, my lord?

Hamlet. Ay, sir. To be honest, as this world goes, is to
be one man picked out of ten thousand.

180 *Polonius.* That's very true, my lord.

Hamlet. For if the sun breed maggots in a dead dog,
being a good kissing carrion°—— Have you a
daughter?

Polonius. I have, my lord.

185 *Hamlet.* Let her not walk i' th' sun. Conception° is a
blessing, but as your daughter may conceive, friend,
look to't.

Polonius. [*Aside*] How say you by that? Still harping
on my daughter. Yet he knew me not at first. 'A said
190 I was a fishmonger. 'A is far gone, far gone. And
truly in my youth I suffered much extremity for
love, very near this. I'll speak to him again.—What
do you read, my lord?

Hamlet. Words, words, words.

195 *Polonius.* What is the matter, my lord?

Hamlet. Between who?

Polonius. I mean the matter° that you read, my lord.

170 *board him presently* accost him at once   174 *fishmonger* dealer
in fish (slang for a procurer)   182 *a good kissing carrion* (perhaps
the meaning is "a good piece of flesh to kiss," but many editors
emend *good* to *god*, taking the word to refer to the sun)   185 *Conception* (1) understanding (2) becoming pregnant   197 *matter*
(Polonius means "subject matter," but Hamlet pretends to take
the word in the sense of "quarrel")

Hamlet. Slanders, sir; for the satirical rogue says here
that old men have gray beards, that their faces are
wrinkled, their eyes purging thick amber and plum- 200
tree gum, and that they have a plentiful lack of wit,
together with most weak hams. All which, sir,
though I most powerfully and potently believe, yet
I hold it not honesty° to have it thus set down; for
you yourself, sir, should be old as I am if, like a 205
crab, you could go backward.

Polonius. [*Aside*] Though this be madness, yet there
is method in't. Will you walk out of the air, my lord?

Hamlet. Into my grave.

Polonius. Indeed, that's out of the air. [*Aside*] How 210
pregnant° sometimes his replies are! A happiness°
that often madness hits on, which reason and sanity
could not so prosperously be delivered of. I will
leave him and suddenly contrive the means of
meeting between him and my daughter.—My lord, 215
I will take my leave of you.

Hamlet. You cannot take from me anything that I will
more willingly part withal—except my life, except
my life, except my life.

　　　　Enter Guildenstern and Rosencrantz.

Polonius. Fare you well, my lord. 220

Hamlet. These tedious old fools!

Polonius. You go to seek the Lord Hamlet? There he
is.

Rosencrantz. [*To Polonius*] God save you, sir!
　　　　　　　　　　　　　　[*Exit Polonius.*]

Guildenstern. My honored lord! 225

Rosencrantz. My most dear lord!

Hamlet. My excellent good friends! How dost thou,
Guildenstern? Ah, Rosencrantz! Good lads, how do
you both?

204 *honesty* decency　211 *pregnant* meaningful　211 *happiness* apt
turn of phrase

230 *Rosencrantz.* As the indifferent° children of the earth.

Guildenstern. Happy in that we are not overhappy.
On Fortune's cap we are not the very button.

Hamlet. Nor the soles of her shoe?

Rosencrantz. Neither, my lord.

235 *Hamlet.* Then you live about her waist, or in the middle
of her favors?

Guildenstern. Faith, her privates° we.

Hamlet. In the secret parts of Fortune? O, most true!
She is a strumpet. What news?

240 *Rosencrantz.* None, my lord, but that the world's
grown honest.

Hamlet. Then is doomsday near. But your news is not
true. Let me question more in particular. What
have you, my good friends, deserved at the hands of
245 Fortune that she sends you to prison hither?

Guildenstern. Prison, my lord?

Hamlet. Denmark's a prison.

Rosencrantz. Then is the world one.

Hamlet. A goodly one, in which there are many
250 confines, wards,° and dungeons, Denmark being
one o' th' worst.

Rosencrantz. We think not so, my lord.

Hamlet. Why, then 'tis none to you, for there is nothing
either good or bad but thinking makes it so. To me
255 it is a prison.

Rosencrantz. Why then your ambition makes it one.
'Tis too narrow for your mind.

Hamlet. O God, I could be bounded in a nutshell and
count myself a king of infinite space, were it not
260 that I have bad dreams.

Guildenstern. Which dreams indeed are ambition, for

230 *indifferent* ordinary   237 *privates* ordinary men (with a pun
on "private parts")   250 *wards* cells

the very substance of the ambitious is merely the
shadow of a dream.

Hamlet. A dream itself is but a shadow.

Rosencrantz. Truly, and I hold ambition of so airy and   265
light a quality that it is but a shadow's shadow.

Hamlet. Then are our beggars bodies, and our
monarchs and outstretched heroes the beggars'
shadows.° Shall we to th' court? For, by my fay,°
I cannot reason.   270

Both. We'll wait upon you.

Hamlet. No such matter. I will not sort you with the
rest of my servants, for, to speak to you like an
honest man, I am most dreadfully attended. But in
the beaten way of friendship, what make you at   275
Elsinore?

Rosencrantz. To visit you, my lord; no other occasion.

Hamlet. Beggar that I am, I am even poor in thanks,
but I thank you; and sure, dear friends, my thanks
are too dear a halfpenny.° Were you not sent for?   280
Is it your own inclining? Is it a free visitation?
Come, come, deal justly with me. Come, come;
nay, speak.

Guildenstern. What should we say, my lord?

Hamlet. Why anything—but to th' purpose. You were   285
sent for, and there is a kind of confession in your
looks, which your modesties have not craft enough
to color. I know the good King and Queen have
sent for you.

Rosencrantz. To what end, my lord?   290

Hamlet. That you must teach me. But let me conjure
you by the rights of our fellowship, by the con-
sonancy of our youth, by the obligation of our ever-

267—69 *Then are . . . beggars' shadows* i.e., by your logic, beggars (lacking ambition) are substantial, and great men are
elongated shadows   269 *fay* faith   280 *too dear a halfpenny* i.e.,
not worth a halfpenny

295   preserved love, and by what more dear a better
        proposer can charge you withal, be even and direct
        with me, whether you were sent for or no.

Rosencrantz. [Aside to Guildenstern] What say you?

Hamlet. [Aside] Nay then, I have an eye of you.—If
        you love me, hold not off.

300 Guildenstern. My lord, we were sent for.

Hamlet. I will tell you why; so shall my anticipation
        prevent your discovery,° and your secrecy to the
        King and Queen molt no feather. I have of late, but
        wherefore I know not, lost all my mirth, forgone all
305   custom of exercises; and indeed, it goes so heavily
        with my disposition that this goodly frame, the
        earth, seems to me a sterile promontory; this most
        excellent canopy, the air, look you, this brave
        o'erhanging firmament, this majestical roof fretted°
310   with golden fire: why, it appeareth nothing to me
        but a foul and pestilent congregation of vapors.
        What a piece of work is a man, how noble in reason,
        how infinite in faculties, in form and moving how
        express° and admirable, in action how like an angel,
315   in apprehension how like a god: the beauty of the
        world, the paragon of animals; and yet to me, what
        is this quintessence of dust? Man delights not me;
        nor woman neither, though by your smiling you
        seem to say so.

320 Rosencrantz. My lord, there was no such stuff in my
        thoughts.

Hamlet. Why did ye laugh then, when I said "Man
        delights not me"?

Rosencrantz. To think, my lord, if you delight not in
325   man, what lenten° entertainment the players shall
        receive from you. We coted° them on the way, and
        hither are they coming to offer you service.

302 prevent your discovery forestall your disclosure 309 fretted
adorned 314 express exact 325 lenten meager 326 coted overtook

Hamlet. He that plays the king shall be welcome; his
  Majesty shall have tribute of me; the adventurous
  knight shall use his foil and target;° the lover shall   330
  not sigh gratis; the humorous man° shall end his
  part in peace; the clown shall make those laugh
  whose lungs are tickle o' th' sere;° and the lady shall
  say her mind freely, or° the blank verse shall halt°
  for't. What players are they?   335

Rosencrantz. Even those you were wont to take such
  delight in, the tragedians of the city.

Hamlet. How chances it they travel? Their residence,
  both in reputation and profit, was better both ways.

Rosencrantz. I think their inhibition° comes by the   340
  means of the late innovation.°

Hamlet. Do they hold the same estimation they did
  when I was in the city? Are they so followed?

Rosencrantz. No indeed, are they not.

Hamlet. How comes it? Do they grow rusty?   345

Rosencrantz. Nay, their endeavor keeps in the wonted
  pace, but there is, sir, an eyrie° of children, little
  eyases, that cry out on the top of question° and are
  most tyrannically° clapped for't. These are now
  the fashion, and so berattle the common stages° (so   350
  they call them) that many wearing rapiers are afraid
  of goosequills° and dare scarce come thither.

Hamlet. What, are they children? Who maintains 'em?
  How are they escoted?° Will they pursue the

330 *target* shield   331 *humorous man* i.e., eccentric man (among
stock characters in dramas were men dominated by a "humor" or
odd trait)   333 *tickle o' th' sere* on hair trigger (*sere* = part of the
gunlock)   334 *or* else   334 *halt* limp   340 *inhibition* hindrance
341 *innovation* (probably an allusion to the companies of child
actors that had become popular and were offering serious compe-
tition to the adult actors)   347 *eyrie* nest   348 *eyases, that . . .
of question* unfledged hawks that cry shrilly above others in matters of debate   349 *tyrannically* violently   350 *berattle the common stages* cry down the public theaters (with the adult acting
companies)   352 *goosequills* pens (of satirists who ridicule the
public theaters and their audiences)   354 *escoted* financially supported

355   quality° no longer than they can sing? Will they not
       say afterwards, if they should grow themselves to
       common players (as it is most like, if their means
       are no better), their writers do them wrong to make
       them exclaim against their own succession?°

360 *Rosencrantz.* Faith, there has been much to-do on
       both sides, and the nation holds it no sin to tarre°
       them to controversy. There was, for a while, no
       money bid for argument° unless the poet and the
       player went to cuffs in the question.

365 *Hamlet.* Is't possible?

    Guildenstern. O, there has been much throwing about
       of brains.

    Hamlet. Do the boys carry it away?

    Rosencrantz. Ay, that they do, my lord—Hercules and
870   his load° too.

    Hamlet. It is not very strange, for my uncle is King of
       Denmark, and those that would make mouths at
       him while my father lived give twenty, forty, fifty,
       a hundred ducats apiece for his picture in little.
875   'Sblood,° there is something in this more than
       natural, if philosophy could find it out.

                                          A flourish.

    Guildenstern. There are the players.

    Hamlet. Gentlemen, you are welcome to Elsinore.
       Your hands, come then. Th' appurtenance of wel-
880   come is fashion and ceremony. Let me comply°
       with you in this garb,° lest my extent° to the players
       (which I tell you must show fairly outwards) should
       more appear like entertainment than yours. You are
       welcome. But my uncle-father and aunt-mother are
885   deceived.

    355 *quality* profession of acting   359 *succession* future   361 *tarre*
    incite   363 *argument* plot of a play   369-70 *Hercules and his load*
    i.e., the whole world (with a reference to the Globe Theatre, which
    had a sign that represented Hercules bearing the globe)   375
    'Sblood by God's blood   380 *comply* be courteous   381 *garb* out-
    ward show   381 *extent* behavior

Guildenstern. In what, my dear lord?

Hamlet. I am but mad north-northwest:° when the
wind is southerly I know a hawk from a handsaw.°

Enter Polonius.

Polonius. Well be with you, gentlemen.

Hamlet. Hark you, Guildenstern, and you too; at each   390
ear a hearer. That great baby you see there is not
yet out of his swaddling clouts.

Rosencrantz. Happily° he is the second time come to
them, for they say an old man is twice a child.

Hamlet. I will prophesy he comes to tell me of the   395
players. Mark it.—You say right, sir; a Monday
morning, 'twas then indeed.

Polonius. My lord, I have news to tell you.

Hamlet. My lord, I have news to tell you. When
Roscius° was an actor in Rome——   400

Polonius. The actors are come hither, my lord.

Hamlet. Buzz, buzz.°

Polonius. Upon my honor——

Hamlet. Then came each actor on his ass——

Polonius. The best actors in the world, either for   405
tragedy, comedy, history, pastoral, pastoral-comical,
historical-pastoral, tragical-historical, tragical-comical-historical-pastoral; scene individable,° or poem
unlimited.° Seneca° cannot be too heavy, nor
Plautus° too light. For the law of writ and the   410
liberty,° these are the only men.

---

387 *north-northwest* i.e., on one point of the compass only
388 *hawk from a handsaw* (*hawk* can refer not only to a bird
but to a kind of pickax; *handsaw*—a carpenter's tool—may in-
volve a similar pun on "hernshaw," a heron)   393 *Happily* perhaps
400 *Roscius* (a famous Roman comic actor)   402 *Buzz, buzz* (an
interjection, perhaps indicating that the news is old)   408 *scene
individable* plays observing the unities of time, place, and action
408–09 *poem unlimited* plays not restricted by the tenets of criticism   409 *Seneca* (Roman tragic dramatist)   410 *Plautus* (Roman
comic dramatist)   410–11 *For the law of writ and the liberty*
(perhaps "for sticking to the text and for improvising"; perhaps
"for classical plays and for modern loosely written plays")

Hamlet. O Jeptha, judge of Israel,° what a treasure
hadst thou!

Polonius. What a treasure had he, my lord?

415 *Hamlet.* Why,
          "One fair daughter, and no more,
               The which he lovèd passing well."

Polonius. [*Aside*] Still on my daughter.

Hamlet. Am I not i' th' right, old Jeptha?

420 *Polonius.* If you call me Jeptha, my lord, I have a
daughter that I love passing well.

Hamlet. Nay, that follows not.

Polonius. What follows then, my lord?

Hamlet. Why,
425   "As by lot, God wot,"
and then, you know,
          "It came to pass, as most like it was."
The first row of the pious chanson° will show you
more, for look where my abridgment° comes.

Enter the Players.

430 You are welcome, masters, welcome, all. I am glad
to see thee well. Welcome, good friends. O, old
friend, why, thy face is valanced° since I saw thee
last. Com'st thou to beard me in Denmark? What,
my young lady° and mistress? By'r Lady, your
435 ladyship is nearer to heaven than when I saw you
last by the altitude of a chopine.° Pray God your
voice, like a piece of uncurrent gold, be not cracked
within the ring.°—Masters, you are all welcome.
We'll e'en to't like French falconers, fly at any-

412 *Jeptha, judge of Israel* (the title of a ballad on the Hebrew
judge who sacrificed his daughter; see Judges 11) 428 *row of
the pious chanson* stanza of the scriptural song 429 *abridgment*
(1) i.e., entertainers, who abridge the time (2) interrupters
432 *valanced* fringed (with a beard) 434 *young lady* i.e., boy
for female roles 436 *chopine* thick-soled shoe 437–38 *like a
piece . . . the ring* (a coin was unfit for legal tender if a crack
extended from the edge through the ring enclosing the monarch's
head. Hamlet, punning on *ring*, refers to the change of voice that
the boy actor will undergo)

thing we see. We'll have a speech straight. Come, 440
give us a taste of your quality. Come, a passionate
speech.

Player. What speech, my good lord?

Hamlet. I heard thee speak me a speech once, but it
was never acted, or if it was, not above once, for 445
the play, I remember, pleased not the million; 'twas
caviary to the general,° but it was (as I received it,
and others, whose judgments in such matters cried
in the top of° mine) an excellent play, well digested
in the scenes, set down with as much modesty as 450
cunning.° I remember one said there were no
sallets° in the lines to make the matter savory;
nor no matter in the phrase that might indict the
author of affectation, but called it an honest method,
as wholesome as sweet, and by very much more 455
handsome than fine.° One speech in't I chiefly loved.
'Twas Aeneas' tale to Dido, and thereabout of it
especially when he speaks of Priam's slaughter. If
it live in your memory, begin at this line—let me
see, let me see: 460

　　"The rugged Pyrrhus, like th' Hyrcanian
　　　　beast°——"

'Tis not so; it begins with Pyrrhus:

　　"The rugged Pyrrhus, he whose sable° arms,
　　Black as his purpose, did the night resemble
　　When he lay couchèd in th' ominous horse,° 465
　　Hath now this dread and black complexion
　　　　smeared
　　With heraldry more dismal.° Head to foot
　　Now is he total gules, horridly tricked°
　　With blood of fathers, mothers, daughters, sons,
　　Baked and impasted° with the parching streets, 470

447 *caviary to the general* i.e., too choice for the multitude　449 *in
the top of* overtopping　450–51 *modesty as cunning* restraint as art
452 *sallets* salads, spicy jests　455–56 *more handsome than fine*
well-proportioned rather than ornamented　461 *Hyrcanian beast*
i.e., tiger (Hyrcania was in Asia)　463 *sable* black　465 *ominous
horse* i.e., wooden horse at the siege of Troy　467 *dismal* ill-
omened　468 *total gules, horridly tricked* all red, horridly adorned
470 *impasted* encrusted

That lend a tyrannous and a damnèd light
To their lord's murder. Roasted in wrath and fire,
And thus o'ersizèd° with coagulate gore,
With eyes like carbuncles, the hellish Pyrrhus
475   Old grandsire Priam seeks."
        So, proceed you.

Polonius. Fore God, my lord, well spoken, with good
    accent and good discretion.

Player.   "Anon he finds him,
480   Striking too short at Greeks. His antique sword,
    Rebellious to his arm, lies where it falls,
    Repugnant to command.° Unequal matched,
    Pyrrhus at Priam drives, in rage strikes wide,
    But with the whiff and wind of his fell sword
485   Th' unnervèd father falls. Then senseless Ilium,°
    Seeming to feel this blow, with flaming top
    Stoops to his base,° and with a hideous crash
    Takes prisoner Pyrrhus' ear. For lo, his sword,
    Which was declining on the milky head
490   Of reverend Priam, seemed i' th' air to stick.
    So as a painted tyrant° Pyrrhus stood,
    And like a neutral to his will and matter°
    Did nothing.
        But as we often see, against° some storm,
495   A silence in the heavens, the rack° stand still,
    The bold winds speechless, and the orb below
    As hush as death, anon the dreadful thunder
    Doth rend the region, so after Pyrrhus' pause,
    A rousèd vengeance sets him new awork,
500   And never did the Cyclops' hammers fall
    On Mars's armor, forged for proof eterne,°
    With less remorse than Pyrrhus' bleeding sword
    Now falls on Priam.
        Out, out, thou strumpet Fortune! All you gods,
505   In general synod° take away her power,

473 *o'ersizèd* smeared over   482 *Repugnant to command* diso-
bedient   485 *senseless Ilium* insensate Troy   487 *Stoops to his
base* collapses (*his* = its)   491 *painted tyrant* tyrant in a picture
492 *matter* task   494 *against* just before   495 *rack* clouds
501 *proof eterne* eternal endurance   505 *synod* council

Break all the spokes and fellies° from her wheel,
And bowl the round nave° down the hill of
heaven,
As low as to the fiends."

Polonius. This is too long.

Hamlet. It shall to the barber's, with your beard.— 510
Prithee say on. He's for a jig or a tale of bawdry,
or he sleeps. Say on; come to Hecuba.

Player. "But who (ah woe!) had seen the mobled°
queen——"

Hamlet. "The mobled queen"?

Polonius. That's good. "Mobled queen" is good. 515

Player. "Run barefoot up and down, threat'ning the
flames
With bisson rheum;° a clout° upon that head
Where late the diadem stood, and for a robe,
About her lank and all o'erteemèd° loins,
A blanket in the alarm of fear caught up— 520
Who this had seen, with tongue in venom steeped
'Gainst Fortune's state would treason have pro-
nounced.
But if the gods themselves did see her then,
When she saw Pyrrhus make malicious sport
In mincing with his sword her husband's limbs, 525
The instant burst of clamor that she made
(Unless things mortal move them not at all)
Would have made milch° the burning eyes of
heaven
And passion in the gods."

Polonius. Look, whe'r° he has not turned his color, 530
and has tears in's eyes. Prithee no more.

Hamlet. 'Tis well. I'll have thee speak out the rest of
this soon. Good my lord, will you see the players
well bestowed?° Do you hear? Let them be well

506 *fellies* rims   507 *nave* hub   513 *mobled* muffled   517 *bisson
rheum* blinding tears   517 *clout* rag   519 *o'erteemèd* exhausted
with childbearing   528 *milch* moist (literally, "milk-giving")
530 *whe'r* whether   534 *bestowed* housed

535 used, for they are the abstract and brief chronicles
of the time. After your death you were better have
a bad epitaph than their ill report while you live.

Polonius. My lord, I will use them according to their
desert.

540 *Hamlet.* God's bodkin,° man, much better! Use every
man after his desert, and who shall scape whipping?
Use them after your own honor and dignity. The
less they deserve, the more merit is in your bounty.
Take them in.

545 *Polonius.* Come, sirs.

Hamlet. Follow him, friends. We'll hear a play tomorrow. [*Aside to Player*] Dost thou hear me, old
friend? Can you play *The Murder of Gonzago*?

Player. Ay, my lord.

550 *Hamlet.* We'll ha't tomorrow night. You could for a
need study a speech of some dozen or sixteen lines
which I would set down and insert in't, could you
not?

Player. Ay, my lord.

555 *Hamlet.* Very well. Follow that lord, and look you
mock him not. My good friends, I'll leave you till
night. You are welcome to Elsinore.
                              Exeunt Polonius and Players.

Rosencrantz. Good my lord.
                         Exeunt [*Rosencrantz and Guildenstern*].

Hamlet. Ay, so, God bye to you.—Now I am alone.
560   O, what a rogue and peasant slave am I!
Is it not monstrous that this player here,
But in a fiction, in a dream of passion,°
Could force his soul so to his own conceit°
That from her working all his visage wanned,
565   Tears in his eyes, distraction in his aspect,
A broken voice, and his whole function° suiting

540 *God's bodkin* by God's little body 562 *dream of passion*
imaginary emotion 563 *conceit* imagination 566 *function* action

With forms° to his conceit? And all for nothing!
For Hecuba!
What's Hecuba to him, or he to Hecuba,
That he should weep for her? What would he do   570
Had he the motive and the cue for passion
That I have? He would drown the stage with tears
And cleave the general ear with horrid speech,
Make mad the guilty and appall the free,°
Confound the ignorant, and amaze indeed   575
The very faculties of eyes and ears.
Yet I,
A dull and muddy-mettled° rascal, peak
Like John-a-dreams,° unpregnant of° my cause,
And can say nothing. No, not for a king,   580
Upon whose property and most dear life
A damned defeat was made. Am I a coward?
Who calls me villain? Breaks my pate across?
Plucks off my beard and blows it in my face?
Tweaks me by the nose? Gives me the lie i' th' throat 585
As deep as to the lungs? Who does me this?
Ha, 'swounds,° I should take it, for it cannot be
But I am pigeon-livered° and lack gall
To make oppression bitter, or ere this
I should ha' fatted all the region kites°   590
With this slave's offal. Bloody, bawdy villain!
Remorseless, treacherous, lecherous, kindless° vil-
     lain!
O, vengeance!
Why, what an ass am I! This is most brave,°
That I, the son of a dear father murdered,   595
Prompted to my revenge by heaven and hell,
Must, like a whore, unpack my heart with words
And fall a-cursing like a very drab,°

---

567 *forms* bodily expressions   574 *appall the free* terrify
(make pale?) the guiltless   578 *muddy-mettled* weak-spirited
578–79 *peak/Like John-a-dreams* mope like a dreamer   579 *unpregnant of* unquickened by   587 *'swounds* by God's wounds
588 *pigeon-livered* gentle as a dove   590 *region kites* kites (scav-
enger birds) of the sky   592 *kindless* unnatural   594 *brave* fine
598 *drab* prostitute

A stallion!° Fie upon't, foh! About,° my brains.
600   Hum——
I have heard that guilty creatures sitting at a play
Have by the very cunning of the scene
Been struck so to the soul that presently°
They have proclaimed their malefactions.
605   For murder, though it have no tongue, will speak
With most miraculous organ. I'll have these players
Play something like the murder of my father
Before mine uncle. I'll observe his looks,
I'll tent° him to the quick. If 'a do blench,°
610   I know my course. The spirit that I have seen
May be a devil, and the devil hath power
T' assume a pleasing shape, yea, and perhaps
Out of my weakness and my melancholy,
As he is very potent with such spirits,
615   Abuses me to damn me. I'll have grounds
More relative° than this. The play's the thing
Wherein I'll catch the conscience of the King. *Exit.*

---

599 *stallion* male prostitute (perhaps one should adopt the Folio
reading, *scullion* = kitchen wench)   599 *About* to work   603 *presently* immediately   609 *tent* probe   609 *blench* flinch   616 *relative*
(probably "pertinent," but possibly "able to be related plausibly")

[ACT III

Scene I. *The castle.*]

Enter King, Queen, Polonius, Ophelia, Rosencrantz,
Guildenstern, Lords.

King. And can you by no drift of conference°
   Get from him why he puts on this confusion,
   Grating so harshly all his days of quiet
   With turbulent and dangerous lunacy?

Rosencrantz. He does confess he feels himself dis-
      tracted,   5
   But from what cause 'a will by no means speak.

Guildenstern. Nor do we find him forward to be
      sounded,°
   But with a crafty madness keeps aloof
   When we would bring him on to some confession
   Of his true state.

Queen.   Did he receive you well?   10

Rosencrantz. Most like a gentleman.

Guildenstern. But with much forcing of his disposi-
      tion.°

Rosencrantz. Niggard of question,° but of our demands
   Most free in his reply.

III.i.1 *drift of conference* management of conversation 7 *forward
to be sounded* willing to be questioned 12 *forcing of his disposition* effort 13 *Niggard of question* uninclined to talk

91

Queen.   Did you assay° him
15   To any pastime?

Rosencrantz. Madam, it so fell out that certain players
   We o'erraught° on the way; of these we told him,
   And there did seem in him a kind of joy
   To hear of it. They are here about the court,
20   And, as I think, they have already order
   This night to play before him.

Polonius.   'Tis most true,
   And he beseeched me to entreat your Majesties
   To hear and see the matter.

King. With all my heart, and it doth much content me
25   To hear him so inclined.
   Good gentlemen, give him a further edge
   And drive his purpose into these delights.

Rosencrantz. We shall, my lord.
             Exeunt Rosencrantz and Guildenstern.

King.   Sweet Gertrude, leave us too,
   For we have closely° sent for Hamlet hither,
30   That he, as 'twere by accident, may here
   Affront° Ophelia.
   Her father and myself (lawful espials°)
   Will so bestow ourselves that, seeing unseen,
   We may of their encounter frankly judge
35   And gather by him, as he is behaved,
   If't be th' affliction of his love or no
   That thus he suffers for.

Queen.   I shall obey you.
   And for your part, Ophelia, I do wish
   That your good beauties be the happy cause
40   Of Hamlet's wildness. So shall I hope your virtues
   Will bring him to his wonted way again,
   To both your honors.

Ophelia.   Madam, I wish it may.
             [Exit Queen.]

14 *assay* tempt   17 *o'erraught* overtook   29 *closely* secretly
31 *Affront* meet face to face   32 *espials* spies

Polonius. Ophelia, walk you here.—Gracious, so please
    you,
  We will bestow ourselves. [*To Ophelia*] Read on this
    book,
  That show of such an exercise may color°   *45*
  Your loneliness. We are oft to blame in this,
  'Tis too much proved, that with devotion's visage
  And pious action we do sugar o'er
  The devil himself.

King.   [*Aside*] O, 'tis too true.
  How smart a lash that speech doth give my con-
    science!   *50*
  The harlot's cheek, beautied with plast'ring art,
  Is not more ugly to the thing that helps it
  Than is my deed to my most painted word.
  O heavy burden!

Polonius. I hear him coming. Let's withdraw, my lord. *55*
             [*Exeunt King and Polonius.*]

          Enter Hamlet.

Hamlet. To be, or not to be: that is the question:
  Whether 'tis nobler in the mind to suffer
  The slings and arrows of outrageous fortune,
  Or to take arms against a sea of troubles,
  And by opposing end them. To die, to sleep—   *60*
  No more—and by a sleep to say we end
  The heartache, and the thousand natural shocks
  That flesh is heir to! 'Tis a consummation
  Devoutly to be wished. To die, to sleep—
  To sleep—perchance to dream: ay, there's the rub,° *65*
  For in that sleep of death what dreams may come
  When we have shuffled off this mortal coil,°
  Must give us pause. There's the respect°
  That makes calamity of so long life:°
  For who would bear the whips and scorns of time, *70*

45 *exercise may color* act of devotion may give a plausible hue to
(the book is one of devotion) 65 *rub* impediment (obstruction
to a bowler's ball) 67 *coil* (1) turmoil (2) a ring of rope (here
the flesh encircling the soul) 68 *respect* consideration 69 *makes
calamity of so long life* (1) makes calamity so long-lived (2)
makes living so long a calamity

Th' oppressor's wrong, the proud man's contumely,
The pangs of despised love, the law's delay,
The insolence of office, and the spurns
That patient merit of th' unworthy takes,
75 When he himself might his quietus° make
With a bare bodkin?° Who would fardels° bear,
To grunt and sweat under a weary life,
But that the dread of something after death,
The undiscovered country, from whose bourn°
80 No traveler returns, puzzles the will,
And makes us rather bear those ills we have,
Than fly to others that we know not of?
Thus conscience° does make cowards of us all,
And thus the native hue of resolution
85 Is sicklied o'er with the pale cast° of thought,
And enterprises of great pitch° and moment,
With this regard° their currents turn awry,
And lose the name of action.—Soft you now,
The fair Ophelia!—Nymph, in thy orisons°
Be all my sins remembered.

90 *Ophelia.*   Good my lord,
How does your honor for this many a day?

Hamlet. I humbly thank you; well, well, well.

Ophelia. My lord, I have remembrances of yours
That I have longèd long to redeliver.
I pray you now, receive them.

95 *Hamlet.*   No, not I,
I never gave you aught.

Ophelia. My honored lord, you know right well you
   did,
And with them words of so sweet breath composed
As made these things more rich. Their perfume lost,
100 Take these again, for to the noble mind

---

75 *quietus* full discharge (a legal term)   76 *bodkin* dagger   76 *fardels* burdens   79 *bourn* region   83 *conscience* self-consciousness, introspection   85 *cast* color   86 *pitch* height (a term from falconry)   87 *regard* consideration   89 *orisons* prayers

Rich gifts wax poor when givers prove unkind.
There, my lord.

Hamlet. Ha, ha! Are you honest?°

Ophelia. My lord?

Hamlet. Are you fair?   105

Ophelia. What means your lordship?

Hamlet. That if you be honest and fair, your honesty
should admit no discourse to your beauty.°

Ophelia. Could beauty, my lord, have better commerce
than with honesty?   110

Hamlet. Ay, truly; for the power of beauty will sooner
transform honesty from what it is to a bawd° than
the force of honesty can translate beauty into his
likeness. This was sometime a paradox, but now
the time gives it proof. I did love you once.   115

Ophelia. Indeed, my lord, you made me believe so.

Hamlet. You should not have believed me, for virtue
cannot so inoculate° our old stock but we shall relish
of it.° I loved you not.

Ophelia. I was the more deceived.   120

Hamlet. Get thee to a nunnery. Why wouldst thou be
a breeder of sinners? I am myself indifferent honest,°
but yet I could accuse me of such things that it were
better my mother had not borne me: I am very
proud, revengeful, ambitious, with more offenses at   125
my beck° than I have thoughts to put them in,
imagination to give them shape, or time to act them
in. What should such fellows as I do crawling between earth and heaven? We are arrant knaves all;
believe none of us. Go thy ways to a nunnery.   130
Where's your father?

103 *Are you honest* (1) are you modest (2) are you chaste (3)
have you integrity 107–08 *your honesty . . . to your beauty*
your modesty should permit no approach to your beauty
112 *bawd* procurer 118 *inoculate* graft 118–19 *relish of it* smack
of it (our old sinful nature) 122 *indifferent honest* moderately
virtuous 126 *beck* call

Ophelia. At home, my lord.

Hamlet. Let the doors be shut upon him, that he may
     play the fool nowhere but in's own house. Farewell.
135 *Ophelia.* O help him, you sweet heavens!

Hamlet. If thou dost marry, I'll give thee this plague
     for thy dowry: be thou as chaste as ice, as pure as
     snow, thou shalt not escape calumny. Get thee to a
     nunnery. Go, farewell. Or if thou wilt needs marry,
140   marry a fool, for wise men know well enough what
     monsters° you make of them. To a nunnery, go,
     and quickly too. Farewell.

Ophelia. Heavenly powers, restore him!

Hamlet. I have heard of your paintings, well enough.
145   God hath given you one face, and you make your-
     selves another. You jig and amble, and you lisp;
     you nickname God's creatures and make your
     wantonness your ignorance.° Go to, I'll no more
     on't; it hath made me mad. I say we will have no
150   moe° marriage. Those that are married already—all
     but one—shall live. The rest shall keep as they are.
     To a nunnery, go.   *Exit.*

Ophelia. O what a noble mind is here o'erthrown!
     The courtier's, soldier's, scholar's, eye, tongue, sword,
155   Th' expectancy and rose° of the fair state,
     The glass of fashion, and the mold of form,°
     Th' observed of all observers, quite, quite down!
     And I, of ladies most deject and wretched,
     That sucked the honey of his musicked vows,
160   Now see that noble and most sovereign reason
     Like sweet bells jangled, out of time and harsh,
     That unmatched form and feature of blown° youth
     Blasted with ecstasy.° O, woe is me
     T' have seen what I have seen, see what I see!

           Enter King and Polonius.

141 *monsters* horned beasts, cuckolds 147–48 *make your wan-
tonness your ignorance* excuse your wanton speech by pretending
ignorance 150 *moe* more 155 *expectancy and rose* i.e., fair hope
156 *The glass . . . of form* the mirror of fashion, and the pattern
of excellent behavior 162 *blown* blooming 163 *ecstasy* madness

King. Love? His affections° do not that way tend,   *165*
   Nor what he spake, though it lacked form a little,
   Was not like madness. There's something in his soul
   O'er which his melancholy sits on brood,
   And I do doubt° the hatch and the disclose
   Will be some danger; which for to prevent,   *170*
   I have in quick determination
   Thus set it down: he shall with speed to England
   For the demand of our neglected tribute.
   Haply the seas, and countries different,
   With variable objects, shall expel   *175*
   This something-settled° matter in his heart,
   Whereon his brains still beating puts him thus
   From fashion of himself. What think you on't?

Polonius. It shall do well. But yet do I believe
   The origin and commencement of his grief   *180*
   Sprung from neglected love. How now, Ophelia?
   You need not tell us what Lord Hamlet said;
   We heard it all. My lord, do as you please,
   But if you hold it fit, after the play,
   Let his queen mother all alone entreat him   *185*
   To show his grief. Let her be round° with him,
   And I'll be placed, so please you, in the ear
   Of all their conference. If she find him not,°
   To England send him, or confine him where
   Your wisdom best shall think.

King.   It shall be so.   *190*
   Madness in great ones must not unwatched go.
                                Exeunt.

---

165 *affections* inclinations 169 *doubt* fear 176 *something-settled*
somewhat settled 186 *round* blunt 188 *find him not* does not
find him out

[Scene II. *The castle*.]

Enter Hamlet and three of the Players.

Hamlet. Speak the speech, I pray you, as I pronounced
it to you, trippingly on the tongue. But if you mouth
it, as many of our players do, I had as lief the town
crier spoke my lines. Nor do not saw the air too much
5 with your hand, thus, but use all gently, for in the
very torrent, tempest, and (as I may say) whirlwind
of your passion, you must acquire and beget a temperance that may give it smoothness. O, it offends
me to the soul to hear a robustious periwig-pated°
10 fellow tear a passion to tatters, to very rags, to split
the ears of the groundlings,° who for the most part
are capable of° nothing but inexplicable dumb
shows° and noise. I would have such a fellow
whipped for o'erdoing Termagant. It out-herods
15 Herod.° Pray you avoid it.

Player. I warrant your honor.

Hamlet. Be not too tame neither, but let your own discretion be your tutor. Suit the action to the word, the
word to the action, with this special observance, that
20 you o'erstep not the modesty of nature. For anything
so o'erdone is from° the purpose of playing, whose
end, both at the first and now, was and is, to hold,
as 'twere, the mirror up to nature; to show virtue
her own feature, scorn her own image, and the very
25 age and body of the time his form and pressure.°

III.ii.9 *robustious periwig-pated* boisterous wig-headed 11 *groundlings* those who stood in the pit of the theater (the poorest and
presumably most ignorant of the audience) 12 *are capable of*
are able to understand 12–13 *dumb shows* (it had been the
fashion for actors to preface plays or parts of plays with silent
mime) 14–15 *Termagant . . . Herod* (boisterous characters in
the old mystery plays) 21 *from* contrary to 25 *pressure* image,
impress

Now, this overdone, or come tardy off, though it
makes the unskillful laugh, cannot but make the
judicious grieve, the censure of the which one must
in your allowance o'erweigh a whole theater of
others. O, there be players that I have seen play,   *30*
and heard others praise, and that highly (not to
speak it profanely), that neither having th' accent of
Christians, nor the gait of Christian, pagan, nor
man, have so strutted and bellowed that I have
thought some of Nature's journeymen° had made   *35*
men, and not made them well, they imitated humanity so abominably.

Player. I hope we have reformed that indifferently°
with us, sir.

Hamlet. O, reform it altogether! And let those that   *40*
play your clowns speak no more than is set down
for them, for there be of them that will themselves
laugh, to set on some quantity of barren spectators to
laugh too, though in the meantime some necessary
question of the play be then to be considered. That's   *45*
villainous and shows a most pitiful ambition in the
fool that uses it. Go make you ready.

                              Exit Players.
　　Enter Polonius, Guildenstern, and Rosencrantz.

How now, my lord? Will the King hear this piece of
work?

Polonius. And the Queen too, and that presently.   *50*

Hamlet. Bid the players make haste.   *Exit Polonius.*
Will you two help to hasten them?

Rosencrantz. Ay, my lord.   *Exeunt they two.*

Hamlet. What, ho, Horatio!

                    Enter Horatio.

Horatio. Here, sweet lord, at your service.   *55*

Hamlet. Horatio, thou art e'en as just a man

35 *journeymen* workers not yet masters of their craft 38 *indif-
ferently* tolerably

As e'er my conversation coped withal.°

Horatio. O, my dear lord——

Hamlet.   Nay, do not think I flatter.
For what advancement° may I hope from thee,
60   That no revenue hast but thy good spirits
To feed and clothe thee? Why should the poor be
     flattered?
No, let the candied° tongue lick absurd pomp,
And crook the pregnant° hinges of the knee
Where thrift° may follow fawning. Dost thou hear?
65   Since my dear soul was mistress of her choice
And could of men distinguish her election,
S' hath sealed thee° for herself, for thou hast been
As one, in suff'ring all, that suffers nothing,
A man that Fortune's buffets and rewards
70   Hast ta'en with equal thanks; and blest are those
Whose blood° and judgment are so well com-
     meddled°
That they are not a pipe for Fortune's finger
To sound what stop she please. Give me that man
That is not passion's slave, and I will wear him
75   In my heart's core, ay, in my heart of heart,
As I do thee. Something too much of this—
There is a play tonight before the King.
One scene of it comes near the circumstance
Which I have told thee, of my father's death.
80   I prithee, when thou seest that act afoot,
Even with the very comment° of thy soul
Observe my uncle. If his occulted° guilt
Do not itself unkennel in one speech,
It is a damnèd ghost that we have seen,
85   And my imaginations are as foul
As Vulcan's stithy.° Give him heedful note,
For I mine eyes will rivet to his face,

57 *coped withal* met with   59 *advancement* promotion   62 *candied*
sugared, flattering   63 *pregnant* (1) pliant (2) full of promise of
good fortune   64 *thrift* profit   67 *S' hath sealed thee* she (the
soul) has set a mark on you   71 *blood* passion   71 *commeddled*
blended   81 *very comment* deepest wisdom   82 *occulted* hidden
86 *stithy* forge, smithy

And after we will both our judgments join
In censure of his seeming.°

Horatio.   Well, my lord.
If 'a steal aught the whilst this play is playing,   90
And scape detecting, I will pay the theft.

*Enter Trumpets and Kettledrums, King, Queen,
Polonius, Ophelia, Rosencrantz, Guildenstern,
and other Lords attendant with his Guard carrying
torches. Danish March. Sound a Flourish.*

Hamlet. They are coming to the play: I must be idle;°
Get you a place.

King. How fares our cousin Hamlet?

Hamlet. Excellent, i' faith, of the chameleon's dish;°   95
I eat the air, promise-crammed; you cannot feed
capons so.

King. I have nothing with this answer, Hamlet; these
words are not mine.

Hamlet. No, nor mine now. [*To Polonius*] My lord, you   101
played once i' th' university, you say?

Polonius. That did I, my lord, and was accounted a good
actor.

Hamlet. What did you enact?

Polonius. I did enact Julius Caesar. I was killed i' th'   105
Capitol; Brutus killed me.

Hamlet. It was a brute part of him to kill so capital a
calf there. Be the players ready?

Rosencrantz. Ay, my lord. They stay upon your
patience.   110

Queen. Come hither, my dear Hamlet, sit by me.

Hamlet. No, good mother. Here's metal more attractive.°

89 *censure of his seeming* judgement on his looks 92 *be idle* play
the fool 95 *the chameleon's dish* air (on which chameleons were
thought to live) 112–13 *attractive* magnetic

Polonius. [*To the King*] O ho! Do you mark that?

115 *Hamlet.* Lady, shall I lie in your lap?

[*He lies at Ophelia's feet.*]

Ophelia. No, my lord.

Hamlet. I mean, my head upon your lap?

Ophelia. Ay, my lord.

Hamlet. Do you think I meant country matters?°

120 *Ophelia.* I think nothing, my lord.

Hamlet. That's a fair thought to lie between maids'
legs.

Ophelia. What is, my lord?

Hamlet. Nothing.

125 *Ophelia.* You are merry, my lord.

Hamlet. Who, I?

Ophelia. Ay, my lord.

Hamlet. O God, your only jig-maker!° What should a
man do but be merry? For look you how cheerfully
130 my mother looks, and my father died within's two
hours.

Ophelia. Nay, 'tis twice two months, my lord.

Hamlet. So long? Nay then, let the devil wear black,
for I'll have a suit of sables.° O heavens! Die two
135 months ago, and not forgotten yet? Then there's
hope a great man's memory may outlive his life half
a year. But, by'r Lady, 'a must build churches then,
or else shall 'a suffer not thinking on, with the hobbyhorse,° whose epitaph is "For O, for O, the hobby-
140 horse is forgot!"

The trumpets sound. Dumb show follows:

119 *country matters* rustic doings (with a pun on the vulgar word
for the pudendum)   128 *jig-maker* composer of songs and dances
(often a Fool, who performed them)   134 *sables* (pun on "black"
and "luxurious furs")   138–39 *hobbyhorse* mock horse worn by a
performer in the morris dance

Enter a King and a Queen very lovingly, the Queen em-
bracing him, and he her. She kneels; and makes show
of protestation unto him. He takes her up, and declines
his head upon her neck. He lies him down upon a bank
of flowers. She, seeing him asleep, leaves him. Anon
come in another man: takes off his crown, kisses it,
pours poison in the sleeper's ears, and leaves him. The
Queen returns, finds the King dead, makes passionate
action. The poisoner, with some three or four, come in
again, seem to condole with her. The dead body is car-
ried away. The poisoner woos the Queen with gifts; she
seems harsh awhile, but in the end accepts love.

Exeunt.

Ophelia. What means this, my lord?

Hamlet. Marry, this is miching mallecho;° it means
   mischief.

Ophelia. Belike this show imports the argument° of
   the play.   *145*

Enter Prologue.

Hamlet. We shall know by this fellow. The players
   cannot keep counsel; they'll tell all.

Ophelia. Will 'a tell us what this show meant?

Hamlet. Ay, or any show that you will show him. Be
   not you ashamed to show, he'll not shame to tell you *150*
   what it means.

Ophelia. You are naught,° you are naught; I'll mark the
   play.

Prologue. For us, and for our tragedy,
          Here stooping to your clemency,
          We beg your hearing patiently.   [*Exit.*]   *155*

Hamlet. Is this a prologue, or the posy of a ring?°

Ophelia. 'Tis brief, my lord.

Hamlet. As woman's love.

142 *miching mallecho* sneaking mischief 144 *argument* plot
152 *naught* wicked, improper 157 *posy of a ring* motto inscribed
in a ring

Enter [two Players as] King and Queen.

Player King. Full thirty times hath Phoebus' cart° gone
160   round
          Neptune's salt wash° and Tellus'° orbèd ground,
          And thirty dozen moons with borrowed sheen
          About the world have times twelve thirties been,
          Since love our hearts, and Hymen did our hands,
165   Unite commutual in most sacred bands.

Player Queen. So many journeys may the sun and
               moon
          Make us again count o'er ere love be done!
          But woe is me, you are so sick of late,
          So far from cheer and from your former state,
170   That I distrust° you. Yet, though I distrust,
          Discomfort you, my lord, it nothing must.
          For women fear too much, even as they love,
          And women's fear and love hold quantity,
          In neither aught, or in extremity.°
175   Now what my love is, proof° hath made you know,
          And as my love is sized, my fear is so.
          Where love is great, the littlest doubts are fear;
          Where little fears grow great, great love grows there.

Player King. Faith, I must leave thee, love, and shortly
               too;
180   My operant° powers their functions leave to do:
          And thou shalt live in this fair world behind,
          Honored, beloved, and haply one as kind
          For husband shalt thou——

Player Queen.   O, confound the rest!
          Such love must needs be treason in my breast.
185   In second husband let me be accurst!
          None wed the second but who killed the first.

160 *Phoebus' cart* the sun's chariot   161 *Neptune's salt wash* the
sea   161 *Tellus* Roman goddess of the earth   170 *distrust* am
anxious about   173–74 *And women's . . . in extremity* (perhaps
the idea is that women's anxiety is great or little in proportion
to their love. The previous line, unrhymed, may be a false start
that Shakespeare neglected to delete)   175 *proof* experience
180 *operant* active

Hamlet. [*Aside*] That's wormwood.°

Player Queen. The instances° that second marriage
  move°
  Are base respects of thrift,° but none of love.
  A second time I kill my husband dead   190
  When second husband kisses me in bed.

Player King. I do believe you think what now you
    speak,
  But what we do determine oft we break.
  Purpose is but the slave to memory,
  Of violent birth, but poor validity,°   195
  Which now like fruit unripe sticks on the tree,
  But fall unshaken when they mellow be.
  Most necessary 'tis that we forget
  To pay ourselves what to ourselves is debt.
  What to ourselves in passion we propose,   200
  The passion ending, doth the purpose lose.
  The violence of either grief or joy
  Their own enactures° with themselves destroy:
  Where joy most revels, grief doth most lament;
  Grief joys, joy grieves, on slender accident.   205
  This world is not for aye, nor 'tis not strange
  That even our loves should with our fortunes
    change,
  For 'tis a question left us yet to prove,
  Whether love lead fortune, or else fortune love.
  The great man down, you mark his favorite flies; 210
  The poor advanced makes friends of enemies;
  And hitherto doth love on fortune tend,
  For who not needs shall never lack a friend;
  And who in want a hollow friend doth try,
  Directly seasons him° his enemy.   215
  But, orderly to end where I begun,
  Our wills and fates do so contrary run
  That our devices still are overthrown;
  Our thoughts are ours, their ends none of our own.

187 *wormwood* a bitter herb 188 *instances* motives 188 *move*
induce 189 *respects of thrift* considerations of profit 195 *validity*
strength 203 *enactures* acts 215 *seasons him* ripens him into

220   So think thou wilt no second husband wed,
       But die thy thoughts when thy first lord is dead.

       Player Queen. Nor earth to me give food, nor heaven
           light,
       Sport and repose lock from me day and night,
       To desperation turn my trust and hope,
225   An anchor's° cheer in prison be my scope,
       Each opposite that blanks° the face of joy
       Meet what I would have well, and it destroy:
       Both here and hence pursue me lasting strife,
       If, once a widow, ever I be wife!

230   *Hamlet.* If she should break it now!

       Player King. 'Tis deeply sworn. Sweet, leave me here
           awhile;
       My spirits grow dull, and fain I would beguile
       The tedious day with sleep.

       Player Queen.   Sleep rock thy brain,
                                          [*He*] *sleeps.*
       And never come mischance between us twain! *Exit.*

233   *Hamlet.* Madam, how like you this play?

       Queen. The lady doth protest too much, methinks.

       Hamlet. O, but she'll keep her word.

       King. Have you heard the argument?° Is there no
       offense in't?

240   *Hamlet.* No, no, they do but jest, poison in jest; no
       offense i' th' world.

       King. What do you call the play?

       Hamlet. The Mousetrap. Marry, how? Tropically.°
       This play is the image of a murder done in Vienna:
243   Gonzago is the Duke's name; his wife, Baptista. You
       shall see anon. 'Tis a knavish piece of work, but
       what of that? Your Majesty, and we that have free°

---

225 *anchor's* anchorite's, hermit's   226 *opposite that blanks* ad-
verse thing that blanches   238 *argument* plot   243 *Tropically* fig-
uratively (with a pun on "trap")   247 *free* innocent

souls, it touches us not. Let the galled jade winch;°
our withers are unwrung.

Enter Lucianus.

This is one Lucianus, nephew to the King.   250

Ophelia. You are as good as a chorus, my lord.

Hamlet. I could interpret° between you and your love,
if I could see the puppets dallying.

Ophelia. You are keen,° my lord, you are keen.

Hamlet. It would cost you a groaning to take off mine   255
edge.

Ophelia. Still better, and worse.

Hamlet. So you mistake° your husbands.—Begin,
murderer. Leave thy damnable faces and begin.
Come, the croaking raven doth bellow for revenge.   260

Lucianus. Thoughts black, hands apt, drugs fit, and
    time agreeing,
Confederate season,° else no creature seeing,
Thou mixture rank, of midnight weeds collected,
With Hecate's ban° thrice blasted, thrice infected,
Thy natural magic and dire property°   265
On wholesome life usurps immediately.

                    Pours the poison in his ears.

Hamlet. 'A poisons him i' th' garden for his estate. His
name's Gonzago. The story is extant, and written in
very choice Italian. You shall see anon how the murderer gets the love of Gonzago's wife.   270

Ophelia. The King rises.

Hamlet. What, frighted with false fire?°

Queen. How fares my lord?

Polonius. Give o'er the play.

248 *galled jade winch* chafed horse wince   252 *interpret* (like a
showman explaining the action of puppets)   254 *keen* (1) sharp
(2) sexually aroused   258 *mistake* err in taking   262 *Confederate
season* the opportunity allied with me   264 *Hecate's ban* the
curse of the goddess of sorcery   265 *property* nature   272 *false
fire* blank discharge of firearms

²⁷⁵ *King.* Give me some light. Away!

Polonius. Lights, lights, lights!

> *Exeunt all but Hamlet and Horatio.*

Hamlet. Why, let the strucken deer go weep,
> The hart ungallèd play:
>> For some must watch, while some must sleep;
²⁸⁰ >> Thus runs the world away.
> Would not this, sir, and a forest of feathers°—if the
> rest of my fortunes turn Turk° with me—with two
> Provincial roses° on my razed° shoes, get me a
> fellowship in a cry° of players?

²⁸⁵ *Horatio.* Half a share.

Hamlet. A whole one, I.
>> For thou dost know, O Damon dear,
>> This realm dismantled was
>> Of Jove himself; and now reigns here
²⁹⁰ >> A very, very—pajock.°

Horatio. You might have rhymed.°

Hamlet. O good Horatio, I'll take the ghost's word for
a thousand pound. Didst perceive?

Horatio. Very well, my lord.

²⁹⁵ *Hamlet.* Upon the talk of poisoning?

Horatio. I did very well note him.

Hamlet. Ah ha! Come, some music! Come, the recorders!°
>> For if the King like not the comedy,
³⁰⁰ >> Why then, belike he likes it not, perdy.°
> Come, some music!

> *Enter Rosencrantz and Guildenstern.*

Guildenstern. Good my lord, vouchsafe me a word
with you.

---

281 *feathers* (plumes were sometimes part of a costume) 282 *turn
Turk* i.e., go bad, treat me badly 283 *Provincial roses* rosettes
like the roses of Provence (?) 283 *razed* ornamented with slashes
284 *cry* pack, company 290 *pajock* peacock 291 *You might have
rhymed* i.e., rhymed "was" with "ass" 297–98 *recorders* flutelike
instruments 300 *perdy* by God (French : *par dieu*)

Hamlet. Sir, a whole history.

Guildenstern. The King, sir——   *805*

Hamlet. Ay, sir, what of him?

Guildenstern. Is in his retirement marvelous distemp'red.

Hamlet. With drink, sir?

Guildenstern. No, my lord, with choler.°   *810*

Hamlet. Your wisdom should show itself more richer to signify this to the doctor, for for me to put him to his purgation would perhaps plunge him into more choler.

Guildenstern. Good my lord, put your discourse into *815* some frame,° and start not so wildly from my affair.

Hamlet. I am tame, sir; pronounce.

Guildenstern. The Queen, your mother, in most great affliction of spirit hath sent me to you.

Hamlet. You are welcome.   *820*

Guildenstern. Nay, good my lord, this courtesy is not of the right breed. If it shall please you to make me a wholesome answer, I will do your mother's commandment: if not, your pardon and my return shall be the end of my business.   *825*

Hamlet. Sir, I cannot.

Rosencrantz. What, my lord?

Hamlet. Make you a wholesome° answer; my wit's diseased. But, sir, such answer as I can make, you shall command, or rather, as you say, my mother. *330* Therefore no more, but to the matter. My mother, you say——

Rosencrantz. Then thus she says: your behavior hath struck her into amazement and admiration.°

---

310 *choler* anger (but Hamlet pretends to take the word in its sense of "biliousness")   316 *frame* order, control   328 *wholesome* sane   334 *admiration* wonder

335 *Hamlet. O* wonderful son, that can so stonish a mother!
But is there no sequel at the heels of this mother's
admiration? Impart.

Rosencrantz. She desires to speak with you in her
closet ere you go to bed.

340 *Hamlet.* We shall obey, were she ten times our mother.
Have you any further trade with us?

Rosencrantz. My lord, you once did love me.

Hamlet. And do still, by these pickers and stealers.°

Rosencrantz. Good my lord, what is your cause of dis-
345 temper? You do surely bar the door upon your own
liberty, if you deny your griefs to your friend.

Hamlet. Sir, I lack advancement.°

Rosencrantz. How can that be, when you have the
voice of the King himself for your succession in
350 Denmark?

Enter the Players with recorders.

Hamlet. Ay, sir, but "while the grass grows"—the
proverb° is something musty. O, the recorders. Let
me see one. To withdraw° with you—why do you
go about to recover the wind° of me as if you would
355 drive me into a toil?°

Guildenstern. O my lord, if my duty be too bold, my
love is too unmannerly.°

Hamlet. I do not well understand that. Will you play
upon this pipe?

360 *Guildenstern.* My lord, I cannot.

Hamlet. I pray you.

Guildenstern. Believe me, I cannot.

Hamlet. I pray you.

Guildenstern. Believe me, I cannot.

343 *pickers and stealers* i.e., hands (with reference to the prayer;
"Keep my hands from picking and stealing") 347 *advancement*
promotion 352 *proverb* ("While the grass groweth, the horse
starveth") 353 *withdraw* speak in private 354 *recover the wind*
get on the windward side (as in hunting) 355 *toil* snare
356–57 *if my duty . . . too unmannerly* i.e., if these questions
seem rude, it is because my love for you leads me beyond good
manners.

Hamlet. I do beseech you.

Guildenstern. I know no touch of it, my lord.

Hamlet. It is as easy as lying. Govern these ventages° 365
with your fingers and thumb, give it breath with your
mouth, and it will discourse most eloquent music.
Look you, these are the stops.

Guildenstern. But these cannot I command to any
utt'rance of harmony; I have not the skill.   370

Hamlet. Why, look you now, how unworthy a thing
you make of me! You would play upon me; you
would seem to know my stops; you would pluck
out the heart of my mystery; you would sound me
from my lowest note to the top of my compass;° 375
and there is much music, excellent voice, in this little
organ,° yet cannot you make it speak. 'Sblood, do
you think I am easier to be played on than a pipe?
Call me what instrument you will, though you can
fret° me, you cannot play upon me.   380

Enter Polonius.

God bless you, sir!

Polonius. My lord, the Queen would speak with you,
and presently.

Hamlet. Do you see yonder cloud that's almost in
shape of a camel?   385

Polonius. By th' mass and 'tis, like a camel indeed.

Hamlet. Methinks it is like a weasel.

Polonius. It is backed like a weasel.

Hamlet. Or like a whale.

Polonius. Very like a whale.   390

Hamlet. Then I will come to my mother by and by.

---

365 *ventages* vents, stops on a recorder 375 *compass* range of
voice 377 *organ* i.e., the recorder 380 *fret* vex (with a pun
alluding to the frets, or ridges, that guide the fingering on some
instruments)

[*Aside*] They fool me to the top of my bent.°—I
will come by and by.°

Polonius. I will say so.   *Exit.*

395 Hamlet. "By and by" is easily said. Leave me, friends.
                                    [*Exeunt all but Hamlet.*]
'Tis now the very witching time of night,
When churchyards yawn, and hell itself breathes out
Contagion to this world. Now could I drink hot
        blood
And do such bitter business as the day
400 Would quake to look on. Soft, now to my mother.
O heart, lose not thy nature; let not ever
The soul of Nero° enter this firm bosom.
Let me be cruel, not unnatural;
I will speak daggers to her, but use none.
405 My tongue and soul in this be hypocrites:
How in my words somever she be shent,°
To give them seals° never, my soul, consent!   *Exit.*

[Scene III. *The castle.*]

Enter King, Rosencrantz, and Guildenstern.

King. I like him not, nor stands it safe with us
To let his madness range. Therefore prepare you.
I your commission will forthwith dispatch,
And he to England shall along with you.
5 The terms° of our estate may not endure
Hazard so near's° as doth hourly grow
Out of his brows.

Guildenstern.   We will ourselves provide.

392 *They fool . . . my bent* they compel me to play the fool to
the limit of my capacity   393 *by and by* very soon   402 *Nero*
(Roman emperor who had his mother murdered)   406 *shent*
rebuked   407 *give them seals* confirm them with deeds
III.iii.5 *terms* conditions   6 *near's* near us

Most holy and religious fear it is
To keep those many many bodies safe
That live and feed upon your Majesty.   *10*

Rosencrantz. The single and peculiar° life is bound
With all the strength and armor of the mind
To keep itself from noyance,° but much more
That spirit upon whose weal depends and rests
The lives of many. The cess of majesty°   *15*
Dies not alone, but like a gulf° doth draw
What's near it with it; or it is a massy wheel
Fixed on the summit of the highest mount,
To whose huge spokes ten thousand lesser things
Are mortised and adjoined, which when it falls,   *20*
Each small annexment, petty consequence,
Attends° the boist'rous ruin. Never alone
Did the King sigh, but with a general groan.

King. Arm° you, I pray you, to this speedy voyage,
For we will fetters put about this fear,   *25*
Which now goes too free-footed.

Rosencrantz.   We will haste us.
                                    Exeunt Gentlemen.

                    Enter Polonius.

Polonius. My lord, he's going to his mother's closet.
Behind the arras I'll convey myself
To hear the process.° I'll warrant she'll tax him
  home,°
And, as you said, and wisely was it said,   *30*
'Tis meet that some more audience than a mother,
Since nature makes them partial, should o'erhear
The speech of vantage.° Fare you well, my liege.
I'll call upon you ere you go to bed
And tell you what I know.

King.   Thanks, dear my lord.   *35*
                                    Exit [Polonius].

11 *peculiar* individual, private 13 *noyance* injury 15 *cess of
majesty* cessation (death) of a king 16 *gulf* whirlpool 22 *Attends*
waits on, participates in 24 *Arm* prepare 29 *process* proceedings
29 *tax him home* censure him sharply 33 *of vantage* from an
advantageous place

O, my offense is rank, it smells to heaven;
It hath the primal eldest curse° upon't,
A brother's murder. Pray can I not,
Though inclination be as sharp as will.
40 My stronger guilt defeats my strong intent,
And like a man to double business bound
I stand in pause where I shall first begin,
And both neglect. What if this cursèd hand
Were thicker than itself with brother's blood,
45 Is there not rain enough in the sweet heavens
To wash it white as snow? Whereto serves mercy
But to confront° the visage of offense?
And what's in prayer but this twofold force,
To be forestallèd ere we come to fall,
50 Or pardoned being down? Then I'll look up.
My fault is past. But, O, what form of prayer
Can serve my turn? "Forgive me my foul murder"?
That cannot be, since I am still possessed
Of those effects° for which I did the murder,
55 My crown, mine own ambition, and my queen.
May one be pardoned and retain th' offense?
In the corrupted currents of this world
Offense's gilded hand may shove by justice,
And oft 'tis seen the wicked prize itself
60 Buys out the law. But 'tis not so above.
There is no shuffling;° there the action lies
In his true nature, and we ourselves compelled,
Even to the teeth and forehead of our faults,
To give in evidence. What then? What rests?°
65 Try what repentance can. What can it not?
Yet what can it when one cannot repent?
O wretched state! O bosom black as death!
O limèd° soul, that struggling to be free
Art more engaged!° Help, angels! Make assay.°
70 Bow, stubborn knees, and, heart with strings of steel,

37 *primal eldest curse* (curse of Cain, who killed Abel) 47 *confront* oppose 54 *effects* things gained 61 *shuffling* trickery 64 *rests* remains 68 *limèd* caught (as with birdlime, a sticky substance spread on boughs to snare birds) 69 *engaged* ensnared 69 *assay* an attempt

Be soft as sinews of the newborn babe.
All may be well.   [*He kneels.*]

Enter Hamlet.

Hamlet. Now might I do it pat, now 'a is a-praying,
And now I'll do't. And so 'a goes to heaven,
And so am I revenged. That would be scanned.°   75
A villain kills my father, and for that
I, his sole son, do this same villain send
To heaven.
Why, this is hire and salary, not revenge.
'A took my father grossly, full of bread,°   80
With all his crimes broad blown,° as flush° as May;
And how his audit° stands, who knows save heaven?
But in our circumstance and course of thought,
'Tis heavy with him; and am I then revenged,
To take him in the purging of his soul,   85
When he is fit and seasoned for his passage?
No.
Up, sword, and know thou a more horrid hent.°
When he is drunk asleep, or in his rage,
Or in th' incestuous pleasure of his bed,   90
At game a-swearing, or about some act
That has no relish° of salvation in't—
Then trip him, that his heels may kick at heaven,
And that his soul may be as damned and black
As hell, whereto it goes. My mother stays.   95
This physic° but prolongs thy sickly days.   *Exit.*

King. [*Rises*] My words fly up, my thoughts remain
    below.
Words without thoughts never to heaven go.   *Exit.*

---

75 *would be scanned* ought to be looked into 80 *bread* i.e.,
worldly gratification 81 *crimes broad blown* sins in full bloom
81 *flush* vigorous 82 *audit* account 88 *hent* grasp (here, occasion
for seizing) 92 *relish* flavor 96 *physic* (Claudius' purgation by
prayer, as Hamlet thinks in line 85)

[Scene IV. *The Queen's closet.*]

Enter [Queen] Gertrude and Polonius.

Polonius. 'A will come straight. Look you lay home°
       to him.
    Tell him his pranks have been too broad° to bear
       with,
    And that your Grace hath screened and stood be-
       tween
    Much heat and him. I'll silence me even here.
5   Pray you be round with him.

Hamlet. (*Within*) Mother, Mother, Mother!

Queen. I'll warrant you; fear me not. Withdraw; I hear
    him coming.   [*Polonius hides behind the arras.*]

                  Enter Hamlet.

Hamlet. Now, Mother, what's the matter?

10 *Queen.* Hamlet, thou hast thy father much offended.

Hamlet. Mother, you have my father much offended.

Queen. Come, come, you answer with an idle° tongue.

Hamlet. Go, go, you question with a wicked tongue.

Queen. Why, how now, Hamlet?

Hamlet.   What's the matter now?

Queen. Have you forgot me?

15 *Hamlet.*   No, by the rood,° not so!
    You are the Queen, your husband's brother's wife,
    And, would it were not so, you are my mother.

Queen. Nay, then I'll set those to you that can speak.

Hamlet. Come, come, and sit you down. You shall not
    budge.

III.iv.1 *lay home* thrust (rebuke) him sharply   2 *broad* unrestrained   12 *idle* foolish   15 *rood* cross

You go not till I set you up a glass°　　　　　20
Where you may see the inmost part of you!

Queen. What wilt thou do? Thou wilt not murder me?
Help, ho!

Polonius. [*Behind*] What, ho! Help!

Hamlet. [*Draws*] How now? A rat? Dead for a ducat,
dead!　　　　　25
　　[*Makes a pass through the arras and*] *kills Polonius.*

Polonius. [*Behind*] O, I am slain!

Queen.　　　　　　　O me, what hast thou done?

Hamlet. Nay, I know not. Is it the King?

Queen. O, what a rash and bloody deed is this!

Hamlet. A bloody deed—almost as bad, good Mother,
As kill a king, and marry with his brother.　　　　　30

Queen. As kill a king?

Hamlet.　　　　　　Ay, lady, it was my word.
　　　　[*Lifts up the arras and sees Polonius.*]
Thou wretched, rash, intruding fool, farewell!
I took thee for thy better. Take thy fortune.
Thou find'st to be too busy is some danger.—
Leave wringing of your hands. Peace, sit you down　　　　　35
And let me wring your heart, for so I shall
If it be made of penetrable stuff,
If damnèd custom have not brazed° it so
That it be proof° and bulwark against sense.°

Queen. What have I done that thou dar'st wag thy
tongue　　　　　40
In noise so rude against me?

Hamlet.　　　　　　Such an act
That blurs the grace and blush of modesty,
Calls virtue hypocrite, takes off the rose
From the fair forehead of an innocent love,
And sets a blister° there, makes marriage vows　　　　　45

20 *glass* mirror　38 *brazed* hardened like brass　39 *proof* armor
39 *sense* feeling　45 *sets a blister* brands (as a harlot)

As false as dicers' oaths. O, such a deed
As from the body of contraction° plucks
The very soul, and sweet religion makes
A rhapsody° of words! Heaven's face does glow
50　O'er this solidity and compound mass
With heated visage, as against the doom
Is thoughtsick at the act.°

Queen.　　　　　　　　　　Ay me, what act,
That roars so loud and thunders in the index?°

Hamlet. Look here upon this picture, and on this,
55　The counterfeit presentment° of two brothers.
See what a grace was seated on this brow:
Hyperion's curls, the front° of Jove himself,
An eye like Mars, to threaten and command,
A station° like the herald Mercury
60　New lighted on a heaven-kissing hill—
A combination and a form indeed
Where every god did seem to set his seal
To give the world assurance of a man.
This was your husband. Look you now what follows.
65　Here is your husband, like a mildewed ear
Blasting his wholesome brother. Have you eyes?
Could you on this fair mountain leave to feed,
And batten° on this moor? Ha! Have you eyes?
You cannot call it love, for at your age
70　The heyday° in the blood is tame, it's humble,
And waits upon the judgment, and what judgment
Would step from this to this? Sense° sure you have,
Else could you not have motion, but sure that sense
Is apoplexed,° for madness would not err,
75　Nor sense to ecstasy° was ne'er so thralled
But it reserved some quantity of choice

47 *contraction* marriage contract　49 *rhapsody* senseless string
49–52 *Heaven's face . . . the act* i.e., the face of heaven blushes
over this earth (compounded of four elements), the face hot, as
if Judgment Day were near, and it is thoughtsick at the act
53 *index* prologue　55 *counterfeit presentment* represented image
57 *front* forehead　59 *station* bearing　68 *batten* feed gluttonously
70 *heyday* excitement　72 *Sense* feeling　74 *apoplexed* paralyzed
75 *ecstasy* madness

To serve in such a difference. What devil was't
That thus hath cozened you at hoodman-blind?°
Eyes without feeling, feeling without sight,
Ears without hands or eyes, smelling sans° all,   *80*
Or but a sickly part of one true sense
Could not so mope.°
O shame, where is thy blush? Rebellious hell,
If thou canst mutine in a matron's bones,
To flaming youth let virtue be as wax   *85*
And melt in her own fire. Proclaim no shame
When the compulsive ardor° gives the charge,
Since frost itself as actively doth burn,
And reason panders will.°

Queen.   O Hamlet, speak no more.
Thou turn'st mine eyes into my very soul,   *90*
And there I see such black and grainèd° spots
As will not leave their tinct.°

Hamlet.   Nay, but to live
In the rank sweat of an enseamèd° bed,
Stewed in corruption, honeying and making love
Over the nasty sty——

Queen.   O, speak to me no more.   *95*
These words like daggers enter in my ears.
No more, sweet Hamlet.

Hamlet.   A murderer and a villain,
A slave that is not twentieth part the tithe°
Of your precedent lord, a vice° of kings,
A cutpurse of the empire and the rule,   *100*
That from a shelf the precious diadem stole
And put it in his pocket——

Queen.   No more.

---

78 *cozened you at hoodman-blind* cheated you at blindman's buff
80 *sans* without   82 *mope* be stupid   87 *compulsive ardor* com-
pelling passion   89 *reason panders will* reason acts as a procurer
for desire   91 *grainèd* dyed in grain (fast dyed)   92 *tinct* color
93 *enseamèd* (perhaps "soaked in grease," i.e., sweaty; perhaps
"much wrinkled")   98 *tithe* tenth part   99 *vice* (like the Vice, a
fool and mischief-maker in the old morality plays)

Enter Ghost.

Hamlet. A king of shreds and patches—
　　Save me and hover o'er me with your wings,
　　You heavenly guards! What would your gracious
105　　　figure?

Queen. Alas, he's mad.

Hamlet. Do you not come your tardy son to chide,
　　That, lapsed in time and passion, lets go by
　　Th' important acting of your dread command?
110　　O, say!

Ghost. Do not forget. This visitation
　　Is but to whet thy almost blunted purpose.
　　But look, amazement on thy mother sits.
　　O, step between her and her fighting soul!
115　　Conceit° in weakest bodies strongest works.
　　Speak to her, Hamlet.

Hamlet.　　　　　　　　How is it with you, lady?

Queen. Alas, how is't with you,
　　That you do bend your eye on vacancy,
　　And with th' incorporal° air do hold discourse?
120　　Forth at your eyes your spirits wildly peep,
　　And as the sleeping soldiers in th' alarm
　　Your bedded hair° like life in excrements°
　　Start up and stand an end.° O gentle son,
　　Upon the heat and flame of thy distemper
125　　Sprinkle cool patience. Whereon do you look?

Hamlet. On him, on him! Look you, how pale he
　　　　glares!
　　His form and cause conjoined, preaching to stones,
　　Would make them capable.°—Do not look upon
　　　　me,
　　Lest with this piteous action you convert
130　　My stern effects.° Then what I have to do
　　Will want true color; tears perchance for blood.

Queen. To whom do you speak this?

115 *Conceit* imagination 119 *incorporal* bodiless 122 *bedded hair* hairs laid flat 122 *excrements* outgrowths (here, the hair) 123 *an end* on end 128 *capable* receptive 129–30 *convert/My stern effects* divert my stern deeds

Hamlet. Do you see nothing there?

Queen. Nothing at all; yet all that is I see.

Hamlet. Nor did you nothing hear?

Queen. No, nothing but ourselves.

Hamlet. Why, look you there! Look how it steals away! 135
My father, in his habit° as he lived!
Look where he goes even now out at the portal!
Exit Ghost.

Queen. This is the very coinage of your brain.
This bodiless creation ecstasy
Is very cunning in.

Hamlet. Ecstasy? 140
My pulse as yours doth temperately keep time
And makes as healthful music. It is not madness
That I have uttered. Bring me to the test,
And I the matter will reword, which madness
Would gambol° from. Mother, for love of grace, 145
Lay not that flattering unction° to your soul,
That not your trespass but my madness speaks.
It will but skin and film the ulcerous place
Whiles rank corruption, mining° all within,
Infects unseen. Confess yourself to heaven, 150
Repent what's past, avoid what is to come,
And do not spread the compost° on the weeds
To make them ranker. Forgive me this my virtue.
For in the fatness of these pursy° times
Virtue itself of vice must pardon beg, 155
Yea, curb° and woo for leave to do him good.

Queen. O Hamlet, thou hast cleft my heart in twain.

Hamlet. O, throw away the worser part of it,
And live the purer with the other half.
Good night—but go not to my uncle's bed. 160
Assume a virtue, if you have it not.

136 *habit* garment (Q1, though a "bad" quarto, is probably correct in saying that at line 102 the ghost enters "in his nightgown," i.e., dressing gown) 145 *gambol* start away 146 *unction* ointment 149 *mining* undermining 152 *compost* fertilizing substance 154 *pursy* bloated 156 *curb* bow low

That monster custom, who all sense doth eat,
Of habits devil, is angel yet in this,
That to the use°of actions fair and good
165 He likewise gives a frock or livery°
That aptly is put on. Refrain tonight,
And that shall lend a kind of easiness
To the next abstinence; the next more easy;
For use almost can change the stamp of nature,
170 And either° the devil, or throw him out
With wondrous potency. Once more, good night,
And when you are desirous to be blest,
I'll blessing beg of you.—For this same lord,
I do repent; but heaven hath pleased it so,
175 To punish me with this, and this with me,
That I must be their° scourge and minister.
I will bestow° him and will answer well
The death I gave him. So again, good night.
I must be cruel only to be kind.
180 Thus bad begins, and worse remains behind.
One word more, good lady.

Queen.   What shall I do?

Hamlet. Not this, by no means, that I bid you do:
Let the bloat King tempt you again to bed,
Pinch wanton on your cheek, call you his mouse,
185 And let him, for a pair of reechy° kisses,
Or paddling in your neck with his damned fingers,
Make you to ravel° all this matter out,
That I essentially am not in madness,
But mad in craft. 'Twere good you let him know,
190 For who that's but a queen, fair, sober, wise,
Would from a paddock,° from a bat, a gib,°
Such dear concernings hide? Who would do so?
No, in despite of sense and secrecy,

---

164 *use* practice 165 *livery* characteristic garment (punning on
"habits" in line 163) 170 *either* (probably a word is missing after
either; among suggestions are "master," "curb," and "house"; but
possibly *either* is a verb meaning "make easier") 176 *their* i.e.,
the heavens' 177 *bestow* stow, lodge 185 *reechy* foul (literally
"smoky") 187 *ravel* unravel, reveal 191 *paddock* toad 191 *gib*
tomcat

Unpeg the basket on the house's top,
Let the birds fly, and like the famous ape,   *195*
To try conclusions,° in the basket creep
And break your own neck down.

Queen. Be thou assured, if words be made of breath,
And breath of life, I have no life to breathe
What thou hast said to me.   *200*

Hamlet. I must to England; you know that?

Queen.   Alack,
I had forgot. 'Tis so concluded on.

Hamlet. There's letters sealed, and my two school-
    fellows,
Whom I will trust as I will adders fanged,
They bear the mandate;° they must sweep my way   *205*
And marshal me to knavery. Let it work;
For 'tis the sport to have the enginer
Hoist with his own petar,° and 't shall go hard
But I will delve one yard below their mines
And blow them at the moon. O, 'tis most sweet   *210*
When in one line two crafts° directly meet.
This man shall set me packing:
I'll lug the guts into the neighbor room.
Mother, good night. Indeed, this counselor
Is now most still, most secret, and most grave,   *215*
Who was in life a foolish prating knave.
Come, sir, to draw toward an end with you.
Good night, Mother.
        [*Exit the Queen. Then*] *exit Hamlet, tugging in*
                                        Polonius.

196 *To try conclusions* to make experiments   205 *mandate* command   208 *petar* bomb   211 *crafts* (1) boats (2) acts of guile,
crafty schemes

[ACT IV

Scene I. *The castle.*]

Enter King and Queen, with Rosencrantz and Guildenstern.

King. There's matter in these sighs. These profound
    heaves
    You must translate; 'tis fit we understand them.
    Where is your son?

Queen. Bestow this place on us a little while.
               [Exeunt Rosencrantz and Guildenstern.]

5   Ah, mine own lord, what have I seen tonight!

King. What, Gertrude? How does Hamlet?

Queen. Mad as the sea and wind when both contend
    Which is the mightier. In his lawless fit,
    Behind the arras hearing something stir,

10   Whips out his rapier, cries, "A rat, a rat!"
    And in this brainish apprehension° kills
    The unseen good old man.

King.   O heavy deed!
    It had been so with us, had we been there.
    His liberty is full of threats to all,

15   To you yourself, to us, to every one.
    Alas, how shall this bloody deed be answered?
    It will be laid to us, whose providence°

IV.i.11 *brainish apprehension* mad imagination 17 *providence*
foresight

124

Should have kept short, restrained, and out of haunt°
This mad young man. But so much was our love
We would not understand what was most fit,   20
But, like the owner of a foul disease,
To keep it from divulging, let it feed
Even on the pith of life. Where is he gone?

Queen. To draw apart the body he hath killed;
O'er whom his very madness, like some ore   25
Among a mineral° of metals base,
Shows itself pure. 'A weeps for what is done.

King. O Gertrude, come away!
The sun no sooner shall the mountains touch
But we will ship him hence, and this vile deed   30
We must with all our majesty and skill
Both countenance and excuse. Ho, Guildenstern!

Enter Rosencrantz and Guildenstern.

Friends both, go join you with some further aid:
Hamlet in madness hath Polonius slain,
And from his mother's closet hath he dragged him.   35
Go seek him out; speak fair, and bring the body
Into the chapel. I pray you haste in this.
                    [*Exeunt Rosencrantz and Guildenstern.*]
Come, Gertrude, we'll call up our wisest friends
And let them know both what we mean to do
And what's untimely done . . .°   40
Whose whisper o'er the world's diameter,
As level as the cannon to his blank°
Transports his poisoned shot, may miss our name
And hit the woundless° air. O, come away!
My soul is full of discord and dismay.   *Exeunt.*   45

18 *out of haunt* away from association with others   25–26 *ore/
Among a mineral* vein of gold in a mine   40 *done* . . . (evidently
something has dropped out of the text. Capell's conjecture, "So,
haply slander," is usually printed)   42 *blank* white center of a
target   44 *woundless* invulnerable

[Scene II. *The castle.*]

Enter Hamlet.

Hamlet. Safely stowed.

Gentlemen. (*Within*) Hamlet! Lord Hamlet!

Hamlet. But soft, what noise? Who calls on Hamlet?
O, here they come.

Enter Rosencrantz and Guildenstern.

Rosencrantz. What have you done, my lord, with the
5   dead body?

Hamlet. Compounded it with dust, whereto 'tis kin.

Rosencrantz. Tell us where 'tis, that we may take it
thence
And bear it to the chapel.

Hamlet. Do not believe it.

10 *Rosencrantz.* Believe what?

Hamlet. That I can keep your counsel and not mine
own. Besides, to be demanded of° a sponge, what
replication° should be made by the son of a king?

Rosencrantz. Take you me for a sponge, my lord?

15 *Hamlet.* Ay, sir, that soaks up the King's countenance,°
his rewards, his authorities. But such officers do the
King best service in the end. He keeps them, like an
ape, in the corner of his jaw, first mouthed, to be
last swallowed. When he needs what you have
20 gleaned, it is but squeezing you and, sponge, you
shall be dry again.

Rosencrantz. I understand you not, my lord.

Hamlet. I am glad of it: a knavish speech sleeps in a
foolish ear.

IV.ii.12 *demanded of* questioned by   13 *replication* reply   15 *countenance* favor

Rosencrantz. My lord, you must tell us where the body   25
is and go with us to the King.

Hamlet. The body is with the King, but the King is not
with the body. The King is a thing——

Guildenstern. A thing, my lord?

Hamlet. Of nothing. Bring me to him. Hide fox, and   30
all after.°   *Exeunt.*

[Scene III. *The castle.*]

Enter King, and two or three.

King. I have sent to seek him and to find the body:
How dangerous is it that this man goes loose!
Yet must not we put the strong law on him:
He's loved of the distracted° multitude,
Who like not in their judgment, but their eyes,   5
And where 'tis so, th' offender's scourge is weighed,
But never the offense. To bear° all smooth and even,
This sudden sending him away must seem
Deliberate pause.° Diseases desperate grown
By desperate appliance are relieved,   10
Or not at all.

Enter Rosencrantz, [Guildenstern,] and all the rest.

How now? What hath befall'n?

Rosencrantz. Where the dead body is bestowed, my
lord,
We cannot get from him.

King.   But where is he?

Rosencrantz. Without, my lord; guarded, to know your
pleasure.

30–31 *Hide fox, and all after* (a cry in a game such as hide-and-
seek; Hamlet runs from the stage) IV.iii.4 *distracted* bewildered,
senseless 7 *bear* carry out 9 *pause* planning

King. Bring him before us.

15 *Rosencrantz.*   Ho! Bring in the lord.

                    They enter.

King. Now, Hamlet, where's Polonius?

Hamlet. At supper.

King. At supper? Where?

Hamlet. Not where he eats, but where 'a is eaten. A
20   certain convocation of politic° worms are e'en at
        him. Your worm is your only emperor for diet. We
        fat all creatures else to fat us, and we fat ourselves
        for maggots. Your fat king and your lean beggar is
        but variable service°—two dishes, but to one table.
25   That's the end.

King. Alas, alas!

Hamlet. A man may fish with the worm that hath eat of
        a king, and eat of the fish that hath fed of that worm.

King. What dost thou mean by this?

30 *Hamlet.* Nothing but to show you how a king may
        go a progress° through the guts of a beggar.

King. Where is Polonius?

Hamlet. In heaven. Send thither to see. If your mes-
        senger find him not there, seek him i' th' other
35   place yourself. But if indeed you find him not
        within this month, you shall nose him as you go
        up the stairs into the lobby.

King. [*To Attendants*] Go seek him there.

Hamlet. 'A will stay till you come.

                    [*Exeunt Attendants.*]

40 *King.* Hamlet, this deed, for thine especial safety,
        Which we do tender° as we dearly grieve
        For that which thou hast done, must send thee hence
        With fiery quickness. Therefore prepare thyself.

20 *politic* statesmanlike, shrewd   24 *variable service* different courses
31 *progress* royal journey   41 *tender* hold dear

  The bark is ready and the wind at help,
  Th' associates tend,° and everything is bent   45
  For England.

Hamlet.   For England?

King.   Ay, Hamlet.

Hamlet.   Good.

King. So is it, if thou knew'st our purposes.

Hamlet. I see a cherub° that sees them. But come, for
  England! Farewell, dear Mother.

King. Thy loving father, Hamlet.   50

Hamlet. My mother—father and mother is man and
  wife, man and wife is one flesh, and so, my mother.
  Come, for England!   *Exit.*

King. Follow him at foot;° tempt him with speed
  aboard.
  Delay it not; I'll have him hence tonight.   55
  Away! For everything is sealed and done
  That else leans° on th' affair. Pray you make haste.
         [Exeunt all but the King.]
  And, England, if my love thou hold'st at aught—
  As my great power thereof may give thee sense,
  Since yet thy cicatrice° looks raw and red   60
  After the Danish sword, and thy free awe°
  Pays homage to us—thou mayst not coldly set
  Our sovereign process,° which imports at full
  By letters congruing to that effect
  The present° death of Hamlet. Do it, England,   65
  For like the hectic° in my blood he rages,
  And thou must cure me. Till I know 'tis done,
  Howe'er my haps,° my joys were ne'er begun.
         Exit.

---

45 *tend* wait 48 *cherub* angel of knowledge 54 *at foot* closely
57 *leans* depends 60 *cicatrice* scar 61 *free awe* uncompelled submission 62–63 *coldly set/Our sovereign process* regard slightly
our royal command 65 *present* instant 66 *hectic* fever 68 *haps*
chances, fortunes

[Scene IV. *A plain in Denmark.*]

Enter Fortinbras with his Army over the stage.

Fortinbras. Go, Captain, from me greet the Danish
      king.
   Tell him that by his license Fortinbras
   Craves the conveyance of° a promised march
   Over his kingdom. You know the rendezvous.
5 If that his Majesty would aught with us,
   We shall express our duty in his eye;°
   And let him know so.

Captain.   I will do't, my lord.

Fortinbras. Go softly° on.
                              [*Exeunt all but the Captain.*]
                  Enter Hamlet, Rosencrantz, &c.

Hamlet. Good sir, whose powers° are these?

10 *Captain.* They are of Norway, sir.

Hamlet. How purposed, sir, I pray you?

Captain. Against some part of Poland.

Hamlet. Who commands them, sir?

Captain. The nephew to old Norway, Fortinbras.

15 *Hamlet.* Goes it against the main° of Poland, sir,
   Or for some frontier?

Captain. Truly to speak, and with no addition,°
   We go to gain a little patch of ground
   That hath in it no profit but the name.
20 To pay five ducats, five, I would not farm it,
   Nor will it yield to Norway or the Pole
   A ranker° rate, should it be sold in fee.°

IV.iv.3 *conveyance of* escort for   6 *in his eye* before his eyes (i.e.,
in his presence)   8 *softly* slowly   9 *powers* forces   15 *main* main
part   17 *with no addition* plainly   22 *ranker* higher   22 *in fee*
outright

Hamlet. Why, then the Polack never will defend it.

Captain. Yes, it is already garrisoned.

Hamlet. Two thousand souls and twenty thousand
    ducats   25
Will not debate° the question of this straw.
This is th' imposthume° of much wealth and peace,
That inward breaks, and shows no cause without
Why the man dies. I humbly thank you, sir.

Captain. God bye you, sir.   [*Exit.*]

Rosencrantz.   Will't please you go, my lord?   30

Hamlet. I'll be with you straight. Go a little before.
                     [*Exeunt all but Hamlet.*]
How all occasions do inform against me
And spur my dull revenge! What is a man,
If his chief good and market° of his time
Be but to sleep and feed? A beast, no more.   35
Sure he that made us with such large discourse,°
Looking before and after, gave us not
That capability and godlike reason
To fust° in us unused. Now, whether it be
Bestial oblivion,° or some craven scruple   40
Of thinking too precisely on th' event°—
A thought which, quartered, hath but one part
    wisdom
And ever three parts coward—I do not know
Why yet I live to say, "This thing's to do,"
Sith I have cause, and will, and strength, and means 45
To do't. Examples gross° as earth exhort me.
Witness this army of such mass and charge,°
Led by a delicate and tender prince,
Whose spirit, with divine ambition puffed,
Makes mouths at the invisible event,°   50
Exposing what is mortal and unsure
To all that fortune, death, and danger dare,

26 *debate* settle 27 *imposthume* abscess, ulcer 34 *market* profit
36 *discourse* understanding 39 *fust* grow moldy 40 *oblivion* forgetfulness 41 *event* outcome 46 *gross* large, obvious 47 *charge*
expense 50 *Makes mouths at the invisible event* makes scornful
faces (is contemptuous of) the unseen outcome

Even for an eggshell. Rightly to be great
Is not° to stir without great argument,°
55 But greatly° to find quarrel in a straw
When honor's at the stake. How stand I then,
That have a father killed, a mother stained,
Excitements° of my reason and my blood,
And let all sleep, while to my shame I see
60 The imminent death of twenty thousand men
That for a fantasy and trick of fame°
Go to their graves like beds, fight for a plot
Whereon the numbers cannot try the cause,
Which is not tomb enough and continent°
65 To hide the slain? O, from this time forth,
My thoughts be bloody, or be nothing worth! *Exit.*

[Scene V. *The castle.*]

Enter Horatio, [Queen] Gertrude, and a Gentleman.

Queen. I will not speak with her.

Gentleman. She is importunate, indeed distract.
Her mood will needs be pitied.

Queen.   What would she have?

Gentleman. She speaks much of her father, says she
        hears
There's tricks i' th' world, and hems, and beats her
5   heart,
Spurns enviously at straws,° speaks things in doubt°
That carry but half sense. Her speech is nothing,
Yet the unshapèd use of it doth move

54 *not* (the sense seems to require "not not") 54 *argument*
reason 55 *greatly* i.e., nobly 58 *Excitements* incentives 61 *fantasy and trick of fame* illusion and trifle of reputation 64 *continent* receptacle, container IV.v.6 *Spurns enviously at straws* objects spitefully to insignificant matters 6 *in doubt* uncertainly

The hearers to collection;° they yawn° at it,
And botch the words up fit to their own thoughts,   10
Which, as her winks and nods and gestures yield them,
Indeed would make one think there might be thought,
Though nothing sure, yet much unhappily.

Horatio. 'Twere good she were spoken with, for she may strew
Dangerous conjectures in ill-breeding minds.   15

Queen. Let her come in.   [*Exit Gentleman.*]
[*Aside*] To my sick soul (as sin's true nature is)
Each toy seems prologue to some great amiss;°
So full of artless jealousy° is guilt
It spills° itself in fearing to be spilt.   20

Enter Ophelia [distracted.]

Ophelia. Where is the beauteous majesty of Denmark?

Queen. How now, Ophelia?

Ophelia. (*She sings.*) How should I your truelove know
          From another one?
      By his cockle hat° and staff   25
      And his sandal shoon.°

Queen. Alas, sweet lady, what imports this song?

Ophelia. Say you? Nay, pray you mark.

      He is dead and gone, lady,   (*Song*)
          He is dead and gone;   30
      At his head a grass-green turf,
          At his heels a stone.

      O, ho!

Queen. Nay, but Ophelia——

Ophelia. Pray you mark.   35

8–9 *Yet the . . . to collection* i.e., yet the formless manner of it moves her listeners to gather up some sort of meaning   9 *yawn* gape (?)   18 *amiss* misfortune   19 *artless jealousy* crude suspicion   20 *spills* destroys   25 *cockle hat* (a cockleshell on the hat was the sign of a pilgrim who had journeyed to shrines overseas. The association of lovers and pilgrims was a common one)   26 *shoon* shoes

    [Sings.] White his shroud as the mountain snow——

                Enter King.

Queen. Alas, look here, my lord.

Ophelia.   Larded°all with sweet flowers *(Song)*
           Which bewept to the grave did not go
40   With truelove showers.

King. How do you, pretty lady?

Ophelia. Well, God dild° you! They say the owl was a
    baker's daughter.° Lord, we know what we are, but
    know not what we may be. God be at your table!

45 *King.* Conceit° upon her father.

Ophelia. Pray let's have no words of this, but when
    they ask you what it means, say you this:
           Tomorrow is Saint Valentine's day.° *(Song)*
           All in the morning betime,
50   And I a maid at your window,
           To be your Valentine.

           Then up he rose and donned his clothes
           And dupped° the chamber door,
           Let in the maid, that out a maid
55   Never departed more.

King. Pretty Ophelia.

Ophelia. Indeed, la, without an oath, I'll make an end
    on't:
    [Sings.] By Gis° and by Saint Charity,
           Alack, and fie for shame!
60   Young men will do't if they come to't,
           By Cock,° they are to blame.
           Quoth she, "Before you tumbled me,
           You promised me to wed."

38 *Larded* decorated   42 *dild* yield, i.e., reward   43 *baker's daughter* (an allusion to a tale of a baker's daughter who begrudged
bread to Christ and was turned into an owl)   45 *Conceit* brooding
48 *Saint Valentine's day* Feb. 14 (the notion was that a bachelor
would become the truelove of the first girl he saw on this day)
53 *dupped* opened (did up)   58 *Gis* (contraction of "Jesus")
61 *Cock* (1) God (2) phallus

He answers:

> "So would I 'a' done, by yonder sun,　　　　65
> 　　An thou hadst not come to my bed."

King. How long hath she been thus?

Ophelia. I hope all will be well. We must be patient, but I cannot choose but weep to think they would lay him i' th' cold ground. My brother shall know　70 of it; and so I thank you for your good counsel. Come, my coach! Good night, ladies, good night. Sweet ladies, good night, good night.　　　　*Exit.*

King. Follow her close; give her good watch, I pray you.　　　　[*Exit Horatio.*]
O, this is the poison of deep grief; it springs　75
All from her father's death—and now behold!
O Gertrude, Gertrude,
When sorrows come, they come not single spies,
But in battalions: first, her father slain;
Next, your son gone, and he most violent author　80
Of his own just remove; the people muddied,°
Thick and unwholesome in their thoughts and
　　whispers
For good Polonius' death, and we have done but
　　greenly°
In huggermugger° to inter him; poor Ophelia
Divided from herself and her fair judgment,　85
Without the which we are pictures or mere beasts;
Last, and as much containing as all these,
Her brother is in secret come from France,
Feeds on his wonder,° keeps himself in clouds,
And wants not buzzers° to infect his ear　90
With pestilent speeches of his father's death,
Wherein necessity, of matter beggared,°
Will nothing stick° our person to arraign
In ear and ear. O my dear Gertrude, this,

---

81 *muddied* muddled　83 *greenly* foolishly　84 *huggermugger* secret haste　89 *wonder* suspicion　90 *wants not buzzers* does not lack talebearers　92 *of matter beggared* unprovided with facts　93 *Will nothing stick* will not hesitate

95 Like to a murd'ring piece,° in many places
    Gives me superfluous death.   *A noise within.*

                Enter a Messenger.

Queen.   Alack, what noise is this?

King. Attend, where are my Switzers?° Let them
    guard the door.
    What is the matter?

Messenger.   Save yourself, my lord.
    The ocean, overpeering of his list,°
100 Eats not the flats with more impiteous haste
    Than young Laertes, in a riotous head,°
    O'erbears your officers. The rabble call him lord,
    And, as the world were now but to begin,
    Antiquity forgot, custom not known,
105 The ratifiers and props of every word,
    They cry, "Choose we! Laertes shall be king!"
    Caps, hands, and tongues applaud it to the clouds,
    "Laertes shall be king! Laertes king!" *A noise within.*

Queen. How cheerfully on the false trail they cry!
110 O, this is counter,° you false Danish dogs!

                Enter Laertes with others.

King. The doors are broke.

Laertes. Where is this king?—Sirs, stand you all
    without.

All. No, let's come in.

Laertes.   I pray you give me leave.

All. We will, we will.

Laertes. I thank you. Keep the door. [*Exeunt his
115   Followers.*] O thou vile King,
    Give me my father.

Queen.   Calmly, good Laertes.

95 *murd'ring piece* (a cannon that shot a kind of shrapnel)
97 *Switzers* Swiss guards 99 *list* shore 101 *in a riotous head*
with a rebellious force 110 *counter* (a hound runs counter when
he follows the scent backward from the prey)

Laertes. That drop of blood that's calm proclaims me
　　bastard,
　　Cries cuckold° to my father, brands the harlot
　　Even here between the chaste unsmirchèd brow
　　Of my true mother.

King.　　　　　　　　What is the cause, Laertes,　　　120
　　That thy rebellion looks so giantlike?
　　Let him go, Gertrude. Do not fear° our person.
　　There's such divinity doth hedge a king
　　That treason can but peep to° what it would,
　　Acts little of his will. Tell me, Laertes,　　　125
　　Why thou art thus incensed. Let him go, Gertrude.
　　Speak, man.

Laertes. Where is my father?

King.　　　　　　　　Dead.

Queen.　　　　　　　　But not by him.

King. Let him demand his fill.

Laertes. How came he dead? I'll not be juggled with.　130
　　To hell allegiance, vows to the blackest devil,
　　Conscience and grace to the profoundest pit!
　　I dare damnation. To this point I stand,
　　That both the worlds I give to negligence,°
　　Let come what comes, only I'll be revenged　　135
　　Most throughly for my father.

King.　　　　　　　　Who shall stay you?

Laertes. My will, not all the world's.
　　And for my means, I'll husband them° so well
　　They shall go far with little.

King.　　　　　　　　Good Laertes,
　　If you desire to know the certainty　　　140
　　Of your dear father, is't writ in your revenge
　　That swoopstake° you will draw both friend and foe,
　　Winner and loser?

118 *cuckold* man whose wife is unfaithful　122 *fear* fear for
124 *peep to* i.e., look at from a distance　134 *That both . . . to
negligence* i.e., I care not what may happen (to me) in this world
or the next　138 *husband them* use them economically　142 *swoopstake* in a clean sweep

Laertes. None but his enemies.

King.   Will you know them then?

Laertes. To his good friends thus wide I'll ope my
145   arms
And like the kind life-rend'ring pelican°
Repast° them with my blood.

King.   Why, now you speak
Like a good child and a true gentleman.
That I am guiltless of your father's death,
150   And am most sensibly° in grief for it,
It shall as level to your judgment 'pear
As day does to your eye.

> *A noise within: "Let her come in."*

Laertes. How now? What noise is that?

> *Enter Ophelia.*

O heat, dry up my brains; tears seven times salt
155   Burn out the sense and virtue° of mine eye!
By heaven, thy madness shall be paid with weight
Till our scale turn the beam.° O rose of May,
Dear maid, kind sister, sweet Ophelia!
O heavens, is't possible a young maid's wits
160   Should be as mortal as an old man's life?
Nature is fine° in love, and where 'tis fine,
It sends some precious instance° of itself
After the thing it loves.

Ophelia.   They bore him barefaced on the bier *(Song)*
165   Hey non nony, nony, hey nony
                 And in his grave rained many a tear——
Fare you well, my dove!

Laertes. Hadst thou thy wits, and didst persuade re-
         venge,
It could not move thus.

170 *Ophelia.* You must sing "A-down a-down, and you call

146 *pelican* (thought to feed its young with its own blood)
147 *Repast* feed 150 *sensibly* acutely 155 *virtue* power 157 *turn the beam* weigh down the bar (of the balance) 161 *fine* refined, delicate 162 *instance* sample

him a-down-a." O, how the wheel° becomes it! It is
the false steward, that stole his master's daughter.

Laertes. This nothing's more than matter.°

Ophelia. There's rosemary, that's for remembrance.
Pray you, love, remember. And there is pansies, 175
that's for thoughts.

Laertes. A document° in madness, thoughts and remembrance fitted.

Ophelia. There's fennel° for you, and columbines.
There's rue for you, and here's some for me. We 180
may call it herb of grace o' Sundays. O, you must
wear your rue with a difference. There's a daisy. I
would give you some violets, but they withered all
when my father died. They say 'a made a good end.
[*Sings*]   For bonny sweet Robin is all my joy.   185

Laertes. Thought and affliction, passion, hell itself,
She turns to favor° and to prettiness.

Ophelia.   And will 'a not come again?   (*Song*)
             And will 'a not come again?
                No, no, he is dead,   190
                Go to thy deathbed,
             He never will come again.

             His beard was as white as snow,
             All flaxen was his poll.°
                He is gone, he is gone,   195
                And we cast away moan.
             God 'a' mercy on his soul!
And of all Christian souls, I pray God. God bye you.
                                          [*Exit.*]

171 *wheel* (of uncertain meaning, but probably a turn or dance of
Ophelia's, rather than Fortune's wheel)   173 *This nothing's more
than matter* this nonsense has more meaning than matters of consequence   177 *document* lesson   179 *fennel* (the distribution of
flowers in the ensuing lines has symbolic meaning, but the meaning
is disputed. Perhaps *fennel*, flattery; *columbines*, cuckoldry; *rue*,
sorrow for Ophelia and repentance for the Queen; *daisy*, dissem-
bling; *violets*, faithfulness. For other interpretations, see J. W.
Lever in *Review of English Studies*, New Series 3 [1952], pp. 123–
29)   187 *favor* charm, beauty   194 *All flaxen was his poll* white
as flax was his head

Laertes. Do you see this, O God?

200 *King.* Laertes, I must commune with your grief,
      Or you deny me right. Go but apart,
      Make choice of whom your wisest friends you will,
      And they shall hear and judge 'twixt you and me.
      If by direct or by collateral° hand
205   They find us touched,° we will our kingdom give,
      Our crown, our life, and all that we call ours,
      To you in satisfaction; but if not,
      Be you content to lend your patience to us,
      And we shall jointly labor with your soul
      To give it due content.

210 *Laertes.*   Let this be so.
      His means of death, his obscure funeral—
      No trophy, sword, nor hatchment° o'er his bones,
      No noble rite nor formal ostentation°—
      Cry to be heard, as 'twere from heaven to earth,
      That I must call't in question.

215 *King.*   So you shall;
      And where th' offense is, let the great ax fall.
      I pray you go with me.   *Exeunt.*

[Scene VI. *The castle.*]

Enter Horatio and others.

Horatio. What are they that would speak with me?

Gentleman. Seafaring men, sir. They say they have
   letters for you.

Horatio. Let them come in.   [*Exit Attendant.*]
5   I do not know from what part of the world
      I should be greeted, if not from Lord Hamlet.

204 *collateral* indirect 205 *touched* implicated 212 *hatchment*
tablet bearing the coat of arms of the dead 213 *ostentation* ceremony

Enter Sailors.

Sailor. God bless you, sir.

Horatio. Let Him bless thee too.

Sailor. 'A shall, sir, an't please Him. There's a letter
for you, sir—it came from th' ambassador that was   10
bound for England—if your name be Horatio, as
I am let to know it is.

Horatio. [*Reads the letter.*] "Horatio, when thou shalt
have overlooked° this, give these fellows some
means to the King. They have letters for him. Ere   15
we were two days old at sea, a pirate of very warlike
appointment° gave us chase. Finding ourselves too
slow of sail, we put on a compelled valor, and in
the grapple I boarded them. On the instant they
got clear of our ship; so I alone became their   20
prisoner. They have dealt with me like thieves of
mercy, but they knew what they did: I am to do a
good turn for them. Let the King have the letters
I have sent, and repair thou to me with as much
speed as thou wouldest fly death. I have words to   25
speak in thine ear will make thee dumb; yet are they
much too light for the bore° of the matter. These
good fellows will bring thee where I am. Rosencrantz and Guildenstern hold their course for England. Of them I have much to tell thee. Farewell.   30
          He that thou knowest thine, HAMLET."
Come, I will give you way for these your letters,
And do't the speedier that you may direct me
To him from whom you brought them.   *Exeunt.*

IV.vi.14 *overlooked* surveyed   17 *appointment* equipment   27 *bore*
caliber (here, "importance")

[Scene VII. *The castle.*]

Enter King and Laertes.

King. Now must your conscience my acquittance seal,
    And you must put me in your heart for friend,
    Sith you have heard, and with a knowing ear,
    That he which hath your noble father slain
    Pursued my life.

5 *Laertes.*   It well appears. But tell me
    Why you proceeded not against these feats
    So criminal and so capital° in nature,
    As by your safety, greatness, wisdom, all things else,
    You mainly° were stirred up.

King.   O, for two special reasons,
10   Which may to you perhaps seem much unsinewed,°
    But yet to me they're strong. The Queen his mother
    Lives almost by his looks, and for myself—
    My virtue or my plague, be it either which—
    She is so conjunctive° to my life and soul,
15   That, as the star moves not but in his sphere,
    I could not but by her. The other motive
    Why to a public count° I might not go
    Is the great love the general gender° bear him,
    Who, dipping all his faults in their affection,
20   Would, like the spring that turneth wood to stone,°
    Convert his gyves° to graces; so that my arrows,
    Too slightly timbered° for so loud a wind,
    Would have reverted to my bow again,
    And not where I had aimed them.

IV.vii.7 *capital* deserving death   9 *mainly* powerfully   10 *unsinewed*
weak   14 *conjunctive* closely united   17 *count* reckoning   18 *general gender* common people   20 *spring that turneth wood to stone*
(a spring in Shakespeare's county was so charged with lime that it
would petrify wood placed in it)   21 *gyves* fetters   22 *timbered*
shafted

Laertes. And so have I a noble father lost,   25
   A sister driven into desp'rate terms,°
   Whose worth, if praises may go back again,°
   Stood challenger on mount of all the age
   For her perfections. But my revenge will come.

King. Break not your sleeps for that. You must not
      think   30
   That we are made of stuff so flat and dull
   That we can let our beard be shook with danger,
   And think it pastime. You shortly shall hear more.
   I loved your father, and we love ourself,
   And that, I hope, will teach you to imagine——   35

         Enter a Messenger with letters.

How now? What news?

Messenger.   Letters, my lord, from Ham-
      let:
   These to your Majesty; this to the Queen.

King. From Hamlet? Who brought them?

Messenger. Sailors, my lord, they say; I saw them not.
   They were given me by Claudio; he received them   40
   Of him that brought them.

King.   Laertes, you shall hear them.——
   Leave us.   *Exit Messenger.*
[*Reads.*] "High and mighty, you shall know I am set
naked° on your kingdom. Tomorrow shall I beg
leave to see your kingly eyes; when I shall (first   45
asking your pardon thereunto) recount the occasion
of my sudden and more strange return.

                              HAMLET."
What should this mean? Are all the rest come back?
Or is it some abuse,° and no such thing?   50

Laertes. Know you the hand?

King.   'Tis Hamlet's character.° "Naked"!

---

26 *terms* conditions   27 *go back again* revert to what is past   44
naked destitute   50 *abuse* deception   51 *character* handwriting

And in a postscript here, he says "alone."
Can you devise° me?

Laertes. I am lost in it, my lord. But let him come.
55   It warms the very sickness in my heart
That I shall live and tell him to his teeth,
"Thus did'st thou."

King.   If it be so, Laertes
(As how should it be so? How otherwise?),
Will you be ruled by me?

Laertes.   Ay, my lord,
60   So you will not o'errule me to a peace.

King. To thine own peace. If he be now returned,
As checking at° his voyage, and that he means
No more to undertake it, I will work him
To an exploit now ripe in my device,
65   Under the which he shall not choose but fall;
And for his death no wind of blame shall breathe,
But even his mother shall uncharge the practice°
And call it accident.

Laertes.   My lord, I will be ruled;
The rather if you could devise it so
That I might be the organ.

70   *King.*   It falls right.
You have been talked of since your travel much,
And that in Hamlet's hearing, for a quality
Wherein they say you shine. Your sum of parts
Did not together pluck such envy from him
75   As did that one, and that, in my regard,
Of the unworthiest siege.°

Laertes.   What part is that, my lord?

King. A very riband in the cap of youth,
Yet needful too, for youth no less becomes
The light and careless livery that it wears
80   Than settled age his sables and his weeds,°
Importing health and graveness. Two months since

53 *devise* advise 62 *checking at* turning away from (a term in
falconry) 67 *uncharge the practice* not charge the device with
treachery 76 *siege* rank 80 *sables and his weeds* i.e., sober attire

Here was a gentleman of Normandy.
I have seen myself, and served against, the French,
And they can° well on horseback, but this gallant
Had witchcraft in't. He grew unto his seat,　　　　85
And to such wondrous doing brought his horse
As had he been incorpsed and deminatured
With the brave beast. So far he topped my thought
That I, in forgery° of shapes and tricks,
Come short of what he did.

Laertes.　　　　　　　　A Norman was't?　　　90

King. A Norman.

Laertes. Upon my life, Lamord.

King.　　　　　　　　The very same.

Laertes. I know him well. He is the brooch° indeed
And gem of all the nation.

King. He made confession° of you,　　　　95
And gave you such a masterly report,
For art and exercise in your defense,
And for your rapier most especial,
That he cried out 'twould be a sight indeed
If one could match you. The scrimers° of their
　　nation　　　　　　　　　　　　　　　100
He swore had neither motion, guard, nor eye,
If you opposed them. Sir, this report of his
Did Hamlet so envenom with his envy
That he could nothing do but wish and beg
Your sudden coming o'er to play with you.　　105
Now, out of this——

Laertes.　　　　　　　What out of this, my lord?

King. Laertes, was your father dear to you?
Or are you like the painting of a sorrow,
A face without a heart?

Laertes.　　　　　　　Why ask you this?

King. Not that I think you did not love your father,　110

84 *can* do　89 *forgery* invention　93 *brooch* ornament　95 *confession* report　100 *scrimers* fencers

But that I know love is begun by time,
And that I see, in passages of proof,°
Time qualifies° the spark and fire of it.
There lives within the very flame of love
115 A kind of wick or snuff° that will abate it,
And nothing is at a like goodness still,°
For goodness, growing to a plurisy,°
Dies in his own too-much. That we would do
We should do when we would, for this "would"
       changes,
120 And hath abatements and delays as many
As there are tongues, are hands, are accidents,
And then this "should" is like a spendthrift sigh,°
That hurts by easing. But to the quick° of th' ulcer—
Hamlet comes back; what would you undertake
125 To show yourself in deed your father's son
More than in words?

Laertes.   To cut his throat i' th' church!

King. No place indeed should murder sanctuarize;°
Revenge should have no bounds. But, good Laertes,
Will you do this? Keep close within your chamber.
130 Hamlet returned shall know you are come home.
We'll put on those° shall praise your excellence
And set a double varnish on the fame
The Frenchman gave you, bring you in fine°
       together
And wager on your heads. He, being remiss,
135 Most generous, and free from all contriving,
Will not peruse the foils, so that with ease,
Or with a little shuffling, you may choose
A sword unbated,° and, in a pass of practice,°
Requite him for your father.

Laertes.   I will do't,

112 *passages of proof* proved cases 113 *qualifies* diminishes
115 *snuff* residue of burnt wick (which dims the light) 116 *still*
always 117 *plurisy* fullness, excess 122 *spendthrift sigh* (sighing
provides ease, but because it was thought to thin the blood and
so shorten life it was spendthrift) 123 *quick* sensitive flesh
127 *sanctuarize* protect 131 *We'll put on those* we'll incite persons
who 133 *in fine* finally 138 *unbated* not blunted 138 *pass of
practice* treacherous thrust

And for that purpose I'll anoint my sword.   140
I bought an unction of a mountebank,°
So mortal that, but dip a knife in it,
Where it draws blood, no cataplasm° so rare,
Collected from all simples° that have virtue°
Under the moon, can save the thing from death   145
That is but scratched withal. I'll touch my point
With this contagion, that, if I gall him slightly,
It may be death.

King.   Let's further think of this,
Weigh what convenience both of time and means
May fit us to our shape.° If this should fail,   150
And that our drift look through° our bad per-
    formance,
'Twere better not assayed. Therefore this project
Should have a back or second, that might hold
If this did blast in proof.° Soft, let me see.
We'll make a solemn wager on your cunnings—   155
I ha't!
When in your motion you are hot and dry—
As make your bouts more violent to that end—
And that he calls for drink, I'll have prepared him
A chalice for the nonce,° whereon but sipping,   160
If he by chance escape your venomed stuck,°
Our purpose may hold there.—But stay, what noise?

Enter Queen.

Queen. One woe doth tread upon another's heel.
So fast they follow. Your sister's drowned, Laertes.

Laertes. Drowned! O, where?   165

Queen. There is a willow grows askant° the brook,
That shows his hoar° leaves in the glassy stream:
Therewith° fantastic garlands did she make
Of crowflowers, nettles, daisies, and long purples,

141 *mountebank* quack   143 *cataplasm* poultice   144 *simplex* medicinal herbs   144 *virtue power* (to heal)   150 *shape* role   151 *drift
look through* purpose show through   154 *blast in proof* burst (fail)
in performance   160 *nonce* occasion   161 *stuck* thrust   166 *askant*
aslant   167 *hoar* silver-gray   168 *Therewith* i.e., with willow twigs

170 That liberal° shepherds give a grosser name,
  But our cold maids do dead men's fingers call them.
  There on the pendent boughs her crownet° weeds
  Clamb'ring to hang, an envious sliver° broke,
  When down her weedy trophies and herself
175 Fell in the weeping brook. Her clothes spread wide,
  And mermaidlike awhile they bore her up,
  Which time she chanted snatches of old lauds,°
  As one incapable° of her own distress,
  Or like a creature native and indued°
180 Unto that element. But long it could not be
  Till that her garments, heavy with their drink,
  Pulled the poor wretch from her melodious lay
  To muddy death.

Laertes.   Alas, then she is drowned?

Queen. Drowned, drowned.

185 *Laertes.* Too much of water hast thou, poor Ophelia,
  And therefore I forbid my tears; but yet
  It is our trick;° nature her custom holds,
  Let shame say what it will: when these are gone,
  The woman° will be out. Adieu, my lord.
190 I have a speech o' fire, that fain would blaze,
  But that this folly drowns it.   *Exit.*

 King.   Let's follow, Gertrude.
  How much I had to do to calm his rage!
  Now fear I this will give it start again;
  Therefore let's follow.   *Exeunt.*

---

170 *liberal* free-spoken, coarse-mouthed 172 *crownet* coronet 173 *envious sliver* malicious branch 177 *lauds* hymns 178 *incapable* unaware 179 *indued* in harmony with 187 *trick* trait, way 189 *woman* i.e., womanly part of me

[ACT V

Scene I. *A churchyard.*]

Enter two Clowns.°

Clown. Is she to be buried in Christian burial when she
willfully seeks her own salvation?

Other. I tell thee she is. Therefore make her grave
straight.° The crowner° hath sate on her, and finds
it Christian burial. 5

Clown. How can that be, unless she drowned herself
in her own defense?

Other. Why, 'tis found so.

Clown. It must be *se offendendo;*° it cannot be else.
For here lies the point: if I drown myself wittingly, 10
it argues an act, and an act hath three branches—
it is to act, to do, to perform. Argal,° she drowned
herself wittingly.

Other. Nay, but hear you, Goodman Delver.

Clown. Give me leave. Here lies the water—good. 15
Here stands the man—good. If the man go to this
water and drown himself, it is, will he nill he,° he
goes; mark you that. But if the water come to him
and drown him, he drowns not himself. Argal, he

V.i.s.d. *Clowns* rustics 4 *straight* straightway 4 *crowner* coroner
9 *se offendendo* (blunder for *se defendendo*, a legal term meaning
"in self-defense") 12 *Argal* (blunder for Latin *ergo*, "therefore")
17 *will he nill he* will he or will he not (whether he will or will
not)

149

20   that is not guilty of his own death, shortens not his
own life.

Other. But is this law?

Clown. Ay marry, is't—crowner's quest° law.

Other. Will you ha' the truth on't? If this had not been
25   a gentlewoman, she should have been buried out
o' Christian burial.

Clown. Why, there thou say'st. And the more pity
that great folk should have count'nance° in this
world to drown or hang themselves more than their
30   even-Christen.° Come, my spade. There is no ancient gentlemen but gard'ners, ditchers, and grave-
makers. They hold up° Adam's profession.

Other. Was he a gentleman?

Clown. 'A was the first that ever bore arms.°

35 *Other*. Why, he had none.

Clown. What, art a heathen? How dost thou understand the Scripture? The Scripture says Adam
digged. Could he dig without arms? I'll put another
question to thee. If thou answerest me not to the
40   purpose, confess thyself——

Other. Go to.

Clown. What is he that builds stronger than either the
mason, the shipwright, or the carpenter?

Other. The gallowsmaker, for that frame outlives a
45   thousand tenants.

Clown. I like thy wit well, in good faith. The gallows
does well. But how does it well? It does well to those
that do ill. Now thou dost ill to say the gallows
is built stronger than the church. Argal, the gallows
50   may do well to thee. To't again, come.

Other. Who builds stronger than a mason, a shipwright, or a carpenter?

23 *quest* inquest   28 *count'nance* privilege   30 *even-Christen* fellow
Christian   32 *hold up* keep up   34 *bore arms* had a coat of arms
(the sign of a gentleman)

Clown. Ay, tell me that, and unyoke.°

Other. Marry, now I can tell.

Clown. To't.   35

Other. Mass,° I cannot tell.

      Enter Hamlet and Horatio afar off.

Clown. Cudgel thy brains no more about it, for your
dull ass will not mend his pace with beating. And
when you are asked this question next, say "a gravemaker." The houses he makes lasts till doomsday.   60
Go, get thee in, and fetch me a stoup° of liquor.
                                   [Exit Other Clown.]

   In youth when I did love, did love,   *(Song)*
     Methought it was very sweet
   To contract—O—the time for—a—my behove,°
    O, methought there—a—was nothing—a—meet.   65

Hamlet. Has this fellow no feeling of his business? 'A
sings in gravemaking.

Horatio. Custom hath made it in him a property of
easiness.°

Hamlet. 'Tis e'en so. The hand of little employment   70
hath the daintier sense.°

Clown.   But age with his stealing steps   *(Song)*
       Hath clawed me in his clutch,
     And hath shipped me into the land,
       As if I had never been such.   75
                              [Throws up a skull.]

Hamlet. That skull had a tongue in it, and could sing
once. How the knave jowls° it to the ground, as if
'twere Cain's jawbone, that did the first murder!
This might be the pate of a politician, which this

53 *unyoke* i.e., stop work for the day   56 *Mass* by the mass   61
stoup tankard   64 *behove* advantage   68–69 *in him a property of
easiness* easy for him   71 *hath the daintier sense* is more sensitive
(because it is not calloused)   77 *jowls* hurls

80 ass now o'erreaches,° one that would circumvent
    God, might it not?

Horatio. It might, my lord.

Hamlet. Or of a courtier, which could say "Good
    morrow, sweet lord! How dost thou, sweet lord?"
85 This might be my Lord Such-a-one, that praised
    my Lord Such-a-one's horse when 'a went to beg
    it, might it not?

Horatio. Ay, my lord.

Hamlet. Why, e'en so, and now my Lady Worm's,
90 chapless,° and knocked about the mazzard° with a
    sexton's spade. Here's fine revolution, an we had
    the trick to see't. Did these bones cost no more
    the breeding but to play at loggets° with them?
    Mine ache to think on't.

95 *Clown.*   A pickax and a spade, a spade,   (*Song*)
                    For and a shrouding sheet;
                 O, a pit of clay for to be made
                    For such a guest is meet.
                              [*Throws up another skull.*]

Hamlet. There's another. Why may not that be the
100 skull of a lawyer? Where be his quiddities° now, his
    quillities,° his cases, his tenures,° and his tricks?
    Why does he suffer this mad knave now to knock
    him about the sconce° with a dirty shovel, and will
    not tell him of his action of battery? Hum! This
105 fellow might be in's time a great buyer of land, with
    his statutes, his recognizances, his fines,° his double
    vouchers, his recoveries. Is this the fine° of his fines,
    and the recovery of his recoveries, to have his fine
    pate full of fine dirt? Will his vouchers vouch him

80 *o'erreaches* (1) reaches over (2) has the advantage over 90
chapless lacking the lower jaw 90 *mazzard* head 93 *loggets* (a
game in which small pieces of wood were thrown at an object)
100 *quiddities* subtle arguments (from Latin *quidditas*, "what-
ness") 101 *quillities* fine distinctions 101 *tenures* legal means of
holding land 103 *sconce* head 106 *his statutes, his recognizances,
his fines* his documents giving a creditor control of a debtor's land,
his bonds of surety, his documents changing an entailed estate into
fee simple (unrestricted ownership) 107 *fine* end

no more of his purchases, and double ones too, than 110
the length and breadth of a pair of indentures?°
The very conveyances° of his lands will scarcely
lie in this box, and must th' inheritor himself have no
more, ha?

Horatio. Not a jot more, my lord. 115

Hamlet. Is not parchment made of sheepskins?

Horatio. Ay, my lord, and of calveskins too.

Hamlet. They are sheep and calves which seek out
assurance° in that. I will speak to this fellow. Whose
grave's this, sirrah? 120

Clown. Mine, sir.
  [*Sings.*]   O, a pit of clay for to be made
           For such a guest is meet.

Hamlet. I think it be thine indeed, for thou liest in't.

Clown. You lie out on't, sir, and therefore 'tis not 125
yours. For my part, I do not lie in't, yet it is mine.

Hamlet. Thou dost lie in't, to be in't and say it is
thine. 'Tis for the dead, not for the quick;° therefore thou liest.

Clown. 'Tis a quick lie, sir; 'twill away again from 130
me to you.

Hamlet. What man dost thou dig it for?

Clown. For no man, sir.

Hamlet. What woman then?

Clown. For none neither. 135

Hamlet. Who is to be buried in't?

Clown. One that was a woman, sir; but, rest her soul,
she's dead.

Hamlet. How absolute° the knave is! We must speak by
the card,° or equivocation° will undo us. By the 140

111 *indentures* contracts 112 *conveyances* legal documents for the
transference of land 119 *assurance* safety 128 *quick* living 139
absolute positive, decided 139–40 *by the card* by the compass card,
i.e., exactly 140 *equivocation* ambiguity

Lord, Horatio, this three years I have took note of
it, the age is grown so picked° that the toe of the
peasant comes so near the heel of the courtier he
galls his kibe.° How long hast thou been a grave-
145 maker?

Clown. Of all the days i' th' year, I came to't that day
that our last king Hamlet overcame Fortinbras.

Hamlet. How long is that since?

Clown. Cannot you tell that? Every fool can tell that. It
150 was that very day that young Hamlet was born—
he that is mad, and sent into England.

Hamlet. Ay, marry, why was he sent into England?

Clown. Why, because 'a was mad. 'A shall recover his
wits there; or, if 'a do not, 'tis no great matter there.

155 *Hamlet.* Why?

Clown. 'Twill not be seen in him there. There the men
are as mad as he.

Hamlet. How came he mad?

Clown. Very strangely, they say.

160 *Hamlet.* How strangely?

Clown. Faith, e'en with losing his wits.

Hamlet. Upon what ground?

Clown. Why, here in Denmark. I have been sexton
here, man and boy, thirty years.

165 *Hamlet.* How long will a man lie i' th' earth ere he rot?

Clown. Faith, if 'a be not rotten before 'a die (as we
have many pocky corses° nowadays that will scarce
hold the laying in), 'a will last you some eight year
or nine year. A tanner will last you nine year.

170 *Hamlet.* Why he, more than another?

Clown. Why, sir, his hide is so tanned with his trade

142 *picked* refined 144 *kibe* sore on the back of the heel 167
pocky corses bodies of persons who had been infected with the
pox (syphilis)

that 'a will keep out water a great while, and your
water is a sore decayer of your whoreson dead body.
Here's a skull now hath lien you i' th' earth three and
twenty years.   175

Hamlet. Whose was it?

Clown. A whoreson mad fellow's it was. Whose do you
think it was?

Hamlet. Nay, I know not.

Clown. A pestilence on him for a mad rogue! 'A poured 180
a flagon of Rhenish on my head once. This same
skull, sir, was, sir, Yorick's skull, the King's jester.

Hamlet. This?

Clown. E'en that.

Hamlet. Let me see. [*Takes the skull.*] Alas, poor 185
Yorick! I knew him, Horatio, a fellow of infinite
jest, of most excellent fancy. He hath borne me on
his back a thousand times. And now how abhorred
in my imagination it is! My gorge rises at it. Here
hung those lips that I have kissed I know not how 190
oft. Where be your gibes now? Your gambols, your
songs, your flashes of merriment that were wont to
set the table on a roar? Not one now to mock your
own grinning? Quite chapfall'n°? Now get you to my
lady's chamber, and tell her, let her paint an inch 195
thick, to this favor° she must come. Make her laugh
at that. Prithee, Horatio, tell me one thing.

Horatio. What's that, my lord?

Hamlet. Dost thou think Alexander looked o' this
fashion i' th' earth?   200

Horatio. E'en so.

Hamlet. And smelt so? Pah!   [*Puts down the skull.*]

Horatio. E'en so, my lord.

---

194 *chapfall'n* (1) down in the mouth (2) jawless 196 *favor*
facial appearance

Hamlet. To what base uses we may return, Horatio!
205   Why may not imagination trace the noble dust of
      Alexander till 'a find it stopping a bunghole?

Horatio. 'Twere to consider too curiously,° to consider
      so.

Hamlet. No, faith, not a jot, but to follow him thither
210   with modesty enough,° and likelihood to lead it; as
      thus: Alexander died, Alexander was buried, Alex-
      ander returneth to dust; the dust is earth; of earth
      we make loam; and why of that loam whereto he was
      converted might they not stop a beer barrel?
215   Imperious Caesar, dead and turned to clay,
      Might stop a hole to keep the wind away.
      O, that that earth which kept the world in awe
      Should patch a wall t' expel the winter's flaw!°
      But soft, but soft awhile! Here comes the King.

*Enter King, Queen, Laertes, and a coffin, with Lords
      attendant [and a Doctor of Divinity].*

220   The Queen, the courtiers. Who is this they follow?
      And with such maimèd° rites? This doth betoken
      The corse they follow did with desp'rate hand
      Fordo it° own life. 'Twas of some estate.°
      Couch° we awhile, and mark. [*Retires with Horatio.*]

Laertes. What ceremony else?

225 *Hamlet.*   That is Laertes,
      A very noble youth. Mark.

Laertes. What ceremony else?

Doctor. Her obsequies have been as far enlarged
      As we have warranty. Her death was doubtful,°
230   And, but that great command o'ersways the order,
      She should in ground unsanctified been lodged
      Till the last trumpet. For charitable prayers,

207 *curiously* minutely   210 *with modesty enough* without exag-
geration   218 *flaw* gust   221 *maimèd* incomplete   223 *Fordo it*
destroy its   223 *estate* high rank   224 *Couch* hide   229 *doubtful*
suspicious

Shards,° flints, and pebbles should be thrown on her.
Yet here she is allowed her virgin crants,°
Her maiden strewments,° and the bringing home   235
Of bell and burial.

Laertes. Must there no more be done?

Doctor.   No more be done.
We should profane the service of the dead
To sing a requiem and such rest to her
As to peace-parted souls.

Laertes.   Lay her i' th' earth,   240
And from her fair and unpolluted flesh
May violets spring! I tell thee, churlish priest,
A minist'ring angel shall my sister be
When thou liest howling!

Hamlet.   What, the fair Ophelia?

Queen. Sweets to the sweet! Farewell.   245

                              [*Scatters flowers.*]
I hoped thou shouldst have been my Hamlet's wife.
I thought thy bride bed to have decked, sweet maid,
And not have strewed thy grave.

Laertes.   O, treble woe
Fall ten times treble on that cursèd head
Whose wicked deed thy most ingenious sense°   250
Deprived thee of! Hold off the earth awhile,
Till I have caught her once more in mine arms.

                              Leaps in the grave.
Now pile your dust upon the quick and dead
Till of this flat a mountain you have made
T'o'ertop old Pelion° or the skyish head   255
Of blue Olympus.

Hamlet.   [*Coming forward*] What is he whose grief

---

233 *Shards* broken pieces of pottery 234 *crants* garlands 235
strewments i.e., of flowers 250 *most ingenious sense* finely endowed mind 255 *Pelion* (according to classical legend, giants in
their fight with the gods sought to reach heaven by piling Mount
Pelion and Mount Ossa on Mount Olympus)

Bears such an emphasis, whose phrase of sorrow
Conjures the wand'ring stars,° and makes them
   stand
Like wonder-wounded hearers? This is I,
Hamlet the Dane.

260 *Laertes.*   The devil take thy soul!
                              [*Grapples with him.*]°

Hamlet. Thou pray'st not well.
   I prithee take thy fingers from my throat,
   For, though I am not splenitive° and rash,
   Yet have I in me something dangerous,
265   Which let thy wisdom fear. Hold off thy hand.

King. Pluck them asunder.

Queen.   Hamlet, Hamlet!

All. Gentlemen!

Horatio.   Good my lord, be quiet.
                              [*Attendants part them.*]

Hamlet. Why, I will fight with him upon this theme
   Until my eyelids will no longer wag.

270 *Queen.* O my son, what theme?

Hamlet. I loved Ophelia. Forty thousand brothers
   Could not with all their quantity of love
   Make up my sum. What wilt thou do for her?

King. O, he is mad, Laertes.

275 *Queen.* For love of God forbear him.

Hamlet. 'Swounds, show me what thou't do.
   Woo't weep? Woo't fight? Woo't fast? Woo't tear
      thyself?
   Woo't drink up eisel?° Eat a crocodile?

258 *wand'ring stars* planets   260 s.d.*Grapples with him* (Q1, a bad
quarto, presumably reporting a version that toured, has a previous
direction saying "Hamlet leaps in after Laertes." Possibly he does
so, somewhat hysterically. But such a direction—absent from the
two good texts, Q2 and F—makes Hamlet the aggressor, somewhat
contradicting his next speech. Perhaps Laertes leaps out of the
grave to attack Hamlet)   263 *splenitive* fiery (the spleen was
thought to be the seat of anger)   278 *eisel* vinegar

I'll do't. Dost thou come here to whine?
To outface me with leaping in her grave?   *280*
Be buried quick with her, and so will I.
And if thou prate of mountains, let them throw
Millions of acres on us, till our ground,
Singeing his pate against the burning zone,°
Make Ossa like a wart! Nay, an thou'lt mouth,   *285*
I'll rant as well as thou.

Queen.   This is mere madness;
And thus a while the fit will work on him.
Anon, as patient as the female dove
When that her golden couplets are disclosed,°
His silence will sit drooping.

Hamlet.   Hear you, sir.   *290*
What is the reason that you use me thus?
I loved you ever. But it is no matter.
Let Hercules himself do what he may,
The cat will mew, and dog will have his day.

King. I pray thee, good Horatio, wait upon him.   *295*
        Exit Hamlet and Horatio.
[*To Laertes*] Strengthen your patience in our last
 night's speech.
We'll put the matter to the present push.°
Good Gertrude, set some watch over your son.
This grave shall have a living° monument.
An hour of quiet shortly shall we see;   *300*
Till then in patience our proceeding be.   *Exeunt.*

284 *burning zone* sun's orbit 289 *golden couplets are disclosed*
(the dove lays two eggs, and the newly hatched [*disclosed*] young
are covered with golden down) 297 *present push* immediate test
299 *living* lasting (with perhaps also a reference to the plot against
Hamlet's life)

[Scene II. *The castle*.]

Enter Hamlet and Horatio.

Hamlet. So much for this, sir; now shall you see the
other.
You do remember all the circumstance?

Horatio. Remember it, my lord!

Hamlet. Sir, in my heart there was a kind of fighting
5   That would not let me sleep. Methought I lay
Worse than the mutines in the bilboes.° Rashly
(And praised be rashness for it) let us know,
Our indiscretion sometime serves us well
When our deep plots do pall,° and that should learn
us
10   There's a divinity that shapes our ends,
Rough-hew them how we will.

Horatio.   That is most certain.

Hamlet. Up from my cabin,
My sea gown scarfed about me, in the dark
Groped I to find out them, had my desire,
15   Fingered° their packet, and in fine° withdrew
To mine own room again, making so bold,
My fears forgetting manners, to unseal
Their grand commission; where I found, Horatio—
Ah, royal knavery!—an exact command,
20   Larded° with many several sorts of reasons,
Importing Denmark's health, and England's too,
With, ho, such bugs and goblins in my life,°
That on the supervise,° no leisure bated,°
No, not to stay the grinding of the ax,

V.ii.6 *mutines in the bilboes* mutineers in fetters   9 *pall* fail   15
Fingered stole   15 *in fine* finally   20 *Larded* enriched   22 *such
bugs and goblins in my life* such bugbears and imagined terrors if
I were allowed to live   23 *supervise* reading   23 *leisure bated*
delay allowed

My head should be struck off.

Horatio.   Is't possible?   25

Hamlet. Here's the commission; read it at more leisure.
But wilt thou hear now how I did proceed?

Horatio. I beseech you.

Hamlet. Being thus benetted round with villains,
Or° I could make a prologue to my brains,   30
They had begun the play. I sat me down,
Devised a new commission, wrote it fair.
I once did hold it, as our statists° do,
A baseness to write fair,° and labored much
How to forget that learning, but, sir, now   35
It did me yeoman's service. Wilt thou know
Th' effect° of what I wrote?

Horatio.   Ay, good my lord.

Hamlet. An earnest conjuration from the King,
As England was his faithful tributary,
As love between them like the palm might flourish,   40
As peace should still her wheaten garland wear
And stand a comma° 'tween their amities,
And many suchlike as's of great charge,°
That on the view and knowing of these contents,
Without debatement further, more or less,   45
He should those bearers put to sudden death,
Not shriving° time allowed.

Horatio.   How was this sealed?

Hamlet. Why, even in that was heaven ordinant.°
I had my father's signet in my purse,
Which was the model° of that Danish seal,   50
Folded the writ up in the form of th' other,
Subscribed it, gave't th' impression, placed it safely,
The changeling never known. Now, the next day
Was our sea fight, and what to this was sequent
Thou knowest already.   55

30 *Or* ere   33 *statists* statesmen   34 *fair* clearly   37 *effect* purport
42 *comma* link   43 *great charge* (1) serious exhortation (2) heavy
burden (punning on *as's* and "asses")   47 *shriving* absolution   48
ordinant ruling   50 *model* counterpart

Horatio. So Guildenstern and Rosencrantz go to't.

Hamlet. Why, man, they did make love to this employ-
      ment.
    They are not near my conscience; their defeat
    Does by their own insinuation° grow.
60 'Tis dangerous when the baser nature comes
    Between the pass° and fell° incensèd points
    Of mighty opposites.

Horatio.   Why, what a king is this!

Hamlet. Does it not, think thee, stand me now upon°—
    He that hath killed my king, and whored my mother,
65 Popped in between th' election° and my hopes,
    Thrown out his angle° for my proper life,°
    And with such coz'nage°—is't not perfect con-
      science
    To quit° him with this arm? And is't not to be
      damned
    To let this canker of our nature come
70 In further evil?

Horatio. It must be shortly known to him from England
    What is the issue of the business there.

Hamlet. It will be short; the interim's mine,
    And a man's life's no more than to say "one."
75 But I am very sorry, good Horatio,
    That to Laertes I forgot myself,
    For by the image of my cause I see
    The portraiture of his. I'll court his favors.
    But sure the bravery° of his grief did put me
    Into a tow'ring passion.

80 *Horatio.*   Peace, who comes here?

                Enter young Osric, a courtier.

Osric. Your lordship is right welcome back to Den-
      mark.

59 *insinuation* meddling   61 *pass* thrust   61 *fell* cruel   63 *stand me
now upon* become incumbent upon me   65 *election* (the Danish
monarchy was elective)   66 *angle* fishing line   66 *my proper life*
my own life   67 *coz'nage* trickery   68 *quit* pay back   79 *bravery*
bravado

Hamlet. I humbly thank you, sir. [*Aside to Horatio*] Dost know this waterfly?

Horatio. [*Aside to Hamlet*] No, my good lord.

Hamlet. [*Aside to Horatio*] Thy state is the more gra-   85
cious, for 'tis a vice to know him. He hath much
land, and fertile. Let a beast be lord of beasts, and
his crib shall stand at the king's mess.° 'Tis a
chough,° but, as I say, spacious° in the possession
of dirt.   90

Osric. Sweet lord, if your lordship were at leisure, I
should impart a thing to you from his Majesty.

Hamlet. I will receive it, sir, with all diligence of spirit.
Put your bonnet to his right use. 'Tis for the head.

Osric. I thank your lordship, it is very hot.   95

Hamlet. No, believe me, 'tis very cold; the wind is
northerly.

Osric. It is indifferent cold, my lord, indeed.

Hamlet. But yet methinks it is very sultry and hot for
my complexion.°   100

Osric. Exceedingly, my lord; it is very sultry, as 'twere
—I cannot tell how. But, my lord, his Majesty bade
me signify to you that 'a has laid a great wager on
your head. Sir, this is the matter——

Hamlet. I beseech you remember.   105
                    [*Hamlet moves him to put on his hat.*]

Osric. Nay, good my lord; for my ease, in good faith.
Sir, here is newly come to court Laertes—believe
me, an absolute gentleman, full of most excellent
differences,° of very soft society and great showing.
Indeed, to speak feelingly° of him, he is the card°   110
or calendar of gentry; for you shall find in him the
continent° of what part a gentleman would see.

---

88 *mess* table   89 *chough* jackdaw (here, chatterer)   89 *spacious*
well off   100 *complexion* temperament   109 *differences* distinguish-
ing characteristics   110 *feelingly* justly   110 *card* chart   112 *continent* summary

Hamlet. Sir, his definement° suffers no perdition° in
you, though, I know, to divide him inventorially
115   would dozy° th' arithmetic of memory, and yet but
yaw neither in respect of his quick sail.° But, in the
verity of extolment, I take him to be a soul of great
article,° and his infusion° of such dearth and rare-
ness as, to make true diction° of him, his semblable°
120   is his mirror, and who else would trace him, his umbrage,° nothing more.

Osric. Your lordship speaks most infallibly of him.

Hamlet. The concernancy,° sir? Why do we wrap the
gentleman in our more rawer breath?

125 *Osric.* Sir?

Horatio. Is't not possible to understand in another
tongue? You will to't,° sir, really.

Hamlet. What imports the nomination of this gentleman?

130 *Osric.* Of Laertes?

Horatio. [*Aside to Hamlet*] His purse is empty already.
All's golden words are spent.

Hamlet. Of him, sir.

Osric. I know you are not ignorant——

135 *Hamlet.* I would you did, sir; yet, in faith, if you did, it
would not much approve° me. Well, sir?

Osric. You are not ignorant of what excellence Laertes
is——

Hamlet. I dare not confess that, lest I should compare
140   with him in excellence; but to know a man well were
to know himself.

---

113 *definement* description 113 *perdition* loss 115 *dozy* dizzy
115–16 *and yet . . . quick sail* i.e., and yet only stagger despite all
(*yaw neither*) in trying to overtake his virtues 118 *article* (literally, "item," but here perhaps "traits" or "importance") 118 *in-
fusion* essential quality 119 *diction* description 119 *semblable*
likeness 120–21 *umbrage* shadow 123 *concernancy* meaning 127
will to't will get there 136 *approve* commend

Osric. I mean, sir, for his weapon; but in the imputa-
tion° laid on him by them, in his meed° he's un-
fellowed.

Hamlet. What's his weapon?   143

Osric. Rapier and dagger.

Hamlet. That's two of his weapons—but well.

Osric. The King, sir, hath wagered with him six Barbary horses, against the which he has impawned,° as
I take it, six French rapiers and poniards, with their   150
assigns,° as girdle, hangers,° and so. Three of the
carriages,° in faith, are very dear to fancy, very re-
sponsive° to the hilts, most delicate carriages, and
of very liberal conceit.°

Hamlet. What call you the carriages?   155

Horatio. [*Aside to Hamlet*] I knew you must be edified
by the margent° ere you had done.

Osric. The carriages, sir, are the hangers.

Hamlet. The phrase would be more germane to the
matter if we could carry a cannon by our sides. I   160
would it might be hangers till then. But on! Six Barbary horses against six French swords, their assigns,
and three liberal-conceited carriages—that's the
French bet against the Danish. Why is this all impawned, as you call it?   165

Osric. The King, sir, hath laid, sir, that in a dozen
passes between yourself and him he shall not exceed
you three hits; he hath laid on twelve for nine, and
it would come to immediate trial if your lordship
would vouchsafe the answer.   170

Hamlet. How if I answer no?

Osric. I mean, my lord, the opposition of your person
in trial.

142–43 *imputation* reputation 143 *meed* merit 149 *impawned*
wagered 151 *assigns* accompaniments 151 *hangers* straps hanging the sword to the belt 152 *carriages* (an affected word for
hangers) 152–53 *responsive* corresponding 154 *liberal conceit*
elaborate design 157 *margent* i.e., marginal (explanatory) comment

Hamlet. Sir, I will walk here in the hall. If it please
175   his Majesty, it is the breathing time of day with me.°
Let the foils be brought, the gentleman willing, and
the King hold his purpose, I will win for him an I
can; if not, I will gain nothing but my shame and
the odd hits.

180 *Osric.* Shall I deliver you e'en so?

Hamlet. To this effect, sir, after what flourish your
nature will.

Osric. I commend my duty to your lordship.

Hamlet. Yours, yours. [*Exit Osric.*] He does well to
185   commend it himself; there are no tongues else for's
turn.

Horatio. This lapwing° runs away with the shell on his
head.

Hamlet. 'A did comply, sir, with his dug° before 'a
190   sucked it. Thus has he, and many more of the
same breed that I know the drossy age dotes on,
only got the tune of the time and, out of an habit of
encounter,° a kind of yeasty° collection, which
carries them through and through the most fanned
195   and winnowed opinions; and do but blow them to
their trial, the bubbles are out.°

Enter a Lord.

Lord. My lord, his Majesty commended him to you by
young Osric, who brings back to him that you
attend him in the hall. He sends to know if your
200   pleasure hold to play with Laertes, or that you will
take longer time.

Hamlet. I am constant to my purposes; they follow the

175 *breathing time of day with me* time when I take exercise   187
lapwing (the new-hatched lapwing was thought to run around with
half its shell on its head)   189 '*A did comply, sir, with his dug* he
was ceremoniously polite to his mother's breast   192–93 *out of an
habit of encounter* out of his own superficial way of meeting and
conversing with people   193 *yeasty* frothy   196 *the bubbles are
out* i.e., they are blown away (the reference is to the "yeasty collection")

King's pleasure. If his fitness speaks, mine is ready;
now or whensoever, provided I be so able as now.

Lord. The King and Queen and all are coming down. 205

Hamlet. In happy time.

Lord. The Queen desires you to use some gentle enter-
tainment° to Laertes before you fall to play.

Hamlet. She well instructs me.   [*Exit Lord.*]

Horatio. You will lose this wager, my lord.   210

Hamlet. I do not think so. Since he went into France
I have been in continual practice. I shall win at the
odds. But thou wouldst not think how ill all's here
about my heart. But it is no matter.

Horatio. Nay, good my lord——   215

Hamlet. It is but foolery, but it is such a kind of gain-
giving° as would perhaps trouble a woman.

Horatio. If your mind dislike anything, obey it. I will
forestall their repair hither and say you are not fit.

Hamlet. Not a whit, we defy augury. There is special 220
providence in the fall of a sparrow.° If it be now,
'tis not to come; if it be not to come, it will be now;
if it be not now, yet it will come. The readiness is
all. Since no man of aught he leaves knows, what
is't to leave betimes?° Let be.   225

A table prepared. [*Enter*] *Trumpets, Drums, and
Officers with cushions; King, Queen,* [*Osric,*] *and
all the State,* [*with*] *foils, daggers,* [*and stoups
of wine borne in*]; *and Laertes.*

King. Come, Hamlet, come, and take this hand from
me.

[*The King puts Laertes' hand into Hamlet's.*]

207–08 *to use some gentle entertainment* to be courteous 217 *gaingiving* misgiving 221 *the fall of a sparrow* (cf. Matthew 10:29
"Are not two sparrows sold for a farthing? and one of them shall
not fall on the ground without your Father") 225 *betimes* early

Hamlet. Give me your pardon, sir. I have done you
    wrong,
    But pardon't, as you are a gentleman.
    This presence° knows, and you must needs have
    heard,
230 How I am punished with a sore distraction.
    What I have done
    That might your nature, honor, and exception°
    Roughly awake, I here proclaim was madness.
    Was't Hamlet wronged Laertes? Never Hamlet.
235 If Hamlet from himself be ta'en away,
    And when he's not himself does wrong Laertes,
    Then Hamlet does it not, Hamlet denies it.
    Who does it then? His madness. If't be so,
    Hamlet is of the faction° that is wronged;
240 His madness is poor Hamlet's enemy.
    Sir, in this audience,
    Let my disclaiming from a purposed evil
    Free me so far in your most generous thoughts
    That I have shot my arrow o'er the house
    And hurt my brother.

245 *Laertes.*   I am satisfied in nature,
    Whose motive in this case should stir me most
    To my revenge. But in my terms of honor
    I stand aloof, and will no reconcilement
    Till by some elder masters of known honor
250 I have a voice and precedent° of peace
    To keep my name ungored. But till that time
    I do receive your offered love like love,
    And will not wrong it.

Hamlet.   I embrace it freely,
    And will this brother's wager frankly play.
    Give us the foils. Come on.

255 *Laertes.*   Come, one for me.

Hamlet. I'll be your foil,° Laertes. In mine ignorance

229 *presence* royal assembly 232 *exception* disapproval 239 *faction* party, side 250 *voice and precedent* authoritative opinion justified by precedent 256 *foil* (1) blunt sword (2) background (of metallic leaf) for a jewel

Your skill shall, like a star i' th' darkest night,
    Stick fiery off° indeed.

Laertes.   You mock me, sir.

Hamlet. No, by this hand.

King. Give them the foils, young Osric. Cousin Hamlet,   260
    You know the wager?

Hamlet.   Very well, my lord.
    Your grace has laid the odds o' th' weaker side.

King. I do not fear it, I have seen you both;
    But since he is bettered,° we have therefore odds.

Laertes. This is too heavy; let me see another.   265

Hamlet. This likes me well. These foils have all a
    length?

                              Prepare to play.

Osric. Ay, my good lord.

King. Set me the stoups of wine upon that table.
    If Hamlet give the first or second hit,
    Or quit° in answer of the third exchange,   270
    Let all the battlements their ordnance fire.
    The King shall drink to Hamlet's better breath,
    And in the cup an union° shall he throw
    Richer than that which four successive kings
    In Denmark's crown have worn. Give me the cups,   275
    And let the kettle° to the trumpet speak,
    The trumpet to the cannoneer without,
    The cannons to the heavens, the heaven to earth,
    "Now the King drinks to Hamlet." Come, begin.

                              Trumpets the while.

    And you, the judges, bear a wary eye.   280

Hamlet. Come on, sir.

Laertes.   Come, my lord.   *They play.*

Hamlet.   One.

Laertes.   No.

258 *Stick fiery off* stand out brilliantly   264 *bettered* has improved
(in France)   270 *quit* repay, hit back   273 *union* pearl   276 *kettle*
kettledrum

Hamlet.   Judgment?

Osric. A hit, a very palpable hit.
    Drum, trumpets, and shot. Flourish; a piece goes off.

Laertes.   Well, again.

King. Stay, give me drink. Hamlet, this pearl is thine.
    Here's to thy health. Give him the cup.

285 *Hamlet.* I'll play this bout first; set it by awhile.
    Come. [*They play.*] Another hit. What say you?

Laertes. A touch, a touch; I do confess't.

King. Our son shall win.

Queen.   He's fat,° and scant of breath.
    Here, Hamlet, take my napkin, rub thy brows.
290 The Queen carouses to thy fortune, Hamlet.

Hamlet. Good madam!

King.   Gertrude, do not drink.

Queen. I will, my lord; I pray you pardon me. [*Drinks.*]

King. [*Aside*] It is the poisoned cup; it is too late.

Hamlet. I dare not drink yet, madam—by and by.

295 *Queen.* Come, let me wipe thy face.

Laertes. My lord, I'll hit him now.

King.   I do not think't.

Laertes. [*Aside*] And yet it is almost against my con-
    science.

Hamlet. Come for the third, Laertes. You do but dally.
    I pray you pass with your best violence;
300 I am sure you make a wanton° of me.

Laertes. Say you so? Come on.   [*They*] *play.*

Osric. Nothing neither way.

Laertes. Have at you now!
                In scuffling they change rapiers, [*and both are
                                              wounded*].

288 *fat* (1) sweaty (2) out of training   300 *wanton* spoiled child

King.   Part them. They are incensed.

Hamlet. Nay, come—again!   [*The Queen falls.*]

Osric.   Look to the Queen there, ho!

Horatio. They bleed on both sides. How is it, my lord?   *305*

Osric. How is't, Laertes?

Laertes. Why, as a woodcock to mine own springe,° Osric.
I am justly killed with mine own treachery.

Hamlet. How does the Queen?

King.   She sounds° to see them bleed.

Queen. No, no, the drink, the drink! O my dear Hamlet!   *310*
The drink, the drink! I am poisoned.   [*Dies.*]

Hamlet. O villainy! Ho! Let the door be locked.
Treachery! Seek it out.   [*Laertes falls.*]

Laertes. It is here, Hamlet. Hamlet, thou art slain;
No med'cine in the world can do thee good.   *315*
In thee there is not half an hour's life.
The treacherous instrument is in thy hand,
Unbated and envenomed. The foul practice°
Hath turned itself on me. Lo, here I lie,
Never to rise again. Thy mother's poisoned.   *320*
I can no more. The King, the King's to blame.

Hamlet. The point envenomed too?
Then, venom, to thy work.   *Hurts the King.*

All. Treason! Treason!

King. O, yet defend me, friends. I am but hurt.   *325*

Hamlet. Here, thou incestuous, murd'rous, damnèd Dane,
Drink off this potion. Is thy union here?
Follow my mother.   *King dies.*

Laertes.   He is justly served.

307 *springe* snare   309 *sounds* swoons   318 *practice* deception

It is a poison tempered° by himself.
330   Exchange forgiveness with me, noble Hamlet.
       Mine and my father's death come not upon thee,
       Nor thine on me!   *Dies.*

Hamlet. Heaven make thee free of it! I follow thee.
       I am dead, Horatio. Wretched Queen, adieu!
335   You that look pale and tremble at this chance,
       That are but mutes° or audience to this act,
       Had I but time (as this fell sergeant,° Death,
       Is strict in his arrest) O, I could tell you—
       But let it be. Horatio, I am dead;
340   Thou livest; report me and my cause aright
       To the unsatisfied.°

Horatio.   Never believe it.
       I am more an antique Roman° than a Dane.
       Here's yet some liquor left.

Hamlet.   As th' art a man,
       Give me the cup. Let go. By heaven, I'll ha't!
345   O God, Horatio, what a wounded name,
       Things standing thus unknown, shall live behind me!
       If thou didst ever hold me in thy heart,
       Absent thee from felicity° awhile,
       And in this harsh world draw thy breath in pain,
       To tell my story.   *A march afar off.* [*Exit Osric.*]
350   What warlike noise is this?

                                        Enter Osric.

Osric. Young Fortinbras, with conquest come from
       Poland,
       To th' ambassadors of England gives
       This warlike volley.

Hamlet.   O, I die, Horatio!
       The potent poison quite o'ercrows° my spirit.
355   I cannot live to hear the news from England,

329 *tempered* mixed   336 *mutes* performers who have no words to
speak   337 *fell sergeant* dread sheriff's officer   341 *unsatisfied* un-
informed   342 *antique Roman* (with reference to the old Roman
fashion of suicide)   348 *felicity* i.e., the felicity of death   354 *o'er-
crows* overpowers (as a triumphant cock crows over its weak
opponent)

But I do prophesy th' election lights
On Fortinbras. He has my dying voice.
So tell him, with th' occurrents,° more and less,
Which have solicited°—the rest is silence. *Dies.*

Horatio. Now cracks a noble heart. Good night, sweet
    Prince,   360
And flights of angels sing thee to thy rest.
                    [*March within.*]
Why does the drum come hither?

   *Enter Fortinbras, with the Ambassadors with
       Drum, Colors, and Attendants.*

Fortinbras. Where is this sight?

Horatio.   What is it you would see?
If aught of woe or wonder, cease your search.

Fortinbras. This quarry° cries on havoc.° O proud
    Death,   365
What feast is toward° in thine eternal cell
That thou so many princes at a shot
So bloodily hast struck?

Ambassador.   The sight is dismal;
And our affairs from England come too late.
The ears are senseless that should give us hearing   370
To tell him his commandment is fulfilled,
That Rosencrantz and Guildenstern are dead.
Where should we have our thanks?

Horatio.   Not from his° mouth,
Had it th' ability of life to thank you.
He never gave commandment for their death.   375
But since, so jump° upon this bloody question,
You from the Polack wars, and you from England,
Are here arrived, give order that these bodies
High on a stage° be placèd to the view,
And let me speak to th' yet unknowing world   380
How these things came about. So shall you hear

358 *occurrents* occurrences 359 *solicited* incited 365 *quarry* heap
of slain bodies 365 *cries on havoc* proclaims general slaughter
366 *toward* in preparation 373 *his* (Claudius') 376 *jump* precisely 379 *stage* platform

Of carnal, bloody, and unnatural acts,
Of accidental judgments, casual° slaughters,
Of deaths put on by cunning and forced cause,
385 And, in this upshot, purposes mistook
Fall'n on th' inventors' heads. All this can I
Truly deliver.

Fortinbras.   Let us haste to hear it,
And call the noblest to the audience.
For me, with sorrow I embrace my fortune.
390 I have some rights of memory° in this kingdom,
Which now to claim my vantage doth invite me.

Horatio. Of that I shall have also cause to speak,
And from his mouth whose voice will draw on°
     more.
But let this same be presently performed,
Even while men's minds are wild, lest more mis-
393   chance
On° plots and errors happen.

Fortinbras.   Let four captains
Bear Hamlet like a soldier to the stage,
For he was likely, had he been put on,°
To have proved most royal; and for his passage°
400 The soldiers' music and the rite of war
Speak loudly for him.
Take up the bodies. Such a sight as this
Becomes the field,° but here shows much amiss.
Go, bid the soldiers shoot.

Exeunt marching; after the which a peal of ordnance
                                        are shot off.

FINIS

---

383 *casual* not humanly planned, chance   390 *rights of memory*
remembered claims   393 *voice will draw on* vote will influence
396 *On* on top of   398 *put on* advanced (to the throne)   399 *passage* death   403 *field* battlefield

Textual Note

Shakespeare's *Hamlet* comes to us in three versions. The first of them, known as the First Quarto, was published in 1603 by N. L. [Nicholas Ling] and John Trundell, who advertised it on the title page as having been played "by his Highness Servants in the City of London, as also in the two universities of Cambridge and Oxford, and elsewhere." This was a pirated edition, published without the consent of the owners, and Shakespeare had nothing to do with it. In the preceding year an attempt had been made to forestall just such a venture. On July 26, 1602, James Roberts, a printer friendly to Shakespeare's company, had entered in the Stationers' Register "A book called The Revenge of Hamlet Prince of Denmark as it was lately acted by the Lord Chamberlain his Servants." This was intended to serve as a kind of copyright. It should be said in passing that "his Highness Servants" were the King's Men and that the Chamberlain's Men became the King's Men on May 19, 1603, when James I took Shakespeare's company under his direct protection.

The copy which Ling and Trundell sent to the printer was an extraordinary hodgepodge, so that the First Quarto gives us a very poor notion of Shakespeare's play. How this copy came into being has been the subject of much investigation, but there is little agreement. In general there are three schools of thought: (1) the First Quarto is a badly reported version of *Hamlet* as Shakespeare wrote it once and for all; (2) it is a badly reported version of an early draft of Shakespeare's play; and (3) it was

175

expanded from some actor's parts of an early version of
the play. This last seems most likely, since some of the lines,
notably those of Marcellus, are accurate, other passages
are partially correct, and still others are sheer invention.
All three levels are to be found in the soliloquy beginning
"To be or not to be."

> To be or not to be, ay there's the point,
> To die, to sleep, is that all? Ay all:
> No, to sleep, to dream, ay marry there it goes,
> For in that dream of death, when we awake,
> And borne before an everlasting judge,
> From whence no passenger ever returned,
> The undiscovered country, at whose sight
> The happy smile, and the accursed damned.
> But for this, the joyful hope of this,
> Who'd bear the scorns and flattery of the world,
> Scorned by the right rich, the rich cursed of the poor?
> The widow being oppressed, the orphan wronged,
> The taste of hunger, or a tyrant's reign,
> And thousand more calamities besides,
> To grunt and sweat under this weary life,
> When that he may his full quietus make,
> With a bare bodkin, who would this endure,
> But for a hope of something after death?
> Which pulses the brain, and doth confound the sense,
> Which makes us rather bear those evils we have,
> Than fly to others that we know not of.
> Ay that, O this conscience makes cowards of us all,
> Lady in thy orisons, be all my sins rememb'red

It is clear that there is a hand other than Shakespeare's in
this. That the First Quarto is a debased version of an early
version of the play is suggested by, most notably, changes
in names. Why should Polonius, for instance, become
Corambis if the copy were based on the version Shakespeare wrote once and for all?

It was not considered good business to publish a play
while it was still popular in the theater, for it could then
be acted in the provinces by other than its owners, reduc-
ing the public for the play when Shakespeare's company

took it on tour. This being so, the publication of the First Quarto had done Shakespeare a double injury: the play was in print, and it misrepresented its author. Shakespeare had some leisure at this time, the theaters being closed because of the plague from March 1603 to April 1604. We may suppose that he decided to revise the play and have it printed. In any case, another edition of *Hamlet* appeared in 1604. The title page seems designed to tell the public that this is the genuine article: "The Tragical History of Hamlet, Prince of Denmark. By William Shakespeare. Newly imprinted and enlarged to almost as much again as it was, according to the true and perfect copy." The statement is literally true. The Second Quarto is almost twice as long as the First Quarto, and although it lacks some passages preserved in the First Folio, the Second Quarto is the fullest and best version of the play.

The third version of *Hamlet* is to be found in the First Folio, 1623, the collected edition of Shakespeare's plays made by his friends and associates in the theater, John Heminges and Henry Condell. Here the text is based on the acting version of the play. The Folio gives us some ninety lines not found in the Second Quarto. These include two passages of considerable length, II.ii.243–74 and II.ii.345–70, but the Folio does not give us some two hundred lines found in the Second Quarto. These are mostly reflective passages, including Hamlet's last soliloquy, "How all occasions do inform against me." As befits an acting version, the Folio stage directions are more numerous and frequently are fuller. Modern editions are made by collation of the Second Quarto and the First Folio and are therefore longer than either of them.

Because the Second Quarto is the longest version, giving us more of the play as Shakespeare conceived it than either of the others, it serves as the basic version for this text. Unfortunately the printers of it often worked carelessly. Words and phrases are omitted, there are plain misreadings of Shakespeare's manuscript, speeches are sometimes wrongly assigned. It was therefore necessary to turn to the First Folio for many readings. Neither the First Quarto nor the Second Quarto is divided into acts or scenes; the Folio indicates only the following: I.i, I.ii, I.iii, II, II.ii. The present edition, to allow for easy reference, follows the traditional divisions of the Globe edition, placing them (as well as indications of locale) in brackets to indicate that they are editorial, not authorial. Punctuation and spelling are modernized (*and* is given as *an* when it means "if"), obvious typographical errors are corrected, abbreviations are expanded, speech prefixes are regularized and the positions of stage directions are slightly altered where necessary. Other departures from the Second Quarto are listed below. First is given the adopted reading, in italic, and then the Second Quarto's reading, in roman. The vast majority of these adopted readings are from the Folio; if an adopted reading is not from the Folio, the fact is indicated by a bracketed remark explaining, for example, that it is drawn from the First Quarto [Q1] or the Second Folio [F2] or an editor's conjecture [ed].

I.i.16 *soldier* souldiers   63 *Polacks* [F has "Pollax"] pollax   68 *my* mine   73 *why* with   73 *cast* cost   88 *those* these   91 *returned* returne   94 *designed* [F2] design   112 *mote* [ed] moth   121 *feared* [ed] feare   138 *you* your   140 *at it* it   142 s.d. *Exit Ghost* [Q2 omits]

I.ii.1 s.d. *Councilors* [ed] Counsaile: as   41 s.d. *Exit Voltemand and Cornelius* [Q2 omits]   58 *He hath* Hath   67 *so* so much   77 *good* coold   82 *shapes* [ed; F has "shewes"] chapes   96 *a mind* or minde   132 *self-slaughter* seale slaughter   133 *weary* wary   137 *to this* thus   143 *would* should   149 *even she* [Q2 omits]   175 *to drink deep* for to drinke   178 *to see* to   209 *Where, as* [ed] Whereas   224 *Indeed, indeed, sirs* Indeede Sirs   237 *Very like, very like* Very like   238 *hundred* hundreth   257 *foul* fonde

I.iii.3 *convoy is* conuay in   12 *bulk* bulkes   18 *For he himself is subject to his birth* [Q2 omits]   49 *like a* a   68 *thine* thy   74 *Are* Or   75 *be* boy   76 *loan* loue   83 *invites* inuests   109 *Tend'ring* [Q1] Wrong [F has "Roaming"]   115 *springes* springs   123 *parley* parle   125 *tether* tider   131 *beguile* beguide

I.iv.1 *shrewdly* shroudly   2 *a nipping* nipping   6 s.d. *go* [ed] goes   19 *clepe* [ed] clip   27 *the* [ed] their   33 *Their* [ed] His   36 *evil* [ed] eale   57 s.d. *Ghost beckons Hamlet* Beckins   69 *my lord* my   70 *summit* [ed] somnet [F has "sonnet"]   82 *artere* [ed] arture [F has "artire"]   87 *imagination* imagion

I.v.47 *what a* what   55 *lust* but   56 *sate* sort   64 *leperous* leaprous
68 *posset* possesse   91 s.d. *Exit* [Q2 omits]   95 *stiffly* swiftly
113 *Horatio and Marcellus (Within)* Enter Horatio and Marcellus
[Q2 gives the speech to Horatio]   116 *bird* and   122 *heaven, my
lord* heauen   132 *Look you, I'll* I will   170 *some'er* [ed] so mere
[F has "so ere"]

II.i. s.d. *Reynaldo* or two   28 *Faith, no* Fayth   38 *warrant* wit
39 *sullies* sallies   40 *i' th'* with   52–53 *at "friend or so," and
"gentleman"* [Q2 omits]   112 *quoted* coted

II.ii.43 *Assure you* I assure   57 *o'erhasty* hastie   58 s.d. *Enter
Polonius, Voltemand, and Cornelius* Enter Embassadors   90 *since
brevity* breuitie   108 s.d. *the letter* [Q2 omits, but has "letter" at
side of line 116]   126 *above* about   137 *winking* working   143
his her   148 *watch* wath   149 *a lightness* lightnes   151 *'tis this*
this   167 s.d. *Enter Hamlet reading on a book* Enter Hamlet
190 *far gone, far gone* far gone   205 *you yourself* your selfe   205
should be shall growe   212 *sanity* sanctity   214–15 *and suddenly
. . . between him* [Q2 omits]   217 *will* will not   227 *excellent* extent   231 *overhappy* euer happy   232 *cap* lap   240 *but that* but
the   243–74 *Let me question . . . dreadfully attended* [Q2 omits]
278 *even* euer   285 *Why anything* Any thing   312 *a piece* peece
318 *woman* women   329 *of me* on me   332–33 *the clown . . .
o' th' sere* [from F, but F has "tickled a" for "tickle o' "; Q2 omits]
334 *blank* black   345–70 *Hamlet. How comes . . . load too* [Q2
omits]   350 *berattle* [ed; F has "be-ratled"; Q2 omits]   357 *most
like* [ed; F has "like most"; Q2 omits]   381 *lest my* let me   407–08
tragical-historical, tragical-comical-historical-pastoral [Q2 omits]
434 *By'r Lady* by lady   439 *French falconers* friendly Fankners
454 *affectation* affection   457 *tale* talke   467 *heraldry* heraldy
485 *Then senseless Ilium* [Q2 omits]   492 *And like* Like   506
fellies [ed] follies   515 *Mobled queen is good* [F has "Inobled"
for "Mobled"; Q2 omits]   525 *husband's* husband   530 *whe'r* [ed]
where   550–51 *a need* neede   551 *or sixteen lines* lines, or six-
teene lines   556 *till* tell   564 *his visage* the visage   569 *to Hecuba*
to her   571 *the cue* that   590 *ha' fatted* [F has "have fatted"] a
fatted   593 *O, vengeance* [Q2 omits]   595 *father* [Q4; Q2 and F
omit]   611 *devil, and the devil* deale, and the deale

III.i.32–33 *myself (lawful espials) Will* myself Wee'le   46 *loneliness* lowliness   55 *Let's withdraw* with-draw   83 *cowards of us
all* cowards   85 *sicklied* sickled   92 *well, well, well* well   107
your honesty you   121 *to a nunnery* a Nunry   129 *knaves all*
knaues   139 *Go, farewell,* farewell   146 *lisp* list   148 *your ignorance* ignorance   155 *expectancy* expectation   160 *that* what

162 *feature* stature   164 [Q2 concludes the line with a stage direction, "Exit"]   191 *unwatched* vnmatcht

III.ii.1 *pronounced* pronound   24 *own feature* feature   28 *the which* which   31 *praise* praysd   39 *us, sir* vs   47 s.d. *Exit Players* [Q2 omits]   51 s.d. *Exit Polonius* [Q2 omits]   54 *ho* [F has "hoa"] howe   91 *detecting* detected   91 s.d. *Rosencrantz . . . Flourish* [Q2 omits]   117–18 *Hamlet. I mean . . . my lord* [Q2 omits]   140 s.d. *sound* [ed] sounds   140 s.d. *very lovingly* [Q2 omits] 140 s.d. *She kneels . . . unto him* [Q2 omits]   140 s.d. *Exeunt* [Q2 omits]   142 *is miching* munching   147 *keep counsel* keepe   161 *ground* the ground   169 *your* our   174 *In neither* Eyther none, in neither   175 *love* Lord   196 *like* the   205 *Grief joys* Greefe ioy   225 *An* [ed] And   229 *a* I be a   233 s.d. *sleeps* [Q2 omits]   234 s.d. *Exit* Exeunt   262 *Confederate* Considerat   264 *infected* inuected   266 s.d. *Pours the poison in his ears* [Q2 omits]   272 *Hamlet. What . . . fire* [Q2 omits]   282–83 *two Provincial* prouinciall   316 *start* stare   325 *my business* busines   366 *and thumb* & the vmber   375 *the top of my* my   379 *you can* you   394–95 *Polonius . . . friends* Leaue me friends. I will, say so. By and by is easily said   397 *breathes* breakes   399 *bitter business as the day* buisnes as the bitter day   404 *daggers* dagger

III.iii.19 *huge* hough   22 *ruin* raine   23 *with a* a   50 *pardoned* pardon   58 *shove* showe   73 *pat* but   79 *hire and salary* base and silly

III.iv.5–6 *with him . . . Mother, Mother, Mother* [Q2 omits]   7 *warrant* wait   21 *inmost* most   23 *ho* [F has "hoa"] how   23 *ho* [F has "hoa"] how   25 s.d. *kills Polonius* [Q2 omits]   53 *That roars . . . index* [Q2 gives to Hamlet]   60 *heaven-kissing* heaue, a kissing   89 *panders* pardons   90 *mine eyes into my very soul* my very eyes into my soule   91 *grainèd* greeued   92 *will not* will   98 *tithe* kyth   140 *Ecstasy* [Q2 omits]   144 *And I* And   159 *live* leaue   166 *Refrain tonight* to refraine night   180 *Thus* This   187 *ravel* rouell   216 *foolish* most foolish   218 s.d. *exit Hamlet, tugging in Polonius* Exit

IV.i.35 *dragged* dreg'd

IV.ii.1 s.d. *Enter Hamlet* Enter Hamlet, Rosencraus, and others   2 *Gentlemen. (Within) Hamlet! Lord Hamlet!* [Q2 omits]   4 s.d. *Enter Rosencrantz and Guildenstern* [Q2 omits]   6 *Compounded* Compound   18 *ape* apple   30–31 *Hide fox, and all after* [Q2 omits]

IV.iii.15 *Ho* [F has "Hoa"] How   43 *With fiery quickness* [Q2 omits]   52 *and so* so   68 *were ne'er begun* will nere begin

IV.v.16 *Queen* [Q2 gives line 16 as part of the previous speech]   20 s.d. *Enter Ophelia distracted* Enter Ophelia [placed after line 16]   39 *grave* ground   42 *God* good   52 *clothes* close   57 *Indeed, la* Indeede   73 s.d. *Exit* [Q2 omits]   82 *in their* in   89 *his* this   96 *Queen. Alack, what noise is this* [Q2 omits]   97 *are* is   106 *They* The   142 *swoopstake* [ed] soopstake   152 s.d. *Let her come in* [Q2 gives to Laertes]   157 *Till* Tell   160 *an old* a poore   161–63 *Nature . . . loves* [Q2 omits]   165 *Hey . . . hey nony* [Q2 omits]   181 *O, you must* you may   186 *affliction* afflictions   194 *All flaxen* Flaxen   198 *Christian souls, I pray God* Christians soules   199 *see this* this

IV.vi.9 *an't* and   23 *good turn* turne   27 *bore* bord   31 *He* So   32 *give you* you

IV.vii.6 *proceeded* proceede   14 *conjunctive* concliue   20 *Would* Worke   22 *loud a wind* loued Arm'd   24 *And* But   24 *had* haue   36 *How now . . . Hamlet* [Q2 omits]   42 s.d. *Exit Messenger* [Q2 omits]   46 *your pardon* you pardon   47 *and more strange return* returne   48 *Hamlet* [Q2 omits]   56 *shall live* liue   62 *checking* the King   88 *my* me   115 *wick* [ed] weeke   119 *changes* change   122 *spendthrift* [ed] spend thirfts   125 *in deed* [ed] indeede   134 *on* ore   138 *pass* pace   140 *for that* for   156 *ha't* hate   159 *prepared* prefard   167 *hoar* horry   171 *cold* cull-cold

V.i.9 *se offendendo* so offended   12 *Argall* or all   35–38 *Other. Why . . . without arms* [Q2 omits]   44 *that frame* that   56 s.d. *Enter Hamlet and Horatio afar off* Enter Hamlet and Horatio [Q2 places after line 65]   61 *stoup* soope   71 *daintier* dintier   90 *mazzard* massene   107–08 *Is this . . . recoveries* [Q2 omits]   109 *his vouchers* vouchers   110 *double ones* doubles   122 *O* or   123 *For such a guest is meet* [Q2 omits]   144–45 *a gravemaker* Graue-maker   146 *all the days* the dayes   167 *corses now-a-days* corses   174–75 *three and twenty* 23   185 *Let me see* [Q2 omits]   187 *borne* bore   195 *chamber* table   210–11 *as thus* [Q2 omits]   218 *winter's* waters   219 s.d. *Enter King . . . Lords attendant* Enter K. Q. Laertes and the corse   233 *Shards, flints* Flints   248 *treble* double   252 s.d. *Leaps in the grave* [Q2 omits]   263 *and rash* rash   279 *Dost thou* doost   287 *thus* this   300 *shortly* thirtie   301 *Till* Tell

V.ii.5 *Methought* my thought   6 *bilboes* bilbo   17 *unseal* vnfold   19 *Ah* [ed; F has "Oh"] A   43 *as's* [F has "assis"] as sir   52 *Sub-*

scribed Subcribe   57 *Why, man . . . employment* [Q2 omits] 68–80 *To quit . . . comes here* [Q2 omits]   78 *court* [ed; F has "count"; Q2 omits]   80 s.d. *Young Osric* [Q2 omits]   81 *Osric* [Q2 prints "Cour" consistently as the speech prefix]   83 *humbly* humble   94 *Put your* your   99 *sultry* sully   99 *for* or   102 *But, my* my   108 *gentleman* [ed] gentlemen   110 *feelingly* [ed] sellingly   142 *his weapon* [ed] this weapon   151 *hangers* [ed] hanger 158 *carriages* carriage   161 *might be* be   164–65 *all impawned, as* all   180 *e'en so* so   184 *Yours, yours.* He Yours   189 *did comply* did   193 *yeasty* histy   194 *fanned* [ed; F has "fond"] prophane 195 *winnowed* trennowed   208 *to Laertes* [ed] Laertes   210 *lose this wager* loose   213 *But thou* thou   217 *gaingiving* gamgiuing 221 *If it be now* if it be   223 *will come* well come   241 *Sir, in this audience* [Q2 omits]   251 *keep my* my   251 *till all*   254 *Come on* [Q2 omits]   264 *bettered* better   266 s.d. *Prepare to play* [Q2 omits]   273 *union* Vnice   281 s.d. *They play* [Q2 omits] 287 *A touch, a touch* [Q2 omits]   301 s.d. *play* [Q2 omits]   303 s.d. *In scuffling they change rapiers* [Q2 omits]   304 *ho* [F has "hoa"] howe   312 *Ho* [ed] how   314 *Hamlet. Hamlet* Hamlet 317 *thy* my   323 s.d. *Hurts the King* [Q2 omits]   326 *murd'rous, damnèd* damned   327 *thy union* the Onixe   328 s.d. *King dies* [Q2 omits]   332 s.d. *Dies* [Q2 omits]   346 *live* I leaue   359 *Dies* [Q2 omits]   362 s.d. *with Drum, Colors, and Attendants* [Q2 omits]   380 *th'* yet yet   384 *forced* for no   393 *on* no   400 *rite* [ed; F has "rites"] right   404 s.d. *marching . . . shot off* [Q2 omits]

The Tragedy of

Othello
The Moor of Venice

◆

EDITED BY
Alvin Kernan

The Names of the Actors

Othello, the Moor
Brabantio, father to Desdemona
Cassio, an honorable lieutenant
Iago, a villain
Roderigo, a gulled gentleman
Duke of Venice
Senators
Montano, Governor of Cyprus
Gentlemen of Cyprus
Lodovico and Gratiano, two noble Venetians
Sailors
Clown
Desdemona, wife to Othello
Emilia, wife to Iago
Bianca, a courtesan
[Messenger, Herald, Officers, Gentlemen,
    Musicians, Attendants
        Scene: Venice and Cyprus]

The Tragedy of Othello

ACT I

Scene I. [*Venice. A street.*]

Enter Roderigo and Iago.

Roderigo. Tush! Never tell me? I take it much un-
        kindly
    That thou, Iago, who hast had my purse
    As if the strings were thine, shouldst know of this.

Iago. 'Sblood,° [1] but you'll not hear me! If ever I did
        dream
    Of such a matter, abhor me.

Roderigo.   Thou told'st me   5
    Thou didst hold him in thy hate.

Iago.   Despise me
    If I do not. Three great ones of the city,
    In personal suit to make me his lieutenant,
    Off-capped° to him; and, by the faith of man,
    I know my price; I am worth no worse a place.   10
    But he, as loving his own pride and purposes,
    Evades them with a bombast circumstance,°

---

[1] The degree sign (°) indicates a footnote, which is keyed to the text by
the line number. Text references are printed in *italic* type; the annotation follows in roman type. I.i.⁴ *'Sblood* by God's blood 9 *Off-capped*
doffed their caps—as a mark of respect 12 *bombast circumstance*
stuffed, roundabout speech

39

Horribly stuffed with epithets of war;
Nonsuits° my mediators. For, "Certes," says he,
"I have already chose my officer." And what was
15   he?
Forsooth, a great arithmetician,°
One Michael Cassio, a Florentine,
(A fellow almost damned in a fair wife)°
That never set a squadron in the field,
20   Nor the division of a battle knows
More than a spinster; unless the bookish theoric,
Wherein the tonguèd° consuls can propose
As masterly as he. Mere prattle without practice
Is all his soldiership. But he, sir, had th' election;
25   And I, of whom his eyes had seen the proof
At Rhodes, at Cyprus, and on other grounds
Christian and heathen, must be belee'd and calmed
By debitor and creditor. This counter-caster,°
He, in good time, must his lieutenant be,
And I—God bless the mark!—his Moorship's an-
30   cient.°

Roderigo. By heaven, I rather would have been his
      hangman.

Iago. Why, there's no remedy. 'Tis the curse of service:
Preferment goes by letter and affection,°
And not by old gradation,° where each second
35   Stood heir to th' first. Now, sir, be judge yourself,
Whether I in any just term am affined°
To love the Moor.

Roderigo.   I would not follow him then.

---

¹⁴ *Nonsuits* rejects   ¹⁶ *arithmetician* theorist (rather than practical)
¹⁸ *A . . . wife* (a much-disputed passage, which is probably best taken as
a general sneer at Cassio as a dandy and a ladies' man. But in the story
from which Shakespeare took his plot the counterpart of Cassio is
married, and it may be that at the beginning of the play Shakespeare
had decided to keep him married but later changed his mind)
²² *tonguèd* eloquent   ²⁸ *counter-caster* i.e., a bookkeeper who *casts*
(reckons up) figures on a *counter* (abacus)   ³⁰ *ancient* standard-bearer;
an underofficer   ³³ *letter and affection* recommendations (from men
of power) and personal preference   ³⁴ *old gradation* seniority
³⁶ *affined* bound

Iago. O, sir, content you.
  I follow him to serve my turn upon him.
  We cannot all be masters, nor all masters   40
  Cannot be truly followed. You shall mark
  Many a duteous and knee-crooking° knave
  That, doting on his own obsequious bondage,
  Wears out his time, much like his master's ass,
  For naught but provender; and when he's old,
    cashiered.   45
  Whip me such honest knaves! Others there are
  Who, trimmed in forms and visages of duty,
  Keep yet their hearts attending on themselves,
  And, throwing but shows of service on their lords,
  Do well thrive by them, and when they have lined
    their coats,   50
  Do themselves homage. These fellows have some
    soul;
  And such a one do I profess myself. For, sir,
  It is as sure as you are Roderigo,
  Were I the Moor, I would not be Iago.
  In following him, I follow but myself.   55
  Heaven is my judge, not I for love and duty,
  But seeming so, for my peculiar° end;
  For when my outward action doth demonstrate
  The native° act and figure of my heart
  In complement extern,° 'tis not long after   60
  But I will wear my heart upon my sleeve
  For daws to peck at; I am not what I am.

Roderigo. What a full fortune does the thick-lips owe°
  If he can carry't thus!

Iago.   Call up her father,
  Rouse him. Make after him, poison his delight,   65
  Proclaim him in the streets, incense her kinsmen,
  And though he in a fertile climate dwell,
  Plague him with flies; though that his joy be joy,

---

⁴² *knee-crooking* bowing ⁵⁷ *peculiar* personal ⁵⁹ *native* natural, innate
⁶⁰ *complement extern* outward appearances ⁶³ *owe* own

Yet throw such chances of vexation on't
70   As it may lose some color.

Roderigo. Here is her father's house. I'll call aloud.

Iago. Do, with like timorous° accent and dire yell
As when, by night and negligence, the fire
Is spied in populous cities.

Roderigo. What, ho, Brabantio! Signior Brabantio,
75   ho!

Iago. Awake! What, ho, Brabantio! Thieves! Thieves!
Look to your house, your daughter, and your bags!
Thieves! Thieves!

          Brabantio above° [*at a window*].

Brabantio. What is the reason of this terrible sum-
          mons?
80   What is the matter there?

Roderigo. Signior, is all your family within?

Iago. Are your doors locked?

Brabantio.   Why, wherefore ask you
          this?

Iago. Zounds, sir, y'are robbed! For shame. Put on
          your gown!
Your heart is burst, you have lost half your soul.
85   Even now, now, very now, an old black ram
Is tupping your white ewe. Arise, arise!
Awake the snorting citizens with the bell,
Or else the devil will make a grandsire of you.
Arise, I say!

Brabantio.   What, have you lost your wits?

Roderigo. Most reverend signior, do you know my
90   voice?

Brabantio. Not I. What are you?

---

⁷² **timorous** frightening   ⁷⁸ s.d. *above* (i.e., on the small upper stage
above and to the rear of the main platform stage, which resembled the
projecting upper story of an Elizabethan house)

Roderigo. My name is Roderigo.

Brabantio.   The worser welcome!
I have charged thee not to haunt about my doors.
In honest plainness thou hast heard me say
My daughter is not for thee; and now, in madness,   95
Being full of supper and distemp'ring draughts,°
Upon malicious knavery dost thou come
To start° my quiet.

Roderigo. Sir, sir, sir——

Brabantio.   But thou must needs be sure
My spirits and my place° have in their power   100
To make this bitter to thee.

Roderigo.   Patience, good sir.

Brabantio. What tell'st thou me of robbing? This is
  Venice;
My house is not a grange.°

Roderigo.   Most grave Brabantio,
In simple and pure soul I come to you.

Iago. Zounds, sir, you are one of those that will not   105
serve God if the devil bid you. Because we come
to do you service and you think we are ruffians,
you'll have your daughter covered with a Barbary°
horse, you'll have your nephews° neigh to you,
you'll have coursers for cousins,° and gennets for   110
germans.°

Brabantio. What profane wretch art thou?

Iago. I am one, sir, that comes to tell you your daughter
and the Moor are making the beast with two backs.

Brabantio. Thou art a villain.

Iago.   You are—a senator.   115

Brabantio. This thou shalt answer. I know thee,
  Roderigo.

96 *distemp'ring draughts* unsettling drinks   98 *start* disrupt   100 *place*
rank, i.e., of senator   108 *grange* isolated house   108 *Barbary* Arabian,
i.e., Moorish   109 *nephews* i.e., grandsons   110 *cousins* relations
110–11 *gennets for germans* Spanish horses for blood relatives

Roderigo. Sir, I will answer anything. But I beseech
      you,
    If't be your pleasure and most wise consent,
    As partly I find it is, that your fair daughter,
120   At this odd-even° and dull watch o' th' night,
    Transported, with no worse nor better guard
    But with a knave of common hire, a gondolier,
    To the gross clasps of a lascivious Moor—
    If this be known to you, and your allowance,
125   We then have done you bold and saucy wrongs;
    But if you know not this, my manners tell me
    We have your wrong rebuke. Do not believe
    That from the sense of all civility°
    I thus would play and trifle with your reverence.
130   Your daughter, if you have not given her leave,
    I say again, hath made a gross revolt,
    Tying her duty, beauty, wit, and fortunes
    In an extravagant° and wheeling stranger
    Of here and everywhere. Straight satisfy yourself.
135   If she be in her chamber, or your house,
    Let loose on me the justice of the state
    For thus deluding you.

Brabantio.   Strike on the tinder, ho!
    Give me a taper! Call up all my people!
    This accident° is not unlike my dream.
140   Belief of it oppresses me already.
    Light, I say! Light!   *Exit [above].*

Iago.   Farewell, for I must leave you.
    It seems not meet, nor wholesome to my place,
    To be produced—as, if I stay, I shall—
    Against the Moor. For I do know the State,
145   However this may gall him with some check,°
    Cannot with safety cast° him; for he's embarked
    With such loud reason to the Cyprus wars,

---

120 *odd-even* between night and morning 128 *sense of all civility* feeling of what is proper 133 *extravagant* vagrant, wandering (Othello is
not Venetian and thus may be considered a wandering soldier of fortune) 139 *accident* happening 145 *check* restraint 146 *cast* dismiss

Which even now stands in act,° that for their souls
Another of his fathom° they have none
To lead their business; in which regard,   150
Though I do hate him as I do hell-pains,
Yet, for necessity of present life,
I must show out a flag and sign of love,
Which is indeed but sign. That you shall surely find
    him,
Lead to the Sagittary° the raisèd search;   155
And there will I be with him. So farewell.   *Exit.*

*Enter Brabantio [in his nightgown], with Servants
                    and torches.*

Brabantio. It is too true an evil. Gone she is;
And what's to come of my despisèd time
Is naught but bitterness. Now, Roderigo,
Where didst thou see her?—O unhappy girl!—   160
With the Moor, say'st thou?—Who would be a
    father?—
How didst thou know 'twas she?—O, she deceives
    me
Past thought!—What said she to you? Get moe°
    tapers!
Raise all my kindred!—Are they married, think
    you?

Roderigo. Truly I think they are.   165

Brabantio. O heaven! How got she out? O treason of
    the blood!
Fathers, from hence trust not your daughters' minds
By what you see them act.° Is there not charms
By which the property° of youth and maidhood
May be abused? Have you not read, Roderigo,   170
Of some such thing?

Roderigo.   Yes, sir, I have indeed.

Brabantio. Call up my brother.—O, would you had
    had her!—

---

¹⁴⁸ *stands in act* takes place ¹⁴⁹ *fathom* ability ¹⁵⁵ *Sagittary* (probably
the name of an inn) ¹⁶³ *moe* more ¹⁶⁸ *act* do ¹⁶⁹ *property* true
nature

Some one way, some another.—Do you know
Where we may apprehend her and the Moor?

175 *Roderigo.* I think I can discover him, if you please
To get good guard and go along with me.

Brabantio. Pray you lead on. At every house I'll call;
I may command at most.—Get weapons, ho!
And raise some special officers of might.—
180   On, good Roderigo; I will deserve your pains.°

                                        Exeunt.

Scene II. [*A street.*]

Enter Othello, Iago, Attendants with torches.

Iago. Though in the trade of war I have slain men,
Yet do I hold it very stuff° o' th' conscience
To do no contrived murder. I lack iniquity
Sometime to do me service. Nine or ten times
I had thought t' have yerked° him here, under the
5   ribs.

Othello. 'Tis better as it is.

Iago.   Nay, but he prated,
And spoke such scurvy and provoking terms
Against your honor, that with the little godliness
I have
I did full hard forbear him. But I pray you, sir,
10   Are you fast married? Be assured of this,
That the magnifico° is much beloved,
And hath in his effect a voice potential
As double as the Duke's.° He will divorce you,
Or put upon you what restraint or grievance

---

180 *deserve your pains* be worthy of (and reward) your efforts
I.ii.² *stuff* essence   ⁵ *yerked* stabbed   ¹¹ *magnifico* nobleman   ¹²⁻¹³ *hath*
. . . *Duke's* i.e., can be as effective as the Duke

The law, with all his might to enforce it on,   15
  Will give him cable.°

Othello.   Let him do his spite.
  My services which I have done the Signiory°
  Shall out-tongue his complaints. 'Tis yet to know° —
  Which when I know that boasting is an honor
  I shall promulgate—I fetch my life and being   20
  From men of royal siege;° and my demerits°
  May speak unbonneted to as proud a fortune
  As this that I have reached.° For know, Iago,
  But that I love the gentle Desdemona,
  I would not my unhousèd° free condition   25
  Put into circumscription and confine
  For the seas' worth. But look, what lights come
      yond?

    Enter Cassio, with [Officers and] torches.

Iago. Those are the raisèd father and his friends.
  You were best go in.

Othello.   Not I. I must be found.
  My parts, my title, and my perfect soul°   30
  Shall manifest me rightly. Is it they?

Iago. By Janus, I think no.

Othello. The servants of the Duke? And my lieutenant?
  The goodness of the night upon you, friends.
  What is the news?

Cassio.   The Duke does greet you, general;   35
  And he requires your haste-posthaste appearance
  Even on the instant.

Othello.   What is the matter, think you?

Cassio. Something from Cyprus, as I may divine.
  It is a business of some heat. The galleys

---

[16] *cable* range, scope   [17] *Signiory* the rulers of Venice   [18] *yet to know* unknown as yet   [21] *siege* rank   [21] *demerits* deserts   [22-23] *May . . . reached,* i.e., are the equal of the family I have married into   [25] *unhousèd* unconfined   [30] *perfect soul* clear, unflawed conscience

40　Have sent a dozen sequent° messengers
　　This very night at one another's heels,
　　And many of the consuls, raised and met,
　　Are at the Duke's already. You have been hotly
　　　called for.
　　When, being not at your lodging to be found,
45　The Senate hath sent about three several° quests
　　To search you out.

Othello.　　　　　　　'Tis well I am found by you.
　　I will but spend a word here in the house,
　　And go with you.　　　　　　　　　　[*Exit.*]

Cassio.　　　　　Ancient, what makes he here?
Iago. Faith, he tonight hath boarded a land carack.°
50　If it prove lawful prize, he's made forever.

Cassio. I do not understand.

Iago.　　　　　　　　　He's married.

Cassio.　　　　　　　　　　　To who?
　　　　　　　　[*Enter Othello.*]

Iago. Marry,° to—Come, captain, will you go?

Othello.　　　　　　　　　Have with you.

Cassio. Here comes another troop to seek for you.

　Enter Brabantio, Roderigo, with Officers and torches.

Iago. It is Brabantio. General, be advised.
　　He comes to bad intent.

55　*Othello.*　　　　　　Holla! Stand there!

Roderigo. Signior, it is the Moor.

Brabantio.　　　　　　Down with him, thief!
　　　　　　　　　[*They draw swords.*]

Iago. You, Roderigo? Come, sir, I am for you.

Othello. Keep up your bright swords, for the dew will
　　rust them.

---

⁴⁰ *sequent* successive　⁴⁵ *several* separate　⁴⁹ *carack* treasure ship
⁵² *Marry* By Mary (an interjection)

Good signior, you shall more command with years
Than with your weapons.   60

Brabantio. O thou foul thief, where hast thou stowed
    my daughter?
Damned as thou art, thou hast enchanted her!
For I'll refer me to all things of sense,°
If she in chains of magic were not bound,
Whether a maid so tender, fair, and happy,   65
So opposite to marriage that she shunned
The wealthy, curlèd darlings of our nation,
Would ever have, t' incur a general mock,°
Run from her guardage to the sooty bosom
Of such a thing as thou—to fear, not to delight.   70
Judge me the world if 'tis not gross in sense°
That thou hast practiced ° on her with foul charms,
Abused her delicate youth with drugs or minerals
That weaken motion.° I'll have't disputed on;
'Tis probable, and palpable to thinking.   75
I therefore apprehend and do attach° thee
For an abuser of the world, a practicer
Of arts inhibited and out of warrant.°
Lay hold upon him. If he do resist,
Subdue him at his peril.

Othello.   Hold your hands,   80
Both you of my inclining and the rest.
Were it my cue to fight, I should have known it
Without a prompter. Whither will you that I go
To answer this your charge?

Brabantio.   To prison, till fit time
Of law and course of direct session   85
Call thee to answer.

Othello.   What if I do obey?
How may the Duke be therewith satisfied,
Whose messengers are here about my side

---

⁶³ *refer . . . sense* i.e., base (my argument) on all ordinary understanding of nature   ⁶⁸ *general mock* public shame   ⁷¹ *gross in sense*
obvious   ⁷² *practiced* used tricks   ⁷⁴ *motion* thought, i.e., reason
⁷⁶ *attach* arrest   ⁷⁸ *inhibited . . . warrant* prohibited and illegal (black
magic)

Upon some present° business of the state
To bring me to him?

90 *Officer.*   'Tis true, most worthy signior.
The Duke's in council, and your noble self
I am sure is sent for.

Brabantio.   How? The Duke in council?
In this time of the night? Bring him away.
Mine's not an idle cause. The Duke himself,
95 Or any of my brothers° of the state,
Cannot but feel this wrong as 'twere their own;
For if such actions may have passage free,
Bondslaves and pagans shall our statesmen be.

Exeunt.

Scene III. [*A council chamber.*]

*Enter Duke, Senators, and Officers [set at a table,
with lights and Attendants].*

Duke. There's no composition° in this news
That gives them credit.°

First Senator.   Indeed, they are disproportioned.
My letters say a hundred and seven galleys.

Duke. And mine a hundred forty.

Second Senator.   And mine two hundred.
5 But though they jump° not on a just accompt° —
As in these cases where the aim° reports
'Tis oft with difference—yet do they all confirm
A Turkish fleet, and bearing up to Cyprus.

Duke. Nay, it is possible enough to judgment.°
10 I do not so secure me in the error,

---

89 *present* immediate   95 *brothers* i.e., the other senators   I.iii.¹ *composition* agreement   ² *gives them credit* makes them believable   ⁵ *jump* agree   ⁵ *just accompt* exact counting   ⁶ *aim* approximation   ⁹ *to judgment* when carefully considered

But the main article I do approve
In fearful sense.°

Sailor. (*Within*) What, ho! What, ho! What, ho!

Enter Sailor.

Officer. A messenger from the galleys.

Duke.   Now? What's the business?

Sailor. The Turkish preparation makes for Rhodes.
So was I bid report here to the State   *15*
By Signior Angelo.

Duke. How say you by this change?

First Senator.   This cannot be
By no assay of reason. 'Tis a pageant°
To keep us in false gaze.° When we consider
Th' importancy of Cyprus to the Turk,   *20*
And let ourselves again but understand
That, as it more concerns the Turk than Rhodes,
So may he with more facile question° bear it,
For that it stands not in such warlike brace,°
But altogether lacks th' abilities   *25*
That Rhodes is dressed in. If we make thought of
    this,
We must not think the Turk is so unskillful
To leave that latest which concerns him first,
Neglecting an attempt of ease and gain
To wake and wage a danger profitless.   *30*

Duke. Nay, in all confidence he's not for Rhodes.

Officer. Here is more news.

Enter a Messenger.

Messenger. The Ottomites, reverend and gracious,
Steering with due course toward the isle of Rhodes,
Have there injointed them with an after° fleet.   *35*

10-12 *I do . . . sense* i.e., just because the numbers disagree in the reports,
I do not doubt that the principal information (that the Turkish fleet is
out) is fearfully true   18 *pageant* show, pretense   19 *in false gaze* looking the wrong way   23 *facile question* easy struggle   24 *warlike brace*
"military posture"   35 *after* following

First Senator. Ay, so I thought. How many, as you
guess?

Messenger. Of thirty sail; and now they do restem
Their backward course, bearing with frank ap-
pearance
Their purposes toward Cyprus. Signior Montano,
40   Your trusty and most valiant servitor,
With his free duty° recommends° you thus,
And prays you to believe him.

Duke. 'Tis certain then for Cyprus.
Marcus Luccicos, is not he in town?

45 *First Senator.* He's now in Florence.

Duke. Write from us to him; post-posthaste dispatch.

First Senator. Here comes Brabantio and the valiant
Moor.

*Enter Brabantio, Othello, Cassio, Iago, Roderigo,
and Officers.*

Duke. Valiant Othello, we must straight° employ you
Against the general° enemy Ottoman.
[*To Brabantio*] I did not see you. Welcome, gentle
50   signior.
We lacked your counsel and your help tonight.

Brabantio. So did I yours. Good your grace, pardon
me.
Neither my place, nor aught I heard of business,
Hath raised me from my bed; nor doth the general
care
55   Take hold on me; for my particular grief
Is of so floodgate and o'erbearing nature
That it engluts and swallows other sorrows,
And it is still itself.

Duke.   Why, what's the matter?

Brabantio. My daughter! O, my daughter!

---

41 *free duty* unlimited respect   41 *recommends* informs   48 *straight* at
once   49 *general* universal

Senators.   Dead?

Brabantio.   Ay, to me.
  She is abused, stol'n from me, and corrupted   60
  By spells and medicines bought of mountebanks;
  For nature so prepost'rously to err,
  Being not deficient, blind, or lame of sense,
  Sans° witchcraft could not.

Duke. Whoe'er he be that in this foul proceeding   65
  Hath thus beguiled your daughter of herself,
  And you of her, the bloody book of law
  You shall yourself read in the bitter letter
  After your own sense; yea, though our proper° son
  Stood in your action.°

Brabantio.   Humbly I thank your Grace.   70
  Here is the man—this Moor, whom now, it seems,
  Your special mandate for the state affairs
  Hath hither brought.

All.   We are very sorry for't.

Duke. [*To Othello*] What in your own part can you
  say to this?

Brabantio. Nothing, but this is so.   75

Othello. Most potent, grave, and reverend signiors,
  My very noble and approved° good masters,
  That I have ta'en away this old man's daughter,
  It is most true; true I have married her.
  The very head and front° of my offending   80
  Hath this extent, no more. Rude am I in my speech,
  And little blessed with the soft phrase of peace,
  For since these arms of mine had seven years' pith°
  Till now some nine moons wasted,° they have used
  Their dearest° action in the tented field;   85
  And little of this great world can I speak

[64] *Sans* without   [69] *proper* own   [70] *Stood in your action* were the accused in your suit   [77] *approved* tested, proven by past performance   [80] *head and front* extreme form (*front* = forehead)   [83] *pith* strength   [84] *wasted* past   [85] *dearest* most important

More than pertains to feats of broils and battle;
And therefore little shall I grace my cause
In speaking for myself. Yet, by your gracious
    patience,
90 I will a round° unvarnished tale deliver
Of my whole course of love—what drugs, what
    charms,
What conjuration, and what mighty magic,
For such proceeding I am charged withal,
I won his daughter—

Brabantio.   A maiden never bold,
95 Of spirit so still and quiet that her motion
Blushed at herself;° and she, in spite of nature,
Of years, of country, credit, everything,
To fall in love with what she feared to look on!
It is a judgment maimed and most imperfect
100 That will confess perfection so could err
Against all rules of nature, and must be driven
To find out practices of cunning hell
Why this should be. I therefore vouch again
That with some mixtures pow'rful o'er the blood,
105 Or with some dram, conjured to this effect,
He wrought upon her.

Duke.   To vouch this is no proof,
Without more wider and more overt test
Than these thin habits° and poor likelihoods
Of modern° seeming do prefer against him.

110 *First Senator.* But, Othello, speak.
Did you by indirect and forcèd courses
Subdue and poison this young maid's affections?
Or came it by request, and such fair question°
As soul to soul affordeth?

Othello.   I do beseech you,
115 Send for the lady to the Sagittary

---

⁹⁰ *round* blunt ⁹⁵⁻⁹⁶ *her motion/Blushed at herself* i.e., she was so
modest that she blushed at every thought (and movement) ¹⁰⁸ *habits*
clothing ¹⁰⁹ *modern* trivial ¹¹³ *question* discussion

And let her speak of me before her father.
If you do find me foul in her report,
The trust, the office, I do hold of you
Not only take away, but let your sentence
Even fall upon my life.

Duke.   Fetch Desdemona hither.   *120*

Othello. Ancient, conduct them; you best know the
    place.
           [*Exit Iago, with two or three Attendants.*]

And till she come, as truly as to heaven
I do confess the vices of my blood,
So justly to your grave ears I'll present
How I did thrive in this fair lady's love,   *125*
And she in mine.

Duke.   Say it, Othello.

Othello. Her father loved me; oft invited me;
Still° questioned me the story of my life
From year to year, the battle, sieges, fortune
That I have passed.   *130*
I ran it through, even from my boyish days
To th' very moment that he bade me tell it.
Wherein I spoke of most disastrous chances,
Of moving accidents by flood and field,
Of hairbreadth scapes i' th' imminent° deadly
    breach,   *135*
Of being taken by the insolent foe
And sold to slavery, of my redemption thence
And portance° in my travel's history,
Wherein of anters° vast and deserts idle,°
Rough quarries, rocks, and hills whose heads touch
    heaven,   *140*
It was my hint to speak. Such was my process.
And of the Cannibals that each other eat,
The Anthropophagi,° and men whose heads

---

[128] *Still* regularly [135] *imminent* threatening [138] *portance* manner of
acting [139] *anters* caves [139] *idle* empty, sterile [143] *Anthropophagi*
man-eaters

Grew beneath their shoulders. These things to hear
145   Would Desdemona seriously incline;
But still the house affairs would draw her thence;
Which ever as she could with haste dispatch,
She'd come again, and with a greedy ear
Devour up my discourse. Which I observing,
150   Took once a pliant hour, and found good means
To draw from her a prayer of earnest heart
That I would all my pilgrimage dilate,°
Whereof by parcels she had something heard,
But not intentively.° I did consent,
155   And often did beguile her of her tears
When I did speak of some distressful stroke
That my youth suffered. My story being done,
She gave me for my pains a world of kisses.
She swore in faith 'twas strange, 'twas passing°
                strange;
160   'Twas pitiful, 'twas wondrous pitiful.
She wished she had not heard it; yet she wished
That heaven had made her such a man. She thanked
                me,
And bade me, if I had a friend that loved her,
I should but teach him how to tell my story,
165   And that would woo her. Upon this hint I spake.
She loved me for the dangers I had passed,
And I loved her that she did pity them.
This only is the witchcraft I have used.
Here comes the lady. Let her witness it.

Enter Desdemona, Iago, Attendants.

170   *Duke.* I think this tale would win my daughter too.
Good Brabantio, take up this mangled matter at the
                best.°
Men do their broken weapons rather use
Than their bare hands.

---

152 *dilate* relate in full   154 *intentively* at length and in sequence
159 *passing* surpassing   171 *Take . . . best* i.e., make the best of this
disaster

Brabantio.   I pray you hear her speak.
 If she confess that she was half the wooer,
 Destruction on my head if my bad blame   *175*
 Light on the man. Come hither, gentle mistress.
 Do you perceive in all this noble company
 Where most you owe obedience?

Desdemona.   My noble father,
 I do perceive here a divided duty.
 To you I am bound for life and education;   *180*
 My life and education both do learn me
 How to respect you. You are the lord of duty,
 I am hitherto your daughter. But here's my husband,
 And so much duty as my mother showed
 To you, preferring you before her father,   *185*
 So much I challenge° that I may profess
 Due to the Moor my lord.

Brabantio.   God be with you. I have done.
 Please it your Grace, on to the state affairs.
 I had rather to adopt a child than get° it.
 Come hither, Moor.   *190*
 I here do give thee that with all my heart
 Which, but thou hast already, with all my heart
 I would keep from thee. For your sake,° jewel,
 I am glad at soul I have no other child,
 For thy escape would teach me tyranny,   *195*
 To hang clogs on them. I have done, my lord.

Duke. Let me speak like yourself and lay a sentence°
 Which, as a grise° or step, may help these lovers.
 When remedies are past, the griefs are ended
 By seeing the worst, which late on hopes depended.° *200*
 To mourn a mischief that is past and gone
 Is the next° way to draw new mischief on.
 What cannot be preserved when fortune takes,

---

¹⁸⁶ *challenge* claim as right ¹⁸⁹ *get* beget ¹⁹³ *For your sake* because of you ¹⁹⁷ *lay a sentence* provide a maxim ¹⁹⁸ *grise* step ²⁰⁰ *late on hopes depended* was supported by hope (of a better outcome) until lately ²⁰² *next* closest, surest

Patience her injury a mock'ry makes.
205 The robbed that smiles, steals something from the
      thief;
      He robs himself that spends a bootless° grief.

      Brabantio. So let the Turk of Cyprus us beguile:
      We lose it not so long as we can smile.
      He bears the sentence well that nothing bears
210   But the free comfort which from thence he hears;
      But he bears both the sentence and the sorrow
      That to pay grief must of poor patience borrow.
      These sentences, to sugar, or to gall,
      Being strong on both sides, are equivocal.
213   But words are words. I never yet did hear
      That the bruisèd heart was piercèd° through the ear.
      I humbly beseech you, proceed to th' affairs of state.

      Duke. The Turk with a most mighty preparation makes
      for Cyprus. Othello, the fortitude° of the place is
220   best known to you; and though we have there a
      substitute° of most allowed sufficiency,° yet opin-
      ion, a more sovereign mistress of effects, throws a
      more safer voice on you.° You must therefore be
      content to slubber° the gloss of your new fortunes
225   with this more stubborn and boisterous° expedition.

      Othello. The tyrant Custom, most grave senators,
      Hath made the flinty and steel couch of war
      My thrice-driven° bed of down. I do agnize°
      A natural and prompt alacrity
230   I find in hardness and do undertake
      This present wars against the Ottomites.

---

²⁰⁶ *bootless* valueless   ²¹⁶ *piercèd* (some editors emend to *pieced,* i.e.,
"healed." But *pierced* makes good sense: Brabantio is saying in effect
that his heart cannot be further hurt [pierced] by the indignity of the
useless, conventional advice the Duke offers him. *Pierced* can also
mean, however, "lanced" in the medical sense, and would then mean
"treated")   ²¹⁹ *fortitude* fortification   ²²¹ *substitute* viceroy   ²²¹ *most
allowed sufficiency* generally acknowledged capability   ²²¹⁻²³ *opinion
. . . you* i.e., the general opinion, which finally controls affairs, is that
you would be the best man in this situation   ²²⁴ *slubber* besmear
²²⁵ *stubborn and boisterous* rough and violent   ²²⁸ *thrice-driven* i.e.,
softest   ²²⁸ *agnize* know in myself

Most humbly, therefore, bending to your state,
I crave fit disposition for my wife,
Due reference of place, and exhibition,°
With such accommodation and besort   235
As levels with° her breeding.

Duke.   Why, at her father's.

Brabantio. I will not have it so.

Othello.   Nor I.

Desdemona.   Nor would I there reside,
To put my father in impatient thoughts
By being in his eye. Most gracious Duke,
To my unfolding° lend your prosperous° ear,   240
And let me find a charter° in your voice,
T' assist my simpleness.

Duke.   What would you, Desdemona?

Desdemona. That I love the Moor to live with him,
My downright violence, and storm of fortunes,
May trumpet to the world. My heart's subdued   245
Even to the very quality of my lord.°
I saw Othello's visage in his mind,
And to his honors and his valiant parts
Did I my soul and fortunes consecrate.
So that, dear lords, if I be left behind,   250
A moth of peace, and he go to the war,
The rites° for why I love him are bereft me,
And I a heavy interim shall support
By his dear absence. Let me go with him.

Othello. Let her have your voice.°   255
Vouch with me, heaven, I therefore beg it not
To please the palate of my appetite,
Nor to comply with heat° —the young affects°

234 *exhibition* grant of funds   236 *levels with* is suitable to   240 *unfolding* explanation   240 *prosperous* favoring   241 *charter* permission   245–46 *My . . . lord* i.e., I have become one in nature and being with the man I married (therefore, I too would go to the wars like a soldier)   252 *rites* (may refer either to the marriage rites or to the rites, formalities, of war)   255 *voice* consent   258 *heat* lust   258 *affects* passions

In me defunct—and proper satisfaction;°
260 But to be free and bounteous to her mind;
And heaven defend° your good souls that you think
I will your serious and great business scant
When she is with me. No, when light-winged toys
Of feathered Cupid seel° with wanton° dullness
265 My speculative and officed instrument,°
That my disports corrupt and taint my business,
Let housewives make a skillet of my helm,
And all indign° and base adversities
Make head° against my estimation!°—

270 *Duke.* Be it as you shall privately determine,
Either for her stay or going. Th' affair cries haste,
And speed must answer it.

First Senator.   You must away tonight.

Othello. With all my heart.

Duke. At nine i' th' morning here we'll meet again
275 Othello, leave some officer behind,
And he shall our commission bring to you,
And such things else of quality and respect
As doth import you.

Othello.   So please your grace, my ancient;
A man he is of honesty and trust.
280 To his conveyance I assign my wife,
With what else needful your good grace shall think
To be sent after me.

Duke.   Let it be so.
Good night to every one. [*To Brabantio*] And, noble
signior,
If virtue no delighted° beauty lack,
285 Your son-in-law is far more fair than black.

First Senator. Adieu, brave Moor. Use Desdemona
well.

---

259 *proper satisfaction* i.e., consummation of the marriage   261 *defend* forbid   264 *seel* sew up   264 *wanton* lascivious   265 *speculative . . . instrument* i.e., sight (and, by extension, the mind)   268 *indign* unworthy   269 *Make head* form an army, i.e., attack   269 *estimation* reputation   284 *delighted* delightful

Brabantio. Look to her, Moor, if thou hast eyes to see:
  She has deceived her father, and may thee.
                    [*Exeunt Duke, Senators, Officers, &c.*]

Othello. My life upon her faith! Honest Iago,
  My Desdemona must I leave to thee.   290
  I prithee let thy wife attend on her,
  And bring them after in the best advantage.°
  Come, Desdemona. I have but an hour
  Of love, of wordly matter, and direction
  To spend with thee. We must obey the time.   295
                    Exit [*Moor with Desdemona*].

Roderigo. Iago?

Iago. What say'st thou, noble heart?

Roderigo. What will I do, think'st thou?

Iago. Why, go to bed and sleep.

Roderigo. I will incontinently° drown myself.   300

Iago. If thou dost, I shall never love thee after. Why,
  thou silly gentleman?

Roderigo. It is silliness to live when to live is torment;
  and then have we a prescription to die when death is
  our physician.   305

Iago. O villainous! I have looked upon the world for
  four times seven years, and since I could distinguish
  betwixt a benefit and an injury, I never found man
  that knew how to love himself. Ere I would say I
  would drown myself for the love of a guinea hen,   310
  I would change my humanity with a baboon.

Roderigo. What should I do? I confess it is my shame
  to be so fond, but it is not in my virtue° to amend it.

Iago. Virtue? A fig! 'Tis in ourselves that we are thus,
  or thus. Our bodies are our gardens, to the which   315
  our wills are gardeners; so that if we will plant
  nettles or sow lettuce, set hyssop and weed up thyme,

───────────────────────────────

²⁹² *advantage* opportunity   ³⁰⁰ *incontinently* at once   ³¹³ *virtue* strength
(Roderigo is saying that his nature controls him)

supply it with one gender of herbs or distract° it
with many—either to have it sterile with idleness or
320   manured with industry—why, the power and corri-
gible° authority of this lies in our wills. If the balance of our lives had not one scale of reason to poise
another of sensuality, the blood and baseness of
our natures would conduct us to most prepost'rous
325   conclusions.° But we have reason to cool our raging
motions, our carnal stings or unbitted° lusts,
whereof I take this that you call love to be a sect
or scion.°

Roderigo. It cannot be.

330   *Iago.* It is merely a lust of the blood and a permission of
the will. Come, be a man! Drown thyself? Drown
cats and blind puppies! I have professed me thy
friend, and I confess me knit to thy deserving with
cables of perdurable toughness. I could never better
335   stead° thee than now. Put money in thy purse.
Follow thou the wars; defeat thy favor° with an
usurped° beard. I say, put money in thy purse.
It cannot be long that Desdemona should continue
her love to the Moor. Put money in thy purse. Nor
340   he his to her. It was a violent commencement in
her and thou shalt see an answerable° sequestra-
tion—put but money in thy purse. These Moors
are changeable in their wills—fill thy purse with
money. The food that to him now is as luscious as
345   locusts° shall be to him shortly as bitter as coloquintida.° She must change for youth; when she is
sated with his body, she will find the errors of her
choice. Therefore, put money in thy purse. If thou
wilt needs damn thyself, do it a more delicate way
350   than drowning. Make all the money thou canst. If

---

³¹⁸ *distract* vary ³²⁰⁻²¹ *corrigible* corrective ³²⁵ *conclusions* ends
³²⁶ *unbitted* i.e., uncontrolled ³²⁷⁻²⁸ *sect or scion* offshoot ³³⁵ *stead*
serve ³³⁶ *defeat thy favor* disguise your face ³³⁷ *usurped* assumed
³⁴¹ *answerable* similar ³⁴⁵ *locusts* (a sweet fruit) ³⁴⁵⁻⁴⁶ *coloquintida*
(a purgative derived from a bitter apple)

sanctimony° and a frail vow betwixt an erring°
barbarian and supersubtle Venetian be not too hard
for my wits, and all the tribe of hell, thou shalt enjoy
her. Therefore, make money. A pox of drowning
thyself, it is clean out of the way. Seek thou rather   *355*
to be hanged in compassing° thy joy than to be
drowned and go without her.

Roderigo. Wilt thou be fast to my hopes, if I depend
on the issue?

Iago. Thou art sure of me. Go, make money. I have   *360*
told thee often, and I retell thee again and again, I
hate the Moor. My cause is hearted;° thine hath no
less reason. Let us be conjunctive° in our revenge
against him. If thou canst cuckold him, thou dost
thyself a pleasure, me a sport. There are many   *365*
events in the womb of time, which will be delivered.
Traverse, go, provide thy money! We will have more
of this tomorrow. Adieu.

Roderigo. Where shall we meet i' th' morning?

Iago. At my lodging.   *370*

Roderigo. I'll be with thee betimes.

Iago. Go to, farewell. Do you hear, Roderigo?

Roderigo. I'll sell all my land.   *Exit.*

Iago. Thus do I ever make my fool my purse;
For I mine own gained knowledge° should profane   *375*
If I would time expend with such snipe
But for my sport and profit. I hate the Moor,
And it is thought abroad that 'twixt my sheets
H'as done my office. I know not if 't be true,
But I, for mere suspicion in that kind,   *380*
Will do, as if for surety.° He holds me well;
The better shall my purpose work on him.

---

³⁵¹ *sanctimony* sacred bond (of marriage) ³⁵¹ *erring* wandering
³⁵⁶ *compassing* encompassing, achieving ³⁶² *hearted* deep-seated in the
heart ³⁶³ *conjunctive* joined ³⁷⁵ *gained knowledge* i.e., practical,
worldly wisdom ³⁸¹ *surety* certainty

Cassio's a proper° man. Let me see now:
To get his place, and to plume up my will°
885 In double knavery. How? How? Let's see.
After some time, to abuse Othello's ears
That he is too familiar with his wife.
He hath a person and a smooth dispose°
To be suspected—framed° to make women false.
890 The Moor is of a free and open nature
That thinks men honest that but seem to be so;
And will as tenderly be led by th' nose
As asses are.
I have't! It is engendered! Hell and night
895 Must bring this monstrous birth to the world's light.
                         [*Exit.*]

---

383 *proper* handsome   384 *plume up my will* (many explanations have been offered for this crucial line, which in Q1 reads "make up my will." The general sense is something like "to make more proud and gratify my ego")   388 *dispose* manner   389 *framed* designed

ACT II

Scene I. [*Cyprus.*]

Enter Montano and two Gentlemen, [one above].°

Montano. What from the cape can you discern at sea?

First Gentleman. Nothing at all, it is a high-wrought
    flood.
    I cannot 'twixt the heaven and the main
    Descry a sail.

Montano. Methinks the wind hath spoke aloud at land;   *5*
    A fuller blast ne'er shook our battlements.
    If it hath ruffianed so upon the sea,
    What ribs of oak, when mountains melt on them,
    Can hold the mortise? What shall we hear of this?

Second Gentleman. A segregation° of the Turkish
    fleet.   *10*
    For do but stand upon the foaming shore,
    The chidden billow seems to pelt the clouds;
    The wind-shaked surge, with high and monstrous
        main,°
    Seems to cast water on the burning Bear
    And quench the guards of th' ever-fixèd pole.°   *15*

II.i. s.d. (the Folio arrangement of this scene requires that the First
Gentleman stand above—on the upper stage—and act as a lookout reporting sights which cannot be seen by Montano standing below on the
main stage) ¹⁰ *segregation* separation ¹³ *main* (both "ocean" and
"strength") ¹⁴⁻¹⁵ *Seems . . . pole* (the constellation Ursa Minor contains two stars which are the *guards*, or companions, of the *pole*, or
North Star)

65

I never did like molestation view
On the enchafèd flood.

Montano.   If that the Turkish fleet
Be not ensheltered and embayed, they are drowned;
It is impossible to bear it out.

Enter a [third] Gentleman.

20 *Third Gentleman.* News, lads! Our wars are done.
The desperate tempest hath so banged the Turks
That their designment halts. A noble ship of Venice
Hath seen a grievous wrack and sufferance°
On most part of their fleet.

Montano. How? Is this true?

25 *Third Gentleman.*   The ship is here put in,
A Veronesa; Michael Cassio,
Lieutenant to the warlike Moor Othello,
Is come on shore; the Moor himself at sea,
And is in full commission here for Cyprus.

30 *Montano.* I am glad on't. 'Tis a worthy governor.

Third Gentleman. But this same Cassio, though he
    speak of comfort
Touching the Turkish loss, yet he looks sadly
And prays the Moor be safe, for they were parted
With foul and violent tempest.

Montano.   Pray heavens he be;
35 For I have served him, and the man commands
Like a full soldier. Let's to the seaside, ho!
As well to see the vessel that's come in
As to throw out our eyes for brave Othello,
Even till we make the main and th' aerial blue
An indistinct regard.°

40 *Third Gentleman.*   Come, let's do so;
For every minute is expectancy
Of more arrivancie.°

23 *sufferance* damage   39–40 *the main . . . regard* i.e., the sea and sky
become indistinguishable   42 *arrivancie* arrivals

Enter Cassio.

Cassio. Thanks, you the valiant of the warlike isle,
   That so approve° the Moor. O, let the heavens
   Give him defense against the elements,   45
   For I have lost him on a dangerous sea.

Montano. Is he well shipped?

Cassio. His bark is stoutly timbered, and his pilot
   Of very expert and approved allowance;°
   Therefore my hopes, not surfeited to death,°   50
   Stand in bold cure.° (*Within*) A sail, a sail, a sail!

Cassio. What noise?

First Gentleman. The town is empty; on the brow o'
      th' sea
   Stand ranks of people, and they cry, "A sail!"

Cassio. My hopes do shape him for the governor.   55
                                            [*A shot.*]

Second Gentleman. They do discharge their shot of
      courtesy:
   Our friends at least.

Cassio.   I pray you, sir, go forth
   And give us truth who 'tis that is arrived.

Second Gentleman. I shall.   *Exit.*

Montano. But, good lieutenant, is your general wived?   60

Cassio. Most fortunately. He hath achieved a maid
   That paragons° description and wild fame;°
   One that excels the quirks of blazoning pens,°
   And in th' essential vesture of creation°
   Does tire the ingener.°

---

⁴⁴ *approve* ("honor" or, perhaps, "are as warlike and valiant as your
governor") ⁴⁹ *approved allowance* known and tested ⁵⁰ *not surfeited
to death* i.e., not so great as to be in danger ⁵¹ *Stand in bold cure* i.e.,
are likely to be restored ⁶² *paragons* exceeds ⁶² *wild fame* extravagant report ⁶³ *quirks of blazoning pens* ingenuities of praising pens
⁶⁴ *essential vesture of creation* i.e., essential human nature as given by
the Creator ⁶⁵ *tire the ingener* (a difficult line which probably means
something like "outdo the human ability to imagine and picture")

Enter [Second] Gentleman.

65   How now? Who has put in?

Second Gentleman. 'Tis one Iago, ancient to the
     general.

Cassio. H'as had most favorable and happy speed:
     Tempests themselves, high seas, and howling winds,
     The guttered° rocks and congregated° sands,
70   Traitors ensteeped° to enclog the guiltless keel,
     As having sense° of beauty, do omit
     Their mortal° natures, letting go safely by
     The divine Desdemona.

Montano.   What is she?

Cassio. She that I spake of, our great captain's captain,
75   Left in the conduct of the bold Iago,
     Whose footing° here anticipates our thoughts
     A se'nnight's° speed. Great Jove, Othello guard,
     And swell his sail with thine own pow'rful breath,
     That he may bless this bay with his tall° ship,
80   Make love's quick pants in Desdemona's arms,
     Give renewed fire to our extincted spirits.

     Enter Desdemona, Iago, Roderigo, and Emilia.

     O, behold! The riches of the ship is come on shore!
     You men of Cyprus, let her have your knees.
                                        [*Kneeling.*]
     Hail to thee, lady! and the grace of heaven,
85   Before, behind thee, and on every hand,
     Enwheel thee round.

Desdemona.   I thank you, valiant Cassio.
     What tidings can you tell of my lord?

Cassio. He is not yet arrived, nor know I aught
     But that he's well and will be shortly here.

90 *Desdemona.* O but I fear. How lost you company?

⁶⁹ *guttered* jagged   ⁶⁹ *congregated* gathered   ⁷⁰ *ensteeped* submerged
⁷¹ *sense* awareness   ⁷² *mortal* deadly   ⁷⁶ *footing* landing   ⁷⁷ *se'nnight's*
week's   ⁷⁹ *tall* brave

Cassio. The great contention of sea and skies
    Parted our fellowship. (*Within*) A sail, a sail!
    [*A shot.*]
                      But hark. A sail!

Second Gentleman. They give this greeting to the
    citadel;
    This likewise is a friend.

Cassio.   See for the news.   95
                    [*Exit Gentleman.*]
    Good ancient, you are welcome. [*To Emilia*] Wel-
    come, mistress.
    Let it not gall your patience, good Iago,
    That I extend° my manners. 'Tis my breeding°
    That gives me this bold show of courtesy. [*Kisses
    Emilia.*]

Iago. Sir, would she give you so much of her lips   100
    As of her tongue she oft bestows on me,
    You would have enough.

Desdemona.   Alas, she has no speech.

Iago. In faith, too much.
    I find it still when I have leave to sleep.°
    Marry, before your ladyship,° I grant,   105
    She puts her tongue a little in her heart
    And chides with thinking.

Emilia.   You have little cause to say so.

Iago. Come on, come on! You are pictures° out of
    door,
    Bells in your parlors, wildcats in your kitchens,
    Saints in your injuries,° devils being offended,   110

---

⁹⁸ *extend* stretch ⁹⁸ *breeding* careful training in manners (Cassio is
considerably more the polished gentleman than Iago, and aware of it)
¹⁰⁴ *still . . . sleep* i.e., even when she allows me to sleep she continues
to scold ¹⁰⁵ *before your ladyship* in your presence ¹⁰⁸ *pictures* models
(of virtue) ¹¹⁰ *in your injuries* when you injure others

Players in your housewifery,° and housewives in
your beds.

Desdemona. O, fie upon thee, slanderer!

Iago. Nay, it is true, or else I am a Turk:
You rise to play, and go to bed to work.

Emilia. You shall not write my praise.

115 *Iago.*   No, let me not.

Desdemona. What wouldst write of me, if thou shouldst
praise me?

Iago. O gentle lady, do not put me to't,
For I am nothing if not critical.

Desdemona. Come on, assay. There's one gone to the
harbor?

Iago. Ay, madam.

120 *Desdemona.* [*Aside*] I am not merry; but I do beguile
The thing I am by seeming otherwise.—
Come, how wouldst thou praise me?

Iago. I am about it; but indeed my invention
Comes from my pate as birdlime° does from
frieze° —

125 It plucks out brains and all. But my Muse labors,
And thus she is delivered:
If she be fair° and wise: fairness and wit,
The one's for use, the other useth it.

Desdemona. Well praised. How if she be black° and
witty?

130 *Iago.* If she be black, and thereto have a wit,
She'll find a white that shall her blackness fit.

Desdemona. Worse and worse!

---

[111] *housewifery* (this word can mean "careful, economical household management," and Iago would then be accusing women of only pretending to be good housekeepers, while in bed they are either [1] economical of their favors, or more likely [2] serious and dedicated workers) [124] *birdlime* a sticky substance put on branches to catch birds [124] *frieze* rough cloth   [127] *fair* light-complexioned   [129] *black* brunette

Emilia. How if fair and foolish?

Iago. She never yet was foolish that was fair,
　For even her folly helped her to an heir.   *135*

Desdemona. These are old fond° paradoxes to make
　fools laugh i' th' alehouse. What miserable praise
　hast thou for her that's foul and foolish?

Iago. There's none so foul, and foolish thereunto,
　But does foul pranks which fair and wise ones do.   *140*

Desdemona. O heavy ignorance. Thou praisest the
　worst best. But what praise couldst thou bestow on
　a deserving woman indeed—one that in the author-
　ity of her merit did justly put on the vouch of very
　malice itself?°   *145*

Iago. She that was ever fair, and never proud;
　Had tongue at will, and yet was never loud;
　Never lacked gold, and yet went never gay;
　Fled from her wish, and yet said "Now I may";
　She that being angered, her revenge being nigh,   *150*
　Bade her wrong stay, and her displeasure fly;
　She that in wisdom never was so frail
　To change the cod's head for the salmon's tail;°
　She that could think, and nev'r disclose her mind;
　See suitors following, and not look behind: *155*
　She was a wight° (if ever such wights were)—

Desdemona. To do what?

Iago. To suckle fools and chronicle small beer.°

Desdemona. O most lame and impotent conclusion.
　Do not learn of him, Emilia, though he be thy hus-   *160*
　band. How say you, Cassio? Is he not a most profane
　and liberal° counselor?

---

¹³⁶ *fond* foolish   ¹⁴³⁻⁴⁵ *one . . . itself* i.e., a woman so honest and
deserving that even malice would be forced to approve of her   ¹⁵³ *To
. . . tail* i.e., to exchange something valuable for something useless
¹⁵⁶ *wight* person   ¹⁵⁸ *chronicle small beer* i.e., keep household accounts
(the most trivial of occupations in Iago's opinion)   ¹⁶² *liberal* licentious

Cassio. He speaks home,° madam. You may relish
him more in° the soldier than in the scholar. [*Takes
Desdemona's hand.*]

165 *Iago.* [*Aside*] He takes her by the palm. Ay, well said,
whisper! With as little a web as this will I ensnare
as great a fly as Cassio. Ay, smile upon her, do! I
will gyve° thee in thine own courtship.—You say
true; 'tis so, indeed!—If such tricks as these strip
170 you out of your lieutenantry, it had been better you
had not kissed your three fingers so oft—which now
again you are most apt to play the sir° in. Very
good! Well kissed! An excellent curtsy!° 'Tis so,
indeed. Yet again your fingers to your lips? Would
175 they were clyster pipes° for your sake! [*Trumpets
within.*] The Moor! I know his trumpet.°

Cassio. 'Tis truly so.

Desdemona. Let's meet him and receive him.

Cassio. Lo, where he comes.

　　　　　　Enter Othello and Attendants.

Othello. O my fair warrior!

180 *Desdemona.*　　　　　　　My dear Othello.

Othello. It gives me wonder great as my content
To see you here before me. O my soul's joy!
If after every tempest come such calms,
May the winds blow till they have wakened death.
185 And let the laboring bark climb hills of seas
Olympus-high, and duck again as low
As hell's from heaven. If it were now to die,
'Twere now to be most happy; for I fear
My soul hath her content so absolute
190 That not another comfort like to this
Succeeds in unknown fate.

---

163 *speaks home* thrusts deeply with his speech   163-64 *relish him more
in* enjoy him more as   168 *gyve* bind   172 *the sir* the fashionable gentleman   173 *curtsy* courtesy, i.e., bow   175 *clyster pipes* enema tubes
176 *his trumpet* (great men had their own distinctive calls)

Desdemona.   The heavens forbid
   But that our loves and comforts should increase
   Even as our days do grow.

Othello.   Amen to that, sweet powers!
   I cannot speak enough of this content;
   It stops me here [*touches his heart*]; it is too much
      of joy.
   And this, and this, the greatest discords be   195

                                        [*They kiss.*]

   That e'er our hearts shall make!

Iago.   [*Aside*] O, you are well tuned now!
   But I'll set down the pegs° that make this music,
   As honest as I am.

Othello.   Come, let us to the castle.
   News, friends! Our wars are done; the Turks are
      drowned.
   How does my old acquaintance of this isle?   200
   Honey, you shall be well desired in Cyprus;
   I have found great love amongst them. O my sweet,
   I prattle out of fashion, and I dote
   In mine own comforts. I prithee, good Iago,   205
   Go to the bay and disembark my coffers.
   Bring thou the master to the citadel;
   He is a good one, and his worthiness
   Does challenge° much respect. Come, Desdemona,
   Once more well met at Cyprus.   210
   Exit Othello and Desdemona [*and all but Iago and
                                              Roderigo*].

Iago. [*To an Attendant*] Do thou meet me presently
   at the harbor. [*To Roderigo*] Come hither. If thou
   be'st valiant (as they say base men being in love
   have then a nobility in their natures more than is
   native to them), list me. The lieutenant tonight   215
   watches on the court of guard.° First, I must tell thee
   this: Desdemona is directly in love with him.

Roderigo. With him? Why, 'tis not possible.

---

¹⁹⁸ *set down the pegs* loosen the strings (to produce discord)   ²⁰⁹ *challenge* require, exact   ²¹⁶ *court of guard* guardhouse

Iago. Lay thy finger thus [*puts his finger to his lips*],
220   and let thy soul be instructed. Mark me with what
violence she first loved the Moor but for bragging
and telling her fantastical lies. To love him still for
prating? Let not thy discreet heart think it. Her
eye must be fed. And what delight shall she have to
225   look on the devil? When the blood is made dull with
the act of sport, there should be a game° to inflame
it and to give satiety a fresh appetite, loveliness in
favor,° sympathy in years,° manners, and beauties;
all which the Moor is defective in. Now for want of
230   these required conveniences,° her delicate tender-
ness will find itself abused, begin to heave the
gorge,° disrelish and abhor the Moor. Very nature
will instruct her in it and compel her to some second
choice. Now, sir, this granted—as it is a most preg-
235   nant° and unforced position—who stands so emi-
nent in the degree of this fortune as Cassio does?
A knave very voluble; no further conscionable°
than in putting on the mere form of civil and hu-
mane° seeming for the better compass of his salt°
240   and most hidden loose° affection. Why, none! Why,
none! A slipper° and subtle knave, a finder of
occasion, that has an eye can stamp and counterfeit
advantages, though true advantage never present
itself. A devilish knave. Besides, the knave is hand-
245   some, young, and hath all those requisites in him
that folly and green minds look after. A pestilent
complete knave, and the woman hath found him
already.

Roderigo. I cannot believe that in her; she's full of
250   most blessed condition.

Iago. Blessed fig's-end! The wine she drinks is made of
grapes. If she had been blessed, she would never

---

²²⁶ *game* sport (with the added sense of "gamey," "rank")   ²²⁸ *favor*
countenance, appearance   ²²⁸ *sympathy in years* sameness of age
²³⁰ *conveniences* advantages   ²³¹⁻³² *heave the gorge* vomit   ²³⁴⁻³⁵ *pregnant* likely   ²³⁷ *no further conscionable* having no more conscience
²³⁸⁻³⁹ *humane* polite   ²³⁹ *salt* lecherous   ²⁴⁰ *loose* immoral   ²⁴¹ *slip-
per* slippery

have loved the Moor. Blessed pudding! Didst thou
not see her paddle with the palm of his hand? Didst
not mark that?   255

Roderigo. Yes, that I did; but that was but courtesy.

Iago. Lechery, by this hand! [*Extends his index finger.*]
An index° and obsure prologue to the history of
lust and foul thoughts. They met so near with their
lips that their breaths embraced together. Villainous   260
thoughts, Roderigo. When these mutualities so
marshal the way, hard at hand comes the master and
main exercise, th' incorporate° conclusion: Pish!
But, sir, be you ruled by me. I have brought you
from Venice. Watch you tonight; for the command,   265
I'll lay't upon you. Cassio knows you not. I'll not be
far from you. Do you find some occasion to anger
Cassio, either by speaking too loud, or tainting°
his discipline, or from what other course you please
which the time shall more favorably minister.   270

Roderigo. Well.

Iago. Sir, he's rash and very sudden in choler,° and
haply may strike at you. Provoke him that he may;
for even out of that will I cause these of Cyprus to
mutiny, whose qualification shall come into no true   275
taste° again but by the displanting of Cassio. So
shall you have a shorter journey to your desires by
the means I shall then have to prefer them; and the
impediment most profitably removed without the
which there were no expectation of our prosperity.   280

Roderigo. I will do this if you can bring it to any
opportunity.

Iago. I warrant thee. Meet me by and by at the citadel.
I must fetch his necessaries ashore. Farewell.

Roderigo. Adieu.   *Exit.* 285

Iago. That Cassio loves her, I do well believe 't;

²⁵⁸ *index* pointer ²⁶³ *incorporate* carnal ²⁶⁸ *tainting* discrediting
²⁷² *choler* anger ²⁷⁵⁻⁷⁶ *qualification . . . taste* i.e., appeasement will not
be brought about (wine was "qualified" by adding water)

That she loves him, 'tis apt and of great credit.
The Moor, howbeit that I endure him not,
Is of a constant, loving, noble nature,
290   And I dare think he'll prove to Desdemona
A most dear° husband. Now I do love her too;
Not out of absolute° lust, though peradventure°
I stand accountant for as great a sin,
But partly led to diet° my revenge,
295   For that I do suspect the lusty Moor
Hath leaped into my seat; the thought whereof
Doth, like a poisonous mineral, gnaw my inwards;
And nothing can or shall content my soul
Till I am evened with him, wife for wife.
300   Or failing so, yet that I put the Moor
At least into a jealousy so strong
That judgment cannot cure. Which thing to do,
If this poor trash of Venice, whom I trace°
For his quick hunting, stand the putting on,
305   I'll have our Michael Cassio on the hip,
Abuse him to the Moor in the right garb°
(For I fear Cassio with my nightcap too),
Make the Moor thank me, love me, and reward me
For making him egregiously an ass
310   And practicing upon° his peace and quiet,
Even to madness. 'Tis here, but yet confused:
Knavery's plain face is never seen till used.   *Exit.*

---

²⁹¹ *dear* expensive   ²⁹² *out of absolute* absolutely out of   ²⁹² *peradventure* perchance   ²⁹⁴ *diet* feed   ³⁰³ *trace* (most editors emend to "trash," meaning to hang weights on a dog to slow his hunting; but "trace" clearly means something like "put on the trace" or "set on the track")   ³⁰⁶ *right garb* i.e., "proper fashion"   ³¹⁰ *practicing upon* scheming to destroy

Scene II. [*A street.*]

Enter Othello's Herald, with a proclamation.

Herald. It is Othello's pleasure, our noble and valiant
 general, that upon certain tidings now arrived importing the mere perdition° of the Turkish fleet,
 every man put himself into triumph. Some to dance,
 some to make bonfires, each man to what sport and   5
 revels his addition° leads him. For, besides these
 beneficial news, it is the celebration of his nuptial.
 So much was his pleasure should be proclaimed.
 All offices° are open, and there is full liberty of
 feasting from this present hour of five till the bell   10
 have told eleven. Bless the isle of Cyprus and our
 noble general Othello!   *Exit.*

Scene III. [*The citadel of Cyprus.*]

Enter Othello, Desdemona, Cassio, and Attendants.

Othello. Good Michael, look you to the guard tonight.
 Let's teach ourselves that honorable stop,
 Not to outsport discretion.

Cassio. Iago hath direction what to do;
 But notwithstanding, with my personal eye   5
 Will I look to't.

Othello.   Iago is most honest.
 Michael, good night. Tomorrow with your earliest
 Let me have speech with you. [*To Desdemona*]
   Come, my dear love,

II.ii.³ *mere perdition* absolute destruction   ⁶ *addition* rank   ⁹ *offices*
kitchens and storerooms of food

The purchase made, the fruits are to ensue,
10 That profit's yet to come 'tween me and you.
Good night.
     Exit [Othello with Desdemona and Attendants].

     Enter Iago.

Cassio. Welcome, Iago. We must to the watch.

Iago. Not this hour, lieutenant; 'tis not yet ten o' th'
clock. Our general cast° us thus early for the love
15 of his Desdemona; who let us not therefore blame.
He hath not yet made wanton the night with her, and
she is sport for Jove.

Cassio. She's a most exquisite lady.

Iago. And, I'll warrant her, full of game.

20 *Cassio.* Indeed, she's a most fresh and delicate creature.

Iago. What an eye she has! Methinks it sounds a parley
to provocation.

Cassio. An inviting eye; and yet methinks right modest.

Iago. And when she speaks, is it not an alarum° to
25 love?

Cassio. She is indeed perfection.

Iago. Well, happiness to their sheets! Come, lieutenant,
I have a stoup° of wine, and here without are a
brace of Cyprus gallants that would fain have a
30 measure to the health of black Othello.

Cassio. Not tonight, good Iago. I have very poor and
unhappy brains for drinking; I could well wish
courtesy would invent some other custom of entertainment.

35 *Iago.* O, they are our friends. But one cup! I'll drink
for you.

Cassio. I have drunk but one cup tonight, and that was
craftily qualified° too; and behold what innovation

II.iii.¹⁴ *cast* dismissed   ²⁴*alarum* the call to action, "general quarters"
²⁸*stoup* two-quart tankard   ³⁸*qualified* diluted

it makes here. I am unfortunate in the infirmity and
dare not task my weakness with any more.   40

Iago. What, man! 'Tis a night of revels, the gallants
desire it.

Cassio. Where are they?

Iago. Here, at the door. I pray you call them in.

Cassio. I'll do't, but it dislikes me.   *Exit.*   45

Iago. If I can fasten but one cup upon him
With that which he hath drunk tonight already,
He'll be as full of quarrel and offense
As my young mistress' dog. Now, my sick fool
  Roderigo,
Whom love hath turned almost the wrong side out,   50
To Desdemona hath tonight caroused
Potations pottle-deep;° and he's to watch.
Three else° of Cyprus, noble swelling spirits,
That hold their honors in a wary distance,°
The very elements of this warlike isle,   55
Have I tonight flustered with flowing cups,
And they watch too. Now, 'mongst this flock of
  drunkards
Am I to put our Cassio in some action
That may offend the isle. But here they come.

     Enter Cassio, Montano, and Gentlemen.

If consequence do but approve my dream,   60
My boat sails freely, both with wind and stream.

Cassio. 'Fore God, they have given me a rouse° already.

Montano. Good faith, a little one; not past a pint, as
I am a soldier.

Iago. Some wine, ho!   65
  [*Sings*] And let me the canakin clink, clink;
        And let me the canakin clink.

---

52 *pottle-deep* to the bottom of the cup   53 *else* others   54 *hold . . .
distance* are scrupulous in maintaining their honor   62 *rouse* drink

                    A soldier's a man;
                    O man's life's but a span,
70   Why then, let a soldier drink.
            Some wine, boys!

Cassio. 'Fore God, an excellent song!

Iago. I learned it in England, where indeed they are
      most potent in potting. Your Dane, your German,
75   and your swag-bellied° Hollander—Drink, ho!—
      are nothing to your English.

Cassio. Is your Englishman so exquisite° in his drink-
      ing?

Iago. Why, he drinks you with facility your Dane dead
80   drunk; he sweats not to overthrow your Almain; he
      gives your Hollander a vomit ere the next pottle can
      be filled.

Cassio. To the health of our general!

Montano. I am for it, lieutenant, and I'll do you justice.

85 *Iago.* O sweet England!
            [*Sings*] King Stephen was and a worthy peer;
                    His breeches cost him but a crown;
                    He held them sixpence all too dear,
                    With that he called the tailor lown.°
90   He was a wight of high renown,
                    And thou art but of low degree:
                    'Tis pride that pulls the country down;
                    And take thine auld cloak about thee.
            Some wine, ho!

95 *Cassio.* 'Fore God, this is a more exquisite song than
      the other.

Iago. Will you hear't again?

Cassio. No, for I hold him to be unworthy of his place
      that does those things. Well, God's above all; and
100   there be souls must be saved, and there be souls
      must not be saved.

---

75 *swag-bellied* hanging   77 *exquisite* superb   89 *lown* lout

Iago. It's true, good lieutenant.

Cassio. For mine own part—no offense to the general,
   nor any man of quality—I hope to be saved.

Iago. And so do I too, lieutenant.   105

Cassio. Ay, but, by your leave, not before me. The lieutenant is to be saved before the ancient. Let's have
   no more of this; let's to our affairs.—God forgive us
   our sins!—Gentlemen, let's look to our business.
   Do not think, gentlemen, I am drunk. This is my   110
   ancient; this is my right hand, and this is my left.
   I am not drunk now. I can stand well enough, and
   I speak well enough.

Gentlemen. Excellent well!

Cassio. Why, very well then. You must not think then   115
   that I am drunk.   *Exit.*

Montano. To th' platform, masters. Come, let's set
   the watch.

Iago. You see this fellow that is gone before.
   He's a soldier fit to stand by Caesar
   And give direction; and do but see his vice.   120
   'Tis to his virtue a just equinox,°
   The one as long as th' other. 'Tis pity of him.
   I fear the trust Othello puts him in,
   On some odd time of his infirmity,
   Will shake this island.

Montano.   But is he often thus?   125

Iago. 'Tis evermore his prologue to his sleep:
   He'll watch the horologe a double set°
   If drink rock not his cradle.

Montano.   It were well
   The general were put in mind of it.
   Perhaps he sees it not, or his good nature   130
   Prizes the virtue that appears in Cassio
   And looks not on his evils. Is not this true?

---

121 *just equinox* exact balance (of dark and light)   127 *watch . . . set*
stay awake twice around the clock

Enter Roderigo.

Iago. [*Aside*] How now, Roderigo?
     I pray you after the lieutenant, go! [*Exit Roderigo.*]

135 *Montano.* And 'tis great pity that the noble Moor
          Should hazard such a place as his own second
          With one of an ingraft° infirmity.
          It were an honest action to say so
          To the Moor.

Iago.   Not I, for this fair island!
140 I do love Cassio well and would do much
     To cure him of this evil.   (Help! Help! *Within.*)
                    But hark? What noise?

Enter Cassio, pursuing Roderigo.

Cassio. Zounds, you rogue! You rascal!

Montano. What's the matter, lieutenant?

Cassio. A knave teach me my duty? I'll beat the knave
145 into a twiggen° bottle.

Roderigo. Beat me?

Cassio. Dost thou prate, rogue?   [*Strikes him.*]

Montano. Nay, good lieutenant! I pray you, sir, hold
     your hand.
                                   [*Stays him.*]

150 *Cassio.* Let me go, sir, or I'll knock you o'er the
          mazzard.°

Montano. Come, come, you're drunk!

Cassio. Drunk?   [*They fight.*]

Iago. [*Aside to Roderigo*] Away, I say! Go out and
155 cry a mutiny!
                              [*Exit Roderigo.*]
     Nay, good lieutenant. God's will, gentlemen!
     Help, ho! Lieutenant. Sir. Montano.
     Help, masters! Here's a goodly watch indeed!
                              [*A bell rung.*]

───────────────────────────────

137 *ingraft* ingrained   145 *twiggen* wicker-covered   151 *mazzard* head

Who's that which rings the bell? Diablo, ho!
The town will rise. God's will, lieutenant,   *160*
You'll be ashamed forever.

    Enter Othello and Attendants.

Othello.   What is the matter here?

Montano. Zounds, I bleed still. I am hurt to the death.
 He dies.   [*He and Cassio fight again.*]

Othello. Hold for your lives!

Iago. Hold, ho! Lieutenant. Sir. Montano. Gentlemen! *165*
 Have you forgot all place of sense and duty?
 Hold! The general speaks to you. Hold, for shame!

Othello. Why, how now, ho? From whence ariseth this?
 Are we turned Turks, and to ourselves do that
 Which heaven hath forbid the Ottomites?°   *170*
 For Christian shame put by this barbarous brawl!
 He that stirs next to carve for his own rage
 Holds his soul light;° he dies upon his motion.
 Silence that dreadful bell! It frights the isle
 From her propriety.° What is the matter, masters? *175*
 Honest Iago, that looks dead with grieving,
 Speak. Who began this? On thy love, I charge thee.

Iago. I do not know. Friends all, but now, even now,
 In quarter° and in terms like bride and groom
 Devesting them for bed; and then, but now— *180*
 As if some planet had unwitted men—
 Swords out, and tilting one at other's breasts
 In opposition bloody. I cannot speak
 Any beginning to this peevish odds,°
 And would in action glorious I had lost   *185*
 Those legs that brought me to a part of it!

Othello. How comes it, Michael, you are thus forgot?

Cassio. I pray you pardon me; I cannot speak.

Othello. Worthy Montano, you were wont to be civil;
 The gravity and stillness of your youth   *190*

---

170 *heaven . . . Ottomites* i.e., by sending the storm which dispersed
the Turks 173 *Holds his soul light* values his soul lightly 175 *propriety*
proper order 179 *In quarter* on duty 184 *odds* quarrel

The world hath noted, and your name is great
In mouths of wisest censure.° What's the matter
That you unlace° your reputation thus
And spend your rich opinion° for the name
195   Of a night-brawler? Give me answer to it.

Montano. Worthy Othello, I am hurt to danger.
    Your officer, Iago, can inform you,
    While I spare speech, which something now offends°
      me,
    Of all that I do know; nor know I aught
200   By me that's said or done amiss this night,
    Unless self-charity be sometimes a vice,
    And to defend ourselves it be a sin
    When violence assails us.

Othello.   Now, by heaven,
    My blood begins my safer guides to rule,
205   And passion, having my best judgment collied,°
    Assays to lead the way. If I once stir
    Or do but lift this arm, the best of you
    Shall sink in my rebuke. Give me to know
    How this foul rout began, who set it on;
210   And he that is approved in this offense,
    Though he had twinned with me, both at a birth,
    Shall lose me. What? In a town of war
    Yet wild, the people's hearts brimful of fear,
    To manage° private and domestic quarrel?
215   In night, and on the court and guard of safety?
    'Tis monstrous. Iago, who began't?

Montano. If partially affined, or leagued in office,°
    Thou dost deliver more or less than truth,
    Thou art no soldier.

Iago.   Touch me not so near.
220   I had rather have this tongue cut from my mouth
    Than it should do offense to Michael Cassio.

---

192 *censure* judgment   193 *unlace* undo (the term refers specifically to
the dressing of a wild boar killed in the hunt)   194 *opinion* reputation
198 *offends* harms, hurts   205 *collied* darkened   214 *manage* conduct
217 *If . . . office* if you are partial because you are related ("affined")
or the brother officer (of Cassio)

Yet I persuade myself to speak the truth
Shall nothing wrong him. This it is, general.
Montano and myself being in speech,
There comes a fellow crying out for help,   225
And Cassio following him with determined sword
To execute upon him. Sir, this gentleman
Steps in to Cassio and entreats his pause.
Myself the crying fellow did pursue,
Lest by his clamor—as it so fell out—   230
The town might fall in fright. He, swift of foot,
Outran my purpose; and I returned then rather
For that I heard the clink and fall of swords,
And Cassio high in oath; which till tonight
I ne'er might say before. When I came back—   235
For this was brief—I found them close together
At blow and thrust, even as again they were
When you yourself did part them.
More of this matter cannot I report;
But men are men; the best sometimes forget.   240
Though Cassio did some little wrong to him,
As men in rage strike those that wish them best,
Yet surely Cassio I believe received
From him that fled some strange indignity,
Which patience could not pass.°

Othello.   I know, Iago,   245
Thy honesty and love doth mince° this matter,
Making it light to Cassio. Cassio, I love thee;
But never more be officer of mine.

                Enter Desdemona, attended.

Look if my gentle love be not raised up.
I'll make thee an example.

Desdemona.   What is the matter, dear.   250

Othello. All's well, sweeting; come away to bed.
  [*To Montano*] Sir, for your hurts, myself will be
    your surgeon.
  Lead him off.   [*Montano led off.*]

───

245 *pass* allow to pass 246 *mince* cut up (i.e., tell only part of)

     Iago, look with care about the town
253 And silence those whom this vile brawl distracted.
     Come, Desdemona: 'tis the soldiers' life
     To have their balmy slumbers waked with strife.
                         Exit [with all but Iago and Cassio].

Iago. What, are you hurt, lieutenant?

Cassio. Ay, past all surgery.

260 *Iago.* Marry, God forbid!

Cassio. Reputation, reputation, reputation! O, I have
     lost my reputation! I have lost the immortal part of
     myself, and what remains is bestial. My reputation,
     Iago, my reputation.

265 *Iago.* As I am an honest man, I had thought you had
     received some bodily wound. There is more sense°
     in that than in reputation. Reputation is an idle and
     most false imposition,° oft got without merit and
     lost without deserving. You have lost no reputation
270 at all unless you repute yourself such a loser. What,
     man, there are more ways to recover the general
     again. You are but now cast in his mood°—a
     punishment more in policy° than in malice—even
     so as one would beat his offenseless dog to affright
275 an imperious lion. Sue to him again, and he's yours.

Cassio. I will rather sue to be despised than to deceive
     so good a commander with so slight, so drunken,
     and so indiscreet an officer. Drunk! And speak
     parrot!° And squabble! Swagger! Swear! and dis-
280 course fustian° with one's own shadow! O thou
     invisible spirit of wine, if thou hast no name to be
     known by, let us call thee devil!

Iago. What was he that you followed with your sword?
     What had he done to you?

285 *Cassio.* I know not.

Iago. Is't possible?

---

²⁶⁶ *sense* physical feeling ²⁶⁸ *imposition* external thing ²⁷² *cast in his
mood* dismissed because of his anger ²⁷³ *in policy* politically necessary
²⁷⁸⁻⁷⁹ *speak parrot* gabble without sense ²⁷⁹⁻⁸⁰ *discourse fustian* speak
nonsense ("fustian" was a coarse cotton cloth used for stuffing)

Cassio. I remember a mass of things, but nothing distinctly: a quarrel, but nothing wherefore. O God,
that men should put an enemy in their mouths to
steal away their brains! that we should with joy, 290
pleasance, revel, and applause transform ourselves
into beasts!

Iago. Why, but you are now well enough. How came
you thus recovered?

Cassio. It hath pleased the devil drunkenness to give 295
place to the devil wrath. One unperfectness shows
me another, to make me frankly despise myself.

Iago. Come, you are too severe a moraler. As the time,
the place, and the condition of this country stands,
I could heartily wish this had not befall'n; but since 300
it is as it is, mend it for your own good.

Cassio. I will ask him for my place again: he shall tell
me I am a drunkard. Had I as many mouths as
Hydra, such an answer would stop them all. To be
now a sensible man, by and by a fool, and presently 305
a beast! O strange! Every inordinate cup is unblest,
and the ingredient is a devil.

Iago. Come, come, good wine is a good familiar
creature if it be well used. Exclaim no more against
it. And, good lieutenant, I think you think I love 310
you.

Cassio. I have well approved it, sir. I drunk?

Iago. You or any man living may be drunk at a time,
man. I tell you what you shall do. Our general's
wife is now the general. I may say so in this respect, 315
for that he hath devoted and given up himself to the
contemplation, mark, and devotement of her parts°
and graces. Confess yourself freely to her; importune
her help to put you in your place again. She is of
so free, so kind, so apt, so blessed a disposition she 320
holds it a vice in her goodness not to do more than

³¹⁷ *devotement of her parts* devotion to her qualities

she is requested. This broken joint between you
and her husband entreat her to splinter;° and my
fortunes against any lay° worth naming, this crack
825   of your love shall grow stronger than it was before.

Cassio. You advise me well.

Iago. I protest, in the sincerity of love and honest
kindness.

Cassio. I think it freely; and betimes in the morning I
830   will beseech the virtuous Desdemona to undertake
for me. I am desperate of my fortunes if they check°
me.

Iago. You are in the right. Good night, lieutenant; I
must to the watch.

833   *Cassio.* Good night, honest Iago.   *Exit Cassio.*

Iago. And what's he then that says I play the villain,
When this advice is free° I give, and honest,
Probal to° thinking, and indeed the course
To win the Moor again? For 'tis most easy
840   Th' inclining° Desdemona to subdue
In any honest suit; she's framed as fruitful°
As the free elements.° And then for her
To win the Moor—were't to renounce his baptism,
All seals and symbols of redeemèd sin—
845   His soul is so enfettered to her love
That she may make, unmake, do what she list,
Even as her appetite° shall play the god
With his weak function.° How am I then a villain
To counsel Cassio to this parallel course,
850   Directly to his good? Divinity of hell!
When devils will the blackest sins put on,°
They do suggest at first with heavenly shows,°
As I do now. For whiles this honest fool
Plies Desdemona to repair his fortune,
855   And she for him pleads strongly to the Moor,

323 *splinter* splint   324 *lay* wager   331 *check* repulse   337 *free* generous
and open   338 *Probal to* provable by   340 *inclining* inclined (to be helpful)   341 *framed as fruitful* made as generous   342 *elements* i.e., basic
nature   347 *appetite* liking   348 *function* thought   351 *put on* advance,
further   352 *shows* appearances

I'll pour this pestilence into his ear:
That she repeals him° for her body's lust;
And by how much she strives to do him good,
She shall undo her credit with the Moor.
So will I turn her virtue into pitch, 360
And out of her own goodness make the net
That shall enmesh them all. How now, Roderigo?

Enter Roderigo.

Roderigo. I do follow here in the chase, not like a
hound that hunts, but one that fills up the cry.° My
money is almost spent; I have been tonight exceed- 365
ingly well cudgeled; and I think the issue will be,
I shall have so much experience for my pains; and
so, with no money at all, and a little more wit,
return again to Venice.

Iago. How poor are they that have not patience! 370
What wound did ever heal but by degrees?
Thou know'st we work by wit, and not by witch-
craft;
And wit depends on dilatory time.
Does't not go well? Cassio hath beaten thee,
And thou by that small hurt hath cashiered Cassio. 375
Though other things grow fair against the sun,
Yet fruits that blossom first will first be ripe.
Content thyself awhile. By the mass, 'tis morning!
Pleasure and action make the hours seem short.
Retire thee; go where thou art billeted. 380
Away, I say! Thou shalt know more hereafter.
Nay, get thee gone! *Exit Roderigo.*
           Two things are to be done:
My wife must move° for Cassio to her mistress;
I'll set her on;
Myself awhile° to draw the Moor apart 385
And bring him jump° when he may Cassio find
Soliciting his wife. Ay, that's the way!
Dull not device by coldness and delay. *Exit.*

---

357 *repeals him* asks for (Cassio's reinstatement)   364 *fills up the cry*
makes up one of the hunting pack, adding to the noise but not actually tracking   383 *move* petition   385 *awhile* at the same time
386 *jump* at the precise moment and place

ACT III

Scene I. [*A street.*]

Enter Cassio [and] Musicians.

Cassio. Masters, play here. I will content your pains.°
Something that's brief; and bid "Good morrow,
general." [*They play.*]

[*Enter Clown.*°]

Clown. Why, masters, have your instruments been in
Naples° that they speak i' th' nose thus?

5 *Musician.* How, sir, how?

Clown. Are these, I pray you, wind instruments?

Musician. Ay, marry, are they, sir.

Clown. O, thereby hangs a tale.

Musician. Whereby hangs a tale, sir?

10 *Clown.* Marry, sir, by many a wind instrument that I
know. But, masters, here's money for you; and the
general so likes your music that he desires you,
for love's sake, to make no more noise with it.

Musician. Well, sir, we will not.

15 *Clown.* If you have any music that may not be heard,
to't again. But, as they say, to hear music the
general does not greatly care.

III.i.¹ *content your pains* reward your efforts   ² s.d. *Clown* fool
⁴ *Naples* (this may refer either to the Neapolitan nasal tone, or to syphilis—rife in Naples—which breaks down the nose)

Musician. We have none such, sir.

Clown. Then put up your pipes in your bag, for I'll
    away. Go, vanish into air, away!   20

                       Exit Musicians.

Cassio. Dost thou hear me, mine honest friend?

Clown. No. I hear not your honest friend. I hear you.

Cassio. Prithee keep up thy quillets.° There's a poor
    piece of gold for thee. If the gentlewoman that
    attends the general's wife be stirring, tell her there's 25
    one Cassio entreats her a little favor of speech.
    Wilt thou do this?

Clown. She is stirring, sir. If she will stir hither, I shall
    seem to notify unto her.°   *Exit Clown.*

              Enter Iago.

Cassio. In happy time, Iago.

Iago.   You have not been abed then?   30

Cassio. Why no, the day had broke before we parted.
    I have made bold, Iago, to send in to your wife;
    My suit to her is that she will to virtuous Desdemona
    Procure me some access.

Iago.   I'll send her to you presently,
    And I'll devise a mean to draw the Moor   35
    Out of the way, that your converse and business
    May be more free.

Cassio. I humbly thank you for 't.   *Exit [Iago].*
                 I never knew
    A Florentine° more kind and honest.

            Enter Emilia.

Emilia. Good morrow, good lieutenant. I am sorry   40
    For your displeasure;° but all will sure be well.
    The general and his wife are talking of it,

---

23 *quillets* puns 29 *seem . . . her* (the Clown is mocking Cassio's
overly elegant manner of speaking) 39 *Florentine* i.e., Iago is as kind
as if he were from Cassio's home town, Florence 41 *displeasure* dis-
comforting

And she speaks for you stoutly. The Moor replies
That he you hurt is of great fame in Cyprus
43 And great affinity,° and that in wholesome wisdom
He might not but refuse you. But he protests he loves
    you,
And needs no other suitor but his likings
To bring you in again.

Cassio.   Yet I beseech you,
If you think fit, or that it may be done,
50 Give me advantage of some brief discourse
With Desdemona alone.

Emilia.   Pray you come in.
I will bestow you where you shall have time
To speak your bosom° freely.

Cassio.   I am much bound to you.
                              [*Exeunt.*]

Scene II. [*The citadel.*]

Enter Othello, Iago, and Gentlemen.

Othello. These letters give, Iago, to the pilot
 And by him do my duties to the Senate.
 That done, I will be walking on the works;
 Repair° there to me.

Iago.   Well, my good lord, I'll do't.

5 *Othello.* This fortification, gentlemen, shall we see't?

Gentlemen. We'll wait upon your lordship.   *Exeunt.*

---

⁴⁵ *affinity* family   ⁵³ *bosom* inmost thoughts   III.ii.⁴ *Repair* go

Scene III. [*The citadel.*]

Enter Desdemona, Cassio, and Emilia.

Desdemona. Be thou assured, good Cassio, I will do
   All my abilities in thy behalf.

Emilia. Good madam, do. I warrant it grieves my hus-
     band
   As if the cause were his.

Desdemona. O, that's an honest fellow. Do not doubt,
    Cassio,   5
   But I will have my lord and you again
   As friendly as you were.

Cassio.   Bounteous madam,
   Whatever shall become of Michael Cassio,
   He's never anything but your true servant.

Desdemona. I know't; I thank you. You do love my   10
    lord.
   You have known him long, and be you well assured
   He shall in strangeness stand no farther off
   Than in a politic distance.°

Cassio.   Ay, but, lady,
   That policy may either last so long,
   Or feed upon such nice° and waterish diet,   15
   Or breed itself so out of circumstances,°
   That, I being absent, and my place supplied,°
   My general will forget my love and service.

Desdemona. Do not doubt° that; before Emilia here
   I give thee warrant of thy place. Assure thee,   20
   If I do vow a friendship, I'll perform it

III.iii.[12-13] *He . . . distance* i.e., he shall act no more distant to you
than is necessary for political reasons   [15] *nice* trivial   [16] *Or . . . circumstances* i.e., or grow so on the basis of accidental happenings and
political needs   [17] *supplied* filled   [19] *doubt* imagine

To the last article. My lord shall never rest;
I'll watch him tame° and talk him out of patience;
His bed shall seem a school, his board a shrift;°
25   I'll intermingle everything he does
With Cassio's suit. Therefore be merry, Cassio,
For thy solicitor shall rather die
Than give thy cause away.

                Enter Othello and Iago [*at a distance*].

Emilia. Madam, here comes my lord.

30   *Cassio.* Madam, I'll take my leave.

Desdemona. Why, stay, and hear me speak.

Cassio. Madam, not now. I am very ill at ease,
   Unfit for mine own purposes.

Desdemona. Well, do your discretion.   *Exit Cassio.*

Iago. Ha! I like not that.

35   *Othello.*   What dost thou say?

Iago. Nothing, my lord; or if—I know not what.

Othello. Was not that Cassio parted from my wife?

Iago. Cassio, my lord? No, sure, I cannot think it
   That he would steal away so guilty-like,
   Seeing your coming.

40   *Othello.*   I do believe 'twas he.

Desdemona. [*Coming to them*] How now, my lord?
   I have been talking with a suitor here,
   A man that languishes in your displeasure.

Othello. Who is't you mean?

Desdemona. Why, your lieutenant, Cassio. Good my
45   lord,
   If I have any grace or power to move you,
   His present° reconciliation take.
   For if he be not one that truly loves you,

---

²³ *watch him tame* (animals were tamed by being kept awake)
²⁴ *board a shrift* table (seem) a confessional   ⁴⁷ *present* immediate

That errs in ignorance, and not in cunning,
I have no judgment in an honest face.   30
I prithee call him back.

Othello.   Went he hence now?

Desdemona. I' sooth so humbled
That he hath left part of his grief with me
To suffer with him. Good love, call him back.

Othello. Not now, sweet Desdemon; some other time.   55

Desdemona. But shall't be shortly?

Othello.   The sooner, sweet, for you.

Desdemona. Shall't be tonight at supper?

Othello.   No, not tonight.

Desdemona. Tomorrow dinner then?

Othello.   I shall not dine at home;
I meet the captains at the citadel.

Desdemona. Why then, tomorrow night, on Tuesday
    morn,   60
On Tuesday noon, or night, on Wednesday morn.
I prithee name the time, but let it not
Exceed three days. In faith, he's penitent;
And yet his trespass, in our common reason
(Save that, they say, the wars must make example   65
Out of her best), is not almost a fault
T' incur a private check.° When shall he come?
Tell me, Othello. I wonder in my soul
What you would ask me that I should deny
Or stand so mamm'ring° on. What? Michael Cassio,   70
That came awooing with you, and so many a time,
When I have spoke of you dispraisingly,
Hath ta'en your part—to have so much to do
To bring him in? By'r Lady, I could do much—

Othello. Prithee no more. Let him come when he will!   75
I will deny thee nothing.

---

⁶⁶⁻⁶⁷ *is . . . check* is almost not serious enough for a private rebuke
(let alone a public disgrace)   ⁷⁰ *mamm'ring* hesitating

Desdemona.   Why, this is not a boon;
'Tis as I should entreat you wear your gloves,
Or feed on nourishing dishes, or keep you warm,
Or sue to you to do a peculiar profit°
80   To your own person. Nay, when I have a suit
Wherein I mean to touch your love indeed,
It shall be full of poise° and difficult weight,
And fearful to be granted.

Othello.   I will deny thee nothing!
Whereon I do beseech thee grant me this,
85   To leave me but a little to myself.

Desdemona. Shall I deny you? No. Farewell, my lord.

Othello. Farewell, my Desdemona: I'll come to thee
straight.°

Desdemona. Emilia, come. Be as your fancies teach
you;
Whate'er you be, I am obedient. *Exit* [*with Emilia*].

90   *Othello.* Excellent wretch! Perdition catch my soul
But I do love thee! And when I love thee not,
Chaos is come again.

Iago. My noble lord——

Othello.   What dost thou say, Iago?

Iago. Did Michael Cassio, when you wooed my lady,
95   Know of your love?

Othello. He did, from first to last. Why dost thou ask?

Iago. But for a satisfaction of my thought,
No further harm.

Othello.   Why of thy thought, Iago?

Iago. I did not think he had been acquainted with her.

100   *Othello.* O, yes, and went between us° very oft.

Iago. Indeed?

Othello. Indeed? Ay, indeed! Discern'st thou aught in
that?

---

79 *peculiar profit*   particularly personal good   82 *poise*   weight
87 *straight* at once   100 *between us* i.e., as messenger

Is he not honest?

Iago.   Honest, my lord?

Othello.   Honest? Ay, honest.

Iago. My lord, for aught I know.

Othello. What dost thou think?

Iago.   Think, my lord?

Othello.   Think, my lord? *105*
By heaven, thou echoest me,
As if there were some monster in thy thought
Too hideous to be shown. Thou dost mean some-
    thing.
I heard thee say even now, thou lik'st not that,
When Cassio left my wife. What didst not like? *110*
And when I told thee he was of my counsel°
Of my whole course of wooing, thou cried'st "In-
    deed?"
And didst contract and purse thy brow together,
As if thou then hadst shut up in thy brain
Some horrible conceit.° If thou dost love me, *115*
Show me thy thought.

Iago. My lord, you know I love you.

Othello.   I think thou dost;
And, for I know thou'rt full of love and honesty
And weigh'st thy words before thou giv'st them
    breath,
Therefore these stops° of thine fright me the more; *120*
For such things in a false disloyal knave
Are tricks of custom;° but in a man that's just
They're close dilations,° working from the heart
That passion cannot rule.

Iago.   For Michael Cassio,
I dare be sworn, I think that he is honest. *125*

Othello. I think so too.

---

¹¹¹ *of my counsel* in my confidence   ¹¹⁵ *conceit* thought   ¹²⁰ *stops*
interruptions   ¹²² *of custom* customary   ¹²³ *close dilations* expressions
of hidden thoughts

Iago.   Men should be what they seem;
 Or those that be not, would they might seem none!

Othello. Certain, men should be what they seem.

Iago. Why then, I think Cassio's an honest man.

130 *Othello.* Nay, yet there's more in this?
 I prithee speak to me as to thy thinkings,
 As thou dost ruminate, and give thy worst of
    thoughts
 The worst of words.

Iago.   Good my lord, pardon me:
 Though I am bound to every act of duty,
135 I am not bound to that all slaves are free to.
 Utter my thoughts? Why, say they are vile and false,
 As where's that palace whereinto foul things
 Sometimes intrude not? Who has that breast so pure
 But some uncleanly apprehensions
140 Keep leets and law days,° and in sessions sit
 With meditations lawful?

Othello. Thou dost conspire against thy friend, Iago,
 If thou but think'st him wronged, and mak'st his ear
 A stranger to thy thoughts.

Iago.   I do beseech you—
145 Though I perchance am vicious in my guess
 (As I confess it is my nature's plague
 To spy into abuses, and of my jealousy
 Shape faults that are not), that your wisdom
 From one that so imperfectly conceits
150 Would take no notice, nor build yourself a trouble
 Out of his scattering and unsure observance.
 It were not for your quiet nor your good,
 Nor for my manhood, honesty, and wisdom,
 To let you know my thoughts.

Othello.   What dost thou mean?

155 *Iago.* Good name in man and woman, dear my lord,
 Is the immediate jewel of their souls.

---

140 *leets and law days* meetings of local courts

Who steals my purse steals trash; 'tis something,
   nothing;
'Twas mine, 'tis his, and has been slave to thousands;
But he that filches from me my good name
Robs me of that which not enriches him   160
And makes me poor indeed.

Othello. By heaven, I'll know thy thoughts!

Iago. You cannot, if my heart were in your hand;
   Nor shall not whilst 'tis in my custody.

Othello. Ha!

Iago.   O, beware, my lord, of jealousy!   165
It is the green-eyed monster, which doth mock
The meat it feeds on. That cuckold lives in bliss
Who, certain of his fate, loves not his wronger;
But O, what damnèd minutes tells° he o'er
Who dotes, yet doubts—suspects, yet fondly° loves!   170

Othello. O misery.

Iago. Poor and content is rich, and rich enough;
But riches fineless° is as poor as winter
To him that ever fears he shall be poor.
Good God the souls of all my tribe defend   175
From jealousy!

Othello.   Why? Why is this?
Think'st thou I'd make a life of jealousy,
To follow still° the changes of the moon
With fresh suspicions? No! To be once in doubt
Is to be resolved. Exchange me for a goat   180
When I shall turn the business of my soul
To such exsufflicate and blown° surmises,
Matching thy inference. 'Tis not to make me jealous
To say my wife is fair, feeds well, loves company,
Is free of speech, sings, plays, and dances;   185
Where virtue is, these are more virtuous.
Nor from mine own weak merits will I draw
The smallest fear or doubt of her revolt,

169 *tells* counts   170 *fondly* foolishly   173 *fineless* infinite   178 *To follow still* to change always (as the phases of the moon)   182 *exsufflicate and blown* inflated and flyblown

For she had eyes, and chose me. No, Iago;
190   I'll see before I doubt; when I doubt, prove;
And on the proof there is no more but this:
Away at once with love or jealousy!

Iago. I am glad of this; for now I shall have reason
To show the love and duty that I bear you
195   With franker spirit. Therefore, as I am bound,
Receive it from me. I speak not yet of proof.
Look to your wife; observe her well with Cassio;
Wear your eyes thus: not jealous nor secure.
I would not have your free and noble nature
200   Out of self-bounty° be abused. Look to't.
I know our country disposition well:
In Venice they do let heaven see the pranks
They dare not show their husbands; their best con-
       science
Is not to leave't undone, but kept unknown.°

205 *Othello.* Dost thou say so?

Iago. She did deceive her father, marrying you;
And when she seemed to shake and fear your looks,
She loved them most.

Othello.   And so she did.

Iago.   Why, go to then!
She that so young could give out such a seeming
210   To seel° her father's eyes up close as oak°—
He thought 'twas witchcraft. But I am much to
       blame.
I humbly do beseech you of your pardon
For too much loving you.

Othello.   I am bound to thee forever.

Iago. I see this hath a little dashed your spirits.

Othello. Not a jot, not a jot.

215 *Iago.*   Trust me, I fear it has.

---

²⁰⁰ *self-bounty* innate kindness (which attributes his own motives to others)   ²⁰³⁻⁴ *their . . . unknown* i.e., their morality does not forbid adultery, but it does forbid being found out   ²¹⁰ *seel* hoodwink   ²¹⁰ *oak* (a close-grained wood)

I hope you will consider what is spoke
Comes from my love. But I do see y' are moved.
I am to pray you not to strain° my speech
To grosser issues, nor to larger reach°
Than to suspicion.   *220*

Othello. I will not.

Iago.   Should you do so, my lord,
My speech should fall into such vile success
Which my thoughts aimed not. Cassio's my worthy
     friend—
My lord, I see y' are moved.

Othello.   No, not much moved.
I do not think but Desdemona's honest.   *225*

Iago. Long live she so. And long live you to think so.

Othello. And yet, how nature erring from itself——

Iago. Ay, there's the point, as (to be bold with you)
Not to affect many proposèd matches
Of her own clime, complexion, and degree,°   *230*
Whereto we see in all things nature tends° —
Foh! one may smell in such a will most rank,
Foul disproportions, thoughts unnatural.
But, pardon me, I do not in position°
Distinctly° speak of her; though I may fear   *235*
Her will, recoiling to her better judgment,
May fall to match° you with her country forms,°
And happily° repent.

Othello.   Farewell, farewell!
If more thou dost perceive, let me know more.
Set on thy wife to observe. Leave me, Iago.   *240*

Iago. My lord, I take my leave.   [*Going.*]

---

[218] *strain* enlarge the meaning of   [219] *reach* meaning   [230] *degree* social station   [231] *in . . . tends* i.e., all things in nature seek out their own kind   [234] *position* general argument   [235] *Distinctly* specifically   [237] *fall to match* happen to compare   [237] *country forms* i.e., the familiar appearances of her countrymen   [238] *happily* by chance

Othello. Why did I marry? This honest creature doubtless
 Sees and knows more, much more, than he unfolds.

Iago. [*Returns*.] My lord, I would I might entreat your
  honor
245 To scan this thing no farther. Leave it to time.
 Although 'tis fit that Cassio have his place,
 For sure he fills it up with great ability,
 Yet, if you please to hold him off awhile,
 You shall by that perceive him and his means.
250 Note if your lady strain his entertainment°
 With any strong or vehement importunity;
 Much will be seen in that. In the meantime
 Let me be thought too busy in my fears
 (As worthy cause I have to fear I am)
255 And hold her free, I do beseech your honor.

Othello. Fear not my government.°

Iago.   I once more take my leave.
             Exit.

Othello. This fellow's of exceeding honesty,
 And knows all qualities,° with a learnèd spirit
 Of human dealings. If I do prove her haggard,°
260 Though that her jesses° were my dear heartstrings,
 I'd whistle her off and let her down the wind°
 To prey at fortune. Haply for° I am black
 And have not those soft parts° of conversation
 That chamberers° have, or for I am declined
265 Into the vale of years—yet that's not much—
 She's gone. I am abused, and my relief
 Must be to loathe her. O curse of marriage,
 That we can call these delicate creatures ours,
 And not their appetites! I had rather be a toad

---

250 *strain his entertainment* urge strongly that he be reinstated
256 *government* self-control 258 *qualities* natures, types of people
259 *haggard* a partly trained hawk which has gone wild again 260 *jesses*
straps which held the hawk's legs to the trainer's wrist 261 *I'd . . .
wind* I would release her (like an untamable hawk) and let her fly free
262 *Haply for* it may be because 263 *soft parts* gentle qualities and
manners 264 *chamberers* courtiers—or perhaps, accomplished seducers

And live upon the vapor of a dungeon   270
Than keep a corner in the thing I love
For others' uses. Yet 'tis the plague to great ones;
Prerogatived are they less than the base.
'Tis destiny unshunnable, like death.
Even then this forkèd° plague is fated to us   275
When we do quicken.° Look where she comes.

      Enter Desdemona and Emilia.

If she be false, heaven mocked itself!
I'll not believe't.

Desdemona.   How now, my dear Othello?
Your dinner, and the generous islanders
By you invited, do attend° your presence.   280

Othello. I am to blame.

Desdemona.   Why do you speak so faintly?
Are you not well?

Othello. I have a pain upon my forehead, here.°

Desdemona. Why, that's with watching; 'twill away
    again.
Let me but bind it hard, within this hour   285
It will be well.

Othello.   Your napkin° is too little;
    [*He pushes the handkerchief away, and it falls.*]
Let it° alone. Come, I'll go in with you.

Desdemona. I am very sorry that you are not well.
                    Exit [*with Othello*].

Emilia. I am glad I have found this napkin;
This was her first remembrance from the Moor.
My wayward husband hath a hundred times   290
Wooed me to steal it; but she so loves the token

---

275 *forkèd* horned (the sign of the cuckold was horns)   276 *do quicken*
are born   280 *attend* wait   283 *here* (he points to his imaginary horns)
286 *napkin* elaborately worked handkerchief   287 *it* (it makes a considerable difference in the interpretation of later events whether this
"it" refers to Othello's forehead or to the handkerchief; nothing in the
text makes the reference clear)

(For he conjured her she should ever keep it)
That she reserves it evermore about her
295 To kiss and talk to. I'll have the work ta'en out°
And give't Iago. What he will do with it,
Heaven knows, not I; I nothing° but to please his
  fantasy.°

Enter Iago.

Iago. How now? What do you here alone?

Emilia. Do not you chide; I have a thing for you.

Iago. You have a thing for me? It is a common
300   thing——

Emilia. Ha?

Iago. To have a foolish wife.

Emilia. O, is that all? What will you give me now
For that same handkerchief?

Iago.   What handkerchief?

305 *Emilia.* What handkerchief!
Why, that the Moor first gave to Desdemona,
That which so often you did bid me steal.

Iago. Hast stol'n it from her?

Emilia. No, but she let it drop by negligence,
310   And to th' advantage,° I, being here, took't up.
Look, here 't is.

Iago.   A good wench. Give it me.

Emilia. What will you do with't, that you have been
  so earnest
To have me filch it?

Iago.   Why, what is that to you?
                                    [*Takes it.*]

Emilia. If it be not for some purpose of import,°
313   Give't me again. Poor lady, she'll run mad
When she shall lack° it.

---

295 *work ta'en out* needlework copied 297 *I nothing* I wish nothing
297 *fantasy* fancy, whim 310 *to th' advantage* being lucky 314 *import*
importance 316 *lack* miss

Iago.   Be not acknown on't.°
I have use for it. Go, leave me.   *Exit Emilia.*
I will in Cassio's lodging lose this napkin
And let him find it. Trifles light as air
Are to the jealous confirmations strong   320
As proofs of Holy Writ. This may do something.
The Moor already changes with my poison:
Dangerous conceits are in their natures poisons,
Which at the first are scarce found to distaste,°
But, with a little,° act upon the blood,   325
Burn like the mines of sulfur. I did say so.

Enter Othello.

Look where he comes! Not poppy nor mandragora,°
Nor all the drowsy syrups of the world,
Shall ever medicine thee to that sweet sleep
Which thou owedst° yesterday.

Othello.   Ha! ha! False to me?   330

Iago. Why, how now, general? No more of that.

Othello. Avaunt! be gone! Thou hast set me on the
    rack.
I swear 'tis better to be much abused
Than but to know't a little.

Iago.   How now, my lord?

Othello. What sense had I of her stol'n hours of lust? 335
I saw't not, thought it not, it harmed not me;
I slept the next night well, fed well, was free and
    merry;
I found not Cassio's kisses on her lips.
He that is robbed, not wanting° what is stol'n,
Let him not know't, and he's not robbed at all.   340

Iago. I am sorry to hear this.

---

³¹⁶ *Be not acknown on't* forget you ever saw it   ³²⁴ *are scarce found
to distaste* scarcely can be tasted   ³²⁵ *with a little* in a short time
³²⁷ *poppy nor mandragora* (soporifics)   ³³⁰ *owedst* possessed   ³³⁹ *want-ing* missing

    Othello. I had been happy if the general camp,
        Pioners° and all, had tasted her sweet body,
        So I had nothing known. O now, forever
345   Farewell the tranquil mind! Farewell content!
        Farewell the plumèd troops, and the big wars
        That makes ambition virtue! O, farewell!
        Farewell the neighing steed and the shrill trump,
        The spirit-stirring drum, th' ear-piercing fife,
350   The royal banner, and all quality,
        Pride, pomp, and circumstance° of glorious war!
        And O you mortal engines° whose rude throats
        Th' immortal Jove's dread clamors° counterfeit,
        Farewell! Othello's occupation's gone!

355 *Iago.* Is't possible, my lord?

    Othello. Villain, be sure thou prove my love a whore!
        Be sure of it; give me the ocular proof;
        Or, by the worth of mine eternal soul,
        Thou hadst been better have been born a dog
        Than answer my waked wrath!

360 *Iago.*   Is't come to this?

    Othello. Make me to see't; or at the least so prove it
        That the probation° bear no hinge nor loop
        To hang a doubt on—or woe upon thy life!

    Iago. My noble lord——

365 *Othello.* If thou dost slander her and torture me,
        Never pray more; abandon all remorse;
        On horror's head horrors accumulate;
        Do deeds to make heaven weep, all earth amazed;
        For nothing canst thou to damnation add
        Greater than that.

370 *Iago.*   O grace! O heaven forgive me!
        Are you a man? Have you a soul or sense?
        God b' wi' you! Take mine office. O wretched fool,
        That lov'st to make thine honesty a vice!
        O monstrous world! Take note, take note, O world,

---

343 *Pioners* (the basest manual laborers in the army, who dug trenches and mines) ³⁵¹ *circumstance* pageantry ³⁵² *mortal engines* lethal weapons, i.e., cannon ³⁵³ *clamors* i.e., thunder ³⁶² *probation* proof

To be direct and honest is not safe.   875
I thank you for this profit, and from hence
I'll love no friend, sith° love breeds such offense.

Othello. Nay, stay. Thou shouldst be honest.

Iago. I should be wise; for honesty's a fool
And loses that it works for.

Othello.   By the world,   880
I think my wife be honest, and think she is not;
I think that thou art just, and think thou art not.
I'll have some proof. My name, that was as fresh
As Dian's° visage, is now begrimed and black
As mine own face. If there be cords, or knives,   885
Poison, or fire, or suffocating streams,
I'll not endure it. Would I were satisfied!

Iago. I see you are eaten up with passion.
I do repent me that I put it to you.
You would be satisfied?

Othello.   Would? Nay, and I will.   890

Iago. And may; but how? How satisfied, my lord?
Would you, the supervisor,° grossly gape on?
Behold her topped?

Othello.   Death and damnation! O!

Iago. It were a tedious° difficulty, I think,
To bring them to that prospect.° Damn them then,   895
If ever mortal eyes do see them bolster°
More than their own! What then? How then?
What shall I say? Where's satisfaction?
It is impossible you should see this,
Were they as prime° as goats, as hot as monkeys,   400
As salt° as wolves in pride,° and fools as gross
As ignorance made drunk. But yet, I say,

---

³⁷⁷ *sith* since ³⁸⁴ *Dian's* Diana's (goddess of the moon and of chastity) ³⁹² *supervisor* onlooker ³⁹⁴ *tedious* hard to arrange ³⁹⁵ *prospect* sight (where they can be seen) ³⁹⁶ *bolster* go to bed ⁴⁰⁰⁻⁰¹ *prime, salt* lustful ⁴⁰¹ *pride* heat

If imputation and strong circumstances
Which lead directly to the door of truth
405 Will give you satisfaction, you might have't.

Othello. Give me a living reason she's disloyal.

Iago. I do not like the office.°
But sith I am entered in this cause so far,
Pricked° to't by foolish honesty and love,
410 I will go on. I lay with Cassio lately,
And being troubled with a raging tooth,
I could not sleep.
There are a kind of men so loose of soul
That in their sleeps will mutter their affairs.
415 One of this kind is Cassio.
In sleep I heard him say, "Sweet Desdemona,
Let us be wary, let us hide our loves!"
And then, sir, would he gripe° and wring my hand,
Cry "O sweet creature!" Then kiss me hard,
420 As if he plucked up kisses by the roots
That grew upon my lips; laid his leg o'er my thigh,
And sigh, and kiss, and then cry, "Cursèd fate
That gave thee to the Moor!"

Othello. O monstrous! monstrous!

Iago.   Nay, this was but his dream.

425 *Othello.* But this denoted a foregone conclusion,°
'Tis a shrewd doubt,° though it be but a dream.

Iago. And this may help to thicken other proofs
That do demonstrate° thinly.

Othello.   I'll tear her all to pieces!

Iago. Nay, yet be wise. Yet we see nothing done;
430 She may be honest yet. Tell me but this:
Have you not sometimes seen a handkerchief
Spotted with strawberries in your wife's hand?

Othello. I gave her such a one; 'twas my first gift.

---

407 *office* duty 409 *Pricked* spurred 418 *gripe* seize 425 *foregone con-*
clusion consummated fact 426 *shrewd doubt* penetrating guess
428 *demonstrate* show, appear

Iago. I know not that; but such a handkerchief—
   I am sure it was your wife's—did I today   435
   See Cassio wipe his beard with.

Othello.   If it be that——

Iago. If it be that, or any that was hers,
   It speaks against her with the other proofs.

Othello. O, that the slave had forty thousand lives!
   One is too poor, too weak for my revenge.   440
   Now do I see 'tis true. Look here, Iago:
   All my fond love thus do I blow to heaven.
   'Tis gone.
   Arise, black vengeance, from the hollow hell!
   Yield up, O Love, thy crown and hearted° throne   445
   To tyrannous hate! Swell, bosom, with thy fraught,°
   For 'tis of aspics'° tongues.

Iago.   Yet be content.°

Othello. O, blood, blood, blood!

Iago. Patience, I say. Your mind may change.

Othello. Never, Iago. Like to the Pontic Sea,°   450
   Whose icy current and compulsive course
   Nev'r keeps retiring ebb, but keeps due on
   To the Propontic and the Hellespont,
   Even so my bloody thoughts, with violent pace,
   Shall nev'r look back, nev'r ebb to humble love,   455
   Till that a capable and wide° revenge
   Swallow them up. [*He kneels.*] Now, by yond mar-
     ble heaven,
   In the due reverence of a sacred vow
   I here engage my words.

Iago.   Do not rise yet.
                         [*Iago kneels.*]
   Witness, you ever-burning lights above,   460

---

445 *hearted* seated in the heart   **446** *fraught* burden   **447** *aspics'* asps'
447 *content* patient, quiet   **450** *Pontic Sea* the Black Sea (famous for
the strong and constant current with which it flows through the Bosporus
into the Mediterranean, where the water level is lower)   **456** *capable
and wide* sufficient and far-reaching

You elements that clip° us round about,
Witness that here Iago doth give up
The execution° of his wit, hands, heart
To wronged Othello's service! Let him command,
465 And to obey shall be in me remorse,°
What bloody business ever.°   [*They rise.*]

Othello.   I greet thy love,
Not with vain thanks but with acceptance boun-
      teous,°
And will upon the instant put thee to't.°
Within these three days let me hear thee say
470 That Cassio's not alive.

Iago. My friend is dead. 'Tis done at your request.
But let her live.

Othello.   Damn her, lewd minx! O, damn her!
Damn her!
Come, go with me apart. I will withdraw
To furnish me with some swift means of death
475 For the fair devil. Now art thou my lieutenant.

Iago. I am your own forever.   *Exeunt.*

Scene IV. [*A street.*]

Enter Desdemona, Emilia, and Clown.

Desdemona. Do you know, sirrah, where Lieutenant
Cassio lies?°

Clown. I dare not say he lies anywhere.

Desdemona. Why, man?

3 *Clown.* He's a soldier, and for me to say a soldier lies,
'tis stabbing.

---

⁴⁶¹ *clip* enfold ⁴⁶³ *execution* workings, action ⁴⁶⁵ *remorse* pity
⁴⁶⁶ *ever* soever ⁴⁶⁷ *bounteous* absolute ⁴⁶⁸ *to't* i.e., to the work you
have said you are prepared to do III.iv.² *lies* lodges

Desdemona. Go to. Where lodges he?

Clown. To tell you where he lodges is to tell you where I lie.

Desdemona. Can anything be made of this?   10

Clown. I know not where he lodges, and for me to devise a lodging, and say he lies here or he lies there, were to lie in mine own throat.°

Desdemona. Can you enquire him out, and be edified° by report?   15

Clown. I will catechize the world for him; that is, make questions, and by them answer.

Desdemona. Seek him, bid him come hither. Tell him I have moved° my lord on his behalf and hope all will be well.   20

Clown. To do this is within the compass° of man's wit, and therefore I will attempt the doing it. *Exit Clown.*

Desdemona. Where should° I lose the handkerchief, Emilia?

Emilia. I know not, madam.

Desdemona. Believe me, I had rather have lost my purse   25
Full of crusadoes.° And but my noble Moor
Is true of mind, and made of no such baseness
As jealous creatures are, it were enough
To put him to ill thinking.

Emilia.   Is he not jealous?

Desdemona. Who? He? I think the sun where he was born   30
Drew all such humors° from him.

Emilia.   Look where he comes.

---

¹³ *lie in mine own throat* (to lie in the throat is to lie absolutely and completely) ¹⁴ *edified* enlightened (Desdemona mocks the Clown's overly elaborate diction) ¹⁹ *moved* pleaded with ²¹ *compass* reach ²³ *should* might ²⁶ *crusadoes* Portuguese gold coins ³¹ *humors* characteristics

Enter Othello.

Desdemona. I will not leave him now till Cassio
    Be called to him. How is't with you, my lord?

Othello. Well, my good lady. [*Aside*] O, hardness to
    dissemble!° —
    How do you, Desdemona?

35 **Desdemona.**   Well, my good lord.

Othello. Give me your hand. This hand is moist,°
    my lady.

Desdemona. It hath felt no age nor known no sorrow.

Othello. This argues° fruitfulness and liberal° heart.
    Hot, hot, and moist. This hand of yours requires
40 A sequester° from liberty; fasting and prayer;
    Much castigation; exercise devout;
    For here's a young and sweating devil here
    That commonly rebels. 'Tis a good hand,
    A frank one.

Desdemona.   You may, indeed, say so;
45 For 'twas that hand that gave away my heart.

Othello. A liberal hand! The hearts of old gave hands,
    But our new heraldry° is hands, not hearts.

Desdemona. I cannot speak of this. Come now, your
    promise!

Othello. What promise, chuck?

Desdemona. I have sent to bid Cassio come speak with
50 you.

Othello. I have a salt and sorry rheum° offends me.
    Lend me thy handkerchief.

---

34 *hardness to dissemble* (Othello may refer here either to the difficulty he has in maintaining his appearance of composure, or to
what he believes to be Desdemona's hardened hypocrisy) 36 *moist*
(a moist, hot hand was taken as a sign of a lustful nature) 38 *argues*
suggests 38 *liberal* free, open (but also with a suggestion of "licentious";
from here on in this scene Othello's words bear a double meaning,
seeming to be normal but accusing Desdemona of being unfaithful)
40 *sequester* separation 47 *heraldry* heraldic symbolism 51 *a salt and
sorry rheum* a heavy, running head cold

Desdemona.   Here, my lord.

Othello. That which I gave you.

Desdemona.   I have it not about me.

Othello. Not?

Desdemona. No, indeed, my lord.

Othello.   That's a fault.
That handkerchief   55
Did an Egyptian to my mother give.
She was a charmer,° and could almost read
The thoughts of people. She told her, while she
    kept it
'Twould make her amiable° and subdue my father
Entirely to her love; but if she lost it   60
Or made a gift of it, my father's eye
Should hold her loathèd, and his spirits should hunt
After new fancies. She, dying, gave it me,
And bid me, when my fate would have me wived,
To give it her. I did so; and take heed on't;   65
Make it a darling like your precious eye.
To lose't or give't away were such perdition
As nothing else could match.

Desdemona.   Is't possible?

Othello. 'Tis true. There's magic in the web° of it.
A sibyl that had numbered in the world   70
The sun to course two hundred compasses,
In her prophetic fury° sewed the work;
The worms were hallowed that did breed the silk,
And it was dyed in mummy° which the skillful
Conserved of maidens' hearts.

Desdemona.   Indeed? Is't true?   75

Othello. Most veritable. Therefore look to't well.

Desdemona. Then would to God that I had never
    seen't!

---

[57] *charmer* magician [59] *amiable* desirable [69] *web* weaving [72] *prophetic fury* seized by the spirit and able to prophesy [74] *mummy* liquid drained from embalmed bodies

Othello. Ha! Wherefore?

Desdemona. Why do you speak so startingly and rash?

80 *Othello.* Is't lost? Is't gone? Speak, is it out o' th' way?

Desdemona. Heaven bless us!

Othello. Say you?

Desdemona. It is not lost. But what an if it were?

Othello. How?

85 *Desdemona.* I say it is not lost.

Othello. Fetch't, let me see't!

Desdemona. Why, so I can; but I will not now.
    This is a trick to put me from my suit:
    Pray you let Cassio be received again.

90 *Othello.* Fetch me the handkerchief! My mind misgives.

Desdemona. Come, come!
    You'll never meet a more sufficient° man——

Othello. The handkerchief!

Desdemona.   A man that all his time
    Hath founded his good fortunes on your love,
95   Shared dangers with you——

Othello. The handkerchief!

Desdemona. I'faith, you are to blame.

Othello. Away!   *Exit Othello.*

Emilia. Is not this man jealous?

100 *Desdemona.* I nev'r saw this before.
    Sure there's some wonder in this handkerchief;
    I am most unhappy in the loss of it.

Emilia. 'Tis not a year or two shows us a man.
    They are all but stomachs, and we all but food;
105   They eat us hungerly, and when they are full,
    They belch us.

---

⁹² *sufficient* complete, with all proper qualities

Enter Iago and Cassio.

    Look you, Cassio and my husband.

Iago. There is no other way; 'tis she must do't.
 And lo the happiness! Go and importune her.

Desdemona. How now, good Cassio? What's the news
 with you?

Cassio. Madam, my former suit. I do beseech you   *110*
 That by your virtuous means I may again
 Exist, and be a member of his love
 Whom I with all the office° of my heart
 Entirely honor. I would not be delayed.
 If my offense be of such mortal kind   *115*
 That nor my service past, nor present sorrows,
 Nor purposed merit in futurity,
 Can ransom me into his love again,
 But to know so must be my benefit.°
 So shall I clothe me in a forced content,   *120*
 And shut myself up in some other course
 To fortune's alms.

Desdemona.   Alas, thrice-gentle Cassio,
 My advocation° is not now in tune.
 My lord is not my lord; nor should I know him
 Were he in favor° as in humor altered.   *125*
 So help me every spirit sanctified
 As I have spoken for you all my best
 And stood within the blank° of his displeasure
 For my free speech. You must awhile be patient.
 What I can do I will; and more I will   *130*
 Than for myself I dare. Let that suffice you.

Iago. Is my lord angry?

Emilia.   He went hence but now,
 And certainly in strange unquietness.

Iago. Can he be angry? I have seen the cannon
 When it hath blown his ranks into the air   *135*
 And, like the devil, from his very arm

---

113 *office* duty 119 *benefit* good 123 *advocation* advocacy 125 *favor*
countenance 128 *blank* bull's-eye of a target

Puffed his own brother. And is he angry?
Something of moment° then. I will go meet him.
There's matter in't indeed if he be angry.

Desdemona. I prithee do so.   *Exit [Iago].*
140   Something sure of state,°
Either from Venice or some unhatched practice°
Made demonstrable here in Cyprus to him,
Hath puddled° his clear spirit; and in such cases
Men's natures wrangle with inferior things,
145   Though great ones are their object. 'Tis even so.
For let our finger ache, and it endues°
Our other, healthful members even to a sense
Of pain. Nay, we must think men are not gods,
Nor of them look for such observancy
150   As fits the bridal. Beshrew me much, Emilia,
I was, unhandsome warrior as I am,
Arraigning his unkindness with my soul;
But now I find I had suborned the witness,
And he's indicted falsely.

Emilia.   Pray heaven it be
155   State matters, as you think, and no conception
Nor no jealous toy° concerning you.

Desdemona. Alas the day! I never gave him cause.

Emilia. But jealous souls will not be answered so;
They are not ever jealous for the cause,
160   But jealous for they're jealous. It is a monster
Begot upon itself, born on itself.

Desdemona. Heaven keep the monster from Othello's
      mind!

Emilia. Lady, amen.

Desdemona. I will go seek him. Cassio, walk here
      about.
165   If I do find him fit,° I'll move your suit
And seek to effect it to my uttermost.

---

138 *moment* importance   140 *of state* state affairs   141 *unhatched prac-*
tice undisclosed plot   143 *puddled* muddied   146 *endues* leads   156 *toy*
trifle   165 *fit* receptive

Cassio. I humbly thank your ladyship.

> *Exit [Desdemona with Emilia].*
>
> *Enter Bianca.*

Bianca. Save you, friend Cassio!

Cassio.   What make you from
    home?
  How is't with you, my most fair Bianca?
  I' faith, sweet love, I was coming to your house.   170

Bianca. And I was going to your lodging, Cassio.
  What, keep a week away? Seven days and nights?
  Eightscore eight hours? And lovers' absent hours
  More tedious than the dial eightscore times?
  O weary reck'ning.°

Cassio.   Pardon me, Bianca.   175
  I have this while with leaden thoughts been pressed,
  But I shall in a more continuate° time
  Strike off this score° of absence. Sweet Bianca,
       [*Gives her Desdemona's handkerchief.*]
  Take me this work out.

Bianca.   O Cassio, whence came this?
  This is some token from a newer friend.   180
  To the felt absence now I feel a cause.
  Is't come to this? Well, well.

Cassio.   Go to, woman!
  Throw your vile guesses in the devil's teeth,
  From whence you have them. You are jealous now
  That this is from some mistress, some remembrance.   185
  No, by my faith, Bianca.

Bianca.   Why, whose is it?

Cassio. I know not neither; I found it in my chamber.
  I like the work well; ere it be demanded,°
  As like enough it will, I would have it copied.
  Take it and do't, and leave me for this time.   190

---

¹⁷⁵ *reck'ning* addition   ¹⁷⁷ *continuate* uninterrupted   ¹⁷⁸ *Strike off this score* i.e., pay this bill (the *score* being the account of drinks kept in a tavern)   ¹⁸⁸ *demanded* asked for (by the person who lost it)

Bianca. Leave you? Wherefore?

Cassio. I do attend here on the general
    And think it no addition, nor my wish,
    To have him see me womaned.

Bianca.   Why, I pray you?

Cassio. Not that I love you not.

195 *Bianca.*   But that you do not love me!
    I pray you bring° me on the way a little,
    And say if I shall see you soon at night.

Cassio. 'Tis but a little way that I can bring you,
    For I attend here; but I'll see you soon.

200 *Bianca.* 'Tis very good. I must be circumstanced.°

                              Exeunt omnes.

---

196 *bring* accompany   200 *circumstanced* accept things as they are

ACT IV

Scene I. [*A street*.]

Enter Othello and Iago.

Iago. Will you think so?

Othello.   Think so, Iago?

Iago.   What,
   To kiss in private?

Othello.   An unauthorized° kiss?

Iago. Or to be naked with her friend in bed
   An hour or more, not meaning any harm?

Othello. Naked in bed, Iago, and not mean harm?   5
   It is hypocrisy against the devil.
   They that mean virtuously, and yet do so,
   The devil their virtue tempts, and they tempt heaven.

Iago. If they do nothing, 'tis a venial slip.
   But if I give my wife a handkerchief——   10

Othello. What then?

Iago. Why, then 'tis hers, my lord; and being hers,
   She may, I think, bestow't on any man.

Othello. She is protectress of her honor too.
   May she give that?   15

Iago. Her honor is an essence that's not seen;
   They have it very oft that have it not.
   But for the handkerchief——

IV.i.² *unauthorized* illicit

119

Othello. By heaven, I would most gladly have forgot it!
20   Thou said'st—O, it comes o'er my memory
As doth the raven° o'er the infected house,
Boding to all—he had my handkerchief.

Iago. Ay, what of that?

Othello.   That's not so good now.

Iago. What if I had said I had seen him do you wrong?
25   Or heard him say—as knaves be such abroad°
Who having, by their own importunate suit,
Or voluntary dotage° of some mistress,
Convincèd or supplied° them, cannot choose
But they must blab——

Othello.   Hath he said anything?

30 *Iago.* He hath, my lord; but be you well assured,
No more than he'll unswear.

Othello.   What hath he said?

Iago. Why, that he did—I know not what he did.

Othello. What? what?

Iago. Lie——

Othello. With her?

35 *Iago.*   With her, on her; what you will.

Othello. Lie with her? Lie on her?—We say lie on her
when they belie her.—Lie with her! Zounds, that's
fulsome.° —Handkerchief—confessions—handkerchief!—To confess, and be hanged for his labor—
40   first to be hanged, and then to confess! I tremble at
it. Nature would not invest herself in such shadow-
ing passion without some instruction.° It is not
words that shakes me thus.—Pish! Noses, ears, and

---

lips? Is't possible?—Confess?—Handkerchief?—O
devil!   *Falls in a trance.*   43

Iago. Work on.
My med'cine works! Thus credulous fools are
    caught,
And many worthy and chaste dames even thus,
All guiltless, meet reproach.° What, ho! My lord!
My lord, I say! Othello!

                    Enter Cassio.

                    How now, Cassio?   50

Cassio. What's the matter?

Iago. My lord is fall'n into an epilepsy.
This is his second fit; he had one yesterday.

Cassio. Rub him about the temples.

Iago. The lethargy° must have his quiet course.   55
If not, he foams at mouth, and by and by
Breaks out to savage madness. Look, he stirs.
Do you withdraw yourself a little while.
He will recover straight. When he is gone,
I would on great occasion° speak with you.   60
                              [*Exit Cassio.*]
How is it, general? Have you not hurt your head?

Othello. Dost thou mock° me?

Iago.   I mock you not, by heaven.
Would you would bear your fortune like a man.

Othello. A hornèd man's a monster and a beast.

Iago. There's many a beast then in a populous city,   65
And many a civil° monster.

Othello. Did he confess it?

Iago.   Good, sir, be a man.
Think every bearded fellow that's but yoked
May draw° with you. There's millions now alive

---

⁴⁹ *reproach* shame ⁵⁵ *lethargy* coma ⁶⁰ *great occasion* very important matter ⁶² *mock* (Othello takes Iago's comment as a reference to
his horns—which it is) ⁶⁶ *civil* city-dwelling ⁶⁹ *draw* i.e., like the
horned ox

70 That nightly lie in those unproper° beds
Which they dare swear peculiar.° Your case is
  better.
O, 'tis the spite of hell, the fiend's arch-mock,
To lip a wanton in a secure couch,
And to suppose her chaste. No, let me know;
75 And knowing what I am, I know what she shall be.

Othello. O, thou art wise! 'Tis certain.

Iago.   Stand you awhile apart;
Confine yourself but in a patient list.°
Whilst you were here, o'erwhelmèd with your
  grief—
A passion most unsuiting such a man—
80 Cassio came hither. I shifted him away°
And laid good 'scuses upon your ecstasy;°
Bade him anon return, and here speak with me;
The which he promised. Do but encave° yourself
And mark the fleers,° the gibes, and notable°
  scorns
85 That dwell in every region of his face.
For I will make him tell the tale anew:
Where, how, how oft, how long ago, and when
He hath, and is again to cope your wife.
I say, but mark his gesture. Marry patience,
90 Or I shall say you're all in all in spleen,°
And nothing of a man.

Othello.   Dost thou hear, Iago?
I will be found most cunning in my patience;
But—dost thou hear?—most bloody.

Iago.   That's not amiss;
But yet keep time in all. Will you withdraw?

[*Othello moves to one side, where his remarks are not
                    audible to Cassio and Iago.*]

---

⁷⁰ *unproper* i.e., not exclusively the husband's ⁷¹ *peculiar* their own alone
⁷⁷ *a patient list* the bounds of patience ⁸⁰ *shifted him away* got rid of
him by a stratagem ⁸¹ *ecstasy* trance (the literal meaning, "outside oneself," bears on the meaning of the change Othello is undergoing)
⁸³ *encave* hide ⁸⁴ *fleers* mocking looks or speeches ⁸⁴ *notable* obvious
⁹⁰ *spleen* passion, particularly anger

Now will I question Cassio of Bianca,   *95*
A huswife° that by selling her desires
Buys herself bread and cloth. It is a creature
That dotes on Cassio, as 'tis the strumpet's plague
To beguile many and be beguiled by one.
He, when he hears of her, cannot restrain   *100*
From the excess of laughter. Here he comes.

Enter Cassio.

As he shall smile, Othello shall go mad;
And his unbookish° jealousy must conster°
Poor Cassio's smiles, gestures, and light behaviors
Quite in the wrong. How do you, lieutenant?   *105*

Cassio. The worser that you give me the addition°
Whose want even kills me.

Iago. Ply Desdemona well, and you are sure on't.
Now, if this suit lay in Bianca's power,
How quickly should you speed!

Cassio.   Alas, poor caitiff!°   *110*

Othello. Look how he laughs already!

Iago. I never knew woman love man so.

Cassio. Alas, poor rogue! I think, i' faith, she loves me.

Othello. Now he denies it faintly, and laughs it out.

Iago. Do you hear, Cassio?

Othello.   Now he importunes him   *115*
To tell it o'er. Go to! Well said, well said!

Iago. She gives it out that you shall marry her.
Do you intend it?

Cassio. Ha, ha, ha!

Othello. Do ye triumph, Roman? Do you triumph?   *120*

Cassio. I marry? What, a customer?° Prithee bear

---

⁹⁶ *huswife* housewife (but with the special meaning here of "prostitute")
¹⁰³ *unbookish* ignorant   ¹⁰⁸ *conster* construe   ¹⁰⁶ *addition* title
¹¹⁰ *caitiff* wretch   ¹²¹ *customer* one who sells, a merchant (here, a prostitute)

some charity to my wit; do not think it so unwholesome. Ha, ha, ha!

Othello. So, so, so, so. They laugh that win.

125 *Iago.* Why, the cry goes that you marry her.

Cassio. Prithee, say true.

Iago. I am a very villain else.

Othello. Have you scored° me? Well.

Cassio. This is the monkey's own giving out. She is
130 persuaded I will marry her out of her own love and
flattery, not out of my promise.

Othello. Iago beckons me; now he begins the story.
[*Othello moves close enough to hear.*]

Cassio. She was here even now; she haunts me in every
place. I was the other day talking on the sea bank
135 with certain Venetians, and thither comes the
bauble,° and falls me thus about my neck——

Othello. Crying "O dear Cassio!" as it were. His gesture imports it.

Cassio. So hangs, and lolls, and weeps upon me; so
140 shakes and pulls me! Ha, ha, ha!

Othello. Now he tells how she plucked him to my
chamber. O, I see that nose of yours, but not that
dog I shall throw it to.

Cassio. Well, I must leave her company.

145 *Iago.* Before me!° Look where she comes.

Enter Bianca.

Cassio. 'Tis such another fitchew!° Marry a perfumed
one? What do you mean by this haunting of me?

Bianca. Let the devil and his dam haunt you! What did
you mean by that same handkerchief you gave me
150 even now? I was a fine fool to take it. I must take

---

128 *scored* marked, defaced   136 *bauble* plaything   145 *Before me!* (an
exclamation of surprise)   146 *fitchew* polecat, i.e., strong-smelling
creature

out the work? A likely piece of work that you should
find it in your chamber and know not who left it
there! This is some minx's token, and I must take
out the work? There! [*She throws down the handkerchief.*] Give it your hobbyhorse.° Wheresoever   155
you had it, I'll take out no work on't.

Cassio. How now, my sweet Bianca? How now? how
now?

Othello. By heaven, that should be my handkerchief!

Bianca. If you'll come to supper tonight, you may; if   160
you will not, come when you are next prepared
for.°   *Exit.*

Iago. After her, after her!

Cassio. Faith, I must; she'll rail in the streets else.

Iago. Will you sup there?   165

Cassio. Yes, I intend so.

Iago. Well, I may chance to see you, for I would very
fain speak with you.

Cassio. Prithee come. Will you?

Iago. Go to, say no more.   [*Exit Cassio.*]   170

Othello. [*Comes forward.*] How shall I murder him,
Iago?

Iago. Did you perceive how he laughed at his vice?

Othello. O Iago!

Iago. And did you see the handkerchief?   175

Othello. Was that mine?

Iago. Yours, by this hand! And to see how he prizes
the foolish woman your wife! She gave it him, and
he hath giv'n it his whore.

Othello. I would have him nine years a-killing!—A   180
fine woman, a fair woman, a sweet woman?

---

155 *hobbyhorse* prostitute   161-62 *next prepared for* next expected—i.e.,
never

Iago. Nay, you must forget that.

Othello. Ay, let her rot, and perish, and be damned
tonight; for she shall not live. No, my heart is turned
185 to stone; I strike it, and it hurts my hand. O, the
world hath not a sweeter creature! She might lie by
an emperor's side and command him tasks.

Iago. Nay, that's not your way.°

Othello. Hang her! I do but say what she is. So deli-
190 cate with her needle. An admirable musician. O, she
will sing the savageness out of a bear! Of so high
and plenteous wit and invention° ——

Iago. She's the worse for all this.

Othello. O, a thousand, a thousand times. And then,
195 of so gentle a condition?°

Iago. Ay, too gentle.

Othello. Nay, that's certain. But yet the pity of it,
Iago. O Iago, the pity of it, Iago.

Iago. If you are so fond over her iniquity, give her
200 patent to offend; for if it touch° not you, it comes
near nobody.

Othello. I will chop her into messes!° Cuckold me!

Iago. O, 'tis foul in her.

Othello. With mine officer!

205 *Iago.* That's fouler.

Othello. Get me some poison, Iago, this night. I'll not
expostulate with her, lest her body and beauty unprovide my mind° again. This night, Iago!

Iago. Do it not with poison. Strangle her in her bed,
210 even the bed she hath contaminated.

Othello. Good, good! The justice of it pleases. Very
good!

188 *way* proper course   192 *invention* imagination   195 *gentle a condition*
(1) well born (2) of a gentle nature   200 *touch* affects   202 *messes* bits
207-08 *unprovide my mind* undo my resolution

Iago. And for Cassio, let me be his undertaker.° You
shall hear more by midnight.

Othello. Excellent good!   [*A trumpet.*]
                    What trumpet is that same?   215

Iago. I warrant something from Venice.

    Enter Lodovico, Desdemona, and Attendants.

                              'Tis Lodovico.
    This comes from the Duke. See, your wife's with
    him.

Lodovico. God save you, worthy general.

Othello.   With° all my heart, sir.

Lodovico. The Duke and the senators of Venice greet
    you.   [*Gives him a letter.*]

Othello. I kiss the instrument of their pleasures.   220
                    [*Opens the letter and reads.*]

Desdemona. And what's the news, good cousin Lodo-
    vico?

Iago. I am very glad to see you, signior.
    Welcome to Cyprus.

Lodovico. I thank you. How does Lieutenant Cassio?

Iago.   Lives, sir.

Desdemona. Cousin, there's fall'n between him and
    my lord   225
    An unkind° breach; but you shall make all well.

Othello. Are you sure of that?

Desdemona. My lord?

Othello. [*Reads*] "This fail you not to do, as you
    will——"

Lodovico. He did not call; he's busy in the paper.   230
    Is there division 'twixt my lord and Cassio?

---

²¹³ *undertaker* (not "burier" but "one who undertakes to do something") ²¹⁸ *With* i.e., I greet you with ²²⁶ *unkind* unnatural

Desdemona. A most unhappy one. I would do much
  T' atone° them, for the love I bear to Cassio.

Othello. Fire and brimstone!

Desdemona.   My lord?

Othello.   Are you wise?

Desdemona. What, is he angry?

235 *Lodovico.*   May be th' letter moved him;
  For, as I think, they do command him home,
  Deputing Cassio in his government.°

Desdemona. Trust me, I am glad on't.

Othello.   Indeed?

Desdemona.   My lord?

Othello. I am glad to see you mad.

Desdemona.   Why, sweet Othello——

240 *Othello.* Devil!   [*Strikes her.*]

Desdemona. I have not deserved this.

Lodovico. My lord, this would not be believed in
    Venice,
  Though I should swear I saw't. 'Tis very much.
  Make her amends; she weeps.

Othello.   O devil, devil!
245 If that the earth could teem° with woman's tears,
  Each drop she falls° would prove a crocodile.°
  Out of my sight!

Desdemona.   I will not stay to offend you.   [*Going.*]

Lodovico. Truly, an obedient lady.
  I do beseech your lordship call her back.

Othello. Mistress!

Desdemona.   My lord?

250 *Othello.*   What would you with her, sir?

---

²³³ *atone* reconcile   ²³⁷ *government* office   ²⁴⁵ *teem* conceive   ²⁴⁶ *falls*
drops   ²⁴⁶ *crocodile* (the crocodile was supposed to shed false tears to
lure its victims)

Lodovico. Who? I, my lord?

Othello. Ay! You did wish that I would make her turn.
    Sir, she can turn, and turn, and yet go on
    And turn again; and she can weep, sir, weep;
    And she's obedient; as you say, obedient.   255
    Very obedient. Proceed you in your tears.
    Concerning this, sir—O well-painted passion!
    I am commanded home.—Get you away;
    I'll send for you anon.—Sir, I obey the mandate
    And will return to Venice.—Hence, avaunt!   260
                           [Exit Desdemona.]
    Cassio shall have my place. And, sir, tonight
    I do entreat that we may sup together.
    You are welcome, sir, to Cyprus.—Goats and mon-
      keys!   *Exit.*

Lodovico. Is this the noble Moor whom our full Senate
    Call all in all sufficient? Is this the nature   265
    Whom passion could not shake? whose solid virtue
    The shot of accident nor dart of chance
    Could neither graze nor pierce?

Iago.   He is much changed.

Lodovico. Are his wits safe? Is he not light of brain?

Iago. He's that he is; I may not breathe my censure.   270
    What he might be (if, what he might, he is not)
    I would to heaven he were!

Lodovico.   What, strike his wife?

Iago. Faith, that was not so well; yet would I knew
    That stroke would prove the worst.

Lodovico.   Is it his use?°
    Or did the letters work upon his blood°   275
    And new-create his fault?

Iago.   Alas, alas!
    It is not honesty in me to speak
    What I have seen and known. You shall observe
      him,

---

²⁷⁴ *use* habit   ²⁷⁵ *blood* passion

And his own courses° will denote him so
280   That I may save my speech. Do but go after
And mark how he continues.

Lodovico. I am sorry that I am deceived in him.

                              Exeunt.

Scene II. [*The citadel.*]

Enter Othello and Emilia.

Othello. You have seen nothing then?

Emilia. Nor ever heard, nor ever did suspect.

Othello. Yes, you have seen Cassio and she together.

Emilia. But then I saw no harm, and then I heard
5   Each syllable that breath made up° between them.

Othello. What, did they never whisper?

Emilia.   Never, my lord.

Othello. Nor send you out o' th' way?

Emilia. Never.

Othello. To fetch her fan, her gloves, her mask, nor
   nothing?

10 *Emilia.* Never, my lord.

Othello. That's strange.

Emilia. I durst, my lord, to wager she is honest,
Lay down my soul at stake.° If you think other,
Remove your thought. It doth abuse your bosom.
15   If any wretch have put this in your head,
Let heaven requite it with the serpent's curse,°
For if she be not honest,° chaste, and true,

---

²⁷⁹ *courses* actions   IV.ii.⁵ *that breath made up* spoken   ¹³ *at stake* as
the wager   ¹⁶ *serpent's curse* (God's curse on the serpent after the fall
in Eden)   ¹⁷ *honest* chaste

There's no man happy. The purest of their wives
Is foul as slander.

Othello.   Bid her come hither. Go.
                                      Exit Emilia.
She says enough; yet she's a simple bawd°   20
That cannot say as much. This is a subtle whore,
A closet lock and key of villainous secrets,
And yet she'll kneel and pray; I have seen her do't.

        Enter Desdemona and Emilia.

Desdemona. My lord, what is your will?

Othello.   Pray you, chuck, come hither.

Desdemona. What is your pleasure?

Othello.   Let me see your eyes.   25
Look in my face.

Desdemona.   What horrible fancy's this?

Othello. [*To Emilia*] Some of your function,° mis-
    tress:
Leave procreants alone and shut the door;
Cough or cry hem if anybody come.
Your mystery,° your mystery! Nay, dispatch!   30
                                      Exit Emilia.

Desdemona. Upon my knee, what doth your speech
    import?
I understand a fury in your words.°

Othello. Why, what art thou?

Desdemona.   Your wife, my lord; your true
And loyal wife.

Othello.   Come, swear it, damn thyself;
Lest, being like one of heaven, the devils themselves 35
Should fear to seize thee. Therefore be double-
    damned:
Swear thou art honest.

Desdemona.   Heaven doth truly know it.

²⁰ *bawd* procuress ²⁷ *Some of your function* do your proper work (as
the operator of a brothel) ³⁰ *mystery* trade ³² *words* (Q1 adds to
this line, "But not the words")

Othello. Heaven truly knows that thou art false as hell.

Desdemona. To whom, my lord? With whom? How am
  I false?

40 *Othello.* Ah, Desdemon! Away! Away! Away!

Desdemona. Alas the heavy day! Why do you weep?
  Am I the motive° of these tears, my lord?
  If haply° you my father do suspect
  An instrument of this your calling back,
45 Lay not your blame on me. If you have lost him,
  I have lost him too.

Othello.   Had it pleased heaven
  To try me with affliction, had they rained
  All kinds of sores and shames on my bare head,
  Steeped° me in poverty to the very lips,
50 Given to captivity me and my utmost hopes,
  I should have found in some place of my soul
  A drop of patience. But, alas, to make me
  The fixèd figure for the time of scorn°
  To point his slow and moving finger at.
55 Yet could I bear that too, well, very well.
  But there where I have garnered up my heart,
  Where either I must live or bear no life,
  The fountain from the which my current runs
  Or else dries up—to be discarded thence,
60 Or keep it as a cistern for foul toads
  To knot and gender° in—turn thy complexion there,
  Patience, thou young and rose-lipped cherubin!
  I here look grim as hell!°

Desdemona. I hope my noble lord esteems me honest.

65 *Othello.* O, ay, as summer flies are in the shambles,°
  That quicken even with blowing.° O thou weed,

---

⁴² *motive* cause ⁴³ *haply* by chance ⁴⁹*Steeped* submerged ⁵³ *The
. . . scorn* the very image of scorn in our time ⁶¹ *knot and gender*
twist in bunches and procreate ⁶¹⁻⁶³ *turn . . . hell* (the rough sense
would seem to be, "even Patience would grow pale, turn complexion, at
Desdemona's perfidy, but that Othello looks grimly on") ⁶⁵ *shambles*
abattoirs ⁶⁶ *quicken even with blowing* become impregnated as soon
as they lay their eggs

Who art so lovely fair, and smell'st so sweet,
That the sense aches at thee, would thou hadst never
    been born!

Desdemona. Alas, what ignorant° sin have I com-
    mitted?

Othello. Was this fair paper, this most goodly book,   70
Made to write "whore" upon? What committed?
Committed? O thou public commoner,°
I should make very forges of my cheeks
That would to cinders burn up modesty,
Did I but speak thy deeds. What committed?   75
Heaven stops the nose at it, and the moon winks;°
The bawdy wind that kisses all it meets
Is hushed within the hollow mine of earth
And will not hear 't. What committed?

Desdemona. By heaven, you do me wrong!   80

Othello. Are not you a strumpet?

Desdemona.   No, as I am a Christian!
If to preserve this vessel for my lord
From any other foul unlawful touch
Be not to be a strumpet, I am none.

Othello. What, not a whore?

Desdemona.   No, as I shall be saved!   85

Othello. Is't possible?

Desdemona. O, heaven forgive us!

Othello.   I cry you mercy° then.
I took you for that cunning whore of Venice
That married with Othello. [*Calling*] You, mistress,

Enter Emilia.

That have the office opposite to Saint Peter   90
And keep the gate of hell! You, you, ay, you!
We have done our course; there's money for your
    pains.   [*Throws her some coins.*]

⁶⁹ *ignorant* unknowing ⁷² *commoner* prostitute ⁷⁶ *winks* closes its
eyes (the moon was the symbol of chastity) ⁸⁷ *cry you mercy* ask
your pardon

I pray you turn the key and keep our counsel.

Exit.

Emilia. Alas, what does this gentleman conceive?
95   How do you, madam? How do you, my good lady?

Desdemona. Faith, half asleep.

Emilia. Good madam, what's the matter with my lord?

Desdemona. With who?

Emilia. Why, with my lord, madam.

Desdemona. Who is thy lord?

100   *Emilia.*   He that is yours, sweet lady.

Desdemona. I have none. Do not talk to me, Emilia.
I cannot weep, nor answers have I none
But what should go by water.° Prithee tonight
Lay on my bed my wedding sheets, remember;
And call thy husband hither.

105   *Emilia.*   Here's a change indeed!

Exit.

Desdemona. 'Tis meet I should be used so, very meet.
How have I been behaved, that he might stick
The small'st opinion on my least misuse?°

Enter Iago and Emilia.

Iago. What is your pleasure, madam? How is't with
you?

Desdemona. I cannot tell. Those that do teach young
110   babes
Do it with gentle means and easy tasks.
He might have chid me so; for, in good faith,
I am a child to chiding.

Iago.   What is the matter, lady?

Emilia. Alas, Iago, my lord hath so bewhored her,

---

103 *water* tears   107-08 *stick . . . misuse* base any doubt on my smallest
fault

Thrown such despite° and heavy terms upon her　　115
That true hearts cannot bear it.

Desdemona. Am I that name, Iago?

Iago.　　　　　　　　　　　What name, fair lady?

Desdemona. Such as she said my lord did say I was.

Emilia. He called her whore. A beggar in his drink
Could not have laid such terms upon his callet.°　　120

Iago. Why did he so?

Desdemona. I do not know; I am sure I am none such.

Iago. Do not weep, do not weep. Alas the day.

Emilia. Hath she forsook so many noble matches,
Her father and her country, and her friends,　　125
To be called whore? Would it not make one weep?

Desdemona. It is my wretched fortune.

Iago.　　　　　　　　　　Beshrew° him for 't!
How comes this trick upon him?

Desdemona.　　　　　　　Nay, heaven doth know.

Emilia. I will be hanged if some eternal villain,
Some busy and insinuating rogue,　　130
Some cogging,° cozening slave, to get some office,
Have not devised this slander. I will be hanged else.

Iago. Fie, there is no such man! It is impossible.

Desdemona. If any such there be, heaven pardon him.

Emilia. A halter pardon him! And hell gnaw his bones!　　135
Why should he call her whore? Who keeps her com-
　　pany?
What place? What time? What form? What likeli-
　　hood?
The Moor's abused by some most villainous knave,
Some base notorious knave, some scurvy fellow.
O heavens, that such companions° thou'dst unfold,°　　140
And put in every honest hand a whip
To lash the rascals naked through the world
Even from the east to th' west!

---

¹¹⁵ *despite* abuse　¹²⁰ *callet* slut　¹²⁷ *Beshrew* curse　¹³¹ *cogging* cheating　¹⁴⁰ *companions* fellows, rogues　¹⁴⁰ *unfold* disclose

Iago.   Speak within door.°

Emilia. O, fie upon them! Some such squire° he was
That turned your wit the seamy side without
And made you to suspect me with the Moor.

Iago. You are a fool. Go to.

Desdemona.   Alas, Iago,
What shall I do to win my lord again?
Good friend, go to him, for, by this light of heaven,
I know not how I lost him. Here I kneel:
If e'er my will did trespass 'gainst his love
Either in discourse of thought° or actual deed,
Or that mine eyes, mine ears, or any sense
Delighted them in any other form;
Or that I do not yet, and ever did,
And ever will (though he do shake me off
To beggarly divorcement) love him dearly,
Comfort forswear me. Unkindness may do much,
And his unkindness may defeat° my life,
But never taint my love. I cannot say "whore."
It does abhor me now I speak the word;
To do the act that might the addition earn
Not the world's mass of vanity could make me.

Iago. I pray you be content. 'Tis but his humor.°
The business of the state does him offense.

Desdemona. If 'twere no other.

Iago.   It is but so, I warrant.
                [*Trumpets within.*]
Hark how these instruments summon to supper.
The messengers of Venice stay the meat.°
Go in, and weep not. All things shall be well.
         [*Exeunt Desdemona and Emilia.*]

Enter Roderigo.

How now, Roderigo?

---

143 *within door* more quietly and moderately   144 *squire* (a term of contempt)   152 *discourse of thought* thinking   159 *defeat* destroy   164 *humor* mood   168 *stay the meat* await the meal

Roderigo. I do not find that thou deal'st justly with me.

Iago. What in the contrary?

Roderigo. Every day thou daff'st° me with some de-
vice,° Iago, and rather, as it seems to me now,
keep'st from me all conveniency° than suppliest me 175
with the least advantage of hope. I will indeed no
longer endure it; nor am I yet persuaded to put up°
in peace what already I have foolishly suffered.

Iago. Will you hear me, Roderigo?

Roderigo. I have heard too much, and your words 180
and performances are no kin together.

Iago. You charge me most unjustly.

Roderigo. With naught but truth. I have wasted myself out of my means. The jewels you have had from
me to deliver Desdemona would half have corrupted 185
a votarist.° You have told me she hath received
them, and returned me expectations and comforts
of sudden respect° and acquaintance; but I find
none.

Iago. Well, go to; very well. 190

Roderigo. Very well? Go to? I cannot go to, man; nor
'tis not very well. Nay, I think it is scurvy, and begin
to find myself fopped° in it.

Iago. Very well.

Roderigo. I tell you 'tis not very well. I will make my- 195
self known to Desdemona. If she will return me
my jewels, I will give over my suit and repent my
unlawful solicitation. If not, assure yourself I will
seek satisfaction of you.

Iago. You have said now? 200

Roderigo. Ay, and said nothing but what I protest°
intendment of doing.

---

¹⁷³ *daff'st* put off   ¹⁷³⁻⁷⁴ *device* scheme   ¹⁷⁵ *conveniency* what is need-
ful   ¹⁷⁷ *put up* accept   ¹⁸⁶ *votarist* nun   ¹⁸⁸ *sudden respect* immediate
consideration   ¹⁹³ *fopped* duped   ²⁰¹ *protest* aver

Iago. Why, now I see there's mettle° in thee, and even
    from this instant do build on thee a better opinion
205   than ever before. Give me thy hand, Roderigo. Thou
    hast taken against me a most just exception;° but
    yet I protest I have dealt most directly° in thy
    affair.

Roderigo. It hath not appeared.

210 *Iago.* I grant indeed it hath not appeared, and your
    suspicion is not without wit and judgment. But,
    Roderigo, if thou hast that in thee indeed which I
    have greater reason to believe now than ever—I
    mean purpose, courage, and valor—this night show
215   it. If thou the next night following enjoy not Desde-
    mona, take me from this world with treachery and
    devise engines for° my life.

Roderigo. Well, what is it? Is it within reason and
    compass?°

220 *Iago.* Sir, there is especial commission come from
    Venice to depute Cassio in Othello's place.

Roderigo. Is that true? Why, then Othello and Desde-
    mona return again to Venice.

Iago. O, no; he goes into Mauritania and taketh away
225   with him the fair Desdemona, unless his abode be
    lingered here by some accident; wherein none can
    be so determinate° as the removing of Cassio.

Roderigo. How do you mean, removing him?

Iago. Why, by making him uncapable of Othello's
230   place—knocking out his brains.

Roderigo. And that you would have me to do?

Iago. Ay, if you dare do yourself a profit and a right.
    He sups tonight with a harlotry,° and thither will I
    go to him. He knows not yet of his honorable for-
235   tune. If you will watch his going thence, which I

---

203 *mettle* spirit   206 *exception* objection   207 *directly* straightforwardly
217 *engines for* schemes against   219 *compass* possibility   227 *determi-
nate* effective   233 *harlotry* female

will fashion to fall out° between twelve and one,
you may take him at your pleasure. I will be near
to second° your attempt, and he shall fall between
us. Come, stand not amazed at it, but go along with
me. I will show you such a necessity in his death 240
that you shall think yourself bound to put it on him.
It is now high supper time, and the night grows
to waste. About it.

Roderigo. I will hear further reason for this.

Iago. And you shall be satisfied.   *Exeunt.* 245

Scene III. [*The citadel.*]

Enter Othello, Lodovico, Desdemona, Emilia, and
Attendants.

Lodovico. I do beseech you, sir, trouble yourself no
further.

Othello. O, pardon me; 'twill do me good to walk.

Lodovico. Madam, good night. I humbly thank your
ladyship.

Desdemona. Your honor is most welcome.

Othello. Will you walk, sir? O, Desdemona.   5

Desdemona. My lord?

Othello. Get you to bed on th' instant; I will be returned forthwith. Dismiss your attendant there.
Look't be done.

Desdemona. I will, my lord.   10
          Exit [Othello, with Lodovico and Attendants].

Emilia. How goes it now? He looks gentler than he did.

236 *fall out* occur   238 *second* support

Desdemona. He says he will return incontinent,°
And hath commanded me to go to bed,
And bade me to dismiss you.

Emilia.   Dismiss me?

15 *Desdemona.* It was his bidding; therefore, good Emilia,
Give me my nightly wearing, and adieu.
We must not now displease him.

Emilia. I would you had never seen him!

Desdemona. So would not I. My love doth so approve
him
That even his stubbornness, his checks,° his
20   frowns—
Prithee unpin me—have grace and favor.

Emilia. I have laid these sheets you bade me on the
bed.

Desdemona. All's one.° Good Father, how foolish
are our minds!
If I do die before, prithee shroud me
In one of these same sheets.

25 *Emilia.*   Come, come! You talk.

Desdemona. My mother had a maid called Barbary.
She was in love; and he she loved proved mad
And did forsake her. She had a song of "Willow";
An old thing 'twas, but it expressed her fortune,
30   And she died singing it. That song tonight
Will not go from my mind; I have much to do
But to go hang my head all at one side
And sing it like poor Barbary. Prithee dispatch.

Emilia. Shall I go fetch your nightgown?

35 *Desdemona.* No, unpin me here.
This Lodovico is a proper man.

Emilia. A very handsome man.

Desdemona. He speaks well.

IV.iii.¹² *incontinent* at once   ²⁰ *checks* rebukes   ²³ *All's one* no matter

Emilia. I know a lady in Venice would have walked
    barefoot to Palestine for a touch of his nether lip.   *40*

Desdemona. [*Sings*]
      "The poor soul sat singing by a sycamore tree,
         Sing all a green willow;
      Her hand on her bosom, her head on her knee,
         Sing willow, willow, willow.
      The fresh streams ran by her and murmured
         her moans;   *45*
         Sing willow, willow, willow;
      Her salt tears fell from her, and soft'ned the
         stones—
         Sing willow, willow, willow—"
    Lay by these.   [*Gives Emilia her clothes.*]
      "Willow, Willow"——   *50*
    Prithee hie° thee; he'll come anon.°
      "Sing all a green willow must be my garland.
      Let nobody blame him; his scorn I approve"——
    Nay, that's not next. Hark! Who is't that knocks?

Emilia. It is the wind.   *55*

Desdemona. [*Sings*]
      "I called my love false love; but what said he
         then?
         Sing willow, willow, willow:
      If I court moe° women, you'll couch with moe
         men."
    So, get thee gone; good night. Mine eyes do itch.
    Doth that bode weeping?

Emilia.   'Tis neither here nor there.   *60*

Desdemona. I have heard it said so. O, these men,
    these men.
    Dost thou in conscience think, tell me, Emilia,
    That there be women do abuse their husbands
    In such gross kind?

Emilia.   There be some such, no question.

---

⁵¹ *hie* hurry   ⁵¹ *anon* at once   ⁵⁸ *moe* more

Desdemona. Wouldst thou do such a deed for all the
65   world?

Emilia. Why, would not you?

Desdemona.   No, by this heavenly light!

Emilia. Nor I neither by this heavenly light.
    I might do't as well i' th' dark.

Desdemona. Wouldst thou do such a deed for all the
    world?

70 *Emilia.* The world's a huge thing; it is a great price for
    a small vice.

Desdemona. In troth, I think thou wouldst not.

Emilia. In troth, I think I should; and undo't when I
    had done. Marry, I would not do such a thing for
75   a joint-ring,° nor for measures of lawn,° nor for
    gowns, petticoats, nor caps, nor any petty exhibi-
    tion,° but for all the whole world? Why, who
    would not make her husband a cuckold to make him
    a monarch? I should venture purgatory for't.

80 *Desdemona.* Beshrew me if I would do such a wrong
    for the whole world.

Emilia. Why, the wrong is but a wrong i' th' world;
    and having the world for your labor, 'tis a wrong
    in your own world, and you might quickly make
85   it right.

Desdemona. I do not think there is any such woman.

Emilia. Yes, a dozen; and as many to th' vantage as
    would store° the world they played for.
    But I do think it is their husbands' faults
90   If wives do fall. Say that they slack their duties
    And pour our treasures into foreign° laps;
    Or else break out in peevish jealousies,
    Throwing restraint upon us; or say they strike us,

---

75 *joint-ring* (a ring with two interlocking halves) 75 *lawn* fine linen
76–77 *exhibition* payment 87–88 *to . . . store* in addition as would fill
91 *foreign* alien, i.e., other than the wife

Or scant our former having in despite°—
Why, we have galls; and though we have some
    grace,   95
Yet have we some revenge. Let husbands know
Their wives have sense like them. They see, and
    smell,
And have their palates both for sweet and sour,
As husbands have. What is it that they do
When they change° us for others? Is it sport?   100
I think it is. And doth affection° breed it?
I think it doth. Is't frailty that thus errs?
It is so too. And have not we affections?
Desires for sport? and frailty? as men have?
Then let them use us well; else let them know,   105
The ills we do, their ills instruct us so.°

Desdemona. Good night, good night. Heaven me such
    uses° send,
Not to pick bad from bad, but by bad mend. *Exeunt.*

---

⁹⁴ *scant . . . despite* reduce, in spite, our household allowance (?)
¹⁰⁰ *change* exchange   ¹⁰¹ *affection* strong feeling, desire   ¹⁰⁶ *instruct us so* teach us to do likewise   ¹⁰⁷ *uses* practices

ACT V

Scene I. [*A street.*]

Enter Iago and Roderigo.

Iago. Here, stand behind this bulk;° straight will he
    come.
    Wear thy good rapier bare, and put it home.
    Quick, quick! Fear nothing; I'll be at thy elbow.
    It makes us, or it mars us, think on that,
5   And fix most firm thy resolution.

Roderigo. Be near at hand; I may miscarry in't.

Iago. Here, at thy hand. Be bold, and take thy stand.
                        [*Moves to one side.*]

Roderigo. I have no great devotion to the deed,
    And yet he hath given me satisfying reasons.
10   'Tis but a man gone. Forth my sword! He dies!

Iago. I have rubbed this young quat° almost to the
    sense,°
    And he grows angry. Now, whether he kill Cassio,
    Or Cassio him, or each do kill the other,
    Every way makes my gain. Live Roderigo,
15   He calls me to a restitution large
    Of gold and jewels that I bobbed° from him
    As gifts to Desdemona.
    It must not be. If Cassio do remain,

V.i.[1] *bulk* projecting stall of a shop   [11] *quat* pimple   [11] *to the sense*
raw [16] *bobbed* swindled

144

He hath a daily beauty in his life
That makes me ugly; and besides, the Moor   20
May unfold me to him; there stand I in much peril.
No, he must die. But so, I hear him coming.

Enter Cassio.

Roderigo. I know his gait. 'Tis he. Villain, thou diest!
                              [*Thrusts at Cassio.*]

Cassio. That thrust had been mine enemy indeed
   But that my coat° is better than thou know'st.   25
   I will make proof of thine.   [*Fights with Roderigo.*]

Roderigo.   O, I am slain!°

Cassio. I am maimed forever. Help, ho! Murder!
   Murder!

Enter Othello [to one side].

Othello. The voice of Cassio. Iago keeps his word.

Roderigo. O, villain that I am!

Othello.   It is even so.

Cassio. O help, ho! Light! A surgeon!   30

Othello. 'Tis he. O brave Iago, honest and just,
   That hast such noble sense of thy friend's wrong!
   Thou teachest me. Minion,° your dear lies dead,
   And your unblest° fate hies.° Strumpet, I come.
   Forth of my heart those charms, thine eyes, are
      blotted.   35
   Thy bed, lust-stained, shall with lust's blood be
      spotted.

                              Exit Othello.

25 *coat* i.e., a mail shirt or bulletproof vest   26 *slain* (most editors add here a stage direction which has Iago wounding Cassio in the leg from behind, but remaining unseen. However, nothing in the text requires this, and Cassio's wound can be given him in the fight with Roderigo, for presumably when Cassio attacks Roderigo the latter would not simply accept the thrust but would parry. Since Iago enters again at line 46, he must exit at some point after line 22)   33 *Minion* hussy, i.e., Desdemona   34 *unblest* unsanctified   34 *hies* approaches swiftly

Enter Lodovico and Gratiano.

Cassio. What, ho? No watch? No passage?° Murder!
Murder!

Gratiano. 'Tis some mischance. The voice is very
direful.

Cassio. O, help!

40   *Lodovico.* Hark!

Roderigo. O wretched villain!

Lodovico. Two or three groan. 'Tis heavy night.
These may be counterfeits. Let's think't unsafe
To come into the cry without more help.

45   *Roderigo.* Nobody come? Then shall I bleed to death.

Lodovico. Hark!

Enter Iago [with a light].

Gratiano. Here's one comes in his shirt, with light and
weapons.

Iago. Who's there? Whose noise is this that cries on
murder?

Lodovico. We do not know.

Iago.   Do not you hear a cry?

Cassio. Here, here! For heaven's sake, help me!

50   *Iago.*   What's the matter?

Gratiano. This is Othello's ancient, as I take it.

Lodovico. The same indeed, a very valiant fellow.

Iago. What are you here that cry so grievously?

Cassio. Iago? O, I am spoiled, undone by villains.
55   Give me some help.

Iago. O me, lieutenant! What villains have done this?

Cassio. I think that one of them is hereabout
And cannot make away.

37 *passage* passers-by

Iago.   O treacherous villains!
   [*To Lodovico and Gratiano*] What are you there?
     Come in, and give some help.

Roderigo. O, help me there!   60

Cassio. That's one of them.

Iago.   O murd'rous slave! O villain!   [*Stabs Roderigo.*]

Roderigo. O damned Iago! O inhuman dog!

Iago. Kill men i' th' dark?—Where be these bloody
     thieves?—
   How silent is this town!—Ho! Murder! Murder!—
   What may you be? Are you of good or evil?   65

Lodovico. As you shall prove us, praise us.

Iago. Signior Lodovico?

Lodovico. He, sir.

Iago. I cry you mercy. Here's Cassio hurt by villains.

Gratiano. Cassio?   70

Iago. How is't, brother?

Cassio. My leg is cut in two.

Iago.   Marry, heaven forbid!
   Light, gentlemen. I'll bind it with my shirt.

           Enter Bianca.

Bianca. What is the matter, ho? Who is't that cried?

Iago. Who is't that cried?   75

Bianca. O my dear Cassio! My sweet Cassio!
   O Cassio, Cassio, Cassio!

Iago. O notable strumpet!—Cassio, may you suspect
   Who they should be that have thus mangled you?

Cassio. No.   80

Gratiano. I am sorry to find you thus. I have been to
     seek you.

Iago. Lend me a garter. So. O for a chair
   To bear him easily hence.

Bianca. Alas, he faints! O Cassio, Cassio, Cassio!

85 *Iago.* Gentlemen all, I do suspect this trash
   To be a party in this injury.—
   Patience awhile, good Cassio.—Come, come.
   Lend me a light. Know we this face or no?
   Alas, my friend and my dear countryman
90 Roderigo? No.—Yes, sure.—Yes, 'tis Roderigo!

Gratiano. What, of Venice?

Iago. Even he, sir. Did you know him?

Gratiano.   Know him? Ay.

Iago. Signior Gratiano? I cry your gentle pardon.
   These bloody accidents must excuse my manners
   That so neglected you.

95 *Gratiano.*   I am glad to see you.

Iago. How do you, Cassio?—O, a chair, a chair!

Gratiano. Roderigo?

Iago. He, he, 'tis he! [*A chair brought in.*] O, that's
   well said;° the chair.
   Some good man bear him carefully from hence.
   I'll fetch the general's surgeon. [*To Bianca*] For you,
100   mistress,
   Save you your labor. [*To Cassio*] He that lies slain
   here, Cassio,
   Was my dear friend. What malice was between you?

Cassio. None in the world; nor do I know the man.

Iago. What, look you pale?—O, bear him out o' th'
   air.   [*Cassio is carried off.*]
   Stay you, good gentlemen.—Look you pale, mis-
105   tress?
   Do you perceive the gastness° of her eye?
   Nay, if you stare, we shall hear more anon.
   Behold her well; I pray you look upon her.

---

⁹⁸ *well said* well done   ¹⁰⁶ *gastness* terror

Do you see, gentlemen? Nay, guiltiness will speak,
Though tongues were out of use.° 110

[Enter Emilia.]

Emilia. Alas, what is the matter? What is the matter,
husband?

Iago. Cassio hath here been set on in the dark
By Roderigo and fellows that are scaped.
He's almost slain, and Roderigo quite dead.

Emilia. Alas, good gentleman! Alas, good Cassio! 115

Iago. This is the fruits of whoring. Prithee, Emilia,
Go know of Cassio where he supped tonight.
[To Bianca] What, do you shake at that?

Bianca. He supped at my house; but I therefore shake
not.

Iago. O, did he so? I charge° you go with me. 120

Emilia. Oh fie upon thee, strumpet!

Bianca. I am no strumpet, but of life as honest
As you that thus abuse me.

Emilia.   As I? Fie upon thee!

Iago. Kind gentlemen, let's go see poor Cassio
dressed.°
[To Bianca] Come, mistress, you must tell's another
tale. 125
Emilia, run you to the citadel
And tell my lord and lady what hath happed.
                    [Exit Emilia.]
Will you go on afore?   *Exeunt [all but Iago].*
            This is the night
That either makes me or fordoes me quite.° *[Exit.]*

¹¹⁰ *tongues were out of use* men no longer spoke ¹²⁰ *charge* command
¹²⁴ *dressed* bandaged ¹²⁹ *fordoes me quite* completely ruins me

Scene II. [*Desdemona's chamber*.]

*Enter Othello [with a light]; and Desdemona
in her bed.*

Othello. It is the cause, it is the cause, my soul.
    Let me not name it to you, you chaste stars.
    It is the cause. Yet I'll not shed her blood,
    Nor scar that whiter skin of hers than snow,
5   And smooth as monumental alabaster.
    Yet she must die, else she'll betray more men.
    Put out the light, and then put out the light.
    If I quench thee, thou flaming minister,°
    I can again thy former light restore,
10   Should I repent me; but once put out thy light,
    Thou cunning'st° pattern of excelling nature,
    I know not where is that Promethean heat°
    That can thy light relume.° When I have plucked
       the rose,
    I cannot give it vital° growth again;
15   It needs must wither. I'll smell thee on the tree.
                     [*He kisses her*.]
    O balmy breath, that dost almost persuade
    Justice to break her sword. One more, one more!
    Be thus when thou art dead, and I will kill thee,
    And love thee after. One more, and that's the last!
20   So sweet was ne'er so fatal. I must weep,
    But they are cruel tears. This sorrow's heavenly;
    It strikes where it doth love. She wakes.

Desdemona. Who's there? Othello?

Othello.   Ay, Desdemona.

V.ii.⁸ *minister* worker, servant ¹¹ *cunning'st* most intricate and skill-
fully wrought (by nature excelling itself) ¹² *Promethean heat* divine
fire (Prometheus is the Titan who stole fire from heaven and gave it to
man) ¹³ *relume* relight ¹⁴ *vital* living

Desdemona. Will you come to bed, my lord?

Othello. Have you prayed tonight, Desdemon?

Desdemona.   Ay, my lord.   25

Othello. If you bethink yourself of any crime
Unreconciled as yet to heaven and grace,
Solicit for it straight.

Desdemona. Alack, my lord, what may you mean by
that?

Othello. Well, do it, and be brief; I will walk by.°   30
I would not kill thy unpreparèd spirit.
No, heavens forfend! I would not kill thy soul.

Desdemona. Talk you of killing?

Othello.   Ay, I do.

Desdemona.   Then heaven
Have mercy on me!

Othello.   Amen, with all my heart.

Desdemona. If you say so, I hope you will not kill me.   35

Othello. Humh.

Desdemona. And yet I fear you; for you're fatal then
When your eyes roll so. Why I should fear I know
not,
Since guiltiness I know not; but yet I feel I fear.

Othello. Think on thy sins.

Desdemona.   They are loves I bear to you.   40

Othello. Ay, and for that thou diest.

Desdemona. That death's unnatural that kills for
loving.
Alas, why gnaw you so your nether lip?
Some bloody passion shakes your very frame.
These are portents; but yet I hope, I hope,   45
They do not point on me.

Othello.   Peace and be still.

30 *by* nearby

Desdemona. I will so. What's the matter?

Othello. That handkerchief which I so loved and gave
thee,
Thou gav'st to Cassio.

Desdemona.   No, by my life and soul!
Send for the man and ask him.

50   *Othello.*   Sweet soul, take heed,
Take heed of perjury; thou art on thy deathbed.

Desdemona. Ay, but not yet to die.

Othello.   Presently.°
Therefore confess thee freely of thy sin,
For to deny each article° with oath
55   Cannot remove nor choke the strong conception
That I do groan withal. Thou art to die.

Desdemona. Then Lord have mercy on me.

Othello.   I say, amen.

Desdemona. And have you mercy too. I never did
Offend you in my life; never loved Cassio
60   But with such general warranty° of heaven
As I might love. I never gave him token.

Othello. By heaven, I saw my handkerchief in's hand!
O perjured woman! thou dost stone° my heart,
And mak'st me call what I intend to do
65   A murder, which I thought a sacrifice.
I saw the handkerchief.

Desdemona.   He found it then.
I never gave it him. Send for him hither.
Let him confess a truth.

Othello.   He hath confessed.

Desdemona. What, my lord?

Othello. That he hath used thee.

Desdemona.   How? Unlawfully?

52 *Presently* immediately   54 *article* item (of the charge of adultery.
Othello makes heavy use of legal terms in this scene)   60 *warranty*
allowance   63 *stone* turn to stone

Othello.   Ay.   70

Desdemona. He will not say so.

Othello.   No, his mouth is stopped.
Honest Iago hath ta'en order for't.°

Desdemona. O, my fear interprets. What, is he dead?

Othello. Had all his hairs been lives, my great revenge
Had stomach° for them all.   75

Desdemona. Alas, he is betrayed, and I undone!

Othello. Out, strumpet! Weep'st thou for him to my
face?

Desdemona. O, banish me, my lord, but kill me not!

Othello. Down, strumpet!

Desdemona. Kill me tomorrow; let me live tonight!   80

Othello. Nay, if you strive——

Desdemona. But half an hour!

Othello.   Being done, there is no pause.

Desdemona. But while I say one prayer!

Othello.   It is too late.
Smothers her.

Emilia at the door.

Emilia. [*Calls within.*] My lord, my lord! What, ho, my
lord, my lord!

Othello. What noise is this? Not dead? Not yet quite
dead?   85
I that am cruel am yet merciful;
I would not have thee linger in thy pain.
So, so.

Emilia. [*Within*] What, ho! My lord, my lord!

Othello.   Who's there?

Emilia. [*Within*] O, good my lord, I would speak a
word with you.

---

⁷² *ta'en order for't* made sure of it   ⁷⁵ *stomach* appetite

90 *Othello.* Yes, 'tis Emilia.—By and by.—She's dead.—
  'Tis like she comes to speak of Cassio's death.
  The noise was high.° Ha! No more moving?
  Still as the grave.—Shall she come in? Were't
    good?—
  I think she stirs again. No.— What's best to do?
95   If she come in, she'll sure speak to my wife.
  My wife! My wife! What wife? I have no wife.
  O, insupportable! O heavy hour!
  Methinks it should be now a huge eclipse
  Of sun and moon, and that th' affrighted globe
  Should yawn° at alteration.

100 *Emilia.*   [*Within*] I do beseech you
  That I may speak with you, O good my lord!

 Othello. I had forgot thee. O, come in, Emilia.
  Soft, by and by.—Let me the curtains draw.—
 [*Draws the bed hangings and then opens the door.*]
  Where art thou?

      Enter Emilia.

     What's the matter with thee now?

105 *Emilia.* O my good lord, yonder's foul murders done!

 Othello. What? Now?

 Emilia. But now, my lord.

 Othello. It is the very error° of the moon.
  She comes more nearer earth than she was wont
110   And makes men mad.

 Emilia. Cassio, my lord, hath killed a young Venetian
  Called Roderigo.

 Othello.   Roderigo killed?
  And Cassio killed?

---

92 *high* loud (Q1 reads "here") 98–100 *Methinks . . . alteration* (the
Elizabethans believed that great changes in human affairs were reflected
by disorders in nature) 100 *yawn* gape open (as in an earthquake)
108 *error* wandering out of regular course (disorders in the heavens
were believed by some to cause disorders on earth, as well as vice
versa)

Emilia.   No, Cassio is not killed.

Othello. Not Cassio killed? Then murder's out of tune,
  And sweet revenge grows harsh.   115

Desdemona. O, falsely, falsely murdered!

Emilia.   O Lord! What cry is that?

Othello. That? What?

Emilia. Out and alas! that was my lady's voice.
  Help! Help, ho! Help! O lady, speak again!
  Sweet Desdemona! O sweet mistress, speak!   120

Desdemona. A guiltless death I die.

Emilia. O, who hath done this deed?

Desdemona. Nobody—I myself. Farewell.
  Commend me to my kind lord. O, farewell!

                          [*She dies.*]

Othello. Why, how should she be murd'red?

Emilia.   Alas, who knows? 125

Othello. You heard her say herself, it was not I.

Emilia. She said so. I must needs report the truth.

Othello. She's like a liar gone to burning hell!
  'Twas I that killed her.

Emilia.   O, the more angel she,
  And you the blacker devil!   130

Othello. She turned to folly, and she was a whore.

Emilia. Thou dost belie her, and thou art a devil.

Othello. She was false as water.

Emilia.   Thou art rash as fire to say
  That she was false. O, she was heavenly true!

Othello. Cassio did top her. Ask thy husband else.   135
  O, I were damned beneath all depth in hell
  But that I did proceed upon just grounds
  To this extremity. Thy husband knew it all.

Emilia. My husband?

Othello.   Thy husband.

Emilia.   That she was false to wedlock?

140 *Othello.* Ay, with Cassio. Had she been true,
      If heaven would make me such another world
      Of one entire and perfect chrysolite,°
      I'd not have sold her for it.

Emilia.   My husband?

Othello. Ay, 'twas he that told me on her first.
145   An honest man he is, and hates the slime
      That sticks on filthy deeds.

Emilia.   My husband?

Othello. What needs this iterance? Woman, I say thy
      husband.

Emilia. O mistress, villainy hath made mocks with
      love!
      My husband say she was false?

Othello.   He, woman.
150   I say, thy husband. Dost understand the word?
      My friend, thy husband; honest, honest Iago.

Emilia. If he say so, may his pernicious soul
      Rot half a grain a day! He lies to th' heart.
      She was too fond of her most filthy bargain.

155 *Othello.* Hah?

Emilia. Do thy worst.
      This deed of thine is no more worthy heaven
      Than thou wast worthy her.

Othello.   Peace, you were best.°

Emilia. Thou hast not half that pow'r to do me harm
160   As I have to be hurt. O gull! O dolt!
      As ignorant as dirt! Thou hast done a deed—
                [*Othello moves to draw his sword.*]
      I care not for thy sword; I'll make thee known,
      Though I lost twenty lives. Help! Help! Ho! Help!
      The Moor hath killed my mistress! Murder! murder!

---

142 *chrysolite* topaz   158 *Peace, you were best* i.e., you had better be
silent

Enter Montano, Gratiano, and Iago [and Others].

Montano. What is the matter? How now, general?   165

Emilia. O, are you come, Iago? You have done well,
That men must lay their murders on your neck.

Gratiano. What is the matter?

Emilia. Disprove this villain, if thou be'st a man.
He says thou told'st him that his wife was false.   170
I know thou didst not; thou'rt not such a villain.
Speak, for my heart is full.

Iago. I told him what I thought, and told no more
Than what he found himself was apt and true.

Emilia. But did you ever tell him she was false?   175

Iago. I did.

Emilia. You told a lie, an odious damnèd lie!
Upon my soul, a lie! A wicked lie!
She false with Cassio? Did you say with Cassio?

Iago. With Cassio, mistress. Go to, charm° your
tongue.   180

Emilia. I will not charm my tongue; I am bound to
speak:
My mistress here lies murdered in her bed.

All. O heavens forfend!

Emilia. And your reports have set the murder on.

Othello. Nay, stare not, masters. It is true indeed.   185

Gratiano. 'Tis a strange truth.

Montano. O monstrous act!

Emilia.   Villainy, villainy, villainy!
I think upon't—I think I smell't!—O villainy!
I thought so then.—I'll kill myself for grief.—
O villainy, villainy!   190

Iago. What, are you mad? I charge you get you home.

Emilia. Good gentlemen, let me have leave to speak.

180 *charm* control

'Tis proper I obey him, but not now.
Perchance, Iago, I will ne'er go home.

Othello. O! O! O!   [*Falls on the bed.*]

195 *Emilia.*   Nay, lay thee down and roar,
For thou hast killed the sweetest innocent
That e'er did lift up eye.

Othello.   O, she was foul!   [*Rises.*]
I scarce did know you, uncle. There lies your niece,
Whose breath, indeed, these hands have newly
      stopped.
200 I know this act shows horrible and grim.

Gratiano. Poor Desdemon! I am glad thy father's dead.
Thy match was mortal to him, and pure grief
Shore his old thread in twain. Did he live now,
This sight would make him do a desperate turn;
205 Yea, curse his better angel from his side,
And fall to reprobation.°

Othello. 'Tis pitiful; but yet Iago knows
That she with Cassio hath the act of shame
A thousand times committed. Cassio confessed it;
210 And she did gratify his amorous works
With that recognizance and pledge of love,
Which I first gave her. I saw it in his hand.
It was a handkerchief, an antique token
My father gave my mother.

215 *Emilia.* O God! O heavenly God!

Iago. Zounds, hold your peace!

Emilia.   'Twill out, 'twill out! I peace?
No, I will speak as liberal as the north.°
Let heaven and men and devils, let them all,
All, all, cry shame against me, yet I'll speak.

Iago. Be wise, and get you home.

220 *Emilia.*   I will not.
                    [*Iago draws and threatens Emilia.*]

---

206 *reprobation* damnation   217 *liberal as the north* freely (and bitingly)
as the north wind blows

Gratiano. Fie! Your sword upon a woman?

Emilia. O thou dull Moor, that handkerchief thou
   speak'st of
   I found by fortune, and did give my husband;
   For often with a solemn earnestness—
   More than indeed belonged to such a trifle—   225
   He begged of me to steal't.

Iago.   Villainous whore!

Emilia. She give it Cassio? No, alas, I found it,
   And I did give't my husband.

Iago.   Filth, thou liest!

Emilia. By heaven, I do not, I do not, gentlemen.
   O murd'rous coxcomb! What should such a fool   230
   Do with so good a wife?

Othello.   Are there no stones° in heaven
   But what serves for the thunder? Precious villain!
[*The Moor runs at Iago, but is disarmed by Montano.
                    Iago kills his wife.*]

Gratiano. The woman falls. Sure he hath killed his
   wife.

Emilia. Ay, ay. O, lay me by my mistress' side.
                    [*Exit Iago.*]

Gratiano. He's gone, but his wife's killed.   235

Montano. 'Tis a notorious° villain. Take you this
   weapon,
   Which I have recovered from the Moor.
   Come, guard the door without. Let him not pass,
   But kill him rather. I'll after that same villain,
   For 'tis a damnèd slave.
                    Exit [*with all but Othello and Emilia*].

Othello.   I am not valiant neither;   240
   But every puny whipster° gets my sword.
   But why should honor outlive honesty?
   Let it go all.

---

²³¹ *stones* thunderbolts ²³⁶ *notorious* out-and-out ²⁴¹ *puny whipster*
small top-whipping boy (?)

Emilia.   What did thy song bode, lady?
Hark, canst thou hear me? I will play the swan,
245   And die in music. [*Sings*] "Willow, willow, willow."
Moor, she was chaste. She loved thee, cruel Moor,
So come my soul to bliss as I speak true.
So speaking as I think, alas, I die.   [*She dies.*]

Othello. I have another weapon in this chamber;
250   It was a sword of Spain, the ice-brook's temper.
O, here it is.—Uncle, I must come forth.

Gratiano. [*Within*] If thou attempt it, it will cost thee
    dear.
Thou hast no weapon, and perforce must suffer.

Othello. Look in upon me then and speak with me,
255   Or, naked as I am, I will assault thee.

                  [*Enter Gratiano.*]

Gratiano. What is the matter?

Othello.   Behold, I have a weapon;
A better never did itself sustain
Upon a soldier's thigh. I have seen the day
That with this little arm and this good sword
260   I have made my way through more impediments
Than twenty times your stop. But O vain boast!
Who can control his fate? 'Tis not so now.
Be not afraid, though you do see me weaponed.
Here is my journey's end, here is my butt,°
265   And very seamark of my utmost sail.°
Do you go back dismayed? 'Tis a lost fear.
Man but a rush° against Othello's breast,
And he retires. Where should Othello go?
Now, how dost thou look now? O ill-starred wench!
270   Pale as thy smock! When we shall meet at compt,°
This look of thine will hurl my soul from heaven,
And fiends will snatch at it. Cold, cold, my girl?
Even like thy chastity.
O cursèd, cursèd slave! Whip me, ye devils,

²⁶⁴ *butt* target, stopping place   ²⁶⁵ *seamark of my utmost sail* marker
of my farthest journey   ²⁶⁷ *Man but a rush* attack with only a reed
²⁷⁰ *compt* Judgment Day

From the possession of° this heavenly sight!   275
Blow me about in winds! roast me in sulfur!
Wash me in steep-down gulfs of liquid fire!
O Desdemon! Dead Desdemon; dead. O! O!

Enter Lodovico, Cassio, Montano, and Iago
[as prisoner,] with Officers.

Lodovico. Where is this rash and most unfortunate
    man?

Othello. That's he that was Othello; Here I am.   280

Lodovico. Where is that viper? Bring the villain forth.

Othello. I look down towards his feet°—but that's a
    fable.
If that thou be'st a devil, I cannot kill thee.
                                    [*Wounds Iago.*]

Lodovico. Wrench his sword from him.
                              [*Othello is disarmed.*]

Iago.   I bleed, sir, but not killed.

Othello. I am not sorry neither. I'd have thee live;   285
For in my sense, 'tis happiness to die.

Lodovico. O thou Othello that was once so good,
Fall'n in the practice° of a cursèd slave,
What shall be said to thee?

Othello.   Why, anything:
An honorable murderer, if you will;   290
For naught I did in hate, but all in honor.

Lodovico. This wretch hath part confessed his villainy.
Did you and he consent in Cassio's death?

Othello. Ay.

Cassio. Dear general, I never gave you cause.   295

Othello. I do believe it, and I ask your pardon.
Will you, I pray, demand that demi-devil
Why he hath thus ensnared my soul and body?

275 *the possession of* being possessed by   282 *towards his feet* i.e., for
his cloven hoofs   288 *practice* plotting

Iago. Demand me nothing. What you know, you know.
800 From this time forth I never will speak word.

Lodovico. What, not to pray?

Gratiano.   Torments will ope your lips.

Othello. Well, thou dost best.

Lodovico. Sir, you shall understand what hath befall'n,
     Which, as I think, you know not. Here is a letter
305 Found in the pocket of the slain Roderigo;
     And here another. The one of them imports
     The death of Cassio to be undertook
     By Roderigo.

Othello. O villain!

Cassio.   Most heathenish and most gross!

310 *Lodovico.* Now here's another discontented paper
     Found in his pocket too; and this, it seems,
     Roderigo meant t' have sent this damnèd villain;
     But that, belike, Iago in the interim
     Came in and satisfied him.

Othello.   O thou pernicious caitiff!
315 How came you, Cassio, by that handkerchief
     That was my wife's?

Cassio.   I found it in my chamber;
     And he himself confessed it but even now
     That there he dropped it for a special purpose
     Which wrought to his desire.

Othello.   O fool! Fool! Fool!

320 *Cassio.* There is besides in Roderigo's letter,
     How he upbraids Iago that he made him
     Brave me upon the watch; whereon it came
     That I was cast; and even but now he spake,
     After long seeming dead—Iago hurt him,
325 Iago set him on.

Lodovico. You must forsake this room and go with
     us.
     Your power and your command is taken off,
     And Cassio rules in Cyprus. For this slave,

If there be any cunning cruelty
That can torment him much and hold him long,   830
It shall be his. You shall close prisoner rest
Till that the nature of your fault be known
To the Venetian state. Come, bring away.

Othello. Soft you, a word or two before you go.
I have done the state some service, and they know't.   835
No more of that. I pray you, in your letters,
When you shall these unlucky deeds relate,
Speak of me as I am. Nothing extenuate,
Nor set down aught in malice. Then must you speak
Of one that loved not wisely, but too well;   840
Of one not easily jealous, but, being wrought,
Perplexed in the extreme; of one whose hand,
Like the base Judean,° threw a pearl away
Richer than all his tribe; of one whose subdued
    eyes,
Albeit unusèd to the melting mood,   845
Drops tears as fast as the Arabian trees
Their med'cinable gum. Set you down this.
And say besides that in Aleppo once,
Where a malignant and a turbaned Turk
Beat a Venetian and traduced the state,   850
I took by th' throat the circumcisèd dog
And smote him—thus.   [*He stabs himself.*]

Lodovico. O bloody period!°

Gratiano.   All that is spoke is marred.

Othello. I kissed thee ere I killed thee. No way but this,
Killing myself, to die upon a kiss.   855
                    [*He falls over Desdemona and dies.*]

Cassio. This did I fear, but thought he had no weapon;
For he was great of heart.

Lodovico.   [*To Iago*] O Spartan dog,
More fell° than anguish, hunger, or the sea!

---

843 *Judean* (most editors use the Q1 reading, "Indian," here, but F is
clear; both readings point toward the infidel, the unbeliever)   **353** *period*
end   **358** *fell* cruel

Look on the tragic loading of this bed.
860　This is thy work. The object poisons sight;
Let it be hid.   [*Bed curtains drawn.*]
　　　　　　Gratiano, keep° the house,
And seize upon the fortunes of the Moor,
For they succeed on you. To you, lord governor,
Remains the censure of this hellish villain,
865　The time, the place, the torture. O, enforce it!
Myself will straight aboard, and to the state
This heavy act with heavy heart relate.   *Exeunt.*

FINIS

861 *keep* remain in

Textual Note

Othello contains some of the most difficult editorial problems of any Shakespearean play. The play was entered in *The Stationer's Register* on 6 October, 1621, and printed in a quarto edition, Q1, by Thomas Walkley in 1622, some eighteen or nineteen years after it was first staged. More curiously, at the time that Walkley printed his quarto edition, the plans for printing the folio edition of Shakespeare's collected works were completed and printing was well along. The Folio, F, appeared in late 1623, and the text of *Othello* included in it differs considerably from Q1. A second quarto, Q2, was printed from F in 1630. The chief differences between the two major texts, Q1 and F, are: (1) There are 160 lines in F that are not in Q1; some of these omissions affect the sense in Q1, but others seem to be either intentional cuts in Q1 or additions in F. (2) There are a number of oaths in Q1 that are not in F; this fact can be interpreted in a number of ways, but all arguments go back to the prohibition in 1606 of swearing on stage—but apparently not in printed editions. (3) The stage directions in Q1 are much fuller than in F. (4) There are a large number of variant readings in the two texts, in single words, in phrases, and in lineation; where Q1, for example, reads "toged" (i.e., wearing a toga), F reads "tongued"; where Q1 reads "Worships," F reads "Moorships."

These may seem petty problems, but they present an editor with a series of most difficult questions about what to print at any given point where the two texts are in disagreement. The usual solution in the past has been for the editor to include all material in F and Q1, and where the two texts are in disagreement to select the reading he prefers. The result is what is known as an eclectic text. But modern bibliographical studies have demonstrated that it is possible to proceed, in some cases at least, in a more precise manner by examining the conflicting texts carefully in order to arrive at something like a reasonable judgment about their relative authority. Shakespearean bibliography has become a most elaborate affair, however, and in most cases it has become necessary to take the word of specialists on these matters. Unfortunately, in the case of *Othello* the experts are not in agreement, and none of their arguments has the ring of certainty. Here is, however, the most general opinion of how the two different texts came into being and how they are related.

After Shakespeare wrote the play, his original draft, usually termed "foul papers," was copied, around 1604, by a scribe and made into what is known as the "promptbook," the official copy of the play used in the theater as the basis for production. This promptbook was the property of the players' company, the King's Men in this case, and remained in their possession to be used, and perhaps revised, whenever they produced *Othello*. Being a repertory company they would present a play for a few performances, then drop it for a time, and then present it again when conditions seemed favorable. At some time around 1620, another copy was made of the original foul papers, or some later copy of them, and this served as the basis for the 1622 Quarto. Later, when the publishers of the Folio got around to printing *Othello*, they took a copy of Q1 and corrected it by the original promptbook, and this corrected copy was then given to the compositors who were setting type for F. There are genuine objections to this theory, the most telling raised by the most recent editor of the play, M. R. Ridley, in *The Arden Shakespeare* edition of *Othello;* but the theory does explain certain difficult facts, and most bibliographers seem to accept some version of it.

The end of this line of argument is to establish fairly

reasonably the authority of the F text as being the closest either to what Shakespeare wrote originally or to the play as he finally left it after playhouse revisions. This agrees with what most scholars find in reading the two texts. Sir Walter Greg puts this common belief in the superiority of F in the strongest terms: "In the great majority of cases there can be no doubt that F has preserved the more Shakespearean reading." (*The Shakespeare First Folio,* Oxford, 1955, p. 365.) For practical purposes what this means is that where an F reading makes sense, then an editor has no choice but to accept it—even though he "likes" the Q reading better and would have used it if he had *written,* instead of only edited, the play. But while an editor may be aided and comforted by the bibliographers' decision that F is more authoritative than Q1, his problems are by no means solved. There are places where F does not make sense but Q1 does, places where F is deficient in some way and Q is clear and complete, and places where both fail to make sense or seem to point to a common failure to transcribe correctly their original. When this occurs an editor must try to understand how the trouble occurred and then fall back on his judgment. This will force him to try to reconstruct the original manuscript from which we are told Q and F both derive, and he must attempt to deduce the original reading which both scribes mangled or which the typesetters in the different printing houses misread or made a mistake in setting.

This editorial process is endlessly complicated, but the general basis of this edition is as follows: F is taken for the copy text and its readings are preserved wherever they make sense. Oaths and stage directions are, however, taken from Q1, since they were presumably part of the original manuscript, but were deleted by the promptbook transcriber to comply with the prohibition against swearing on stage and because the prompt copy did not require such elaborate stage directions as a reading version—somewhat contrary to common sense, this last, but the bibliographers insist upon it. Where mislineation occurs in F, but Q1 has it correctly, the Q1 lineation is used on the theory that it has a better chance of being the original than any hypothetical reconstruction of my own. Finally, where F and Q1 both produce nonsense, changes, based on the above theory about the transmission of the text and on the work of previous editors, have been made.

Where F is deficient, the reading adopted and printed in this text is given below first in italics; unless otherwise stated it is taken from Q1. The original F reading that has been changed follows in roman. Obvious typographical errors in F, expansions of abbreviations, spelling variants ("murder," "murther"), and changes in punctuation and lineation are not noted. The act and scene divisions are translated from Latin, and the division at II.iii is from the Globe edition rather than from F; otherwise the divisions of F and the Globe edition are identical. "The Names of the Actors," here printed at the beginning of the play, in F follows the play.

I.i.1 *Tush! Never* Never 4 *'Sblood, but* But 26 *other* others 27 *Christian* Christen'd 30 *God bless* blesse 63 *full* fall *thicklips* Thicks-lips 83 *Zounds, sir* Sir 105 *Zounds, sir* Sir 111 *germans* Germaines 143 *produced* producted 151 *hell pains* (emendation) hell apines [hells paines Q1]

I.ii.33 *Duke* Dukes 37 *Even* enen 49 *carack* (emendation) Carract [Carrick Q1] 50 *he's made* he' made 57 *Come* Cme 67 *darlings* Deareling 74 *weaken* weakens 83 *Whither* Whether 86 *if I do* if do

I.iii.53 *nor* hor 74 *your* yonr 99 *maimed* main'd 106 *Duke* [F omits] 107 *overt test* oer Test 110 *First Senator* Sen. 122 *till* tell 138 *travel's* trauellours 140 *rocks, and hills* Rocks, Hills *heads* head 142 *other* others 146 *thence* hence 154 *intentively* instinctively 203 *preserved* presern'd 227 *couch* (emendation) Coach [Cooch Q1] 229 *alacrity* Alacartie 259 *me* my [F and Q1] 273 *First Senator* Sen. 286 *First Senator* Sen. 321–22 *balance* braine 328 *scion* (emendation) Seyen [seyen Q1] 376 *snipe* snpe 379 *H'as* She ha's

II.i.9 *mortise* (emendation) morties [morties Q1] 33 *prays* praye 40 *Third Gentleman* Gent. 53 *First Gentleman* Gent. 56 *Second Gentleman* Gent. 59 *Second Gentleman* Gent. 65 *ingener* Ingeniuer 66 *Second Gentleman* Gent. 94 *Second Gentleman* Gent. 168 *gyve* (emendation) giue [catch Q1] 173 *an* and 175 *clyster* cluster 212 *hither* thither 242 *has* he's 261 *mutualities* mutabilities 299 *wife* wist 307 *nightcap* Night-Cape

II.iii.39 *unfortunate* infortunate 57 *to put* put to 61 *God*
heauen 72 *God* Heauen 77 *Englishman* Englishmen 93 *thine*
thy 95 *'Fore God* Why 99 *God's* heaven's 108 *God forgive* For-
giue 141 *Within . . . help* [F omits; Q1 reads "Helpe, helpe,
within"] 142 *Zounds, you* You 156 *God's will* Alas 160 *God's
will* Fie, fie 162 *Zounds, I* I 217 *leagued* (emendation) [league
F and Q1] 260 *God* Heauen 274 *to* ro 288 *O God* Oh
343 *were 't* were to 362 *enmesh* en-mash 378 *By the mass* In
troth

III.i.1s.d. [F includes the Clown] 20 *Exeunt Musicians* Exit Mu.
25 *general's wife* Generall 30 *Cassio* [no speech ascription in F]

III.ii.6 *We'll* Well

III.iii.74 *By'r Lady* Trust me 94 *you* he 106 *By heaven* Alas
135 *free to* free 136 *vile* vild 139 *But some* Wherein 148 *Shape*
(emendation) Shapes 162 *By heaven I'll* Ile 170 *fondly* (emendation) soundly [strongly Q1] 175 *God* heauen 182 *exsufflicate*
(emendation) exufflicate (F and Q1) *blown* blowd 217 *my* your
222 *vile* vilde 248 *hold him* him 258 *qualities* Quantities
259 *human* humane 281 *to* too 335 *of* in 347 *make* makes
372 *b' wi'* buy 392 *supervisor* supervision 437 *that was* (Malone's
emendation) it was [F and Q1]

III.iv.77 *God* Heauen 81 *Heaven* Blesse 97 *I'faith* In sooth
170 *I'faith* Indeed 186 *by my faith* in good troth

IV.i.21 *infected* infectious 37 *Zounds, that's* that's 79 *unsuiting*
resulting 103 *conster* conserue 109 *power* dowre 113 *i'faith*
indeed 124 *win* winnes 132 *beckons* becomes 164 *Faith, I* I
218 *God save* Save 248 *an obedient* obedient

IV.ii.16 *requite* requit 30 *Nay* May 48 *kinds* kind 154 *in* [Q2]
or 168 *stay* stays

IV.iii.14 *bade* bid 51 *hie* high

V.i.1 *bulk* Barke 22 *hear* heard 34 *hies* highes 35 *Forth* For
50 *heaven's* heaven 104 *out o' th'* o' th'

V.ii.13 *the rose* thy Rose 35 *say so* say 57 *Then Lord* O Heauen
100 *Should* Did 116 *O Lord* Alas 126 *heard* heare 206 *reprobation* Reprobance 215 *O God! O heavenly God* O Heauen! Oh
heauenly powres 216 *Zounds* Come

The Tragedy of
King Lear

◆

EDITED BY
Russell Fraser

The Tragedy of King Lear

ACT I

Scene I.   [*King Lear's palace.*]

Enter Kent, Gloucester, and Edmund.

Kent. I thought the King had more affected°¹ the Duke
of Albany° than Cornwall.

Gloucester. It did always seem so to us; but now, in
the division of the kingdom, it appears not which
of the dukes he values most, for equalities are so   5
weighed that curiosity in neither can make choice
of either's moiety.°

Kent. Is not this your son, my lord?

Gloucester. His breeding,° sir, hath been at my
charge. I have so often blushed to acknowledge   10
him that now I am brazed° to't.

Kent. I cannot conceive° you.

Gloucester. Sir, this young fellow's mother could;
whereupon she grew round-wombed, and had in-
deed, sir, a son for her cradle ere she had a hus-   15
band for her bed. Do you smell a fault?

---

1 The degree sign (°) indicates a footnote, which is keyed to the text by
line number. Text references are printed in *italic* type; the annotation
follows in roman type.
I.i. 1 *affected* loved   2 *Albany* Albanacte, whose domain extended "from
the river Humber to the point of Caithness" (Holinshed)   5-7 *equalities . . . moiety* i.e., shares are so balanced against one another that
careful examination by neither can make him wish the other's portion
9 *breeding* upbringing   11 *brazed* made brazen, hardened   12 *conceive*
understand (pun follows)

39

Kent. I cannot wish the fault undone, the issue° of it being so proper.°

Gloucester. But I have a son, sir, by order of law,
20 some year elder than this, who yet is no dearer in my account:° though this knave° came something saucily° to the world before he was sent for, yet was his mother fair, there was good sport at his making, and the whoreson° must be acknowl-
25 edged. Do you know this noble gentleman, Edmund?

Edmund. No, my lord.

Gloucester. My Lord of Kent. Remember him hereafter as my honorable friend.

30 *Edmund.* My services to your lordship.

Kent. I must love you, and sue° to know you better.

Edmund. Sir, I shall study deserving.

Gloucester. He hath been out° nine years, and away he shall again. The King is coming.

Sound a sennet.° Enter one bearing a coronet,° then King Lear, then the Dukes of Cornwall and Albany, next Goneril, Regan, Cordelia, and Attendants.

35 *Lear.* Attend the lords of France and Burgundy, Gloucester.

Gloucester. I shall, my lord.   *Exit [with Edmund].*

Lear. Meantime we shall express our darker purpose.°
     Give me the map there. Know that we have divided
40 In three our kingdom; and 'tis our fast° intent
     To shake all cares and business from our age,
     Conferring them on younger strengths, while we

17 *issue* result (child) 18 *proper* handsome 21 *account* estimation
21 *knave* fellow (without disapproval) 22 *saucily* (1) insolently (2) lasciviously 24 *whoreson* fellow (lit., son of a whore) 31 *sue* entreat 33 *out* away, abroad 34 s.d. *sennet* set of notes played on a trumpet, signalizing the entrance or departure of a procession 34 s.d. *coronet* small crown, intended for Cordelia 38 *darker purpose* hidden intention 40 *fast* fixed

Unburthened crawl toward death. Our son of
    Cornwall,
And you our no less loving son of Albany,
We have this hour a constant will to publish°   45
Our daughters' several° dowers, that future strife
May be prevented° now. The Princes, France and
    Burgundy,
Great rivals in our youngest daughter's love,
Long in our court have made their amorous sojourn,
And here are to be answered. Tell me, my daughters   50
(Since now we will divest us both of rule,
Interest° of territory, cares of state),
Which of you shall we say doth love us most,
That we our largest bounty may extend
Where nature doth with merit challenge.° Goneril,   55
Our eldest-born, speak first.

Goneril. Sir, I love you more than word can wield°
    the matter;
Dearer than eyesight, space° and liberty;
Beyond what can be valued, rich or rare;
No less than life, with grace, health, beauty, honor;   60
As much as child e'er loved, or father found;
A love that makes breath° poor, and speech
    unable:
Beyond all manner of so much° I love you.

Cordelia. [*Aside*] What shall Cordelia speak? Love,
    and be silent.

Lear. Of all these bounds, even from this line to this,   65
With shadowy forests, and with champains riched,°
With plenteous rivers, and wide-skirted meads,°
We make thee lady. To thine and Albany's issues°
Be this perpetual.° What says our second daughter,

---

45 *constant will to publish* fixed intention to proclaim   46 *several* separate   47 *prevented* forestalled   52 *Interest* legal right   55 *nature . . .
challenge* i.e., natural affection contends with desert for (or lays claim
to) bounty   57 *wield* handle   58 *space* scope   62 *breath* language
62 *unable* impotent   63 *Beyond . . . much* beyond all these comparisons
66 *champains riched* enriched plains   67 *wide-skirted meads* extensive
grasslands   68 *issues* descendants   69 *perpetual* in perpetuity

70   Our dearest Regan, wife of Cornwall? Speak.

Regan. I am made of that self mettle° as my sister,
    And prize me at her worth.° In my true heart
    I find she names my very deed of love;°
    Only she comes too short, that° I profess
75   Myself an enemy to all other joys
    Which the most precious square of sense
        professes,°
    And find I am alone felicitate°
    In your dear Highness' love.

Cordelia.   [*Aside*] Then poor Cordelia!
    And yet not so, since I am sure my love's
80   More ponderous° than my tongue.

Lear. To thee and thine hereditary ever
    Remain this ample third of our fair kingdom,
    No less in space, validity,° and pleasure
    Than that conferred on Goneril. Now, our joy,
85   Although our last and least;° to whose young love
    The vines of France and milk° of Burgundy
    Strive to be interest;° what can you say to draw
    A third more opulent than your sisters? Speak.

Cordelia. Nothing, my lord.

90   *Lear.* Nothing?

Cordelia. Nothing.

Lear. Nothing will come of nothing. Speak again.

Cordelia. Unhappy that I am, I cannot heave
    My heart into my mouth. I love your Majesty
95   According to my bond,° no more nor less.

Lear. How, how, Cordelia? Mend your speech a little,
    Lest you may mar your fortunes.

---

71 *self mettle* same material or temperament   72 *prize . . . worth* value
me the same (imperative)   73 *my . . . love* what my love really is (a
legalism)   74 *that* in that   76 *Which . . . professes* which the choicest
estimate of sense avows   77 *felicitate* made happy   80 *ponderous* weighty
83 *validity* value   85 *least* youngest, smallest   86 *milk* i.e., pastures
87 *interest* closely connected, as interested parties   95 *bond* i.e., filial
obligation

Cordelia.   Good my lord,
 You have begot me, bred me, loved me. I
 Return those duties back as are right fit,°
 Obey you, love you, and most honor you.   *100*
 Why have my sisters husbands, if they say
 They love you all? Haply,° when I shall wed,
 That lord whose hand must take my plight° shall
   carry
 Half my love with him, half my care and duty.
 Sure I shall never marry like my sisters,   *105*
 To love my father all.

Lear. But goes thy heart with this?

Cordelia.   Ay, my good lord.

Lear. So young, and so untender?

Cordelia. So young, my lord, and true.

Lear. Let it be so, thy truth then be thy dower!   *110*
 For, by the sacred radiance of the sun,
 The mysteries of Hecate° and the night,
 By all the operation of the orbs°
 From whom we do exist and cease to be,
 Here I disclaim all my paternal care,   *115*
 Propinquity and property of blood,°
 And as a stranger to my heart and me
 Hold thee from this for ever. The barbarous
   Scythian,°
 Or he that makes his generation messes°
 To gorge his appetite, shall to my bosom   *120*
 Be as well neighbored, pitied, and relieved,
 As thou my sometime° daughter.

Kent.   Good my liege——

Lear. Peace, Kent!

---

⁹⁹ *Return . . . fit* i.e., am correspondingly dutiful   ¹⁰² *Haply* perhaps
¹⁰³ *plight* troth plight   ¹¹² *mysteries of Hecate* secret rites of Hecate
(goddess of the infernal world, and of witchcraft)   ¹¹³ *operation of
the orbs* astrological influence   ¹¹⁶ *Propinquity and property of blood*
relationship and common blood   ¹¹⁸ *Scythian* (type of the savage)
¹¹⁹ *makes his generation messes* eats his own offspring   ¹²² *sometime*
former

Come not between the Dragon° and his wrath.
125 I loved her most, and thought to set my rest°
On her kind nursery.° Hence and avoid my sight!
So be my grave my peace, as here I give
Her father's heart from her! Call France. Who stirs?
Call Burgundy. Cornwall and Albany,
130 With my two daughters' dowers digest° the third;
Let pride, which she calls plainness, marry her.°
I do invest you jointly with my power,
Pre-eminence, and all the large effects
That troop with majesty.° Ourself,° by monthly
            course,
135 With reservation° of an hundred knights,
By you to be sustained, shall our abode
Make with you by due turn. Only we shall retain
The name, and all th' addition° to a king. The sway,
Revènue, execution of the rest,
140 Belovèd sons, be yours; which to confirm,
This coronet° part between you.

Kent.   Royal Lear,
Whom I have ever honored as my king,
Loved as my father, as my master followed,
As my great patron thought on in my prayers——

Lear. The bow is bent and drawn; make from the
145   shaft.°

Kent. Let it fall° rather, though the fork° invade
The region of my heart. Be Kent unmannerly
When Lear is mad. What wouldst thou do, old
            man?
Think'st thou that duty shall have dread to speak

---

124 *Dragon* (1) heraldic device of Britain (2) emblem of ferocity
125 *set my rest* (1) stake my all (a term from the card game of primero)
(2) find my rest   126 *nursery* care, nursing   130 *digest* absorb
131 *Let . . . her* i.e., let her pride be her dowry and gain her a husband   133–34 *effects/That troop with majesty* accompaniments that go with
kingship   134 *Ourself* (the royal "we")   135 *reservation* the action of
reserving a privilege (a legalism)   138 *addition* titles and honors   141 *coronet* (the crown which was to have been Cordelia's)   145 *make from
the shaft* avoid the arrow   146 *fall* strike   146 *fork* forked head of the
arrow

When power to flattery bows? To plainness honor's
   bound   *150*
When majesty falls to folly. Reserve thy state,°
And in thy best consideration° check
This hideous rashness. Answer my life my
   judgment,°
Thy youngest daughter does not love thee least,
Nor are those empty-hearted whose low sounds   *155*
Reverb° no hollowness.°

Lear.   Kent, on thy life, no more!

Kent. My life I never held but as a pawn°
   To wage° against thine enemies; nor fear to lose it,
   Thy safety being motive.°

Lear.   Out of my sight!

Kent. See better, Lear, and let me still° remain   *160*
   The true blank° of thine eye.

Lear. Now by Apollo——

Kent.   Now by Apollo, King,
   Thou swear'st thy gods in vain.

Lear.   O vassal! Miscreant!°
                     [*Laying his hand on his sword.*]

Albany, Cornwall. Dear sir, forbear!

Kent. Kill thy physician, and the fee bestow   *165*
   Upon the foul disease. Revoke thy gift,
   Or, whilst I can vent clamor° from my throat,
   I'll tell thee thou dost evil.

Lear.   Hear me, recreant!°
   On thine allegiance,° hear me!
   That thou hast sought to make us break our vows,   *170*

---

151 *Reserve thy state* retain your kingly authority   152 *best consideration* most careful reflection   153 *Answer . . . judgment* I will stake my
life on my opinion   156 *Reverb* reverberate   156 *hollowness* (1) empti-
ness (2) insincerity   157 *pawn* stake in a wager   158 *wage* (1) wager
(2) carry on war   159 *motive* moving cause   160 *still* always   161 *blank*
the white spot in the center of the target (at which Lear should aim)
163 *vassal! Miscreant!* base wretch! Misbeliever!   167 *vent clamor* utter
a cry   168 *recreant* traitor   169 *On thine allegiance* (to forswear, which
is to commit high treason)

Which we durst never yet, and with strained° pride
To come betwixt our sentence° and our power,
Which nor our nature nor our place can bear,
Our potency made good,° take thy reward.
175   Five days we do allot thee for provision°
To shield thee from diseases° of the world,
And on the sixth to turn thy hated back
Upon our kingdom. If, on the tenth day following,
Thy banished trunk° be found in our dominions,
180   The moment is thy death. Away! By Jupiter,
This shall not be revoked.

Kent. Fare thee well, King. Sith° thus thou wilt appear,
Freedom lives hence, and banishment is here.
[*To Cordelia*] The gods to their dear shelter take
thee, maid,
185   That justly think'st, and hast most rightly said.
[*To Regan and Goneril*] And your large speeches
may your deeds approve,°
That good effects° may spring from words of love.
Thus Kent, O Princes, bids you all adieu;
He'll shape his old course° in a country new.   *Exit.*

*Flourish.° Enter Gloucester, with France and
Burgundy; Attendants.*

190   *Gloucester.* Here's France and Burgundy, my noble
lord.

Lear. My Lord of Burgundy,
We first address toward you, who with this king
Hath rivaled for our daughter. What in the least
Will you require in present° dower with her,
Or cease your quest of love?

195   *Burgundy.*   Most royal Majesty,
I crave no more than hath your Highness offered,

---

171 *strained* forced (and so excessive)   172 *sentence* judgment, decree
174 *Our potency made good* my royal authority being now asserted
175 *for provision* for making preparation   176 *diseases* troubles
179 *trunk* body   182 *Sith* since   186*approve* prove true   187 *effects* results
189 *shape . . . course* pursue his customary way   189 s.d. *Flourish* trumpet
fanfare   194 *present* immediate

Nor will you tender° less.

Lear.   Right noble Burgundy,
When she was dear° to us, we did hold her so;
But now her price is fallen. Sir, there she stands.
If aught within that little seeming substance,°   200
Or all of it, with our displeasure pieced,°
And nothing more, may fitly like° your Grace,
She's there, and she is yours.

Burgundy.   I know no answer.

Lear. Will you, with those infirmities she owes,°
Unfriended, new adopted to our hate,   205
Dow'red with our curse, and strangered° with our
    oath,
Take her, or leave her?

Burgundy.   Pardon me, royal sir.
Election makes not up° on such conditions.

Lear. Then leave her, sir; for, by the pow'r that made
    me,
I tell you all her wealth. [*To France.*] For you,
    great King,   210
I would not from your love make such a stray
To° match you where I hate; therefore beseech°
    you
T' avert your liking a more worthier way°
Than on a wretch whom nature is ashamed
Almost t' acknowledge hers.

France.   This is most strange,   215
That she whom even but now was your best object,°
The argument° of your praise, balm of your age,
The best, the dearest, should in this trice of time
Commit a thing so monstrous to dismantle°

---

197 *tender* offer   198 *dear* (1) beloved (2) valued at a high price
200 *little seeming substance* person who is (1) inconsiderable (2) out-
spoken   201 *pieced* added to it   202 *fitly like* please by its fitness
204 *owes* possesses   206 *strangered* made a stranger   208 *Election makes
not up* no one can choose   211-12 *make such a stray/To* stray so far as to
212 *beseech* I beseech   213 *avert . . . way* turn your affections from her
and bestow them on a better person   216 *best object* i.e., the one you
loved most   217 *argument* subject   219 *dismantle* strip off

220   So many folds of favor. Sure her offense
        Must be of such unnatural degree
        That monsters it,° or your fore-vouched° affection
        Fall into taint;° which to believe of her
        Must be a faith that reason without miracle
        Should never plant in me.°

225 *Cordelia.*   I yet beseech your Majesty,
        If for° I want that glib and oily art
        To speak and purpose not,° since what I well intend
        I'll do't before I speak, that you make known
        It is no vicious blot, murder, or foulness,
230   No unchaste action or dishonored step,
        That hath deprived me of your grace and favor;
        But even for want of that for which I am richer,
        A still-soliciting° eye, and such a tongue
        That I am glad I have not, though not to have it
        Hath lost° me in your liking.

235 *Lear.*   Better thou
        Hadst not been born than not t' have pleased me
           better.

France. Is it but this? A tardiness in nature°
        Which often leaves the history unspoke°
        That it intends to do. My Lord of Burgundy,
240   What say you° to the lady? Love's not love
        When it is mingled with regards° that stands
        Aloof from th' entire point.° Will you have her?
        She is herself a dowry.

Burgundy.   Royal King,
        Give but that portion which yourself proposed,
245   And here I take Cordelia by the hand,
        Duchess of Burgundy.

222 *That monsters it* as makes it monstrous, unnatural   222 *fore-vouched* previously sworn   223 *Fall into taint* must be taken as having been unjustified all along i.e., Cordelia was unworthy of your love from the first   224-25 *reason . . . me* my reason would have to be supported by a miracle to make me believe   226 *for* because   227 *purpose not* not mean to do what I promise   233 *still-soliciting* always begging   235 *lost* ruined   237 *tardiness in nature* natural reticence   238 *leaves the history unspoke* does not announce the action   240 *What say you* i.e., will you have   241 *regards* considerations (the dowry)   241-42 *stands . . . point* have nothing to do with the essential question (love)

Lear. Nothing. I have sworn. I am firm.

Burgundy. I am sorry then you have so lost a father
    That you must lose a husband.

Cordelia.   Peace be with Burgundy.
    Since that respects of fortune° are his love,   250
    I shall not be his wife.

France. Fairest Cordelia, that art most rich being
        poor,
    Most choice forsaken, and most loved despised,
    Thee and thy virtues here I seize upon.
    Be it lawful I take up what's cast away.   255
    Gods, gods! 'Tis strange that from their cold'st
        neglect
    My love should kindle to inflamed respect.°
    Thy dow'rless daughter, King, thrown to my
        chance,°
    Is Queen of us, of ours, and our fair France.
    Not all the dukes of wat'rish° Burgundy   260
    Can buy this unprized precious° maid of me.
    Bid them farewell, Cordelia, though unkind.
    Thou losest here, a better where° to find.

Lear. Thou hast her, France; let her be thine, for we
    Have no such daughter, nor shall ever see   265
    That face of hers again. Therefore be gone,
    Without our grace, our love, our benison.°
    Come, noble Burgundy.

    *Flourish. Exeunt [Lear, Burgundy, Cornwall,
        Albany, Gloucester, and Attendants].*

France. Bid farewell to your sisters.

Cordelia. The jewels of our father,° with washed°
    eyes   270
    Cordelia leaves you. I know you what you are,

---

250 *respects of fortune* mercenary considerations   257 *inflamed respect*
more ardent affection   258 *chance* lot   260 *wat'rish* (1) with many
rivers (2) weak, diluted   261 *unprized precious* unappreciated by others, and yet precious   263 *here . . . where* in this place, in another
place   267 *benison* blessing   270 *The jewels of our father* you creatures
prized by our father   270 *washed* (1) weeping (2) clear-sighted

And, like a sister,° am most loath to call
Your faults as they are named.° Love well our
    father.
To your professèd° bosoms I commit him.
275 But yet, alas, stood I within his grace,
I would prefer° him to a better place.
So farewell to you both.

Regan. Prescribe not us our duty.

Goneril.   Let your study
Be to content your lord, who hath received you
280 At Fortune's alms.° You have obedience scanted,°
And well are worth the want that you have wanted.°

Cordelia. Time shall unfold what plighted° cunning
    hides,
Who covers faults, at last shame them derides.°
Well may you prosper.

France.   Come, my fair Cordelia.
                    Exit France and Cordelia.

285 *Goneril.* Sister, it is not little I have to say of what
    most nearly appertains to us both. I think our
    father will hence tonight.

Regan. That's most certain, and with you; next month
    with us.

290 *Goneril.* You see how full of changes his age is. The
    observation we have made of it hath not been lit-
    tle. He always loved our sister most, and with
    what poor judgment he hath now cast her off ap-
    pears too grossly.°

295 *Regan.* 'Tis the infirmity of his age; yet he hath ever
    but slenderly known himself.

---

272 *like a sister* because I am a sister i.e., loyal, affectionate 273 *as they are named* i.e., by their right and ugly names 274 *professèd* pretending to love 276 *prefer* recommend 280 *At Fortune's alms* as a charitable bequest from Fortune (and so, by extension, as one beggared or cast down by Fortune) 280 *scanted* stinted 281 *worth . . . wanted* deserve to be denied, even as you have denied 282 *plighted* pleated, enfolded 283 *Who . . . derides* those who hide their evil are finally exposed and shamed ("He that hideth his sins, shall not prosper") 294 *grossly* obviously

Goneril. The best and soundest of his time° hath
been but rash; then must we look from his age to
receive not alone the imperfections of long-in-
grafted° condition,° but therewithal° the unruly   300
waywardness that infirm and choleric years bring
with them.

Regan. Such unconstant starts° are we like to have
from him as this of Kent's banishment.

Goneril. There is further compliment° of leave-taking   305
between France and him. Pray you, let's hit° to-
gether; if our father carry authority with such disposition as he bears,° this last surrender° of his
will but offend° us.

Regan. We shall further think of it.   310

Goneril. We must do something, and i' th' heat.°

                              Exeunt.

Scene II.   [*The Earl of Gloucester's castle.*]

Enter Edmund [with a letter].

Edmund. Thou, Nature,° art my goddess; to thy law
My services are bound. Wherefore should I
Stand in the plague of custom,° and permit
The curiosity° of nations to deprive me,
For that° I am some twelve or fourteen
   moonshines °   5

---

²⁹⁷ *of his time* period of his life up to now   ²⁹⁹⁻³⁰⁰ *long-ingrafted* im-
planted for a long time   ³⁰⁰ *condition* disposition   ³⁰⁰ *therewithal*
with them   ³⁰³ *unconstant starts* impulsive whims   ³⁰⁵ *compliment*
formal courtesy   ³⁰⁶ *hit* agree   ³⁰⁷⁻⁸ *carry . . . bears* continues, and
in such frame of mind, to wield the sovereign power   ³⁰⁸ *last surrender* recent abdication   ³⁰⁹ *offend* vex   ³¹¹ *i' th' heat* while the iron is
hot   I.ii.   ¹ *Nature* (Edmund's conception of Nature accords with our
description of a bastard as a natural child)   ³ *Stand . . . custom*
respect hateful convention   ⁴ *curiosity* nice distinctions   ⁵ *For that*
because   ⁵ *moonshines* months

Lag of° a brother? Why bastard? Wherefore base?
When my dimensions are as well compact,°
My mind as generous,° and my shape as true,
As honest° madam's issue? Why brand they us
10   With base? With baseness? Bastardy? Base? Base?
Who, in the lusty stealth of nature, take
More composition° and fierce° quality
Than doth, within a dull, stale, tired bed,
Go to th' creating a whole tribe of fops°
15   Got° 'tween asleep and wake? Well then,
Legitimate Edgar, I must have your land.
Our father's love is to the bastard Edmund
As to th' legitimate. Fine word, "legitimate."
Well, my legitimate, if this letter speed,°
20   And my invention° thrive, Edmund the base
Shall top th' legitimate. I grow, I prosper.
Now, gods, stand up for bastards.

Enter Gloucester.

Gloucester. Kent banished thus? and France in choler
          parted?
          And the King gone tonight? prescribed° his pow'r?
25   Confined to exhibition?° All this done
          Upon the gad?° Edmund, how now? What news?

Edmund. So please your lordship, none.

Gloucester. Why so earnestly seek you to put up°
          that letter?

30   *Edmund.* I know no news, my lord.

Gloucester. What paper were you reading?

Edmund. Nothing, my lord.

Gloucester. No? What needed then that terrible dis-
          patch° of it into your pocket? The quality of noth-

---

6 *Lag of* short of being (in age)   7 *compact* framed   8 *generous* gallant   9 *honest* chaste   12 *composition* completeness   12 *fierce* energetic
14 *fops* fools   15 *Got* begot   19 *speed* prosper   20 *invention* plan
24 *prescribed* limited   25 *exhibition* an allowance or pension   26 *Upon
the gad* on the spur of the moment (as if pricked by a gad or goad)
28 *put up* put away, conceal   33-34 *terrible dispatch* hasty putting away

ing hath not such need to hide itself. Let's see. 35
Come, if it be nothing, I shall not need spectacles.

Edmund. I beseech you, sir, pardon me. It is a letter
from my brother that I have not all o'er-read; and
for so much as I have perused, I find it not fit
for your o'erlooking.° 40

Gloucester. Give me the letter, sir.

Edmund. I shall offend, either to detain or give it.
The contents, as in part I understand them, are
to blame.°

Gloucester. Let's see, let's see. 45

Edmund. I hope, for my brother's justification, he
wrote this but as an essay or taste° of my virtue.

Gloucester. (*Reads*) "This policy and reverence° of
age makes the world bitter to the best of our
times;° keeps our fortunes from us till our oldness 50
cannot relish° them. I begin to find an idle and
fond° bondage in the oppression of aged tyranny,
who sways, not as it hath power, but as it is suffered.° Come to me, that of this I may speak more.
If our father would sleep till I waked him, you 55
should enjoy half his revenue° for ever, and live
the beloved of your brother,   EDGAR."
Hum! Conspiracy? "Sleep till I waked him, you
should enjoy half his revenue." My son Edgar! Had
he a hand to write this? A heart and brain to 60
breed it in? When came you to this? Who brought
it?

Edmund. It was not brought me, my lord; there's the
cunning of it. I found it thrown in at the casement of my closet.° 65

---

40 *o'erlooking* inspection 44 *to blame* blameworthy 47 *essay or taste*
test 48 *policy and reverence* policy of reverencing (hendiadys)
49-50 *best of our times* best years of our lives (i.e., our youth) 51 *relish*
enjoy 51-52 *idle and fond* foolish 53-54 *who . . . suffered* which rules,
not from its own strength, but from our allowance 56 *revenue* income
64-65 *casement of my closet* window of my room

Gloucester. You know the character° to be your brother's?

Edmund. If the matter were good, my lord, I durst swear it were his; but in respect of that,° I would
70   fain° think it were not.

Gloucester. It is his.

Edmund. It is his hand, my lord; but I hope his heart is not in the contents.

Gloucester. Has he never before sounded° you in this
75   business?

Edmund. Never, my lord. But I have heard him oft maintain it to be fit that, sons at perfect° age, and fathers declined, the father should be as ward to the son, and the son manage his revenue.

80 *Gloucester.* O villain, villain! His very opinion in the letter. Abhorred villain, unnatural, detested,° brutish villain; worse than brutish! Go, sirrah,° seek him. I'll apprehend him. Abominable villain! Where is he?

85 *Edmund.* I do not well know, my lord. If it shall please you to suspend your indignation against my brother till you can derive from him better testimony of his intent, you should run a certain course;° where, if you violently proceed against
90   him, mistaking his purpose, it would make a great gap° in your own honor and shake in pieces the heart of his obedience. I dare pawn down° my life for him that he hath writ this to feel° my affection to your honor, and to no other pretense of
95   danger.°

Gloucester. Think you so?

---

66 *character* handwriting   69 *in respect of that* in view of what it is
70 *fain* prefer to   74 *sounded* sounded you out   77 *perfect* mature
81 *detested* detestable   82 *sirrah* sir (familiar form of address)   88-89 *run a certain course* i.e., proceed safely, know where you are going   91 *gap* breach   92 *pawn down* stake   93 *feel* test   94-95 *pretense of danger* dangerous purpose

Edmund. If your honor judge it meet,° I will place
   you where you shall hear us confer of this, and
   by an auricular assurance° have your satisfaction,
   and that without any further delay than this very   *100*
   evening.

Gloucester. He cannot be such a monster.

Edmund. Nor is not, sure.

Gloucester. To his father, that so tenderly and entirely loves him. Heaven and earth! Edmund, seek   *105*
   him out; wind me into him,° I pray you; frame°
   the business after your own wisdom. I would unstate myself to be in a due resolution.°

Edmund. I will seek him, sir, presently;° convey° the
   business as I shall find means, and acquaint you   *110*
   withal.°

Gloucester. These late° eclipses in the sun and moon
   portend no good to us. Though the wisdom of Na-
   ture° can reason° it thus and thus, yet Nature
   finds itself scourged by the sequent effects.° Love   *115*
   cools, friendship falls off,° brothers divide. In
   cities, mutinies;° in countries, discord; in palaces,
   treason; and the bond cracked 'twixt son and
   father. This villain of mine comes under the prediction,° there's son against father; the King falls   *120*
   from bias of nature,° there's father against child.
   We have seen the best of our time.° Machinations,
   hollowness,° treachery, and all ruinous disorders
   follow us disquietly° to our graves. Find out this

---

⁹⁷ *meet* fit   ⁹⁹ *auricular assurance* proof heard with your own ears
¹⁰⁶ *wind me into him* insinuate yourself into his confidence for me
¹⁰⁶ *frame* manage   ¹⁰⁷⁻⁰⁸ *unstate . . . resolution* forfeit. my earldom
to know the truth   ¹⁰⁹ *presently* at once   ¹⁰⁹ *convey* manage   ¹¹¹ *withal*
with it   ¹¹² *late* recent   ¹¹³⁻¹⁴ *wisdom of Nature* scientific learning   ¹¹⁴ *reason* explain   ¹¹⁴⁻¹⁵ *yet . . . effects* nonetheless our world
is punished with subsequent disasters   ¹¹⁶ *falls off* revolts   ¹¹⁷ *mutinies*
riots   ¹¹⁹⁻²⁰ *This . . . prediction* i.e., my son's villainous behavior is
included in these portents, and bears them out   ¹²¹ *bias of nature*
natural inclination (the metaphor is from the game of bowls)   ¹²² *best
of our time* our best days   ¹²³ *hollowness* insincerity   ¹²⁴ *disquietly*
unquietly

125   villain, Edmund; it shall lose thee nothing.° Do it
       carefully. And the noble and true-hearted Kent
       banished; his offense, honesty. 'Tis strange.

                                                    Exit.

       Edmund. This is the excellent foppery° of the world,
       that when we are sick in fortune, often the surfeits
130   of our own behavior,° we make guilty of our dis-
       asters the sun, the moon, and stars; as if we were
       villains on° necessity; fools by heavenly compul-
       sion; knaves, thieves, and treachers by spherical
       predominance;° drunkards, liars, and adulterers by
135   an enforced obedience of planetary influence;° and
       all that we are evil in, by a divine thrusting on.°
       An admirable evasion of whoremaster° man, to
       lay his goatish° disposition on the charge of a
       star. My father compounded° with my mother
140   under the Dragon's Tail,° and my nativity° was
       under Ursa Major,° so that it follows I am rough
       and lecherous. Fut!° I should have been that° I
       am, had the maidenliest star in the firmament twin-
       kled on my bastardizing. Edgar——

                         Enter Edgar.

145   and pat he comes, like the catastrophe° of the old
       comedy. My cue is villainous melancholy, with a
       sigh like Tom o' Bedlam.°—O, these eclipses do
       portend these divisions. Fa, sol, la, mi.°

       Edgar. How now, brother Edmund; what serious con-
150   templation are you in?

125 *it . . . nothing* you will not lose by it   128 *foppery* folly
129-30 *often . . . behavior* often caused by our own excesses   132 *on* of
133-34 *treachers . . . predominance* traitors because of the ascen-
dancy of a particular star at our birth   134-35 *by . . . influence* because
we had to submit to the influence of our star   136 *divine thrusting on*
supernatural compulsion   137 *whoremaster* lecherous   138 *goatish* lascivious   139 *compounded* (1) made terms (2) formed (a child)
140 *Dragon's Tail* the constellation Draco   140 *nativity* birthday
141 *Ursa Major* the Great Bear   142 *Fut!* 's foot (an impatient oath)
142 *that* what   145 *catastrophe* conclusion   146-47 *My . . . Bedlam* I must
be doleful, like a lunatic beggar out of Bethlehem (Bedlam) Hospital, the
London madhouse   148 *Fa, sol, la, mi* (Edmund's humming of the
musical notes is perhaps prompted by his use of the word "division,"
which describes a musical variation)

Edmund. I am thinking, brother, of a prediction I
read this other day, what should follow these
eclipses.

Edgar. Do you busy yourself with that?

Edmund. I promise you, the effects he writes of suc- 155
ceed° unhappily: as of unnaturalness° between the
child and the parent, death, dearth, dissolutions of
ancient amities,° divisions in state, menaces and
maledictions against King and nobles, needless diffidences,° banishment of friends, dissipation of co- 160
horts,° nuptial breaches, and I know not what.

Edgar. How long have you been a sectary astronomical?°

Edmund. Come, come, when saw you my father last?

Edgar. Why, the night gone by. 165

Edmund. Spake you with him?

Edgar. Ay, two hours together.

Edmund. Parted you in good terms? Found you no
displeasure in him by word nor countenance?°

Edgar. None at all. 170

Edmund. Bethink yourself wherein you may have offended him; and at my entreaty forbear his pres-
ence° until some little time hath qualified° the heat
of his displeasure, which at this instant so rageth
in him that with the mischief of your person it 175
would scarcely allay.°

Edgar. Some villain hath done me wrong.

Edmund. That's my fear, brother I pray you have a
continent forbearance° till the speed of his rage
goes slower; and, as I say, retire with me to my 180

155-56 *succeed* follow   157 *unnaturalness* unkindness   158 *amities* friend-
ships   159-60 *diffidences* distrusts   160-61 *dissipation of cohorts* falling
away of supporters   162-63 *sectary astronomical* believer in astrology
169 *countenance* expression   172-73 *forbear his presence* keep away from
him   173 *qualified* lessened   175-76 *with . . . allay* even an injury to you
would not appease his anger   178-79 *have a continent forbearance* be restrained and keep yourself withdrawn

lodging, from whence I will fitly° bring you to hear
my lord speak. Pray ye, go; there's my key. If
you do stir abroad, go armed.

Edgar. Armed, brother?

185 *Edmund.* Brother, I advise you to the best. Go armed.
I am no honest man if there be any good meaning
toward you. I have told you what I have seen and
heard; but faintly, nothing like the image and hor-
ror° of it. Pray you, away.

190 *Edgar.* Shall I hear from you anon?°

Edmund. I do serve you in this business.

Exit Edgar.

A credulous father, and a brother noble,
Whose nature is so far from doing harms
That he suspects none; on whose foolish honesty
195 My practices° ride easy. I see the business.
Let me, if not by birth, have lands by wit.
All with me's meet° that I can fashion fit.° *Exit.*

Scene III. [*The Duke of Albany's palace.*]

Enter Goneril, and [Oswald, her] Steward.

Goneril. Did my father strike my gentleman for chiding of his Fool?°

Oswald. Ay, madam.

Goneril. By day and night he wrongs me. Every hour
5 He flashes into one gross crime° or other

---

181 *fitly* at a fit time 188-89 *image and horror* true horrible picture
190 *anon* in a little while 195 *practices* plots 197 *meet* proper 197 *fashion*
fit shape to my purpose I.iii. 2 *Fool* court jester 5 *crime* offense

That sets us all at odds. I'll not endure it.
His knights grow riotous,° and himself upbraids us
On every trifle. When he returns from hunting,
I will not speak with him. Say I am sick.
If you come slack of former services,°   10
You shall do well; the fault of it I'll answer.°

                                   [*Horns within.*]

Oswald. He's coming, madam; I hear him.

Goneril. Put on what weary negligence you please,
You and your fellows. I'd have it come to question.°
If he distaste° it, let him to my sister,   15
Whose mind and mine I know in that are one,
Not to be overruled. Idle° old man,
That still would manage those authorities
That he hath given away. Now, by my life,
Old fools are babes again, and must be used   20
With checks as flatteries, when they are seen
     abused.°
Remember what I have said.

Oswald.   Well, madam.

Goneril. And let his knights have colder looks among
     you.
What grows of it, no matter; advise your fellows so.
I would breed from hence occasions, and I shall,   25
That I may speak.° I'll write straight° to my sister
To hold my course. Go, prepare for dinner.

                                        Exeunt.

---

7 *riotous* dissolute 10 *come . . . services* are less serviceable to him
than formerly 11 *answer* answer for 14 *come to question* be discussed
openly 15 *distaste* dislike 17 *Idle* foolish 21 *With . . . abused*
with restraints as well as soothing words when they are misguided
25-26 *breed . . . speak* find in this opportunities for speaking out
26 *straight* at once

Scene IV.   [*A hall in the same.*]

Enter Kent [disguised].

Kent. If but as well I other accents borrow
    That can my speech defuse,° my good intent
    May carry through itself to that full issue°
    For which I razed my likeness.° Now, banished
      Kent,
    If thou canst serve where thou dost stand
5   condemned,
    So may it come,° thy master whom thou lov'st
    Shall find thee full of labors.

      *Horns within.° Enter Lear, [Knights] and
        Attendants.*

Lear. Let me not stay° a jot for dinner; go, get it
    ready. [*Exit an Attendant.*] How now, what art
10   thou?

Kent. A man, sir.

Lear. What dost thou profess?° What wouldst thou
    with us?

Kent. I do profess° to be no less than I seem, to
15   serve him truly that will put me in trust, to love
    him that is honest, to converse with him that is
    wise and says little, to fear judgment,° to fight
    when I cannot choose, and to eat no fish.°

I.iv. 2 *defuse* disguise 3 *full issue* perfect result 4 *razed my likeness*
shaved off, disguised my natural appearance 6 *So may it come* so may
it fall out 7 s.d. *within* offstage 8 *stay* wait 12 *What dost thou profess* what do you do 14 *profess* claim 17 *judgment* (by a heavenly or
earthly judge) 18 *eat no fish* i.e., (1) I am no Catholic, but a loyal
Protestant (2) I am no weakling (3) I use no prostitutes

Lear. What art thou?

Kent. A very honest-hearted fellow, and as poor as   20
  the King.

Lear. If thou be'st as poor for a subject as he's for a
  king, thou art poor enough. What wouldst thou?

Kent. Service.

Lear. Who wouldst thou serve?   25

Kent. You.

Lear. Dost thou know me, fellow?

Kent. No, sir, but you have that in your countenance°
  which I would fain° call master.

Lear. What's that?   30

Kent. Authority.

Lear. What services canst thou do?

Kent. I can keep honest counsel,° ride, run, mar a
  curious tale in telling it,° and deliver a plain message bluntly. That which ordinary men are fit for, I   35
  am qualified in, and the best of me is diligence.

Lear. How old art thou?

Kent. Not so young, sir, to love a woman for singing, nor so old to dote on her for anything. I have
  years on my back forty-eight.   40

Lear. Follow me; thou shalt serve me. If I like thee
  no worse after dinner, I will not part from thee
  yet. Dinner, ho, dinner! Where's my knave?° my
  Fool? Go you and call my Fool hither.

　　　　　　　　　　　　　　[Exit an Attendant.]

　　　　　　　Enter Oswald.

You, you, sirrah, where's my daughter?   45

Oswald. So please you——   *Exit.*

---

²⁸ *countenance* bearing ²⁹ *fain* like to ³³ *honest counsel* honorable
secrets ³³⁻³⁴ *mar . . . it* i.e., I cannot speak like an affected courtier
("curious" = "elaborate," as against "plain") ⁴³ *knave* boy

Lear. What says the fellow there? Call the clotpoll°
back. [*Exit a Knight.*] Where's my Fool? Ho, I
think the world's asleep.

[*Re-enter Knight.*]

50 How now? Where's that mongrel?

Knight. He says, my lord, your daughter is not well.

Lear. Why came not the slave back to me when I
called him?

Knight. Sir, he answered me in the roundest° manner,
55 he would not.

Lear. He would not?

Knight. My lord, I know not what the matter is;
but to my judgment your Highness is not enter-
tained° with that ceremonious affection as you
60 were wont. There's a great abatement of kindness
appears as well in the general dependants° as in the
Duke himself also and your daughter.

Lear. Ha? Say'st thou so?

Knight. I beseech you pardon me, my lord, if I be
65 mistaken; for my duty cannot be silent when I
think your Highness wronged.

Lear. Thou but rememb'rest° me of mine own conception.° I have perceived a most faint neglect°
of late, which I have rather blamed as mine own
70 jealous curiosity° than as a very pretense° and
purpose of unkindness. I will look further into't.
But where's my Fool? I have not seen him this two
days.

Knight. Since my young lady's going into France, sir,
75 the Fool hath much pined away.

Lear. No more of that; I have noted it well. Go you

---

47 *clotpoll* clodpoll, blockhead   54 *roundest* rudest   58-59 *entertained*
treated   61 *dependants* servants   67 *rememb'rest* remindest   67-68 *conception* idea   68 *faint neglect* i.e., "weary negligence" (I.iii.13)
69-70 *mine own jealous curiosity* suspicious concern for my own dignity
70 *very pretense* actual intention

and tell my daughter I would speak with her. Go
you, call hither my Fool.   [*Exit an Attendant.*]
                    Enter Oswald.

O, you, sir, you! Come you hither, sir. Who am I,
sir?   80

Oswald. My lady's father.

Lear. "My lady's father"? My lord's knave, you
whoreson dog, you slave, you cur!

Oswald. I am none of these, my lord; I beseech your
pardon.   85

Lear. Do you bandy° looks with me, you rascal?
                                        [*Striking him.*]

Oswald. I'll not be strucken,° my lord.

Kent. Nor tripped neither, you base football° player.
                                  [*Tripping up his heels.*]

Lear. I thank thee, fellow. Thou serv'st me, and I'll
love thee.   90

Kent. Come, sir, arise, away. I'll teach you differences.° Away, away. If you will measure your lubber's° length again, tarry; but away. Go to!° Have
you wisdom?° So.°   [*Pushes Oswald out.*]

Lear. Now, my friendly knave, I thank thee. There's   93
earnest° of thy service.   [*Giving Kent money.*]
                    Enter Fool.

Fool. Let me hire him too. Here's my coxcomb.°
                              [*Offering Kent his cap.*]

Lear. How now, my pretty knave? How dost thou?

Fool. Sirrah, you were best° take my coxcomb.

Kent. Why, Fool?   100

---

86 *bandy* exchange insolently (metaphor from tennis) 87 *strucken*
struck 88 *football* (a low game played by idle boys to the scandal of
sensible men) 91-92 *differences* (of rank) 92-93 *lubber's* lout's 93 *Go
to* (expression of derisive incredulity) 93-94 *Have you wisdom* i.e., do
you know what's good for you 94 *So* good 96 *earnest* money for services rendered 97 *coxcomb* professional fool's cap, shaped like a coxcomb 99 *you were best* you had better

Fool. Why? For taking one's part that's out of favor.
Nay, an° thou canst not smile as the wind sits,°
thou'lt catch cold shortly. There, take my coxcomb.
Why, this fellow has banished° two on's daughters,
105 and did the third a blessing against his will. If thou
follow him, thou must needs wear my coxcomb.
—How now, Nuncle?° Would I had two coxcombs
and two daughters.

Lear. Why, my boy?

110 *Fool.* If I gave them all my living,° I'd keep my coxcombs myself. There's mine; beg another of thy
daughters.

Lear. Take heed, sirrah—the whip.

Fool. Truth's a dog must to kennel; he must be
115 whipped out, when Lady the Brach° may stand by
th' fire and stink.

Lear. A pestilent gall° to me.

Fool. Sirrah, I'll teach thee a speech.

Lear. Do.

120 *Fool.* Mark it, Nuncle.
         Have more than thou showest,
         Speak less than thou knowest,
         Lend less than thou owest,°
         Ride more than thou goest,°
125   Learn more than thou trowest,°
         Set less than thou throwest;°
         Leave thy drink and thy whore,
         And keep in-a-door,
         And thou shalt have more
130   Than two tens to a score.°

Kent. This is nothing, Fool.

---

102 *an* if   102 *smile . . . sits* ingratiate yourself with those in power
104 *banished* alienated (by making them independent)   107 *Nuncle*
(contraction of "mine uncle")   110 *living* property   115 *Brach* bitch
117 *gall* sore   123 *owest* ownest   124 *goest* walkest   125 *trowest* knowest
126 *Set . . . throwest* bet less than you play for (get odds from your
opponent)   129-30 *have . . . score* i.e., come away with more than you
had (two tens, or twenty shillings, make a score, or one pound)

Fool. Then 'tis like the breath of an unfeed° lawyer
—you gave me nothing for't. Can you make no use
of nothing, Nuncle?

Lear. Why, no, boy. Nothing can be made out of   *135*
nothing.

Fool. [*To Kent*] Prithee tell him, so much the
rent of his land comes to; he will not believe a
Fool.

Lear. A bitter° Fool.   *140*

Fool. Dost thou know the difference, my boy, between
a bitter Fool and a sweet one?

Lear. No, lad; teach me.

Fool.

> That lord that counseled thee
> > To give away thy land,   *145*
>
> Come place him here by me,
> > Do thou for him stand.
>
> The sweet and bitter fool
> > Will presently appear;
>
> The one in motley° here,   *150*
> > The other found out° there.°

Lear. Dost thou call me fool, boy?

Fool. All thy other titles thou hast given away; that
thou wast born with.

Kent. This is not altogether fool, my lord.   *155*

Fool. No, faith; lords and great men will not let me.°
If I had a monopoly° out, they would have part
on't. And ladies too, they will not let me have all
the fool to myself; they'll be snatching. Nuncle,
give me an egg, and I'll give thee two crowns.   *160*

---

132 unfeed unpaid for   *140 bitter* satirical   *150 motley* the drab costume
of the professional jester   *151 found out* revealed   *151 there* (the Fool
points at Lear, as a fool in the grain)   *156 let me* (have all the folly to
myself)   *157 monopoly* (James I gave great scandal by granting to his
"snatching" courtiers royal patents to deal exclusively in some com-
modity)

Lear. What two crowns shall they be?

Fool. Why, after I have cut the egg i' th' middle
and eat up the meat, the two crowns of the egg.
When thou clovest thy crown i' th' middle and
165   gav'st away both parts, thou bor'st thine ass on
thy back o'er the dirt.° Thou hadst little wit in thy
bald crown when thou gav'st thy golden one away.
If I speak like myself° in this, let him be whipped°
that first finds it so.
170   [*Singing*] Fools had ne'er less grace in a year,
            For wise men are grown foppish,
        And know not how their wits to wear,
            Their manners are so apish.°

Lear. When were you wont to be so full of songs,
175   sirrah?

Fool. I have used° it, Nuncle, e'er since thou mad'st
thy daughters thy mothers; for when thou gav'st
them the rod, and put'st down thine own breeches,
[*Singing*] Then they for sudden joy did weep,
180   And I for sorrow sung,
        That such a king should play bo-peep°
            And go the fools among.
Prithee, Nuncle, keep a schoolmaster that can teach
thy Fool to lie. I would fain learn to lie.

185   *Lear.* And° you lie, sirrah, we'll have you whipped.

Fool. I marvel what kin thou and thy daughters are.
They'll have me whipped for speaking true; thou'lt
have me whipped for lying; and sometimes I am
whipped for holding my peace. I had rather be any
190   kind o' thing than a Fool, and yet I would not be

165–66 *bor'st . . . dirt* (like the foolish and unnatural countryman in
Aesop's fable) 168 *like myself* like a Fool 168 *let him be whipped* i.e.,
let the man be whipped for a Fool who thinks my true saying to be
foolish 170–73 *Fools . . . apish* i.e., fools were never in less favor than
now, and the reason is that wise men, turning foolish, and not knowing
how to use their intelligence, imitate the professional fools and so make
them unnecessary 176 *used* practiced 181 *play bo-peep* (1) act like a
child (2) blind himself 185 *And* if

thee, Nuncle: thou hast pared thy wit o' both sides
and left nothing i' th' middle. Here comes one o'
the parings.

Enter Goneril.

Lear. How now, daughter? What makes that frontlet°
on? Methinks you are too much of late i' th'   193
frown.

Fool. Thou wast a pretty fellow when thou hadst no
need to care for her frowning. Now thou art an O
without a figure.° I am better than thou art now: I
am a Fool, thou art nothing. [*To Goneril.*] Yes,   200
forsooth, I will hold my tongue. So your face bids
me, though you say nothing. Mum, mum,
     He that keeps nor crust nor crum,°
     Weary of all, shall want° some.

[*Pointing to Lear*] That's a shealed peascod.°   205

Goneril. Not only, sir, this your all-licensed° Fool,
But other° of your insolent retinue
Do hourly carp and quarrel, breaking forth
In rank° and not-to-be-endurèd riots. Sir,
I had thought by making this well known unto you   210
To have found a safe° redress, but now grow
     fearful,
By what yourself too late° have spoke and done,
That you protect this course, and put it on
By your allowance;° which if you should, the fault
Would not 'scape censure, nor the redresses sleep,°   215
Which, in the tender of° a wholesome weal,°
Might in their working do you that offense,
Which else were shame, that then necessity
Will call discreet proceeding.°

194 *frontlet* frown (lit., ornamental band)   199 *figure* digit, to give
value to the cipher (Lear is a nought)   203 *crum* soft bread inside
the loaf   204 *want* lack   205 *shealed peascod* empty pea pod   206 *all-
licensed* privileged to take any liberties   207 *other* others   209 *rank*
gross   211 *safe* sure   212 *too late* lately   213-14 *put . . . allowance*
promote it by your approval   214 *allowance* approval   215 *redresses
sleep* correction fail to follow   216 *tender of* desire for   216 *weal* state
217-19 *Might . . . proceeding* as I apply it, the correction might humili-
iate you; but the need to take action cancels what would otherwise be
unfilial conduct in me

220 *Fool.* For you know, Nuncle,
         The hedge-sparrow fed the cuckoo° so long
         That it had it head bit off by it° young.
      So out went the candle, and we were left darkling.°

Lear. Are you our daughter?

225 *Goneril.* Come, sir,
         I would you would make use of your good wisdom
         Whereof I know you are fraught° and put away
         These dispositions° which of late transport you
         From what you rightly are.

230 *Fool.* May not an ass know when the cart draws the
         horse? Whoop, Jug,° I love thee!

Lear. Does any here know me? This is not Lear.
         Does Lear walk thus? Speak thus? Where are his
            eyes?
         Either his notion° weakens, or his discernings°
235   Are lethargied°—Ha! Waking? 'Tis not so.
         Who is it that can tell me who I am?

Fool. Lear's shadow.

Lear. I would learn that; for, by the marks of sover-
         eignty,° knowledge, and reason, I should be false°
240   persuaded I had daughters.

Fool. Which° they will make an obedient father.

Lear. Your name, fair gentlewoman?

Goneril. This admiration,° sir, is much o' th' savor°
         Of other your° new pranks. I do beseech you
245   To understand my purposes aright.
         As you are old and reverend, should be wise.
         Here do you keep a hundred knights and squires,

---

221 *cuckoo* (who lays its eggs in the nests of other birds)   222 *it* its
223 *darkling* in the dark   227 *fraught* endowed   228 *dispositions* moods
231 *Jug* Joan (? a quotation from a popular song)   234 *notion* understanding   234 *discernings* faculties   235 *lethargied* paralyzed   238-39 *marks
of sovereignty* i.e., tokens that Lear is king, and hence father to his
daughters   239 *false* falsely   241 *Which* whom (Lear)   243 *admiration*
(affected) wonderment   243 *is much o' th' savor* smacks much
244 *other your* others of your

Men so disordered, so deboshed,° and bold,
That this our court, infected with their manners,
Shows° like a riotous inn. Epicurism° and lust   250
Makes it more like a tavern or a brothel
Than a graced° palace. The shame itself doth speak
For instant remedy. Be then desired°
By her, that else will take the thing she begs,
A little to disquantity your train,°   255
And the remainders° that shall still depend,°
To be such men as may besort° your age,
Which know themselves, and you.

Lear.   Darkness and devils!
Saddle my horses; call my train together.
Degenerate° bastard, I'll not trouble thee: 260
Yet have I left a daughter.

Goneril. You strike my people, and your disordered
     rabble
Make servants of their betters.

Enter Albany.

Lear. Woe, that too late repents. O, sir, are you
     come?
Is it your will? Speak, sir. Prepare my horses.   265
Ingratitude! thou marble-hearted fiend,
More hideous when thou show'st thee in a child
Than the sea-monster.

Albany.   Pray, sir, be patient

Lear. Detested kite,° thou liest.
My train are men of choice and rarest parts,°   270
That all particulars of duty know,
And, in the most exact regard,° support
The worships° of their name. O most small fault,

---

²⁴⁸ *deboshed* debauched   ²⁵⁰ *Shows* appears   ²⁵⁰ *Epicurism* riotous living   ²⁵² *graced* dignified   ²⁵³ *desired* requested   ²⁵⁵ *disquantity your train* reduce the number of your dependents   ²⁵⁶ *remainders* those who remain   ²⁵⁶ *depend* attend on you   ²⁵⁷ *besort* befit   ²⁶⁰ *Degenerate* unnatural   ²⁶⁹ *kite* scavenging bird of prey   ²⁷⁰ *parts* accomplishments ²⁷² *exact regard* strict attention to detail   ²⁷³ *worships* honor

How ugly didst thou in Cordelia show!
Which, like an engine,° wrenched my frame of
275   nature
From the fixed place;° drew from my heart all love,
And added to the gall.° O Lear, Lear, Lear!
Beat at this gate that let thy folly in [*Striking
   his head.*]
And thy dear judgment out. Go, go, my people.

280 *Albany.* My lord, I am guiltless, as I am ignorant
Of what hath moved you.

Lear.   It may be so, my lord.
Hear, Nature, hear; dear Goddess, hear:
Suspend thy purpose if thou didst intend
To make this creature fruitful.
285 Into her womb convey sterility,
Dry up in her the organs of increase,°
And from her derogate° body never spring
A babe to honor her. If she must teem,°
Create her child of spleen,° that it may live
290 And be a thwart disnatured° torment to her.
Let it stamp wrinkles in her brow of youth,
With cadent° tears fret° channels in her cheeks,
Turn all her mother's pains and benefits°
To laughter and contempt, that she may feel
295 How sharper than a serpent's tooth it is
To have a thankless child. Away, away!   *Exit.*

Albany. Now, gods that we adore, whereof comes
    this?

Goneril. Never afflict yourself to know the cause,
But let his disposition° have that scope
300 As° dotage gives it.

Enter Lear.

Lear. What, fifty of my followers at a clap?°

---

275 *engine* destructive contrivance 274-76 *wrenched . . . place* i.e.,
disordered my natural self 277 *gall* bitterness 286 *increase* childbearing 287 *derogate* degraded 288 *teem* conceive 289 *spleen* ill humor
290 *thwart disnatured* perverse unnatural 292 *cadent* falling 292 *fret*
wear 293 *benefits* the mother's beneficent care of her child 299 *disposition* mood 300 *As* that 301 *at a clap* at one stroke

Within a fortnight?

Albany.   What's the matter, sir?

Lear. I'll tell thee. [*To Goneril*] Life and death,
    I am ashamed
    That thou hast power to shake my manhood°
      thus!
    That these hot tears, which break from me
      perforce,°   305
    Should make thee worth them. Blasts and fogs
      upon thee!
    Th' untented woundings° of a father's curse
    Pierce every sense about thee! Old fond° eyes,
    Beweep° this cause again, I'll pluck ye out
    And cast you, with the waters that you loose,°   310
    To temper° clay. Yea, is it come to this?
    Ha! Let it be so. I have another daughter,
    Who I am sure is kind and comfortable.°
    When she shall hear this of thee, with her nails
    She'll flay thy wolvish visage. Thou shalt find   315
    That I'll resume the shape° which thou dost think
    I have cast off for ever.
              Exit [*Lear with Kent and Attendants*].

Goneril.   Do you mark that?

Albany. I cannot be so partial, Goneril,
    To the great love I bear you°——

Goneril. Pray you, content. What, Oswald, ho!   320
    [*To the Fool*] You, sir, more knave than fool,
    after your master!

Fool. Nuncle Lear, Nuncle Lear, tarry. Take the Fool°
    with thee.

---

804 *shake my manhood* i.e., with tears   305 *perforce* involuntarily, against my will   307 *untented woundings* wounds too deep to be probed with a tent (a roll of lint)   308 *fond* foolish   309 *Beweep* if you weep over   310 *loose* (1) let loose (2) lose, as of no avail   311 *temper* mix with and soften   313 *comfortable* ready to comfort   316 *shape* i.e., kingly role   318-19 *I cannot . . . you* i.e., even though my love inclines me to you, I must protest   322 *Fool* (1) the Fool himself (2) the epithet or character of "fool"

                A fox, when one has caught her,
325   And such a daughter,
                Should sure to the slaughter,
                If my cap would buy a halter.°
                So the Fool follows after.°   *Exit.*

Goneril. This man hath had good counsel. A hundred
        knights!
330   'Tis politic° and safe to let him keep
        At point° a hundred knights: yes, that on every
                dream,
        Each buzz,° each fancy, each complaint, dislike,
        He may enguard° his dotage with their pow'rs
        And hold our lives in mercy.° Oswald, I say!

Albany. Well, you may fear too far.

335 *Goneril.*   Safer than trust too far.
        Let me still take away the harms I fear,
        Not fear still to be taken.° I know his heart.
        What he hath uttered I have writ my sister.
        If she sustain him and his hundred knights,
        When I have showed th' unfitness——

                        Enter Oswald.
340   How now, Oswald?
        What, have you writ that letter to my sister?

Oswald. Ay, madam.

Goneril. Take you some company,° and away to
        horse.
        Inform her full of my particular° fear,
345   And thereto add such reasons of your own
        As may compact° it more. Get you gone,
        And hasten your return. [*Exit Oswald.*] No, no,
                my lord,
        This milky gentleness and course° of yours,
        Though I condemn not,° yet under pardon,

327-28 *halter, after* pronounced "hauter," "auter"   330 *politic* good
policy   331 *At point* armed   332 *buzz* rumor   333 *enguard* protect
334 *in mercy* at his mercy   337 *Not . . . taken* rather than remain fearful of being overtaken by them   343 *company* escort   344 *particular*
own   346 *compact* strengthen   348 *milky . . . course* mild and gentle
way (hendiadys)   349 *condemn not* condemn it not

You are much more attasked° for want of wisdom   350
   Than praised for harmful mildness.°

Albany. How far your eyes may pierce I cannot tell;
   Striving to better, oft we mar what's well.

Goneril. Nay then——

Albany. Well, well, th' event.°   *Exeunt.* 353

Scene V.   [*Court before the same.*]

Enter Lear, Kent, and Fool.

Lear. Go you before to Gloucester with these letters.
   Acquaint my daughter no further with anything
   you know than comes from her demand out of
   the letter.° If your diligence be not speedy, I shall
   be there afore you.   5

Kent. I will not sleep, my lord, till I have delivered
   your letter.   *Exit.*

Fool. If a man's brains were in's heels, were't° not
   in danger of kibes?°

Lear. Ay, boy.   10

Fool. Then I prithee be merry. Thy wit shall not go
   slipshod.°

Lear. Ha, ha, ha.

Fool. Shalt° see thy other daughter will use thee
   kindly;° for though she's as like this as a crab's°   15
   like an apple, yet I can tell what I can tell.

---

350 *attasked* taken to task, blamed   351 *harmful mildness* dangerous in-
dulgence   355 *th' event* i.e., we'll see what happens   I.v.   3-4 *than . . .
letter* than her reading of the letter brings her to ask   8 *were't* i.e., the
brains   9 *kibes* chilblains   11-12 *Thy . . . slipshod* your brains shall not
go in slippers (because you have no brains to be protected from chilblains)   14 *Shalt* thou shalt   15 *kindly* (1) affectionately (2) after her
kind or nature   15 *crab* crab apple

Lear. Why, what canst thou tell, my boy?

Fool. She will taste as like this as a crab does to a
crab. Thou canst tell why one's nose stands i' th'
20   middle on's° face?

Lear. No.

Fool. Why, to keep one's eyes of° either side's nose,
that what a man cannot smell out, he may spy
into.

25   *Lear.* I did her wrong.

Fool. Canst tell how an oyster makes his shell?

Lear. No.

Fool. Nor I neither; but I can tell why a snail has a
house.

80   *Lear.* Why?

Fool. Why, to put 's head in; not to give it away to
his daughters, and leave his horns° without a case.

Lear. I will forget my nature.° So kind a father! Be
my horses ready?

85   *Fool.* Thy asses are gone about 'em. The reason why
the seven stars° are no moe° than seven is a pretty°
reason.

Lear. Because they are not eight.

Fool. Yes indeed. Thou wouldst make a good Fool.

40   *Lear.* To take't again perforce!° Monster ingratitude!

Fool. If thou wert my Fool, Nuncle, I'd have thee
beaten for being old before thy time.

Lear. How's that?

Fool. Thou shouldst not have been old till thou hadst
45   been wise.

---

20 *on's* of his   22 *of* on   32 *horns* (1) snail's horns (2) cuckold's
horns   33 *nature* paternal instincts   36 *seven stars* the Pleiades   36 *moe*
more   36 *pretty* apt   40 *To . . . perforce* (1) of Goneril, who has
forcibly taken away Lear's privileges; or (2) of Lear, who meditates
a forcible resumption of authority

Lear. O, let me not be mad, not mad, sweet heaven!
   Keep me in temper;° I would not be mad!

             [*Enter Gentleman.*]

   How now, are the horses ready?

Gentleman. Ready, my lord.

Lear. Come, boy.   50

Fool. She that's a maid now, and laughs at my
       departure,
   Shall not be a maid long, unless things be cut
       shorter.°   *Exeunt.*

---

⁴⁷ *in temper* sane   ⁵¹⁻⁵² *She . . . shorter* the maid who laughs, missing
the tragic implications of this quarrel, will not have sense enough to
preserve her virginity ("things" = penises)

ACT II

Scene I. [*The Earl of Gloucester's castle.*]

Enter Edmund and Curan, severally.°

Edmund. Save° thee, Curan.

Curan. And you, sir. I have been with your father,
and given him notice that the Duke of Cornwall
and Regan his duchess will be here with him this
5   night.

Edmund. How comes that?

Curan. Nay, I know not. You have heard of the news
abroad? I mean the whispered ones, for they are
yet but ear-kissing arguments.°

10   *Edmund.* Not I. Pray you, what are they?

Curan. Have you heard of no likely° wars toward,°
'twixt the Dukes of Cornwall and Albany?

Edmund. Not a word.

Curan. You may do, then, in time. Fare you well,
15   sir.   *Exit.*

Edmund. The Duke be here tonight? The better!°
best!

II.i. ¹ s.d. *severally* separately (from different entrances on stage)
¹ *Save* God save   ⁹ *ear-kissing arguments* subjects whispered in the
ear   ¹¹ *likely* probable   ¹¹ *toward* impending   ¹⁶ *The better* so much
the better

This weaves itself perforce° into my business.
My father hath set guard to take my brother,
And I have one thing of a queasy question°
Which I must act. Briefness° and Fortune, work!   20
Brother, a word; descend. Brother, I say!

Enter Edgar.

My father watches. O sir, fly this place.
Intelligence° is given where you are hid.
You have now the good advantage of the night.
Have you not spoken 'gainst the Duke of Cornwall?   25
He's coming hither, now i' th' night, i' th' haste,°
And Regan with him. Have you nothing said
Upon his party° 'gainst the Duke of Albany?
Advise yourself.°

Edgar.   I am sure on't,° not a word.

Edmund. I hear my father coming. Pardon me: 30
In cunning° I must draw my sword upon you.
Draw, seem to defend yourself; now quit you° well.
Yield! Come before my father! Light ho, here!
Fly, brother. Torches, torches! —So farewell.

                              Exit Edgar.

Some blood drawn on me would beget opinion°   35

                              [Wounds his arm]

Of my more fierce endeavor. I have seen drunkards
Do more than this in sport. Father, father!
Stop, stop! No help?

    Enter Gloucester, and Servants with torches.

Gloucester. Now, Edmund, where's the villain?

Edmund. Here stood he in the dark, his sharp sword
    out,   40
Mumbling of wicked charms, conjuring the moon
To stand auspicious mistress.

Gloucester.   But where is he?

---

17 *perforce* necessarily   19 *of a queasy question* that requires delicate
handling (to be "queasy" is to be on the point of vomiting)   20 *Brief-
ness* speed   23 *Intelligence* information   26 *i' th' haste* in great haste
28 *Upon his party* censuring his enmity   29 *Advise yourself* reflect
29 *on't* of it   31 *In cunning* as a pretense   32 *quit you* acquit yourself
35 *beget opinion* create the impression

Edmund. Look, sir, I bleed.

Gloucester.   Where is the villain, Edmund?

Edmund. Fled this way, sir, when by no means he
      could——

Gloucester. Pursue him, ho! Go after.

                              [*Exeunt some Servants.*]

⁴³   By no means what?

Edmund. Persuade me to the murder of your lordship;
      But that I told him the revenging gods
      'Gainst parricides did all the thunder bend;°
      Spoke with how manifold and strong a bond
⁵⁰   The child was bound to th' father. Sir, in fine,°
      Seeing how loathly opposite° I stood
      To his unnatural purpose, in fell° motion°
      With his preparèd sword he charges home
      My unprovided° body, latched° mine arm;
⁵⁵   But when he saw my best alarumed° spirits
      Bold in the quarrel's right,° roused to th'
          encounter,
      Or whether gasted° by the noise I made,
      Full suddenly he fled.

Gloucester.   Let him fly far.
      Not in this land shall he remain uncaught;
⁶⁰   And found—dispatch.° The noble Duke my master,
      My worthy arch° and patron, comes tonight.
      By his authority I will proclaim it,
      That he which finds him shall deserve our thanks,
      Bringing the murderous coward to the stake.
⁶⁵   He that conceals him, death.°

Edmund. When I dissuaded him from his intent,
      And found him pight° to do it, with curst° speech
      I threatened to discover° him. He replied,

---

⁴⁸ *bend* aim   ⁵⁰ *in fine* finally   ⁵¹ *loathly opposite* bitterly opposed
⁵² *fell* deadly   ⁵² *motion* thrust (a term from fencing)   ⁵⁴ *unprovided*
unprotected   ⁵⁴ *latched* wounded (lanced)   ⁵⁵ *best alarumed* wholly
aroused   ⁵⁶ *Bold . . . right* confident in the rightness of my cause
⁵⁷ *gasted* struck aghast   ⁶⁰ *dispatch* i.e., he will be killed   ⁶¹ *arch* chief
⁶⁵ *death* (the same elliptical form that characterizes "dispatch," 1.60)
⁶⁷ *pight* determined   ⁶⁷ *curst* angry   ⁶⁸ *discover* expose

"Thou unpossessing° bastard, dost thou think,
If I would stand against thee, would the reposal°   70
Of any trust, virtue, or worth in thee
Make thy words faithed?° No. What I should
        deny—
As this I would, ay, though thou didst produce
My very character°—I'd turn it all
To thy suggestion,° plot, and damnèd practice.°   75
And thou must make a dullard of the world,°
If they not thought° the profits of my death
Were very pregnant° and potential spirits°
To make thee seek it."

Gloucester.   O strange and fastened° villain!
Would he deny his letter, said he? I never got° him.   80

                    Tucket° within.

Hark, the Duke's trumpets. I know not why he
        comes.
All ports° I'll bar; the villain shall not 'scape;
The Duke must grant me that. Besides, his picture
I will send far and near, that all the kingdom
May have due note of him; and of my land,   85
Loyal and natural° boy, I'll work the means
To make thee capable.°

        Enter Cornwall, Regan, and Attendants.

Cornwall. How now, my noble friend! Since I came
        hither,
Which I can call but now, I have heard strange
        news.

Regan. If it be true, all vengeance comes too short   90
Which can pursue th' offender. How dost, my lord?

Gloucester. O madam, my old heart is cracked, it's
        cracked.

---

⁶⁹ *unpossessing* beggarly (landless)   ⁷⁰ *reposal* placing   ⁷² *faithed* believed   ⁷⁴ *character* handwriting   ⁷⁵ *suggestion* instigation   ⁷⁵ *practice*
device   ⁷⁶ *make . . . world* think everyone stupid   ⁷⁷ *not thought* did
not think   ⁷⁸ *pregnant* teeming with incitement   ⁷⁸ *potential spirits*
powerful evil spirits   ⁷⁹ *fastened* hardened   ⁸⁰ *got* begot   ⁸⁰ s.d. *Tucket* (Cornwall's special trumpet call)   ⁸² *ports* exits, of whatever sort
⁸⁶ *natural* (1) kind (filial) (2) illegitimate   ⁸⁷ *capable* able to inherit

Regan. What, did my father's godson seek your life?
He whom my father named, your Edgar?

95 *Gloucester.* O lady, lady, shame would have it hid.

Regan. Was he not companion with the riotous knights
That tended upon my father?

Gloucester. I know not, madam. 'Tis too bad, too bad.

Edmund. Yes, madam, he was of that consort.°

100 *Regan.* No marvel then, though he were ill affected.°
'Tis they have put° him on the old man's death,
To have th' expense and waste° of his revenues.
I have this present evening from my sister
Been well informed of them, and with such cautions
105 That, if they come to sojourn at my house,
I'll not be there.

Cornwall.   Nor I, assure thee, Regan.
Edmund, I hear that you have shown your father
A childlike° office.

Edmund. It was my duty, sir.

110 *Gloucester.* He did bewray his practice,° and received
This hurt you see, striving to apprehend him.

Cornwall. Is he pursued?

Gloucester.   Ay, my good lord.

Cornwall. If he be taken, he shall never more
Be feared of doing° harm. Make your own purpose,
115 How in my strength you please.° For you, Edmund,
Whose virtue and obedience° doth this instant
So much commend itself, you shall be ours.
Natures of such deep trust we shall much need;
You we first seize on.

Edmund.   I shall serve you, sir,
Truly, however else.

120 *Gloucester.*   For him I thank your Grace.

---

99 *consort* company 100 *ill affected* disposed to evil 101 *put* set
102 *expense and waste* squandering 108 *childlike* filial 110 *bewray his
practice* disclose his plot 114 *of doing* because he might do
114-15 *Make . . . please* use my power freely, in carrying out your plans
for his capture 116 *virtue and obedience* virtuous obedience

Cornwall. You know not why we came to visit you?

Regan. Thus out of season, threading dark-eyed night.
 Occasions, noble Gloucester, of some prize,°
 Wherein we must have use of your advice.
 Our father he hath writ, so hath our sister,   125
 Of differences,° which° I best thought it fit
 To answer from° our home. The several
    messengers
 From hence attend dispatch.° Our good old friend,
 Lay comforts to your bosom,° and bestow
 Your needful° counsel to our businesses,   130
 Which craves the instant use.°

Gloucester.   I serve you, madam.
 Your Graces are right welcome.

                                   Exeunt. Flourish.

Scene II.   [*Before Gloucester's castle.*]

              Enter Kent and Oswald, severally.

Oswald. Good dawning° to thee, friend. Art of this
 house?°

Kent. Ay.

Oswald. Where may we set our horses?

Kent. I' th' mire.   5

Oswald. Prithee, if thou lov'st me, tell me.

Kent. I love thee not.

---

122 *prize* importance   125 *differences* quarrels   125 *which* (referring not
to "differences," but to the letter Lear has written)   126 *from* away
from   127 *attend dispatch* are waiting to be sent off   128 *Lay . . .
bosom* console yourself (about Edgar's supposed treason)   129 *needful*
needed   131 *craves the instant use* demands immediate transaction
II.ii. 1 *dawning* (dawn is impending, but not yet arrived)   1-2 *Art of
this house* i.e., do you live here

Oswald. Why then, I care not for thee.

Kent. If I had thee in Lipsbury Pinfold,° I would make
10   thee care for me.

Oswald. Why dost thou use me thus? I know thee not.

Kent. Fellow, I know thee.

Oswald. What dost thou know me for?

Kent. A knave, a rascal, an eater of broken meats;°
15   a base, proud, shallow, beggarly, three-suited,°
hundred-pound,° filthy worsted-stocking° knave;
a lily-livered, action-taking,° whoreson, glass-gazing,° superserviceable,° finical° rogue; one-trunk-
inheriting° slave; one that wouldst be a bawd in
20   way of good service,° and art nothing but the com-
position° of a knave, beggar, coward, pander, and
the son and heir of a mongrel bitch; one whom I
will beat into clamorous whining if thou deniest the
least syllable of thy addition.°

25   *Oswald.* Why, what a monstrous fellow art thou, thus
to rail on one that is neither known of thee nor
knows thee!

Kent. What a brazen-faced varlet art thou to deny
thou knowest me! Is it two days since I
30   tripped up thy heels and beat thee before the
King? [*Drawing his sword*] Draw, you rogue,
for though it be night, yet the moon shines. I'll
make a sop o' th' moonshine° of you. You whoreson cullionly barbermonger,° draw!

9 *Lipsbury Pinfold* a pound or pen in which strayed animals are enclosed ("Lipsbury" may denote a particular place, or may be slang for
"between my teeth")   14 *broken meats* scraps of food   15 *three-suited*
(the wardrobe permitted to a servant or "knave")   16 *hundred-pound*
(the extent of Oswald's wealth, and thus a sneer at his aspiring to
gentility)   16 *worsted-stocking* (worn by servants)   17 *action-taking*
one who refuses a fight and goes to law instead   17-18 *glass-gazing*
conceited   18 *superserviceable* sycophantic, serving without principle.
18 *finical* overfastidious   18-19 *one-trunk-inheriting* possessing only a
trunkful of goods   19-20 *bawd . . . service* pimp, to please his master
20-21 *composition* compound   24 *addition* titles   33 *sop o' th' moonshine*
i.e., Oswald will admit the moonlight, and so sop it up, through the
open wounds Kent is preparing to give him   34 *cullionly barbermonger*
base patron of hairdressers (effeminate man)

Goose, if I had you upon Sarum Plain,°
I'd drive ye cackling home to Camelot.°

Cornwall. What, art thou mad, old fellow?

Gloucester. How fell you out? Say that.

Kent. No contraries° hold more antipathy
Than I and such a knave.   90

Cornwall. Why dost thou call him knave? What is his
fault?

Kent. His countenance likes° me not.

Cornwall. No more perchance does mine, nor his, nor
hers.

Kent. Sir, 'tis my occupation to be plain:
I have seen better faces in my time   95
Than stands on any shoulder that I see
Before me at this instant.

Cornwall.   This is some fellow
Who, having been praised for bluntness, doth
    affect
A saucy roughness, and constrains the garb
Quite from his nature.° He cannot flatter, he;   100
An honest mind and plain, he must speak truth.
And° they will take it, so; if not, he's plain.
These kind of knaves I know, which in this
    plainness
Harbor more craft and more corrupter ends
Than twenty silly-ducking observants°   105
That stretch their duties nicely.°

Kent. Sir, in good faith, in sincere verity,
Under th' allowance° of your great aspect,°
Whose influence,° like the wreath of radiant fire

---

85 *Sarum Plain* Salisbury Plain   86 *Camelot* the residence of King
Arthur (presumably a particular point, now lost, is intended here)
89 *contraries* opposites   92 *likes* pleases   99-100 *constrains . . . nature*
forces the manner of candid speech to be a cloak, not for candor but
for craft   102 *And* if   105 *silly-ducking observants* ridiculously obsequious attendants   106 *nicely* punctiliously   108 *allowance* approval
108 *aspect* (1) appearance (2) position of the heavenly bodies   109 *influence* astrological power

On flick'ring Phoebus' front°——

110   *Cornwall.*   What mean'st by this?

Kent. To go out of my dialect,° which you discommend
     so much. I know, sir, I am no flatterer. He° that
     beguiled you in a plain accent was a plain knave,
     which, for my part, I will not be, though I should
115 win your displeasure to entreat me to't.°

Cornwall. What was th' offense you gave him?

Oswald. I never gave him any.
     It pleased the King his master very late°
     To strike at me, upon his misconstruction;°
120 When he, compact,° and flattering his displeasure,
     Tripped me behind; being down, insulted, railed,
     And put upon him such a deal of man°
     That worthied him,° got praises of the King
     For him attempting who was self-subdued;°
125 And, in the fleshment° of this dread exploit,
     Drew on me here again.

Kent.   None of these rogues and cowards
     But Ajax is their fool.°

Cornwall.   Fetch forth the stocks!
     You stubborn° ancient knave, you reverent°
        braggart,
     We'll teach you.

Kent.   Sir, I am too old to learn.

---

110 *Phoebus' front* forehead of the sun   111 *dialect* customary manner
of speaking   112 *He* i.e., the sort of candid-crafty man Cornwall has
been describing   114-15 *though . . . to't* even if I were to succeed in
bringing your graceless person ("displeasure" personified) and in lieu
of the expected form, "your grace") to beg me to be a plain knave
118 *very late* recently   119 *misconstruction* misunderstanding   120 *compact* in league with the king   122 *put . . . man* pretended such manly
behavior   123 *worthied him* made him seem heroic   124 *For . . . self-
subdued* for attacking a man (Oswald) who offered no resistance
125 *fleshment* the bloodthirstiness excited by his first success or "flesh-
ing"   126-27 *None . . . fool* i.e., cowardly rogues like Oswald always
impose on fools like Cornwall (who is likened to Ajax: [1] the brag-
gart Greek warrior [2] a jakes or privy)   128 *stubborn* rude   128 *rev-
erent* old

Call not your stocks for me, I serve the King,   130
On whose employment I was sent to you.
You shall do small respect, show too bold malice
Against the grace and person° of my master,
Stocking his messenger.

Cornwall. Fetch forth the stocks. As I have life and
     honor,   135
There shall he sit till noon.

Regan. Till noon? Till night, my lord, and all night
     too.

Kent. Why, madam, if I were your father's dog,
You should not use me so.

Regan.   Sir, being his knave, I will.

Cornwall. This is a fellow of the selfsame color°   140
Our sister speaks of. Come, bring away° the stocks.
                   Stocks brought out.

Gloucester. Let me beseech your Grace not to do so.
His fault is much, and the good King his master
Will check° him for't. Your purposed° low
     correction
Is such as basest and contemnèd'st° wretches   145
For pilf'rings and most common trespasses
Are punished with.
The King his master needs must take it ill
That he, so slightly valued in° his messenger,
Should have him thus restrained.

Cornwall.   I'll answer° that.   150

Regan. My sister may receive it much more worse,
To have her gentleman abused, assaulted,
For following her affairs. Put in his legs.
              [Kent is put in the stocks.]
Come, my good lord, away!
            [Exeunt all but Gloucester and Kent.]

---

133 *grace and person* i.e., Lear as sovereign and in his personal character   140 *color* kind   141 *away* out   144 *check* correct   144 *purposed*
intended   145 *contemnèd'st* most despised   149 *slightly valued in* little
honored in the person of   150 *answer* answer for

Gloucester. I am sorry for thee, friend. 'Tis the Duke's
155   pleasure,
Whose disposition° all the world well knows
Will not be rubbed° nor stopped. I'll entreat for
thee.

Kent. Pray do not, sir. I have watched° and traveled
hard.
Some time I shall sleep out, the rest I'll whistle.
160   A good man's fortune may grow out at heels.°
Give° you good morrow.

Gloucester. The Duke's to blame in this. 'Twill be
ill taken.°   *Exit.*

Kent. Good King, that must approve° the common
saw,°
Thou out of Heaven's benediction com'st
165   To the warm sun.°
Approach, thou beacon to this under globe,°
That by thy comfortable° beams I may
Peruse this letter. Nothing almost sees miracles
But misery.° I know 'tis from Cordelia,
170   Who hath most fortunately been informed
Of my obscurèd° course. And shall find time
From this enormous state, seeking to give
Losses their remedies.° All weary and o'erwatched,
Take vantage,° heavy eyes, not to behold
175   This shameful lodging. Fortune, good night;
Smile once more, turn thy wheel.°

                            Sleeps.

---

156 *disposition* inclination   157 *rubbed* diverted (metaphor from the
game of bowls)   158 *watched* gone without sleep   160 *A . . . heels*
even a good man may have bad fortune   161 *Give* God give   162 *taken*
received   163 *approve* confirm   163 *saw* proverb   164-65 *Thou . . . sun*
i.e., Lear goes from better to worse, from Heaven's blessing or shelter
to lack of shelter   166 *beacon . . . globe* i.e., the sun, whose rising
Kent anticipates   167 *comfortable* comforting   168-69 *Nothing . . .
misery* i.e., true perception belongs only to the wretched   171 *obscurèd*
disguised   171-73 *shall . . . remedies* (a possible reading: Cordelia,
away from this monstrous state of things, will find occasion to right
the wrongs we suffer)   174 *vantage* advantage (of sleep)   176 *turn thy
wheel* i.e., so that Kent, who is at the bottom, may climb upward

[Scene III. *A wood*.]

Enter Edgar.

Edgar. I heard myself proclaimed,
  And by the happy° hollow of a tree
  Escaped the hunt. No port is free, no place
  That guard and most unusual vigilance
  Does not attend my taking.° Whiles I may 'scape,   *5*
  I will preserve myself; and am bethought°
  To take the basest and most poorest shape
  That ever penury, in contempt of man,
  Brought near to beast;° my face I'll grime with filth,
  Blanket° my loins, elf° all my hairs in knots,   *10*
  And with presented° nakedness outface°
  The winds and persecutions of the sky.
  The country gives me proof° and precedent
  Of Bedlam° beggars, who, with roaring voices,
  Strike° in their numbed and mortified° bare arms   *15*
  Pins, wooden pricks,° nails, sprigs of rosemary;
  And with this horrible object,° from low° farms,
  Poor pelting° villages, sheepcotes, and mills,
  Sometimes with lunatic bans,° sometime with
    prayers,
  Enforce their charity. Poor Turlygod, Poor Tom,°   *20*
  That's something yet: Edgar I nothing am.° *Exit.*

II.iii. ²*happy* lucky ⁵*attend my taking* watch to capture me ⁶*am bethought* have decided ⁸⁻⁹*penury . . . beast* poverty, to show how contemptible man is, reduced to the level of a beast ¹⁰*Blanket* cover only with a blanket ¹⁰*elf* tangle (into "elflocks," supposed to be caused by elves) ¹¹*presented* the show of ¹¹*outface* brave ¹³*proof* example ¹⁴*Bedlam* (see I.ii.r. ¹⁴⁶⁻⁴⁷) ¹⁵*strike* stick ¹⁵*mortified* not alive to pain ¹⁶*pricks* skewers ¹⁷*object* spectacle ¹⁷*low* humble ¹⁸*pelting* paltry ¹⁹*bans* curses ²⁰*Poor . . . Tom* (Edgar recites the names a Bedlam beggar gives himself) ²¹*That's . . . am* there's a chance for me in that I am no longer known for myself

[Scene IV.   *Before Gloucester's castle. Kent in
the stocks.*]

Enter Lear, Fool, and Gentleman.

Lear. 'Tis strange that they should so depart from
    home,
    And not send back my messenger.

Gentleman.   As I learned,
    The night before there was no purpose° in them
    Of this remove.°

Kent.   Hail to thee, noble master.

5 *Lear.* Ha!
    Mak'st thou this shame thy pastime?°

Kent.   No, my lord.

Fool. Ha, ha, he wears cruel° garters. Horses are tied
    by the heads, dogs and bears by th' neck, monkeys
    by th' loins, and men by th' legs. When a man's over-
10   lusty at legs,° then he wears wooden netherstocks.°

Lear. What's he that hath so much thy place mistook
    To set thee here?

Kent.   It is both he and she,
    Your son and daughter.

Lear. No.

15 *Kent.* Yes.

Lear. No, I say.

Kent. I say yea.

II.iv. 3 *purpose* intention   4 *remove* removal   6 *Mak'st . . . pastime* i.e.,
are you doing this to amuse yourself   7 *cruel* (1) painful (2)
"crewel," a worsted yarn used in garters   9-10 *overlusty at legs* (1) a
vagabond (2) ? sexually promiscuous   10 *netherstocks* stockings (as
opposed to knee breeches or upperstocks)

Lear. No, no, they would not.

Kent. Yes, they have.

Lear. By Jupiter, I swear no! 20

Kent. By Juno, I swear ay!

Lear. They durst not do't;
They could not, would not do't. 'Tis worse than
    murder
To do upon respect° such violent outrage.
Resolve° me with all modest° haste which way
Thou mightst deserve or they impose this usage, 25
Coming from us.

Kent. My lord, when at their home
I did commend° your Highness' letters to them,
Ere I was risen from the place that showed
My duty kneeling, came there a reeking post,°
Stewed° in his haste, half breathless, panting forth 30
From Goneril his mistress salutations,
Delivered letters, spite of intermission,°
Which presently° they read; on° whose contents
They summoned up their meiny,° straight took
    horse,
Commanded me to follow and attend 35
The leisure of their answer, gave me cold looks,
And meeting here the other messenger,
Whose welcome I perceived had poisoned mine,
Being the very fellow which of late
Displayed° so saucily against your Highness, 40
Having more man than wit° about me, drew;
He raised° the house, with loud and coward cries.
Your son and daughter found this trespass worth°
The shame which here it suffers.

23 *upon respect* (1) on the respect due to the King (2) deliberately
24 *Resolve* inform 24 *modest* becoming 27 *commend* deliver 29 *reeking post* sweating messenger 30 *stewed* steaming 32 *spite of intermission* in spite of the interrupting of my business 33 *presently* at once
33 *on* on the strength of 34 *meiny* retinue 40 *Displayed* showed off
41 *more man than wit* more manhood than sense 42 *raised* aroused
43 *worth* deserving

⁴⁵ *Fool.* Winter's not gone yet, if the wild geese fly that
            way.°
                    Fathers that wear rags
                        Do make their children blind,°
                    But fathers that bear bags°
⁵⁰   Shall see their children kind.
                    Fortune, that arrant whore,
                        Ne'er turns the key° to th' poor.
            But for all this, thou shalt have as many dolors° for
            thy daughters as thou canst tell° in a year.

⁵³ *Lear.* O, how this mother° swells up toward my heart!
            Hysterica passio,° down, thou climbing sorrow,
            Thy element's° below. Where is this daughter?

Kent. With the Earl, sir, here within.

Lear.   Follow me not;
            Stay here.   *Exit.*

Gentleman. Made you no more offense but what you
⁶⁰   speak of?

Kent. None.
            How chance° the King comes with so small a
                number?

Fool. And° thou hadst been set i' th' stocks for that
            question, thou'dst well deserved it.

⁶⁵ *Kent.* Why, Fool?

Fool. We'll set thee to school to an ant, to teach thee
            there's no laboring i' th' winter.° All that follow

---

45-46 *Winter's . . . way* i.e., more trouble is to come, since Cornwall
and Regan act so ("geese" is used contemptuously, as in Kent's quarrel with Oswald, II.ii. 85-6)   48 *blind* i.e., indifferent   49 *bags* money-
bags   52 *turns the key* i.e., opens the door   53 *dolors* (1) sorrows (2)
dollars (English name for Spanish and German coins)   54 *tell* (1) tell
about (2) count   55-56 *mother . . . Hysterica passio* hysteria, causing
suffocation or choking   57 *element* proper place   62 *How chance* how
does it happen that   63 *And if*   66-67 *We'll . . . winter* (in the popular
fable the ant, unlike the improvident grasshopper, anticipates the winter
when none can labor by laying up provisions in the summer. Lear,
trusting foolishly to summer days, finds himself unprovided for, and
unable to provide, now that "winter" has come)

their noses are led by their eyes but blind men,
and there's not a nose among twenty but can smell
him that's stinking.° Let go thy hold when a great   70
wheel runs down a hill, lest it break thy neck with
following. But the great one that goes upward,
let him draw thee after. When a wise man gives
thee better counsel, give me mine again. I would
have none but knaves follow it since a Fool gives   75
it.

    That sir, which serves and seeks for gain,
        And follows but for form,°
    Will pack,° when it begins to rain,
        And leave thee in the storm.   80
    But I will tarry; the Fool will stay,
        And let the wise man fly.
    The knave turns Fool that runs away,
        The Fool no knave,° perdy.°

Kent. Where learned you this, Fool?   85

Fool. Not i' th' stocks, fool.

        Enter Lear and Gloucester.

Lear. Deny° to speak with me? They are sick, they
    are weary,
They have traveled all the night? Mere fetches,°
The images° of revolt and flying off!°
Fetch me a better answer.

Gloucester.   My dear lord,   90
You know the fiery quality° of the Duke,
How unremovable and fixed he is
In his own course.

Lear.   Vengeance, plague, death, confusion!
Fiery? What quality? Why, Gloucester, Gloucester,
I'd speak with the Duke of Cornwall and his wife.   95

67-70 *All . . . stinking* i.e., all can smell out the decay of Lear's fortunes 78 *form* show 79 *pack* be off 83-84 *The . . . knave* i.e., the
faithless man is the true fool, for wisdom requires fidelity. Lear's Fool,
who remains faithful, is at least no knave 84 *perdy* by God (Fr. *par
Dieu*) 87 *Deny* refuse 88 *fetches* subterfuges, acts of tacking (nautical
metaphor) 89 *images* exact likenesses 89 *flying off* desertion 91 *quality* temperament

Gloucester. Well, my good lord, I have informed them
    so.

Lear. Informed them? Dost thou understand me,
    man?

Gloucester. Ay, my good lord.

Lear. The King would speak with Cornwall. The dear
    father
100   Would with his daughter speak, commands—tends°
    —service.
    Are they informed of this? My breath and blood!
    Fiery? The fiery Duke, tell the hot Duke that—
    No, but not yet. May be he is not well.
    Infirmity doth still neglect all office
105   Whereto our health is bound.° We are not
    ourselves
    When nature, being oppressed, commands the
    mind
    To suffer with the body. I'll forbear;
    And am fallen out° with my more headier will°
    To take the indisposed and sickly fit
    For the sound man. [*Looking on Kent*] Death on
110   my state!° Wherefore
    Should he sit here? This act persuades me
    That this remotion° of the Duke and her
    Is practice° only. Give me my servant forth.°
    Go tell the Duke and's wife I'd speak with them!
    Now, presently!° Bid them come forth and hear
115   me,
    Or at their chamber door I'll beat the drum
    Till it cry sleep to death.°

Gloucester. I would have all well betwixt you.

                    Exit.

---

100 *tends* attends (i.e., awaits); with, possibly, an ironic second meaning, "tenders," or "offers"   105 *Whereto . . . bound* duties which we
are required to perform, when in health   108 *fallen out* angry   108 *head-
ier will* headlong inclination   110 *state* royal condition   112 *remotion*
(1) removal (2) remaining aloof   113 *practice* pretense   113 *forth* i.e.,
out of the stocks   115 *presently* at once   117 *cry . . . death* follow
sleep, like a cry or pack of hounds, until it kills it

Lear. O me, my heart, my rising heart! But down!

Fool. Cry to it, Nuncle, as the cockney° did to 120
the eels when she put 'em i' th' paste° alive. She
knapped° 'em o' th' coxcombs° with a stick and
cried, "Down, wantons,° down!" 'Twas her brother
that, in pure kindness to his horse, buttered his
hay.°   125

Enter Cornwall, Regan, Gloucester, Servants.

Lear. Good morrow to you both.

Cornwall.   Hail to your Grace.

                    Kent here set at liberty.

Regan. I am glad to see your Highness.

Lear. Regan, I think you are. I know what reason
I have to think so. If thou shouldst not be glad,
I would divorce me from thy mother's tomb,   130
Sepulchring an adultress.° [*To Kent*] O, are you
    free?
Some other time for that. Beloved Regan,
Thy sister's naught.° O Regan, she hath tied
Sharp-toothed unkindness, like a vulture, here.

                    [*Points to his heart.*]

I can scarce speak to thee. Thou'lt not believe   135
With how depraved a quality°——O Regan!

Regan. I pray you, sir, take patience. I have hope
You less know how to value her desert
Than she to scant her duty.°

Lear.   Say? how is that?

---

120 *cockney* Londoner (ignorant city dweller) 121 *paste* pastry pie
122 *knapped* rapped 122 *coxcombs* heads 123 *wantons* i.e., playful
things (with a sexual implication) 125 *buttered his hay* i.e., the city
dweller does from ignorance what the dishonest ostler does from craft:
greases the hay the traveler has paid for, so that the horse will not
eat 130-31 *divorce . . . adultress* i.e., repudiate your dead mother as
having conceived you by another man 133 *naught* wicked 136 *quality*
nature 137-39 *I . . . duty* (despite the double negative, the passage
means, "I believe that you fail to give Goneril her due, rather than
that she fails to fulfill her duty")

140 *Regan.* I cannot think my sister in the least
      Would fail her obligation. If, sir, perchance
      She have restrained the riots of your followers,
      'Tis on such ground, and to such wholesome end,
      As clears her from all blame.

   Lear. My curses on her!

145 *Regan.*   O, sir, you are old,
      Nature in you stands on the very verge
      Of his confine.° You should be ruled, and led
      By some discretion that discerns your state
      Better than you yourself.° Therefore I pray you
150   That to our sister you do make return,
      Say you have wronged her.

   Lear.   Ask her forgiveness?
      Do you but mark how this becomes the house:°
      "Dear daughter, I confess that I am old.

                                   [*Kneeling.*]

      Age is unnecessary. On my knees I beg
155   That you'll vouchsafe me raiment, bed, and food."

   Regan. Good sir, no more. These are unsightly tricks.
      Return you to my sister.

   Lear.   [*Rising*] Never, Regan.
      She hath abated° me of half my train,
      Looked black upon me, struck me with her tongue,
160   Most serpentlike, upon the very heart.
      All the stored vengeances of heaven fall
      On her ingrateful top!° Strike her young bones,°
      You taking° airs, with lameness.

   Cornwall.   Fie, sir, fie!

   Lear. You nimble lightnings, dart your blinding flames
165   Into her scornful eyes! Infect her beauty,

146-47 *Nature . . . confine* i.e., you are nearing the end of your life
148-49 *some . . . yourself* some discreet person who understands your
condition more than you do   152 *becomes the house* suits my royal and
paternal position   158 *abated* curtailed   162 *top* head   162 *young bones*
(the reference may be to unborn children, rather than to Goneril herself)   163 *taking* infecting

You fen-sucked° fogs, drawn by the pow'rful sun,
To fall and blister° her pride.

Regan.   O the blest gods!
So will you wish on me when the rash mood is on.

Lear. No, Regan, thou shalt never have my curse.
Thy tender-hefted° nature shall not give   *170*
Thee o'er to harshness. Her eyes are fierce, but thine
Do comfort, and not burn. 'Tis not in thee
To grudge my pleasures, to cut off my train,
To bandy° hasty words, to scant my sizes,°
And, in conclusion, to oppose the bolt°   *175*
Against my coming in. Thou better know'st
The offices of nature, bond of childhood,°
Effects° of courtesy, dues of gratitude.
Thy half o' th' kingdom hast thou not forgot,
Wherein I thee endowed.

Regan.   Good sir, to th' purpose.°   *180*

                   Tucket within.

Lear. Who put my man i' th' stocks?

Cornwall.   What trumpet's that?

Regan. I know't—my sister's. This approves° her letter,
That she would soon be here.

            Enter Oswald.

                Is your lady come?

Lear. This is a slave, whose easy borrowed° pride
Dwells in the fickle grace° of her he follows.   *185*
Out, varlet,° from my sight.

Cornwall.   What means your Grace?

---

166 *fen-sucked* drawn up from swamps by the sun   167 *fall and blister* fall upon and raise blisters   170 *tender-hefted* gently framed   174 *bandy* volley (metaphor from tennis)   174 *scant my sizes* reduce my allowances   175 *oppose the bolt* i.e., bar the door   177 *offices . . . childhood* natural duties, a child's duty to its parent   178 *Effects* manifestations   180 *to th' purpose* come to the point   182 *approves* confirms   184 *easy borrowed* (1) facile and taken from another (2) acquired without anything to back it up (like money borrowed without security)   185 *grace* favor   186 *varlet* base fellow

Lear. Who stocked my servant? Regan, I have good
     hope
Thou didst not know on't.

                    Enter Goneril.

                         Who comes here? O heavens!
If you do love old men, if your sweet sway
190   Allow° obedience, if you yourselves are old,
Make it° your cause. Send down, and take my part.
[*To Goneril*] Art not ashamed to look upon
     this beard?
O Regan, will you take her by the hand?

Goneril. Why not by th' hand, sir? How have I
     offended?
195   All's not offense that indiscretion finds°
And dotage terms so.

Lear.   O sides,° you are too tough!
Will you yet hold? How came my man i' th' stocks?

Cornwall. I set him there, sir; but his own disorders°
Deserved much less advancement.°

Lear.   You? Did you?

200   *Regan.* I pray you, father, being weak, seem so.°
If till the expiration of your month
You will return and sojourn with my sister,
Dismissing half your train, come then to me.
I am now from home, and out of that provision
205   Which shall be needful for your entertainment.°

Lear. Return to her, and fifty men dismissed?
No, rather I abjure all roofs, and choose
To wage° against the enmity o' th' air,
To be a comrade with the wolf and owl,
210   Necessity's sharp pinch.° Return with her?
Why, the hot-blooded° France, that dowerless
     took

---

190 *Allow* approve of   191 *it* i.e., my cause   195 *finds* judges   196 *sides*
breast   198 *disorders* misconduct   199 *advancement* promotion   200 *seem
so* i.e., act weak   205 *entertainment* maintenance   208 *wage* fight
210 *Necessity's sharp pinch* (a summing up of the hard choice he has
just announced)   211 *hot-blooded* passionate

Our youngest born, I could as well be brought
To knee° his throne, and, squirelike,° pension beg
To keep base life afoot. Return with her?
Persuade me rather to be slave and sumpter°   215
To this detested groom. [*Pointing at Oswald.*]

Goneril.   At your choice, sir.

Lear. I prithee, daughter, do not make me mad.
I will not trouble thee, my child; farewell.
We'll no more meet, no more see one another.
But yet thou art my flesh, my blood, my daughter,   220
Or rather a disease that's in my flesh,
Which I must needs call mine. Thou art a boil,
A plague-sore, or embossèd carbuncle°
In my corrupted blood. But I'll not chide thee.
Let shame come when it will, I do not call it.   225
I do not bid the Thunder-bearer° shoot,
Nor tell tales of thee to high-judging° Jove.
Mend when thou canst, be better at thy leisure,
I can be patient, I can stay with Regan,
I and my hundred knights.

Regan.   Not altogether so.   230
I looked not for you yet, nor am provided
For your fit welcome. Give ear, sir, to my sister,
For those that mingle reason with your passion°
Must be content to think you old, and so—
But she knows what she does.

Lear.   Is this well spoken?   235

Regan. I dare avouch° it, sir. What, fifty followers?
Is it not well? What should you need of more?
Yea, or so many, sith that° both charge° and
    danger
Speak 'gainst so great a number? How in one house

---

²¹³ *knee* kneel before   ²¹³ *squirelike* like a retainer   ²¹⁵ *sumpter* pack
horse   ²²³ *embossèd carbuncle* swollen boil   ²²⁶ *Thunder-bearer* i.e.,
Jupiter   ²²⁷ *high-judging* (1) supreme (2) judging from heaven
²³³ *mingle . . . passion* i.e., consider your turbulent behavior coolly
and reasonably   ²³⁶ *avouch* swear by   ²³⁸ *sith that* since   ²³⁸ *charge*
expense

240   Should many people, under two commands,
       Hold° amity? 'Tis hard, almost impossible.

Goneril. Why might not you, my lord, receive attendance
       From those that she calls servants, or from mine?

Regan. Why not, my lord? If then they chanced to slack° ye,
245   We could control them. If you will come to me
       (For now I spy a danger), I entreat you
       To bring but five-and-twenty. To no more
       Will I give place or notice.°

Lear. I gave you all.

Regan.   And in good time you gave it.

250 *Lear.* Made you my guardians, my depositaries,°
       But kept a reservation° to be followed
       With such a number. What, must I come to you
       With five-and-twenty? Regan, said you so?

Regan. And speak't again, my lord. No more with me.

Lear. Those wicked creatures yet do look well-
255   favored°
       When others are more wicked; not being the worst
       Stands in some rank of praise.° [*To Goneril*] I'll
          go with thee.
       Thy fifty yet doth double five-and-twenty,
       And thou art twice her love.°

Goneril.   Hear me, my lord.
260   What need you five-and-twenty? ten? or five?
       To follow° in a house where twice so many
       Have a command to tend you?

Regan.   What need one?

Lear. O reason° not the need! Our basest beggars

---

241 *hold* preserve   244 *slack* neglect   248 *notice* recognition   250 *depositaries* trustees   251 *reservation* condition   255 *well-favored* handsome   256-57 *not . . . praise* i.e., that Goneril is not so bad as Regan is one thing in her favor   259 *her love* i.e., as loving as she   261 *follow* attend on you   263 *reason* scrutinize

Are in the poorest thing superfluous.°
Allow not nature more than nature needs,°   265
Man's life is cheap as beast's. Thou art a lady:
If only to go warm were gorgeous,
Why, nature needs not what thou gorgeous wear'st,
Which scarcely keeps thee warm.° But, for true
    need—
You heavens, give me that patience, patience I
    need.   270
You see me here, you gods, a poor old man,
As full of grief as age, wretched in both.
If it be you that stirs these daughters' hearts
Against their father, fool° me not so much
To bear° it tamely; touch me with noble anger,   275
And let not women's weapons, water drops,
Stain my man's cheeks. No, you unnatural hags!
I will have such revenges on you both
That all the world shall—I will do such things—
What they are, yet I know not; but they shall be   280
The terrors of the earth. You think I'll weep.
No, I'll not weep.

                Storm and tempest.

I have full cause of weeping, but this heart
Shall break into a hundred thousand flaws°
Or ere° I'll weep. O Fool, I shall go mad!   285

        Exeunt Lear, Gloucester, Kent, and Fool.

Cornwall. Let us withdraw, 'twill be a storm.

Regan. This house is little; the old man and's people
Cannot be well bestowed.°

Goneril. 'Tis his own blame; hath° put himself from
    rest°
And must needs taste his folly.   290

---

264 *Are . . . superfluous* i.e., have some trifle not absolutely necessary
265 *needs* i.e., to sustain life   267-69 *If . . . warm* i.e., if to satisfy the
need for warmth were to be gorgeous, you would not need the clothing you wear, which is worn more for beauty than warmth   274 *fool*
humiliate   275 *To bear* as to make me bear   284 *flaws* (1) pieces (2)
cracks (3) gusts of passion   285 *Or ere* before   288 *bestowed* lodged
289 *hath* he hath   289 *rest* (1) place of residence (2) repose of mind

Regan. For his particular,° I'll receive him gladly,
But not one follower.

Goneril.   So am I purposed.°
Where is my Lord of Gloucester?

Cornwall. Followed the old man forth.

                    Enter Gloucester.

                              He is returned.

Gloucester. The King is in high rage.

295 *Cornwall.*   Whither is he going?

Gloucester. He calls to horse, but will I know not
whither.

Cornwall. 'Tis best to give him way, he leads himself.°

Goneril. My lord, entreat him by no means to stay.

Gloucester. Alack, the night comes on, and the high
winds
300   Do sorely ruffle.° For many miles about
There's scarce a bush.

Regan.   O, sir, to willful men
The injuries that they themselves procure
Must be their schoolmasters. Shut up your doors.
He is attended with a desperate train,
305   And what they may incense° him to, being apt
To have his ear abused,° wisdom bids fear.

Cornwall. Shut up your doors, my lord; 'tis a wild
night.
My Regan counsels well. Come out o' th' storm.
                              Exeunt.

---

291 *his particular* himself personally   292 *purposed* determined   297 *give
. . . himself* let him go; he insists on his own way   300 *ruffle* rage
305 *incense* incite   305-06 *being . . . abused* he being inclined to harken
to bad counsel

ACT III

Scene I.   [*A heath.*]

Storm still.° *Enter Kent and a Gentleman severally.*

Kent. Who's there besides foul weather?

Gentleman. One minded like the weather most
   unquietly.°

Kent. I know you. Where's the King?

Gentleman. Contending with the fretful elements;
   Bids the wind blow the earth into the sea,   5
   Or swell the curlèd waters 'bove the main,°
   That things might change,° or cease; tears his white
      hair,
   Which the impetuous blasts, with eyeless° rage,
   Catch in their fury, and make nothing of;
   Strives in his little world of man° to outscorn   10
   The to-and-fro-conflicting wind and rain.
   This night, wherein the cub-drawn° bear would
      couch,°
   The lion, and the belly-pinchèd° wolf
   Keep their fur dry, unbonneted° he runs,

III.i.s.d. *still* continually   2 *minded . . . unquietly* disturbed in mind,
like the weather   6 *main* land   7 *change* (1) be destroyed (2) be ex-
changed (i.e., turned upside down) (3) change for the better   8 *eyeless* (1) blind (2) invisible   10 *little world of man* (the microcosm, as
opposed to the universe or macrocosm, which it copies in little)
12 *cub-drawn* sucked dry by her cubs, and so ravenously hungry
12 *couch* take shelter in its lair   13 *belly-pinchèd* starved   14 *unbonneted*
hatless

And bids what will take all.°

15   *Kent.*   But who is with him?
      Gentleman. None but the Fool, who labors to outjest
            His heart-struck injuries.

      Kent.   Sir, I do know you,
            And dare upon the warrant of my note°
            Commend a dear thing° to you. There is division,
20   Although as yet the face of it is covered
            With mutual cunning, 'twixt Albany and Cornwall;
            Who have—as who have not, that° their great
                  stars
            Throned° and set high?—servants, who seem no
                  less,°
            Which are to France the spies and speculations
25   Intelligent° of our state. What hath been seen,
            Either in snuffs and packings° of the Dukes,
            Or the hard rein which both of them hath borne°
            Against the old kind King, or something deeper,
            Whereof, perchance, these are but furnishings°—
30   But, true it is, from France there comes a power°
            Into this scattered° kingdom, who already,
            Wise in our negligence, have secret feet
            In some of our best ports, and are at point°
            To show their open banner. Now to you:
35   If on my credit you dare build° so far
            To make your speed to Dover, you shall find
            Some that will thank you, making° just° report
            Of how unnatural and bemadding° sorrow
            The King hath cause to plain.°
40   I am a gentleman of blood and breeding,°

¹⁵ *take all* (like the reckless gambler, staking all he has left) ¹⁸ *war-rant of my note* strength of what I have taken note (of you) ¹⁹ *Commend . . . thing* entrust important business ²² *that* whom ²²⁻²³ *stars /Throned* destinies have throned ²³ *seem no less* seem to be so ²⁴⁻²⁵ *speculations/Intelligent* giving intelligence ²⁶ *snuffs and packings* quarrels and plots ²⁷ *hard . . . borne* close and cruel control they have exercised ²⁹ *furnishings* excuses ³⁰ *power* army ³¹ *scattered* dis-united ³³ *at point* ready ³⁵ *If . . . build* if you can trust me, proceed ³⁶ *To* as to ³⁷ *making* for making ³⁷ *just* accurate ³⁸ *bemadding* mad-dening ³⁹ *plain* complain of ⁴⁰ *blood and breeding* noble family

And from some knowledge and assurance° offer
This office° to you.

Gentleman. I will talk further with you.

Kent.   No, do not.
For confirmation that I am much more
Than my out-wall,° open this purse and take   45
What it contains. If you shall see Cordelia,
As fear not but you shall, show her this ring,
And she will tell you who that fellow° is
That yet you do not know. Fie on this storm!
I will go seek the King.   50

Gentleman. Give me your hand. Have you no more to
say?

Kent. Few words, but, to effect,° more than all yet:
That when we have found the King—in which your
pain°
That way, I'll this—he that first lights on him,
Holla the other.   *Exeunt [severally].*   53

Scene II.   [*Another part of the heath.*]

Storm still.

Enter Lear and Fool.

Lear. Blow, winds, and crack your cheeks. Rage, blow!
You cataracts and hurricanoes,° spout
Till you have drenched our steeples, drowned the
cocks.°

---

41 *knowledge and assurance* sure and trustworthy information   42 *office*
service (i.e., the trip to Dover)   45 *out-wall* superficial appearance
48 *fellow* companion   52 *to effect* in their importance   53 *pain* labor
III.ii. 2 *hurricanoes* waterspouts   3 *cocks* weathercocks

You sulph'rous and thought-executing° fires,
5 Vaunt-couriers° of oak-cleaving thunderbolts,
Singe my white head. And thou, all-shaking thunder,
Strike flat the thick rotundity° o' th' world,
Crack Nature's molds,° all germains spill° at once,
That makes ingrateful° man.

10 *Fool.* O Nuncle, court holy-water° in a dry house is
better than this rain water out o' door. Good
Nuncle, in; ask thy daughters blessing. Here's a
night pities neither wise man nor fools.

Lear. Rumble thy bellyful. Spit, fire. Spout, rain!
15 Nor rain, wind, thunder, fire are my daughters.
I tax° not you, you elements, with unkindness.
I never gave you kingdom, called you children,
You owe me no subscription.° Then let fall
Your horrible pleasure.° Here I stand your slave,
20 A poor, infirm, weak, and despised old man.
But yet I call you servile ministers,°
That will with two pernicious daughters join
Your high-engendered battles° 'gainst a head
So old and white as this. O, ho! 'tis foul.

25 *Fool.* He that has a house to put 's head in has a good
headpiece.°
          The codpiece° that will house
          Before the head has any,
          The head and he° shall louse:
30   So beggars marry many.°
          The man that makes his toe

---

4 *thought-executing* (1) doing execution as quick as thought (2) exe-
cuting or carrying out the thought of him who hurls the lightning
5 *Vaunt-couriers* heralds, scouts who range before the main body of the
army 7 *rotundity* i.e., not only the sphere of the globe, but the round-
ness of gestation (Delius) 8 *Nature's molds* the molds or forms in
which men are made 8 *all germains spill* destroy the basic seeds of
life 9 *ingrateful* ungrateful 10 *court holy-water* flattery 16 *tax* accuse
18 *subscription* allegiance, submission 19 *pleasure* will 21 *ministers*
agents 23 *high-engendered battles* armies formed in the heavens
26 *headpiece* (1) helmet (2) brain 27 *codpiece* penis (lit., padding
worn at the crotch of a man's hose) 29 *he* it 30 *many* i.e., lice
27-30 *The . . . many* i.e., the man who gratifies his sexual appetites
before he has a roof over his head will end up a lousy beggar

What he his heart should make
Shall of a corn cry woe,
And turn his sleep to wake.°
For there was never yet fair woman but she made   35
mouths in a glass.°

Enter Kent.

Lear. No, I will be the pattern of all patience,
I will say nothing.

Kent. Who's there?

Fool. Marry,° here's grace and a codpiece; that's a   40
wise man and a fool.°

Kent. Alas, sir, are you here? Things that love night
Love not such nights as these. The wrathful skies
Gallow° the very wanderers of the dark
And make them keep° their caves. Since I was man,   45
Such sheets of fire, such bursts of horrid° thunder,
Such groans of roaring wind and rain, I never
Remember to have heard. Man's nature cannot
carry°
Th' affliction nor the fear.

Lear.   Let the great gods
That keep this dreadful pudder° o'er our heads   50
Find out their enemies now.° Tremble, thou wretch,
That hast within thee undivulgèd crimes
Unwhipped of justice. Hide thee, thou bloody
hand,
Thou perjured,° and thou simular° of virtue

31-34 *The . . . wake* i.e., the man who, ignoring the fit order of things,
elevates what is base above what is noble, will suffer for it as Lear
has, in banishing Cordelia and enriching her sisters   **35-36** *made mouths
in a glass* posed before a mirror (irrelevant nonsense, except that it
calls to mind the general theme of vanity and folly)   **40** *Marry* by the
Virgin Mary   **40-41** *here's . . . fool* (Kent's question is answered: The
King ("grace") is here, and the Fool—who customarily wears an ex-
aggerated codpiece. But which is which is left ambiguous, since Lear
has previously been called a codpiece)   **44** *Gallow* frighten   **45** *keep*
remain inside   **46** *horrid* horrible   **48** *carry* endure   **50** *pudder* turmoil.
51 *Find . . . now* i.e., discover sinners by the terror they reveal
54 *perjured* perjurer   **54** *simular* counterfeiter

55   That art incestuous. Caitiff,° to pieces shake,
        That under covert and convenient seeming°
        Has practiced on° man's life. Close° pent-up guilts,
        Rive° your concealing continents° and cry
        These dreadful summoners grace.° I am a man
        More sinned against than sinning.

60 *Kent*.   Alack, bareheaded?
        Gracious my lord,° hard by here is a hovel;
        Some friendship will it lend you 'gainst the
            tempest.
        Repose you there, while I to this hard house
        (More harder than the stones whereof 'tis raised,
65   Which even but now, demanding after° you,
        Denied me to come in) return, and force
        Their scanted° courtesy.

    Lear.   My wits begin to turn.
        Come on, my boy. How dost, my boy? Art cold?
        I am cold myself. Where is this straw, my fellow?
70   The art° of our necessities is strange,
        That can make vile things precious. Come, your
            hovel.
        Poor Fool and knave, I have one part in my heart
        That's sorry yet for thee.

    Fool. [*Singing*]
            He that has and a little tiny wit,
75   With heigh-ho, the wind and the rain,
            Must make content with his fortunes fit,°
            Though the rain it raineth every day.

    Lear. True, my good boy. Come, bring us to this hovel.
                                        Exit [*with Kent*].

----

55 *Caitiff* wretch   **56** *seeming* hypocrisy   **57** *practiced on* plotted against
57 *Close* hidden   **58** *Rive* split open   **58** *continents* containers   **58-59** *cry
. . . grace* beg mercy from the vengeful gods (here figured as officers
who summoned a man charged with immorality before the ecclesiastical
court)   **61** *Gracious my lord* my gracious lord   **65** *demanding after*
asking for   **67** *scanted* stinted   **70** *art* magic powers of the alchemists,
who sought to transmute base metals into precious   **76** *Must . . . fit*
must be satisfied with a fortune as tiny as his wit

Fool. This is a brave° night to cool a courtesan. I'll
    speak a prophecy ere I go: *80*

> When priests are more in word than matter;
> When brewers mar their malt with water;
> When nobles are their tailors' tutors,
> No heretics burned, but wenches' suitors;°
> When every case in law is right,   *85*
> No squire in debt nor no poor knight;
> When slanders do not live in tongues;
> Nor cutpurses come not to throngs;
> When usurers tell their gold i' th' field,°
> And bawds and whores do churches build,°   *90*
> Then shall the realm of Albion°
> Come to great confusion.
> Then comes the time, who lives to see't,
> That going shall be used with feet.°

This prophecy Merlin° shall make, for I live before *95*
his time.   *Exit.*

Scene III.   [*Gloucester's castle.*]

Enter Gloucester and Edmund.

Gloucester. Alack, alack, Edmund, I like not this unnatural dealing. When I desired their leave that I
might pity° him, they took from me the use of mine

---

79 *brave* fine   81-84 *When . . . suitors* (the first four prophecies are
fulfilled already, and hence "confusion" has come to England. The
priest does not suit his action to his words. The brewer adulterates
his beer. The nobleman is subservient to his tailor [i.e., cares only for
fashion]. Religious heretics escape, and only those burn [i.e., suffer]
who are afflicted with venereal disease)   89 *tell . . . field* count their
money in the open   85-90 *When . . . build* (the last six prophecies, as
they are Utopian, are meant ironically. They will never be fulfilled)
91 *Albion* England   94 *going . . . feet* people will walk on their feet
95 *Merlin* King Arthur's great magician who, according to Holinshed's
Chronicles, lived later than Lear III.iii.   3 *pity* show pity to

5 own house, charged me on pain of perpetual displeasure neither to speak of him, entreat for him,
or any way sustain° him.

Edmund. Most savage and unnatural.

Gloucester. Go to; say you nothing. There is division°
between the Dukes, and a worse° matter than that.
10 I have received a letter this night—'tis dangerous
to be spoken°—I have locked the letter in my
closet.° These injuries the King now bears will be
revenged home;° there is part of a power° already
footed;° we must incline to° the King. I will look°
15 him and privily° relieve him. Go you and maintain
talk with the Duke, that my charity be not of° him
perceived. If he ask for me, I am ill and gone to
bed. If I die for it, as no less is threatened me, the
King my old master must be relieved. There is
20 strange things toward,° Edmund; pray you be careful.   *Exit.*

Edmund. This courtesy forbid° thee shall the Duke
Instantly know, and of that letter too.
This seems a fair deserving,° and must draw me
25 That which my father loses—no less than all.
The younger rises when the old doth fall.
                                      Exit.

III.iii. 6 *sustain* care for   8 *division* falling out   9 *worse* more serious
(i.e., the French invasion)   11 *spoken* spoken of   12 *closet* room
13 *home* to the utmost   13 *power* army   14 *footed* landed   14 *incline to*
take the side of   14 *look* search for   15 *privily* secretly   16 *of* by
20 *toward* impending   22 *courtesy forbid* kindness forbidden (i.e., to
Lear)   24 *fair deserving* an action deserving reward

Scene IV.   [*The heath. Before a hovel.*]

Enter Lear, Kent, and Fool.

Kent. Here is the place, my lord. Good my lord,
    enter.
The tyranny of the open night's too rough
For nature to endure.

                                    Storm still.

Lear.   Let me alone.

Kent. Good my lord, enter here.

Lear.   Wilt break my heart?°

Kent. I had rather break mine own. Good my lord,
    enter.   *5*

Lear. Thou think'st 'tis much that this contentious
    storm
Invades us to the skin: so 'tis to thee;
But where the greater malady is fixed,°
The lesser is scarce felt. Thou'dst shun a bear;
But if thy flight lay toward the roaring sea,   *10*
Thou'dst meet the bear i' th' mouth.° When the
    mind's free,°
The body's delicate. The tempest in my mind
Doth from my senses take all feeling else,
Save what beats there. Filial ingratitude,
Is it not as° this mouth should tear this hand   *15*
For lifting food to't? But I will punish home.°
No, I will weep no more. In such a night
To shut me out! Pour on, I will endure.

III.iv. 4 *break my heart* i.e., by shutting out the storm which distracts
me from thinking 8 *fixed* lodged (in the mind) 11 *i' th' mouth* in the
teeth 11 *free* i.e., from care 15 *as* as if 16 *home* to the utmost

In such a night as this! O Regan, Goneril,
Your old kind father, whose frank° heart gave
　　all—
20
O, that way madness lies; let me shun that.
No more of that.

Kent.　　　　　　　Good my lord, enter here.

Lear. Prithee go in thyself; seek thine own ease.
This tempest will not give me leave to ponder
On things would hurt me more, but I'll go in.
25
[*To the Fool*] In, boy; go first. You houseless
　　poverty°—
Nay, get thee in. I'll pray, and then I'll sleep.

　　　　　　　　　　　　　　　Exit [*Fool*].

Poor naked wretches, wheresoe'er you are,
That bide° the pelting of this pitiless storm,
30
How shall your houseless heads and unfed sides,
Your looped and windowed° raggedness, defend
　　you
From seasons such as these? O, I have ta'en
Too little care of this! Take physic, pomp;°
Expose thyself to feel what wretches feel,
35
That thou mayst shake the superflux° to them,
And show the heavens more just.

Edgar. [*Within*] Fathom and half, fathom and half!°
Poor Tom!

　　　　　　　　　　　Enter Fool.

Fool. Come not in here, Nuncle, here's a spirit. Help
40
me, help me!

Kent. Give me thy hand. Who's there?

Fool. A spirit, a spirit. He says his name's Poor Tom.

Kent. What art thou that dost grumble there i' th'
　　straw?
　　Come forth.

---

20 *frank* liberal (magnanimous)　**26** *houseless poverty* (the unsheltered
poor, abstracted)　**29** *bide* endure　**31** *looped and windowed* full of
holes　**33** *Take physic, pomp* take medicine to cure yourselves, you
great men　**35** *superflux* superfluity　**37** *Fathom and half* (Edgar, because of the downpour, pretends to take soundings)

Enter Edgar [disguised as a madman].

Edgar. Away! the foul fiend follows me. Through the ⁴³
sharp hawthorn blows the cold wind.° Humh! Go
to thy cold bed, and warm thee.°

Lear. Didst thou give all to thy daughters? And art
thou come to this?

Edgar. Who gives anything to Poor Tom? Whom the ⁵⁰
foul fiend hath led through fire and through flame,
through ford and whirlpool, o'er bog and quag-
mire; that hath laid knives under his pillow and
halters in his pew,° set ratsbane° by his porridge,°
made him proud of heart, to ride on a bay trotting ⁵⁵
horse over four-inched bridges,° to course° his
own shadow for° a traitor. Bless thy five wits,°
Tom's a-cold. O, do, de, do, de, do, de. Bless thee
from whirlwinds, star-blasting,° and taking.° Do
Poor Tom some charity, whom the foul fiend vexes. ⁶⁰
There could I have him now—and there—and
there again—and there.

Storm still.

Lear. What, has his daughters brought him to this
pass?°
Couldst thou save nothing? Wouldst thou give 'em
all?

Fool. Nay, he reserved a blanket,° else we had been ⁶⁵
all shamed.

Lear. Now all the plagues that in the pendulous° air
Hang fated o'er° men's faults light on thy
daughters!

---

⁴⁵⁻⁴⁶ *Through . . . wind* (a line from the ballad of "The Friar of
Orders Gray") ⁴⁶⁻⁴⁷ *go . . . thee* (a reminiscence of *The Taming of
the Shrew,* Induction, 1.10) ⁵³⁻⁵⁴ *knives . . . halters . . . ratsbane* (the
fiend tempts Poor Tom to suicide) ⁵⁴ *pew* gallery or balcony outside
a window ⁵⁴ *porridge* broth ⁵⁵⁻⁵⁶ *ride . . . bridges* i.e., risk his life
⁵⁶ *course* chase ⁵⁷ *for* as ⁵⁷ *five wits* i.e., common wit, imagination,
fantasy, estimation, memory ⁵⁹ *star-blasting* the evil caused by malignant stars ⁵⁹ *taking* pernicious influences ⁶³ *pass* wretched condition
⁶⁵ *blanket* i.e., to cover his nakedness ⁶⁷ *pendulous* overhanging
⁶⁸ *fated o'er* destined to punish

Kent. He hath no daughters, sir.

Lear. Death, traitor; nothing could have subdued°
70   nature
To such a lowness but his unkind daughters.
Is it the fashion that discarded fathers
Should have thus little mercy on° their flesh?
Judicious punishment—'twas this flesh begot
75   Those pelican° daughters.

Edgar. Pillicock sat on Pillicock Hill.° Alow, alow,
loo, loo!°

Fool. This cold night will turn us all to fools and
madmen.

80   *Edgar.* Take heed o' th' foul fiend; obey thy parents;
keep thy word's justice;° swear not; commit not°
with man's sworn spouse; set not thy sweet heart
on proud array. Tom's a-cold.

Lear. What hast thou been?

85   *Edgar.* A servingman, proud in heart and mind; that
curled my hair, wore gloves in my cap;° served the
lust of my mistress' heart, and did the act of darkness with her; swore as many oaths as I spake
words, and broke them in the sweet face of
90   heaven. One that slept in the contriving of lust,
and waked to do it. Wine loved I deeply, dice
dearly; and in woman out-paramoured the Turk.°
False of heart, light of ear,° bloody of hand; hog
in sloth, fox in stealth, wolf in greediness, dog in
95   madness, lion in prey.° Let not the creaking° of
shoes nor the rustling of silks betray thy poor

---

70 *subdued* reduced   73 *on* i.e., shown to   75 *pelican* (supposed to feed
on its parent's blood)   76 *Pillicock . . . Hill* (probably quoted from a
nursery rhyme, and suggested by "pelican." *Pillicock* is a term of
endearment and the phallus)   76-77 *Alow . . . loo* (? a hunting call,
or the refrain of the song)   81 *keep . . . justice* i.e., do not break thy
word   81 *commit not* i.e., adultery   86 *gloves in my cap* i.e., as a pledge
from his mistress   92 *out-paramoured the Turk* had more concubines
than the Sultan   93 *light of ear* ready to hear flattery and slander
95 *prey* preying   95 *creaking* (deliberately cultivated, as fashionable)

heart to woman. Keep thy foot out of brothels,
thy hand out of plackets,° thy pen from lenders'
books,° and defy the foul fiend. Still through the
hawthorn blows the cold wind; says suum, mun,   100
nonny.° Dolphin° my boy, boy, sessa!° let him trot
by.

                                      Storm still.

Lear. Thou wert better in a grave than to answer°
with thy uncovered body this extremity° of the
skies. Is man no more than this? Consider him   105
well. Thou ow'st° the worm no silk, the beast no
hide, the sheep no wool, the cat° no perfume. Ha!
here's three on's° are sophisticated.° Thou art the
thing itself; unaccommodated° man is no more
but such a poor, bare, forked° animal as thou art.   110
Off, off, you lendings!° Come, unbutton here.
                            [*Tearing off his clothes.*]

Fool. Prithee, Nuncle, be contented, 'tis a naughty°
night to swim in. Now a little fire in a wild° field
were like an old lecher's heart—a small spark, all
the rest on's body, cold. Look, here comes a walk-   115
ing fire.

                Enter Gloucester, with a torch.

Edgar. This is the foul fiend Flibbertigibbet.° He begins at curfew,° and walks till the first cock.° He
gives the web and the pin,° squints° the eye, and
makes the harelip; mildews the white° wheat, and   120
hurts the poor creature of earth.

---

⁹⁸ *plackets* openings in skirts ⁹⁶⁻⁹⁹ *pen . . . books* i.e., do not enter
your name in the moneylender's account book ¹⁰⁰⁻⁰¹ *suum, mun, nonny*
the noise of the wind ¹⁰¹ *Dolphin* the French Dauphin (identified by
the English with the devil. Poor Tom is presumably quoting from a
ballad) ¹⁰¹ *sessa* an interjection: "Go on!" ¹⁰³ *answer* confront, bear
the brunt of ¹⁰⁴ *extremity* extreme severity ¹⁰⁶ *ow'st* have taken from
¹⁰⁷ *cat* civet cat, whose glands yield perfume ¹⁰⁸ *on's* of us ¹⁰⁸ *sophisticated* adulterated, made artificial ¹⁰⁹ *unaccommodated* uncivilized
¹¹⁰ *forked* i.e., two-legged ¹¹¹ *lendings* borrowed garments ¹¹² *naughty*
wicked ¹¹³ *wild* barren ¹¹⁷ *Flibbertigibbet* (a figure from Elizabethan
demonology) ¹¹⁸ *curfew:* 9 P.M. ¹¹⁸ *first cock* midnight ¹¹⁹ *web and
the pin* cataract ¹¹⁹ *squints* crosses ¹²⁰ *white* ripening

Swithold footed thrice the old;°
He met the nightmare,° and her nine fold;°
　　Bid her alight°
125　　And her troth plight,°
And aroint° thee, witch, aroint thee!

Kent. How fares your Grace?

Lear. What's he?

Kent. Who's there? What is't you seek?

130　*Gloucester.* What are you there? Your names?

Edgar. Poor Tom, that eats the swimming frog, the
toad, the todpole, the wall-newt and the water;°
that in the fury of his heart, when the foul fiend
rages, eats cow-dung for sallets,° swallows the old
135　rat and the ditch-dog,° drinks the green mantle°
of the standing° pool; who is whipped from tithing°
to tithing, and stocked, punished, and imprisoned;
who hath had three suits to his back, six shirts to
his body,
140　　　Horse to ride, and weapon to wear,
　　　But mice and rats, and such small deer,°
　　　Have been Tom's food for seven long year.°
Beware my follower!° Peace, Smulkin,° peace,
thou fiend!

Gloucester. What, hath your Grace no better com-
145　pany?

Edgar. The Prince of Darkness is a gentleman.
Modo° he's called, and Mahu.°

122 *Swithold . . . old* Withold (an Anglo-Saxon saint who subdued
demons) walked three times across the open country　123 *nightmare*
demon　123 *fold* offspring　124 *alight* i.e., from the horse she had
possessed　125 *her troth plight* pledge her word　126 *aroint* be gone
132 *todpole . . . water* tadpole, wall lizard, water newt　134 *sallets*
salads　135 *ditch-dog* dead dog in a ditch　135 *mantle* scum　136 *standing* stagnant　136 *tithing* a district comprising ten families　141-42 *But
. . . year* (adapted from a popular romance, "Bevis of Hampton")
141 *deer* game　143 *follower* familiar　143, 147 *Smulkin, Modo, Mahu*
(Elizabethan devils, from Samuel Harsnett's *Declaration* of 1603)

Gloucester. Our flesh and blood, my Lord, is grown
    so vile
  That it doth hate what gets° it.

Edgar. Poor Tom's a-cold.   *150*

Gloucester. Go in with me. My duty cannot suffer°
  T' obey in all your daughters' hard commands.
  Though their injunction be to bar my doors
  And let this tyrannous night take hold upon you,
  Yet have I ventured to come seek you out   *155*
  And bring you where both fire and food is ready.

Lear. First let me talk with this philosopher.
  What is the cause of thunder?

Kent. Good my lord, take his offer; go into th' house.

Lear. I'll talk a word with this same learnèd Theban.° *160*
  What is your study?°

Edgar. How to prevent° the fiend, and to kill vermin.

Lear. Let me ask you one word in private.

Kent. Importune him once more to go, my lord.
  His wits begin t' unsettle.

Gloucester.   Canst thou blame him?   *165*

                          Storm still.

His daughters seek his death. Ah, that good Kent,
He said it would be thus, poor banished man!
Thou say'st the King grows mad—I'll tell thee,
    friend,
I am almost mad myself. I had a son,
Now outlawed from my blood;° he sought my life *170*
But lately, very late.° I loved him, friend,
No father his son dearer. True to tell thee,
The grief hath crazed my wits. What a night's this!

---

149 *gets* begets   151 *suffer* permit me   160 *Theban* i.e., Greek philosopher   161 *study* particular scientific study   162 *prevent* balk   170 *outlawed from my blood* disowned and tainted, like a carbuncle in the
corrupted blood   171 *late* recently

I do beseech your Grace——

Lear.   O, cry you mercy,° sir.
175   Noble philosopher, your company.

Edgar. Tom's a-cold.

Gloucester. In, fellow, there, into th' hovel; keep thee
    warm.

Lear. Come, let's in all.

Kent.   This way, my lord.

Lear.   With him!
    I will keep still with my philosopher.

Kent. Good my lord, soothe° him; let him take the
180   fellow.

Gloucester. Take him you on.°

Kent. Sirrah, come on; go along with us.

Lear. Come, good Athenian.°

Gloucester. No words, no words! Hush.

185 *Edgar.* Child Rowland to the dark tower came;°
    His word was still,° "Fie, foh, and fum,
    I smell the blood of a British man."°   *Exeunt.*

---

174 *cry you mercy* I beg your pardon   180 *soothe* humor   181 *you on*
with you   183 *Athenian* i.e., philosopher (like "Theban")   185 *Child
. . . came* (? from a lost ballad; "child"=a candidate for knighthood;
Rowland was Charlemagne's nephew, the hero of *The Song of Roland*)
186 *His . . . still* his motto was always   186-87 *Fie . . . man* (a deliberately absurd linking of the chivalric hero with the nursery tale of
Jack the Giant-Killer)

Scene V. [*Gloucester's castle.*]

Enter Cornwall and Edmund.

Cornwall. I will have my revenge ere I depart his house.

Edmund. How, my lord, I may be censured,° that nature thus gives way to loyalty, something fears° me to think of.   5

Cornwall. I now perceive it was not altogether your brother's evil disposition made him seek his death; but a provoking merit, set a-work by a reprovable badness in himself.°

Edmund. How malicious is my fortune that I must   10 repent to be just! This is the letter which he spoke of, which approves° him an intelligent party° to the advantages° of France. O heavens, that his treason were not! or not I the detector!

Cornwall. Go with me to the Duchess.   15

Edmund. If the matter of this paper be certain, you have mighty business in hand.

Cornwall. True or false, it hath made thee Earl of Gloucester. Seek out where thy father is, that he may be ready for our apprehension.°   20

Edmund. [*Aside*] If I find him comforting° the King, it will stuff his suspicion more fully.—I will persever° in my course of loyalty, though the conflict be sore between that and my blood.°

III.v. 3 *censured* judged   4 *something fears* somewhat frightens   8-9 *a provoking . . . himself* a stimulating goodness in Edgar, brought into play by a blamable badness in Gloucester   12 *approves* proves   12 *intelligent party* (1) spy (2) well-informed person   13 *to the advantages* on behalf of   20 *apprehension* arrest   21 *comforting* supporting (a legalism)   23 *persever* persevere   24 *blood* natural feelings

25 *Cornwall.* I will lay trust upon° thee, and thou
shalt find a dearer father in my love.   *Exeunt.*

Scene VI.   [*A chamber in a farmhouse
adjoining the castle.*]

Enter Kent and Gloucester.

Gloucester. Here is better than the open air; take it
thankfully. I will piece out the comfort with what
addition I can. I will not be long from you.

5 *Kent.* All the power of his wits have given way to his
impatience.° The gods reward your kindness.
                    Exit [Gloucester].

Enter Lear, Edgar, and Fool.

Edgar. Frateretto° calls me, and tells me Nero° is
an angler in the lake of darkness. Pray, innocent,°
and beware the foul fiend.

10 *Fool.* Prithee, Nuncle, tell me whether a madman be a
gentleman or a yeoman.°

Lear. A king, a king.

Fool. No, he's a yeoman that has a gentleman to his
son; for he's a mad yeoman that sees his son a gentleman before him.

15 *Lear.* To have a thousand with red burning spits
Come hizzing° in upon 'em——

---

25 *lay trust upon* (1) trust (2) advance III.vi. 5 *impatience* raging
6 *Frateretto* Elizabethan devil, from Harsnett's *Declaration* 6 *Nero*
(who is mentioned by Harsnett, and whose angling is reported by
Chaucer in "The Monk's Tale") 7 *innocent* fool 10 *yeoman* farmer
(just below a gentleman in rank. The Fool asks what class of man has
most indulged his children, and thus been driven mad) 16 *hizzing*
hissing

Edgar. The foul fiend bites my back.

Fool. He's mad that trusts in the tameness of a wolf,
a horse's health, a boy's love, or a whore's oath.

Lear. It shall be done; I will arraign° them straight.°   20
    [*To Edgar*] Come, sit thou here, most learned
        justice.°
    [*To the Fool*] Thou, sapient° sir, sit here. Now,
        you she-foxes——

Edgar. Look, where he° stands and glares. Want'st
thou eyes at trial, madam?°
    Come o'er the bourn,° Bessy, to me.   25

Fool. Her boat hath a leak,
        And she must not speak
        Why she dares not come over to thee.°

Edgar. The foul fiend haunts Poor Tom in the voice
of a nightingale.° Hoppedance° cries in Tom's belly   30
for two white herring.° Croak° not, black angel; I
have no food for thee.

Kent. How do you, sir? Stand you not so amazed.°
Will you lie down and rest upon the cushions?

Lear. I'll see their trial first. Bring in their evidence.   85
    [*To Edgar*] Thou, robèd man of justice, take
        thy place.
    [*To the Fool*] And thou, his yokefellow of equity,°
    Bench° by his side. [*To Kent*] You are o' th'
        commission;°
    Sit you too.

Edgar. Let us deal justly.   40

---

²⁰ *arraign* bring to trial ²⁰ *straight* straightaway ²¹ *justice* justicer,
judge ²² *sapient* wise ²³ *he* i.e., a fiend ²³⁻²⁴ *Want'st . . . madam* (to
Goneril) i.e., do you want eyes to look at you during your trial?
The fiend serves that purpose ²⁵ *bourn* brook (Edgar quotes from a
popular ballad) ²⁶⁻²⁸ *Her . . . thee* (the Fool parodies the ballad)
³⁰ *nightingale* i.e., the Fool's singing ³⁰ *Hoppedance* Hoberdidance
(another devil from Harsnett's *Declaration*) ³¹ *white herring* un-
smoked (? as against the black and sulfurous devil) ³¹ *Croak* rumble
(because his belly is empty) ³³ *amazed* astonished ³⁵ *evidence* the
evidence of witnesses against them ³⁷ *yokefellow of equity* partner in
justice ³⁸ *Bench* sit on the bench ³⁸ *commission* those commissioned
as king's justices

Sleepest or wakest thou, jolly shepherd?
   Thy sheep be in the corn;°
And for one blast of thy minikin° mouth
   \ Thy sheep shall take no harm.°

45   Purr, the cat is gray.°

Lear. Arraign her first. 'Tis Goneril, I here take my
oath before this honorable assembly, she kicked
the poor King her father.

Fool. Come hither, mistress. Is your name Goneril?

50 *Lear.* She cannot deny it.

Fool. Cry you mercy, I took you for a joint stool.°

Lear. And here's another, whose warped looks
      proclaim
What store° her heart is made on. Stop her there!
Arms, arms, sword, fire! Corruption in the place!°
55   False justicer, why hast thou let her 'scape?

Edgar. Bless thy five wits!

Kent. O pity! Sir, where is the patience now
That you so oft have boasted to retain?

Edgar. [*Aside*] My tears begin to take his part so
      much
60   They mar my counterfeiting.°

Lear. The little dogs and all,
Tray, Blanch, and Sweetheart—see, they bark at
      me.

Edgar. Tom will throw his head at them. Avaunt, you
      curs.
   Be thy mouth or black or° white,

41-44 *Sleepest . . . harm* (probably quoted or adapted from an Elizabethan song) **42** *corn* wheat **43** *minikin* shrill **45** *gray* (devils were
thought to assume the shape of a gray cat) **51** *Cry . . . joint stool*
(proverbial and deliberately impudent apology for overlooking a person. A joint stool was a low stool made by a joiner, perhaps here a
stage property to represent Goneril and in line 52, Regan. "Joint stool"
can also suggest the judicial bench; hence Goneril may be identified
by the Fool, ironically, with those in power, who judge) **53** *store*
stuff **54** *Corruption . . . place* bribery in the court **60** *counterfeiting*
i.e., feigned madness **64** *or . . . or* either . . . or

Tooth that poisons if it bite;   65
Mastiff, greyhound, mongrel grim,
Hound or spaniel, brach° or lym,°
Or bobtail tike, or trundle-tail°—
Tom will make him weep and wail;
For, with throwing° thus my head,   70
Dogs leaped the hatch,° and all are fled.

Do, de, de, de. Sessa!° Come, march to wakes°
and fairs and market towns. Poor Tom, thy horn°
is dry.

Lear. Then let them anatomize Regan. See what breeds   75
about her heart.° Is there any cause in nature that
make° these hard hearts? [*To Edgar*] You, sir,
I entertain° for one of my hundred;° only I do not
like the fashion of your garments. You will say
they are Persian;° but let them be changed.   80

Kent. Now, good my lord, lie here and rest awhile.

Lear. Make no noise, make no noise; draw the
curtains.°
So, so. We'll go to supper i' th' morning.

Fool. And I'll go to bed at noon.°

Enter Gloucester.

Gloucester. Come hither, friend. Where is the King
my master?   85

Kent. Here, sir, but trouble him not; his wits are gone.

Gloucester. Good friend, I prithee take him in thy
arms.

---

⁶⁷ *brach* bitch ⁶⁷ *lym* bloodhound (from the liam or leash with
which he was led) ⁶⁸ *bobtail . . . trundle-tail* short-tailed or long-
tailed cur ⁷⁰ *throwing* jerking (as a hound lifts its head from the
ground, the scent having been lost) ⁷¹ *leaped the hatch* leaped over
the lower half of a divided door (i.e., left in a hurry) ⁷² *Sessa* be off
⁷² *wakes* feasts attending the dedication of a church ⁷³ *horn* horn
bottle which the Bedlam used in begging a drink (Edgar is suggesting that he is unable to play his role any longer) ⁷⁵⁻⁷⁶ *Then . . .
heart* i.e., if the Bedlam's horn is dry, let Regan, whose heart has
become as hard as horn, be dissected ⁷⁷ *make* (subjunctive) ⁷⁸ *enter-
tain* engage ⁷⁸ *hundred* i.e., Lear's hundred knights ⁸⁰ *Persian*
gorgeous (ironically of Edgar's rags) ⁸² *curtains* (Lear imagines
himself in bed) ⁸⁴ *And . . . noon* (the Fool's last words)

I have o'erheard a plot of death upon him.
There is a litter ready; lay him in't
And drive toward Dover, friend, where thou shalt
90   meet
Both welcome and protection. Take up thy master.
If thou shouldst dally half an hour, his life,
With thine and all that offer to defend him,
Stand in assurèd loss. Take up, take up,
95   And follow me, that will to some provision°
Give thee quick conduct.°

Kent.   Oppressèd nature sleeps.
This rest might yet have balmed thy broken
        sinews,°
Which, if convenience° will not allow,
Stand in hard cure.° [*To the Fool*] Come, help
        to bear thy master.
Thou must not stay behind.

100 *Gloucester.*   Come, come, away!
                              Exeunt [all but Edgar].

Edgar. When we our betters see bearing our woes,
We scarcely think our miseries our foes.°
Who alone suffers suffers most i' th' mind,
Leaving free° things and happy shows° behind;
105   But then the mind much sufferance° doth o'erskip
When grief hath mates, and bearing fellowship.°
How light and portable° my pain seems now,
When that which makes me bend makes the
        King bow.
He childed as I fathered. Tom, away.
110   Mark the high noises,° and thyself bewray°
When false opinion, whose wrong thoughts° defile
        thee,

---

95 *provision* maintenance 96 *conduct* direction 97 *balmed thy broken*
sinews soothed thy racked nerves 98 *convenience* fortunate occasion
99 *Stand . . . cure* will be hard to cure 102 *our foes* enemies peculiar
to ourselves 104 *free* carefree 104 *shows* scenes 105 *sufferance* suffering 106 *bearing fellowship* suffering has company 107 *portable* able to
be supported or endured 110 *Mark the high noises* observe the rumors
of strife among those in power 110 *bewray* reveal 111 *wrong thoughts*
misconceptions

In thy just proof repeals and reconciles thee.°
What will hap more° tonight, safe 'scape the King!
Lurk,° lurk.   [*Exit.*]

Scene VII.   [*Gloucester's castle.*]

*Enter Cornwall, Regan, Goneril, Edmund, and
Servants.*

Cornwall. [*To Goneril*] Post speedily to my Lord
  your husband; show him this letter. The army of
  France is landed. [*To Servants*] Seek out the
  traitor Gloucester. [*Exeunt some of the Servants.*]

Regan. Hang him instantly.   5

Goneril. Pluck out his eyes.

Cornwall. Leave him to my displeasure. Edmund, keep
  you our sister company. The revenges we are
  bound° to take upon your traitorous father are not
  fit for your beholding. Advise the Duke where you   10
  are going, to a most festinate° preparation. We are
  bound to the like. Our posts° shall be swift and
  intelligent° betwixt us. Farewell, dear sister; farewell, my Lord of Gloucester.°

Enter Oswald.

How now? Where's the King?   15

Oswald. My Lord of Gloucester hath conveyed him
  hence.

---

112 *In . . . thee* on the manifesting of your innocence recalls you
from outlawry and restores amity between you and your father
113 *What . . . more* whatever else happens 114 *Lurk* hide III.vii.
9 *bound* (1) forced (2) purposing to 11 *festinate* speedy 12 *posts*
messengers 13 *intelligent* full of information 14 *Lord of Gloucester*
i.e., Edmund, now elevated to the title

Some five or six and thirty of his knights,
Hot questrists° after him, met him at gate;
Who, with some other of the lords dependants,°
20   Are gone with him toward Dover, where they
            boast
To have well-armèd friends.

Cornwall.   Get horses for your mistress.
                              [*Exit Oswald.*]

Goneril. Farewell, sweet lord, and sister.

Cornwall. Edmund, farewell.
                    [*Exeunt Goneril and Edmund.*]

                    Go seek the traitor Gloucester,
Pinion him like a thief, bring him before us.
                    [*Exeunt other Servants.*]
25   Though well we may not pass upon° his life
Without the form of justice, yet our power
Shall do a court'sy to° our wrath, which men
May blame, but not control.

    Enter Gloucester, brought in by two or three.

                    Who's there, the traitor?

Regan. Ingrateful fox, 'tis he.

30   *Cornwall.* Bind fast his corky° arms.

Gloucester. What means your Graces? Good my
            friends, consider
    You are my guests. Do me no foul play, friends.

Cornwall. Bind him, I say.

                    [*Servants bind him.*]
Regan.   Hard, hard! O filthy traitor.

Gloucester. Unmerciful lady as you are, I'm none.

Cornwall. To this chair bind him. Villain, thou shalt
35   find——

---

18 *questrists* searchers   19 *lords dependants* attendant lords (members of Lear's retinue)   25 *pass upon* pass judgment on   27 *do a
court'sy to* indulge   30 *corky* sapless (because old)

[Regan plucks his beard.°]

Gloucester. By the kind gods, 'tis mostly ignobly done
  To pluck me by the beard.

Regan. So white, and such a traitor?

Gloucester.   Naughty° lady,
  These hairs which thou dost ravish from my chin
  Will quicken° and accuse thee. I am your host.   40
  With robber's hands my hospitable favors°
  You should not ruffle° thus. What will you do?

Cornwall. Come, sir, what letters had you late° from
    France?

Regan. Be simple-answered,° for we know the truth.

Cornwall. And what confederacy have you with the
    traitors   45
  Late footed in the kingdom?

Regan. To whose hands you have sent the lunatic
    King:
  Speak.

Gloucester. I have a letter guessingly° set down,
  Which came from one that's of a neutral heart,
  And not from one opposed.

Cornwall.   Cunning.

Regan.   And false.   50

Cornwall. Where hast thou sent the King?

Gloucester. To Dover.

Regan. Wherefore to Dover? Wast thou not charged
  at peril°——

Cornwall. Wherefore to Dover? Let him answer that.

---

³⁵ s.d. *plucks his beard* (a deadly insult)   ³⁸ *Naughty* wicked   ⁴⁰ *quicken* come to life   ⁴¹ *hospitable favors* face of your host   ⁴² *ruffle* tear at violently   ⁴³ *late* recently   ⁴⁴ *simple-answered* straightforward in answering   ⁴⁸ *guessingly* without certain knowledge   ⁵³ *charged at peril* ordered under penalty

Gloucester. I am tied to th' stake, and I must stand
55   the course.°

Regan. Wherefore to Dover?

Gloucester. Because I would not see thy cruel nails
         Pluck out his poor old eyes; nor thy fierce sister
         In his anointed° flesh rash° boarish fangs.
60   The sea, with such a storm as his bare head
         In hell-black night endured, would have buoyed° up
         And quenched the stellèd° fires.
         Yet, poor old heart, he holp° the heavens to rain.
         If wolves had at thy gate howled that dearn° time,
         Thou shouldst have said, "Good porter, turn the
65   key."°
         All cruels else subscribe.° But I shall see
         The wingèd° vengeance overtake such children.

Cornwall. See't shalt thou never. Fellows, hold the
           chair.
         Upon these eyes of thine I'll set my foot.

Gloucester. He that will think° to live till he be
70   old,
         Give me some help. —O cruel! O you gods!

Regan. One side will mock° another. Th' other too.

Cornwall. If you see vengeance——

First Servant.   Hold your hand, my lord!
         I have served you ever since I was a child;
75   But better service have I never done you
         Than now to bid you hold.

Regan.   How now, you dog?

First Servant. If you did wear a beard upon your chin,

---

55 *course* coursing (in which a relay of dogs baits a bull or bear
tied in the pit)   59 *anointed* holy (because king)   59 *rash* strike with
the tusk, like a boar   61 *buoyed* risen   62 *stellèd* (1) fixed (as opposed to the planets or wandering stars)   (2) starry   63 *holp* helped
64 *dearn* dread   65 *turn the key* i.e., unlock the gate   66 *All cruels else
subscribe* all cruel creatures but man are compassionate   67 *wingèd*
(1) heavenly (2) swift   70 *will think* expects   72 *mock* make ridic-
ulous (because of the contrast)

I'd shake it° on this quarrel. What do you mean!°

Cornwall. My villain!°

Draw and fight.

First Servant. Nay, then, come on, and take the
    chance of·anger.   80

Regan. Give me thy sword. A peasant stand up thus?

She takes a sword and runs at him behind,
kills him.

First Servant. O, I am slain! my lord, you have one
    eye left
To see some mischief° on him. O!

Cornwall. Lest it see more, prevent it. Out, vile jelly.
    Where is thy luster now?   85

Gloucester. All dark and comfortless. Where's my son
    Edmund?
Edmund, enkindle all the sparks of nature°
To quit° this horrid act.

Regan.   Out, treacherous villain,
Thou call'st on him that hates thee. It was he
That made the overture° of thy treasons to us;   90
Who is too good to pity thee.

Gloucester. O my follies! Then Edgar was abused.°
Kind gods, forgive me that, and prosper him.

Regan. Go thrust him out at gates, and let him smell
His way to Dover.   *Exit [one] with Gloucester.*
           How is't, my lord? How look you?°   95

Cornwall. I have received a hurt. Follow me, lady.
Turn out that eyeless villain. Throw this slave
Upon the dunghill. Regan, I bleed apace.

---

78 *shake it* (an insult comparable to Regan's plucking of Gloucester's
beard)   78 *What . . . mean* i.e., what terrible thing are you doing
79 *villain* serf (with a suggestion of the modern meaning)   83 *mis-*
chief injury   87 *enkindle . . . nature* fan your natural feeling into
flame   88 *quit* requite   90 *overture* disclosure   92 *abused* wronged
95 *How look you* how are you

Untimely comes this hurt. Give me your arm.

Exeunt.

100 *Second Servant*. I'll never care what wickedness I do,
If this man come to good.

Third Servant.   If she live long,
And in the end meet the old course of death,°
Women will all turn monsters.

Second Servant. Let's follow the old Earl, and get the
Bedlam
105   To lead him where he would. His roguish madness
Allows itself to anything.°

Third Servant. Go thou. I'll fetch some flax and
whites of eggs
To apply to his bleeding face. Now heaven help
him.   [*Exeunt severally.*]

---

102 *meet . . . death* die the customary death of old age   105-6 *His
. . . anything* his lack of all self-control leaves him open to any
suggestion

ACT IV

Scene I.   [*The heath.*]

Enter Edgar.

Edgar. Yet better thus, and known to be contemned,°
    Than still contemned and flattered. To be worst,
    The lowest and most dejected° thing of fortune,
    Stands still in esperance,° lives not in fear:
    The lamentable change is from the best,   *5*
    The worst returns to laughter.° Welcome then,
    Thou unsubstantial air that I embrace!
    The wretch that thou hast blown unto the worst
    Owes° nothing to thy blasts.

Enter Gloucester, led by an Old Man.

                      But who comes here?
    My father, poorly led?° World, world, O world!   *10*
    But that thy strange mutations make us hate thee,
    Life would not yield to age.°

Old Man. O, my good lord, I have been your tenant,
    and your father's tenant, these fourscore years.

Gloucester. Away, get thee away; good friend, be
    gone: *15*

IV.i. 1 *known to be contemned* conscious of being despised   3 *dejected*
abased 4 *esperance* hope 6 *returns to laughter* changes for the better
9 *Owes* is in debt for 10 *poorly led* (1) led like a poor man, with
only one attendant (2) led by a poor man 11-12 *But . . . age* we
should not agree to grow old and hence die, except for the hateful
mutability of life

Thy comforts° can do me no good at all;
Thee they may hurt.°

Old Man.   You cannot see your way.

Gloucester. I have no way and therefore want° no
        eyes;
    I stumbled when I saw. Full oft 'tis seen,
20 Our means secure us, and our mere defects
    Prove our commodities.° Oh, dear son Edgar,
    The food° of thy abusèd° father's wrath!
    Might I but live to see thee in° my touch,
    I'd say I had eyes again!

Old Man.   How now! Who's there?

Edgar. [*Aside*] O gods! Who is 't can say "I am at
25   the worst"?
    I am worse than e'er I was.

Old Man.   'Tis poor mad Tom.

Edgar. [*Aside*] And worse I may be yet: the worst
        is not
    So long as we can say "This is the worst."°

Old Man. Fellow, where goest?

Gloucester.   Is it a beggar-man?

30 *Old Man.* Madman and beggar too.

Gloucester. He has some reason,° else he could not
        beg.
    I' th' last night's storm I such a fellow saw,
    Which made me think a man a worm. My son
    Came then into my mind, and yet my mind
    Was then scarce friends with him. I have heard
35   more since.
    As flies to wanton° boys, are we to th' gods,

---

16 *comforts* ministrations 17 *hurt* injure 18 *want* require 20-21 *Our
. . . commodities* our resources make us overconfident, while our
afflictions make for our advantage 22 *food* i.e., the object on which
Gloucester's anger fed 22 *abusèd* deceived 23 *in* i.e., with, by means
of 27-28 *the . . . worst* so long as a man continues to suffer (i.e., is
still alive), even greater suffering may await him 31 *reason* faculty
of reasoning 36 *wanton* (1) playful (2) reckless

They kill us for their sport.

Edgar. [*Aside*]   How should this be?°
  Bad is the trade that must play fool to sorrow,
  Ang'ring° itself and others. Bless thee, master!

Gloucester. Is that the naked fellow?

Old Man.   Ay, my lord.   40

Gloucester. Then, prithee, get thee gone: if for my
    sake
  Thou wilt o'ertake us hence a mile or twain
  I' th' way toward Dover, do it for ancient° love,
  And bring some covering for this naked soul,
  Which I'll entreat to lead me.

Old Man.   Alack, sir, he is mad.   45

Gloucester. 'Tis the times' plague,° when madmen
    lead the blind.
  Do as I bid thee, or rather do thy pleasure;°
  Above the rest,° be gone.

Old Man. I'll bring him the best 'parel° that I have,
  Come on 't what will.   *Exit.*   50

Gloucester. Sirrah, naked fellow——

Edgar. Poor Tom's a-cold. [*Aside*] I cannot daub
  it° further.

Gloucester. Come hither, fellow.

Edgar. [*Aside*] And yet I must. ——Bless thy sweet
    eyes, they bleed.   55

Gloucester. Know'st thou the way to Dover?

Edgar. Both stile and gate, horse-way and footpath.
  Poor Tom hath been scared out of his good wits.
  Bless thee, good man's son, from the foul fiend!
  Five fiends have been in Poor Tom at once; of lust,   60

---

37 *How should this be* i.e., how can this horror be? 39 *Ang'ring*
offending 43 *ancient* (1) the love the Old Man feels, by virtue of
his long tenancy (2) the love that formerly obtained between master
and man 46 *times' plague* characteristic disorder of this time 47 *thy
pleasure* as you like 48 *the rest* all 49 *'parel* apparel 52-53 *daub it* lay
it on (figure from plastering mortar)

as Obidicut;° Hobbididence, prince of dumbness;° Mahu, of stealing; Modo, of murder; Flibbertigibbet, of mopping and mowing;° who since
possesses chambermaids and waiting-women. So,
65   bless thee, master!

Gloucester. Here, take this purse, thou whom the
          heavens' plagues
Have humbled to all strokes:° that I am wretched
Makes thee the happier. Heavens, deal so still!
Let the superfluous° and lust-dieted° man,
70   That slaves° your ordinance,° that will not see
Because he does not feel, feel your pow'r quickly;
So distribution should undo excess,°
And each man have enough. Dost thou know
          Dover?

Edgar. Ay, master.

Gloucester. There is a cliff whose high and bending°
75   head
Looks fearfully° in the confinèd deep:°
Bring me but to the very brim of it,
And I'll repair the misery thou dost bear
With something rich about me: from that place
I shall no leading need.

80   *Edgar.*   Give me thy arm:
Poor Tom shall lead thee.   *Exeunt.*

---

61 *Obidicut* Hoberdicut, a devil (like the four that follow, from Harsnett's *Declaration*)   61-62 *dumbness* muteness (like the crimes and
afflictions in the next lines, the result of diabolic possession)
63 *mopping and mowing* grimacing and making faces   67 *humbled to
all strokes* brought so low as to bear anything humbly   69 *superfluous*
possessed of superfluities   69 *lust-dieted* whose lust is gratified (like
Gloucester's)   70 *slaves* (1) tramples, spurns like a slave (2) ?
tears, rends (Old English *slaefan*)   70 *ordinance* law   72 *So . . . excess*
then the man with too much wealth would distribute it among those
with too little   75 *bending* overhanging   76 *fearfully* occasioning fear
76 *confinèd deep* the sea, hemmed in below

Scene II.   [*Before the Duke of Albany's palace.*]

Enter Goneril and Edmund.

Goneril. Welcome, my lord: I marvel our mild
    husband
Not met° us on the way.

               Enter Oswald.

                    Now, where's your master?

Oswald. Madam, within; but never man so changed.
I told him of the army that was landed:
He smiled at it. I told him you were coming;   5
His answer was, "The worse." Of Gloucester's
    treachery,
And of the loyal service of his son
When I informed him, then he called me sot,°
And told me I had turned the wrong side out:
What most he should dislike seems pleasant to him;   10
What like,° offensive.

Goneril. [*To Edmund*] Then shall you go no
    further.
It is the cowish° terror of his spirit,
That dares not undertake:° he'll not feel wrongs,
Which tie him to an answer.° Our wishes on the
    way
May prove effects.° Back, Edmund, to my brother;   15
Hasten his musters° and conduct his pow'rs.°

IV.ii. 2 *Not met* did not meet   8 *sot* fool   11 *What like* what he
should like   12 *cowish* cowardly   13 *undertake* venture   14 *tie him to
an answer* oblige him to retaliate   14-15 *Our . . . effects* our desires
(that you might be my husband), as we journeyed here, may be
fulfilled   16 *musters* collecting of troops   16 *conduct his pow'rs* lead
his army

I must change names° at home and give the
  distaff°
Into my husband's hands. This trusty servant
Shall pass between us: ere long you are like to hear,
20   If you dare venture in your own behalf,
A mistress's° command. Wear this; spare speech;

                    [*Giving a favor*]

Decline your head.° This kiss, if it durst speak,
Would stretch thy spirits up into the air:
Conceive,° and fare thee well.

Edmund. Yours in the ranks of death.

25   *Goneril.*   My most dear Gloucester!
                         Exit [*Edmund*].

O, the difference of man and man!
To thee a woman's services are due:
My fool usurps my body.°

Oswald.   Madam, here comes my lord.
                              Exit.

                    Enter Albany.

Goneril. I have been worth the whistle.°

Albany.   O Goneril!
30   You are not worth the dust which the rude wind
Blows in your face. I fear your disposition:°
That nature which contemns° its origin
Cannot be bordered certain in itself;°
She that herself will sliver and disbranch°

---

17 *change names* i.e., exchange the name of "mistress" for that of
"master"   17 *distaff* spinning stick (wifely symbol)   21 *mistress's* lover's (and also, Albany having been disposed of, lady's or wife's)
22 *Decline your head* i.e., that Goneril may kiss him   24 *Conceive*
understand (with a sexual implication, that includes "stretch thy
spirits," l. 23; and "death," l. 25: "to die," meaning "to experience
sexual intercourse")   28 *My fool usurps body* my husband wrong-
fully enjoys me   29 *I . . . whistle* i.e., once you valued me (the
proverb is implied, "It is a poor dog that is not worth the whistling")
31 *disposition* nature   32 *contemns* despises   33 *bordered . . . itself*
kept within its normal bounds   34 *sliver and disbranch* cut off

From her material sap,° perforce must wither   *35*
And come to deadly use.°

Goneril. No more; the text° is foolish.

Albany. Wisdom and goodness to the vile seem vile:
Filths savor but themselves.° What have you done?
Tigers, not daughters, what have you performed?   *40*
A father, and a gracious agèd man,
Whose reverence even the head-lugged bear°
     would lick,
Most barbarous, most degenerate, have you
     madded.°
Could my good brother suffer you to do it?
A man, a prince, by him so benefited!   *45*
If that the heavens do not their visible spirits°
Send quickly down to tame these vile offenses,
It will come,
Humanity must perforce prey on itself,
Like monsters of the deep.

Goneril.   Milk-livered° man!   *50*
That bear'st a cheek for blows, a head for wrongs;
Who hast not in thy brows an eye discerning
Thine honor from thy suffering;° that not know'st
Fools do those villains pity who are punished
Ere they have done their mischief.° Where's thy
     drum?   *55*
France spreads his banners in our noiseless°
     land,
With plumèd helm° thy state begins to threat,°

---

³⁵ *material sap* essential and life-giving sustenance ³⁶ *come to deadly use* i.e., be as a dead branch for the burning ³⁷ *text* i.e., on which your sermon is based ³⁹ *Filths savor but themselves* the filthy relish only the taste of filth ⁴² *head-lugged bear* bear-baited by the dogs, and hence enraged ⁴³ *madded* made mad ⁴⁶ *visible spirits* avenging spirits in material form ⁵⁰ *Milk-livered* lily-livered (hence cowardly, the liver being regarded as the seat of courage) ⁵²⁻⁵³ *discerning . . . suffering* able to distinguish between insults that ought to be resented, and ordinary pain that is to be borne ⁵⁴⁻⁵⁵ *Fools . . . mischief* only fools are sorry for criminals whose intended criminality is prevented by punishment ⁵⁶ *noiseless* i.e., the drum, signifying preparation for war, is silent ⁵⁷ *helm* helmet ⁵⁷ *thy . . . threat* France begins to threaten Albany's realm

Whilst thou, a moral° fool, sits still and cries
"Alack, why does he so?"

Albany.   See thyself, devil!
60 Proper° deformity seems not in the fiend
So horrid as in woman.

Goneril.   O vain fool!

Albany. Thou changèd and self-covered° thing,
    for shame,
Be-monster not thy feature.° Were 't my fitness°
To let these hands obey my blood,°
65 They are apt enough to dislocate and tear
Thy flesh and bones: howe'er° thou art a fiend,
A woman's shape doth shield thee.

Goneril. Marry,° your manhood mew°——

                Enter a Messenger.

Albany. What news?

Messenger. O, my good lord, the Duke of Cornwall's
70   dead,
Slain by his servant, going to° put out
The other eye of Gloucester.

Albany.   Gloucester's eyes!

Messenger. A servant that he bred,° thrilled with
    remorse,°
Opposed against the act, bending his sword
75 To his great master, who thereat enraged
Flew on him, and amongst them felled° him dead,
But not without that harmful stroke which since

---

58 *moral* moralizing; but also with the implication that morality and
folly are one   60 *Proper* (1) natural (to a fiend) (2) fair-appearing
62 *changèd and self-covered* i.e., transformed, by the contorting of
her woman's face, on which appears the fiendish behavior she has
allowed herself. (Goneril has disguised nature by wickedness)   63 *Be-
monster not thy feature* do not change your appearance into a
fiend's   63 *my fitness* appropriate for me   64 *blood* passion   66 *howe'er*
but even if   68 *Marry* by the Virgin Mary   68 *your manhood mew*
(1) coop up or confine your (pretended) manhood (2) molt or shed
it, if that is what is supposed to "shield" me from you   71 *going to*
as he was about to   73 *bred* reared   73 *thrilled with remorse* pierced
by compassion   76 *amongst them felled* others assisting, they felled

Hath plucked him after.°

Albany.   This shows you are above,
Y   justicers,° that these our nether° crimes
S   ly can venge.° But, O poor Gloucester!   80
I   his other eye?

Messenger.   Both, both, my lord.
This   ter, madam, craves° a speedy answer;
'Tis from your sister.

Goneril.   [*Aside*] One way I like this well;
But being widow, and my Gloucester with her,
May all the building in my fancy pluck   85
Upon my hateful life.° Another way,°
The news is not so tart.°—I'll read, and answer.
                                          Exit.

Albany. Where was his son when they did take his
     eyes?

Messenger. Come with my lady hither.

Albany.   He is not here.

Messenger. No, my good lord; I met him back° again.   90

Albany. Knows he the wickedness?

Messenger. Ay, my good lord; 'twas he informed
     against him,
And quit the house on purpose, that their punish-
     ment
Might have the freer course.

Albany.   Gloucester, I live
To thank thee for the love thou showed'st the
     King,   95
And to revenge thine eyes. Come hither, friend:
Tell me what more thou know'st.   *Exeunt.*

---

⁷⁸ *plucked him after* i.e., brought Cornwall to death with his servant ⁷⁹ *justicers* judges ⁷⁹ *nether* committed below (on earth)
⁸⁰ *venge* avenge ⁸² *craves* demands ⁸⁵⁻⁸⁶ *May . . . life* these things
(1.84) may send my future hopes, my castles in air, crashing down
upon the hateful (married) life I lead now ⁸⁶ *Another way* looked
at another way ⁸⁷ *tart* sour ⁹⁰ *back* going back

[Scene III.   *The French camp near Dover.*]

Enter Kent and a Gentleman.

Kent. Why the King of France is so suddenly gone
  back, know you no reason?

Gentleman. Something he left imperfect in the
  state,° which since his coming forth is thought of,
5 which imports° to the kingdom so much fear and
  danger that his personal return was most required
  and necessary.

Kent. Who hath he left behind him general?

Gentleman. The Marshal of France, Monsieur La Far.

10 *Kent.* Did your letters pierce° the queen to any dem-
  onstration of grief?

Gentleman. Ay, sir; she took them, read them in my
    presence,
  And now and then an ample tear trilled° down
  Her delicate cheek: it seemed she was a queen
15 Over her passion, who most rebel-like
  Sought to be king o'er her.

Kent.   O, then it moved her.

Gentleman. Not to a rage: patience and sorrow
    strove
  Who should express her goodliest.° You have seen
  Sunshine and rain at once: her smiles and tears
20 Were like a better way:° those happy smilets°
  That played on her ripe lip seemed not to know
  What guests were in her eyes, which parted thence

IV.iii. ³⁻⁴ *imperfect in the state* unsettled in his own kingdom   ⁵ *im-ports* portends   ¹⁰ *pierce* impel   ¹³ *trilled* trickled   ¹⁸ *Who . . . goodliest* which should give her the most becoming expression   ²⁰ *Were like a better way* i.e., improved on that spectacle   ²⁰ *smilets* little smiles

As pearls from diamonds dropped. In brief,
Sorrow would be a rarity most belovèd,
If all could so become it.°

Kent.   Made she no verbal question?   25

Gentleman. Faith, once or twice she heaved° the name
    of "father"
Pantingly forth, as if it pressed her heart;
Cried "Sisters! Sisters! Shame of ladies! Sisters!
Kent! Father! Sisters! What, i' th' storm? i' th'
    night?
Let pity not be believed!"° There she shook   30
The holy water from her heavenly eyes,
And clamor moistened:° then away she started
To deal with grief alone.

Kent.   It is the stars,
The stars above us, govern our conditions;°
Else one self mate and make could not beget   35
Such different issues.° You spoke not with her
    since?

Gentleman. No.

Kent. Was this before the King returned?

Gentleman.   No, since.

Kent. Well, sir, the poor distressèd Lear's i' th'
    town;
Who sometime in his better tune° remembers   40
What we are come about, and by no means
Will yield to see his daughter.

Gentleman.   Why, good sir?

Kent. A sovereign° shame so elbows° him: his own
    unkindness

24-25 *Sorrow . . . it* sorrow would be a coveted jewel if it became
others as it does her   26 *heaved* expressed with difficulty   30 *Let pity
not be believed* let it not be believed for pity   32 *clamor moistened*
moistened clamor, i.e., mixed (and perhaps assuaged) her outcries
with tears   34 *govern our conditions* determine what we are
35-36 *Else . . . issues* otherwise the same husband and wife could
not produce such different children   40 *better tune* composed, less
jangled intervals   43 *sovereign* overpowering   43 *elbows* jogs his elbow
i.e., reminds him

That stripped her from his benediction, turned her
45 To foreign casualties,° gave her dear rights
To his dog-hearted daughters: these things sting
His mind so venomously that burning shame
Detains him from Cordelia.

Gentleman.   Alack, poor gentleman!

Kent. Of Albany's and Cornwall's powers you heard
not?

50 *Gentleman.* 'Tis so;° they are afoot.

Kent. Well, sir, I'll bring you to our master Lear,
And leave you to attend him: some dear cause°
Will in concealment wrap me up awhile;
When I am known aright, you shall not grieve
55 Lending me this acquaintance. I pray you, go
Along with me.   [*Exeunt.*]

[Scene IV.   *The same. A tent.*]

*Enter, with drum and colors, Cordelia, Doctor,
and Soldiers.*

Cordelia. Alack, 'tis he: why, he was met even now
As mad as the vexed sea; singing aloud;
Crowned with rank femiter and furrow-weeds,
With hardocks, hemlock, nettles, cuckoo-flow'rs,
5 Darnel,° and all the idle weeds that grow
In our sustaining corn.° A century° send forth;
Search every acre in the high-grown field,

45 *casualties* chances   50 *'Tis so* i.e., I have heard of them   52 *dear cause* important reason   IV.iv. 3-5 *femiter . . . Darnel: femiter* fumitory, whose leaves and juice are bitter; *furrow-weeds* weeds that grow in the furrow; or plowed land; *hardocks* ? hoar or white docks, burdocks, harlocks; *hemlock* a poison; *nettles* plants which sting and burn; *cuckoo-flow'rs* identified with a plant employed to remedy diseases of the brain; *Darnel* tares, noisome weeds   6 *sustaining corn* life-maintaining wheat   6 *century* ? sentry; troop of a hundred soldiers

And bring him to our eye [*Exit an Officer.*] What
    can man's wisdom°
In the restoring his bereavèd° sense?
He that helps him take all my outward° worth.   10

Doctor. There is means, madam:
    Our foster-nurse° of nature is repose,
    The which he lacks: that to provoke° in him,
    Are many simples operative,° whose power
    Will close the eye of anguish.

Cordelia.   All blest secrets,   15
    All you unpublished virtues° of the earth,
    Spring with my tears! be aidant and remediate°
    In the good man's distress! Seek, seek for him,
    Lest his ungoverned rage dissolve the life
    That wants the means to lead it.°

                Enter Messenger.

Messenger.   News, madam;   20
    The British pow'rs are marching hitherward.

Cordelia. 'Tis known before. Our preparation stands
    In expectation of them. O dear father,
    It is thy business that I go about;
    Therefore° great France   25
    My mourning and importuned° tears hath pitied.
    No blown° ambition doth our arms incite,
    But love, dear love, and our aged father's right:
    Soon may I hear and see him!   *Exeunt.*

---

8 *What can man's wisdom* what can science accomplish   9 *bereavèd*
impaired   10 *outward* material   12 *foster-nurse* fostering nurse   13 *provoke* induce   14 *simples operative* efficacious medicinal herbs   16 *un-
published virtues* i.e., secret remedial herbs   17 *remediate* remedial
20 *wants . . . it* i.e., lacks the reason to control the rage   25 *Therefore* because of that   26 *importuned* importunate   27 *blown* puffed up

[Scene V. *Gloucester's castle.*]

Enter Regan and Oswald.

Regan. But are my brother's pow'rs set forth?

Oswald.   Ay, madam.

Regan. Himself in person there?

Oswald.   Madam, with much ado:°
Your sister is the better soldier.

Regan. Lord Edmund spake not with your lord at
        home?

5 *Oswald.* No, madam.

Regan. What might import° my sister's letter to him?

Oswald. I know not, lady.

Regan. Faith, he is posted° hence on serious matter.
It was great ignorance,° Gloucester's eyes being
        out,
10   To let him live. Where he arrives he moves
All hearts against us: Edmund, I think, is gone,
In pity of his misery, to dispatch
His nighted° life; moreover, to descry
The strength o' th' enemy.

Oswald. I must needs after him, madam, with my
15   letter.

Regan. Our troops set forth tomorrow: stay with us;
The ways are dangerous.

Oswald.   I may not, madam:
My lady charged my duty° in this business.

IV.v. 2 *ado* bother and persuasion 6 *import* purport, carry as its
message 8 *is posted* has ridden speedily 9 *ignorance* folly 13 *nighted*
(1) darkened, because blinded (2) benighted 18 *charged my duty*
ordered me as a solemn duty

Regan. Why should she write to Edmund? Might not
   you
   Transport her purposes° by word? Belike,°   20
   Some things I know not what. I'll love thee much,
   Let me unseal the letter.

Oswald.   Madam, I had rather——

Regan. I know your lady does not love her husband;
   I am sure of that: and at her late° being here
   She gave strange eliads° and most speaking looks   25
   To noble Edmund. I know you are of her bosom.°

Oswald. I, madam?

Regan. I speak in understanding: y'are; I know 't:
   Therefore I do advise you, take this note:°
   My lord is dead; Edmund and I have talked;   30
   And more convenient° is he for my hand
   Than for your lady's: you may gather more.°
   If you do find him, pray you, give him this;°
   And when your mistress hears thus much from you,
   I pray, desire her call° her wisdom to her.   35
   So, fare you well.
   If you do chance to hear of that blind traitor,
   Preferment° falls on him that cuts him off.

Oswald. Would I could meet him, madam! I should
   show
   What party I do follow.

Regan.   Fare thee well.   40

               Exeunt.

---

[20] *Transport her purposes* convey her intentions [20] *Belike* probably
[24] *late* recently [25] *eliads* amorous looks [26] *of her bosom* in her
confidence [29] *take this note* take note of this [31] *convenient* fitting
[32] *gather more* surmise more yourself [33] *this* this advice [35] *call*
recall [38] *Preferment* promotion

[Scene VI.   *Fields near Dover.*]

Enter Gloucester and Edgar.

Gloucester. When shall I come to th' top of that same
    hill?
Edgar. You do climb up it now. Look, how we labor.
Gloucester. Methinks the ground is even.
Edgar.   Horrible steep.
    Hark, do you hear the sea?
Gloucester.   No, truly.
5   *Edgar.* Why then your other senses grow imperfect
    By your eyes' anguish.°
Gloucester.   So may it be indeed.
    Methinks thy voice is altered, and thou speak'st
    In better phrase and matter than thou didst.
Edgar. Y'are much deceived: in nothing am I changed
    But in my garments.
10 *Gloucester.*   Methinks y'are better spoken.
Edgar. Come on, sir; here's the place: stand still. How
    fearful
    And dizzy 'tis to cast one's eyes so low!
    The crows and choughs° that wing the midway air°
    Show scarce so gross° as beetles. Half way down
15 Hangs one that gathers sampire,° dreadful trade!
    Methinks he seems no bigger than his head.
    The fishermen that walk upon the beach
    Appear like mice; and yond tall anchoring° bark
    Diminished to her cock;° her cock, a buoy

IV.vi. ⁶ *anguish* pain ¹³ *choughs* a kind of crow ¹³ *midway air* i.e.,
halfway down the cliff ¹⁴ *gross* large ¹⁵ *sampire* samphire, an aromatic
herb associated with Dover Cliffs ¹⁸ *anchoring* anchored ¹⁹ *cock* cock-
boat, a small boat usually towed behind the ship

Almost too small for sight. The murmuring surge   20
That on th' unnumb'red idle pebble° chafes
Cannot be heard so high. I'll look no more,
Lest my brain turn and the deficient sight
Topple° down headlong.

Gloucester.   Set me where you stand.

Edgar. Give me your hand: you are now within a foot   25
Of th' extreme verge: for all beneath the moon
Would I not leap upright.°

Gloucester.   Let go my hand.
Here, friend, 's another purse; in it a jewel
Well worth a poor man's taking. Fairies° and gods
Prosper it with thee! Go thou further off;   30
Bid me farewell, and let me hear thee going.

Edgar. Now fare ye well, good sir.

Gloucester.   With all my heart.

Edgar. [*Aside*] Why I do trifle thus with his despair
Is done to cure it.°

Gloucester.   O you mighty gods!

                              He kneels.

This world I do renounce, and in your sights   35
Shake patiently my great affliction off:
If I could bear it longer and not fall
To quarrel° with your great opposeless° wills,
My snuff° and loathèd part of nature should
Burn itself out. If Edgar live, O bless him!   40
Now, fellow, fare thee well.

                              He falls.

Edgar.   Gone, sir, farewell.

---

²¹ *unnumb'red idle pebble* innumerable pebbles, moved to and fro
by the waves to no purpose   ²³⁻²⁴ *the deficient sight/Topple* my failing
sight topple me   ²⁷ *upright* i.e., even up in the air, to say nothing
of forward, over the cliff   ²⁹ *Fairies* (who are supposed to guard
and multiply hidden treasure)   ³³⁻³⁴ *Why . . . it* I play on his despair
in order to cure it   ³⁷⁻³⁸ *fall/To quarrel with* rebel against   ³⁸ *oppose-
less* not to be, and not capable of being, opposed   ³⁹ *snuff* the gutter-
ing (and stinking) wick of a burnt-out candle

And yet I know not how° conceit° may rob
The treasury of life, when life itself
Yields to° the theft. Had he been where he thought,
45   By this had thought been past. Alive or dead?
Ho, you sir! friend! Hear you, sir! speak!
Thus might he pass° indeed: yet he revives.
What are you, sir?

Gloucester.   Away, and let me die.

Edgar. Hadst thou been aught but gossamer, feathers, air,
50   So many fathom down precipitating,°
Thou'dst shivered like an egg: but thou dost breathe;
Hast heavy substance; bleed'st not; speak'st; art sound.
Ten masts at each° make not the altitude
Which thou hast perpendicularly fell:
55   Thy life's° a miracle. Speak yet again.

Gloucester. But have I fall'n, or no?

Edgar. From the dread summit of this chalky bourn.°
Look up a-height;° the shrill-gorged° lark so far
Cannot be seen or heard: do but look up.

60   *Gloucester.* Alack, I have no eyes.
Is wretchedness deprived that benefit,
To end itself by death? 'Twas yet some comfort,
When misery could beguile° the tyrant's rage
And frustrate his proud will.

Edgar.   Give me your arm.
65   Up, so. How is 't? Feel you° your legs? You stand.

Gloucester. Too well, too well.

Edgar.   This is above all strangeness.
Upon the crown o' th' cliff, what thing was that

---

42 *how* but what 42 *conceit* imagination 44 *Yields to* allows 47 *pass* die 50 *precipitating* falling 53 *at each* one on top of the other 55 *life's* survival 57 *bourn* boundary 58 *a-height* on high 58 *gorged* throated, voiced 63 *beguile* cheat (i.e., by suicide) 65 *Feel you* have you any feeling in

Which parted from you?

Gloucester.   A poor unfortunate beggar.

Edgar. As I stood here below, methought his eyes
   Were two full moons; he had a thousand noses,   70
   Horns whelked° and waved like the enridgèd° sea:
   It was some fiend; therefore, thou happy father,°
   Think that the clearest° gods, who make them
      honors
   Of men's impossibilities,° have preserved thee.

Gloucester. I do remember now: henceforth I'll bear   75
   Affliction till it do cry out itself
   "Enough, enough," and die. That thing you speak
      of,
   I took it for a man; often 'twould say
   "The fiend, the fiend"—he led me to that place.

Edgar. Bear free° and patient thoughts.
        *Enter Lear [fantastically dressed with wild
                flowers].*
                        But who comes here?   80
   The safer° sense will ne'er accommodate°
   His master thus.

Lear. No, they cannot touch me for coining;° I am
   the King himself.

Edgar. O thou side-piercing sight!   85

Lear. Nature's above art in that respect.° There's
   your press-money.° That fellow handles his bow

---

71 *whelked* twisted   71 *enridgèd* i.e., furrowed into waves   72 *happy father* fortunate old man   73 *clearest* purest   73-74 *who . . . impossibilities* who cause themselves to be honored and revered by performing miracles of which men are incapable   80 *free* i.e., emancipated from grief and despair, which fetter the soul   81 *safer* sounder, saner   81 *accommodate* dress, adorn   83 *touch me for coining* arrest me for minting coins (the king's prerogative)   86 *Nature's . . . respect* i.e., a born king is superior to legal (and hence artificial) inhibition. There is also a glance here at the popular Renaissance debate, concerning the relative importance of nature (inspiration) and art (training)   87 *press-money* (paid to conscripted soldiers)

like a crow-keeper;° draw me a clothier's yard.°
Look, look, a mouse! Peace, peace; this piece of
90 toasted cheese will do 't. There's my gauntlet;° I'll
prove it on° a giant. Bring up the brown bills.° O,
well flown,° bird! i' th' clout, i' th' clout:° hewgh!°
Give the word.°

Edgar. Sweet marjoram.°

95 *Lear.* Pass.

Gloucester. I know that voice.

Lear. Ha! Goneril, with a white beard! They flattered
me like a dog,° and told me I had white hairs
in my beard ere the black ones were there.° To
100 say "ay" and "no" to everything that I said! "Ay"
and "no" too was no good divinity.° When the
rain came to wet me once and the wind to make
me chatter; when the thunder would not peace at
my bidding; there I found 'em, there I smelt 'em
105 out. Go to, they are not men o' their words: they
told me I was everything; 'tis a lie, I am not ague-
proof.°

Gloucester. The trick° of that voice I do well remember: Is't not the king?

Lear.   Ay, every inch a king.
110 When I do stare, see how the subject quakes.
I pardon that man's life. What was thy cause?°

°°crow-keeper a farmer scaring away crows °°clothier's yard (the
standard English arrow was a cloth-yard long. Here the injunction is
to draw the arrow back, like a powerful archer, a full yard to the ear)
°°gauntlet armored glove, thrown down as a challenge °¹prove it on
maintain my challenge even against °¹brown bills halberds varnished
to prevent rust (here the reference is to the soldiers who carry them)
°²well flown (falconer's cry; and perhaps a reference to the flight of
the arrow) °²clout the target shot at °²hewgh ? imitating the whizzing
of the arrow °³word password °⁴Sweet marjoram herb, used as a
remedy for brain disease °⁸⁻°⁹I . . .
there I was wise before I had even grown a beard ¹⁰¹no good divinity
(bad theology, because contrary to the Biblical saying [II Corinthians
1:18], "Our word toward you was not yea and nay." See also James
5:12 "But let your yea be yea, and your nay, nay; lest ye fall into condemnation"; and Matthew 5:36-37) ¹⁰⁶⁻⁰⁷ague-proof secure against
fever ¹⁰⁸trick intonation ¹¹¹cause offense

Adultery?
Thou shalt not die: die for adultery! No:
The wren goes to 't, and the small gilded fly
Does lecher° in my sight.   *115*
Let copulation thrive; for Gloucester's bastard son
Was kinder to his father than my daughters
Got° 'tween the lawful sheets.
To 't, luxury,° pell-mell! for I lack soldiers.°
Behold yond simp'ring dame,   *120*
Whose face between her forks presages snow,°
That minces° virtue and does shake the head
To hear of pleasure's name.°
The fitchew,° nor the soilèd° horse, goes to 't
With a more riotous appetite.   *125*
Down from the waist they are Centaurs,°
Though women all above:
But to the girdle° do the gods inherit,°
Beneath is all the fiend's.
There's hell, there's darkness, there is the
     sulphurous pit,   *130*
Burning, scalding, stench, consumption; fie, fie, fie!
pah, pah! Give me an ounce of civet;° good apothe-
cary, sweeten my imagination: there's money for thee.

Gloucester. O, let me kiss that hand!

Lear. Let me wipe it first; it smells of mortality.°   *135*

Gloucester. O ruined piece of nature! This great world
     Shall so wear out to nought.° Dost thou know me?

---

[115] *lecher* copulate [118] *Got* begot [119] *luxury* lechery [119] *for . . .
soldiers* i.e., ? (1) whom copulation will supply (2) and am therefore powerless [121] *Whose . . . snow* whose cold demeanor seems to
promise chaste behavior ("forks": legs) [122] *minces* squeamishly pretends to [123] *pleasure's name* the very name of sexual pleasure
[124] *fitchew* polecat (and slang for "prostitute") [124] *soilèd* put to
pasture, and hence wanton with feeding [126] *Centaurs* lustful creatures,
half man and half horse [128] *girdle* waist [128] *inherit* possess [132] *civet*
perfume [135] *mortality* (1) death (2) existence [136-37] *This . . . nought*
i.e., the universe (macrocosm) will decay to nothing in the same way
as the little world of man (microcosm)

Lear. I remember thine eyes well enough. Dost thou
squiny° at me? No, do thy worst, blind Cupid;° I'll
140   not love. Read thou this challenge;° mark but the
penning of it.

Gloucester. Were all thy letters suns, I could not see.

Edgar. I would not take° this from report: it is,
And my heart breaks at it.

145   *Lear.* Read.

Gloucester. What, with the case° of eyes?

Lear. O, ho, are you there with me?° No eyes in your
head, nor no money in your purse? Your eyes are
in a heavy case,° your purse in a light,° yet you
150   see how this world goes.

Gloucester. I see it feelingly.°

Lear. What, art mad? A man may see how this world
goes with no eyes. Look with thine ears: see how
yond justice rails upon yond simple° thief. Hark,
155   in thine ear: change places, and, handy-dandy,°
which is the justice, which is the thief? Thou hast
seen a farmer's dog bark at a beggar?

Gloucester. Ay, sir.

Lear. And the creature run from the cur? There thou
160   mightst behold the great image of authority:° a
dog's obeyed in office.°
Thou rascal beadle,° hold thy bloody hand!
Why dost thou lash that whore? Strip thy own
back;
Thou hotly lusts to use her in that kind°

---

139 *squiny* squint, look sideways, like a prostitute   139 *blind Cupid*
the sign hung before a brothel   140 *challenge* a reminiscence of
ll. 89-90   143 *take* believe   146 *case* empty sockets   147 *are . . . me* is
that what you tell me   149 *heavy case* sad plight (pun on l. 146)
149 *light* i.e., empty   151 *feelingly* (1) by touch (2) by feeling pain
(3) with emotion   154 *simple* common, of low estate   155 *handy-dandy*
i.e., choose, guess (after the children's game—"Handy-dandy, prickly
prandy"—of choosing the right hand)   160 *image of authority* symbol revealing the true meaning of authority   160-61 *a . . . office* i.e.,
whoever has power is obeyed   162 *beadle* parish constable   164 *kind*
i.e., sexual act

For which thou whip'st her. The usurer hangs the
  cozener.°   *165*
Through tattered clothes small vices do appear;
Robes and furred gowns° hide all. Plate sin with
  gold,
And the strong lance of justice hurtless° breaks;
Arm it in rags, a pygmy's straw does pierce it.
None does offend, none, I say, none; I'll able°
  'em: *170*
Take that° of me, my friend, who have the power
To seal th' accuser's lips. Get thee glass eyes,°
And, like a scurvy politician,° seem
To see the things thou dost not. Now, now, now,
  now.
Pull off my boots: harder, harder: so.   *175*

Edgar. O, matter and impertinency° mixed!
  Reason in madness!

Lear. If thou wilt weep my fortunes, take my eyes.
  I know thee well enough; thy name is Gloucester:
  Thou must be patient; we came crying hither: *180*
  Thou know'st, the first time that we smell the air
  We wawl and cry. I will preach to thee: mark.

Gloucester. Alack, alack the day!

Lear. When we are born, we cry that we are come
  To this great stage of fools. This'° a good block.° *185*

---

¹⁶⁴⁻⁶⁵ *The usurer . . . cozener* i.e., the powerful moneylender, in his
role as judge, puts to death the petty cheat   ¹⁶⁷ *Robes and furred
gowns* (worn by a judge)   ¹⁶⁸ *hurtless* i.e., without hurting the sinner
¹⁷⁰ *able* vouch for   ¹⁷¹ *that* (the immunity just conferred) (l. 170)
¹⁷² *glass eyes* spectacles   ¹⁷³ *scurvy politician* vile politic man
¹⁷⁶ *matter and impertinency* sense and nonsense   ¹⁸⁵ *This'* this is
¹⁸⁵ *block* (various meanings have been suggested, for example, the
stump of a tree, on which Lear is supposed to climb; a mounting-
block, which suggests "horse" l. 187; a hat [which Lear or another
must be made to wear], from the block on which a felt hat is mold-
ed, and which would suggest a "felt" l. 187. The proposal here is
that "block" be taken to denote the quintain, whose function is to bear
blows, "a mere lifeless block" [*As You Like It*, I.ii.263], an object
shaped like a man and used for tilting practice. See also *Much Ado*,
II.i.246-7, "she misused me past the endurance of a block!" and, in
the same passage, the associated reference, "I stood like a man at
a mark [target]" [l. 253])

It were a delicate° stratagem, to shoe
A troop of horse with felt: I'll put 't in proof;°
And when I have stol'n upon these son-in-laws,
Then, kill, kill, kill, kill, kill, kill!

Enter a Gentleman [with Attendants].

190 **Gentleman.** O, here he is: lay hand upon him. Sir,
Your most dear daughter——

Lear. No rescue? What, a prisoner? I am even
The natural fool° of fortune. Use me well;
You shall have ransom. Let me have surgeons;
I am cut° to th' brains.

195 **Gentleman.**   You shall have anything.

Lear. No seconds?° all myself?
Why, this would make a man a man of salt,°
To use his eyes for garden water-pots,
Ay, and laying autumn's dust.

200 **Gentleman.** Good sir——

Lear. I will die bravely,° like a smug° bridegroom.°
What!
I will be jovial: come, come; I am a king;
Masters, know you that?

Gentleman. You are a royal one, and we obey you.

205 **Lear.** Then there's life in 't.° Come, and you get it,
you shall get it by running. Sa, sa, sa, sa.°

Exit [running; Attendants follow].

Gentleman. A sight most pitiful in the meanest wretch,
Past speaking of in a king! Thou hast one daughter
Who redeems nature from the general curse
210 Which twain have brought her to.°

---

186 *delicate* subtle 187 *put 't in proof* test it 193 *natural fool* born
sport (with pun on "natural": "imbecile") 195 *cut* wounded 196 *seconds* supporters 197 *man of salt* i.e., all (salt) tears 201 *bravely* (1)
smartly attired (2) courageously 201 *smug* spick and span 201 *bridegroom* whose "brave" sexual feats are picked up in the pun on "die"
205 *there's life in 't* there's still hope 206 *Sa . . . sa* hunting and
rallying cry; also an interjection of defiance 209-10 *general . . .
to* (1) universal condemnation which Goneril and Regan have made
for (2) damnation incurred by the original sin of Adam and Eve

Edgar. Hail, gentle° sir.

Gentleman.   Sir, speed° you: what's your will?

Edgar. Do you hear aught, sir, of a battle toward?°

Gentleman. Most sure and vulgar:° every one hears that,
   Which can distinguish sound.

Edgar.   But, by your favor,
   How near's the other army?   213

Gentleman. Near and on speedy foot; the main descry
   Stands on the hourly thought.°

Edgar.   I thank you, sir: that's all.

Gentleman. Though that the Queen on special cause is here,
   Her army is moved on.

Edgar.   I thank you, sir.

          Exit [Gentleman].

Gloucester. You ever-gentle gods, take my breath from me;   220
   Let not my worser spirit° tempt me again
   To die before you please.

Edgar.   Well pray you, father.

Gloucester. Now, good sir, what are you?

Edgar. A most poor man, made tame° to fortune's blows;
   Who, by the art of known and feeling sorrows,°   225
   Am pregnant° to good pity. Give me your hand,
   I'll lead you to some biding.°

Gloucester.   Hearty thanks;

---

²¹¹ *gentle* noble ²¹¹ *speed* God speed ²¹² *toward* impending ²¹³ *vulgar* common knowledge ²¹⁶⁻¹⁷ *the . . . thought* we expect to see the main body of the army any hour ²²¹ *worser spirit* bad angel, evil side of my nature ²²⁴ *tame* submissive ²²⁵ *art . . . sorrows* instruction of sorrows painfully experienced ²²⁶ *pregnant* disposed ²²⁷ *biding* place of refuge

The bounty and the benison° of heaven
To boot, and boot.°

Enter Oswald.

Oswald.   A proclaimed prize°! Most happy!°
230 That eyeless head of thine was first framed° flesh
To raise my fortunes. Thou old unhappy traitor,
Briefly thyself remember:° the sword is out
That must destroy thee.

Gloucester.   Now let thy friendly° hand
Put strength enough to 't.

[*Edgar interposes.*]

Oswald.   Wherefore, bold peasant,
235 Dar'st thou support a published° traitor? Hence!
Lest that th' infection of his fortune take
Like hold on thee. Let go his arm.

Edgar. Chill° not let go, zir, without vurther 'casion.°

Oswald. Let go, slave, or thou diest!

240 *Edgar.* Good gentleman, go your gait,° and let poor
volk° pass. And chud ha' bin zwaggered° out of my
life, 'twould not ha' bin zo long as 'tis by a vort-
night. Nay, come not near th' old man; keep out,
che vor' ye,° or I'se° try whether your costard°
245 or my ballow° be the harder: chill be plain with
you.

Oswald. Out, dunghill!

They fight.

---

²²⁸ *benison* blessing ²²⁹ *To boot, and boot* also, and in the highest degree
²²⁹ *proclaimed prize* i.e., one with a price on his head ²²⁹ *happy* fortunate (for Oswald) ²³⁰ *framed* created ²³² *thyself remember* i.e., pray,
think of your sins ²³³ *friendly* i.e., because it offers the death Gloucester
covets ²³⁵ *published* proclaimed ²³⁸ *Chill . . .* (Edgar speaks in rustic
dialect) ²³⁸ *Chill* I will ²³⁸ *vurther 'casion* further occasion ²⁴⁰ *gait*
way ²⁴¹ *volk* folk ²⁴¹ *And chud ha' bin zwaggered* if I could have been
swaggered ²⁴⁴ *Che vor' ye* I warrant you ²⁴⁴ *I'se* I shall ²⁴⁴ *costard*
head (literally, "apple") ²⁴⁵ *ballow* cudgel

Edgar. Chill pick your teeth,° zir: come; no matter
    vor your foins.°

                   [*Oswald falls.*]

Oswald. Slave, thou hast slain me. Villain, take my
    purse: 250
    If ever thou wilt thrive, bury my body,
    And give the letters which thou find'st about° me
    To Edmund Earl of Gloucester; seek him out
    Upon the English party.° O, untimely death!
    Death!   253

                            He dies.

Edgar. I know thee well. A serviceable° villain,
    As duteous° to the vices of thy mistress
    As badness would desire.

Gloucester.   What, is he dead?

Edgar. Sit you down, father; rest you.
    Let's see these pockets: the letters that he speaks
      of   260
    May be my friends. He's dead; I am only sorry
    He had no other deathsman.° Let us see:
    Leave,° gentle wax;° and, manners, blame us not:
    To know our enemies' minds, we rip their hearts;
    Their papers° is more lawful.   265

              Reads the letter.

    "Let our reciprocal vows be remembered. You
have many opportunities to cut him off: if your
will want not,° time and place will be fruitfully
offered. There is nothing done, if he return the conqueror: then am I the prisoner, and his bed my   270
jail; from the loathed warmth whereof deliver me,
and supply the place for your labor.
    "Your—wife, so I would° say—affectionate

servant, and for you her own for venture,°
275   'Goneril.' "
O indistinguished space of woman's will!°
A plot upon her virtuous husband's life;
And the exchange° my brother! Here in the sands
Thee I'll rake up,° the post unsanctified°
280 Of murderous lechers; and in the mature° time,
With this ungracious paper° strike° the sight
Of the death-practiced° Duke: for him 'tis well
That of thy death and business I can tell.

Gloucester. The King is mad: how stiff° is my vile
    sense,°
285 That I stand up, and have ingenious° feeling
Of my huge sorrows! Better I were distract:°
So should my thoughts be severed from my griefs,
And woes by wrong imaginations° lose
The knowledge of themselves.
                            Drum afar off.

Edgar.   Give me your hand:
290 Far off, methinks, I hear the beaten drum.
Come, father, I'll bestow° you with a friend.
                            Exeunt.

Scene VII. [*A tent in the French camp.*]

Enter Cordelia, Kent, Doctor, and Gentleman.

Cordelia. O thou good Kent, how shall I live and
    work,

---

²⁷⁴ *and . . . venture* i.e., and one who holds you her own for venturing (Edmund had earlier been promised union by Goneril, "If you dare venture in your own behalf," IV.ii.20). ²⁷⁶ *indistinguished . . . will* unlimited range of woman's lust ²⁷⁸ *exchange* substitute ²⁷⁹ *rake up* cover up, bury ²⁷⁹ *post unsanctified* unholy messenger ²⁸⁰ *mature* ripe ²⁸¹ *ungracious paper* wicked letter ²⁸¹ *strike* blast ²⁸² *death-practiced* whose death is plotted ²⁸⁴ *stiff* unbending ²⁸⁴ *vile sense* hateful capacity for feeling ²⁸⁵ *ingenious* conscious ²⁸⁶ *distract* distracted, mad ²⁸⁸ *wrong imaginations* delusions ²⁹¹ *bestow* lodge

To match thy goodness? My life will be too short,
And every measure fail me.

Kent. To be acknowledged, madam, is o'erpaid.
All my reports go° with the modest truth,   5
Nor more nor clipped,° but so.

Cordelia.   Be better suited:°
These weeds° are memories° of those worser
    hours:
I prithee, put them off.

Kent.   Pardon, dear madam;
Yet to be known shortens my made intent:°
My boon I make it,° that you know me not   10
Till time and I think meet.°

Cordelia. Then be 't so, my good lord. [*To the Doctor.*] How does the King?

Doctor. Madam, sleeps still.

Cordelia. O you kind gods!
Cure this great breach in his abusèd° nature.   15
Th' untuned and jarring senses, O, wind up°
Of this child-changèd° father.

Doctor.   So please your Majesty
That we may wake the King: he hath slept long.

Cordelia. Be governed by your knowledge, and
    proceed
I' th' sway of° your own will. Is he arrayed?   20

> *Enter Lear in a chair carried by Servants.*

IV.vii. ⁵ *go* conform ⁶ *clipped* curtailed ⁶ *suited* attired ⁷ *weeds*
clothes ⁷ *memories* reminders ⁹ *Yet . . . intent* to reveal myself just
yet interferes with the plan I have made ¹⁰ *My boon I make it* I ask
this reward ¹¹ *meet* fitting ¹⁵ *abusèd* disturbed ¹⁶ *wind up* tune
¹⁷ *child-changèd* changed, deranged (and also, reduced to a child) by
the cruelty of his children ²⁰ *I' th' sway of* according to

Gentleman. Ay, madam; in the heaviness of sleep
    We put fresh garments on him.

Doctor. Be by, good madam, when we do awake him;
    I doubt not of his temperance.°

Cordelia.   Very well.

Doctor. Please you, draw near. Louder the music
25   there!

Cordelia. O my dear father, restoration hang
    Thy medicine on my lips, and let this kiss
    Repair those violent harms that my two sisters
    Have in thy reverence° made.

Kent.   Kind and dear Princess.

Cordelia. Had you not been their father, these white
30   flakes°
    Did challenge° pity of them. Was this a face
    To be opposed against the warring winds?
    To stand against the deep dread-bolted° thunder?
    In the most terrible and nimble stroke
    Of quick, cross° lightning to watch—poor
35   perdu!°—
    With this thin helm?° Mine enemy's dog,
    Though he had bit me, should have stood that night
    Against my fire; and wast thou fain,° poor father,
    To hovel thee with swine and rogues° forlorn,
40   In short° and musty straw? Alack, alack!
    'Tis wonder that thy life and wits at once
    Had not concluded all.° He wakes; speak to him.

Doctor. Madam, do you; 'tis fittest.

---

24 *temperance* sanity 29 *reverence* revered person 30 *flakes* hairs (in long strands) 31 *challenge* claim 33 *deep dread-bolted* deep-voiced and furnished with the dreadful thunderbolt 35 *cross* zigzag 35 *perdu* (1) sentry in a forlorn position (2) lost one 36 *helm* helmet (his scanty hair) 38 *fain* pleased 39 *rogues* vagabonds 40 *short* (when straw is freshly cut, it is long, and suitable for bedding, given its flexibility and crispness. As it is used, it becomes musty, shreds into pieces, is "short." In contemporary Maine usage, "short manure" refers to dung mixed with straw that has been broken up; "long manure" to dung mixed with coarse new straw) 42 *concluded all* come to a complete end

Cordelia. How does my royal lord? How fares your
     Majesty?

Lear. You do me wrong to take me out o' th' grave: **45**
     Thou art a soul in bliss; but I am bound
     Upon a wheel of fire,° that mine own tears
     Do scald like molten lead.

Cordelia.   Sir, do you know me?

Lear. You are a spirit, I know. Where did you die?

Cordelia. Still, still, far wide.°   **50**

Doctor. He's scarce awake: let him alone awhile.

Lear. Where have I been? Where am I? Fair daylight?
     I am mightily abused.° I should ev'n die with pity,
     To see another thus. I know not what to say.
     I will not swear these are my hands: let's see;   **55**
     I feel this pin prick. Would I were assured
     Of my condition.

Cordelia.   O, look upon me, sir,
     And hold your hand in benediction o'er me.
     You must not kneel.

Lear.   Pray, do not mock me:
     I am a very foolish fond° old man,   **60**
     Fourscore and upward, not an hour more nor less;
     And, to deal plainly,
     I fear I am not in my perfect mind.
     Methinks I should know you and know this man,
     Yet I am doubtful; for I am mainly° ignorant   **65**
     What place this is, and all the skill I have
     Remembers not these garments, nor I know not
     Where I did lodge last night. Do not laugh at me,
     For, as I am a man, I think this lady
     To be my child Cordelia.

Cordelia.   And so I am, I am.   **70**

Lear. Be your tears wet? Yes, faith. I pray, weep not.
     If you have poison for me, I will drink it.

---

47 *wheel of fire* (torment associated by the Middle Ages with Hell,
where Lear thinks he is)   **50** *wide* i.e., of the mark (of sanity)
53 *abused* deluded   **60** *fond* in dotage   **65** *mainly* entirely

I know you do not love me; for your sisters
Have, as I do remember, done me wrong.
You have some cause, they have not.

75 *Cordelia.*   No cause, no cause.

Lear. Am I in France?

Kent.   In your own kingdom, sir.

Lear. Do not abuse° me.

Doctor. Be comforted, good madam: the great rage,°
You see, is killed in him: and yet it is danger
80 To make him even o'er° the time he has lost.
Desire him to go in; trouble him no more
Till further settling.°

Cordelia. Will 't please your Highness walk?°

Lear. You must bear with me. Pray you now, forget
85 and forgive. I am old and foolish.

                    Exeunt. Mane[n]t° Kent and Gentleman.

Gentleman. Holds it true, sir, that the Duke of Cornwall was so slain?

Kent. Most certain, sir.

Gentleman. Who is conductor of his people?

90 *Kent.* As 'tis said, the bastard son of Gloucester.

Gentleman. They say Edgar, his banished son, is with
the Earl of Kent in Germany.

Kent. Report is changeable.° 'Tis time to look about;
the powers° of the kingdom approach apace.

95 *Gentleman.* The arbitrement° is like to be bloody.
Fare you well, sir.   [*Exit.*]

Kent. My point and period will be throughly
        wrought,°
Or well or ill, as this day's battle's fought.

                                        Exit.

---

77 *abuse* deceive   78 *rage* frenzy   80 *even o'er* smooth over by filling
in; and hence, "recollect"   82 *settling* calming   83 *walk* (perhaps in
the sense of "withdraw")   85 s.d. *Mane[n]t* remain   93 *Report is
changeable* rumors are unreliable   94 *powers* armies   95 *arbitrement*
deciding encounter   97 *My . . . wrought* the aim and end, the close of
my life will be completely worked out

ACT V

Scene I. [*The British camp near Dover.*]

*Enter, with drum and colors, Edmund, Regan,
Gentlemen, and Soldiers.*

Edmund. Know° of the Duke if his last purpose hold,°
    Or whether since he is advised° by aught
    To change the course: he's full of alteration
    And self-reproving: bring his constant pleasure.°

                    [*To a Gentleman, who goes out.*]

Regan. Our sister's man is certainly miscarried.°   5

Edmund. 'Tis to be doubted,° madam.

Regan.   Now, sweet lord,
    You know the goodness I intend upon you:
    Tell me, but truly, but then speak the truth,
    Do you not love my sister?

Edmund.   In honored° love.

Regan. But have you never found my brother's way   10
    To the forfended° place?

Edmund.   That thought abuses° you.

V.i. 1 *Know* learn 1 *last purpose hold* most recent intention (to fight)
be maintained 2 *advised* induced 4 *constant pleasure* fixed (final)
decision 5 *miscarried* come to grief 6 *doubted* feared 9 *honored*
honorable 11 *forfended* forbidden 11 *abuses* (1) deceives (2) de-
means, is unworthy of

163

Regan. I am doubtful that you have been conjunct
    And bosomed with her, as far as we call hers.°

Edmund. No, by mine honor, madam.

15 *Regan.* I shall never endure her: dear my lord,
    Be not familiar with her.

Edmund.   Fear° me not.—
    She and the Duke her husband!

    Enter, with drum and colors, Albany, Goneril
        [and] Soldiers.

Goneril. [*Aside*] I had rather lose the battle than
      that sister
    Should loosen° him and me.

20 *Albany.* Our very loving sister, well be-met.°
    Sir, this I heard, the King is come to his daughter,
    With others whom the rigor of our state°
    Forced to cry out. Where I could not be honest,°
    I never yet was valiant: for this business,
25   It touches us, as° France invades our land,
    Not bolds the King, with others, whom, I fear,
    Most just and heavy causes make oppose.°

Edmund. Sir, you speak nobly.

Regan.   Why is this reasoned?°

Goneril. Combine together 'gainst the enemy;
30   For these domestic and particular broils°
    Are not the question° here.

Albany.   Let's then determine
    With th' ancient of war° on our proceeding.

Edmund. I shall attend you presently at your tent.

12-13 *I . . . hers* I fear that you have united with her intimately, in the
fullest possible way   16 *Fear* distrust   19 *loosen* separate   20 *be-met* met
22 *rigor . . . state* tyranny of our government   23 *honest* honorable
25 *touches us, as* concerns me, only in that   26-27 *Not . . . oppose* and
not in that France emboldens the King and others, who have been
led, by real and serious grievances, to take up arms against us
28 *reasoned* argued   30 *particular broils* private quarrels   31 *question*
issue   32 *th' ancient of war* experienced commanders

Regan. Sister, you'll go with us?°

Goneril. No.   35

Regan. 'Tis most convenient;° pray you, go with us.

Goneril. [*Aside*] O, ho, I know the riddle.°—I
     will go.

     Exeunt both the Armies. Enter Edgar [disguised].

Edgar. If e'er your Grace had speech with man so
     poor,
Hear me one word.

Albany. [*To those going out*] I'll overtake you. [*To
     Edgar*] Speak.

                    Exeunt [all but Albany and Edgar].

Edgar. Before you fight the battle, ope this letter.   40
If you have victory, let the trumpet sound
For° him that brought it: wretched though I seem,
I can produce a champion that will prove°
What is avouchèd° there. If you miscarry,
Your business of° the world hath so an end,   45
And machination° ceases. Fortune love you.

Albany. Stay till I have read the letter.

Edgar.   I was forbid it.
When time shall serve, let but the herald cry,
And I'll appear again.

Albany. Why, fare thee well: I will o'erlook° thy
     paper.   *Exit [Edgar].*   50

                    Enter Edmund.

Edmund. The enemy's in view: draw up your powers.
Here is the guess° of their true strength and
     forces
By diligent discovery;° but your haste

---

³⁴ *us* me (rather than Edmund)   ³⁶ *convenient* fitting, desirable   ³⁷ *riddle* real reason (for Regan's curious request)   ⁴¹⁻⁴² *sound/For* summon   ⁴³ *prove* i.e., by trial of combat   ⁴⁴ *avouchèd* maintained   ⁴⁵ *of* in   ⁴⁶ *machination* plotting   ⁵⁰ *o'erlook* read over   ⁵² *guess* estimate   ⁵³ *By diligent discovery* obtained by careful reconnoitering

Is now urged on you.

Albany.   We will greet° the time.   *Exit.*

55 *Edmund.* To both these sisters have I sworn my love;
     Each jealous° of the other, as the stung
     Are of the adder. Which of them shall I take?
     Both? One? Or neither? Neither can be enjoyed,
     If both remain alive: to take the widow
60   Exasperates, makes mad her sister Goneril;
     And hardly° shall I carry out my side,°
     Her husband being alive. Now then, we'll use
     His countenance° for the battle; which being done,
     Let her who would be rid of him devise
65   His speedy taking off. As for the mercy
     Which he intends to Lear and to Cordelia,
     The battle done, and they within our power,
     Shall never see his pardon; for my state
     Stands on me to defend, not to debate.°   *Exit.*

Scene II.   [*A field between the two camps.*]

*Alarum° within. Enter, with drum and colors,
Lear, Cordelia, and Soldiers, over the stage; and
exeunt.*
          Enter Edgar and Gloucester.

Edgar. Here, father,° take the shadow of this tree
     For your good host; pray that the right may thrive.
     If ever I return to you again,
     I'll bring you comfort.

Gloucester.   Grace go with you, sir.
                                        Exit [Edgar].

---

54 *greet* i.e., meet the demands of   56 *jealous* suspicious   61 *hardly* with
difficulty   61 *carry . . . side* (1) satisfy my ambition (2) fulfill my
bargain (with Goneril)   63 *countenance* authority   68-69 *for . . . debate*
my position requires me to act, not to reason about right and wrong
V.ii. s.d. *Alarum* a trumpet call to battle   1 *father* i.e., venerable
old man (Edgar has not yet revealed his identity)

Alarum and retreat° within. [Re-]enter Edgar.   5

Edgar. Away, old man; give me thy hand; away!
    King Lear hath lost, he and his daughter ta'en:°
    Give me thy hand; come on.

Gloucester. No further, sir; a man may rot even here.

Edgar. What, in ill thoughts again? Men must endure
    Their going hence, even as their coming hither: 10
    Ripeness° is all. Come on.

Gloucester.   And that's true too.
                                                    Exeunt.

Scene III.   [*The British camp near Dover.*]

*Enter, in conquest, with drum and colors, Ed-
mund; Lear and Cordelia, as prisoners; Soldiers,
Captain.*

Edmund. Some officers take them away: good guard,°
    Until their greater pleasures° first be known
    That are to censure° them.

Cordelia.   We are not the first
    Who with best meaning° have incurred the worst.
    For thee, oppressèd King, I am cast down;   5
    Myself could else out-frown false fortune's frown.
    Shall we not see these daughters and these sisters?

Lear. No, no, no, no! Come, let's away to prison:
    We two alone will sing like birds i' th' cage:
    When thou dost ask me blessing, I'll kneel down   10
    And ask of thee forgiveness: so we'll live,
    And pray, and sing, and tell old tales, and laugh

---

4 s.d. *retreat* (signaled by a trumpet)   6 *ta'en* captured   11 *Ripeness*
maturity, as of fruit that is ready to fall   V.iii.   1 *good guard* let there
be good guard   2 *their greater pleasures* the will of those in command,
the great ones   3 *censure* pass judgment on   4 *meaning* intentions

At gilded butterflies,° and hear poor rogues
Talk of court news; and we'll talk with them too,
15 Who loses and who wins, who's in, who's out;
And take upon's the mystery of things,
As if we were God's spies:° and we'll wear out,°
In a walled prison, packs and sects of great ones
That ebb and flow by th' moon.°

Edmund.   Take them away.

20 *Lear.* Upon such sacrifices, my Cordelia,
The gods themselves throw incense.° Have I caught
    thee?
He that parts us shall bring a brand from heaven,
And fire us hence like foxes.° Wipe thine eyes;
The good years° shall devour them,° flesh and fell,°
Ere they shall make us weep. We'll see 'em starved
25 first.
Come.   [*Exeunt Lear and Cordelia, guarded.*]

Edmund. Come hither, captain; hark.
Take thou this note: go follow them to prison:
One step I have advanced thee; if thou dost
30 As this instructs thee, thou dost make thy way
To noble fortunes: know thou this, that men
Are as the time is:° to be tender-minded
Does not become a sword:° thy great employment
Will not bear question;° either say thou'lt do 't,
Or thrive by other means.

35 *Captain.*   I'll do 't, my lord.

---

13 *gilded butterflies* i.e., gorgeously attired courtiers, fluttering after
nothing 16-17 *take . . . spies* profess to read the riddle of existence, as
if endowed with divine omniscience 17 *wear out* outlast 18-19 *packs
. . . moon* intriguing and partisan cliques of those in high station,
whose fortunes change every month 20-21 *Upon . . . incense* i.e., the
gods approve our renunciation of the world 22-23 *He . . . foxes* no human agency can separate us, but only divine interposition, as of a
heavenly torch parting us like foxes who are driven from their place of
refuge by fire and smoke 24 *good years* plague and pestilence ("unde-
fined malefic power or agency," *N.E.D.*) 24 *them* i.e., the enemies of
Lear and Cordelia 24 *fell* skin 32 *as the time is* i.e., absolutely determined by the exigencies of the moment 33 *become a sword* befit a soldier
34 *bear question* admit of discussion

Edmund. About it; and write happy° when th' hast
   done.
   Mark; I say, instantly, and carry it so°
   As I have set it down.

Captain. I cannot draw a cart, nor eat dried oats;
   If it be man's work, I'll do 't.   *Exit Captain.*   40

> *Flourish. Enter Albany, Goneril, Regan [another
>   Captain, and] Soldiers.*

Albany. Sir, you have showed today your valiant
   strain,°
   And fortune led you well: you have the captives
   Who were the opposites of° this day's strife:
   I do require them of you, so to use them
   As we shall find their merits° and our safety   45
   May equally determine.

Edmund.   Sir, I thought it fit
   To send the old and miserable King
   To some retention and appointed guard;°
   Whose° age had charms in it, whose title more,
   To pluck the common bosom on his side,°   50
   And turn our impressed lances in our eyes°
   Which do command them. With him I sent the
      Queen:
   My reason all the same; and they are ready
   Tomorrow, or at further space,° t' appear
   Where you shall hold your session.° At this time   55
   We sweat and bleed: the friend hath lost his friend;
   And the best quarrels, in the heat, are cursed
   By those that feel their sharpness.°
   The question of Cordelia and her father

---

³⁶ *write happy* style yourself fortunate   ³⁷ *carry it so* manage the affair
in exactly that manner (as if Cordelia had taken her own life)
⁴¹ *strain* (1) stock (2) character   ⁴³ *opposites of* opponents in   ⁴⁵ *merits*
deserts   ⁴⁸ *retention . . . guard* confinement under duly appointed
guard   ⁴⁹ *Whose* i.e., Lear's   ⁵⁰ *pluck . . . side* win the sympathy of
the people to himself   ⁵¹ *turn . . . eyes* turn our conscripted lancers
against us   ⁵⁴ *further space* a later time   ⁵⁵ *session* trial   ⁵⁷⁻⁵⁸ *the . . .
sharpness* the worthiest causes may be judged badly by those who have
been affected painfully by them, and whose passion has not yet cooled

Requires a fitter place.

60 *Albany.*   Sir, by your patience,
I hold you but a subject of° this war,
Not as a brother.

Regan.   That's as we list to grace° him.
Methinks our pleasure might have been demanded,
Ere you had spoke so far. He led our powers,
65 Bore the commission of my place and person;
The which immediacy may well stand up
And call itself your brother.°

Goneril.   Not so hot:
In his own grace he doth exalt himself
More than in your addition.°

Regan.   In my rights,
70 By me invested, he compeers° the best.

Goneril. That were the most,° if he should husband
you.°

Regan. Jesters do oft prove prophets.

Goneril.   Holla, holla!
That eye that told you so looked but a-squint.°

Regan. Lady, I am not well; else I should answer
75 From a full-flowing stomach.° General,
Take thou my soldiers, prisoners, patrimony;°
Dispose of them, of me; the walls is thine:°
Witness the world, that I create thee here
My lord, and master.

Goneril.   Mean you to enjoy him?

80 *Albany.* The let-alone° lies not in your good will.

---

61 *subject of* subordinate in   62 *list to grace* wish to honor   65-67 *Bore
. . . brother* was authorized, as my deputy, to take command; his
present status, as my immediate representative, entitles him to be considered your equal   69 *your addition* honors you have bestowed on
him   70 *compeers* equals   71 *most* most complete investing in your
rights   71 *husband you* become your husband   73 *a-squint* cross-eyed
75 *From . . . stomach* angrily   76 *patrimony* inheritance   77 *walls is
thine* i.e., Regan's person, which Edmund has stormed and won
80 *let-alone* power to prevent

Edmund. Nor in thine, lord.

Albany. Half-blooded° fellow, yes.

Regan. [*To Edmund*] Let the drum strike, and prove
    my title thine.°

Albany. Stay yet; hear reason. Edmund, I arrest thee
    On capital treason; and in thy attaint°
    This gilded serpent [*pointing to Goneril*]. For
        your claim, fair sister,   85
    I bar it in the interest of my wife.
    'Tis she is subcontracted° to this lord,
    And I, her husband, contradict your banes.°
    If you will marry, make your loves° to me;
    My Lady is bespoke.°

Goneril. An interlude!°   90

Albany. Thou art armed, Gloucester: let the trumpet
      sound:
    If none appear to prove upon thy person
    Thy heinous, manifest, and many treasons,
    There is my pledge° [*throwing down a glove*]:
    I'll make° it on thy heart,
    Ere I taste bread, thou art in nothing less   95
    Than I have here proclaimed thee.

Regan. Sick, O, sick!

Goneril. [*Aside*] If not, I'll ne'er trust medicine.°

Edmund. [*Throwing down a glove*] There's my
    exchange:° what in the world he is
    That names me traitor, villain-like he lies:°
    Call by the trumpet:° he that dares approach,   *100*

---

81 *Half-blooded* bastard, and so only half noble   82 *prove . . . thine*
prove by combat your entitlement to my rights   84 *in thy attaint* as a
sharer in the treason for which you are impeached   87 *subcontracted*
pledged by a contract which is called into question by the existence
of a previous contract (Goneril's marriage)   88 *contradict your banes*
forbid your announced intention to marry (by citing the precontract)
89 *loves* love-suits   90 *bespoke* already pledged   90 *interlude* play
94 *pledge* gage   94 *make* prove   97 *medicine* poison   98 *exchange* (tech-
nical term, denoting the glove Edmund throws down)   99 *villain-like he
lies* (the lie direct, a challenge to mortal combat)   100 *trumpet* trumpeter

On him, on you—who not?—I will maintain
My truth and honor firmly.

Albany. A herald, ho!

Edmund.   A herald, ho, a herald!

Albany. Trust to thy single virtue;° for thy soldiers,
105   All levied in my name, have in my name
Took their discharge.

Regan.   My sickness grows upon me.

Albany. She is not well; convey her to my tent.

                              [*Exit Regan, led.*]

                    Enter a Herald.

Come hither, herald. Let the trumpet sound—
And read out this.

110 *Captain.* Sound, trumpet!

                    A trumpet sounds.

Herald. (*Reads.*) "If any man of quality or degree°
within the lists° of the army will maintain upon Edmund, supposed Earl of Gloucester, that he is a
manifold traitor, let him appear by the third sound
115   of the trumpet: he is bold in his defense."

Edmund. Sound!

                    First trumpet.

Herald. Again!

                    Second trumpet.

Herald. Again!

                    Third trumpet.

          *Trumpet answers within. Enter Edgar, at the
          third sound, armed, a trumpet before him.°*

Albany. Ask him his purposes, why he appears
Upon this call o' th' trumpet.

120 *Herald.*   What are you?

---

104 *single virtue* unaided valor   111 *quality or degree* rank or position
112 *lists* rolls   118 s.d. *trumpet before him* trumpeter preceding him

Your name, your quality,° and why you answer
This present summons?

Edgar.   Know, my name is lost;
By treason's tooth bare-gnawn and canker-bit:°
Yet am I noble as the adversary
I come to cope.°

Albany.   Which is that adversary?   *125*

Edgar. What's he that speaks for Edmund, Earl of
    Gloucester?

Edmund. Himself: what say'st thou to him?

Edgar.   Draw thy sword,
That if my speech offend a noble heart,
Thy arm may do thee justice: here is mine.
Behold it is my privilege,   *130*
The privilege of mine honors,
My oath, and my profession.° I protest,
Maugre° thy strength, place, youth, and eminence,
Despite thy victor sword and fire-new° fortune,
Thy valor and thy heart,° thou art a traitor,   *135*
False to thy gods, thy brother, and thy father,
Conspirant° 'gainst this high illustrious prince,
And from th' extremest upward° of thy head
To the descent and dust below thy foot,°
A most toad-spotted traitor.° Say thou "No,"   *140*
This sword, this arm and my best spirits are bent°
To prove upon thy heart, whereto I speak,°
Thou liest.

Edmund.   In wisdom° I should ask thy name,
But since thy outside looks so fair and warlike,

121 *quality* rank   123 *canker-bit* eaten by the caterpillar   125 *cope* encounter   130-32 *it . . . profession* my knighthood entitles me to challenge you, and to have my challenge accepted   133 *Maugre* despite
134 *fire-new* fresh from the forge or mint   135 *heart* courage   137 *Con-
spirant* conspiring, a conspirator   138 *extremest upward* the very top
139 *the . . . foot* your lowest part (sole) and the dust beneath it
140 *toad-spotted traitor* spotted with treason (and hence venomous, as
the toad is allegedly marked with spots that exude venom)   141 *bent* di-
rected   142 *whereto I speak* (Edgar speaks from the heart, and speaks
to the heart of Edmund)   143 *wisdom* prudence (since he is not obliged
to fight with one of lesser rank)

And that thy tongue some say° of breeding
145   breathes,
What safe and nicely° I might well delay°
By rule of knighthood, I disdain and spurn:
Back do I toss these treasons° to thy head;
With the hell-hated° lie o'erwhelm thy heart;
150   Which for they yet glance by and scarcely bruise,
This sword of mine shall give them instant way,
Where they shall rest for ever.° Trumpets, speak!

     Alarums. [They] fight. [Edmund falls.]

Albany. Save° him, save him!

Goneril.   This is practice,° Gloucester:
By th' law of war thou wast not bound to answer
155   An unknown opposite;° thou art not vanquished,
But cozened and beguiled.

Albany.   Shut your mouth, dame,
Or with this paper shall I stop it. Hold, sir;°
Thou° worse than any name, read thine own evil.
No tearing, lady; I perceive you know it.

160 *Goneril.* Say, if I do, the laws are mine, not thine:
Who can arraign me for 't?

Albany.   Most monstrous! O!
Know'st thou this paper?

Goneril.   Ask me not what I know.

                               Exit.

Albany. Go after her; she's desperate; govern° her.

Edmund. What you have charged me with, that have
     I done;
165   And more, much more; the time will bring it out.
'Tis past, and so am I. But what art thou

---

145 *say* assay (i.e., touch, sign) 146 *safe and nicely* cautiously and
punctiliously 146 *delay* i.e., avoid 148 *treasons* accusations of treason
149 *hell-hated* hated like hell 150-52 *Which . . . ever* which accusations
of treason, since as yet they do no harm, even though I have hurled
them back, I now thrust upon you still more forcibly, with my sword,
so that they may remain with you permanently 153 *Save* spare
153 *practice* trickery 155 *opposite* opponent 157 *Hold, sir* (to Edmund:
"Just a moment!") 158 *Thou* (probably Goneril) 163 *govern* control

That hast this fortune on° me? If thou 'rt noble,
I do forgive thee.

Edgar.   Let's exchange charity.°
I am no less in blood° than thou art, Edmund;
If more,° the more th' hast wronged me.   170
My name is Edgar, and thy father's son.
The gods are just, and of our pleasant° vices
Make instruments to plague us:
The dark and vicious place° where thee he got°
Cost him his eyes.

Edmund.   Th' hast spoken right, 'tis true;   175
The wheel is come full circle; I am here.°

Albany. Methought thy very gait did prophesy°
A royal nobleness: I must embrace thee:
Let sorrow split my heart, if ever I
Did hate thee or thy father!

Edgar.   Worthy° Prince, I know 't. 180

Albany. Where have you hid yourself?
How have you known the miseries of your father?

Edgar. By nursing them, my lord. List a brief tale;
And when 'tis told, O, that my heart would burst!
The bloody proclamation to escape°   185
That followed me so near—O, our lives' sweetness,
That we the pain of death would hourly die
Rather than die at once!°—taught me to shift
Into a madman's rags, t' assume a semblance
That very dogs disdained: and in this habit°   190
Met I my father with his bleeding rings,°
Their precious stones new lost; became his guide,
Led him, begged for him, saved him from despair;

---

167 *fortune on* victory over   168 *charity* forgiveness and love   169 *blood*
lineage   170 *If more* if I am more noble (since legitimate)   172 *of our
pleasant* out of our pleasurable   174 *place* i.e., the adulterous bed
174 *got* begot   176 *Wheel . . . here* i.e., Fortune's wheel, on which
Edmund ascended, has now, in its downward turning, deposited him
at the bottom, whence he began   177 *gait did prophesy* carriage did
promise   180 *Worthy* honorable   185 *to escape* (my wish) to escape the
sentence of death   186-88 *O . . . once* how sweet is life, that we choose
to suffer death every hour rather than make an end at once   190 *habit*
attire   191 *rings* sockets

Never—O fault!—revealed myself unto him,
195 Until some half-hour past, when I was armed,
Not sure, though hoping, of this good success,
I asked his blessing, and from first to last
Told him our pilgrimage.° But his flawed° heart—
Alack, too weak the conflict to support—
200 'Twixt two extremes of passion, joy and grief,
Burst smilingly.

Edmund.   This speech of yours hath moved me,
And shall perchance do good: but speak you on;
You look as you had something more to say.

Albany. If there be more, more woeful, hold it in;
205 For I am almost ready to dissolve,°
Hearing of this.

Edgar.   This would have seemed a period°
To such as love not sorrow; but another,
To amplify too much, would make much more,
And top extremity.°
210 Whilst I was big in clamor,° came there in a man,
Who, having seen me in my worst estate,°
Shunned my abhorred° society; but then, finding
Who 'twas that so endured, with his strong arms
He fastened on my neck, and bellowed out
215 As he'd burst heaven; threw him on my father;
Told the most piteous tale of Lear and him
That ever ear received: which in recounting
His grief grew puissant,° and the strings of life
Began to crack: twice then the trumpets sounded,
And there I left him tranced.°

220 *Albany.*   But who was this?

Edgar. Kent, sir, the banished Kent; who in disguise
Followed his enemy° king, and did him service
Improper for a slave.

198 *our pilgrimage* of our (purgatorial) journey 198 *flawed* cracked
205 *dissolve* i.e., into tears 206 *period* limit 207-09 *but . . . extremity*
just one woe more, described too fully, would go beyond the extreme
limit 210 *big in clamor* loud in lamentation 211 *estate* condition
212 *abhorred* abhorrent 218 *puissant* overmastering 220 *tranced* insensible 222 *enemy* hostile

Enter a Gentleman, with a bloody knife.

Gentleman. Help, help, O, help!

Edgar.   What kind of help?

Albany.   Speak, man.

Edgar. What means this bloody knife?

Gentleman.   'Tis hot, it smokes;° 225
   It came even from the heart of—O, she's dead!

Albany. Who dead? Speak, man.

Gentleman. Your lady, sir, your lady: and her
      sister
   By her is poisoned; she confesses it.

Edmund. I was contracted° to them both: all three   230
   Now marry° in an instant.

Edgar.   Here comes Kent.

Albany. Produce the bodies, be they alive or dead.

                          [Exit Gentleman.]

   This judgment of the heavens, that makes us
      tremble,
   Touches us not with pity.

                     Enter Kent.

                  O, is this he?
   The time will not allow the compliment°   235
   Which very manners° urges.

Kent.   I am come
   To bid my king and master aye° good night:
   Is he not here?

Albany.   Great thing of° us forgot!
   Speak, Edmund, where's the King? and where's
      Cordelia?
   Seest thou this object,° Kent?   240

The bodies of Goneril and Regan are brought in.

Kent. Alack, why thus?

---

225 *smokes* steams 230 *contracted* betrothed 231 *marry* i.e., unite in
death 235 *compliment* ceremony 236 *very manners* ordinary civility
237 *aye* forever 238 *thing of* matter by 240 *object* sight (the bodies
of Goneril and Regan)

Edmund.   Yet° Edmund was beloved:
  The one the other poisoned for my sake,
  And after slew herself.

Albany. Even so. Cover their faces.

245 *Edmund.* I pant for life:° some good I mean to do,
  Despite of mine own nature. Quickly send,
  Be brief in it, to th' castle; for my writ°
  Is on the life of Lear and on Cordelia:
  Nay, send in time.

Albany.   Run, run, O, run!

250 *Edgar.* To who, my lord? Who has the office?° Send
  Thy token of reprieve.°

Edmund. Well thought on: take my sword,
  Give it the captain.

Edgar.   Haste thee, for thy life.

                              [*Exit Messenger.*]

Edmund. He hath commission from thy wife and me
255 To hang Cordelia in the prison, and
  To lay the blame upon her own despair,
  That she fordid° herself.

Albany. The gods defend her! Bear him hence awhile.

                              [*Edmund is borne off.*]

  *Enter Lear, with Cordelia in his arms [Gentle-
  man, and others following].*

Lear. Howl, howl, howl, howl! O, you are men of
      stones:
260 Had I your tongues and eyes, I'd use them so
  That heaven's vault should crack. She's gone for
      ever.
  I know when one is dead and when one lives;
  She's dead as earth. Lend me a looking-glass;
  If that her breath will mist or stain the stone,°
  Why, then she lives.

241 *Yet* in spite of all   245 *pant for life* gasp for breath   247 *writ* command (ordering the execution)   250 *office* commission   251 *token of
reprieve* sign that they are reprieved   257 *fordid* destroyed   264 *stone*
i.e., the surface of the crystal looking glass

Kent.   Is this the promised end?°   265

Edgar. Or image° of that horror?

Albany.   Fall and cease.°

Lear. This feather stirs; she lives. If it be so,
It is a chance which does redeem° all sorrows
That ever I have felt.

Kent.   O my good master.

Lear. Prithee, away.

Edgar.   'Tis noble Kent, your friend.   270

Lear. A plague upon you, murderers, traitors all!
I might have saved her; now she's gone for ever.
Cordelia, Cordelia, stay a little. Ha,
What is 't thou say'st? Her voice was ever soft,
Gentle and low, an excellent thing in woman.   275
I killed the slave that was a-hanging thee.

Gentleman. 'Tis true, my lords, he did.

Lear.   Did I not, fellow?
I have seen the day, with my good biting falchion°
I would have made them skip: I am old now,
And these same crosses° spoil me.° Who are you?   280
Mine eyes are not o' th' best: I'll tell you straight.°

Kent. If Fortune brag of two° she loved and hated,
One of them we behold.

Lear. This is a dull sight.° Are you not Kent?

Kent.   The same,
Your servant Kent. Where is your servant Caius?°   285

Lear. He's a good fellow, I can tell you that;
He'll strike, and quickly too: he's dead and rotten.

Kent. No, my good lord; I am the very man.

---

265 *promised end* Doomsday   266 *image* exact likeness   266 *Fall and cease* i.e., let the heavens fall, and all things finish   268 *redeem* make good   278 *falchion* small curved sword   280 *crosses* troubles   280 *spoil me* i.e., my prowess as a swordsman   281 *tell you straight* recognize you straightway   282 *two* i.e., Lear, and some hypothetical second, who is also a prime example of Fortune's inconstancy ("loved and hated")   284 *dull sight* (1) melancholy spectacle (2) faulty eyesight (Lear's own, clouded by weeping)   285 *Caius* (Kent's name, in disguise)

Lear. I'll see that straight.°

290 *Kent.* That from your first of difference and decay°
Have followed your sad steps.

Lear.   You are welcome hither.

Kent. Nor no man else:° all's cheerless, dark and
deadly.
Your eldest daughters have fordone° themselves,
And desperately° are dead.

Lear.   Ay, so I think.

295 *Albany.* He knows not what he says, and vain is it
That we present us to him.

Edgar.   Very bootless.°

Enter a Messenger.

Messenger. Edmund is dead, my lord.

Albany.   That's but a trifle here.
You lords and noble friends, know our intent.
What comfort to this great decay may come°
300 Shall be applied. For us, we° will resign,
During the life of this old majesty,
To him our absolute power: [*To Edgar and Kent*]
you, to your rights;
With boot,° and such addition° as your honors
Have more than merited. All friends shall taste
305 The wages of their virtue, and all foes
The cup of their deservings. O, see, see!

Lear. And my poor fool° is hanged: no, no, no
life?
Why should a dog, a horse, a rat, have life,

289 *see that straight* attend to that in a moment   290 *your . . . decay*
beginning of your decline in fortune   292 *Nor no man else* no, I am
not welcome, nor is anyone else   293 *fordone* destroyed   294 *desper-
ately* in despair   296 *bootless* fruitless   299 *What . . . come* whatever
aid may present itself to this great ruined man   300 *us, we* (the royal
"we")   303 *boot* good measure   303 *addition* additional titles and rights
307 *fool* Cordelia ("fool" being a term of endearment. But it is perfectly possible to take the word as referring also to the Fool)

And thou no breath at all? Thou'lt come no more,
Never, never, never, never, never.   *310*
Pray you, undo this button.° Thank you, sir.
Do you see this? Look on her. Look, her lips,
Look there, look there.

He dies.

Edgar.   He faints. My lord, my lord!

Kent. Break, heart; I prithee, break.

Edgar.   Look up, my lord.

Kent. Vex not his ghost:° O, let him pass! He hates
    him   *315*
That would upon the rack° of this tough world
Stretch him out longer.°

Edgar.   He is gone indeed.

Kent. The wonder is he hath endured so long:
He but usurped° his life.

Albany. Bear them from hence. Our present business   *320*
Is general woe. [*To Kent and Edgar*] Friends of
    my soul, you twain,
Rule in this realm and the gored state sustain.

Kent. I have a journey, sir, shortly to go;
My master calls me, I must not say no.

Edgar. The weight of this sad time we must obey,°   *325*
Speak what we feel, not what we ought to say.
The oldest hath borne most: we that are young
Shall never see so much, nor live so long.

Exeunt, with a dead march.

FINIS

---

³¹¹ *undo this button* i.e., to ease the suffocation Lear feels   ³¹⁵ *Vex
. . . ghost* do not trouble his departing spirit   ³¹⁶ *rack* instrument of
torture, stretching the victim's joints to dislocation   ³¹⁷ *longer* (1) in
time (2) in bodily length   ³¹⁹ *usurped* possessed beyond the allotted
term   ³²⁵ *obey* submit to

Textual Note

The earliest extant version of Shakespeare's *King Lear* is the First Quarto of 1608. This premier edition is known as the Pied Bull Quarto, after the sign which hung before the establishment of the printer. The title page reads as follows: "M. William Shak-speare: / HIS / True Chronicle Historie of the life and / death of King Lear and his three / Daughters. / *With the vnfortunate life of* Edgar, *sonne* / and heire to the Earle of Gloster, and his / sullen and assumed humor of / Tom of Bedlam: / *As it was played before the Kings Maiestie at Whitehall vpon* / S. Stephans *night in Christmas Hollidayes.* / By his Maiesties seruants playing vsually at the Gloabe / on the Bancke-side. / LONDON, / Printed for *Nathaniel Butter,* and are to be sold at his shop in *Pauls* / Church-yard at the signe of the Pide Bull neere / S^t. *Austin's* Gate. 1608." Twelve copies of the First Quarto survive. They are, however, in ten different states, because proofreading, and hence correcting, took place as the play was being printed. The instances (167 in all) in which these copies of Q1 differ one from another have been enumerated by contemporary scholarship.[1]

In 1619 appeared the Second Quarto, known as the N. Butter Quarto, and falsely dated in the same year as

[1] W. W. Greg, *The Variants in the First Quarto of "King Lear,"* London, 1940 (for 1939).

the first (the title page reads: "Printed for Nathaniel Butter. 1608"). The source of Q2 was apparently a copy of Q1 in which a number of sheets had been corrected.

Four years later *King Lear* was reprinted once more, this time in the first collection of Shakespeare's works, the First Folio of 1623. The source of the Folio text seems to have been, again, a corrected copy of Q1. The corrections in this copy, however, do not duplicate those in the presumptive source of Q2, but are at once more and less extensive. In some cases the Quarto which lies behind the Folio offers corrections not found in the source of Q2. In other cases, corrections incorporated in the course of Q2 are not included in the source of F1. The Folio text, moreover, omits some 300 lines found in the Quarto, and thus leads to the supposition that the copy used in preparing the Folio had been collated with the prompt book—a shorter, acting version of the play—in the possession of Shakespeare's company. The Folio text would seem, then, to stand in close relation to Shakespeare's play as it was actually performed. On the other hand, the Folio does include some 100 lines not found in the Quarto.

It is now very generally, though not unanimously, agreed that the Folio is superior to the Quarto, and ought to serve as the basis of any modern edition. The present text of *King Lear* is based, therefore, on the First Folio of 1623, except when the Folio is guilty of an obvious misprinting, or when it omits pertinent material found in the Quarto, or when its version seems to the editor so inferior to the Quarto version as to demand precedence for the latter, or when an emendation, even though perhaps unnecessary (like Edwards' "top th' legitimate"), has been canonized by use and wont.

In the preparation of this text, the spelling of Folio and Quarto has been modernized; punctuation and capitalization have been altered, when alteration seemed suitable; character designations have been expanded or clarified (F "Cor." becomes "Cordelia," F "Bastard" and "Steward" become "Edmund" and "Oswald"); contractions not affecting pronunciation have been eliminated

(F "banish'd" becomes "banished"); necessary quotation marks (as in the reading of a letter) have been supplied; as have diacritical marks whenever a syllable that is normally unemphasized must be stressed (as in "oppressèd"). These changes are not recorded.

All other departures from the Folio appearing in this text are recorded here in italic type. Unless specifically noted, these departures derive in every case from the First Quarto [Q]. If some other source is levied on, such as the Second Quarto [Q2] or Second Folio [F2] or the conjecture of an editor (for example, [Theobald]), that source is given, within brackets, immediately after the reading. There follows next, in roman type, the Folio reading which has been superseded. If an editor's emendation has been preferred to both Folio and Quarto readings, the emendation, with its provenance, is followed by the Folio and Quarto readings it replaces.

Stage directions are not given lineation. Reference to them in these notes is determined, therefore, by the line of text they follow. If a stage direction occurs at the beginning of a scene, reference is to the line of text it precedes. On occasion, the stage direction in the present text represents a conflation of Folio and Quarto. In that case, both Folio and Quarto readings are set down in the notes. Stage directions and notations of place, printed within brackets, are, unless otherwise noted, substantially from the Globe edition. The list of Dramatis Personae, first given by Rowe, is taken also from the Globe edition.

I.i. *Act 1. Scene 1* Actus Primus. Scaena Prima 5 *equalities* qualities 34 s.d. *Sound . . . Attendants* Sennet. Enter King Lear, Cornwall, Albany, Gonerill, Regan, Cordelia, and attendants [F] Sound a Sennet, Enter one bearing a Coronet, then Lear, then the Dukes of Albany, and Cornwall, next Gonerill, Regan, Cordelia, with followers [Q] 70 *speak* [F omits] 98 *loved me. I* loved me 99 *Return* I return 106 *To love my father all* [F omits] 112 *mysteries* [F2] miseries [F] mistress [Q] 157 *as a pawn* as pawn 158 *nor* nere [i.e., "ne'er"] 165 *the* thy 172 *sentence* sentences 176 *diseases* disasters 190 *Gloucester* Cor[delia]

208 *on* in 216 *best object* object 227 *well* will 235 *Better thou*
Better thou hadst 250 *respects of fortune* respect and Fortunes
268 s.d. *Lear . . . Attendants* [Capell] Exit Lear and Burgundy
[Q] 283 *shame them derides* with shame derides 291 *hath not
been* hath been 299-300 *ingrafted* ingraffed 306 *let's hit* let us sit

I.ii. *Scene II* Scena Secunda 21 *top th'* [Edwards] to' th' [F]
tooth' [Q] 103-05 *Edmund . . . earth* [F omits] 142 *Fut* [F
omits] 144 *Edgar* [F omits] 145 *and pat* [Steevens] Pat [F]
and out [Q] 156-64 *as . . . come* [F omits] 165 *Why, the* The
178 *brother* [F omits] 185 *Go armed* [F omits] 191 s.d. *Exit
Edgar* Exit

I.iii. *Scene III* Scena Tertia 17-21 *Not . . . abused* [F omits]
25-26 *I would . . . speak* [F omits] 27 *Go, prepare* prepare

I.iv. *Scene IV* Scena Quarta 1 *well* will 51 *daughter* Daughters 100 *Fool* my Boy 115 *Lady the Brach* [Steevens] the
Lady Brach [F] Ladie oth'e brach [Q] 144-59 *That . . . snatching* [F omits] 158 *on't* [Q2] [F omits] an't [Q] 158 *ladies*
[Q corrected] [F omits] lodes [Q uncorrected] 167 *crown*
Crownes 182 *fools* Foole 195 *Methinks* [F omits] 222 *it
had* it's had 225 *Come, Sir* [F omits] 234 *or his* his 237-41
I . . . father [F omits] 264 *O . . . come* [F omits] 298 *the
cause* more of it 311 *Yea . . . this* [F omits] 350 *You are*
[F2] Your are [F] Y'are [Q] 350 *attasked for* [Q corrected:
"attaskt"] at task for [F] alapt [Q uncorrected]

I.v. *Scene V* Scena Quinta 1 s.d. *Enter . . . Fool* [Q2] Enter
Lear, Kent, Gentleman, and Foole 17 *Why . . . boy* What can'st
tell Boy

II.i. *Act II. Scene I* Actus Secundus. Scena Prima 21 s.d. *Enter
Edgar* [placed by Theobald] [F prints after l. 20] 55 *But* And
72 *I should* should I 73 *ay* [F omits] 80 *I . . . him* [F omits]
80 s.d. *Tucket within* [placed by Malone] [F prints after l. 79]
81 *why* wher 89 *strange news* strangenesse

II.ii. *Scene II* Scena Secunda 23 *clamorous* [Q corrected] clam-
ours [F] clamarous [Q uncorrected] 44 s.d. *Enter . . . drawn*
Enter Bastard, Cornewall, Regan, Gloster, Servants [F] Enter
Edmund with his rapier drawne, Gloster the Duke and Dutchesse
[Q] 77 *too t'* 80 *Renege* Revenge 81 *gale* gall 110 *flick'ring*
[Pope: "flickering"] flicking [F] flitkering [Q] 125 *dread* dead
132 *respect* respects 141 s.d. *Stocks brought out* [placed by
Dyce] [F prints after l. 139] [Q omits] 143-47 *His . . . with*
[F omits] 145 *contemnèd'st* [Capell] [F omits] contaned [Q un-

corrected] temnest [Q corrected]   153 *For . . . legs* [F omits]
154 *Come . . . away* [F assigns to Cornwall]   154 *my good Lord*
my Lord   154 s.d. *Exeunt . . . Kent* Exit [F] [Q omits]
155 *Duke's* Duke   176 s.d. *Sleeps* [F omits]

II.iii. *Scene III* [Steevens] [F, Q omit]   4 *unusual* unusall   15
mortified bare arms mortified Armes   18 *sheepcotes* Sheeps-Cotes

II.iv.1 s.d. *Scene IV* [Steevens] [F, Q omit]   2 *messenger* Messengers   6 *thy* ahy   9 *man's* man   18-19 *No . . . have* [F omits]
30 *panting* painting   33 *whose* those   61 *the* the the   75 *have*
hause   86 s.d. *Enter . . . Gloucester* [F prints after 1. 84]
130 *mother's* Mother   167 *her pride* [F omits]   183 s.d. *Enter
Oswald* [placed by Dyce] [F and Q print after 1. 181]   185 *fickle*
fickly   188 s.d. *Enter Goneril* [placed by Johnson] [F and Q print
after 1. 186]   282 s.d. *Storm and tempest* [F prints after 1. 283]
[Q omits]   285 s.d. *Exeunt . . . Fool* [Q2] Exeunt [F] Exeunt
Lear, Leister, Kent, and Foole [Q]   294 s.d. *Enter Gloucester* [F
and Q print after 1. 293]

III.i. *Act III. Scene 1* Actus Tertius. Scena Prima   7-14 *tears
. . . all* [F omits]   30-42 *But . . . you* [F omits]

III.ii. *Scene II* Scena Secunda   3 *drowned* drown   71 *That* And
78 *True . . . boy* True boy

III.iii. *Scene III* Scaena Tertia

III.iv. *Scene IV* Scena Quarta   7 *skin: so* [Rowe] skinso [F] skin,
so [Q]   10 *thy* they   27 s.d. *Exit* [placed by Johnson] [F prints
after 1. 26] [Q omits]   38 s.d. *Enter Fool* [Duthie] Enter Edgar,
and Foole [F, which prints after 1. 36] [Q omits]   44 s.d. *Enter
Edgar* Enter Edgar, and Foole [F, which prints after 1. 36] [Q
omits]   46 *blows . . . wind* blow the windes   47 *thy cold bed*
thy bed   52 *ford* Sword   57 *Bless* Blisse   58 *Bless* blisse   63
What, has Ha's   91 *deeply* deerely   101 *sessa* [Malone] Sesey
[F] caese [Q] cease [Q2]   116 s.d. *Enter . . . torch* [F prints
after 1. 111] Enter Gloster [Q, which prints after 1. 116]   117
foul fiend Flibbertigibbet foule Flibbertigibbet   118 *till . . . cock*
at first Cocke   138 *hath* had hath

III.v. *Scene V* Scena Quinta   13 *his* this   26 *dearer* deere

III.vi. *Scene VI* Scena Sexta   5 s.d. *Exit* [placed by Capell] [F
prints after 1. 3]   17-55 *The . . . 'scape* [F omits]   22 *Now*
[Q2] [F omits] no [Q]   25 *bourn* [Capell] [F omits] broome [Q]

34 *cushions* [F omits] cushings [Q]   **47** *she kicked* [Q2] [F omits]
kicked [Q]   **53** *made on* [Capell] [F omits] made an [Q]   **67**
lym [Hanmer] Hym [F] him [Q]   **68** *tike, or trundle* tight, or
Troudle   **72** *Sessa!* [Malone] sese [F] [Q omits]   **84** s.d. *Enter
Gloucester* [placed by Capell] [F prints after 1. 80]   **97-100** *Oppressèd . . . behind* [F omits]   **101-14** *When . . . lurk* [F omits]

III.vii. *Scene VII* Scena Septima   **21** s.d. *Exit Oswald* [Staunton]
[F and Q omit]   **23** s.d. *Exeunt . . . Edmund* [Staunton] [F
(Exit) and Q (Exit Gon. and Bast.) print after 1. 22]   **28** s.d.
Enter . . . three [Q, which prints after "traitor"] Enter Gloucester,
and Servants [F, which prints as here after "control"]   **59** *rash*
sticke   **64** *dearn* sterne   **79** s.d. *Draw and fight* [F omits]   **81**
s.d. *She . . . him* Killes him [F] Shee . . . behind [Q]   **100-108**
I'll . . . him [F omits]   **100** *Second Servant* [Capell] [F omits]
Servant [Q]   **101** *Third Servant* [Capell] [F omits]   **2** Servant
[Q]   **104** *Second Servant* [Capell] [F omits] 1 Ser. [Q]   **105**
roguish [Q2] [Q omits]   **107** *Third Servant* [Capell] [F omits]
2 Ser. [Q]   **108** s.d. *Exeunt severally* [F omits] Exit [Q]

IV.i. *Act IV Scene 1* Actus Quartus. Scena Prima   **9** s.d. *led by
an Old Man* [Q, which prints after 1. 12] and an Old man [F,
which places after 1. 9, as here]   **41** *Then, prithee, get thee gone*
Get thee away   **60-65** *Five . . . master* [F omits]   **62-63** *Flibbertigibbet* [Pope] Stiberdigebit [Q]   **63** *mopping and mowing* [Theo-
bald] Mobing, & Mohing [Q]

IV.ii. *Scene II* Scena Secunda   **1** s.d. *Enter Goneril and Edmund*
Enter Gonerill, Bastard, and Steward   **2** s.d. [after "way"] *Enter
Oswald* [placed by Theobald] [Q prints after "master," 1.2] [F
omits]   **25** s.d. *Exit Edmund* [placed by Rowe] Exit [F, which
prints after "death"] [Q omits]   **28** s.d. *Exit* [F omits] Exit Stew.
[Q]   **31-50** *I . . . deep* [F omits]   **32** *its* ith [Q]   **45** *benefited*
[Q corrected] benificted [Q uncorrected]   **47** *these* [Jennens; Heath
conj.] the [Q uncorrected] this [Q corrected]   **49** *Humanity* [Q cor-
rected] Humanly [Q uncorrected]   **53-59** *that . . . so* [F omits]   **56**
noiseless [Q corrected] noystles [Q uncorrected]   **57** *thy state
begins to threat* [Jennens] thy slayer begin threats [Q uncorrected]
thy state begins thereat [Q corrected] thy slaier begins threats
[Q2]   **58** *Whilst* [Q corrected] Whil's [Q uncorrected]   **62-69**
Thou . . . news [F omits]   **65** *dislocate* [Q3] dislecate [Qq.1,2]
68 *mew* [Q corrected] now [Q uncorrected]   **68** s.d. *Enter a
Messenger* [F prints after 1. 61] Enter a Gentleman [Q, which
prints after 1. 69; and Q2, which prints after 1. 68, as here]   **75**
thereat enraged threat-enrag'd   **79** *justicers* [Q corrected] Iustices
[F, Q]   **87** s.d. *Exit* [F omits]

IV.iii. *Scene III* Scena Tertia [for Scene IV] 1 s.d. *Enter . . . Gentleman* [F omits the entire scene] 12 *sir* [Theobald] say 17 *strove* [Pope] streme 21 *seemed* [Pope: "seem'd"] seeme 30 *believed* [Q2] beleeft 32 *moistened* [Capell] moystened her 56 *Exeunt* [Pope] Exit

IV.iv. *Scene IV* [Pope] Scena Tertia [F] [Q omits] 1 s.d. *Cordelia, Doctor, and Soldiers* Cordelia, Gentlemen, and Souldiours [F] Cordelia, Doctor and others [Q] 3 *femiter* Fenitar 6 *century* Centery 18 *distress* desires 28 *right* Rite

IV.v. *Scene V* [Pope] Scena Quarta [F] [Q omits] 39 *meet him* meet

IV.vi. *Scene VI* [Pope] Scena Quinta [Q omits] 17 *walk* walk'd 34 s.d. *He kneels* [F omits] 41 s.d. *He falls* [F omits] 71 *whelked* wealk'd 71 *enridgèd* enraged 83 *coining* crying 97 *had white* had the white 166 *Through* Thorough *small* great 167 *Plate sin* [Theobald] Place sinnes [Q omits] 199 *Ay . . . dust* [F omits] 200 *Good sir* [Q2] [F and Q omit] 206 s.d. *Exit . . . follow* Exit [F] Exit King running [Q] 208 *one* a 244 *I'se* [Johnson: "Ise"] ice [F] ile [Q] 247 s.d. *They fight* [F omits] 255 s.d. *He dies* [F omits] 274 *and . . . venture* [Q reads "Venter"] [F omits] [This line, from the First Quarto, is almost universally omitted from editions of the play] 276 *indistinguished* indinguish'd 289 s.d. *Drum afar off* [F prints after l. 287] A drum a farre off [Q, which prints as here]

IV.vii. *Scene VII* Scaena Septima 1 s.d. *Enter . . . Gentleman* Enter Cordelia, Kent, and Gentleman [F] Enter Cordelia, Kent, and Doctor [Q] 24 *doubt not* doubt 24-25 *Very . . . there* [F omits] 32 *warring* iarring 33-36 *To . . . helm* [F omits] 79-80 *and . . . lost* [F omits] 85 s.d. *Exeunt . . . Gentleman* Exeunt 86-98 *Holds . . . fought* [F omits]

V.i. *Act V Scene I* Actus Quintus. Scena Prima 11-13 *That . . . hers* [F omits] 16 *Fear me not* Feare not 18-19 *I . . . me* [F omits] 23-28 *Where . . . nobly* [F omits] 33 *I . . . tent* [F omits] 36 *pray you* pray 39 s.d. *To those going out* [F and Q omit] *To Edgar* [F and Q omit] *Exeunt* [placed by Cambridge edition] [Q prints after "word," l. 39] [F omits] 46 *love* loues 50 s.d. *Exit* [placed by Dyce] [F and Q print after l. 49]

V.ii. *Scene II* Scena Secunda

V.iii. *Scene III* Scena Tertia 13 *hear poor rogues* heere (poore Rogues) [reference in F is to Lear and Cordelia] 26 s.d. *Exeunt*

. . . *guarded* Exit [F] [Q omits]   39-40 *I . . . do't* [F omits]   40
s.d. *Exit Captain* [F prints after 1. 38] [Q omits]   48 *and appointed guard* [Q corrected, and Q2] [F and Q omit]   55-60 *At
. . . place* [F omits]   56 *We* [Q corrected, and Q2] mee [Q]   58
sharpness [Q corrected, and Q2] sharpes [Q]   84 *attaint* arrest
85 *sister* Sisters   98 *he is* hes   103 *Edmund . . . ho, a herald*
[F omits]   108 s.d. *Enter a Herald* [placed by Hanmer] [F prints
after 1. 102] [Q omits]   110 *Sound, trumpet* [F omits]   110 s.d.
A trumpet sounds [F prints after 1. 109] [Q omits] trumpet [F2]
Tumpet   116 *Sound* [F omits]   116 s.d. *First trumpet* [F prints
after 1. 115] [Q omits]   118 s.d. *Enter . . . him* Enter Edgar
armed [F] Enter Edgar at the third sound, a trumpet before him
[Q]   137 *illustrious* illustirous   145 *some say* (some say)   152
s.d. *fight* Fights [F, which prints after 1. 153, "him"] [Q omits]
162 *Ask . . . know* [F gives to Edmund]   162 s.d. *Exit* [placed
here by Q: "Exit. Gonorill"] [F prints after 1. 161, "for't"]
206-23 *This . . . slave* [F omits]   215 *him* [Theobald] me [Q]
[F omits]   223 s.d. *Enter . . . knife* Enter a Gentleman [F]
Enter one with a bloudie knife [Q]   234 s.d. *Enter Kent* [placed
by Q2] [F prints after 1. 231, "Kent"] [Q prints after "allow"
in 1. 235]   240 s.d. *The . . . in* Gonerill and Regans bodies
brought out [F, which prints after 1. 232]   253 s.d. *Exit Messenger* [Theobald] [F and Q omit]   259 *Howl, howl, howl, howl*
Howle, howle, howle *you are* your are   279 *them* him   291
You are [Q2] Your are [F] You'r [Q]   296 s.d. *Enter a Messenger* [F, which prints after "him"] Enter Captaine [Q, placed as
here]

The Tragedy of
Macbeth

♦

EDITED BY
Sylvan Barnet

[*Dramatis Personae*

Duncan, King of Scotland
Malcolm ⎫
Donalbain ⎬ his sons

Macbeth
Banquo
Macduff
Lennox
Ross ⎬ noblemen of Scotland
Menteith
Angus
Caithness

Fleance, son to Banquo
Siward, Earl of Northumberland, general of the
    English forces
Young Siward, his son
Seyton, an officer attending on Macbeth
Son to Macduff
An English Doctor
A Scottish Doctor
A Porter
An Old Man
Three Murderers
Lady Macbeth
Lady Macduff
A Gentlewoman attending on Lady Macbeth
Hecate
Witches
Apparitions
Lords, Officers, Soldiers, Attendants, and Mes-
    sengers

Scene: Scotland; England]

The Tragedy of Macbeth

ACT I

Scene I.   [An open place.]

Thunder and lightning. Enter Three Witches.

First Witch. When shall we three meet again?
    In thunder, lightning, or in rain?

Second Witch. When the hurlyburly's done,
    When the battle's lost and won.

Third Witch. That will be ere the set of sun.   5

First Witch. Where the place?

Second Witch.   Upon the heath.

Third Witch. There to meet with Macbeth.

First Witch. I come, Graymalkin.° ¹

Second Witch. Paddock° calls.

Third Witch.   Anon!°

All. Fair is foul, and foul is fair.   10

    Hover through the fog and filthy air.

                                        Exeunt.

¹ The degree sign (°) indicates a footnote, which is keyed to the text by
line number. Text references are printed in *italic* type; the annotation
follows in roman type.
I.i. ⁸ *Graymalkin* (the witch's attendant spirit, a gray cat)   ⁹ *Paddock*
toad   ⁹ *Anon* at once

Scene II.   [*A camp.*]

Alarum within.° Enter King [Duncan], Mal-
colm, Donalbain, Lennox, with Attendants, meet-
ing a bleeding Captain.

King. What bloody man is that? He can report,
　　As seemeth by his plight, of the revolt
　　The newest state.

Malcolm.　　　　　This is the sergeant°
　　Who like a good and hardy soldier fought
5　　'Gainst my captivity. Hail, brave friend!
　　Say to the king the knowledge of the broil°
　　As thou didst leave it.

Captain.　　　　　　Doubtful it stood,
　　As two spent swimmers, that do cling together
　　And choke their art.° The merciless Macdonwald—
10　　Worthy to be a rebel for to that
　　The multiplying villainies of nature
　　Do swarm upon him—from the Western Isles°
　　Of kerns and gallowglasses° is supplied;
　　And Fortune, on his damnèd quarrel° smiling,
15　　Showed like a rebel's whore:° but all's too weak:
　　For brave Macbeth—well he deserves that name—
　　Disdaining Fortune, with his brandished steel,
　　Which smoked with bloody execution,
　　Like valor's minion° carved out his passage

I.ii.s.d. *Alarum within* trumpet call offstage   **3** *sergeant* i.e., officer
(he is called, perhaps with no inconsistency in Shakespeare's day,
a captain in the s.d. and speech prefixes. *Sergeant* is trisyllabic)
6 *broil* quarrel   **9** *choke their art* hamper each other's doings   **12** *West-*
ern Isles Hebrides   **13** *Of kerns and gallowglasses* with lightly armed
Irish foot soldiers and heavily armed ones   **14** *damnèd quarrel* accursed
cause   **15** *Showed like a rebel's whore* i.e., falsely appeared to favor
Macdonwald   **19** *minion* (trisyllabic) favorite

  20

Till he faced the slave;
Which nev'r shook hands, nor bade farewell to him,
Till he unseamed him from the nave to th' chops,°
And fixed his head upon our battlements.

King. O valiant cousin! Worthy gentleman!

Captain. As whence the sun 'gins his reflection°   25
Shipwracking storms and direful thunders break,
So from that spring whence comfort seemed to come
Discomfort swells. Mark, King of Scotland, mark:
No sooner justice had, with valor armed,
Compelled these skipping kerns to trust their heels   30
But the Norweyan lord, surveying vantage,°
With furbished arms and new supplies of men,
Began a fresh assault.

King.   Dismayed not this
Our captains, Macbeth and Banquo?

Captain.   Yes;
As sparrows eagles, or the hare the lion.   35
If I say sooth,° I must report they were
As cannons overcharged with double cracks;°
So they doubly redoubled strokes upon the foe.
Except° they meant to bathe in reeking wounds,
Or memorize another Golgotha,°   40
I cannot tell—
But I am faint; my gashes cry for help.

King. So well thy words become thee as thy wounds;
They smack of honor both. Go get him surgeons.

                         [*Exit Captain, attended.*]

        Enter Ross and Angus.
Who comes here?

---

22 *nave to th' chops* navel to the jaws   25 *reflection* (four syllables;
the ending—*ion* here and often elsewhere in the play— is disyllabic)
31 *surveying vantage* seeing an opportunity   36 *sooth* truth   37 *cracks*
explosives   39 *Except* unless   40 *memorize another Golgotha* make
the place as memorable as Golgotha, "the place of the skull"

45 *Malcolm.*   The worthy Thane° of Ross.

Lennox. What a haste looks through his eyes! So
      should he look
   That seems to° speak things strange.

Ross.   God save the king!

King. Whence cam'st thou, worthy Thane?

Ross.   From Fife, great King;
   Where the Norweyan banners flout the sky
50 And fan our people cold.
   Norway° himself, with terrible numbers,
   Assisted by that most disloyal traitor
   The Thane of Cawdor, began a dismal° conflict;
55 Till that Bellona's bridegroom, lapped in proof,°
   Confronted him with self-comparisons,°
   Point against point, rebellious arm 'gainst arm,
   Curbing his lavish° spirit: and, to conclude,
   The victory fell on us.

King.   Great happiness!

Ross.   That now
   Sweno, the Norways' king, craves composition;°
60 Nor would we deign him burial of his men
   Till he disbursèd, at Saint Colme's Inch,°
   Ten thousand dollars° to our general use.

King. No more that Thane of Cawdor shall deceive
   Our bosom interest:° go pronounce his present°
      death,
65 And with his former title greet Macbeth.

Ross. I'll see it done.

King. What he hath lost, noble Macbeth hath won.
                              Exeunt.

---

⁴⁵ *Thane* (a Scottish title of nobility) ⁴⁷ *seems to* seems about to
⁵¹ *Norway* the King of Norway ⁵³ *dismal* threatening ⁵⁴ *Bellona's
. . . proof* the mate of the goddess of war, clad in tested (proved)
armor ⁵⁵ *self-comparisons* counter-movements ⁵⁷ *lavish* insolent
⁵⁹ *composition* terms of peace ⁶¹ *Inch* island ⁶² *dollars* (Spanish and
Dutch currency) ⁶⁴ *Our bosom interest* my (plural of royalty)
heart's trust ⁶⁴ *present* immediate

Scene III.   [*A heath.*]

Thunder. Enter the Three Witches.

First Witch. Where hast thou been, sister?

Second Witch. Killing swine.

Third Witch. Sister, where thou?

First Witch. A sailor's wife had chestnuts in her lap,
   And mounched, and mounched, and mounched.
      "Give me," quoth I.   **5**
   "Aroint thee,° witch!" the rump-fed ronyon° cries.
   Her husband's to Aleppo gone, master o' th' Tiger:
   But in a sieve I'll thither sail,
   And, like a rat without a tail,
   I'll do, I'll do, and I'll do.   **10**

Second Witch. I'll give thee a wind.

First Witch. Th' art kind.

Third Witch. And I another.

First Witch. I myself have all the other;
   And the very ports they blow,°   **15**
   All the quarters that they know
   I' th' shipman's card.°
   I'll drain him dry as hay:
   Sleep shall neither night nor day
   Hang upon his penthouse lid;°   **20**
   He shall live a man forbid:°
   Weary sev'nights nine times nine
   Shall he dwindle, peak,° and pine:

I.iii. ⁶ *Aroint thee* begone   ⁶ *rump-fed ronyon* fat-rumped scabby creature   ¹⁵ *ports they blow* harbors to which the winds blow (?)
¹⁷ *card* compass card   ²⁰ *penthouse lid* eyelid (the figure is of a lean-to)
²¹ *forbid* cursed   ²³ *peak* waste away

Though his bark cannot be lost,
25   Yet it shall be tempest-tossed.
Look what I have.

Second Witch. Show me, show me.

First Witch. Here I have a pilot's thumb,
Wracked as homeward he did come.

Drum within.

30   *Third Witch.* A drum, a drum!
Macbeth doth come.

All. The weïrd° sisters, hand in hand,
Posters° of the sea and land,
Thus do go about, about:
35   Thrice to thine, and thrice to mine,
And thrice again, to make up nine.
Peace! The charm's wound up.

Enter Macbeth and Banquo.

Macbeth. So foul and fair a day I have not seen.

Banquo. How far is 't called to Forres? What are these
40   So withered, and so wild in their attire,
That look not like th' inhabitants o' th' earth,
And yet are on 't? Live you, or are you aught
That man may question?° You seem to understand
me,
By each at once her choppy° finger laying
45   Upon her skinny lips. You should be women,
And yet your beards forbid me to interpret
That you are so.

Macbeth.   Speak, if you can: what are you?

First Witch. All hail, Macbeth! Hail to thee, Thane of
Glamis!

Second Witch. All hail, Macbeth! Hail to thee, Thane of
Cawdor!

32 *weïrd* destiny-serving (?)   33 *Posters* swift travelers   43 *question* talk
to   44 *choppy* chapped

Third Witch. All hail, Macbeth, that shalt be King
    hereafter!   50

Banquo. Good sir, why do you start, and seem to fear
    Things that do sound so fair? I' th' name of truth,
    Are ye fantastical,° or that indeed
    Which outwardly ye show? My noble partner
    You greet with present grace° and great prediction   55
    Of noble having° and of royal hope,
    That he seems rapt withal:° to me you speak not.
    If you can look into the seeds of time,
    And say which grain will grow and which will not,
    Speak then to me, who neither beg nor fear   60
    Your favors nor your hate.

First Witch. Hail!

Second Witch. Hail!

Third Witch. Hail!

First Witch. Lesser than Macbeth, and greater.   65

Second Witch. Not so happy,° yet much happier.

Third Witch. Thou shalt get° kings, though thou be
    none.
    So all hail, Macbeth and Banquo!

First Witch. Banquo and Macbeth, all hail!

Macbeth. Stay, you imperfect° speakers, tell me more: 70
    By Sinel's° death I know I am Thane of Glamis;
    But how of Cawdor? The Thane of Cawdor lives,
    A prosperous gentleman; and to be King
    Stands not within the prospect of belief,
    No more than to be Cawdor. Say from whence   75
    You owe° this strange intelligence?° Or why
    Upon this blasted heath you stop our way

---

53 *fantastical* imaginary   55 *grace* honor   56 *having* possession   57 *rapt
withal* entranced by it   66 *happy* fortunate   67 *get* beget   70 *imperfect*
incomplete   71 *Sinel* (Macbeth's father)   76 *owe* own, have   76 *intelligence* information

With such prophetic greeting? Speak, I charge
   you.

                              Witches vanish.

Banquo. The earth hath bubbles as the water has,
80   And these are of them. Whither are they vanished?

Macbeth. Into the air, and what seemed corporal°
   melted
      As breath into the wind. Would they had stayed!

Banquo. Were such things here as we do speak about?
      Or have we eaten on the insane° root
85   That takes the reason prisoner?

Macbeth. Your children shall be kings.

Banquo.   You shall be King.

Macbeth. And Thane of Cawdor too. Went it not so?
Banquo. To th' selfsame tune and words. Who's here?

               Enter Ross and Angus.

Ross. The King hath happily received, Macbeth,
90   The news of thy success; and when he reads°
      Thy personal venture in the rebels' fight,
      His wonders and his praises do contend
      Which should be thine or his.° Silenced with that,
      In viewing o'er the rest o' th' selfsame day,
95   He finds thee in the stout Norweyan ranks,
      Nothing afeard of what thyself didst make,
      Strange images of death. As thick as tale
      Came post with post,° and every one did bear
      Thy praises in his kingdom's great defense,
      And poured them down before him.

100 *Angus.*   We are sent
      To give thee, from our royal master, thanks;

81 *corporal* corporeal   84 *insane* insanity-producing   90 *reads* considers
92–93 *His* wonders . . . *his* i.e., Duncan's speechless admiration, appropriate to him, contends with his desire to praise you (?)   97–98 *As
thick . . . post* as fast as could be counted came messenger after messenger

Only to herald thee into his sight,
Not pay thee.

Ross. And for an earnest° of a greater honor,
    He bade me, from him, call thee Thane of Cawdor;   *105*
    In which addition,° hail, most worthy Thane!
    For it is thine.

Banquo.   What, can the devil speak true?

Macbeth. The Thane of Cawdor lives: why do you dress
    me
    In borrowed robes?

Angus.   Who was the thane lives yet,
    But under heavy judgment bears that life   *110*
    Which he deserves to lose. Whether he was com-
      bined°
    With those of Norway, or did line° the rebel
    With hidden help and vantage,° or that with both
    He labored in his country's wrack,° I know not;
    But treasons capital, confessed and proved,   *115*
    Have overthrown him.

Macbeth.   [*Aside*] Glamis, and Thane of Cawdor:
    The greatest is behind.° [*To Ross and Angus*] Thanks
      for your pains.
    [*Aside to Banquo*] Do you not hope your children
      shall be kings,
    When those that gave the Thane of Cawdor to me
    Promised no less to them?

Banquo. [*Aside to Macbeth*] That, trusted home,°   *120*
    Might yet enkindle you unto the crown,
    Besides the Thane of Cawdor. But 'tis strange:
    And oftentimes, to win us to our harm,
    The instruments of darkness tell us truths,
    Win us with honest trifles, to betray 's   *125*

104 *earnest* pledge   106 *addition* title   111 *combined* allied   112 *line* support   113 *vantage* opportunity   114 *wrack* ruin   117 *behind* i.e., to follow   120 *home* all the way

In deepest consequence.°
Cousins,° a word, I pray you.

Macbeth.   [*Aside*] Two truths are told,
As happy prologues to the swelling° act
Of the imperial theme.—I thank you, gentlemen.—
130   [*Aside*] This supernatural soliciting°
Cannot be ill, cannot be good. If ill,
Why hath it given me earnest of success,
Commencing in a truth? I am Thane of Cawdor:
If good, why do I yield to that suggestion
135   Whose horrid image doth unfix my hair
And make my seated° heart knock at my ribs,
Against the use of nature?° Present fears
Are less than horrible imaginings.
My thought, whose murder yet is but fantastical,°
140   Shakes so my single° state of man that function
Is smothered in surmise, and nothing is
But what is not.

Banquo.   Look, how our partner's rapt.

Macbeth. [*Aside*] If chance will have me King, why,
        chance may crown me,
Without my stir.

Banquo.   New honors come upon him,
Like our strange° garments, cleave not to their
145   mold
But with the aid of use.

Macbeth.   [*Aside*] Come what come may,
Time and the hour runs through the roughest day.

Banquo. Worthy Macbeth, we stay upon your leisure.°

Macbeth. Give me your favor.° My dull brain was
        wrought

126 *In deepest consequence* in the most significant sequel   127 *Cousins*
i.e., fellow noblemen   128 *swelling* stately   130 *soliciting* inviting
136 *seated* fixed   137 *Against the use of nature* contrary to my natural
way   139 *fantastical* imaginary   140 *single* unaided, weak (or "entire"?)
145 *strange* new   148 *stay upon your leisure* await your convenience
149 *favor* pardon

With things forgotten. Kind gentlemen, your pains 150
Are registered where every day I turn
The leaf to read them. Let us toward the King.
[*Aside to Banquo*] Think upon what hath
   chanced, and at more time,
The interim having weighed it,° let us speak
Our free hearts° each to other.

Banquo.   Very gladly. 155

Macbeth. Till then, enough. Come, friends.

                              Exeunt.

Scene IV.   [*Forres. The palace.*]

*Flourish.° Enter King [Duncan], Lennox,
   Malcolm, Donalbain, and Attendants.*

King. Is execution done on Cawdor? Are not
   Those in commission° yet returned?

Malcolm.   My liege,
They are not yet come back. But I have spoke
With one that saw him die, who did report
That very frankly he confessed his treasons,
Implored your Highness' pardon and set forth 5
A deep repentance: nothing in his life
Became him like the leaving it. He died
As one that had been studied° in his death,
To throw away the dearest thing he owed° 10
As 'twere a careless° trifle.

---

154 *The interim having weighed it* i.e., when we have had time to
think   155 *Our free hearts* our minds freely   I.iv.s.d. *Flourish* fanfare
2 *in commission* i.e., commissioned to oversee the execution   9 *studied*
rehearsed   10 *owed* owned   11 *careless* uncared-for

King.   There's no art
To find the mind's construction in the face:
He was a gentleman on whom I built
An absolute trust.

Enter Macbeth, Banquo, Ross, and Angus.

                      O worthiest cousin!
15 The sin of my ingratitude even now
Was heavy on me: thou art so far before,
That swiftest wing of recompense is slow
To overtake thee. Would thou hadst less deserved,
That the proportion° both of thanks and payment
20 Might have been mine! Only I have left to say,
More is thy due than more than all can pay.

Macbeth. The service and the loyalty I owe,
In doing it, pays itself.° Your Highness' part
Is to receive our duties: and our duties
25 Are to your throne and state children and servants;
Which do but what they should, by doing every
      thing
Safe toward° your love and honor.

King.   Welcome hither.
I have begun to plant thee, and will labor
To make thee full of growing. Noble Banquo,
30 That hast no less deserved, nor must be known
No less to have done so, let me enfold thee
And hold thee to my heart.

Banquo.   There if I grow,
The harvest is your own.

King.   My plenteous joys,
Wanton° in fullness, seek to hide themselves
35 In drops of sorrow. Sons, kinsmen, thanes,
And you whose places are the nearest, know,
We will establish our estate° upon
Our eldest, Malcolm, whom we name hereafter

19 *proportion* preponderance   23 *pays itself* is its own reward   27 *Safe toward* safeguarding (?)   34 *Wanton* unrestrained   37 *establish our estate* settle the succession

 The Prince of Cumberland: which honor must
 Not unaccompanied invest him only,   40
 But signs of nobleness, like stars, shall shine
 On all deservers. From hence to Inverness,
 And bind us further to you.

Macbeth. The rest is labor, which is not used for you.°
 I'll be myself the harbinger, and make joyful   45
 The hearing of my wife with your approach;
 So, humbly take my leave.

King.   My worthy Cawdor!

Macbeth. [*Aside*] The Prince of Cumberland! That
       is a step
 On which I must fall down, or else o'erleap,
 For in my way it lies. Stars, hide your fires;   50
 Let not light see my black and deep desires:
 The eye wink at the hand;° yet let that be
 Which the eye fears, when it is done, to see.

                                           Exit.

King. True, worthy Banquo; he is full so valiant,
 And in his commendations° I am fed;   55
 It is a banquet to me. Let's after him,
 Whose care is gone before to bid us welcome.
 It is a peerless kinsman.   *Flourish. Exeunt.*

 Scene V.   [*Inverness. Macbeth's castle.*]

 Enter Macbeth's wife, alone, with a letter.

Lady Macbeth. [*Reads*] "They met me in the day
 of success; and I have learned by the perfect'st

---

44 *The rest . . . you* i.e., repose is laborious when not employed for
you   52 *wink at the hand* i.e., be blind to the hand's deed   55 *his commendations* commendations of him

report they have more in them than mortal knowledge. When I burned in desire to question them
further, they made themselves air, into which they
vanished. Whiles I stood rapt in the wonder of it,
came missives° from the King, who all-hailed me
'Thane of Cawdor'; by which title, before, these
weïrd sisters saluted me, and referred me to the
coming on of time, with 'Hail, King that shalt
be!' This have I thought good to deliver thee,° my
dearest partner of greatness, that thou mightst not
lose the dues of rejoicing, by being ignorant of
what greatness is promised thee. Lay it to thy heart,
and farewell."

Glamis thou art, and Cawdor, and shalt be
What thou art promised. Yet do I fear thy nature;
It is too full o' th' milk of human kindness°
To catch the nearest way. Thou wouldst be great,
Art not without ambition, but without
The illness° should attend it. What thou wouldst
    highly,
That wouldst thou holily; wouldst not play false,
And yet wouldst wrongly win. Thou'dst have,
    great Glamis,
That which cries "Thus thou must do" if thou have
    it;
And that which rather thou dost fear to do
Than wishest should be undone. Hie thee hither,
That I may pour my spirits in thine ear,
And chastise with the valor of my tongue
All that impedes thee from the golden round°
Which fate and metaphysical° aid doth seem
To have thee crowned withal.°

Enter Messenger.

I.v. 7 *missives* messengers 11 *deliver thee* report to you 18 *milk of human kindness* i.e., gentle quality of human nature 21 *illness* wickedness 29 *round* crown 30 *metaphysical* supernatural 31 *withal* with

                    What is your tidings?

Messenger. The King comes here tonight.

Lady Macbeth.   Thou'rt mad to say it!
Is not thy master with him, who, were 't so,
Would have informed for preparation?

Messenger. So please you, it is true. Our thane is
    coming.   35
One of my fellows had the speed of him,°
Who, almost dead for breath, had scarcely more
Than would make up his message.

Lady Macbeth.   Give him tending;
He brings great news.   *Exit Messenger.*
               The raven himself is hoarse
That croaks the fatal entrance of Duncan   40
Under my battlements. Come, you spirits
That tend on mortal° thoughts, unsex me here,
And fill me, from the crown to the toe, top-full
Of direst cruelty! Make thick my blood,
Stop up th' access and passage to remorse,°   45
That no compunctious visitings of nature°
Shake my fell° purpose, nor keep peace between
Th' effect° and it! Come to my woman's breasts,
And take my milk for° gall, you murd'ring ministers,°
Wherever in your sightless° substances   50
You wait on° nature's mischief! Come, thick night,
And pall° thee in the dunnest° smoke of hell,
That my keen knife see not the wound it makes,
Nor heaven peep through the blanket of the dark,
To cry "Hold, hold!"

              Enter Macbeth.

           Great Glamis! Worthy Cawdor!   55
Greater than both, by the all-hail hereafter!°

---

36 *had the speed of him* outdistanced him 42 *mortal* deadly 45 *remorse* compassion 46 *compunctious visitings of nature* natural feelings of compassion 47 *fell* savage 48 *effect* fulfillment 49 *for* in exchange for 49 *ministers* agents 50 *sightless* invisible 51 *wait on* assist 52 *pall* enshroud 52 *dunnest* darkest 56 *all-hail hereafter* the third all-hail (?) the all-hail of the future(?)

    Thy letters have transported me beyond
    This ignorant° present, and I feel now
    The future in the instant.°

Macbeth.   My dearest love,
    Duncan comes here tonight.

60 *Lady Macbeth.*   And when goes hence?

Macbeth. Tomorrow, as he purposes.

Lady Macbeth.   O, never
    Shall sun that morrow see!
    Your face, my Thane, is as a book where men
    May read strange matters. To beguile the time,°
65   Look like the time; bear welcome in your eye,
    Your hand, your tongue: look like th' innocent
       flower,
    But be the serpent under 't. He that's coming
    Must be provided for: and you shall put
    This night's great business into my dispatch;°
70   Which shall to all our nights and days to come
    Give solely sovereign sway and masterdom.

Macbeth. We will speak further.

Lady Macbeth.   Only look up clear.°
    To alter favor ever is to fear.°
    Leave all the rest to me.   *Exeunt.*

---

58 *ignorant* unknowing 59 *instant* present 64 *To beguile the time* i.e.,
to deceive people of the day 69 *dispatch* management 72 *look up clear*
appear undisturbed 73 *To alter . . . fear* to show a disturbed face is
dangerous

Scene VI.   [*Before Macbeth's castle.*]

Hautboys° and torches. Enter King [*Duncan*]
*Malcolm, Donalbain, Banquo, Lennox, Macduff,
Ross, Angus, and Attendants.*

King. This castle hath a pleasant seat;° the air
    Nimbly and sweetly recommends itself
    Unto our gentle° senses.

Banquo.   This guest of summer,
    The temple-haunting martlet,° does approve°
    By his loved mansionry° that the heaven's breath   5
    Smells wooingly here. No jutty,° frieze,
    Buttress, nor coign of vantage,° but this bird
    Hath made his pendent bed and procreant° cradle.
    Where they most breed and haunt,° I have observed
    The air is delicate.

Enter Lady [*Macbeth*].

King.   See, see, our honored hostess!   10
    The love that follows us sometime is our trouble,
    Which still we thank as love.° Herein I teach you
    How you shall bid God 'ield° us for your pains
    And thank us for your trouble.

Lady Macbeth.   •   All our service
    In every point twice done, and then done double,   15
    Were poor and single business° to contend
    Against those honors deep and broad wherewith

I.vi.s.d. *Hautboys* oboes 1 *seat* site 3 *gentle* soothed 4 *temple-haunt-
ing martlet* martin (swift) nesting in churches 4 *approve* prove
5 *mansionry* nests 6 *jutty* projection 7 *coign of vantage* advantageous
corner 8 *procreant* breeding 9 *haunt* visit 11-12 *The love . . . love*
the love offered me sometimes inconveniences me, but still I value it
as love 13 *'ield* reward 16 *single business* feeble service

Your Majesty loads our house: for those of old,
And the late dignities heaped up to them,
We rest your hermits.°

20 *King.*   Where's the Thane of Cawdor?
We coursed° him at the heels, and had a purpose
To be his purveyor:° but he rides well,
And his great love, sharp as his spur, hath holp°
    him
To his home before us. Fair and noble hostess,
We are your guest tonight.

25 *Lady Macbeth.*   Your servants ever
Have theirs, themselves, and what is theirs, in
    compt,°
To make their audit at your Highness' pleasure,
Still° to return your own.

King.   Give me your hand.
Conduct me to mine host: we love him highly,
30 And shall continue our graces towards him.
By your leave, hostess.   *Exeunt.*

Scene VII.   [*Macbeth's castle.*]

*Hautboys. Torches. Enter a Sewer,° and diverse
Servants with dishes and service over the stage.
Then enter Macbeth.*

Macbeth. If it were done° when 'tis done, then 'twere
    well
It were done quickly. If th' assassination

20 *your hermits* dependents bound to pray for you   21 *coursed* pursued
22 *purveyor* advance-supply officer   23 *holp* helped   26 *Have theirs . . .
compt* have their dependents, themselves, and their possessions in trust
28 *Still* always   I.vii.s.d. *Sewer* chief butler   1 *done* over and done
with

Could trammel up° the consequence, and catch,
With his surcease,° success;° that but this blow
Might be the be-all and the end-all—here,   5
But here, upon this bank and shoal of time,
We'd jump° the life to come. But in these cases
We still° have judgment here; that we but teach
Bloody instructions, which, being taught, return
To plague th' inventor: this even-handed° justice   10
Commends° th' ingredients of our poisoned
    chalice
To our own lips. He's here in double trust:
First, as I am his kinsman and his subject,
Strong both against the deed; then, as his host,
Who should against his murderer shut the door,   15
Not bear the knife myself. Besides, this Duncan
Hath borne his faculties° so meek, hath been
So clear° in his great office, that his virtues
Will plead like angels trumpet-tongued against
The deep damnation of his taking-off;   20
And pity, like a naked newborn babe,
Striding° the blast, or heaven's cherubin horsed
Upon the sightless couriers° of the air,
Shall blow the horrid deed in every eye,
That° tears shall drown the wind. I have no spur   25
To prick the sides of my intent, but only
Vaulting ambition, which o'erleaps itself
And falls on th' other——

                    Enter Lady [Macbeth].

                            How now! What news?

Lady Macbeth. He has almost supped. Why have you
    left the chamber?

---

8 *trammel up* catch in a net 4 *his surcease* Duncan's death(?) the
consequence's cessation(?) 4 *success* what follows 7 *jump* risk 8 *still*
always 10 *even-handed* impartial 11 *Commends* offers 17 *faculties*
powers 18 *clear* spotless 22 *Striding* bestriding 23 *sightless couriers*
invisible coursers (i.e., the winds) 25 *That* so that

Macbeth. Hath he asked for me?

30 *Lady Macbeth.*   Know you not he has?

Macbeth. We will proceed no further in this business:
He hath honored me of late, and I have bought°
Golden opinions from all sorts of people,
Which would be worn now in their newest gloss,
Not cast aside so soon.

35 *Lady Macbeth.*   Was the hope drunk
Wherein you dressed yourself? Hath it slept since?
And wakes it now, to look so green° and pale
At what it did so freely? From this time
Such I account thy love. Art thou afeard
40 To be the same in thine own act and valor
As thou art in desire? Wouldst thou have that
Which thou esteem'st the ornament of life,
And live a coward in thine own esteem,
Letting "I dare not" wait upon° "I would,"
Like the poor cat° i' th' adage?

45 *Macbeth.*   Prithee, peace!
I dare do all that may become a man;
Who dares do more is none.

Lady Macbeth.   What beast was 't then
That made you break° this enterprise to me?
When you durst do it, then you were a man;
50 And to be more than what you were, you would
Be so much more the man. Nor time nor place
Did then adhere,° and yet you would make both.
They have made themselves, and that their° fitness
   now
Does unmake you. I have given suck, and know
55 How tender 'tis to love the babe that milks me:
I would, while it was smiling in my face,
Have plucked my nipple from his boneless gums,

---

32 *bought* acquired   37 *green* sickly   44 *wait upon* follow   45 *cat* (who
wants fish but fears to wet its paws)   48 *break* broach   52 *adhere* suit
53 *that their* their very

And dashed the brains out, had I so sworn as you
Have done to this.

Macbeth.   If we should fail?

Lady Macbeth.   We fail?
But° screw your courage to the sticking-place,°   60
And we'll not fail. When Duncan is asleep—
Whereto the rather shall his day's hard journey
Soundly invite him—his two chamberlains
Will I with wine and wassail° so convince,°
That memory, the warder° of the brain,   65
Shall be a fume, and the receipt of reason
A limbeck only:° when in swinish sleep
Their drenchèd natures lies° as in a death,
What cannot you and I perform upon
Th' unguarded Duncan, what not put upon   70
His spongy° officers, who shall bear the guilt
Of our great quell?°

Macbeth.   Bring forth men-children only;
For thy undaunted mettle° should compose
Nothing but males. Will it not be received,
When we have marked with blood those sleepy two   75
Of his own chamber, and used their very daggers,
That they have done 't?

Lady Macbeth.   Who dares receive it other,°
As we shall make our griefs and clamor roar
Upon his death?

Macbeth.   I am settled, and bend up
Each corporal agent to this terrible feat.   80
Away, and mock the time° with fairest show:
False face must hide what the false heart doth know.

                         Exeunt.

---

60 *But* only   60 *sticking place* notch (holding the bowstring of a taut crossbow)   64 *wassail* carousing   64 *convince* overpower   65 *warder* guard   66-67 *receipt . . . only* i.e., the receptacle (*receipt*), which should collect the distillate of thought—reason—will be a mere vessel (*limbeck*) of undistilled liquids   68 *lies* lie   71 *spongy* sodden   72 *quell* killing   73 *mettle* substance   77 *other* otherwise   81 *mock the time* beguile the world

ACT II

Scene I.   [*Inverness. Court of Macbeth's castle.*]

Enter Banquo, and Fleance, with a torch before him.

Banquo. How goes the night, boy?

Fleance. The moon is down; I have not heard the clock.

Banquo. And she goes down at twelve.

Fleance.   I take't, 'tis later, sir.

Banquo. Hold, take my sword. There's husbandry° in heaven.

5   Their candles are all out. Take thee that too.
A heavy summons° lies like lead upon me,
And yet I would not sleep. Merciful powers,
Restrain in me the cursèd thoughts that nature
Gives way to in repose!

Enter Macbeth, and a Servant with a torch.

                            Give me my sword!
10   Who's there?

Macbeth. A friend.

Banquo. What, sir, not yet at rest? The King's a-bed:
He hath been in unusual pleasure, and
Sent forth great largess to your offices:°
15   This diamond he greets your wife withal,
By the name of most kind hostess; and shut up°
In measureless content.

II.i. 4 *husbandry* frugality   6 *summons* call (to sleep)   14 *largess to your offices* gifts to your servants' quarters   16 *shut up* concluded

Macbeth.   Being unprepared,
Our will became the servant to defect,°
Which else should free have wrought.

Banquo.   All's well.
I dreamt last night of the three weïrd sisters: 20
To you they have showed some truth.

Macbeth.   I think not of them.
Yet, when we can entreat an hour to serve,
We would spend it in some words upon that
   business,
If you would grant the time.

Banquo.   At your kind'st leisure.

Macbeth. If you shall cleave to my consent, when
   'tis,°   25
It shall make honor for you.

Banquo.   So° I lose none
In seeking to augment it, but still keep
My bosom franchised° and allegiance clear,°
I shall be counseled.

Macbeth.   Good repose the while!

Banquo. Thanks, sir. The like to you!   30

                    Exit Banquo [with Fleance].

Macbeth. Go bid thy mistress, when my drink is ready,
She strike upon the bell. Get thee to bed.

                    Exit [Servant].

Is this a dagger which I see before me,
The handle toward my hand? Come, let me clutch
   thee.
I have thee not, and yet I see thee still.   35
Art thou not, fatal vision, sensible°
To feeling as to sight, or art thou but
A dagger of the mind, a false creation,

18 *Our . . . defect* our good will was hampered by our deficient preparations   25 *cleave . . . 'tis* join my cause, when the time comes
26 *So* provided that   28 *franchised* free (from guilt)   28 *clear* spotless
36 *sensible* perceptible

Proceeding from the heat-oppressèd brain?
40 I see thee yet, in form as palpable
As this which now I draw.
Thou marshal'st me the way that I was going;
And such an instrument I was to use.
Mine eyes are made the fools o' th' other senses,
45 Or else worth all the rest. I see thee still;
And on thy blade and dudgeon° gouts° of blood,
Which was not so before. There's no such thing.
It is the bloody business which informs°
Thus to mine eyes. Now o'er the one half-world
50 Nature seems dead, and wicked dreams abuse°
The curtained sleep; witchcraft celebrates
Pale Hecate's offerings;° and withered murder,
Alarumed° by his sentinel, the wolf,
Whose howl's his watch, thus with his stealthy pace,
55 With Tarquin's° ravishing strides, towards his design
Moves like a ghost. Thou sure and firm-set earth,
Hear not my steps, which way they walk, for fear
Thy very stones prate of my whereabout,
And take the present horror from the time,
Which now suits with it.° Whiles I threat, he
60   lives:
Words to the heat of deeds too cold breath gives.

A bell rings.

I go, and it is done: the bell invites me.
Hear it not, Duncan, for it is a knell
That summons thee to heaven, or to hell.

Exit.

46 *dudgeon* wooden hilt   46 *gouts* large drops   48 *informs* gives shape
(?)   50 *abuse* deceive   52 *Hecate's offerings* offerings to Hecate (goddess of sorcery)   53 *Alarumed* called to action   55 *Tarquin* (Roman
tyrant who ravished Lucrece)   59-60*take . . . it* remove (by noise) the
horrible silence attendant on this moment and suitable to it (?)

Scene II.   [*Macbeth's Castle.*]

Enter Lady [Macbeth].

Lady Macbeth. That which hath made them drunk hath
    made me bold;
  What hath quenched them hath given me fire. Hark!
    Peace!
  It was the owl that shrieked, the fatal bellman,
  Which gives the stern'st good-night.° He is about it.
  The doors are open, and the surfeited grooms   5
  Do mock their charge with snores. I have drugged
    their possets,°
  That death and nature° do contend about them,
  Whether they live or die.

Macbeth.   [*Within*] Who's there? What, ho?

Lady Macbeth. Alack, I am afraid they have awaked
  And 'tis not done! Th' attempt and not the deed   10
  Confounds° us. Hark! I laid their daggers ready;
  He could not miss 'em. Had he not resembled
  My father as he slept, I had done 't.

Enter Macbeth.

                      My husband!

Macbeth. I have done the deed. Didst thou not hear a
  noise?

Lady Macbeth. I heard the owl scream and the crickets
  cry.   15
  Did not you speak?

Macbeth.   When?

II.ii.3-4 *bellman . . . good-night* i.e., the owl's call, portending death,
is like the town crier's call to a condemned man   6 *possets* (bedtime
drinks)   7 *nature* natural vitality   11 *Confounds* ruins

Lady Macbeth.   Now.

Macbeth.   As I descended?

Lady Macbeth. Ay.

Macbeth. Hark!
  Who lies i' th' second chamber?

Lady Macbeth.   Donalbain.

20 *Macbeth.* This is a sorry° sight.

Lady Macbeth. A foolish thought, to say a sorry sight.

Macbeth. There's one did laugh in 's sleep, and one
      cried "Murder!"
  That they did wake each other. I stood and heard
      them.
  But they did say their prayers, and addressed them
  Again to sleep.

25 *Lady Macbeth.*   There are two lodged together.

Macbeth. One cried "God bless us!" and "Amen" the
      other,
  As they had seen me with these hangman's° hands:
  List'ning their fear, I could not say "Amen,"
  When they did say "God bless us!"

Lady Macbeth.   Consider it not so deeply.

Macbeth. But wherefore could not I pronounce
30   "Amen"?
  I had most need of blessing, and "Amen"
  Stuck in my throat.

Lady Macbeth.   These deeds must not be thought
  After these ways; so, it will make us mad.

Macbeth. Methought I heard a voice cry "Sleep no
      more!
35   Macbeth does murder sleep"—the innocent sleep,
  Sleep that knits up the raveled sleave° of care,

20 *sorry* miserable   27 *hangman's* executioner's (i.e., bloody)   36 *knits up the raveled sleave* straightens out the tangled skein

The death of each day's life, sore labor's bath,
Balm of hurt minds, great nature's second course,°
Chief nourisher in life's feast——

Lady Macbeth.   What do you mean?

Macbeth. Still it cried "Sleep no more!" to all the
    house: 40
"Glamis hath murdered sleep, and therefore
    Cawdor
Shall sleep no more: Macbeth shall sleep no more."

Lady Macbeth. Who was it that thus cried? Why,
    worthy Thane,
You do unbend° your noble strength, to think
So brainsickly of things. Go get some water,   45
And wash this filthy witness° from your hand.
Why did you bring these daggers from the place?
They must lie there: go carry them, and smear
The sleepy grooms with blood.

Macbeth.   I'll go no more.
I am afraid to think what I have done;   50
Look on 't again I dare not.

Lady Macbeth.   Infirm of purpose!
Give me the daggers. The sleeping and the dead
Are but as pictures. 'Tis the eye of childhood
That fears a painted° devil. If he do bleed,
I'll gild° the faces of the grooms withal,   55
For it must seem their guilt.

                         Exit. Knock within.

Macbeth.   Whence is that knocking?
How is 't with me, when every noise appalls me?
What hands are here? Ha! They pluck out mine
    eyes!
Will all great Neptune's ocean wash this blood
Clean from my hand? No; this my hand will rather   60

---

88 *second course* i.e., sleep (the less substantial first course is food)
44 *unbend* relax 46 *witness* evidence 54 *painted* depicted 55 *gild* paint

The multitudinous seas incarnadine,°
Making the green one red.°

Enter Lady [Macbeth].

Lady Macbeth. My hands are of your color, but I
shame
To wear a heart so white. (*Knock.*) I hear a
knocking
65   At the south entry. Retire we to our chamber.
A little water clears us of this deed:
How easy is it then! Your constancy
Hath left you unattended.° (*Knock.*) Hark! more
knocking.
Get on your nightgown,° lest occasion call us
70   And show us to be watchers.° Be not lost
So poorly° in your thoughts.

Macbeth. To know my deed, 'twere best not know
myself. (*Knock.*)
Wake Duncan with thy knocking! I would thou
couldst!   *Exeunt.*

Scene III.   [*Macbeth's Castle.*]

Enter a Porter. Knocking within.

Porter. Here's a knocking indeed! If a man were
porter of hell gate, he should have old° turning the
key. (*Knock.*) Knock, knock, knock! Who's there,

61 *incarnadine* redden 62 *the green one red* (perhaps "the green one"
means "the ocean," but perhaps "one" here means "totally," "uniform-
ly") 67-68 *Your . . . unattended* your firmness has deserted you
69 *nightgown* dressing-gown 70 *watchers* i.e., up late 71 *poorly* weakly
II.iii. 2 *should have old* would certainly have plenty of

i' th' name of Beelzebub? Here's a farmer, that
hanged himself on th' expectation of plenty.° Come   5
in time! Have napkins enow° about you; here you'll
sweat for 't. (*Knock.*) Knock, knock! Who's there,
in th' other devil's name? Faith, here's an equivocator,° that could swear in both the scales against
either scale; who committed treason enough for   10
God's sake, yet could not equivocate to heaven. O,
come in, equivocator. (*Knock.*) Knock, knock,
knock! Who's there? Faith, here's an English tailor
come hither for stealing out of a French hose:°
come in, tailor. Here you may roast your goose.°   15
(*Knock.*) Knock, knock; never at quiet! What are
you? But this place is too cold for hell. I'll devil-
porter it no further. I had thought to have let in
some of all professions that go the primrose way
to th' everlasting bonfire. (*Knock.*) Anon, anon!   20
[*Opens an entrance.*] I pray you, remember the
porter.

Enter Macduff and Lennox.

Macduff. Was it so late, friend, ere you went to bed,
That you do lie so late?

Porter. Faith, sir, we were carousing till the second   25
cock:° and drink, sir, is a great provoker of three
things.

Macduff. What three things does drink especially provoke?

Porter. Marry, sir, nose-painting, sleep, and urine.   30
Lechery, sir, it provokes and unprovokes; it provokes the desire, but it takes away the performance: therefore much drink may be said to be an
equivocator with lechery: it makes him and it mars

4-5 *farmer . . . plenty* (the farmer hoarded so he could later sell high,
but when it looked as though there would be a crop surplus he hanged
himself)   6 *enow* enough   8-9 *equivocator* i.e., Jesuit (who allegedly
employed deceptive speech to further God's ends)   14 *French hose* tight-
fitting hose   15 *goose* pressing iron   25-26 *second cock* (about 3 a.m.)

35   him; it sets him on and it takes him off; it per-
      suades him and disheartens him; makes him stand
      to and not stand to; in conclusion, equivocates
      him in a sleep, and giving him the lie, leaves him.

Macduff. I believe drink gave thee the lie° last night.

40 *Porter.* That it did, sir, i' the very throat on me: but
      I requited him for his lie, and, I think, being too
      strong for him, though he took up my legs some-
      time, yet I make a shift to cast° him.

Macduff. Is thy master stirring?

                    Enter Macbeth.

45   Our knocking has awaked him; here he comes.

Lennox. Good morrow, noble sir.

Macbeth.   Good morrow, both.

Macduff. Is the king stirring, worthy Thane?

Macbeth.   Not yet.

Macduff. He did command me to call timely° on him:
      I have almost slipped° the hour.

Macbeth.   I'll bring you to him.

50 *Macduff.* I know this is a joyful trouble to you;
      But yet 'tis one.

Macbeth. The labor we delight in physics pain.°
      This is the door.

Macduff.   I'll make so bold to call,
      For 'tis my limited service.°

                              Exit Macduff.

Lennox. Goes the king hence today?

55 *Macbeth.*   He does: he did appoint so.

---

³⁹ *gave thee the lie* called you a liar (with a pun on "stretched you
out") ⁴³ *cast* (with a pun on "cast," meaning "vomit") ⁴⁸ *timely*
early ⁴⁹ *slipped* let slip ⁵² *The labor . . . pain* labor that gives us
pleasure cures discomfort ⁵⁴ *limited service* appointed duty

Lennox. The night has been unruly. Where we lay,
  Our chimneys were blown down, and, as they say,
  Lamentings heard i' th' air, strange screams of
    death,
  And prophesying with accents terrible
  Of dire combustion° and confused events   60
  New hatched to th' woeful time: the obscure bird°
  Clamored the livelong night. Some say, the earth
  Was feverous and did shake.

Macbeth.   'Twas a rough night.

Lennox. My young remembrance cannot parallel
  A fellow to it.   65

Enter Macduff.

Macduff. O horror, horror, horror! Tongue nor heart
  Cannot conceive nor name thee.

Macbeth and Lennox.   ·What's the matter?

Macduff. Confusion° now hath made his masterpiece.
  Most sacrilegious murder hath broke ope
  The Lord's anointed temple, and stole thence   70
  The life o' th' building.

Macbeth.   What is 't you say? The life?

Lennox. Mean you his Majesty?

Macduff. Approach the chamber, and destroy your
    sight
  With a new Gorgon:° do not bid me speak;
  See, and then speak yourselves. Awake, awake!   75

Exeunt Macbeth and Lennox.

  Ring the alarum bell. Murder and Treason!
  Banquo and Donalbain! Malcolm! Awake!
  Shake off this downy sleep, death's counterfeit,°
  And look on death itself! Up, up, and see
  The great doom's image!° Malcolm! Banquo!   80

---

60 *combustion* tumult   61 *obscure bird* bird of darkness, i.e., the owl
68 *Confusion* destruction   74 *Gorgon* (creature capable of turning be-
holders to stone)   78 *counterfeit* imitation   80 *great doom's image* likeness of Judgment Day

As from your graves rise up, and walk like sprites,°
To countenance° this horror. Ring the bell.

Bell rings. Enter Lady [Macbeth].

Lady Macbeth. What's the business,
  That such a hideous trumpet calls to parley
  The sleepers of the house? Speak, speak!

85 *Macduff.*   O gentle lady,
  'Tis not for you to hear what I can speak:
  The repetition,° in a woman's ear,
  Would murder as it fell.

Enter Banquo.

                         O Banquo, Banquo!
  Our royal master's murdered.

Lady Macbeth.   Woe, alas!
  What, in our house?

90 *Banquo.*   Too cruel anywhere.
  Dear Duff, I prithee, contradict thyself,
  And say it is not so.

Enter Macbeth, Lennox, and Ross.

Macbeth. Had I but died an hour before this chance,
  I had lived a blessèd time; for from this instant
95 There's nothing serious in mortality:°
  All is but toys.° Renown and grace is dead,
  The wine of life is drawn, and the mere lees°
  Is left this vault° to brag of.

Enter Malcolm and Donalbain.

Donalbain. What is amiss?

Macbeth.   You are, and do not know 't.
100 The spring, the head, the fountain of your blood
  Is stopped; the very source of it is stopped.

Macduff. Your royal father's murdered.

---

81 *sprites* spirits 82 *countenance* be in keeping with 87 *repetition* report 95 *serious in mortality* worthwhile in mortal life 96 *toys* trifles 97 *lees* dregs 98 *vault* (1) wine vault (2) earth, with the sky as roof (?)

Malcolm   O, by whom?

Lennox. Those of his chamber, as it seemed, had
    done 't:
  Their hands and faces were all badged° with blood;
  So were their daggers, which unwiped we found   105
  Upon their pillows. They stared, and were
      distracted.
  No man's life was to be trusted with them.

Macbeth. O, yet I do repent me of my fury,
  That I did kill them.

Macduff.   Wherefore did you so?

Macbeth. Who can be wise, amazed,° temp'rate and
      furious,   110
  Loyal and neutral, in a moment? No man.
  The expedition° of my violent love
  Outrun the pauser, reason. Here lay Duncan,
  His silver skin laced with his golden blood,
  And his gashed stabs looked like a breach in nature   115
  For ruin's wasteful entrance: there, the murderers,
  Steeped in the colors of their trade, their daggers
  Unmannerly breeched with gore.° Who could
      refrain,°
  That had a heart to love, and in that heart
  Courage to make 's love known?

Lady Macbeth.   Help me hence, ho!   120

Macduff. Look to° the lady.

Malcolm. [*Aside to Donalbain*] Why do we hold
      our tongues,
  That most may claim this argument for ours?°

Donalbain. [*Aside to Malcolm*] What should be
      spoken here,
  Where our fate, hid in an auger-hole,°

---

104 *badged* marked   110 *amazed* bewildered   112 *expedition* h a s t e
118 *Unmannerly breeched with gore* covered with unseemly breeches of
blood   118 *refrain* check oneself   121 *Look to* look after   123 *That
most . . . ours?* who are the most concerned with this topic   124 *auger-
hole* i.e., unsuspected place

125   May rush, and seize us? Let's away:
            Our tears are not yet brewed.

    Malcolm. [*Aside to Donalbain*] Nor our strong
                sorrow
            Upon the foot of motion.°
    Banquo.   Look to the lady.

                        [*Lady Macbeth is carried out.*]

            And when we have our naked frailties hid,°
            That suffer in exposure, let us meet
130   And question° this most bloody piece of work,
            To know it further. Fears and scruples° shake us.
            In the great hand of God I stand, and thence
            Against the undivulged pretense° I fight
            Of treasonous malice.

    Macduff.   And so do I.

    All.   So all.

135 Macbeth. Let's briefly° put on manly readiness,
            And meet i' th' hall together.

    All.   Well contented.

                    Exeunt [all but Malcolm and Donalbain].

    Malcolm. What will you do? Let's not consort with
                them.
            To show an unfelt sorrow is an office°
            Which the false man does easy. I'll to England.

140 Donalbain. To Ireland, I; our separated fortune
            Shall keep us both the safer. Where we are
            There's daggers in men's smiles; the near in blood,
            The nearer bloody.

    Malcolm.   This murderous shaft that's shot
            Hath not yet lighted, and our safest way

    ¹²⁶⁻²⁷ *Our tears . . . motion* i.e., we have not yet had time for tears
    nor to express our sorrows in action (?) ¹²⁸ *naked frailties hid* poor
    bodies clothed ¹³⁰ *question* discuss ¹³¹ *scruples* suspicions ¹³³ *un-
    divulged pretense* hidden purpose ¹³⁵ *briefly* quickly ¹³⁸ *office* func-
    tion

Is to avoid the aim. Therefore to horse; 145
And let us not be dainty of° leave-taking,
But shift away. There's warrant° in that theft
Which steals itself° when there's no mercy left.

Exeunt.

Scene IV.　[*Outside Macbeth's castle.*]

Enter Ross with an Old Man.

Old Man. Threescore and ten I can remember well:
Within the volume of which time I have seen
Hours dreadful and things strange, but this sore°
　　night
Hath trifled former knowings.°

Ross.　　　　　　　　Ha, good father,
Thou seest the heavens, as troubled with man's act, 5
Threatens his bloody stage. By th' clock 'tis day,
And yet dark night strangles the traveling lamp:°
Is 't night's predominance,° or the day's shame,
That darkness does the face of earth entomb,
When living light should kiss it?

Old Man.　　　　　　　'Tis unnatural, 10
Even like the deed that's done. On Tuesday last
A falcon, tow'ring in her pride of place,°
Was by a mousing° owl hawked at and killed.

Ross. And Duncan's horses—a thing most strange
　　and certain—
Beauteous and swift, the minions° of their race, 15

146 *dainty of* fussy about 147 *warrant* justification 148 *steals itself*
steals oneself away II.iv. 3 *sore* grievous 4 *trifled former knowings*
made trifles of former experiences 7 *traveling lamp* i.e., the sun 8 *predominance* astrological supremacy 12 *tow'ring . . . place* soaring at
her summit 13 *mousing* i.e., normally mouse-eating 15 *minions* darlings

Turned wild in nature, broke their stalls, flung out,°
Contending 'gainst obedience, as they would make
War with mankind.

Old Man.   'Tis said they eat° each other.

Ross. They did so, to th' amazement of mine eyes,
That looked upon 't.

Enter Macduff.

20   Here comes the good Macduff.
How goes the world, sir, now?

Macduff.   Why, see you not?

Ross. Is 't known who did this more than bloody deed?

Macduff. Those that Macbeth hath slain.

Ross.   Alas, the day!
What good could they pretend?°

Macduff.   They were suborned:°
25 Malcolm and Donalbain, the king's two sons,
Are stol'n away and fled, which puts upon them
Suspicion of the deed.

Ross.   'Gainst nature still.
Thriftless° ambition, that will ravin up°
Thine own life's means! Then 'tis most like
30 The sovereignty will fall upon Macbeth.

Macduff. He is already named,° and gone to Scone
To be invested.°

Ross.   Where is Duncan's body?

Macduff. Carried to Colmekill,
The sacred storehouse of his predecessors
And guardian of their bones.

35 *Ross.*   Will you to Scone?

Macduff. No, cousin, I'll to Fife.

---

16 *flung out* lunged wildly   18 *eat* ate   24 *pretend* hope for   24 *suborned* bribed   28 *Thriftless* wasteful   28 *ravin up* greedily devour
31 *named* elected   32 *invested* installed as king

Ross.   Well, I will thither.

Macduff. Well, may you see things well done there.
    Adieu,
    Lest our old robes sit easier than our new!

Ross. Farewell, father.

Old Man. God's benison° go with you, and with those   *40*
    That would make good of bad, and friends of foes!

                                    Exeunt omnes.

ACT III

Scene I.   [*Forres. The palace.*]

Enter Banquo.

Banquo. Thou hast it now: King, Cawdor, Glamis, all,
As the weïrd women promised, and I fear
Thou play'dst most foully for 't. Yet it was said
It should not stand° in thy posterity,
5 But that myself should be the root and father
Of many kings. If there come truth from them—
As upon thee, Macbeth, their speeches shine—
Why, by the verities on thee made good,
May they not be my oracles as well
10 And set me up in hope? But hush, no more!

   Sennet° sounded. Enter Macbeth as King, Lady
   [Macbeth], Lennox, Ross, Lords, and Attendants

Macbeth. Here's our chief guest.

Lady Macbeth.   If he had been forgotten,
It had been as a gap in our great feast,
And all-thing° unbecoming.

Macbeth. Tonight we hold a solemn° supper, sir,
And I'll request your presence.

15 *Banquo.*   Let your Highness
Command upon me, to the which my duties

III.i 4 *stand* continue   s.d. *Sennet* trumpet call   13 *all-thing* altogether
14 *solemn* ceremonious

74

Are with a most indissoluble tie
For ever knit.

Macbeth. Ride you this afternoon?

Banquo.   Ay, my good lord.

Macbeth. We should have else desired your good advice   20
    (Which still° hath been both grave and
      prosperous°)
    In this day's council; but we'll take tomorrow.
    Is 't far you ride?

Banquo. As far, my lord, as will fill up the time
    'Twixt this and supper. Go not my horse the
      better,°   25
    I must become a borrower of the night
    For a dark hour or twain.

Macbeth.   Fail not our feast.

Banquo. My lord, I will not.

Macbeth. We hear our bloody cousins are bestowed°
    In England and in Ireland, not confessing   30
    Their cruel parricide, filling their hearers
    With strange invention.° But of that tomorrow,
    When therewithal we shall have cause of state
    Craving us jointly.° Hie you to horse. Adieu,
    Till you return at night. Goes Fleance with you?   35

Banquo. Ay, my good lord: our time does call upon 's.

Macbeth. I wish your horses swift and sure of foot,
    And so I do commend you to their backs.
    Farewell.   *Exit Banquo.*
    Let every man be master of his time   40
    Till seven at night. To make society
    The sweeter welcome, we will keep ourself

---

21 *still* always   21 *grave and prosperous* weighty and profitable   25*Go
. . . better* unless my horse goes better than I expect   29 *are bestowed*
have taken refuge   32 *invention* lies   33-34 *cause . . . jointly* matters of
state demanding our joint attention

Till supper-time alone. While° then, God be with
  you!

    Exeunt Lords [and all but Macbeth and a Servant].

43 Sirrah,° a word with you: attend° those men
  Our pleasure?

Attendant. They are, my lord, without° the palace
  gate.

Macbeth. Bring them before us.   *Exit Servant.*
  To be thus is nothing, but° to be safely thus—
  Our fears in° Banquo stick deep,
50 And in his royalty of nature reigns that
  Which would° be feared. 'Tis much he dares;
  And, to° that dauntless temper° of his mind,
  He hath a wisdom that doth guide his valor
  To act in safety. There is none but he
55 Whose being I do fear: and under him
  My genius is rebuked,° as it is said
  Mark Antony's was by Cæsar. He chid the sisters,
  When first they put the name of King upon me,
  And bade them speak to him; then prophetlike
60 They hailed him father to a line of kings.
  Upon my head they placed a fruitless crown
  And put a barren scepter in my gripe,°
  Thence to be wrenched with an unlineal hand,
  No son of mine succeeding. If 't be so,
65 For Banquo's issue have I filed° my mind;
  For them the gracious Duncan have I murdered;
  Put rancors° in the vessel of my peace
  Only for them, and mine eternal jewel°
  Given to the common enemy of man,°
70 To make them kings, the seeds of Banquo kings!

---

43 *While* until 44 *Sirrah* (common address to an inferior) 44 *attend*
await 46 *without* outside 48 *but* unless 49 *in* about 51 *would* must
52 *to* added to 52 *temper* quality 56 *genius is rebuked* guardian spirit
is cowed 62 *gripe* grasp 65 *filed* defiled 67 *rancors* bitter enmities
68 *eternal jewel* i.e., soul 69 *common enemy of man* i.e., the Devil

Rather than so, come, fate, into the list,°
And champion me to th' utterance!° Who's there?

Enter Servant and Two Murderers.

Now go to the door, and stay there till we call.

                         Exit Servant.

Was it not yesterday we spoke together?

Murderers. It was, so please your Highness.

Macbeth   Well then, now   75
Have you considered of my speeches? Know
That it was he in the times past, which held you
So under fortune,° which you thought had been
Our innocent self: this I made good to you
In our last conference; passed in probation° with
    you,   80
How you were born in hand,° how crossed;° the
    instruments,°
Who wrought with them, and all things else that
    might
To half a soul° and to a notion° crazed
Say "Thus did Banquo."

First Murderer.   You made it known to us.

Macbeth. I did so; and went further, which is now   85
Our point of second meeting. Do you find
Your patience so predominant in your nature,
That you can let this go? Are you so gospeled,°
To pray for this good man and for his issue,
Whose heavy hand hath bowed you to the grave   90
And beggared yours for ever?

First Murderer.   We are men, my liege.

Macbeth. Ay, in the catalogue ye go for° men;

---

71 *list* lists   72 *champion me to th' utterance* fight against me to the
death   77-78 *held . . . fortune* kept you from good fortune (?)   80 *passed
in probation* reviewed the proofs   81 *borne in hand* deceived   81 *crossed*
thwarted   81 *instruments* tools   83 *half a soul* a halfwit   83 *notion* mind
88 *gospeled* i.e., made meek by the gospel   92 *go for* pass as

As hounds and greyhounds, mongrels, spaniels,
        curs,
Shoughs, water-rugs° and demi-wolves, are clept°
95 All by the name of dogs: the valued file°
Distinguishes the swift, the slow, the subtle,
The housekeeper,° the hunter, every one
According to the gift which bounteous nature
Hath in him closed,° whereby he does receive
100 Particular addition, from the bill°
That writes them all alike: and so of men.
Now if you have a station in the file,
Not i' th' worst rank of manhood, say 't,
And I will put that business in your bosoms
105 Whose execution takes your enemy off,
Grapples you to the heart and love of us,
Who wear our health but sickly in his life,°
Which in his death were perfect.

Second Murderer.   I am one, my liege,
Whom the vile blows and buffets of the world
110 Hath so incensed that I am reckless what
I do to spite the world.

First Murderer.   And I another
So weary with disasters, tugged with fortune,
That I would set° my life on any chance,
To mend it or be rid on 't.

Macbeth.   Both of you
Know Banquo was your enemy.

115 *Both Murderers.*   True, my lord.

Macbeth. So is he mine, and in such bloody distance°
That every minute of his being thrusts
Against my near'st of life:° and though I could

---

94 *Shoughs, water-rugs* shaggy dogs, long-haired water dogs 94 *clept*
called 95 *valued file* classification by valuable traits 97 *housekeeper*
watchdog 99 *closed* enclosed 100 *Particular addition, from the bill*
special distinction in opposition to the list 107 *wear . . . life* have
only imperfect health while he lives 113 *set* risk 116 *distance* quarrel
118 *near'st of life* most vital spot

With barefaced power sweep him from my sight
And bid my will avouch° it, yet I must not,   120
For° certain friends that are both his and mine,
Whose loves I may not drop, but wail his fall°
Who I myself struck down: and thence it is
That I to your assistance do make love,
Masking the business from the common eye   125
For sundry weighty reasons.

Second Murderer.   We shall, my lord,
  Perform what you command us.

First Murderer.   Though our lives——

Macbeth. Your spirits shine through you. Within this
    hour at most
  I will advise you where to plant yourselves,
  Acquaint you with the perfect spy° o' th' time,   130
  The moment on 't;° for 't must be done tonight,
  And something° from the palace; always thought°
  That I require a clearness:° and with him—
  To leave no rubs° nor botches in the work—
  Fleance his son, that keeps him company,   135
  Whose absence is no less material to me
  Than is his father's, must embrace the fate
  Of that dark hour. Resolve yourselves apart:°
  I'll come to you anon.

Murderers.   We are resolved, my lord.

Macbeth. I'll call upon you straight.° Abide within.   140
  It is concluded: Banquo, thy soul's flight,
  If it find heaven, must find it out tonight.   *Exeunt.*

---

¹²⁰ *avouch* justify   ¹²¹ *For* because of   ¹²² *wail his fall* bewail his death
¹³⁰ *perfect spy* exact information (?) (*spy* literally means "observation";
apparently Macbeth already has the Third Murderer in mind)   ¹³¹ *on 't*
of it   ¹³² *something* some distance   ¹³² *thought* remembered   ¹³³ *clearness* freedom from suspicion   ¹³⁴ *rubs* flaws   ¹³⁸ *Resolve yourselves apart* decide by yourself   ¹⁴⁰ *straight* immediately

Scene II.   [*The palace.*]

Enter Macbeth's Lady and a Servant.

Lady Macbeth. Is Banquo gone from court?

Servant. Ay, madam, but returns again tonight.

Lady Macbeth. Say to the King, I would attend his
    leisure
For a few words.

Servant.   Madam, I will.   *Exit.*

Lady Macbeth.   Nought's had, all's spent,
5   Where our desire is got without content:
'Tis safer to be that which we destroy
Than by destruction dwell in doubtful joy.

Enter Macbeth.

How now, my lord! Why do you keep alone,
Of sorriest° fancies your companions making,
Using those thoughts which should indeed have
10   died
With them they think on? Things without° all
    remedy
Should be without regard: what's done is done.

Macbeth. We have scorched° the snake, not killed it:
She'll close° and be herself, whilst our poor malice°
15   Remains in danger of her former tooth.
But let the frame of things disjoint,° both the
    worlds° suffer,
Ere we will eat our meal in fear, and sleep
In the affliction of these terrible dreams

III.ii. 9 *sorriest* most despicable 11 *without* beyond 13 *scorched*
slashed, scored 14 *close* heal 14 *poor malice* feeble enmity 16 *frame*
of things disjoint universe collapse 16 *both the worlds* heaven and
earth (?)

That shake us nightly: better be with the dead,
Whom we, to gain our peace, have sent to peace,   20
Than on the torture° of the mind to lie
In restless ecstasy.° Duncan is in his grave;
After life's fitful fever he sleeps well.
Treason has done his° worst: nor steel, nor poison,
Malice domestic,° foreign levy, nothing,   25
Can touch him further.

Lady Macbeth.   Come on.
Gentle my lord, sleek° o'er your rugged° looks;
Be bright and jovial among your guests tonight.

Macbeth. So shall I, love; and so, I pray, be you:
Let your remembrance apply to Banquo;°   30
Present him eminence,° both with eye and tongue:
Unsafe the while, that we must lave°
Our honors in these flattering streams
And make our faces vizards° to our hearts,
Disguising what they are.

Lady Macbeth.   You must leave this.   35

Macbeth. O, full of scorpions is my mind, dear wife!
Thou know'st that Banquo, and his Fleance, lives.

Lady Macbeth. But in them nature's copy's° not eterne.

Macbeth. There's comfort yet; they are assailable.
Then be thou jocund. Ere the bat hath flown   40
His cloistered flight, ere to black Hecate's summons
The shard-borne° beetle with his drowsy hums
Hath rung night's yawning peal, there shall be done
A deed of dreadful note.

Lady Macbeth.   What's to be done?

---

21 *torture* i.e., rack 22 *ecstasy* frenzy 24 *his* its 25 *Malice domestic*
civil war 27 *sleek* smooth 27 *rugged* furrowed 30 *Let . . . Banquo*
focus your thoughts on Banquo 31 *Present him eminence* honor him
32 *Unsafe . . . lave* i.e., you and I are unsafe because we must dip
34 *vizards* masks 38 *nature's copy* nature's lease (?) imitation (i.e., a
son) made by nature (?) 42 *shard-borne* borne on scaly wings (?)
dung-bred (?)

Macbeth. Be innocent of the knowledge, dearest
45   chuck,°
        Till thou applaud the deed. Come, seeling° night,
        Scarf up° the tender eye of pitiful day,
        And with thy bloody and invisible hand
        Cancel and tear to pieces that great bond°
50   Which keeps me pale! Light thickens, and the crow
        Makes wing to th' rooky° wood.
        Good things of day begin to droop and drowse,
        Whiles night's black agents to their preys do rouse.
        Thou marvel'st at my words: but hold thee still;
55   Things bad begun make strong themselves by ill:
        So, prithee, go with me.   *Exeunt.*

Scene III.   [*Near the palace.*]

Enter Three Murderers.

First Murderer. But who did bid thee join with us?

Third Murderer.   Macbeth.

Second Murderer. He needs not our mistrust; since he
    delivers
    Our offices and what we have to do
    To the direction just.°

First Murderer.   Then stand with us.
5   The west yet glimmers with some streaks of day.
    Now spurs the lated° traveler apace
    To gain the timely inn, and near approaches
    The subject of our watch.

---

45 *chuck* chick (a term of endearment)   46 *seeling* eye-closing   47 *Scarf up* blindfold   49 *bond* i.e., between Banquo and fate (?) Banquo's lease on life (?) Macbeth's link to humanity (?)   51 *rooky* full of rooks   III.iii.   2-4 *He needs . . . just* we need not mistrust him (i.e., the Third Murderer) since he describes our duties according to our exact directions   6 *lated* belated

Third Murderer.   Hark! I hear horses.

Banquo. (*Within*) Give us a light there, ho!

Second Murderer.   Then 'tis he. The rest
That are within the note of expectation°   10
Already are i' th' court.

First Murderer.   His horses go about.

Third Murderer. Almost a mile: but he does usually—
So all men do—from hence to th' palace gate
Make it their walk.

          Enter Banquo and Fleance, with a torch.

Second Murderer. A light, a light!

Third Murderer.   'Tis he.

First Murderer.   Stand to 't.   15

Banquo. It will be rain tonight.

First Murderer.   Let it come down.

          [*They set upon Banquo.*]

Banquo. O, treachery! Fly, good Fleance, fly, fly, fly!

          [*Exit Fleance.*]

     Thou mayst revenge. O slave! [*Dies.*]

Third Murderer. Who did strike out the light?

First Murderer.   Was 't not the way?°

Third Murderer. There's but one down; the son is fled.   20

Second Murderer. We have lost best half of our affair.

First Murderer. Well, let's away and say how much is
     done.   *Exeunt.*

---

10 *within the note of expectation* on the list of expected guests   19 *way*
i.e., thing to do

Scene IV. [*The palace.*]

*Banquet prepared. Enter Macbeth, Lady [Mac-
beth], Ross, Lennox, Lords, and Attendants.*

Macbeth. You know your own degrees;° sit down:
At first and last, the hearty welcome.

Lords. Thanks to your Majesty.

Macbeth. Ourself will mingle with society°
5 And play the humble host.
Our hostess keeps her state,° but in best time
We will require° her welcome.

Lady Macbeth. Pronounce it for me, sir, to all our
friends,
For my heart speaks they are welcome.

Enter First Murderer.

Macbeth. See, they encounter° thee with their hearts'
10 thanks.
Both sides are even: here I'll sit i' th' midst:
Be large in mirth; anon we'll drink a measure°
The table round. [*Goes to Murderer*] There's
blood upon thy face.

Murderer. 'Tis Banquo's then.

15 *Macbeth.* 'Tis better thee without than he within.°
Is he dispatched?

Murderer. My lord, his throat is cut; that I did for
him.

Macbeth. Thou art the best o' th' cutthroats.

III.iv. 1 *degrees* ranks 4 *society* the company 6 *keeps her state* remains seated in her chair of state 7 *require* request 10 *encounter* meet
12 *measure* goblet 15 *thee without than he within* outside you than
inside him

Yet he's good that did the like for Fleance;
If thou didst it, thou art the nonpareil.   20

Murderer. Most royal sir, Fleance is 'scaped.

Macbeth. [*Aside*] Then comes my fit again: I had
     else been perfect,
Whole as the marble, founded° as the rock,
As broad and general as the casing° air:
But now I am cabined, cribbed,° confined, bound in   25
To saucy° doubts and fears.—But Banquo's safe?

Murderer. Ay, my good lord: safe in a ditch he bides,
With twenty trenchèd° gashes on his head,
The least a death to nature.

Macbeth.   Thanks for that.
     [*Aside*] There the grown serpent lies; the worm°
     that's fled   30
Hath nature that in time will venom breed,
No teeth for th' present. Get thee gone. Tomorrow
We'll hear ourselves° again.   *Exit Murderer.*

Lady Macbeth.   My royal lord,
You do not give the cheer.° The feast is sold
That is not often vouched, while 'tis a-making,   35
'Tis given with welcome. To feed were best at
     home;°
From thence, the sauce to meat° is ceremony;
Meeting were bare without it.

            *Enter the Ghost of Banquo, and sits in
                 Macbeth's place.*

Macbeth.   Sweet remembrancer!°
Now good digestion wait on appetite,
And health on both!

---

²³*founded* firmly based   ²⁴ *broad . . . casing* unconfined as the sur-
rounding   ²⁵ *cribbed* penned up   ²⁶ *saucy* insolent   ²⁸ *trenchèd* trench-
like   ³⁰ *worm* serpent   ³³ *hear ourselves* talk it over   ³⁴ *the cheer* a
sense of cordiality   ³⁴⁻³⁶ *The feast . . . home* i.e., the feast seems sold
(not given) during which the host fails to welcome the guests. Mere eat-
ing is best done at home   ³⁷ *meat* food   ³⁸ *remembrancer* reminder

Lennox.   May 't please your Highness sit.

Macbeth. Here had we now our country's honor
    roofed,°
    Were the graced person of our Banquo present—
    Who may I rather challenge for unkindness
    Than pity for mischance!°

Ross.   His absence, sir,
    Lays blame upon his promise. Please 't your
        Highness
    To grace us with your royal company?

Macbeth. The table's full.

Lennox.   Here is a place reserved, sir.

Macbeth. Where?

Lennox. Here, my good lord. What is 't that moves
    your Highness?

Macbeth. Which of you have done this?

Lords.   What, my good lord?

Macbeth. Thou canst not say I did it. Never shake
    Thy gory locks at me.

Ross. Gentlemen, rise, his Highness is not well.

Lady Macbeth. Sit, worthy friends. My lord is often
    thus,
    And hath been from his youth. Pray you, keep seat.
    The fit is momentary; upon a thought°
    He will again be well. If much you note him,
    You shall offend him and extend his passion.°
    Feed, and regard him not.—Are you a man?

Macbeth. Ay, and a bold one, that dare look on that
    Which might appall the devil.

Lady Macbeth.   O proper stuff!
    This is the very painting of your fear.
    This is the air-drawn dagger which, you said,

41 *our country's honor roofed* our nobility under one roof   43-44 *Who
. . . mischance* whom I hope I may reprove because he is unkind rather
than pity because he has encountered an accident   56 *upon a thought*
as quick as thought   58 *extend his passion* lengthen his fit

Led you to Duncan. O, these flaws° and starts,
Impostors to° true fear, would well become   65
A woman's story at a winter's fire,
Authorized° by her grandam. Shame itself!
Why do you make such faces? When all's done,
You look but on a stool.

Macbeth.   Prithee, see there!
Behold! Look! Lo! How say you?   70
Why, what care I? If thou canst nod, speak too.
If charnel houses° and our graves must send
Those that we bury back, our monuments
Shall be the maws of kites.°   [*Exit Ghost.*]

Lady Macbeth.   What, quite unmanned in folly?

Macbeth. If I stand here, I saw him.

Lady Macbeth.   Fie, for shame!   75

Macbeth. Blood hath been shed ere now, i' th' olden
    time,
Ere humane statute purged the gentle weal;°
Ay, and since too, murders have been performed
Too terrible for the ear. The times has been
That, when the brains were out, the man would die,   80
And there an end; but now they rise again,
With twenty mortal murders on their crowns,°
And push us from our stools. This is more strange
Than such a murder is.

Lady Macbeth.   My worthy lord,
Your noble friends do lack you.

Macbeth.   I do forget.   85
Do not muse at me, my most worthy friends;
I have a strange infirmity, which is nothing
To those that know me. Come, love and health to
    all!

64 *flaws* gusts, outbursts 65 *to* compared with 67 *Authorized* vouched
for 72 *charnel houses* vaults containing bones 73-74 *our . . . kites*
our tombs shall be the bellies of rapacious birds 77 *purged the gentle
weal* i.e., cleansed the state and made it gentle 82 *mortal murders on
their crowns* deadly wounds on their heads

Then I'll sit down. Give me some wine, fill full.

Enter Ghost.

90   I drink to th' general joy o' th' whole table,
   And to our dear friend Banquo, whom we miss;
   Would he were here! To all and him we thirst,°
   And all to all.°

Lords.   Our duties, and the pledge.

Macbeth. Avaunt! and quit my sight! Let the earth hide
   thee!
95   Thy bones are marrowless, thy blood is cold;
   Thou hast no speculation° in those eyes
   Which thou dost glare with.

Lady Macbeth.   Think of this, good peers,
   But as a thing of custom; 'tis no other.
   Only it spoils the pleasure of the time.

100 *Macbeth.* What man dare, I dare.
   Approach thou like the rugged Russian bear,
   The armed rhinoceros, or th' Hyrcan° tiger;
   Take any shape but that, and my firm nerves°
   Shall never tremble. Or be alive again,
105   And dare me to the desert° with thy sword.
   If trembling I inhabit then, protest me
   The baby of a girl.° Hence, horrible shadow!
   Unreal mock'ry, hence!   *[Exit Ghost.]*
                 Why, so: being gone,
   I am a man again. Pray you, sit still.

Lady Macbeth. You have displaced the mirth, broke the
110   good meeting,
   With most admired° disorder.

Macbeth.   Can such things be,
   And overcome us° like a summer's cloud,

---

92 *thirst* desire to drink 93 *all to all* everything to everybody (?) let
everybody drink to everybody (?) 96 *speculation* sight 102 *Hyrcan* of
Hyrcania (near the Caspian Sea) 103 *nerves* sinews 105 *the desert* a
lonely place 106-07 *If . . . girl* if then I tremble, proclaim me a baby
girl 111 *admired* amazing 112 *overcome us* come over us

Without our special wonder? You make me strange
Even to the disposition that I owe,°
When now I think you can behold such sights,   *115*
And keep the natural ruby of your cheeks,
When mine is blanched with fear.

Ross.   What sights, my lord?

Lady Macbeth. I pray you, speak not: he grows worse
      and worse;
Question enrages him: at once, good night.
Stand not upon the order of your going,°   *120*
But go at once.

Lennox.   Good night; and better health
Attend his Majesty!

Lady Macbeth.   A kind good night to all!

                              Exeunt Lords.

Macbeth. It will have blood, they say: blood will have
      blood.
Stones have been known to move and trees to
      speak;
Augures and understood relations° have   *125*
By maggot-pies and choughs and rooks brought
      forth°
The secret'st man of blood. What is the night?°

Lady Macbeth. Almost at odds° with morning, which is
      which.

Macbeth. How say'st thou, that Macduff denies his
      person
At our great bidding?

Lady Macbeth.   Did you send to him, sir?   *130*

Macbeth. I hear it by the way,° but I will send:

---

¹¹³⁻¹⁴ *You . . . owe* i.e., you make me wonder what my nature is
¹²⁰ *Stand . . . going* do not insist on departing in your order of rank
¹²⁵ *Augures and understood relations* auguries and comprehended reports   ¹²⁶ *By . . . forth* by magpies, choughs, and rooks (telltale
birds) revealed   ¹²⁷ *What is the night* what time of night is it
¹²⁸ *at odds* striving   ¹³¹ *by the way* incidentally

There's not a one of them but in his house
I keep a servant fee'd.° I will tomorrow,
And betimes° I will, to the weïrd sisters:
135   More shall they speak, for now I am bent° to know
By the worst means the worst. For mine own good
All causes° shall give way. I am in blood
Stepped in so far that, should I wade no more,
Returning were as tedious as go o'er.
140   Strange things I have in head that will to hand,
Which must be acted ere they may be scanned.°

Lady Macbeth. You lack the season of all natures,°
    sleep.

Macbeth. Come, we'll to sleep. My strange and self-
    abuse°
Is the initiate fear that wants hard use.°
145   We are yet but young in deed.   *Exeunt.*

Scene V. [*A Witches' haunt.*]

*Thunder. Enter the Three Witches, meeting
Hecate.*

First Witch. Why, how now, Hecate! you look
    angerly.

Hecate. Have I not reason, beldams° as you are,
    Saucy and overbold? How did you dare
    To trade and traffic with Macbeth
5   In riddles and affairs of death;

133 *fee'd* i.e., paid to spy 134 *betimes* quickly 135 *bent* determined
137 *causes* considerations 141 *may be scanned* can be examined
142 *season of all natures* seasoning (preservative) of all living creatures
143 *My strange and self-abuse* my strange delusion 144 *initiate . . .
use* beginner's fear that lacks hardening practice III.v. 2 *beldams* hags

And I, the mistress of your charms,
The close contriver° of all harms,
Was never called to bear my part,
Or show the glory of our art?
And, which is worse, all you have done   10
Hath been but for a wayward son,
Spiteful and wrathful; who, as others do,
Loves for his own ends, not for you.
But make amends now: get you gone,
And at the pit of Acheron°   15
Meet me i' th' morning: thither he
Will come to know his destiny.
Your vessels and your spells provide,
Your charms and everything beside.
I am for th' air; this night I'll spend   20
Unto a dismal and a fatal end:
Great business must be wrought ere noon.
Upon the corner of the moon
There hangs a vap'rous drop profound;°
I'll catch it ere it come to ground: 25
And that distilled by magic sleights°
Shall raise such artificial sprites°
As by the strength of their illusion
Shall draw him on to his confusion.°
He shall spurn fate, scorn death, and bear   30
His hopes 'bove wisdom, grace, and fear:
And you all know security°
Is mortals' chiefest enemy.

Music and a song.

Hark! I am called; my little spirit, see,
Sits in a foggy cloud and stays for me.   [*Exit.*]   35
   Sing within, "Come away, come away," &c.

First Witch. Come, let's make haste; she'll soon be
   back again.   *Exeunt.*

---

7 *close contriver* secret inventor 15 *Acheron* (river of Hades) 24 *profound* heavy 26 *sleights* arts 27 *artificial sprites* spirits created by magic arts (?) artful (cunning) spirits. (?) 29 *confusion* ruin 32 *security* overconfidence

Scene VI.   [*The palace.*]

Enter Lennox and another Lord.

Lennox. My former speeches have but hit your
          thoughts,°
          Which can interpret farther. Only I say
          Things have been strangely borne.° The gracious
          Duncan
          Was pitied of Macbeth: marry, he was dead.
5   And the right-valiant Banquo walked too late;
          Whom, you may say, if 't please you, Fleance
          killed,
          For Fleance fled. Men must not walk too late.
          Who cannot want the thought,° how monstrous
          It was for Malcolm and for Donalbain
10   To kill their gracious father? Damnèd fact!°
          How it did grieve Macbeth! Did he not straight,
          In pious rage, the two delinquents tear,
          That were the slaves of drink and thralls° of sleep?
          Was not that nobly done? Ay, and wisely too;
15   For 'twould have angered any heart alive
          To hear the men deny 't. So that I say
          He has borne° all things well: and I do think
          That, had he Duncan's sons under his key—
          As, an 't° please heaven, he shall not—they should
          find
20   What 'twere to kill a father. So should Fleance.
          But, peace! for from broad words,° and 'cause he
          failed
          His presence at the tyrant's feast, I hear,

III.vi. 1 *My . . . thoughts* i.e., my recent words have only coincided
with what you have in your mind   3 *borne* managed   8 *cannot want
the thought* can fail to think   10 *fact* evil deed   13 *thralls* slaves
17 *borne* managed   19 *an 't* if it   21 *for from broad words* because of
frank talk

Macduff lives in disgrace. Sir, can you tell
Where he bestows himself?

Lord.   The son of Duncan,
From whom this tyrant holds the due of birth,°   25
Lives in the English court, and is received
Of the most pious Edward° with such grace
That the malevolence of fortune nothing
Takes from his high respect.° Thither Macduff
Is gone to pray the holy King, upon his aid°   30
To wake Northumberland° and warlike Siward;
That by the help of these, with Him above
To ratify the work, we may again
Give to our tables meat, sleep to our nights,
Free from our feasts and banquets bloody knives,   35
Do faithful homage and receive free° honors:
All which we pine for now. And this report
Hath so exasperate the King that he
Prepares for some attempt of war.

Lennox.   Sent he to Macduff?

Lord. He did: and with an absolute "Sir, not I,"   40
The cloudy° messenger turns me his back,
And hums, as who should say "You'll rue the time
That clogs° me with this answer."

Lennox.   And that well might
Advise him to a caution, t' hold what distance
His wisdom can provide. Some holy angel   45
Fly to the court of England and unfold
His message ere he come, that a swift blessing
May soon return to this our suffering country
Under a hand accursed!

Lord.   I'll send my prayers with him.

                         Exeunt.

---

25 *due of birth* birthright   27 *Edward* Edward the Confessor (reigned
1042–1066)   28-29 *nothing . . . respect* does not diminish the high respect in which he is held   30 *upon his aid* to aid him (Malcolm)
31 *To wake Northumberland* i.e., to arouse the people in an English
county near Scotland   36 *free* freely granted   41 *cloudy* disturbed
43 *clogs* burdens

ACT IV

Scene I. [*A Witches' haunt.*]

Thunder. Enter the Three Witches.

First Witch. Thrice the brinded° cat hath mewed.

Second Witch. Thrice and once the hedge-pig°
    whined.

Third Witch. Harpier° cries. 'Tis time, 'tis time.

First Witch. Round about the caldron go:
5   In the poisoned entrails throw.
    Toad, that under cold stone
    Days and nights has thirty-one
    Swelt'red venom sleeping got,°
    Boil thou first i' th' charmèd pot.

10 *All.* Double, double, toil and trouble;
    Fire burn and caldron bubble.

Second Witch. Fillet° of a fenny° snake,
    In the caldron boil and bake;
    Eye of newt and toe of frog,
15   Wool of bat and tongue of dog,
    Adder's fork° and blindworm's° sting,
    Lizard's leg and howlet's° wing,

IV.i. 1 *brinded* brindled 2 *hedge-pig* hedgehog 3 *Harpier* (an attendant spirit, like Graymalkin and Paddock in I.i) 8 *Swelt'red venom sleeping got* venom sweated out while sleeping 12 *Fillet* slice 12 *fenny* from a swamp 16 *fork* forked tongue 16 *blindworm* (a legless lizard) 17 *howlet* owlet

For a charm of pow'rful trouble,
Like a hell-broth boil and bubble.

All. Double, double, toil and trouble;   20
Fire burn and caldron bubble.

Third Witch. Scale of dragon, tooth of wolf,
Witch's mummy,° maw and gulf°
Of the ravined° salt-sea shark,
Root of hemlock digged i' th' dark,   25
Liver of blaspheming Jew,
Gall of goat, and slips of yew
Slivered in the moon's eclipse,
Nose of Turk and Tartar's lips,
Finger of birth-strangled babe   30
Ditch-delivered by a drab,°
Make the gruel thick and slab:°
Add thereto a tiger's chaudron,°
For th' ingredience of our caldron.

All. Double, double, toil and trouble;   35
Fire burn and caldron bubble.

Second Witch. Cool it with a baboon's blood,
Then the charm is firm and good.

   Enter Hecate and the other Three Witches.

Hecate. O, well done! I commend your pains;
And every one shall share i' th' gains: 40
And now about the caldron sing,
Like elves and fairies in a ring,
Enchanting all that you put in.

   Music and a song: "Black Spirits," &c.

   [*Exeunt Hecate and the other Three Witches.*]

Second Witch. By the pricking of my thumbs,
Something wicked this way comes: 45
      Open, locks,
      Whoever knocks!

---

23 *Witch's mummy* mummified flesh of a witch   23 *maw and gulf*
stomach and gullet   24 *ravined* ravenous   31 *Ditch-delivered by a drab*
born in a ditch of a harlot   32 *slab* viscous   33 *chaudron* entrails

Enter Macbeth.

Macbeth. How now, you secret, black, and midnight
    hags!
    What is 't you do?

All.   A deed without a name.

50 **Macbeth.** I conjure you, by that which you profess,
    Howe'er you come to know it, answer me:
    Though you untie the winds and let them fight
    Against the churches; though the yesty° waves
    Confound° and swallow navigation up;
    Though bladed corn be lodged° and trees blown
55   down;
    Though castles topple on their warders' heads;
    Though palaces and pyramids do slope°
    Their heads to their foundations; though the treas-
    ure
    Of nature's germens° tumble all together,
60   Even till destruction sicken,° answer me
    To what I ask you.

First Witch.   Speak.

Second Witch.   Demand.

Third Witch.   We'll answer.

First Witch. Say, if th' hadst rather hear it from our
    mouths,
    Or from our masters?

Macbeth.   Call 'em, let me see 'em.

First Witch. Pour in sow's blood, that hath eaten
65   Her nine farrow;° grease that's sweaten°
    From the murderer's gibbet throw
    Into the flame.

All.   Come, high or low,
    Thyself and office° deftly show!

---

53 *yesty* foamy   54 *Confound* destroy   55 *bladed corn be lodged* grain
in the ear be beaten down   57 *slope* bend   59 *nature's germens* seeds
of all life   60 *sicken* i.e., sicken at its own work   65 *farrow* young pigs
65 *sweaten* sweated   68 *office* function

Thunder. First Apparition: an Armed Head.

Macbeth. Tell me, thou unknown power——

First Witch.   He knows thy thought:
    Hear his speech, but say thou nought.   70

First Apparition. Macbeth! Macbeth! Macbeth! Beware
    Macduff!
    Beware the Thane of Fife. Dismiss me: enough.

                           He descends.

Macbeth. Whate'er thou art, for thy good caution
    thanks:
    Thou hast harped° my fear aright. But one word
    more——

First Witch. He will not be commanded. Here's an-
    other,   75
    More potent than the first.

    Thunder. Second Apparition: a Bloody Child.

Second Apparition. Macbeth! Macbeth! Macbeth!

Macbeth. Had I three ears, I'd hear thee.

Second Apparition. Be bloody, bold, and resolute!
    Laugh to scorn
    The pow'r of man, for none of woman born   80
    Shall harm Macbeth.   *Descends.*

Macbeth. Then live, Macduff: what need I fear of
    thee?
    But yet I'll make assurance double sure,
    And take a bond of fate.° Thou shalt not live;
    That I may tell pale-hearted fear it lies,   85
    And sleep in spite of thunder.

    Thunder. Third Apparition: a Child Crowned,
            with a tree in his hand.

---

74 *harped* hit upon, struck the note of   84 *take a bond of fate* get a
guarantee from fate (i.e., he will kill Macduff and thus will compel
fate to keep its word)

                                        What is this,
        That rises like the issue° of a king,
        And wears upon his baby-brow the round
        And top of sovereignty?°

    All.   Listen, but speak not to 't.

    Third Apparition. Be lion-mettled, proud, and take
90   no care
        Who chafes, who frets, or where conspirers are:
        Macbeth shall never vanquished be until
        Great Birnam Wood to high Dunsinane Hill
        Shall come against him.   *Descends.*

    Macbeth.   That will never be.
95   Who can impress° the forest, bid the tree
        Unfix his earth-bound root? Sweet bodements,°
            good!
        Rebellious dead,° rise never, till the Wood
        Of Birnam rise, and our high-placed Macbeth
        Shall live the lease of nature,° pay his breath
100   To time and mortal custom.° Yet my heart
        Throbs to know one thing. Tell me, if your art
        Can tell so much: shall Banquo's issue ever
        Reign in this kingdom?

    All.   Seek to know no more.

    Macbeth. I will be satisfied.° Deny me this,
105   And an eternal curse fall on you! Let me know.
        Why sinks that caldron? And what noise° is this?

                        Hautboys.

    First Witch. Show!

    Second Witch. Show!

    Third Witch. Show!

    _____

    87 *issue* offspring 88-89 *round/And top of sovereignty* i.e., crown
    95 *impress* conscript 96 *bodements* prophecies 97 *Rebellious dead*
    (perhaps a reference to Banquo; but perhaps a misprint for "rebellion's
    head") 99 *lease of nature* natural lifespan 100 *mortal custom* natural
    death 104 *satisfied* i.e., fully informed 106 *noise* music

All. Show his eyes, and grieve his heart;   110
    Come like shadows, so depart!

> *A show of eight Kings and Banquo, last [King]
>   with a glass° in his hand.*

Macbeth. Thou art too like the spirit of Banquo.
        Down!
    Thy crown does sear mine eyelids. And thy hair,
    Thou other gold-bound brow, is like the first.
    A third is like the former. Filthy hags!   115
    Why do you show me this? A fourth! Start,° eyes!
    What, will the line stretch out to th' crack of
        doom?°
    Another yet! A seventh! I'll see no more.
    And yet the eighth appears, who bears a glass
    Which shows me many more; and some I see   120
    That twofold balls and treble scepters° carry:
    Horrible sight! Now I see 'tis true;
    For the blood-boltered° Banquo smiles upon me,
    And points at them for his. What, is this so?

First Witch. Ay, sir, all this is so. But why   125
    Stands Macbeth thus amazedly?
    Come, sisters, cheer we up his sprites,°
    And show the best of our delights:
    I'll charm the air to give a sound,
    While you perform your antic round,°   130
    That this great king may kindly say
    Our duties did his welcome pay.

> *Music. The Witches dance, and vanish.*

Macbeth. Where are they? Gone? Let this pernicious
        hour
    Stand aye accursèd in the calendar!
    Come in, without there!

III.s.d. *glass* mirror [116] *Start* i.e., from the sockets [117] *crack of doom*
blast (of a trumpet?) at doomsday [121] *twofold balls and treble
scepters* (coronation emblems) [123] *blood-boltered* matted with blood
[127] *sprites* spirits [130] *antic round* grotesque circular dance

Enter Lennox.

135 *Lennox.*   What's your Grace's will?

Macbeth. Saw you the weïrd sisters?

Lennox.   No, my lord.

Macbeth. Came they not by you?

Lennox.   No indeed, my lord.

Macbeth. Infected be the air whereon they ride,
    And damned all those that trust them! I did hear
140 The galloping of horse.° Who was 't came by?

Lennox. 'Tis two or three, my lord, that bring you
        word
    Macduff is fled to England.

Macbeth.   Fled to England?

Lennox. Ay, my good lord.

Macbeth. [*Aside*] Time, thou anticipat'st° my
        dread exploits.
145 The flighty purpose never is o'ertook
    Unless the deed go with it.° From this moment
    The very firstlings of my heart° shall be
    The firstlings of my hand. And even now,
    To crown my thoughts with acts, be it thought and
        done:
150 The castle of Macduff I will surprise;°
    Seize upon Fife; give to th' edge o' th' sword
    His wife, his babes, and all unfortunate souls
    That trace him in his line.° No boasting like a fool;
    This deed I'll do before this purpose cool:
155 But no more sights!—Where are these gentlemen?
    Come, bring me where they are.   *Exeunt.*

---

140 *horse* horses (or "horsemen")   144 *anticipat'st* foretold   145-46 *The
flighty . . . it* the fleeting plan is never fulfilled unless an action ac-
companies it   147 *firstlings of my heart* i.e., first thoughts, impulses
150 *surprise* attack suddenly   153 *trace him in his line* are of his lineage

Scene II.   [*Macduff's castle.*]

Enter Macduff's wife, her Son, and Ross.

Lady Macduff. What had he done, to make him fly the
    land?

Ross. You must have patience, madam.

Lady Macduff.   He had none:
    His flight was madness. When our actions do not,
    Our fears do make us traitors.

Ross.   You know not
    Whether it was his wisdom or his fear.   5

Lady Macduff. Wisdom! To leave his wife, to leave his
    babes,
    His mansion and his titles,° in a place
    From whence himself does fly? He loves us not;
    He wants the natural touch:° for the poor wren,
    The most diminutive of birds, will fight,   10
    Her young ones in her nest, against the owl.
    All is the fear and nothing is the love;
    As little is the wisdom, where the flight
    So runs against all reason.

Ross.   My dearest coz,°
    I pray you, school° yourself. But, for your husband,   15
    He is noble, wise, judicious, and best knows
    The fits o' th' season.° I dare not speak much
        further:
    But cruel are the times, when we are traitors
    And do not know ourselves; when we hold rumor
    From what we fear,° yet know not what we fear,   20

IV.ii.   ⁷ *titles* possessions   ⁹ *wants the natural touch* i.e., lacks natural
affection for his wife and children   ¹⁴ *coz* cousin   ¹⁵ *school* control
¹⁷ *fits o' th' season* disorders of the time   ¹⁹⁻²⁰ *hold rumor/From what
we fear* believe rumors because we fear

But float upon a wild and violent sea
Each way and move. I take my leave of you.
Shall not be long but I'll be here again.
Things at the worst will cease,° or else climb up-
　　ward
25　To what they were before. My pretty cousin,
Blessing upon you!

Lady Macduff. Fathered he is, and yet he's fatherless.

Ross. I am so much a fool, should I stay longer,
It would be my disgrace° and your discomfort.
I take my leave at once.　　　　　　*Exit Ross.*

30　*Lady Macduff.*　　　　　　Sirrah,° your father's dead:
And what will you do now? How will you live?

Son. As birds do, mother.

Lady Macduff.　　　　　What, with worms and flies?

Son. With what I get, I mean; and so do they.

Lady Macduff. Poor bird! thou'dst never fear the net
　　nor lime,°
35　The pitfall nor the gin.°

Son. Why should I, mother? Poor birds they are not
　　set for.
My father is not dead, for all your saying.

Lady Macduff. Yes, he is dead: how wilt thou do for a
　　father?

Son. Nay, how will you do for a husband?

Lady Macduff. Why, I can buy me twenty at any
40　　market.

Son. Then you'll buy 'em to sell° again.

Lady Macduff. Thou speak'st with all thy wit, and yet,
　　i' faith,
With wit enough for thee.°

---

24 *cease* i.e., cease worsening　29 *It would be my disgrace* i.e., I would
weep　30 *Sirrah* (here an affectionate address to a child)　34 *lime* birdlime (smeared on branches to catch birds)　35 *gin* trap　41 *sell* betray
43 *for thee* i.e., for a child

Son. Was my father a traitor, mother?

Lady Macduff. Ay, that he was.   45

Son. What is a traitor?

Lady Macduff. Why, one that swears and lies.°

Son. And be all traitors that do so?

Lady Macduff. Every one that does so is a traitor, and must be hanged.

Son. And must they all be hanged that swear and lie? 50

Lady Macduff. Every one.

Son. Who must hang them?

Lady Macduff. Why, the honest men.

Son. Then the liars and swearers are fools; for there are liars and swearers enow° to beat the honest 55 men and hang up them.

Lady Macduff. Now, God help thee, poor monkey! But how wilt thou do for a father?

Son. If he were dead, you'd weep for him. If you would not, it were a good sign that I should quickly 60 have a new father.

Lady Macduff. Poor prattler, how thou talk'st!

Enter a Messenger.

Messenger. Bless you, fair dame! I am not to you known,
Though in your state of honor I am perfect.°
I doubt° some danger does approach you nearly: 65
If you will take a homely° man's advice,
Be not found here; hence, with your little ones.
To fright you thus, methinks I am too savage;
To do worse to you were fell° cruelty,
Which is too nigh your person. Heaven preserve you! 70

⁴⁷ *swears and lies* i.e., takes an oath and breaks it ⁵⁵ *enow* enough
⁶⁴ *in . . . perfect* I am fully informed of your honorable rank ⁶⁵ *doubt*
fear ⁶⁶ *homely* plain ⁶⁹ *fell* fierce

I dare abide no longer.   *Exit Messenger.*

Lady Macduff.   Whither should I fly?
I have done no harm. But I remember now
I am in this earthly world, where to do harm
Is often laudable, to do good sometime
75   Accounted dangerous folly. Why then, alas,
Do I put up that womanly defense,
To say I have done no harm?—What are these faces?

                   Enter Murderers.

Murderer. Where is your husband?

Lady Macduff. I hope, in no place so unsanctified
   Where such as thou mayst find him.

80   *Murderer.*   He's a traitor.

Son. Thou li'st, thou shag-eared° villain!

Murderer.   What, you egg!

                   [*Stabbing him.*]

   Young fry° of treachery!

Son.   He has killed me, mother:
   Run away, I pray you!

                   [*Dies.*]
            Exit [*Lady Macduff*], *crying "Murder!"* [*fol-
                  lowed by Murderers*].

Scene III.   [*England. Before the King's palace.*]

            Enter Malcolm and Macduff.

Malcolm. Let us seek out some desolate shade, and
      there
   Weep our sad bosoms empty.

81 *shag-eared* hairy-eared (?), with shaggy hair hanging over the ears
(?)   82 *fry* spawn

Macduff.   Let us rather
Hold fast the mortal° sword, and like good men
Bestride our down-fall'n birthdom.° Each new
    morn
New widows howl, new orphans cry, new sorrows   5
Strike heaven on the face, that° it resounds
As if it felt with Scotland and yelled out
Like syllable of dolor.°

Malcolm.   What I believe, I'll wail;
What know, believe; and what I can redress,
As I shall find the time to friend,° I will.   10
What you have spoke, it may be so perchance.
This tyrant, whose sole° name blisters our tongues,
Was once thought honest:° you have loved him
    well;
He hath not touched you yet. I am young; but
    something
You may deserve of him through me;° and wisdom°   15
To offer up a weak, poor, innocent lamb
T' appease an angry god.

Macduff. I am not treacherous.

Malcolm.   But Macbeth is.
A good and virtuous nature may recoil
In° an imperial charge. But I shall crave your
    pardon;   20
That which you are, my thoughts cannot
    transpose:°
Angels are bright still, though the brightest° fell:
Though all things foul would wear° the brows of
    grace,
Yet grace must still look so.°

IV.iii. 3 *mortal* deadly 4 *Bestride our down-fall'n birthdom* protectively
stand over our native land 6 *that* so that 8 *Like syllable of dolor*
similar sound of grief 10 *to friend* friendly, propitious 12 *sole* very
13 *honest* good 15 *deserve of him through me* i.e., earn by betraying
me to Macbeth 15 *wisdom* it may be wise 19-20 *recoil/In* give way
under 21 *transpose* transform 22 *the brightest* i.e., Lucifer 23 *would
wear* desire to wear 24 *so* i.e., like itself

Macduff.   I have lost my hopes.

Malcolm. Perchance even there where I did find my
25   doubts.
    Why in that rawness° left you wife and child,
    Those precious motives, those strong knots of
        love,
    Without leave-taking? I pray you,
    Let not my jealousies° be your dishonors,
30   But mine own safeties. You may be rightly just°
    Whatever I shall think.

Macduff.   Bleed, bleed, poor country:
    Great tyranny, lay thou thy basis° sure,
    For goodness dare not check° thee: wear thou thy
        wrongs;
    The title is affeered.° Fare thee well, lord:
35   I would not be the villain that thou think'st
    For the whole space that's in the tyrant's grasp
    And the rich East to boot.

Malcolm.   Be not offended:
    I speak not as in absolute fear of you.
    I think our country sinks beneath the yoke;
40   It weeps, it bleeds, and each new day a gash
    Is added to her wounds. I think withal°
    There would be hands uplifted in my right;°
    And here from gracious England° have I offer
    Of goodly thousands: but, for° all this,
45   When I shall tread upon the tyrant's head,
    Or wear it on my sword, yet my poor country
    Shall have more vices than it had before,
    More suffer, and more sundry ways than ever,
    By him that shall succeed.

Macduff.   What should he be?

50 *Malcolm.* It is myself I mean, in whom I know

---

26 *rawness* unprotected condition   29 *jealousies* suspicions   30 *rightly just* perfectly honorable   32 *basis* foundation   33 *check* restrain   34 *affeered* legally confirmed   41 *withal* moreover   42 *in my right* on behalf of my claim   43 *England* i.e., the King of England   44 *for* despite

All the particulars° of vice so grafted°
That, when they shall be opened,° black Macbeth
Will seem as pure as snow, and the poor state
Esteem him as a lamb, being compared
With my confineless harms.°

Macduff.   Not in the legions   55
Of horrid hell can come a devil more damned
In evils to top Macbeth.

Malcolm.   I grant him bloody,
Luxurious,° avaricious, false, deceitful,
Sudden,° malicious, smacking of every sin
That has a name: but there's no bottom, none,   60
In my voluptuousness:° your wives, your daughters,
Your matrons and your maids, could not fill up
The cistern of my lust, and my desire
All continent° impediments would o'erbear,
That did oppose my will. Better Macbeth   65
Than such an one to reign.

Macduff.   Boundless intemperance
In nature° is a tyranny; it hath been
Th' untimely emptying of the happy throne,
And fall of many kings. But fear not yet
To take upon you what is yours: you may   70
Convey° your pleasures in a spacious plenty,
And yet seem cold, the time° you may so hoodwink.
We have willing dames enough. There cannot be
That vulture in you, to devour so many
As will to greatness dedicate themselves,   75
Finding it so inclined.

Malcolm.   With this there grows
In my most ill-composed affection° such

---

⁵¹ *particulars* special kinds ⁵¹ *grafted* engrafted ⁵² *opened* in bloom,
i.e., revealed ⁵⁵ *confineless harms* unbounded evils ⁵⁸ *Luxurious* lecherous ⁵⁹ *Sudden* violent ⁶¹ *voluptuousness* lust ⁶⁴ *continent* restraining
⁶⁷ *In nature* in man's nature ⁷¹ *Convey* secretly manage ⁷² *time* age,
i.e., people ⁷⁷ *ill-composed affection* evilly compounded character

A stanchless° avarice that, were I King,
I should cut off the nobles for their lands,
80   Desire his jewels and this other's house:
And my more-having would be as a sauce
To make me hunger more, that I should forge
Quarrels unjust against the good and loyal,
Destroying them for wealth.

Macduff.   This avarice
85   Sticks deeper, grows with more pernicious root
Than summer-seeming° lust, and it hath been
The sword of our slain kings.° Yet do not fear.
Scotland hath foisons to fill up your will
Of your mere own.° All these are portable,°
90   With other graces weighed.

Malcolm. But I have none: the king-becoming graces,
As justice, verity, temp'rance, stableness,
Bounty, perseverance, mercy, lowliness,
Devotion, patience, courage, fortitude,
95   I have no relish of° them, but abound
In the division of each several crime,°
Acting it many ways. Nay, had I pow'r, I should
Pour the sweet milk of concord into hell,
Uproar° the universal peace, confound
All unity on earth.

100 *Macduff.*   O Scotland, Scotland!

Malcolm. If such a one be fit to govern, speak:
I am as I have spoken.

Macduff.   Fit to govern!
No, not to live. O nation miserable!
With an untitled tyrant bloody-sceptered,
105   When shalt thou see thy wholesome days again,

Since that the truest issue of thy throne
By his own interdiction° stands accursed,
And does blaspheme his breed?° Thy royal father
Was a most sainted king: the queen that bore thee,
Oft'ner upon her knees than on her feet,   *110*
Died° every day she lived. Fare thee well!
These evils thou repeat'st upon thyself
Hath banished me from Scotland. O my breast,
Thy hope ends here!

Malcolm.   Macduff, this noble passion,
Child of integrity, hath from my soul   *115*
Wiped the black scruples,° reconciled my thoughts
To thy good truth and honor. Devilish Macbeth
By many of these trains° hath sought to win me
Into his power; and modest wisdom° plucks me
From over-credulous haste: but God above   *120*
Deal between thee and me! For even now
I put myself to° thy direction, and
Unspeak mine own detraction; here abjure
The taints and blames I laid upon myself,
For° strangers to my nature. I am yet   *125*
Unknown to woman, never was forsworn,
Scarcely have coveted what was mine own,
At no time broke my faith, would not betray
The devil to his fellow, and delight
No less in truth than life. My first false speaking   *130*
Was this upon myself. What I am truly,
Is thine and my poor country's to command:
Whither indeed, before thy here-approach,
Old Siward, with ten thousand warlike men,
Already at a point,° was setting forth.   *135*
Now we'll together, and the chance of goodness
Be like our warranted quarrel!° Why are you
      silent?

---

107 *interdiction* curse, exclusion 108 *breed* ancestry 111 *Died* i.e., prepared for heaven 116 *scruples* suspicions 118 *trains* plots 119 *modest
wisdom* i.e., prudence 122 *to* under 125 *For* as 135 *at a point* prepared
136-37 *the chance . . . quarrel* i.e., may our chance of success equal the
justice of our cause

Macduff. Such welcome and unwelcome things at once
'Tis hard to reconcile.

Enter a Doctor.

Malcolm. Well, more anon. Comes the King forth, I
140   pray you?

Doctor. Ay, sir. There are a crew of wretched souls
That stay° his cure: their malady convinces
The great assay of art;° but at his touch,
Such sanctity hath heaven given his hand,
They presently amend.°

145 *Malcolm.*   I thank you, doctor.

Exit [Doctor].

Macduff. What's the disease he means?

Malcolm.   'Tis called the evil:°
A most miraculous work in this good King,
Which often since my here-remain in England
I have seen him do. How he solicits heaven,
150   Himself best knows: but strangely-visited° people,
All swoll'n and ulcerous, pitiful to the eye,
The mere° despair of surgery, he cures,
Hanging a golden stamp° about their necks,
Put on with holy prayers: and 'tis spoken,
155   To the succeeding royalty he leaves
The healing benediction. With this strange virtue°
He hath a heavenly gift of prophecy,
And sundry blessings hang about his throne
That speak° him full of grace.

Enter Ross.

Macduff.   See, who comes here?

160 *Malcolm.* My countryman; but yet I know him not.

---

142 *stay* await   142-43 *convinces/The great assay of art* i.e., defies the
efforts of medical science   145 *presently amend* immediately recover
146 *evil* (scrofula, called "the king's evil" because it could allegedly be
cured by the king's touch)   150 *strangely-visited* oddly afflicted
152 *mere* utter   153 *stamp* coin   156 *virtue* power   159 *speak* proclaim

Macduff. My ever gentle° cousin, welcome hither.

Malcolm. I know him now: good God, betimes°
      remove
   The means that makes us strangers!

Ross.   Sir, amen.

Macduff. Stands Scotland where it did?

Ross.   Alas, poor country!
   Almost afraid to know itself! It cannot   165
   Be called our mother but our grave, where nothing°
   But who knows nothing is once seen to smile;
   Where sighs and groans, and shrieks that rent the
      air,
   Are made, not marked;° where violent sorrow seems
   A modern ecstasy.° The dead man's knell   170
   Is there scarce asked for who, and good men's lives
   Expire before the flowers in their caps,
   Dying or ere they sicken.

Macduff.   O, relation
   Too nice,° and yet too true!

Malcolm.   What's the newest grief?

Ross. That of an hour's age doth hiss the speaker;°   175
   Each minute teems° a new one.

Macduff.   How does my wife?

Ross. Why, well.

Macduff.   And all my children?

Ross.   Well too.

Macduff. The tyrant has not battered at their peace?

Ross. No; they were well at peace when I did leave
      'em.

---

161 *gentle* noble 162 *betimes* quickly 166 *nothing* no one 169 *marked*
noticed 170 *modern ecstasy* i.e., ordinary emotion 173-74 *relation/Too
nice* tale too accurate 175 *That . . . speaker* i.e., the report of the
grief of an hour ago is hissed as stale news 176 *teems* gives birth to

180 *Macduff.* Be not a niggard of your speech: how goes 't?

Ross. When I came hither to transport the tidings,
　　　　Which I have heavily° borne, there ran a rumor
　　　　Of many worthy fellows that were out;°
　　　　Which was to my belief witnessed° the rather,
185　　For that I saw the tyrant's power° afoot.
　　　　Now is the time of help. Your eye in Scotland
　　　　Would create soldiers, make our women fight,
　　　　To doff their dire distresses.

Malcolm. 　　　　　　　　　　Be 't their comfort
　　　　We are coming thither. Gracious England hath
190　　Lent us good Siward and ten thousand men;
　　　　An older and a better soldier none
　　　　That Christendom gives out.°

Ross. 　　　　　　　　　　　　Would I could answer
　　　　This comfort with the like! But I have words
　　　　That would° be howled out in the desert air,
　　　　Where hearing should not latch° them.

195 *Macduff.* 　　　　　　　　　　What concern they?
　　　　The general cause or is it a fee-grief
　　　　Due to some single breast?°

Ross. 　　　　　　　　　　No mind that's honest
　　　　But in it shares some woe, though the main part
　　　　Pertains to you alone.

Macduff. 　　　　　　If it be mine,
200　　Keep it not from me, quickly let me have it.

Ross. Let not your ears despise my tongue for ever,
　　　　Which shall possess them with the heaviest sound
　　　　That ever yet they heard.

Macduff. 　　　　　　　　Humh! I guess at it.

Ross. Your castle is surprised;° your wife and babes

---

182 *heavily* sadly 183 *out* i.e., up in arms 184 *witnessed* attested
185 *power* army 192 *gives out* reports 194 *would* should 195 *latch*
catch 196-97 *fee-grief / Due to some single breast* i.e., a personal grief
belonging to an individual 204 *surprised* suddenly attacked

Savagely slaughtered. To relate the manner,   205
Were, on the quarry° of these murdered deer,
To add the death of you.

Malcolm.   Merciful heaven!
What, man! Ne'er pull your hat upon your brows;
Give sorrow words. The grief that does not speak
Whispers the o'er-fraught heart,° and bids it break.   210

Macduff. My children too?

Ross.   Wife, children, servants, all
That could be found.

Macduff.   And I must be from thence!
My wife killed too?

Ross.   I have said.

Malcolm.   Be comforted.
Let's make us med'cines of our great revenge,
To cure this deadly grief.   215

Macduff. He has no children. All my pretty ones?
Did you say all? O hell-kite!° All?
What, all my pretty chickens and their dam
At one fell swoop?

Malcolm. Dispute° it like a man.

Macduff.   I shall do so;   220
But I must also feel it as a man.
I cannot but remember such things were,
That were most precious to me. Did heaven look on,
And would not take their part? Sinful Macduff,
They were all struck for thee! Naught° that I am,   225
Not for their own demerits but for mine
Fell slaughter on their souls. Heaven rest them now!

Malcolm. Be this the whetstone of your sword. Let
    grief
Convert to anger; blunt not the heart, enrage it.

206 *quarry* heap of slaughtered game   210 *Whispers the o'er-fraught heart*
whispers to the overburdened heart   217 *hell-kite* hellish bird of prey
220 *Dispute* counter   225 *Naught* wicked

230 *Macduff.* O, I could play the woman with mine eyes,
      And braggart with my tongue! But, gentle heavens,
      Cut short all intermission;° front to front°
      Bring thou this fiend of Scotland and myself;
      Within my sword's length set him. If he 'scape,
      Heaven forgive him too!

235 *Malcolm.*   This time goes manly.
      Come, go we to the King. Our power is ready;
      Our lack is nothing but our leave.° Macbeth
      Is ripe for shaking, and the pow'rs above
      Put on their instruments.° Receive what cheer you
        may.

240   The night is long that never finds the day.   *Exeunt.*

---

232 *intermission* interval   232 *front to front* forehead to forehead i.e.,
face to face   237 *Our lack is nothing but our leave* i.e., we need only
to take our leave   239 *Put on their instruments* arm themselves (?)
urge us, their agents, onward (?)

ACT V

Scene I.   [*Dunsinane. In the castle.*]

*Enter a Doctor of Physic and a
Waiting-Gentlewoman.*

Doctor. I have two nights watched with you, but can
perceive no truth in your report. When was it she
last walked?

Gentlewoman. Since his Majesty went into the field, I
have seen her rise from her bed, throw her night-   5
gown upon her, unlock her closet,° take forth
paper, fold it, write upon 't, read it, afterwards seal
it, and again return to bed; yet all this while in a
most fast sleep.

Doctor. A great perturbation in nature, to receive at   10
once the benefit of sleep and do the effects of
watching!° In this slumb'ry agitation, besides her
walking and other actual performances,° what, at
any time, have you heard her say?

Gentlewoman. That, sir, which I will not report after   15
her.

Doctor. You may to me, and 'tis most meet° you
should.

Gentlewoman. Neither to you nor anyone, having no
witness to confirm my speech.   20

Enter Lady [*Macbeth*], *with a taper.*

V.i.   6 *closet* chest   11-12 *effects of watching* deeds of one awake
13 *actual performance* deeds   17 *meet* suitable

Lo you, here she comes! This is her very guise,° and, upon my life, fast asleep! Observe her; stand close.°

Doctor. How came she by that light?

25 *Gentlewoman.* Why, it stood by her. She has light by her continually. 'Tis her command.

Doctor. You see, her eyes are open.

Gentlewoman. Ay, but their sense° are shut.

Doctor. What is it she does now? Look, how she rubs
30   her hands.

Gentlewoman. It is an accustomed action with her, to seem thus washing her hands: I have known her continue in this a quarter of an hour.

Lady Macbeth. Yet here's a spot.

35 *Doctor.* Hark! she speaks. I will set down what comes from her, to satisfy° my remembrance the more strongly.

Lady Macbeth. Out, damned spot! Out, I say! One: two: why, then 'tis time to do 't. Hell is murky.
40   Fie, my lord, fie! A soldier, and afeard? What need we fear who knows it, when none can call our pow'r to accompt?° Yet who would have thought the old man to have had so much blood in him?

Doctor. Do you mark that?

45 *Lady Macbeth.* The Thane of Fife had a wife. Where is she now? What, will these hands ne'er be clean? No more o' that, my lord, no more o' that! You mar all with this starting.

Doctor. Go to,° go to! You have known what you
50   should not.

Gentlewoman. She has spoke what she should not, I

---

21 *guise* custom   23 *close* hidden   28 *sense* i.e., powers of sight   36 *satisfy* confirm   42 *to accompt* into account   49 *Go to* (an exclamation)

am sure of that. Heaven knows what she has known.

Lady Macbeth. Here's the smell of the blood still. All
the perfumes of Arabia will not sweeten this little
hand. Oh, oh, oh! 55

Doctor. What a sigh is there! The heart is sorely
charged.°

Gentlewoman. I would not have such a heart in my
bosom for the dignity° of the whole body.

Doctor. Well, well, well—— 60

Gentlewoman. Pray God it be, sir.

Doctor. This disease is beyond my practice.° Yet I
have known those which have walked in their sleep
who have died holily in their beds.

Lady Macbeth. Wash your hands; put on your night- 65
gown; look not so pale! I tell you yet again, Banquo's buried. He cannot come out on 's° grave.

Doctor. Even so?

Lady Macbeth. To bed, to bed! There's knocking at
the gate. Come, come, come, come, give me your 70
hand! What's done cannot be undone. To bed, to
bed, to bed!   *Exit Lady [Macbeth].*

Doctor. Will she go now to bed?

Gentlewoman. Directly.

Doctor. Foul whisp'rings are abroad. Unnatural deeds 75
Do breed unnatural troubles. Infected minds
To their deaf pillows will discharge their secrets.
More needs she the divine than the physician.
God, God forgive us all! Look after her;
Remove from her the means of all annoyance,° 80
And still° keep eyes upon her. So good night.

---

⁵⁷ *charged* burdened ⁵⁹ *dignity* worth, rank ⁶² *practice* professional
skill ⁶⁷ *on 's* of his ⁸⁰ *annoyance* injury ⁸¹ *still* continuously

My mind she has mated° and amazed my sight:
I think, but dare not speak.

Gentlewoman.   Good night, good doctor.

                                        Exeunt.

Scene II.   [*The country near Dunsinane.*]

Drum and colors. Enter Menteith, Caithness,
Angus, Lennox, Soldiers.

Menteith. The English pow'r° is near, led on by
      Malcolm,
   His uncle Siward and the good Macduff.
   Revenges burn in them; for their dear° causes
   Would to the bleeding and the grim alarm
   Excite the mortified man.°

5 *Angus.*   Near Birnam Wood
   Shall we well meet them; that way are they coming.

Caithness. Who knows if Donalbain be with his
      brother?

Lennox. For certain, sir, he is not. I have a file°
   Of all the gentry: there is Siward's son,
10   And many unrough° youths that even now
   Protest° their first of manhood.

Menteith.   What does the tyrant?

Caithness. Great Dunsinane he strongly fortifies.
   Some say he's mad; others, that lesser hate him,
   Do call it valiant fury: but, for certain,

82 *mated* baffled   V.ii.   1 *pow'r* army   3 *dear* heartfelt   4-5 *Would . . .*
man i.e., would incite a dead man (or "a paralyzed man") to join the
bloody and grim call to battle   8 *file* list   10 *unrough* i.e., beardless
11 *Protest* assert

He cannot buckle his distempered° cause   15
Within the belt of rule.°

Angus.   Now does he feel
His secret murders sticking on his hands;
Now minutely revolts upbraid° his faith-breach.
Those he commands move only in command,
Nothing in love. Now does he feel his title   20
Hang loose about him, like a giant's robe
Upon a dwarfish thief.

Menteith.   Who then shall blame
His pestered° senses to recoil and start,
When all that is within him does condemn
Itself for being there?

Caithness.   Well, march we on,   25
To give obedience where 'tis truly owed.
Meet we the med'cine° of the sickly weal,°
And with him pour we, in our country's purge,
Each drop of us.°

Lennox.   Or so much as it needs
To dew° the sovereign° flower and drown the
          weeds.   30
Make we our march towards Birnam.

                              Exeunt, marching.

Scene III.   [*Dunsinane. In the castle.*]

Enter Macbeth, Doctor, and Attendants.

Macbeth. Bring me no more reports; let them fly all!
Till Birnam Wood remove to Dunsinane
I cannot taint° with fear. What's the boy Malcolm?

---

15 *distempered* swollen by dropsy 16 *rule* self-control 18 *minutely
revolts upbraid* rebellions every minute rebuke 23 *pestered* tormented
27 *med'cine* i.e., Malcolm 27 *weal* commonwealth 29 *Each drop of
us* i.e., every last drop of our blood (?) 30 *dew* bedew, water (and
thus make grow) 30 *sovereign* (1) royal (2) remedial V.iii. 3 *taint*
become infected

Was he not born of woman? The spirits that know
All mortal consequences° have pronounced me
5   thus:
"Fear not, Macbeth; no man that's born of woman
Shall e'er have power upon thee." Then fly, false
      thanes,
And mingle with the English epicures.
The mind I sway° by and the heart I bear
10   Shall never sag with doubt nor shake with fear.

Enter Servant.

The devil damn thee black, thou cream-faced loon!°
Where got'st thou that goose look?

Servant. There is ten thousand——

Macbeth.   Geese, villain?

Servant.   Soldiers, sir.

Macbeth. Go prick thy face and over-red° thy fear,
15   Thou lily-livered boy. What soldiers, patch?°
Death of° thy soul! Those linen° cheeks of thine
Are counselors to fear. What soldiers, whey-face?

Servant. The English force, so please you.

Macbeth. Take thy face hence.   [*Exit Servant.*]
                    Seyton!—I am sick at heart,
20   When I behold—Seyton, I say!—This push°
Will cheer me ever, or disseat° me now.
I have lived long enough. My way of life
Is fall'n into the sear,° the yellow leaf,
And that which should accompany old age,
25   As honor, love, obedience, troops of friends,
I must not look to have; but, in their stead,
Curses not loud but deep, mouth-honor, breath,
Which the poor heart would fain deny, and dare not.
Seyton!

---

5 *mortal consequences* future human events 9 *sway* move 11 *loon*
fool 14 *over-red* cover with red 15 *patch* fool 16 *of* upon 16 *linen*
i.e., pale 20 *push* effort 21 *disseat* i.e., unthrone (with wordplay on
"cheer," pronounced "chair") 23 *sear* withered

Enter Seyton.

Seyton. What's your gracious pleasure?

Macbeth.   What news more?   *30*

Seyton. All is confirmed, my lord, which was reported.

Macbeth. I'll fight, till from my bones my flesh be
     hacked.
     Give me my armor.

Seyton.   'Tis not needed yet.

Macbeth. I'll put it on.
     Send out moe° horses, skirr° the country round.   *35*
     Hang those that talk of fear. Give me mine armor.
     How does your patient, doctor?

Doctor.   Not so sick, my lord,
     As she is troubled with thick-coming fancies
     That keep her from her rest.

Macbeth.   Cure her of that.
     Canst thou not minister to a mind diseased,   *40*
     Pluck from the memory a rooted sorrow,
     Raze out° the written troubles of the brain,
     And with some sweet oblivious° antidote
     Cleanse the stuffed bosom of that perilous stuff
     Which weighs upon the heart?

Doctor.   Therein the patient   *45*
     Must minister to himself.

Macbeth. Throw physic° to the dogs, I'll none of it.
     Come, put mine armor on. Give me my staff.
     Seyton, send out.——Doctor, the thanes fly from
          me.——
     Come, sir, dispatch.° If thou couldst, doctor, cast   *50*
     The water° of my land, find her disease
     And purge it to a sound and pristine health,
     I would applaud thee to the very echo,

---

³⁵ *moe* more   ³⁵ *skirr* scour   ⁴² *Raze out* erase   ⁴³ *oblivious* causing
forgetfulness   ⁴⁷ *physic* medical science   ⁵⁰ *dispatch* hurry   ⁵⁰⁻⁵¹ *cast/
The water* analyze the urine

        That should applaud again.—Pull 't off, I say.—
55   What rhubarb, senna, or what purgative drug,
        Would scour these English hence? Hear'st thou of
            them?

    Doctor. Ay, my good lord; your royal preparation
        Makes us hear something.

    Macbeth.   Bring it° after me.
        I will not be afraid of death and bane°
60   Till Birnam Forest come to Dunsinane.

    Doctor. [*Aside*] Were I from Dunsinane away
            and clear,
        Profit again should hardly draw me here.   *Exeunt.*

        Scene IV.   [*Country near Birnam Wood.*]

        *Drum and colors. Enter Malcolm, Siward, Mac-
        duff, Siward's Son, Menteith, Caithness, Angus,
        and Soldiers, marching.*

    Malcolm. Cousins, I hope the days are near at hand
        That chambers will be safe.°

    Menteith.   We doubt it nothing.°

    Siward. What wood is this before us?

    Menteith.   The Wood of Birnam.

    Malcolm. Let every soldier hew him down a bough
5   And bear 't before him. Thereby shall we shadow
        The numbers of our host, and make discovery°
        Err in report of us.

    Soldiers.   It shall be done.

    ---

    58 *it* i.e., the armor 59 *bane* destruction V.iv. 2 *That chambers will
    be safe* i.e., that a man will be safe in his bedroom   2 *nothing* not at
    all   6 *discovery* reconnaisance

Siward. We learn no other but° the confident tyrant
    Keeps still in Dunsinane, and will endure°
    Our setting down before 't.

Malcolm.   'Tis his main hope,   *10*
    For where there is advantage to be given°
    Both more and less° have given him the revolt,
    And none serve with him but constrainèd things
    Whose hearts are absent too.

Macduff.   Let our just censures
    Attend the true event,° and put we on   *15*
    Industrious soldiership.

Siward.   The time approaches,
    That will with due decision make us know
    What we shall say we have and what we owe.°
    Thoughts speculative their unsure hopes relate,
    But certain issue strokes must arbitrate:°   *20*
    Towards which advance the war.°

                           Exeunt, marching.

Scene V.   [*Dunsinane. Within the castle.*]

*Enter Macbeth, Seyton, and Soldiers, with drum
and colors.*

Macbeth. Hang out our banners on the outward walls.
    The cry is still "They come!" Our castle's strength
    Will laugh a siege to scorn. Here let them lie
    Till famine and the ague° eat them up.
    Were they not forced° with those that should be
      ours,   *5*

---

8 *no other but* nothing but that   9 *endure* allow   11 *advantage to
be given* afforded an opportunity   12 *more and less* high and low
14-15 *just censures/Attend the true event* true judgment await the actual
outcome   18 *owe* own (the contrast is between "what we shall say we
have" and "what we shall really have")   20 *certain issue strokes must
arbitrate* the definite outcome must be decided by battle   21 *war* army
V.v. 4 *ague* fever   5 *forced* reinforced

We might have met them dareful,° beard to beard,
And beat them backward home.

A cry within of women.

What is that noise?

Seyton. It is the cry of women, my good lord. [*Exit.*]

Macbeth. I have almost forgot the taste of fears:
10   The time has been, my senses would have cooled
To hear a night-shriek, and my fell° of hair
Would at a dismal treatise° rouse and stir
As life were in 't. I have supped full with horrors.
Direness, familiar to my slaughterous thoughts,
Cannot once start° me.

[*Enter Seyton.*]

15   Wherefore was that cry?

Seyton. The Queen, my lord, is dead.

Macbeth. She should° have died hereafter;
There would have been a time for such a word.°
Tomorrow, and tomorrow, and tomorrow
20   Creeps in this petty pace from day to day,
To the last syllable of recorded time;
And all our yesterdays have lighted fools
The way to dusty death. Out, out, brief candle!
Life's but a walking shadow, a poor player
25   That struts and frets his hour upon the stage
And then is heard no more. It is a tale
Told by an idiot, full of sound and fury
Signifying nothing.

Enter a Messenger.

Thou com'st to use thy tongue; thy story quickly!

30 *Messenger.* Gracious my lord,
I should report that which I say I saw,
But know not how to do 't.

Macbeth.   Well, say, sir.

---

6 *met them dareful* i.e., met them in the battlefield boldly   11 *fell* pelt
12 *treatise* story   15 *start* startle   17 *should* inevitably would (?)
18 *word* message

Messenger. As I did stand my watch upon the hill,
    I looked toward Birnam, and anon, methought,
    The wood began to move.

Macbeth.   Liar and slave!   35

Messenger. Let me endure your wrath, if 't be not so.
    Within this three mile may you see it coming;
    I say a moving grove.

Macbeth.   If thou speak'st false,
    Upon the next tree shalt thou hang alive,
    Till famine cling° thee. If thy speech be sooth,°   40
    I care not if thou dost for me as much.
    I pull in resolution,° and begin
    To doubt° th' equivocation of the fiend
    That lies like truth: "Fear not, till Birnam Wood
    Do come to Dunsinane!" And now a wood   45
    Comes toward Dunsinane. Arm, arm, and out!
    If this which he avouches° does appear,
    There is nor flying hence nor tarrying here.
    I 'gin to be aweary of the sun,
    And wish th' estate° o' th' world were now undone.   50
    Ring the alarum bell! Blow wind, come wrack!
    At least we'll die with harness° on our back.

                                    Exeunt.

Scene VI.   [*Dunsinane. Before the castle.*]

    Drum and colors. Enter Malcolm, Siward,
      Macduff, and their army, with boughs.

Malcolm. Now near enough. Your leavy° screens
    throw down,
  And show like those you are. You, worthy uncle,

---

⁴⁰ *cling* wither   ⁴⁰ *sooth* truth   ⁴² *pull in resolution* restrain confidence
⁴³ *doubt* suspect   ⁴⁷ *avouches* asserts   ⁵⁰ *th' estate* the orderly condition   ⁵² *harness* armor   V.vi. ¹ *leavy* leafy

     Shall, with my cousin, your right noble son,
     Lead our first battle.° Worthy Macduff and we°
5   Shall take upon 's what else remains to do,
     According to our order.°

Siward.   Fare you well.
     Do we° but find the tyrant's power° tonight,
     Let us be beaten, if we cannot fight.

Macduff. Make all our trumpets speak; give them all
      breath,
10   Those clamorous harbingers of blood and death.

                   Exeunt. Alarums continued.

Scene VII.   [*Another part of the field.*]

Enter Macbeth.

Macbeth. They have tied me to a stake; I cannot fly,
     But bearlike I must fight the course.° What's he
     That was not born of woman? Such a one
     Am I to fear, or none.

            Enter Young Siward.

Young Siward. What is thy name?

5 *Macbeth.*   Thou'lt be afraid to hear it.

Young Siward. No; though thou call'st thyself a hotter
      name
     Than any is in hell.

Macbeth.   My name's Macbeth.

---

4 *battle* battalion   4 *we* (Malcolm uses the royal "we")   6 *order* plan
7 *Do we* if we do 7 *power* forces V.vii. 2 *course* bout, round (he has
in mind an attack of dogs or men upon a bear chained to a stake)

Young Siward. The devil himself could not pronounce
    a title
  More hateful to mine ear.

Macbeth.   No, nor more fearful.

Young Siward. Thou liest, abhorrèd tyrant; with my
    sword   10
  I'll prove the lie thou speak'st.

        Fight, and Young Siward slain.

Macbeth.   Thou wast born of woman.
  But swords I smile at, weapons laugh to scorn,
  Brandished by man that's of a woman born.

                             Exit.

       Alarums. Enter Macduff.

Macduff. That way the noise is. Tyrant, show thy face!
  If thou be'st slain and with no stroke of mine,   15
  My wife and children's ghosts will haunt me still.
  I cannot strike at wretched kerns,° whose arms
  Are hired to bear their staves.° Either thou,
    Macbeth,
  Or else my sword, with an unbattered edge,
  I sheathe again undeeded.° There thou shouldst
    be;   20
  By this great clatter, one of greatest note
  Seems bruited.° Let me find him, Fortune!
  And more I beg not.   *Exit. Alarums.*

       Enter Malcolm and Siward.

Siward. This way, my lord. The castle's gently
    rend'red:°
  The tyrant's people on both sides do fight;   25
  The noble thanes do bravely in the war;
  The day almost itself professes° yours,
  And little is to do.

---

17 *kerns* foot soldiers (contemptuous) 18 *staves* spears 20 *undeeded*
i.e., having done nothing 22 *bruited* reported 24 *gently rend'red* sur-
rendered without a struggle 27 *itself professes* declares itself

Malcolm.   We have met with foes
  That strike beside us.°

Siward.   Enter, sir, the castle.

                                Exeunt. Alarum.

            [Scene VIII.   *Another part of the field.*]

                    Enter Macbeth.

Macbeth. Why should I play the Roman fool, and die
  On mine own sword? Whiles I see lives,° the gashes
  Do better upon them.

                    Enter Macduff.

Macduff.   Turn, hell-hound, turn!

Macbeth. Of all men else I have avoided thee.
5   But get thee back! My soul is too much charged°
  With blood of thine already.

Macduff.   I have no words:
  My voice is in my sword, thou bloodier villain
  Than terms can give thee out!°

                    Fight. Alarum.

Macbeth.   Thou losest labor:
  As easy mayst thou the intrenchant° air
10   With thy keen sword impress° as make me bleed:
  Let fall thy blade on vulnerable crests;
  I bear a charmèd life, which must not yield
  To one of woman born.

29 *beside us* i.e., deliberately miss us (?) as our comrades (?)   V.viii.
2 *Whiles I see lives* so long as I see living men   5 *charged* burdened
8 *terms can give thee out* words can describe you   9 *intrenchant*
incapable of being cut   10 *impress* make an impression on

Macduff.   Despair° thy charm,
And let the angel° whom thou still hast served
Tell thee, Macduff was from his mother's womb   *15*
Untimely ripped.

Macbeth. Accursèd be that tongue that tells me so,
For it hath cowed my better part of man!°
And be these juggling fiends no more believed,
That palter° with us in a double sense;   *20*
That keep the word of promise to our ear,
And break it to our hope. I'll not fight with thee.

Macduff. Then yield thee, coward,
And live to be the show and gaze o' th' time:°
We'll have thee, as our rarer monsters° are,   *25*
Painted upon a pole,° and underwrit,
"Here may you see the tyrant."

Macbeth.   I will not yield,
To kiss the ground before young Malcolm's feet,
And to be baited° with the rabble's curse.
Though Birnam Wood be come to Dunsinane,   *30*
And thou opposed, being of no woman born,
Yet I will try the last. Before my body
I throw my warlike shield. Lay on, Macduff;
And damned be him that first cries "Hold,
     enough!"   *Exeunt, fighting. Alarums.*

[*Re-*]*enter fighting, and Macbeth slain.* [*Exit
Macduff, with Macbeth.*] *Retreat and flour-
ish.*° *Enter, with drum and colors, Malcolm,
Siward, Ross, Thanes, and Soldiers.*

Malcolm. I would the friends we miss were safe
     arrived.   *35*

Siward. Some must go off;° and yet, by these I see,
So great a day as this is cheaply bought.

---

¹³ *Despair* despair of   ¹⁴ *angel* i.e., fallen angel, fiend   ¹⁸ *better part
of man* manly spirit   ²⁰ *palter* equivocate   ²⁴ *gaze o' th' time* spectacle
of the age   ²⁵ *monsters* freaks   ²⁶ *Painted upon a pole* i.e., pictured
on a banner set by a showman's booth   ²⁹ *baited* assailed (like a bear
by dogs)   ³⁴ s.d. *Retreat and flourish* trumpet call to withdraw, and
fanfare   ³⁶ *go off* die (theatrical metaphor)

Malcolm. Macduff is missing, and your noble son.

Ross. Your son, my lord, has paid a soldier's debt:
40 He only lived but till he was a man;
    The which no sooner had his prowess confirmed
    In the unshrinking station° where he fought,
    But like a man he died.

Siward.   Then he is dead?

Ross. Ay, and brought off the field. Your cause of
        sorrow
45 Must not be measured by his worth, for then
    It hath no end.

Siward.   Had he his hurts before?

Ross. Ay, on the front.

Siward.   Why then, God's soldier be he!
    Had I as many sons as I have hairs,
    I would not wish them to a fairer death:
    And so his knell is knolled.

50 *Malcolm.*   He's worth more sorrow,
    And that I'll spend for him.

Siward.   He's worth no more:
    They say he parted well and paid his score:°
    And so God be with him! Here comes newer
        comfort.

            Enter Macduff, with Macbeth's head.

Macduff. Hail, King! for so thou art: behold, where
        stands
55 Th' usurper's cursèd head. The time is free.°
    I see thee compassed° with thy kingdom's pearl,
    That speak my salutation in their minds,
    Whose voices I desire aloud with mine:
    Hail, King of Scotland!

All.   Hail, King of Scotland!

---

42 *unshrinking station* i.e., place at which he stood firmly   52 *parted well and paid his score* departed well and settled his account   55 *The time is free* the world is liberated   56 *compassed* surrounded

Flourish.

Malcolm. We shall not spend a large expense of time   60
    Before we reckon with your several loves,°
    And make us even with you. My thanes and
      kinsmen,
    Henceforth be earls, the first that ever Scotland
    In such an honor named. What's more to do,
    Which would be planted newly with the time°—   65
    As calling home our exiled friends abroad
    That fled the snares of watchful tyranny,
    Producing forth the cruel ministers°
    Of this dead butcher and his fiendlike queen,
    Who, as 'tis thought, by self and violent° hands   70
    Took off her life—this, and what needful else
    That calls upon us,° by the grace of Grace
    We will perform in measure, time, and place:°
    So thanks to all at once and to each one,
    Whom we invite to see us crowned at Scone.   75

Flourish. Exeunt Omnes.

FINIS

---

61 *reckon with your several loves* reward the devotion of each of you
64-65 *What's more . . . time* i.e., what else must be done which should
be newly established in this age   68 *ministers* agents   70 *self and vio-lent* her own violent   72 *calls upon us* demands my attention   73 *in measure, time and place* fittingly, at the appropriate time and place

Textual Note

Macbeth, never printed during Shakespeare's lifetime, was first printed in the Folio of 1623. The play is remarkably short, and it may be that there has been some cutting. That in I.v Lady Macbeth apparently proposes to kill Duncan, and that later in the play Macbeth kills him, is scarcely evidence that a scene had been lost, but the inconsistent stage directions concerning Macbeth's death (one calls for him to be slain on stage, another suggests he is both slain and decapitated off stage) indicate some sort of revision. Nevertheless, when one reads the account of Macbeth in Holinshed (Shakespeare's source) one does not feel that the play as it has come down to us omits anything of significance. If, as seems likely, the play was presented at court, its brevity may well be due to King James's known aversion to long plays. On the other hand, it is generally believed that Hecate is a non-Shakespearean addition to the play (she dominates III.v and has a few lines in IV.i), but the evidence is not conclusive, although the passages (along with IV.i.125-32) sound un-Shakespearean.

The present division into acts and scenes is that of the Folio except for V.viii, a division added by the Globe editors. The present edition silently modernizes spelling and punctuation, regularizes speech prefixes, and translates into English the Folio's Latin designations of act and scene. Other departures from the Folio are listed below. The reading of the present text is given first, in italics, and then the reading of the Folio (F) in roman.

I.i.9 *Second Witch . . . Anon* [F attributes to "All," as part of the ensuing speech]

I.ii.13 *gallowglasses* gallowgrosses   14 *quarrel* Quarry   26 *thunders break* Thunders   33-34 *Dismayed . . . Banquo* [one line in F]   33-35 *Dismayed . . . lion* [three lines in F, ending: Banquoh, Eagles, Lyon]   42 *But . . . faint* [F gives to previous line]   46 *So . . . look* [F gives to next line]   59 *Sweno . . . king* [F gives to previous line]

I.iii.5 *Give . . . I* [F prints as a separate line]

32 *weïrd* weyward [also at I.v.9; II.i.20; "weyard" at III.i.2; III.iv.134; IV.i.136]   39 *Forres* Soris   78 *Speak . . . you* [F prints as a separate line]   81-82 *Into . . . stayed* [three lines in F, ending: corporall, Winde, stay'd]   98 *Came* can   108 *why . . . me* [F gives to next line]   111-14 *Which . . . not* [five lines in F, ending: loose, Norway, helpe, labour'd, not]   131 *If ill* [F gives to next line]   140-42 *Shakes . . . not* [F's lines end: Man, surmise, not]   143 *If . . . crown me* [two lines in F, ending: King, crown me]   149-53 *Give . . . time* [seven lines in F, ending: fauour, forgotten, registred, Leafe, them, vpon, time]   156 *Till . . . friends* [two lines in F, ending: enough, friends]

I.iv.1 *Are not* Or not [given in F to next line]   2-8 *My . . . died* [seven lines in F, ending: back, die, hee, Pardon, Repentance, him, dy'de]   23-27 *In . . . honor* [six lines in F, ending: selfe, Duties, State, should, Loue, Honor]

I.v.23-24 *And yet . . . have it* [three lines in F, ending: winne, cryes, haue it]

I.vi.1 *the air* [F gives to next line]   4 *martlet* Barlet   9 *most* must   17-20 *Against . . . hermits* [F's lines end: broad, House, Dignities, Ermites]

I. vii.6 *shoal* Schoole [variant spelling]   47 *do* no   58 *as you* [F gives to next line]

II.i.4 *Hold . . . heaven* [two lines in F, ending: Sword, Heauen]   7-9 *And . . . repose* [F's endings: sleepe, thoughts, repose]   13-17 *He . . . content* [F's endings: Pleasure, Offices, withall, Hostesse, content]   25 *when 'tis* [F gives to next line]   55 *strides* sides   56 *sure* sowre   57 *way they* they may

II.ii.2-6 *What . . . possets* [6 lines in F, ending: fire, shriek'd, good-night, open, charge, Possets] 13 s.d. *Enter Macbeth* [F places after "die" in 1.8] 14 *I . . . noise* [two lines in F, ending: deed, noyse] 18-19 *Hark . . . chamber* [one line in F] 22-25 *There's . . . sleep* [F's endings: sleepe, other, Prayers, sleepe] 32 *Stuck . . . throat* [F gives to previous line] 64-65 *To wear . . . chamber* [three lines in F, ending: white, entry, Chamber] 68 *Hath . . . knocking* [two lines in F, ending: vnattended, knocking] 72-73 *To . . . couldst* [four lines in F, ending: deed, my selfe, knocking, could'st. The s.d. "Knock" appears after "deed"]

II.iii.25-27 *Faith . . . things* [two lines of verse in F, the second beginning "And"] 44 s.d. *Enter Macbeth* [F places after 1.43] 53-54 *I'll . . . service* [one line of prose in F] 56-63 *The night . . . shake* [10 lines in F, ending: vnruly, downe, Ayre, Death, terrible, Euents, time, Night, feuorous, shake] 66 *Tongue nor heart* [F gives to next line] 88-89 *O . . . murdered* [one line in F] 137-43 *What . . . bloody* [nine lines in F, ending: doe, them, Office, easie, England, I, safer, Smiles, bloody]

II.iv.14 *And . . . horses* [F prints as a separate line] 17 *make* [F gives to next line] 19 *They . . . so* [F prints as a separate line]

III.i.34-35 *Craving . . . with you* [three lines in F, ending: Horse, Night, you] 42-43 *The sweeter . . . you* [three lines in F, ending: welcome, alone, you] 72 *Who's there* [F prints as a separate line] 75-82 *Well . . . might* [ten lines in F, ending: then, speeches, past, fortune, selfe, conference, with you, crost, them, might] 85-91 *I . . . ever* [nine lines in F, ending: so, now, meeting, predominant, goe, man, hand, begger'd, euer] 111 *I do* [F gives to previous line] 114-15 *Both . . . enemy* [one line in F] 128 *Your . . . most* [two lines in F, ending: you, most]

III.ii.16 *But . . . suffer* [two lines in F, ending: dis-ioynt, suffer] 22 *Duncan . . . grave* [F prints as a separate line] 43 *there . . . done* [F gives to next line] 50 *and . . . crow* [F gives to next line]

III.iii.9 *The rest* [F gives to next line] 17 *O . . . fly, fly, fly* [two lines in F, the first ending: Trecherie] 21 *We . . . affair* [two lines in F, ending: lost, Affaire]

III.iv.21-22 *Most . . . perfect* [four lines in F, ending: Sir, scap'd, againe, perfect] 49 *Here . . . Highness* [two lines in F, ending: Lord, Highness] 110 *broke . . . meeting* [F gives to next line]

122 s.d. *Exeunt* Exit   123 *blood will have blood* [F prints as a separate line]   145 *in deed* indeed

III.v.36 *back again* [F prints as a separate line]

III.vi.1 *My . . . thoughts* [two lines in F, ending: Speeches, Thoughts]   24 *son* Sonnes   38 *the* their

IV.i.46-47 *Open . . . knocks* [one line in F]   59 *germens* Germaine   71 *Beware Macduff* [F prints as a separate line]   79 *Laugh to scorn* [F prints as a separate line]   86 *What is this* [F gives to next line]   93 *Dunsinane* Dunsmane   98 *Birnam* Byrnan [this F spelling, or with *i* for *y* or with a final *e*, occurs at V.ii.5, 31; V.iii.2, 60; V.iv.3; V.v.34, 44; V.viii.30]   119 *eighth* eight   133 *Let . . . hour* [F prints as a separate line]

IV.ii.27 *Fathered . . . fatherless* [two lines in F, ending: is, Father-lesse] IV.ii.34 *Poor bird* [F prints as a separate line]   36-43 *Why . . . for thee* [ten lines in F, ending: Mother, for, saying, is, dead, Father, Husband, Market, againe, wit, thee]   48-49 *Every . . . hanged* [two lines of verse in F, ending: Traitor, hang'd]   57-58 [two lines of verse in F, ending: Monkie, Father]   77 *What . . . faces* [F prints as a separate line]

IV.iii.4 *down-fall'n* downfall   15 *deserve* discerne   25 *where . . . doubts* [F prints as a separate line]   102 *Fit to govern* [F gives to next line]   107 *accursed* accust   133 *thy* they   140 *I pray you* [F prints as a separate line]   173 *O relation* [F gives to next line]   211-12 *Wife . . . found* [one line in F]   212-13 *And . . . too* [one line in F]

V.iii.39 *Cure her* Cure   55 *senna* Cyme

V.vi.1 *Your . . . down* [F prints as a separate line]

V.viii.54 *behold . . . stands* [F prints as a separate line]

Suggested References

◆

SUGGESTED REFERENCES

1. SHAKESPEARE

Barnet, Sylvan. *A Short Guide to Shakespeare*. New York: Harcourt Brace Jovanovich, Inc., 1974. An introduction to all of the works and to the traditions behind them.

Bently, Gerald E. *Shakespeare: A Biographical Handbook*. New Haven, Conn.: Yale University Press, 1961. The facts about Shakespeare, with virtually no conjecture intermingled.

Chambers, E. K. *William Shakespeare: A Study of Facts and Problems*. 2 vols., London: Oxford University Press, 1930. An invaluable, detailed reference work; not for the casual reader.

Chute, Marchette, *Shakespeare of London*. New York: E. P. Dutton & Co., Inc., 1949. A readable biography fused with portraits of Stratford and London life.

Harbage, Alfred. *As They Liked It*. New York: The Macmillan Company, 1947. A sensitive, long essay on Shakespeare, morality, and the audience's expectations.

————. *William Shakespeare: A Reader's Guide*. New York: Farrar, Straus, 1963. Extensive comments, scene by scene, on fourteen plays.

Schoenbaum, S. *William Shakespeare: A Compact Documentary Life*. New York: Oxford University Press, 1977. A readable presentation of all that the documents tell us about Shakespeare.

Traversi, D. A. *An Approach to Shakespeare*. Rev. ed. New York: Doubleday & Co., Inc., 1956. An analysis of the plays, beginning with words, images, and themes, rather than with characters.

Van Doren, Mark. *Shakespeare*. New York: Henry Holt & Company, Inc., 1939. Brief, perceptive readings of all of the plays.

2. SHAKESPEARE'S THEATER

Gurr, Andrew. *The Shakespearean Stage 1574–1642*. Cambridge: Cambridge University Press, 1970. On the acting companies, the actors, the playhouses, the stages, and the audiences.

Kernodle, George R. *From Art to Theatre: Form and Convention in the Renaissance*. Chicago: University of Chicago Press, 1944. Pioneering and stimulating work on the symbolic and cultural meanings of theater construction.

Nagler, A. M. *Shakespeare's Stage*. Tr. Ralph Manheim. New Haven, Conn.: Yale University Press, 1958. An excellent brief introduction to the physical aspect of the playhouse.

3. MISCELLANEOUS REFERENCE WORKS

Bullough, Geoffrey. *Narrative and Dramatic Sources of Shakespeare*. 8 vols. New York: Columbia University Press, 1957–75. A collection of many of the books Shakespeare drew upon.

Campbell, Oscar James, and Edward G. Quinn. *The Reader's Encyclopedia of Shakespeare*. New York: Thomas Y. Crowell Co., 1966. More than 2,700 entries, from a few sentences to a few pages on everything related to Shakespeare.

Kökeritz, Helge. *Shakespeare's Names*. New Haven, Conn.: Yale University Press, 1959. A guide to the pronunciation of some 1,800 names appearing in Shakespeare.

Onions, C. T. *A Shakespeare Glossary*. London: Oxford University Press, 1911; 2nd ed., rev., with enlarged addenda, 1953. Definitions of words (or senses of words) now obsolete.

Spevack, Marvin. *The Harvard Concordance to Shakespeare*. Cambridge, Mass.: Harvard University Press, 1973. An index to Shakespeare's words.

Wells, Stanley, ed. *Shakespeare: Select Bibliographies*. London: Oxford University Press, 1973. Seventeen essays surveying scholarship and criticism of Shakespeare's life, work, and theater.

4. THE TRAGEDIES

Bradley, A. C. *Shakespearean Tragedy*. London: Macmillan and Co., 1904.

Brower, Reuben Arthur. *Hero and Saint: Shakespeare and*

the Greco-Roman Heroic Tradition. New York: Oxford University Press, 1970.

Champion, Larry S. *Shakespeare's Tragic Perspective.* Athens, Georgia: University of Georgia Press, 1976.

Granville-Barker, Harley. *Prefaces to Shakespeare,* 2 vols. Princeton: Princeton University Press, 1946-47.

Holloway, John. *The Story of the Night.* London: Routledge and Kegan Paul, 1961.

Nevo, Ruth. *Tragic Form in Shakespeare.* Princeton: Princeton University Press, 1972.

Rosen, William. *Shakespeare and the Craft of Tragedy.* Cambridge, Mass.: Harvard University Press, 1960.

5. HAMLET

Alexander, Nigel. *Poison, Play and Duel: A Study of "Hamlet."* Lincoln, Nebraska: University of Nebraska, 1971.

Alexander, Peter. *Hamlet: Father and Son.* New York and London: Oxford University Press, 1955.

Bevington, David (ed.) *Twentieth-Century Interpretations of "Hamlet."* Englewood Cliffs, N. J.: Prentice-Hall, 1968.

Brown, John Russell, and Bernard Harris (ed.). *Stratford-upon-Avon Studies 5: "Hamlet."* London: Edward Arnold, Publ., 1963.

Charney, Maurice. *Style in Hamlet,* Princeton, N. J.: Princeton University Press, 1969.

Jones, Ernest. *Hamlet and Oedipus.* New York: Doubleday & Company, Inc. (Anchor Books), 1954.

Kitto, H. D. F. *Form and Meaning in Drama.* London: Methuen & Co., Ltd., 1956; New York: Barnes & Noble, Inc., 1960.

Levin, Harry. *The Question of Hamlet,* New York and London: Oxford University Press, 1959.

Mander, Raymond, and Joe Mitchenson (comps.). *Hamlet Through the Ages. A Pictorial Record from 1709.* London: Rockliff Publishing Corporation, 1952.

Nicoll, Allardyce (ed.). *Shakespeare Survey 9.* London: Cambridge University Press, 1956.

Walker, Roy. *The Time Is out of Joint: A Study of Hamlet.* New York: The Macmillan Company; London: Andrew Dakers, Ltd., 1948.

Wilson, J. Dover. *What Happens in "Hamlet."* New York: The Macmillan Company; London: Cambridge University Press, 1935; 3rd ed., New York and London: Cambridge University Press, 1951.

6. KING LEAR

Fraser, Russell A. *Shakespeare's Poetics in Relation to "King Lear."* London: Routledge & Kegan Paul, Ltd., 1962.

Heilman, Robert B. *This Great Stage: Image and Structure in "King Lear."* Baton Rouge, La.: Louisiana State University Press, 1948.

Knight, G. Wilson. *The Wheel of Fire.* New York and London: Oxford University Press, 1930; 5th rev. ed., New York: Meridian Books, Inc., 1957.

Mack, Maynard. *King Lear in Our Time.* Berkeley and Los Angeles University of California Press, 1965.

7. OTHELLO

Bayley, John. *The Characters of Love.* New York: Basic Books, Inc.; London: Constable & Co., Ltd., 1961.

Eliot, T. S. "Shakespeare and the Stoicism of Seneca," *Selected Essays, 1917–1932.* New York: Harcourt, Brace & Company, Inc.; London; Faber & Faber, Ltd., 1932.

Gardner, Helen. *The Noble Moor.* London: Oxford University Press, 1956.

————. *"Othello:* A Retrospect, 1900–67," *Shakespeare Survey 21,* ed. Kenneth Muir. Cambridge: Cambridge University Press, 1968.

Heilman, Robert B. *Magic in the Web, Action & Language in Othello,* Lexington, Ky.: University of Kentucky Press, 1956.

Rosenberg, Marvin. *The Masks of Othello.* Berkeley, Calif.: University of California Press, 1961.

8. MACBETH

Farnham, Williard. *Shakespeare's Tragic Frontier.* Berkeley: University of California Press, 1950.

Mack, Maynard Jr. *Killing the King.* New Haven: Yale University Press, 1973.

Muir, Kenneth, ed. *Shakespeare Survey 19.* Cambridge: Cambridge University Press, 1966.

Rosenberg, Marvin. *The Masks of Macbeth.* Berkeley: University of California, 1978.

Walker, Roy. *The Time Is Free.* New York: The Macmillan Company. 1949.